Chaz Brenchley has made a living as a writer since he was eighteen; this year he turned forty. He is the author of a dozen novels for adults, and one book of short stories; he has also published three books for children and some poetry. He lives in Newcastle upon Tyne, with two cats and a famous teddy bear.

Also by Chaz Brenchley

The First Book of Outremer:
TOWER OF THE KING'S DAUGHTER

Visit the series' web-site at:
www.outremer.co.uk

Feast of the King's Shadow

THE SECOND BOOK OF OUTREMER

Chaz Brenchley

ORBIT

An *Orbit* Book

First published in Great Britain by Orbit 2000

A CIP catalogue record for this book is
available from the British Library.

ISBN 1 85723 745 5

Typeset in Adobe Garamond by M Rules
Printed and bound in Great Britain
by Mackays of Chatham PLC

Orbit
A Division of
Little, Brown and Company (UK)
Brettenham House
Lancaster Place
London WC2E 7EN

Big hearts are big houses,
with a spare room for friends.
This one's for Richard and Jane.

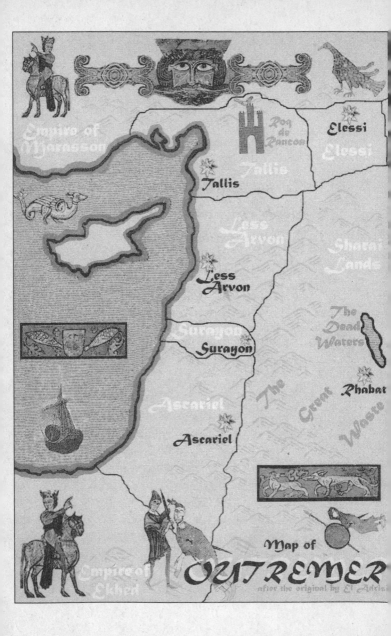

Empire of Mjarasson

Elessi
Elessi

Roq de Rancon

Tallis
Tallis

Less Arvon
Less Arvon

Sharai Lands

Surayon
Surayon

The Dead Waters

Ascariel
Ascariel

The Great Waste

Rhabat

Empire of Ekhed

Map of
OUTREMER
after the original by El Adrim

Qul 'a 'uuzu bi Rabbin Naas,
Malikin Naas,
'Ilaahin Naas,
Minsharril waswaasil khan Naas,
'Allazii yuwas wisu fii suduurin Naasi,
Minal Jinnati wan Naas.

Al-Qur'aan, 114, Naas, 1–6

He had come out of the west in the early morning, running now as he had run all night, hard on their trail. Four horses and one afoot, it had been simple – he'd said – in these soft lands, even in the dark. He had done what he could to hide or mask that trail, though, against anyone else's following.

His name was Jemel, he'd said, the women knew him. He had sworn to guide them safely to Rhabat. Then the Patric horsemen had come and taken them the other way, back to the castle. He'd followed then – and did not say why – and had followed again this night when they'd burst the gate and come riding out, a party of four and one. He'd tried to keep up with that one at least, the one on foot, the runner; but that one had outrun the horses, and Jemel could not. So he had followed, at his best pace.

And had found them in a gully, resting and watering their horses. Dismounted, they had faced him as a group, and yet they were not; not even four and one, the runner divided from the riders, though certainly that was true.

There had been tensions everywhere. That had made it easier.

The old man, the crippled man had asked him what he wanted. He'd said that he was oath-bound to the women, to take them to Rhabat. The bearded man had laughed shortly, though he'd said nothing.

'But if we know the way, they do not need your guidance now.'

'You need my help, perhaps,' I said. 'I have disguised your trail for you, which you could not. You would have been caught by now, without me.'

'If we don't want you,' from the bearded man, 'why do you want to come?'

His eyes had moved of themselves, inexorably sideways to the one young man of their party, the one who kept his distance from the horses; the one who kept his silence, his head lowered, his eyes hooded and hidden.

Too late to hide them from Jemel. He had seen, he knew.

'Your road lies with mine,' was all he'd said, as mild as he could make it. And then, when that had seemed not to be enough, 'We can be useful to each other. You need another sword, and one who is of the desert; I would be stupid to travel alone, here where your soldiers boil like bees at my back, or there where a man alone can die of a single bee-sting . . .'

'Enough of this.' The bearded man again, brutally abrupt. 'Tell the truth, boy. You want to come because of him, don't you?' A jerk of his head, towards the silent one. 'Because of what he is.'

'He is not yours.'

'Indeed not. I don't want him, never did. We're stuck with him now, though – so yes, I think we'll take him to Rhabat. Why not? It should be interesting, if nothing more. You'll excuse me if I decline to follow you, though. I suspect I know the way there at least as well as you, and likely better.'

'I think Jemel should come,' one of the women had said instantly: not the one he'd saved from the 'ifrit, the other, the one who spoke his tongue and had shown some signs of decency, half-veiling her face when he'd appeared, though she'd let that veil slip mind and fingers soon. The other had simply gazed at him bare-faced, judgemental.

'Oh heavens, girl, so do I think he should come. Why not?' Again, as though it had been all a bitter joke. 'He'll make the perfect addition to our party. We've already got the escaped prisoner, condemned to death for heresy and tortured till he can barely move, till he must use another's strength to ride with; we've got the runaway baroness who rides to Rhabat because a djinni told her to, and her companion who goes to spite her father.'

'The djinni sent me too,' the girl objected. 'And I'd go in any case, to be with Julianne.'

'Of course: the girl who goes for loyalty, obedience and love, and so to spite her father. That father himself, who goes to prevent a war, if he is able; and who takes in his baggage, running at his stirrup-rein, the very weapon which can win that war. Who is a boy from the one side, possessed by a spirit from the other; whatever he does, he will betray himself. All we need now is another boy, and one who wants that war more than he wants any other thing in life, am I right?'

No, he had not been right, he was too late for that. A month before, yes, certainly; but not by then. By then what Jemel had wanted most was vengeance. But he'd said nothing of that, and so the bearded man had nodded, sure of his own cynical judgement.

'Join us, Jemel,' he'd said, 'and welcome. We are a party of fools; there's always room for a little more foolishness.'

PART ONE

The Road to Rhabat

1

Sand Dancers

At this distance she thought they looked like dancers, blurred figures who swirled and stamped and left strange trails in the sand. Black silhouettes, hazed by the heat so that they would flicker and jerk, vanish almost for moments too brief to count.

At this distance, she couldn't see the swords that were the focus and the purpose of all that dancing.

Weeks into their journey, this was the first sand that they had come to; and even this, she'd been told, was not the true sand, the drifting dry of the desert ocean, the *mul'abarta*, what Jemel called simply the Sands: only a wind-blown herald of what awaited them days further to the south.

'Look at it, Julianne,' Elisande had said, scuffing at the trail with her boot, digging the sand aside to show glassy black lava beneath. 'This is a dusting, no more. We could take an ox-cart over this, no need for camels. The sand just smooths the ridges here. You wait until you wade in it, until you swim in it, until you think you could sink and sink and never touch bottom . . .'

Well, she would wait, then; and not be afraid, though she thought her friend wanted her to be. *Anywhere you can go, I can go too*; and Elisande had been that way already, more than once. There were things ahead to be afraid of, Julianne knew that, and those she would fear when she needed to – but not the journey, no. Only what lay beyond the journey, what had caused them to travel this way . . .

They were travelling with a caravan for cloak, for safety, certainly not for speed. *If my father need speed*, Julianne thought, *if his cloak, his safety lie in our speed to reach him, then I have no father.* She wasn't sure about Elisande's ox-carts, there had been cruel ruts in the lava-bed before they reached the sand, that wheels must have balked at; but their horses had picked their way across that, and certainly they could have ridden hard across this ground, this demi-desert. Other parties had done just that, indeed, sweeping by the laden camel-train with cries and cracking whips.

But Rudel was master of their own small party, even Elisande had had to accept that; and when they'd met this caravan of northern tribespeople at a well on the margin of the lava plain, he had paid over silver and jewels from their small stock of wealth for the right to travel at its tail, to share its food and fires.

'News blows on the wind,' he'd said, when Elisande – inevitably, Elisande – had challenged him, 'and all the winds blow southerly from here. You know that, daughter. We have need of haste, perhaps – but our need for secrecy outweighs it. What we carry with us we must hide, for as long as we can.'

And his gaze had fallen inexorably, inevitably, on Marron where that boy sat at a little distance from their fire, from themselves; and even Elisande had had no further argument to offer.

After some days with the caravan, Julianne thought that it had perhaps not been the wisest decision he might have made. To be sure, the rest of them could hide to some extent within the milling crowd at every halt, they could conceal their own origins beneath rough woollen clothes bartered from their new companions; but the quality of their horseflesh could not be disguised, nor emphatically could Marron's strangeness.

A boy who held himself apart, a boy who walked while his friends had fine beasts to ride; more, a boy who could not come close to any animal in the train without that animal backing or shying or bellowing its terror . . .

No, such a boy would stand out in any company. The greater the number, the more was he isolated against it. It might after all have been better to have travelled fast and few, to let the rumour fly ahead of them, *a party of riders well-mounted, and one boy who runs beside and never falters* . . .

They'd have needed a mount for Jemel, of course, better than the scruffy pony he rode now; but there were other beasts among the caravan they might have bought for him. Better to have spent their money thus, and gone ahead . . .

But the decision had been taken, well or ill. Too late to revoke it now. Their immediate goal, the oasis of Bar'ath

Tazore, lay only one further day's journey down the trail. There this trail ended, there they would part company with the caravan and strike on alone. They'd leave behind the questioning glances of even these uncurious folk, the murmurs that neither Rudel nor Jemel could understand; with luck, they just might avoid all company else, and outride the rumour.

She didn't expect such luck, but she could hope. There was nothing else indeed that she could do.

For now, while men and women and beasts rested under the sun's height, she sat and shaded her eyes against the glare and watched two shadows, two stick-figures dance and spin.

Marron, and Jemel. Two boys, and neither seemed to feel any need of rest. Jemel was scornful of this midday lethargy, promising them hotter days by far before they reached Rhabat; while Marron—

Marron, she thought, was ice-cold in his spirit now, and no external warmth could touch him; or else his blood was fire, and there was nothing any sun or fire could do to heat it further. Wherever the truth lay, he was inexhaustible.

And so the two boys fenced while others dozed. Properly they were men, she supposed, young men who had loved and killed and carried the weight of that with them always; but it was their youth she saw, in Jemel's anger and Marron's silent pain. She was younger by a year or so and had never had a brother, but sometimes she felt like elder sister to them both.

Sometimes not. As now, watching them at swordplay and flinching even at this distance from the ferocity of it:

play perhaps but no game as she understood the word. Games should not be deadly.

The sand lay thicker away from the age-worn trail, rising in billows that looked soft and were not. Hard-packed by time and their own weight, baked like mud by the occasional rains and the sun that came after, they made good ground to fence on, seemingly. Not so good for sitting, hot enough to scorch where her hand fell; she shifted uncomfortably, and yearned for shade.

And had it for a moment, as a shadow fell across her; she glanced up, and saw Elisande.

'Julianne. What are you doing?'

'Resting.'

'You don't look very restful.'

Julianne sighed, as her friend settled beside her. 'Well, no. I was watching them,' with a jerk of her head. 'They don't exactly inspire ease in my mind. I worry about them both.'

Elisande's face twisted in sympathy. 'We all do. I keep telling myself that it's good that they're together, that they find some comfort in each other; but I don't know . . .'

'No.' The opposite might be true; Julianne couldn't tell, any more than Elisande. Jemel was a bitter companion, and she thought that it was not truly comfort that he found with Marron. Awe and fear she was certain of; more there must be, to make the one boy dog the other so determinedly, but when she was honest with herself she thought that neither found much comfort in it.

'Are they trying to kill each other out there?' Elisande murmured, after a few moments' pause to watch.

Julianne chuckled, dry-mouthed from more than heat. 'Not them,' she said. 'Jemel would never do anything to harm the Ghost Walker, even if he was able; and Marron – well, Marron wants never to kill anything, ever again.' Too many bodies in that boy's past, she thought; more than she'd seen herself, she thought, though he wouldn't speak about it. Nor willingly about anything, any more. Perhaps that was why he accepted Jemel's company where he shunned theirs: he was spending time with the one member of the party he could barely exchange six words with. Perhaps.

'Even so,' Elisande said. 'There can be accidents at practice, even with bated blades; Marron knows that.' *That's how he got to be the Ghost Walker.* 'Someone should stop them—'

And she stood up to be that someone, but Julianne gripped her sleeve and tugged her down again.

'Leave them. Marron wouldn't allow an accident. Supposedly, Jemel's teaching him to use a scimitar – but it's Jemel who's taking lessons. Marron's the master, even where he doesn't know the weapon. He's faster, stronger, a lot more careful.'

'You call that care?'

'Sit and watch. You'll see.'

Even from this distance, even with the tricks played by heat and light against her eyes, she'd seen; and so did Elisande, with a little unnatural patience.

'All right. He won't hurt Jemel, and he won't let Jemel hurt him. But someone should stop them anyway. I don't know about Marron's body any more, since he took the Daughter into him – but Jemel can't ride all day on a mouthful of water and an hour's fight at noon.'

'Yes, he can. He's a boy. You let them be, Elisande. If you try to call a halt, they'll fight another hour just to show you.'

Elisande snorted. 'I'm not picking him up, mind, if he falls off that pony. And he will, sooner or later. He doesn't eat enough to feed a snake.'

Neither did Marron, but that was a different matter. 'Jemel's still grieving for the death of his friend.'

'Hating, more like. And I'm the one that killed him . . .'

'No. It was d'Escrivey that killed him.' They'd established that cautiously, obliquely, largely by dint of encouraging Jemel to spit his anger at the fire night after night.

'My knife that gave him space to do it, though. It's my burden, Julianne, let me carry it.'

'So long as you don't try to share it with Jemel.'

'I won't,' though silence was clearly costing her; how much, only Elisande could know. 'Jemel's teaching Marron to speak Catari too, did you know?'

'No . . .' It wasn't a mutual and enforced silence that drew the two boys together, then. 'That's good, though.'

'It is. And it reminds me, I'm supposed to be teaching you. Tell me what you see, Julianne.'

I see trouble, and danger, and uncertainty – but she couldn't say any of that in Catari yet, and the lessons did at least help to pass the time. Even when the heat lay like a smothering blanket across her head, fuzzing her mind into stupidity. She took a breath – and even the air was hot, parching her throat and her lungs, doing her no good – and fumbled for words she could barely pronounce or understand, a language she couldn't think in.

And found shelter in that, a relief from constant anxiety. When she couldn't think, she couldn't worry either.

They talked also as they rode, side by side and a little lag of the caravan proper, not to breathe its dust or the smell of it; but they talked only in Catari. Elisande insisted on that. Slow talk, then, and slipping soon into a weary silence. It was possible almost to sleep ahorseback under so much weight of sun, to slide into a half-doze and touch the borders of dream before jerking back and staring wildly for a moment, before realising or remembering what and who and where she was and so slouching in the saddle again and slowly, slowly losing grip . . .

When they came to where they would camp that night, she thought for a short while that they were a day ahead of themselves, that they had come to Bar'ath Tazore already.

What else? This was her abiding picture of an oasis, from a thousand childhood stories: stars pricking through the sky above as darkness swept across it, just at the moment when the trail dropped into an unexpected valley, glimpses of green before the last light fled. And then the glimmer of fires below, to match the glimmers overhead; and a song sung from two dozen tribal throats to announce them to the watchers at those fires, to say they were peaceful folk and no bandits come to steal and slay; and cries of welcome from left and right as the path brought them down to the valley bottom, and then the shimmer of dark water ahead, a pool knee-deep to beasts and men both, and what could this be but an oasis . . .?

Elisande laughed at her. 'Oh, Julianne, this is a happenstance, no more. This is lava country, remember? The ground cannot drink the rain, and it must go somewhere; so it floods any dip or hollow it can find. Here is more than a dip, it goes deep and it takes a lot of water. And the water lingers in the shadow of the cleft, where the sun can't bake it dry in a day. What's left now seems like a treasure to you, but it's little to what was here before, and every mouthful your horse drinks reduces it further. In a fortnight, there'll be nothing; and what's green here will die back till the next rain come, and those who camp here will feed their camels on the husks and then look for somewhere else. No, my love, this is no oasis. Wait till tomorrow.'

And so she would, though she was glad enough of this tonight: water to drink and to wash in, despite the animals who had waded and perhaps wallowed in it first, bathing dust and dung from their pads and hooves and hides. Perhaps adding a little water of their own, before they were done. She didn't care; it tasted better and far better than a warm and stale drink from a dubious goatskin.

This night as every night the six of them sat around their own fire, though it was made up of dung-cakes from the caravan's store. This night as every night a woman brought them food. Her headdress was sewn with silver rings and her arms clashed with bangles; she kept her face so low that Julianne was never sure if it were the same woman every night, or if the duty were shared around.

Tonight, it seemed, they were feasting: a plate of boiled meat and greens, and a basket of flat breads. Rudel reached for a fleshy rib, bit and chewed, chewed and swallowed;

spat gristle into the flames and said, 'Ah, well. All things are comparative. At least it's better than preserved eggs.'

Jemel frowned. 'This is good food.'

'Then why don't you eat it?' Elisande demanded. Receiving nothing but a shrug in response, she scowled momentously and went on, 'And you, Marron. Here . . .'

She folded two breads around generous portions of meat and vegetable and thrust them into the boys' hands, didn't serve herself until she'd seen both begin to eat.

Julianne hid a smile behind sudden activity, picking out what tender pieces she could find for the elderly Redmond. His broken hands were healing now, but were too badly damaged to manage such work without pain.

He thanked her kindly; she helped herself and then settled down beside him to eat, finding him far the most restful of her companions.

The meat was stringy; there was sand in the greens, and more in the bread. She worked her way through it till her jaw ached with chewing, and her lips were raw from the grit. It was hard to be grateful: hard to remember that they had eaten less and worse already, or that there would likely be shorter commons still in the journey to come. Sometimes, though – when she tried – she could still find some pleasure in this adventure, in discovering the pampered and privileged daughter of the King's Shadow fallen so far from grace.

No, not fallen – jumped, rather. Jumped and run deliberately from her secure and comfortable existence, for the sake of a djinni's word against her father's life . . .

She was also of course the Baroness Julianne von und zu Karlheim these days; she should be Countess of Elessi in days to come, and had run also from someone who offered more than security or comfort – but there was no pleasure in that particular memory. She jerked her eyes away from the fire, where they could so easily have seen his face form in the flames.

And looked instead at the ground before the fire, and saw instead how the air seemed to flicker with more than the flicker of the firelight. She narrowed her gaze and bent a little closer, and saw a black line drawn above the sand: thicker than a hair, finer than a wire, snagging her eye like a hook. It was there, and then it was not there; for a moment she thought *djinni* . . .

But then there was another, and then there were two at once and she lost them both by trying to watch them both; and there had only ever been one djinni, and it had never played games with her this way. It had come, had done and said what it meant to do and say and then it had gone again.

So no, not the djinni; but—

'What *are* those things, do you see them?'

Surprisingly Redmond laughed, though there was a harsh and knowing ring to it that she liked not at all. 'The insects? The Sharai call them sand dancers. Try to catch one.'

She made a cup of her hand, and grabbed; and opened her closed hand to find it empty. And tried again, and failed again; and tried to snare one between her two clapping hands, and still failed.

'You could sit all night,' Redmond said, stilling her with a touch on her shoulder, 'and still come up with nothing. The Sharai say that they slip between two worlds, this and another, which is why they call them sand dancers. One reason why.'

'I don't understand,' she said.

'No. Be grateful.'

She swallowed her irritation and said, 'Well, I will try. Since you ask it. But what is the other reason?'

'They are killers,' Redmond said. 'If you set a beetle on the sand there, they would destroy it. If you set a nest of ants there, they would destroy them all.'

The day's heat dissipated quickly; after an hour of darkness, they found themselves shifting closer to the fire. Except for Marron, of course, who apparently felt neither cold nor heat; and except for Jemel also, who felt or at least said that the nights were as warm as the days were cool. If he had another reason for keeping a touch of distance – as for example that he hated so much the place and the people they had come from, it was an effort to him not to hate them also, and he would not risk his knife too close to their throats – then he did not say so; neither if he had rather a reason for staying quite close to Marron.

Julianne felt that she had reasons in plenty for staying as far as possible from Marron, and yet she couldn't do it. As a Ransomer boy he had charmed her with his naïvety, and a little with his blushful beauty too; as a creature out of nightmare, slaying and slaying with a flicker of his eyes or a gesture of his bleeding arm, he had terrified her. She tried deliberately to remember that terror sometimes, to use his red eyes and his inexhaustible, inhuman energy as a reminder that he was not what he used to be. She wished that she could react to him as her palfrey Merissa did or any animal else, bucking and screaming; but it seemed that she could not. She still looked at him and saw the boy that he had been, in many ways the boy that he still was, only dreadfully burdened now.

And she was not even Sharai, she hadn't grown up eyeing the night's shadows for any hint of the Ghost Walker, while a hundred stories thundered in her head. No blame to Jemel if he'd chosen to run the other way that night or the morning following, if he'd kept all the distance he could between himself and Marron; but he was Sharai, and so he had not.

Also, of course, he'd not seen that skein of red that killed, that was the Ghost Walker's wicked will; all he'd seen of Marron was the eyes and the energy and the flesh that contained them, the silence and withdrawal. She thought that probably what he saw was also mostly boy. And boys will cling together, she thought, against girls or against authority, against the world itself . . .

When the flames died to a glimmer among white ashes and the cold pressed in at their backs as the day lay heavy on their bones, they wrapped themselves in blankets and lay down two by two around the circle of the fire: the older men Rudel and Redmond, the girls Julianne and Elisande, the boys Marron and Jemel.

Except that Marron slept as little as he ate, and Jemel also. Julianne was accustomed now to seeing them still sitting silhouetted against the stars as she closed her eyes; she knew they would be up and about before her in the morning. She hoped tonight that all their long nights were full of talking, that the excuse of language lessons would teach them both to share their troubles; only then she thought of what each might have to say to the other when they could talk as equals, and rather wished they would not.

Something else to which Julianne had become accustomed: Elisande's being wakeful and watchful also, restless at her side. Wakeful for many reasons, Julianne thought, but watchful only over Marron.

Between them all, they made it precious hard for a girl to get any sleep herself . . .

But sleep she did, and wake she did, and watched them all through their morning rituals.

Jemel – who had kept to his Sharai dress and Sharai habits also – would walk some distance away and kneel, and pray towards the rising sun: alone, he said, because the tribespeople they travelled with were untrue in their words, following bastard rites. Elisande said that it was Sharai pride, that he thought himself superior; Julianne thought it another expression of his anger.

Marron made a great point of saying no prayers at all. No longer a brother of the Ransomers, no longer squire to a religious master and not at all certain what he had become, he would sit apart and do nothing until Elisande took him bread, and stood over him until he had eaten it.

Rudel had discarded his jongleur's garb for the anonymity of the simple clothes the others wore, but he still practised his juggling for half an hour every morning.

Redmond had been too much hurt in his hands and his feet to do anything active. He would sit over the fire, warming his bones for the day ahead, he said; his eyes watched them all, though, and his wise tongue soothed any quarrels that might be building.

Elisande saw to everyone's breakfast, though Marron was her special charge and her father Rudel her hardest, seemingly. They were the two most likely to stretch Redmond's peacemaking.

Which left Julianne to see to the horses, a duty she took on willingly, and more than ever so this morning. They were all of them friends by now and Merissa had always been special, a wilful and occasionally difficult companion but a confidante too when they were both young in Marasson, sometimes closer in her affections than any of her circle. Julianne had a building ache in her heart, as each day's journey brought them that much nearer to a certain parting. There was nothing she could do to prevent it, they could not take horses into the true desert nor keep them alive if they had tried to; but soon it would be another's hands that brought bridle and saddle, hopefully sweets and petting. Julianne had known too many hard separations in recent weeks; she wasn't sure that she could tolerate another.

She wasn't sure either that it was truly the loss of Merissa that grieved her so, but she was determined to think it. Otherwise she might still be crying herself to sleep every night over a pair of green-grey eyes, blond hair and a devastating smile . . .

So this one time more – and trying not to torment herself with the thought that it might be the last time – she fetched all the horses from where they foraged fresh greenstuff by the water's edge. She stroked their soft noses and pulled their ears, and promised them more and better

eating that evening. She spent longer with Merissa, murmuring secrets that only the palfrey could hear and would
not spread around. Then she burdened them one by one
with saddle and harness, glanced around for her human
companions and called softly to say their mounts were
ready. The caravan was on the move already, filing up the
shadowed path into the early sun's light above. Julianne
would have preferred another hour's rest and then a fast
gallop to catch it, but Rudel was firm about that, they must
do nothing to attract attention.

No more than they could help, at least. Nothing, she
thought, would keep the quiet tribespeople from gossiping
at journey's end. Their best hope would be hardly to pause
at Bar'ath Tazore, to trade their horses for camels tonight or
tomorrow and be away before the rumour spread.

And so another day of weary riding at a walker's pace,
weary for herself and Merissa both: the horse was as restless
as she was, sidling and jerking and tossing her head. As
keen for speed too, Julianne thought, and a cool wind running. That they'd never find on this baking plain; when the
breeze came it brought only more heat with it. Marasson
summers were worse, though, not so purely hot perhaps
but stickier and far more draining, and they'd both enjoyed
the freedom of a gallop then.

This trailing of the caravan was nothing but dull, sucking at reserves of patience. As the sun rose higher, so
conversation flagged. She covered her head with a fold of
cloth to shade her eyes from the pale sky's glare, and
focused her gaze between Merissa's ears. Marron was a
shimmering dot away to the side, as ever. Jemel rode as

close to him as he dared, which was not close at all; Rudel and Redmond rode ahead, Elisande at her side. Julianne worried about them all, in turn: Marron for the burden he carried or else the creature he had become, the thing that infested his blood had made the two indistinguishable; Jemel for his grief and loss and anger, which could not be allayed; Redmond for his physical weakness, the cruelties worked against him by the Ransomers' questioners; Rudel and Elisande for the gulf between them that she still did not understand, that they would not talk about, that should not so divide father and daughter.

Betweentimes she worried about her own father, whom she was travelling so far to find and to rescue, according to the djinni's word, though she did not know how. It had refused to tell her; sometimes, often, she doubted herself and her ability.

And when she was worrying about none of them, when she occasionally found space to think about her future, that too was nothing but worry and grief, a loss as great as Jemel's. Or greater, she dared to think sometimes, because it was her own choice that had caused it. She had deliberately fled the man she'd married, the one young man she would happily have given herself to for the rest of her days; she thought he would never take her back now.

And yet – despite boredom and discomfort and the ache in her bones, despite anxiety and sorrow and the ache in her heart – yet she was happy. Happier than she had been before, she thought, perhaps.

In the past, in Marasson, happiness had always been contingent: she was happy *but* her father was in Outremer, as he almost always was; she was happy *but* she was afraid of falling, and dared not climb; she was happy *but* she was to be married to an unknown lordling in a far-distant province.

Now all that was turned around. Her father was in Rhabat, in the hands of the Sharai, in danger; but she was happy. She was afraid of many things now, and afraid for many people for many different reasons; but she was happy. She was married to her lordling, and she had fallen desperately, dangerously in love with her husband, and had fled him for her father's sake for whom her love was far more complex and far less all-engulfing – and still, bizarrely, treacherously almost, she was happy.

She pulled her mettlesome mount into line again, for the hundredth time already today, and tried to understand herself. It might be the freedom, she supposed, that she so relished: to ride untrammelled – better yet, unveiled; these people did not cloak their women's faces – under wide skies, to sleep in a blanket beneath the stars with no other guard than her own and her companions' watchfulness. To make her own decisions, or at least to have an equal voice among the company. Perhaps. Or it might be the prospect of action, the chance to do what she felt to be right or necessary, to be more than a quiet voice sequestered in her lord's ear. She was afraid of making mistakes, afraid of failure, but still it might be better to try and fail than not to have the opportunity to try.

Perhaps.

Or perhaps it was simply to be riding into doubt and mystery with these particular few, these dubious and mysterious folk her friends. If friends they were. One at least she was sure of, Elisande who rode beside her and kept far fewer secrets now. The others still kept more of their own counsel than they shared with her. That was fair, though; so did she. It was only Elisande to whom she whispered the truths of her heart, and not all even to her. Some she held back, though the other girl had seen enough surely to guess at those also.

The sun climbed to its highest and moved on, as they moved on beneath it. For the first time in many days, the caravan did not pause to rest despite the heat. There was no place, the endless plain offered no hope of shade nor water beyond what they carried in bags slung below the bellies of their beasts; even so, Julianne thought there was another reason today. Even these trading tribes must grow tired of the road, must press with added urgency when their goal came close, eager to arrive even an hour earlier than they might . . .

Despite that, she did not recognise the signs when they first appeared, she was only confused. The sky was green, and she thought that meant a storm. She thought it had to. In Marasson, when the sky was porridge-yellow and porridge-thick, even the animals sought shelter against the coming deluge.

None of that heaviness here: the sky ahead was green but glimmering with it, like a fine translucent glaze on a good pot. It couldn't be rain, surely. She had heard that it rained even in the true desert, but not from such a sky. There were other kinds of storm, though; she had heard that also. A dust-storm, a sand-storm might somehow look like this from a distance, if a rain-storm looked like porridge.

Green, and glimmering like water as they rode through heat that made the air dance above the sand; and Elisande at her side but not so much watching the road ahead or the sky above it, much more watching her and smiling, smiling in anticipation . . .

At last the egg broke, she cracked it, and all but choked on her sudden rush of understanding.

'That's it, isn't it? That's the oasis doing that . . .'

'Bar'ath Tazore,' Elisande confirmed, grinning. 'Pastures of the Sky, they call it; but any oasis can seem so from a distance. The Sharai say that it's the generosity of their God, to guide them to water and good grazing.'

'Do they?'

'Well, that's what they tell their children. Maybe it's what most of them believe. If you can read the mind of a Sharai, then you explain it to me. I spoke to a man once who said the mirage was all to do with light and reflection and the heat, but I didn't understand him either.'

'You didn't understand him. Right . . .'

'Well, I can draw his diagrams for you, then you can explain that too. He was Sharai himself. Now watch, you're going to enjoy this.'

Did she enjoy it? She wasn't sure, that didn't seem quite the word. Elisande enjoyed it, no doubt of that – but Elisande again was watching her more than she watched the road or the sky.

She could hardly have seen, that moment when the air rippled and closed like a curtain, hiding the long stretch of the caravan ahead and blurring even the near figures of Rudel and Redmond to a single shifting silhouette; though even Elisande, even without looking, could hardly have missed that moment when the masking air shivered to a mirror. Briefly Julianne found herself staring at a smudged, wild image of herself, that hung perhaps an arm's length above the road, though it seemed to have a road of its own to ride on.

Whatever Merissa saw, with those large and wide-set eyes that could take in half the horizon at a glance, it must have been something other than herself. The horse snorted as though there really were some barrier drawn across the sand, something more real than the nonsense Julianne's eyes reported; but she didn't shy or startle, as she would have if she'd thought there were a sky-horse coming down to meet her, nose to nose.

She walked steadily forward and met that horse, nose to nose. Only when they touched did the image jar and vanish, like a reflection in water shattered by a stone.

And the curtain lifted, the air cleared, Julianne could see for miles ahead – and for miles ahead all she could see was green. The sky was sere blue again as it should have been all day; but where there had been yellow-white sand and the odd black lava outcrop all around them all day and nothing else to fix the eyes on, nor the mind, now there were trees and simple houses and more trees. There was pasture and cultivated land, and trees; and there were people moving among the houses, people and animals flowing this way and that through narrow alleys and wide avenues, and all the avenues were lined with trees.

Julianne chanced a glance behind, fearful of magic; at her back she saw the endless desert of the day, a vista of sand and occasional rock blurring too soon with the heat.

Here there was no blurring, and the heat was less too, she thought, though as yet they were only on the margin of Bar'ath Tazore and still a long way from any shade.

'Elisande? What happened there? Is there some kind of protection, that hides this place from those who mean it harm?' Some kind of priestly magic, she meant – though if there were, it should have hesitated long before it let them through. She thought that this little party carried harm very much within its shadow.

'No, none,' Elisande said with a chuckle. 'It's the mirage, love, that's all. The hand of God, or the hand of mystery that some men think they've solved. Unless it's desert magic, like the djinni. *I* don't know. It's desert charm, to me – and you're seeing some of it even before we reach the desert proper. That was the mirage, and this, Julianne, is an oasis. Forget that puddle where we camped last night . . .'

Julianne had forgotten it already, as she gulped at cool beauty with sore dry eyes, drinking and drinking.

The oasis lay in a broad shallow bowl below them, though she hadn't realised they'd been climbing a ridge to reach it; that might explain something of how it had been hidden till now, though not all. Certainly it explained how she could see so much of it at a glance, even the great pool at its heart like a gleaming jewel set in a cloth of green. The trees were date-palms and there must be thousands of them, to make such a canopy. On the far side of the water, she could see the roofs of one grand building rising up through their cover; she'd like a closer look at that, though she doubted that she'd have the chance.

The caravan they'd followed so far was moving on

already, but Rudel held his mount rock-steady, breaking that easy link. A sudden flight of birds drew Julianne's attention, the first she'd seen for weeks; it burst from the treetops, wheeled screaming above her head and then dived back out of sight. She turned her head to find Marron, standing away to one side as he always was. The older man was right in his stillness, he didn't need to speak; they couldn't risk taking that deadly boy into the busy traffic below.

Between the desert and the trees, around the rim of the bowl was a broad band of rock and gravel that made for easy riding. Rudel led them that way with a gesture, as though he meant to circle the oasis and strike straight out into the desert again. Not possible if they meant to go further, but at least he wanted that option, Julianne thought, if things should go badly here: a quick escape through the heat-curtain and away to rethink, retreat or reroute. They could go back to the wild country, or else they could go west and find their way into Outremer again. Skirt Elessi – *please?* – but come to Tallis or Less Arvon and so sneak south, perhaps even as far as fabled Surayon, accursed Surayon which was home to Rudel and to Elisande . . .

Not that things would go badly here, of course. Why should they? Travellers seeking to change horses for camels could hardly be unknown at this oasis; they ought to be its lifeblood. Any border trading-post subsists on what passes through, and the rich trade here must be from Outremer to Rhabat and back again. She had heard that Rhabat had links with tribes and peoples far further to the east, strange empires with stranger goods to bargain with; she knew that silks and ivory came that way to the courts of Outremer and Marasson.

So there ought to be no cause for Rudel's caution, but she applauded it anyway. After so long mewed up in the castle at the Roq, desperately trying to get away and being balked at every turn, she favoured open spaces and no walls. Redmond at least, she thought, must feel the same.

Whoever lived in the palace whose roofs she'd seen, whoever ruled Bar'ath Tazore favoured palm-tree walls to his territory. His people worked the land within the circle of trees, irrigating the soil with a complex system of dykes that must somehow draw its water up from the central pool.

Long ago, Julianne thought, when the lava of the plain had been boiling rock, it must have flowed all around this bowl and found no way inside. Its cooling had killed all the surrounding land but left this living, fertile but isolated, a tiny kingdom only waiting for its king.

Eventually they came to a spot where the trees seemed sick, their great leaves brown and drooping. The mud walls of the dykes beyond were broken, the channels dry; nothing grew in the land around.

There was a simple hut between the dykes, one of many that they'd passed. The others had all been occupied, people busy among their crops or tending goats or preparing a meal in the doorway of their home, all of them pausing to watch the riders through the shadows of the trees. Here, though, the hut door was cast down and they could see black shadows within, no signs of life.

Rudel called back, 'Wait,' and guided his horse between

the trees. He rode to the hut and called again, 'Hullo in there!'

When there was no answer, he dismounted and walked inside.

After a moment he reappeared in the doorway, beckoning.

The hut was as abandoned as the land it served. It seemed strange to Julianne, as to the others; where viable ground was so sparse and precious, even death or disgrace should simply have opened the way for another family to claim it.

But the hut was here, and unclaimed. 'We'll use this,' Rudel said flatly. 'There's no forage for the horses, but we've grain enough for tonight. Water we can fetch. The girls can sleep in the hut while we men stand guard outside, in turns. Marron must stay here, and Redmond too; the market will be too far for you to walk, old friend. The rest of us, though — if the girls will veil themselves, we can all go down and taste the life here, listen to the gossip and hope not to find ourselves the theme of it.'

'I will stay with Marron,' Jemel said, predictably.

'No. Please, Jemel, we may need you. There will be Sharai among the traders; they will deal fairly with you, but not with me in this garb,' with a gesture at the discreet plainstuff that he wore, 'and I had rather not declare my true name here.'

'I will stay with Marron.' Jemel's words again, but this time it was Elisande who spoke them. She was perhaps simply being convenient, helping the young Sharai to choose her father's way; more likely, Julianne thought, she preferred not to walk with her father.

Jemel hesitated, before nodding reluctantly.

*

It was a party of three, then, who left the hut and the horses and their friends, to find out the heart of Bar'ath Tazore. There were signs of a path, sun-cracked mud with a dusting of blown sand, running beside the dry water-course; that led them shortly to another line of palms, and beyond it a sudden change, almost a different world. Here the air was full of birdsong and goat-cries, the smells of moisture and growing; the irrigation channels ran with clean water; beside the narrow path the ground was green with crops.

This land too had its hut, well-kept and busy; children stood gaping by the wall. A man rose from among the crops, muddy to the knees before his robe fell down to cover them. He had mud on his hands too, and held them self-consciously at his sides as he strode forward.

'What are you seeking, strangers?' He spoke in Catari, of course, but he spoke it slowly, out of courtesy, and Julianne was only a beat behind his words in understanding.

'The best way forward,' Rudel said mildly. 'I regret walking on your land, but we are newly arrived here, and do not know where we are free to go and where not.'

'The land is the Sultan's,' the reply was brisk and corrective, 'and not my own. All land here is the Sultan's. Walk where you will. But the resting-place for travellers is on the further side of the oasis.'

'Is it? Ah. I did not know.' It seemed likely to Julianne that he was lying, she thought he must have been here before; but he did it wonderfully well, so that even she found it hard not to believe him.

'There you will be made welcome. Take the highway past the pool, anyone will show you . . .'

'We have come a long way, and our beasts are tired. We've settled them now; I think we'll not move on again today. Unless the Sultan would object to our staying where we are . . .?'

'The Sultan provides water and a roof for all travellers,' *in the proper place*, he was saying, *where they can be watched*. Julianne understood him very well. The Sultan would indeed object to their camping where they were, if he heard about it; and she was reasonably sure that he would, that a child would be running the news to the palace any minute now. 'Where else have you found, to halt?'

'Why, just here, through the trees,' Rudel told him, with an expansive wave. 'There was a hut that seemed abandoned, to give shade and shelter to our womenfolk; and space enough for men and horses, if you wouldn't mind our fetching in a little of your water . . .?'

But the man was backing off suddenly, taking hurried little steps that crushed his plants in their tidy rows. When he was five or six paces distant, he lifted his hands in a gesture of denial. 'Keep away! Keep away from me and mine . . .!'

'Well, if you wish it. Though we will still need water. What is the matter, have we profaned holy ground?'

'Diseased ground, infected ground! Touch nothing and no one, you are corrupt . . .'

He turned and hustled his watching family within the safety of their hut, leaving the door only a crack ajar so that wary eyes could follow what strangers did.

'Well. If we're corrupt, I suspect the Sultan would not welcome us in his caravanserai; and just as well, I think. We could neither leave Marron nor take him into company.

But if that land truly harbours disease . . . Jemel? What do you think?'

'I saw no sign of it. Nothing grows, but nothing has water. Even the palms are thirsty.'

'Mmm. We'll ask questions, I think, around the market-place; but no one speak of empty huts, until we know. There must be some reason why it was abandoned, the land and the trees left to die. No one wastes good land, where it lies so sparse . . .'

They had to cross another man's fields before they found a wider path, a wagon-road in a shaded aisle. That led in turn to a broad highway which ran straight as the spoke of a wheel, between fields and houses and directly to the pool that was the jewel of Bar'ath Tazore.

The nearer they approached the water, the more traffic they met and mixed with. No one asked questions of them now, no one seemed to look at them twice; certainly there were more interesting people for the old men squatting in doorways or the children playing in the narrow alleys to look at. There were men in rich dress on horseback or camelback, cursing and cracking whips to clear a way through the throng; there were servants in simple tunics, running errands or carrying sacks or dripping water-skins. There were black men in gorgeous robes, reminding Julianne of the slaves who'd borne her in the palanquin from Tallis, though these were surely free; there were men who might be slave or free who carried similar litters here, which perhaps hid girls like herself behind their concealing curtains. Other women walked as she did, some in swathes of black with only their eyes showing, some in gossamer veils and silks that clung like a shadowy second skin to the body beneath, teasing and revealing.

Some of the riders were Sharai in tribal robes, whose dark gaze found Jemel and then dismissed him, either for his own tribal allegiance or his companions, or both. He stiffened each time that happened, and his hand twitched towards his scimitar's hilt; each time, though, he fixed his eyes blindly ahead and strode on.

Once, passing a large house with an inner court, Julianne glanced in through the open gateway and stiffened momentarily herself, before hurrying on. She gripped Rudel's sleeve and whispered, 'You may think me mad, but I swear I saw Ransomers in there, Knights Ransomers . . .' Tall young men with light hair and sun-bronzed skins, at least, wearing white robes with black cloaks thrown over, and what else could they be . . .?

'Outremer trades with the Sharai, child,' he murmured, and she thought he was laughing at her, almost. 'How else would the lords of the Kingdom have their silks and salt and spices? They meet often on neutral ground, places such as this. Some of the lords are brazen, some are discreet; a great many come, or send their agents. They come warily, though, and often with an escort of knights. Not the brothers, they are not permitted to dabble their fingers so close to heresy; and not I think from Elessi, if that's your fear.'

That was the worst of her fears, to be seen and known; sought for, even, even here. She was reassured, but not completely. He added, 'The lords come, but not their women, Julianne; keep a hand on your veil, and be discreet with your eyes.' That gave her the excuse she needed. She walked closer in Rudel's shadow thereafter, and held her head lower, and wished that he would do the same. He came from a proscribed state, but still his face and beard had been seen widely throughout Outremer, in many guises; she dreaded a chance encounter that might carry news of her back to Elessi, and believed the God or fate or perhaps that damned djinni malign enough to allow it. Even to arrange it, perhaps . . .

The great pool at Bar'ath Tazore must presumably have been a natural occurrence, but men's hands had worked it extensively, so that now it was a broad, wide rectangle, as deep and dark as myth in the centre but shallow at its paved edges, and shadowed by the inevitable palms. At intervals, steps led down into the water; the water-carriers filled their skins there while naked children splashed and shrilled, while men in decent loin-cloths immersed themselves in a ritual cleansing. Further out, squads of small brown birds ripped the air with their shrieking and the water with their beaks, drinking aflight and then darting, twisting, diving after invisible insects.

All along the nearest side of the pool was a noisy marketplace. Gaudy awnings shielded rank after rank of stalls from the sun; other traders spread their goods on a carpet or on the bare sandy ground. Julianne saw sacks of maize and millet, tables laden with still-dripping meat or piled high with vegetables strange in both shape and colour; she saw jewellery and carved ivory, bolts of silk and bales of plainer cloth; in one distant corner, she saw near-naked people squatting disconsolately or standing to be bargained for like any other goods.

Mostly, though, she was still watching faces in the

crowds, watching for light-coloured eyes or sunburned skin, any sign of Outremer; and so it was she who first saw a small group of men gathered by the bole of a palm, men in robes such as the Sharai wore but that the robes were black rather than midnight blue. The men were silent, watchful; she met the intensity of one man's gaze, and shuddered.

Two of their number were squatted at the others' feet, seeming to play some simple game with stones; puzzled, she watched for a moment. Both set their stones left-handed, and there was something strange about those hands. It took a moment longer to register with her, but each man was missing the smallest finger from that hand.

Again, she tugged at Rudel's sleeve.

'Those men – what are they?'

He followed the nod of her head, saw them and turned swiftly away; Jemel was a little slower, and his eyes were wide and anxious as he hurried after.

'Who are they?' Julianne asked again.

Rudel said nothing; it was Jemel who told her, in his own language, and though she understood the words she still felt little wiser.

'They are Sand Dancers. Beware of them . . .'

2

Taking Rice

Even at his loneliest, at his most frightened and depressed, Marron had never felt so alone as he did these days.

Always at his back, two ghost-voices whispered against the wind from the desert, the wind of his running: Aldo and Sieur Anton, friend and master, boy and man. Both had invaded his heart, his life, his bed; and now Aldo was dead – by Marron's own hand, yet: literally by his hand flung up, by the bleeding wound on his arm – and Sieur Anton was betrayed. Marron ran from the dead and the living both, and could not escape them.

And though he ran in company, almost in the company of friends, he could not come close to any of them. Where they were riding, it was their animals that shied at his approach; where they walked or sat or lay down, they lacked that excuse, and still they shied. Not meaning to, not knowingly, but still. He saw it in the flinch of an eye before the smile followed; he heard it in their firm, deliberate voices when they spoke to him, how determined they were to sound warm and welcoming.

Only Jemel was different, and perhaps Elisande – and Marron shied himself from both of those, for different reasons.

And so found himself unbearably alone, even in company; felt himself in another world, almost, isolated from those who moved around him, shadow to their substance unless it was the other way about.

In ways, of course, that was true. He did walk with one foot in another world. His blood beat with a strange inhabitant. He dared not wake that creature, but when he ran its strength was added to his own, when he fenced its speed led his arm – and always, always he saw at least a little through its eyes, or else it infected his. He saw the world through a red haze, though he saw by night and day far more clearly than ever he had before.

Actually he was growing accustomed to that haze, as he was to the seemingly inexhaustible strength and the furious speed and the immunity to physical pain. His soul hurt exceedingly, but never his body now. These gifts were all of them borrowed, not owned; owed though, perhaps, a payment in kind for his carrying a passenger in his blood. When he looked at a thing he could see its true colour, his eyes had adapted that much. Sometimes he almost forgot that red cast, he had become so used to it.

What he never could forget was what other people saw, whenever they looked at him. They saw the unnatural redness of his eyes, and even after weeks of it his companions had not learned to hide the disquiet that they felt.

*

As now, as Elisande came over to where he stood among the slow-dying palms, gazing back across the many miles that they'd covered: gazing north and west, towards the castle where he'd left Aldo dead and Sieur Anton abandoned, along with love and duty.

He didn't turn his head, he didn't consciously turn even his mind towards her, but he knew that she was coming. Almost before she did, perhaps; certainly as soon as she started to move his way. His hearing was as much sharper as his eyesight now. Only his mind was fogged and grieving, doubtful and distressed and not really able to remember why he was here, even, where or how this had started, which step it was that had set him on an inevitable pathway to destruction . . .

Destroyed was how he felt, despite his new-come powers; he was still Marron, and Marron had lost everything he valued, and was trapped now in a body he could not own and on a course he wanted neither to follow nor to leave.

He might have left regardless, although he knew nowhere else to go; he might have left days ago, weeks ago, if it weren't for Jemel and Elisande.

Jemel had gone away for a rarity, which made things easier, which made things harder; in the absence of that boy's watchfulness, here came Elisande, with her own.

With things also, for excuse; with water-skin and bread, with bowl and cloth.

'Marron, here. A long dry day for you, I brought you water . . .'

He tried to say thank you for memory's sake, for manners, and could not. Realised that she was right, his throat was too parched for speech; and took the skin and drank, and tried again.

'Thank you, Elisande.'

She shrugged awkwardly. 'You're stupid, you forget if someone doesn't tell you; and that Jemel's gone off, so . . . Will you eat? If I tell you to?'

He did think about it for a moment, before he shook his head. 'No. I don't need to.'

'You mean you're not hungry. That's not the same thing. You weren't thirsty either, were you? But you needed water. And you need food too, you were always scrawny but you're all bone now . . .'

'I'll eat when Jemel eats,' which meant at dawn and sunset, and scantily. Once he'd loved to eat, but now it was only a chore, chew and swallow with no savour.

'He's as bad as you are. It's a conspiracy of boys. I'll break you both, eventually – if you don't break yourselves first. If you'd eat more, then so would he – and he needs to, even if you don't. For his sake, Marron, you could make the effort. Well,' taking the water-skin back and pouring into the bowl, moistening the cloth, 'you'll let me bathe your arm, at least, and have a look at it. I know Jemel won't do that.'

'There's no point, it doesn't change.' Not even Redmond or Rudel could change it now, they'd both tried and they'd tried both together, though they'd said all along that it was hopeless. Elisande had tried and tried.

'I know,' she sighed, 'but show me anyway.'

Like a ragged range of hills Marron thought his wound was now, if ever hills had been so brutal: thrusts and folds of scar tissue ripping across the smooth skin of his forearm where it had been slashed and torn and let half heal before it was torn again.

And torn a final time, and this time there would be no healing. Like a chasm sundering a range of hills, an open mouth of raw flesh cut through the scarring, fresh and glistening wet. It did not bleed, it could not hurt, but neither could it mend. New leather stitches were knotted through it to draw the lips together, to close it somewhat against filth and infection; those had not hurt either, but neither could they help. Marron had told Rudel so, he and Jemel together; the older man had grunted, had said, 'I know,' and had sewn the stitches regardless.

Each evening Elisande brought water to bathe the wound, and there was no purpose to that either, but he bore it patiently. For her sake, for her deep regret that was so clear and unscarred by the others' darker emotions: Julianne's fear of him, Rudel's distrust, Redmond's almost-envy. What Jemel felt, Marron was uncertain; he knew only that it was darker yet, and hungry.

Cool water washed across his arm, carrying away little particles of sand and grit that had lodged within the wound. It could have been soothing, if he could have been soothed by any service so small and meaningless. Cool fingers held firmly to his wrist; uncool eyes, dark and fiery eyes lifted to seek his face, hesitated, and then were distracted. Were almost glad, he thought, to find some other interest.

'What's this?' She reached with her other hand, the one that still held the cloth; he felt it touch his neck.

'I don't know. What?'

'There's a bruise . . .'

'Oh. Yes. A child threw a stone, I didn't see it . . .' He had already turned away, after straying too close to the tribe's small herd of goats. They had scattered in terror, and so had the children who drove them. One had been brave with a slingshot; he'd heard the buzz of the stone in the air, but understood too late to do more than twist so that it struck his neck and not his temple. It hadn't hurt.

'You should be careful,' Elisande said anxiously. 'If it had cut . . .'

If it had cut, the Daughter would have flowed out of him with his blood, a red mist, lethal in his anger; but he had not been angry, so the child would have been safe. What matter?

He said all of that, patiently. Elisande was still fretful, though. 'Would it have healed, after?'

'I think so, yes.' If he had nicked his arm again, to take the Daughter back. The open wound on his arm was the Daughter's gateway, in and out, sealed to that purpose. It might escape through any break in his skin, any window to the world, but there was no need to let it back in the same way.

The cloth dropped, to lie wetly on the shoulder of his tunic; it was her hand now that lay against his neck.

'You make an interesting companion,' she murmured, trying to be teasing and falling short by a distance, her voice betraying her, 'but – oh, I do miss Marron . . .'

'I'm still Marron,' though none of them would believe him if she did not.

'You look like Marron,' she allowed, and he could feel the effort she made to stay light, not to break completely.

'And you talk like Marron too, sometimes, when I can get you to talk at all. Though you don't say the right things any more. But the old Marron used to fall asleep after a glass of wine and you don't, you hardly seem to sleep at all; and the old Marron would never have let me do this,' and her fingers stroked his cheek, deliberately sensuous, 'without the blood rising until he'd blushed himself to death. And you just sit there now and look at me, and don't react at all . . .'

That wasn't true, only that his reactions didn't show in his face any more. 'Something else has charge of my blood now, Elisande.'

'I know, I know. And – oh, Marron, I'm so sorry . . .'

He knew that, she'd told him time and again. That it was in no sense her fault, she knew. He might have blamed himself – or she might have blamed him, volubly, viciously – except that it had been no choice of his either, he hadn't known in the least what he was doing.

And so they were stranded here, nowhere further to go; and so they stood as silent as they always did, until she sniffed and tossed her head and took the bowl and left him.

Left him with the water-skin, half full still. Slowly, thoughtfully, he lifted it to his mouth and drank again.

When the others came back from the marketplace, Julianne was carrying a brace of black-feathered chickens and a bag of other purchases while Rudel and Jemel struggled with sacks of fresh and dried produce, as much as they could carry on one trip. They brought news too, as much perhaps as they could glean on one trip, more perhaps than any of them had wanted to hear.

'Sickness and miracles,' Rudel said wearily, slumping to the ground as though the weight of the tale he bore had exhausted him. 'That's all they want to talk about. Redmond, old friend, try if you can to make sense of this, for I cannot. People fell sick and silent, they say, dozens of them, with a dreadful wasting disease. The old and the weak turned their faces to the wall and died, and it seemed that the hale would follow them; there was no remedy that anyone could find. Until a holy man came out of Outremer, they say, a wild priest with the mummified hand of a saint in his possession. He preached the God in the market here, and the Sultan would have sent him forth or silenced him, I think, he has done that before; except that this holy man touched those who were sick with his saint's hand, and they were made well again. Others came to him with other ills, those lame or blind from birth, and those too he cured. He left here a fortnight since, and in his train he took all those his hand had touched. They followed him like slaves, it's said, with all their households too. We must just have missed this circus on the road. Have you ever heard the like?'

Redmond breathed once, in and out; and said, 'No. If it had been one man healed, in another place and time, I might have thought about the Daughter,' as he thought about himself, as Marron guessed, and what the Daughter might have done for him: *if any of us had to bear that thing*, Marron suspected was the constant burden of the old man's thoughts, *it should have been me . . .* 'But as things stand, here and now – no, I have no answers for you.'

'No. Well. The Sultan has declared them all apostate, who followed the miracle-worker; he says it was the work of devils, to deceive the faithful. He may be right, I cannot say. The people watch their health, and pray, and avoid the houses of those who were sick. They want their priests to purify them; their priests are as afraid as they are. Which is why we can rest here undisturbed, though our neighbours may spit at our shadows.'

'Will they share their water with us?' Elisande demanded, practical as ever, awkward as ever in any exchange with her father. 'We cannot drink their spit.'

'I think we can take an allowance of water; they wouldn't pollute themselves to prevent it. If our doing so pollutes the water in their eyes – well, it's their problem and not our own.'

'Unless they fetch out dogs to drive us off,' Julianne suggested.

'What, and kill the beasts afterwards, for fear their bites may bring corruption back? I doubt it. No, we'll be shunned, no worse than that. And Jemel and I both doubt there's any true sickness here, that we might catch. I think you can rest easy in that hut, if not quite comfortably.'

Jemel stirred, but didn't speak; they all knew what he would have said, that the hut was luxurious quarters next to what awaited them in the desert. Better than half the company had travelled that desert already, and knew the truth of it; Julianne would learn; Marron didn't care.

Marron was keeping his usual distance from the group, listening but saying nothing, little concerned by talk of disease. If it were true, it still couldn't touch him; the Daughter wouldn't allow it. And if it did, still he wouldn't care. His life was not his own. Sworn to Sieur Anton and forsworn shortly after, possessed now by magic, it would be no loss to him if he did die. Two, perhaps three of his companions would mourn him, he thought. No more than that, no one else in the world. Rudel certainly would be relieved; perhaps the whole world ought to be.

Elisande built and lit a fire by the doorway of the hut, fetched pots from their baggage, set Julianne to plucking the chickens and sent Jemel for water. He went unprotesting, with only one backward glance at Marron. When he was gone, Elisande produced a meaningful glance of her own. Marron made a gesture, *all right, I will eat. For his sake*, or for hers.

It might have been for his sake and Jemel's that she fussed so over her cooking, jointing the fowls and slicing vegetables, rummaging in Julianne's bag for salt and spices; it might equally have been to show her father what she could do, or else simply because she was weary of desert food.

Whatever the cause, she produced a savoury stew, serving it in wooden bowls as the sun set, with fresh bread warmed at the fire's edge. Marron sat and ate with Jemel, matching the young Sharai mouthful for mouthful. That much was duty; it was something more – perhaps only an appetite unexpectedly rediscovered, but he thought something even more than that – that had him standing, taking both his bowl and Jemel's back to the fire to be refilled. Elisande gave him a glad smile, to season the food the better. Jemel didn't smile, but he did accept the second helping, and before he ate it he did tap the rim of his bowl against Marron's in token of thanks or again perhaps something more.

And he didn't do as he usually did, he didn't murmur his

dead lover's name over the food like a blessing or a vow renewed, a promise kept. Marron thought that was progress, an improvement, a definite step taken towards a private peace; he thought Elisande would have been pleased to hear of it, though nobody would tell her.

The stew was delicious, he thought, sucking at a chicken bone before tossing it neatly into the fire. At his side, Jemel did the same; their eyes caught, and this time Jemel did smile briefly.

Rudel was determined that they should move on the following day. They would need to return to the market, he said, to buy more essential provisions; they would need to take the horses to the livestock market on the far side of the oasis, to sell them and find camels fit to tackle the *mul'abarta*. Six beasts to ride, and two more to act as pack animals initially, but also to keep in reserve against disaster. Disaster was inevitable, he said, in the high desert. They couldn't hope to come through it without loss; if they lost no more than a camel or two, they'd be lucky.

Jemel twitched, and made a soft noise in his throat; Marron glanced sideways at him, thinking that the Sharai would once again be dwelling on his own loss, his love-sworn partner Jazra who had died on the wall at the Roq.

Had died at Sieur Anton's hand, with Marron just a further pace away; had died with Elisande's knife in his side also, and though it was the knight's sword that had slain him, that other slim blade was guilty too, as was the hand that had thrown it.

No one had said as much to Jemel, of course; no one had spoken of it at all, or not directly. None of them was stupid enough to cut loose the bindings on that particular fury. But he must know some of the story at least, he must have seen Marron fighting beside his master on the wall; he might already have put a name to the knight who killed Jazra.

There was no sullen louring in his eyes now, though, no dark thoughts imprinted on his face; he was gazing at Marron with a fierce determination. His hand left his side and touched against Marron's for a moment, knuckle to knuckle; it felt like a promise, an oath heard and witnessed, *whatever we may lose in the desert, Ghost Walker, I will not lose you.*

Or was Marron misreading? He'd assumed that the message was for him as Ghost Walker, that figure of myth and magic, rather than for him as fleshbound boy and journey's companion; of a sudden, as Jemel turned his head sharply away, he wasn't sure any more.

But that made only one more question, one more doubt to lie unresolved among the many others in his head. Marron was becoming used to those. Ever since his coming to the Sanctuary Land, certainties had been stolen or worn away, confusion had fed and flourished. Now he believed in nothing, trusted nothing: not his own strength nor his strength of will, not the oaths nor intentions of those he ran with, not the God of his own people nor the God of the Sharai. If he could have done it, he would have doubted the ground beneath his feet and the sky above, the sun's rising and the mirror of the moon.

Even in the dense dark that surrounded the circle of firelight, though, and even with the horses' shuffling and the murmur of voices and the cries of distant birds, he had to trust his eyes and his ears both. An alteration in the noises of the night alerted him; he lifted his head and stared east and west, north and south.

'What is it, Marron?' Redmond asked, the first to notice.

'Men. Moving silently, two at each quarter . . .'

Rudel cursed and rose slowly to his feet, his hand on his belt-knife. 'If they're moving silently, how do you hear them?'

'Their bones creak. But I can see them too,' crimson shadows in a starlit haze; the red cast to his sight seemed to shine more clearly in the night, as his eyes did. 'Shall I point them out?'

'No, don't do that. They'll announce themselves, I'm sure. Keep your weapon in its sheath, Jemel. We don't want a fight, if we can avoid it.' Rudel folded his arms deliberately.

They were all standing now, Julianne stooping to help Redmond to his feet; it was inevitably Elisande's voice that murmured, 'I thought you said we would be left undisturbed here?'

'I thought we would be. I was wrong. Be quiet.'

They waited, in a growing tension; at last, 'One is coming forward,' Marron muttered. 'From the west there . . .'

From between the palms, a figure approached: a tall man in flowing robes and turban, with a sword undrawn at his belt and his hands spread wide in sign of peace even before the firelight had touched him. Marron lowered his head, not to let his eyes betray the passenger he carried.

'Greetings,' the man said softly. 'I am Raben ib' Taraffi, and I have the honour to be chamberlain at the palace here. It is the Sultan's express wish that you should take your rice with him tonight.'

It was a command, barely veiled as an invitation; Rudel nodded slowly. 'Your master is most gracious. Is it his custom to offer hospitality to all travellers who pause here at his waterhole? Or to send his own chamberlain in person, to extend it?'

'No, it is not. Will you come now? You need not concern yourselves with your beasts or your baggage; my men will attend to all.'

His men had stepped up out of the shadows now, forming almost a circle about them, armed and silent. The chamberlain made an elegant, sweeping gesture, *will you walk?*

Rudel said, 'No lights? One of us is old, and others may be nervous in the dark, in a place strange to them . . .'

'Not strange to you, I think; though you have perhaps forgotten our ways? We do not carry torches, in Bar'ath Tazore. It is an order of the Sultan; we may not rival the stars. They give us light enough. Your friends should find it so, once the fire has died from their eyes. Till then, those with younger sight could offer an arm for guidance . . .?'

Marron needed no torch to see by, the stars were a glory. In fact, all the party seemed to see well enough; and Rudel, he thought, forgot nothing of others' customs. The older man had been bargaining, he thought, or making a point, trying to make them all out as strangers here. If so, he had missed his mark. Julianne perhaps was nervous, as he'd suggested; she busied herself with helping Redmond, though, and it was not for Marron to speculate which of those two offered more support to the other.

The chamberlain walked ahead with two of his men,

two more walked behind. They could be an honour guard, in form at least; Marron determined to think so.

Jemel strode watchfully at his side. Marron murmured, 'We have eaten already; the Sultan's invitation comes late. Must we eat again?' If so it would help Elisande, he supposed, in her campaign to force food into them.

Astonishingly, Jemel chuckled. 'A little, yes. Taking rice is a Sharai custom, it means more than it says. We may feast with our sheikhs or other lords, but we go back to our tents to eat rice with our own kin before we sleep. To take rice with a stranger is to accept his protection, his hospitality for that night. The Sultan means that we must sleep within the walls of his palace.'

Well, that would mean greater comfort in one sense at least, though greater cause for concern also. Julianne would be glad of a bed, he thought, and Redmond also.

Unless the Sultan's hospitality meant the Sultan's cells, or worse. It would be hard to keep his eyes hidden, even if the palace were kept as dark as the streets. He said, 'Who is he, then, this Sultan? What do you know of him?'

'You should ask Rudel, I know little. Only that his family was of the Sharai, which tribe I have not heard; but they came to this place many generations since, and settled here. And built houses and took taxes from the traders, and they planted palms, they call him the date-king now . . .' Which made the Sultan no longer Sharai, so much was clear from the contempt in his voice. Marron wasn't clear whether it was the settling, the building, the taxing or the planting which was the worst offence. He only hoped that Jemel would govern his scorn, anywhere they could be overheard.

He wanted to know more, what kind of man the Sultan was, how he was likely to treat reluctant guests, whether he might delay or forbid their journey. Jemel was right, he should ask Rudel; that man had evidently been here before, though it was evident too that he hadn't expected to be recognised.

Rudel was walking almost in the star-shadow of their guards, though, almost on the chamberlain's heels: making a point again, Marron guessed. This was no time to be asking him questions. Elisande might know more than Jemel, but she was laggard, dawdling behind Julianne and Redmond, going so slowly that the guards who followed her were stumbling over their own feet as they tried to match her pace. They were frustrated, silently furious, barely holding themselves back from shoving her forward; she was normally so brisk, she must be making a point of her own. These were dangerous games, Marron thought, but he would not interfere.

The wide avenues were quiet now; lights burned in the houses, sometimes a wash of laughter or loud voices leaked out, but there was no movement beyond the flight of bats and night-birds, clouds of insects, the occasional giant moth. Perhaps there was a curfew after dark; perhaps the people simply preferred their bright-lit homes to the dark of the streets. There might be thieves about or worse, to supply another reason for this armed guard.

Marron didn't believe it, though. All his stretched senses could find no human presence lurking in the shadows; if it was fear that kept the people withindoors, it was not fear of robbery or assault. Fear of the Sultan was his better guess.

*

They passed the vast pool, the heart of the oasis. Its waters were still and restful, reflecting the patterns of the stars in crystal, clouded only by stirring masses of tiny nightflies and disturbed only when a great fish rose from the dark centre of the water to gulp at something on the surface. The marketplace alongside was quite deserted: empty stalls and folded awnings, not even a few bruised leaves or a scatter of nut-husks left on the stone flags, not a smear of wine or oil spilled. Such tidiness was unnatural, Marron thought, remembering the markets of his childhood where men lingered late, long after the light was gone, and no one swept or scrubbed until the following day. There were always pickings to be found on the ground for beggars.

But there were no beggars here either. That was strange, too. He wondered again what kind of man the Sultan must be, to rule his territory so strictly.

From the pool, all roads led upward. The way they took was another broad avenue, lined with the inevitable palms. There were large houses on either side, but it was the palace ahead that drew the eye now.

A wide blank wall closed off the further end of the avenue. There was only one narrow gate that he could see, and that was guarded. Beyond the wall, beyond a fringe of trees, lights burned in many windows; there seemed to be several buildings within the complex, rising two or three storeys to steep tiled roofs.

The chamberlain took them to the gate; the guards there swung it open without a word, and stepped back to let them pass through.

They stepped from a dry, chill, bright-lit desert night

into a garden. Heavy, damp foliage brushed at Marron's arm; overhead, a tangle of low-hanging branches blotted out the sky. The air was thick with competing scents, scarred by the jagged cries of insects, soothed with bird-song.

The path under Marron's boots was a little slippery with mud. He wondered vaguely if this were magic, if he'd stepped into another world through that misleading gate. Rudel ahead of him was blundering a little, with the loss of light; Jemel took Marron's arm, his good right arm, with a fingertip touch.

'What is this place?' he asked, in a hissing whisper. 'I can see nothing . . .'

'It's just a garden,' Marron murmured. 'The trees hide the stars, that's all. There's light ahead . . .'

There was, although the path took a twisting way to find it. The chamberlain and his guards clearly knew every turn, and Marron could see well enough, but his compan-ions were all but blind, fumbling and shuffling. Julianne took a grip on his tunic from behind, while she kept her other arm linked with Redmond's, so that he was guide to three until they reached the light.

For a moment, Marron thought that too might be magic, the moon ensnared in water; but it was man's work, no more than that. A creamy, perfect globe of glass was set on a plinth above a pond; inside the globe an oil-lamp burned, and the water shimmered under the weight of the globe's reflection.

Beyond the globe was a walled terrace; beyond the ter-race, the palace waited.

*

They waited too, for lingering Elisande and her train of guards. A boy came past them, carrying a bucket and a scoop; as Marron watched, he took a dip of water and sprayed it into the foliage with a practised flick of the wrist. None of this was magic, then, it was only wealth. Great wealth, deliberately exploited to make a different world within the Sultan's walls. Once more, what kind of man . . .?

Elisande joined them at last, playing with plucked fronds between her fingers. The chamberlain made a gentle gesture, *shall we proceed?* She made a lavish gesture in return, *by all means*, and scattered what she carried across the terrace at her feet.

As the chamberlain led them forward, Marron saw another boy scurry and stoop to retrieve each shredded frond.

There were many windows to the buildings that made the palace, but they were high and narrow, and barred with elaborate iron traceries. There seemed to be no doors. Marron remembered the narrow, guarded gate in the outer wall, and thought, *this Sultan is a cautious man, and comes of a cautious family*. With reason, though, most likely; Bar'ath Tazore was a jewel beyond price, and must have been the target of many an acquisitive eye. Even the nature of its value made it vulnerable. Not water alone had made this place so rich, but its situation, a crossing-point between two cultures. Without constant caravans, the passage of many men with goods to trade, it would be all but worthless; every man who came was a potential threat.

Which was presumably why they had been summoned here, to be examined. Though why a small party of men and girls should be judged such a risk, Marron couldn't guess. Even if Rudel had been seen and known, there was little in that. A wandering prince he might be, but by his own assertion he came from a peaceable princedom. His own people might not accept that, but the Sharai surely did . . .

Not Rudel was the danger, then. Marron reminded himself once more to keep his head low, and hope.

There was an inner court, faced by all the buildings in the complex; all the doors were here, where they and their guards could watch each other. One was opened at the chamberlain's approach; the men who walked with him stepped back to either side. He walked within, and Rudel followed. Jemel's finger-touch urged Marron forward: his turn to act as guide now, with Marron's eyes so firmly fixed on his feet. He seemed to know it.

The Sultan might allow no torches in his dark streets, but the corridors of his palace were ablaze with light. Even the floor was dazzling, a gorgeous mosaic of many-coloured stone chips that glittered and seemed almost to spark as the chamberlain's robes swept across them. Briefly, Marron worried about the condition of his boots, whether he might be leaving muddy tracks. Then he remembered that he had more and far more to worry about; then he remembered the boy in the garden, whose only apparent role was to rush and tidy. There were sure to be others in the house. Perhaps if he looked back he'd see one at work already, down on his knees with water and cloth . . .

He didn't look back. Didn't look anywhere but down, relied on Rudel's heels and Jemel's touch to keep him walking straight.

He breathed through his nose, using scents as substitute for what his eyes were missing. The air had been moist and exotic in the garden, heady with too much perfume; in here it was easier, drier and spicier, less overladen. Someone had been burning incense, someone had brought cut flowers and boughs indoors. Closer, fresher, someone was nervous: he could smell sweat cutting through an aromatic bodywash that might have been meant to disguise it. Not Julianne: she was nervous, but she was also behind him and he was walking into this air, this information. Besides, when did she last have a chance to wash in perfumed water?

It must be the chamberlain, ib' Taraffi sweating cold this close to his master; and again, what kind of master could rouse so much fear in his most favoured servant, this mature and cultured and elegant man . . .?

Marron's ears were also busy, sorting and sifting. He heard the distant sounds of many people, guards and servants and slaves at their many duties. More closely he heard a strange music, drum and flute, only that the flute wailed almost like a human voice under its incurable weight of sorrow.

The feet that Marron followed slowed, and turned; Jemel's hand on his elbow urged him to do the same.

Now the floor was tiled in blue and white, in intricate patterning; it was hard not to lift his head, not to see how far it stretched away ahead and to either side. All his other senses were telling him how vast this space was that they had entered, but still he wanted his eyes to say it for certain.

Not only broad, but high also; a hand-clap sang like a bell. The music stilled, and hurried, barefoot steps set up a whisper that took a long time to subside. The sounds of their own boots rang and echoed back like drumbeats all out of rhythm with themselves.

He could smell sweat here too, the sweat of a hard dance interrupted; but more, the sweat of fear again. There were perhaps two dozen bodies in this massive chamber, and most of them were fearful.

There might be a reason for that: he could smell blood also. And roasted meats, and cold meats, and breads and fruits and herbal drinks; but the blood had been recently spilled, and he didn't think it was animal. He felt the Daughter react to the tang of it, stirring within his own blood, and was certain.

The chamberlain brought them to the foot of a dais, over-hung with carpets; it was high enough to make an awkward step up for the girls, but that they were not invited to take the step. They were arrayed, rather, stood in line two paces short, where they could be well looked over.

There were men on the dais, and men standing to either side; further off men and women mixed, Marron's nose – or the Daughter's use of his nose – could tell so much. Those were the musicians and dancers, and oddly, they were not afraid. All the fear was closer set about him, among the robes and perfumes of this rich court.

Ib' Taraffi dropped to his knees; Rudel emphatically did not, so neither did the others.

'Excellence, I have brought—'

'So I see.' The voice that interrupted him was high and cool; Marron shivered at its touch. 'A Sharai' – Jemel stiffened; Marron's turn to touch his sleeve, to warn him, *keep your temper, temper your pride in this place* – 'and a full hand of the Patric. An odd company, where none of them has any goods to trade. Nor even decent clothing, it would seem – except the Sharai boy, of course, and he is Saren. Rudel, how does your father?'

'Well enough, excellence, I thank you for asking. When last I saw him, he was well enough. For a man whose age has softened his skull, I hear.'

There was a smile in the Sultan's answer – a thin smile, Marron suspected though he did not look to see, a thin smile from a thin and dangerous man. 'Did I say that? Well, well. He has charge of a soft country, perhaps he can afford to be so. Some cannot.'

'These times are not soft for anyone, excellence.'

'No. Perhaps not. When last we saw you, Rudel, you wore other dress in other company, and paid me the honour of a visit uninvited. Today it seems you prefer to travel in disguise through my territory, and camp in plaguespots, and keep me from meeting your friends. How is it that I have so offended you?'

'Excellence, the offence is all mine, and I ask your pardon for it. Our mission is secret, and urgent; I chose not to impose on your hospitality, for fear that the comforts of your palace and the pleasures of your company delay us. You have forestalled our intent; I wish I could regret that, but . . .'

'Well. The silver in the beard is new; the silver on the tongue, I see, is as smooth as ever. We will talk, and I hope you will not offer me any reason to delay you beyond this one night. First, though, you must name your companions to me. I am intrigued.'

'A duty can be a privilege, excellence – but do you not recognise Redmond? He too has passed this way before, and tasted your generosity.'

'Indeed, though he was in better health that time, if I remember. Your pardon, Redmond – my eyes were distracted by the beauty of your handmaid.'

'More by the shadows of my age, I think, excellence,' Redmond said, with a soft chuckle. 'Though she is beautiful behind her veil, and not alas my handmaid. This child is Julianne de Rance, daughter of the King's Shadow.'

'Lady, a delight to offer you welcome here. Your father of course I know; I had never hoped to see his daughter grace my house.'

'Excellence, you are courtesy itself, but you know the delight is all my own. To be ushered from a hard bed to such a gracious house is a kindness quite unlooked-for.' Her voice was tight, but her words matched these careful, neutral, meaningless manners exactly; Marron hoped she could sense the others' approval, and his also. 'Nor am I the only daughter you should greet tonight; here is Elisande, who is Rudel's own child.'

That, Marron thought, was wicked; but it served the trick. More effusive expressions of welcome, delivered crisply; more self-effacing rebuttals, in a tone that carried only a hint of Elisande's normally needle-sharp tongue.

'Father and daughter ride together, how charming. And the Surayonnaise, of course, are famously friendly with the Sharai.'

'That is true.' Rudel's voice once more. 'This is Jemel, of the Saren as you have observed; he is our guide, as well as our companion.'

'A guide, is it? You used not to need a guide, Rudel.'

'Times change; the wise man takes assistance where he may find it.'

'Truly. Jemel of what family?'

'I am of no family now, excellence,' Jemel said shortly.

'Ah. You are Saren, of course. Which leaves us only with the shy boy at your side . . .?'

Again, Rudel stepped in. 'His name is Marron. He was once a brother of the Ransomers, but he has fled them; he travels under my protection now.'

'And stands under mine, for so long as he stands within my house. But I will entertain no guest who has not looked me once directly in the eye . . .'

A rustle of silken robes, a bulky figure moving in the periphery of Marron's vision, stepping lightly down from the dais, coming to stand before him. No possible escape. A big, pudgy hand rising, heavy rings on every finger; those fingers strong beneath his chin, forcing his head up, not to be denied. Those fingers also smelled of blood; Marron wanted to wrench his head away, and did not.

A fat face trimly bearded under a jewelled turban, and everything about this man belied his slender voice. His dark eyes widened momentarily, as they met Marron's; then he breathed out slowly, and stepped back.

'Yes. I see why such a boy would flee the Ransomers. We must talk of this, Rudel, and also of your mission. But first, Redmond is exhausted, and in pain; all of you are dirty, and should rest. And yet I insist that you take rice with me, it is my custom and I will not break it for any friendship, old or new. How shall we resolve this? In a manner satisfactory to none, alas; such is the way of the world. However I choose, I must deny myself and insult you. But let us part for a little hour, too long for me and too brief for you; let my doctors attend Redmond and my slaves you all. Wash, bathe if you will, seek what comforts my poor house can offer; but then return, I beg you, and we will eat a little and talk at least a little more than that.'

Marron thought that Rudel might object, on the girls' behalf at least if not his own, although the Sultan clearly meant to keep him all night talking. They really had no choice, though, and Rudel only bowed a silent acquiescence as barefoot attendants in pure white gowns and turbans beckoned them away. One took Redmond's arm, displacing Julianne; neither made any demur.

Although he was gazing about him freely now, drinking in the decorated walls of the palace, the bowls of cut blooms and the pots of greenery, Marron didn't see where Redmond was taken, only that the old man was suddenly gone from the company. The rest of them were led to a suite of interconnected rooms, luxuriously furnished with couches and tables and beds; from a doorway at the far end, steam was leaking.

Julianne collapsed with a groan, stretching out full-length on a bed; Elisande touched her shoulder, laughing.

'Go away, let me sleep . . .'

'No, sweet, not yet. You heard the man. Up you come, and let me help you off with that scratchy stuff. Look, there's a hammam, concentrate on being warm and clean;

and see, here comes a girl with fresh clothes, we can dress up after. *After* we have bathed . . .'

Briefly, Marron thought she meant to strip Julianne there and then; but a procession of slaves had followed them, and with Elisande's assistance two women soon had the other girl on her feet again, and were ushering them both through into the steam.

One of the male attendants made a gesture, inviting the men of the party to follow. Rudel laughed shortly.

'No, we'll let the ladies have their privacy, thank you. If you could bring us bowls of water, we'll wash out here. And change our clothing, gladly . . .'

Marron had too many questions burning in his head, and there were too many of the Sultan's slaves too close, he dared not risk being overheard. One of those questions should be safe, though; he shared a great copper bowl of scalding water with Jemel, and as they splashed he hissed, 'Why did he call us Patric, what does that mean?'

'It is the Sharai word for your people. I think it is because you call your God your father, is that right?'

Right it was when they prayed in the old tongue, as they always did; and 'Pater' to 'Patric' was not so far a leap. Marron grunted, and cast about for a towel. One was handed to him, by an elderly man – a man with blue eyes below his turban, and a skin that must once have been pale beneath its age-old tan.

'I have not prayed to the God for many years,' the man murmured, 'it is forbidden to us, and the Sultan is my father now; but yes, they call us Patric for that reason. Should I summon a doctor, lad, to look at that hurt on your arm?'

Marron blinked, to be sure the man had seen his eyes. When there was no reaction, only a patient waiting for an answer, he said, 'No. Thank you, but it does not hurt.' *Except my soul, and that is beyond the reach of any doctor . . .*

The man bowed, and stepped away; Marron reminded himself again not to ask any question where the answer might be important, if the Sultan's slaves were the Sultan's children. Good children always carried news to their father, and no language that he knew could be secret here.

When they had washed, they dressed in cool, shimmering gowns that felt slippery against the skin, after the rough stuff they had worn before. For Jemel, who would have refused any dress else, there was a new Sharai robe which he could tie in his tribal style. Their old clothes were borne away; the neutral expressions on the faces of the men who took them suggested that they might be bound for a furnace. Marron tried to regret that, and could not. He owned little enough – and less that he valued, the sword Dard and a good knife, no more than those, and he hoped never to use either one of them again – but he would happily see the number of his possessions reduced further, if it meant not having to wear those clothes again. Even if it meant that they were dangerously beholden to the Sultan: what's given can be taken away, and a naked man is half a prisoner already, but Marron would run naked and grateful not to have to hide again, either his white skin or his burning eyes.

While they waited for the girls to join them, they sat on couches and sipped at beakers of crushed iced fruit. And it wasn't a question, it was a flat statement and any listening slave must know it already, and his companions he thought would need to; and so Marron said, 'The Sultan has blood on his hands.'

'Show me any leader of men in these days who has not,' Rudel countered.

'I mean new blood, I mean that he has killed today. Himself, not his executioner; and with his hands, I think, no weapon else. He had scrubbed his fingers with rose-water, but I could scent it still. And all the lords of his court are afraid of him, but his slaves are not . . .'

'Ah. Yes. The Sultan is a singular man, and he keeps a singular grip upon his people. It's no secret,' with a nod towards Marron's caution, 'that he doesn't keep an execu-tioner; when he feels that a death is needed, he sees to it himself, and where it will have the most effect. If one of his lords had offended him, the whole court would have watched that man die; but I don't believe that he would kill a slave.'

'What of the people outside the palace?' Jemel asked. 'They are not Sharai, but they are said to have that blood, or to claim it. And yet they are all in their houses by sunset, the doors are closed, the marketplace is abandoned . . . Where are the fires, the songs, the tales? Where are the young men dancing?'

'I don't know,' Rudel admitted. 'They did dance, when I was here last; though that was long ago. Perhaps the Sultan grew displeased with it. His people obey him in the least particular, or he casts them out.'

'And will he cast us out also?' Julianne demanded as she and Elisande came through, swathed and veiled in folds of falling silk.

'That I do not know, my lady,' Rudel said, rising and bowing to her, teasing gently without mockery. His daughter as usual he ignored. 'He might forbid us to go further, if he feels there is danger in it for him and his.'

'Has he the authority to do that?'

'Within Bar'ath Tazore, he is master; well, you have seen that. Beyond the lip, then no, he has no authority at all; but his word here denies us camels, denies us food and water for the trip. He could deny us freedom too, and he might yet do that; he could imprison us or kill us, and answer to no one for it. Power gives him the authority he lacks by right.'

'So how should we talk to him?'

'Truthfully, I would suggest. He knows more than you might think, in any case; half the world passes through this little point, and brings its news with it. He may play the ignorant tyrant, but he is not. He will know of your marriage, Julianne, and of your fleeing it; he will have heard rumours of that night, and of our party on the road. He may even have been expecting to see the Daughter come this way, though not perhaps with such a host as Marron. Nor will he have been idle this last hour; giving us time to rest is the least of it. If he didn't know before that the Ghost Walker was abroad in his territory, he knows now. There will be message-birds flying to Rhabat and other places; we have no hope of arriving unannounced. He will also be taking advice from his lords perhaps, his astrologers certainly. So step carefully, and say as little as you can; but don't lie to him. If he asks a direct question, answer it. And don't ask any on your own account, a clever man can learn a lot from what is asked of him.'

'I knew it,' Julianne muttered aside to Elisande. 'It's going to be like talking to the djinni again.' And then, direct to Rudel, 'Should I tell him about the djinni?'

'I think you must. It's hard to explain your journey else; and even the Sultan might be impressed by a djinni. We'll see. Are you ready to face him?'

'No.' But she was rising, smoothing needlessly at the gleaming gossamer fabric of her dress before reaching for Elisande's hand. 'If we must do it, let's do it now. Rice and cool drink and conversation, what could be more pleasant of an evening . . .?'

'Eat with the right hand only,' Redmond murmured, one last swatch of advice before they reached the corridor where servants waited, 'and don't talk of weighty matters till the meal is done . . .'

When Jemel had spoken of taking rice with the family, Marron had thought he'd meant that literally, a bowl of cooked rice and no more.

Looking at Jemel's face now, he was sure of it. That was the Sharai custom, what was dictated by centuries of usage, what spoke to the nomad's soul.

Taking rice with the Sultan of Bar'ath Tazore, it seemed, was something else entirely: a noble custom corrupted, by Jemel's expression, a beautiful vessel broken.

The Sultan's rice was a precious mountain, a heaped and steaming dish of jewelled gold. The rice had been cooked with saffron, and was flecked with bright peppers and spice-pods, preserved peels, coloured shreds of smoked meat and fish, all gleaming with a buttery sheen. Around it was set a circle of smaller dishes containing boiled eggs, salted lemons, vegetables pickled in vinegar or drenched in oil.

This was on the dais, the divan they called it here, at the far end of the great chamber where the Sultan held his court. The first time they had stood before it, and been examined; this time they had been beckoned up by the man himself, and had arranged themselves upon his carpets, side by side with His Excellence and the lords of this small state. Slaves had brought and poured scented water above great copper vessels, so that guests might wash their hands; they had proffered towels; they had brought the giant platter in and all its attendant dishes, and had set them in the centre of the dining circle. Marron's mind had been distracted by those white robes they wore, too reminiscent of the Sharai boys burned at the Roq, their white tunics and the white shifts of the penitents which he had worn himself and dyed with other men's blood . . .

Following that thought, Marron looked at Jemel's face and saw his scorn again, and understood it; and so like all his party he was surprised by what that young man did next, and perhaps he was more surprised than most, although he'd spent most time with the Sharai, or the Sharai with him.

'Excellence,' Jemel said, staring darkly while one of his hands clenched hard on the skirts of his robe, 'will you hear my oath?'

It seemed as though the Sultan were startled also, the way his hand stilled in its reaching for a bowl of crystal fruits. He blinked his wide, deceptive eyes, and smiled as if at a victory won, and not a small one.

'If you wish me to,' he said, 'I must; it is my burden, to

carry young men's oaths. Along with the souls of all my own people. But not till we have eaten, youth, I beg you.'

'An oath should be made on an empty belly,' Jemel growled. 'There is little virtue in a well-fed man.'

'But you have not yet taken rice with me; there is no obligation between us, till you do.'

Jemel's fingers twitched, and Marron was briefly afraid for him; he thought he might do something extravagant and stupid, take a single grain of rice on his tongue and so insult his host in the same moment that he claimed his protection.

Sharai manners won the day, though. Jemel bowed his head, hiding his face as he accepted the Sultan's ruling; diplomatic Redmond stretched awkwardly forward with his twisted fingers to scoop a handful of rice from the platter, and Elisande spoke lightly, gratefully of the comforts of the palace.

And so they ate, though they were not hungry; and so they spoke meaninglessly of what mattered not at all; and all the while they were only waiting for what must come later, Jemel's revelation and the Sultan's doom on their expedition.

Music was played softly in the shadows. Under its veil and the buzz of louder voices, Marron murmured, 'What oath is that, Jemel? And why must the Sultan hear it?'

'It is the tradition. He claims to be Sharai, though he is not; there is no other sheikh here that has a better claim, at least, and this will not wait. Be patient, you will hear.'

Marron thought Jemel could listen to himself, could show a little patience in this, above all could and should both talk and listen to his companions before launching himself into whatever private venture he had in mind. But there was no talking to him here; nor would any words have served a purpose, by his set face and his intense scowl. He meant to have his say, to swear his oath in public and before a prince of his people, or the nearest to it that he could find. If he wouldn't speak to Marron, he would speak to no one.

Nor would he wait past the niceties, the conventions of his culture. The food-dishes were removed, and he fidgeted but was silent yet; coffee was brought and served in tiny cups which were twice refilled, and still he said nothing.

As the slaves withdrew, though, the Sultan turned once more to Rudel at his right-hand side; and for the first time there was purpose in his voice as he said, 'So now. You are far from your lands, my friend, and trying to whisper through my own, though your footsteps betray you. Tell me why.'

'No!' Jemel shrugged off Marron's vain and belated touch, leaping to his feet to stand centre-circle before the Sultan. 'First, my oath! It is my right, excellence, and your duty to hear it . . .'

The Sultan made a shrug of apology to Rudel, *forgive me, but young men will be impetuous*; and followed it with a gesture to Jemel. 'It is your right, and my duty. Continue, then. Is it an oath of blood?'

'It is.'

For the briefest moment, the Sultan's eyes seemed to say, *it would be*. But his voice said, 'Let all bear witness, then, that I who am Sultan of Bar'ath Tazore and lord of the tribe of the Buresset as my father was before me, I who have taken this Jemel of the tribe of the Saren into my house and offered him the protection of my name, in the absence of his own lord I will hear his oath; and if he fail or forswear it I will take vengeance on his body, for the sake of his tribe's honour and my own.'

Jemel bowed low; Rudel touched a hand to his forehead, as though he knew what was coming and despaired. Marron was simply bewildered, watching the young Sharai as he straightened, as he began to speak.

'Excellence, I am Saren, as you have seen and said; but here in your presence I will renounce my tribe and live outside their tents or any man's, until this oath I make now be fulfilled.'

He unwound the silken rope that tied his headdress and threw it down, twisting the cloth instead into a simple knot to hold it. He drew his dagger and cut away the silver ends to the rope that was his belt, and let them fall; he tugged at his robes until he had unmade that particular style of wear that declared him Saren. His way would be hard in the desert, without a tribe to claim him as its own: that much Marron knew, though little more.

'Excellence, when I was Saren I was sworn blood-brother to a man, Jazra of my tribe. You know the strength and meaning of those vows. Jazra died at the castle of the Roq; he was first wounded and then slain, while I was prevented from going to his aid. I could name the one who prevented me, who made me break my vow; for our peoples' sake, though, I will not. I could name the one who wounded him, who broke his stroke and guard; for her own sake, though, and for the sake of mysteries I do not understand, again I will not. I can and I will name the man who killed him, and this I swear: that when I have done the service I am bound to now, I will hunt down that man and challenge him, blade to blade and to the death, for Jazra's honour and my own.'

'The oath is heard and witnessed, Jemel of the Sharai. Name the man.'

'His name is Anton d'Escrivey, a Patric knight of the Ransomers. This I have learned, and it is sure.'

Sure it was, Marron had been there on the walls with Sieur Anton at the time. He didn't remember Jemel, but he remembered the Sharai who had come close perhaps to killing his master. Elisande's knife had taken him in the side, and Sieur Anton's sword had finished him; Jemel must have heard the name and worked out the truth of it in these weeks of travelling, though his companions had tried so hard to keep it from him.

Marron stared down at the intricate knotting of the rug he sat on, and swore a private, secret vow of his own: that he would keep Jemel at his side if he could and go with him if he could not, and that one way or another – whatever way lay in his power, once he had learned where his power lay and how to use it – he would cause this oath also to be broken.

When he lifted his head there were other people in the hall, though only he perhaps had heard their coming. They walked softly, to the rhythm of the music, and they came through a hidden door at the further end. That was what he'd heard to alert him first, the snick of its lock sounding; then he strained to listen to their progress.

The others seemed oblivious, even Jemel, who dropped

into place again beside him and gave him a stubborn, challenging glare. Marron just looked back at him, with all the advantages of his new eyes that no one could read. He wouldn't say anything about the men at his back, unless or until there seemed a need. They must be making their way behind the pillars that supported the gallery, all but invisible to anyone on the divan; some servant or guard must have shouted the alarm by now, though, if they were unknown or unwelcome here. And Marron thought perhaps there had been the faintest movement on the Sultan's face to acknowledge their arrival, though if so it was subtle beyond expectation for such an obvious man.

He was speaking to Rudel again, speaking of their journey; and now the thing was said, the truth was told, simple and direct.

'We are travelling towards Rhabat,' Rudel said, 'though we may not all go so far together. Redmond has been a guest of the Ransomers, and he still feels the effects of their hospitality; well, you have seen, and your doctors have seen more. Him I would like to see safe in Surayon, but I must take him this long loop from Outremer, to be sure. I also want to watch over these young people, as far as possible in their journey.'

'Indeed. The young can always bear watching. And why do they travel to Rhabat?'

'Marron because of what he carries, that he does not know how to guard or use; there are those who can teach him, there. Julianne because a djinni sends her.'

'A djinni? Which djinni would that be?' His voice was not – quite – incredulous, but the question stung none the less; and it stung Julianne into answering for herself.

'It said its name was Shaban Ra'isse Khaldor.'

'Then I think we must believe it, my lady Julianne. The djinn do not lie about such matters.' He sounded impressed, despite himself.

'I had heard that the djinn do not lie at all?'

'Yes. I have heard that, also. Why does Djinni Khaldor send you to Rhabat?'

It seemed she was taking her attitude from the djinn, because she did not lie at all, even by omission. 'I am uncertain, what it truly wants. It said to me that I must go where I am sent, and marry where I must; and it sends me to Rhabat, though I am married already. It said also that I would find my father there, and that he would be in peril, but that I might save him. Though it might be better if I did not, it said that too.'

So much information, so much honesty: the Sultan took a while to mull it over and weigh its value. The men on the floor of the hall were quite still now; a servant had lit a burner, now that the meal was over, and a waft of incense hid even the hard, dusty smell of them from Marron.

'There is a gathering, at Rhabat,' the Sultan said at last, trading truth for truth. 'I have heard that much. Hasan passed this way a week since,' *after his failure at the Roq* he did not add, nor need to, 'and he was on his way there, to meet with tribal leaders. I will not go myself, I have my charge and am not free to travel,' which likely meant he hadn't been invited, Marron thought, 'but you will find it busy. Perhaps that is your father's work?'

'Perhaps it is,' Julianne agreed neutrally. 'The King's Shadow does the King's will; he does not discuss it with me.'

'Neither with me. He can be as mysterious as the djinn. Why one of them would send you from your husband, and on such a long and chancy journey – well, it may be that we will both learn the answer to that, in time to come. I for one will not delay you, when such powers are pushing at your back. Indeed, I will do what I can to haste you on your way.'

'That is generous, excellence,' Rudel said gruffly.

'No, not generous. Sensible, I feel. I had as soon see such a party move on quickly from my land. One of your company, though, may not need to go so far as he thinks. There are those here who can test what he carries, and teach him the proper use of it . . .'

And now there was movement at Marron's back, as those men strode out into the centre of the hall. He saw sudden anxiety on Rudel's face, fear on Julianne's; he heard the rasp of steel as swords were drawn, and felt Jemel stiffen at his side. A touch of his hand on that young man's knee was enough to still him, though.

Marron stood, bowed his head to the Sultan, and turned to face whatever had come, for surely it had come for him.

3

Company for the Road

It was Elisande's profound conviction, based on a lifetime of observation, that men were by nature perverse. The only exceptions she allowed were Redmond and her grandfather, who were both of them kind, sensible and wise. Her father was the prime exemplar of her belief: leave Rudel to make a decision, any decision that mattered, and he would be sure to choose wrongly.

If anything, boys could be worse than men; after a few short weeks of knowing him, she thought that Marron was worse than any boy she'd met. Give him the chance and he'd not only do the wrong thing, he'd do the stupid thing. The most stupid thing that it was in his power to do . . .

As now, when four armed and deadly men had arrayed themselves in a semicircle across the floor of the hall; when he had friends on the divan there who would do their best to shelter him from any threat, two at least who would die for him if necessary; when he had a terrible gift in his blood that could counter any enemy, the mere sight of which should be enough to still any man who understood it.

Marron stood, and she thought he would back away from the danger, into the circle of his friends.

He walked the other way, to the edge of the divan, and drew his sword; she thought then that he would touch that to the wound on his arm and free the Daughter, only to show it, to have it seen and known.

He stepped down from the divan, and walked to meet those four lethal blades with only his own to answer them.

Stupid, *stupid* . . .

She jerked and tried to rise, to go after him; and was held back by her father's strong arm, his clamping hand about her wrist, his hissed whisper, 'Sit still!'

'But—'

She still had one hand free, she could work one of her throwing-knives out of the harness beneath her bodice and maybe drop one man with it, give that stupid boy better odds to play against . . .

Except that Julianne took hold of her other arm, and muttered frantically, 'Elisande, aren't those Sand Dancers? We saw them in the market, I don't know what they are but Jemel said to beware of them . . .'

Right, Jemel knew best what Sand Dancers were, and how deadly; and Jemel was only sitting there opposite, watching while the Ghost Walker, his friend Marron went down to meet their silent challenge.

'Yes,' she said to Julianne, 'Sand Dancers is just what they are. See those robes, those mutilated hands? They have mutilated hearts too. No one can hope to fight four of them, not even Rudel, and,' grudgingly, 'Rudel is the best and the smartest and the sneakiest swordsman I've ever seen. Marron needs help, and between the two of you, you and Rudel are preventing me from giving it . . .'

She had time for the speech, because Marron seemed to be speaking to one of the four, in his slow and careful Catari. Or slow and distant, perhaps, because he'd seemed so detached from them all since the Roq; but he couldn't be distant or detached now, his life hung like silk against a blade's edge. One twitch and it was cut and gone, if those men truly meant his death.

Which they would, for sure. Red eyes or no, unhealing wound or no: they had seen convincing frauds before. They would kill him to test him, and if he died and was true, no matter. The Daughter would be there, for the first who dared to claim it; there would be another Ghost Walker this night, one of their own, seen and acclaimed . . .

'Child, be still,' Rudel said again, into her ear. 'In this, even you cannot interfere.'

'But he could have stood back and shown them, one drop of blood, no more; doesn't he *know* that?'

'He knows. He chose another way. Why can you never trust?'

'Because my trust is always betrayed,' she said bitterly, furiously. Rudel caught his breath, and then released her; Julianne had already freed her other arm. She did draw her knives, both of them, but kept them hidden uselessly in her sleeves, only for her own comfort. Rudel was right, for once; she had no place in this. Marron had made his choice, and must live or die by it.

Stupid, *stupid* choice . . .

*

Marron and his opponent had finished their talking, it seemed. Each took a step back, and now all blades were raised in earnest. The soft, insidious music faltered and fell silent; she was glad of that. This dance needed no accompaniment, and Marron should not die to the beat of an alien tune.

It was his good sword he carried, the straight Patric blade that he called Dard, not the scimitar he fenced with against Jemel. She was glad of that, too. It felt right to her, although she knew something of how complex his own feelings were about that sword.

Steel glinted in the light of many lamps; steel whispered, grated, sang to other steel. This truly was a dance, that made its own harsh music. It had grace and strength and a distressful beauty, and the wonder of it was how well Marron knew the steps, and how he seemed to lead all four of his adversaries although they were men grown and he was still so very much a boy.

She'd seen him fence day after day with Jemel and yet hadn't realised how fast he could be, how certain in his body. It must be the Daughter, she thought, taking strange control. The Ghost Walker was not invulnerable, very far from that; but hard to kill, yes, that was the tradition. Now she could see why.

Marron spun and blocked and thrust, and leaped away; and he made those four deadly warriors look wooden, like poppets jerked by strings. Again and again he could have killed one, and did not.

Julianne beside her let out a breath she'd been holding, and whispered, 'Tell me what they are, these Sand Dancers?'

'They are men sworn to a brotherhood,' Elisande replied, without taking her eyes from the dance, 'sworn to serve the Ghost Walker, if he should come. They give a finger to their God, in witness; and they live apart from the tribes, in little groups together. For centuries now, they have lived with each other and their vows and nothing more. Now the Ghost Walker has come again, he stands among them, and they are trying to slay him . . .'

Trying, and failing; and yet not dying as they ought, because Marron had made vows also, and would not kill. So many high oaths he'd broken, and yet this, this newest and least of all his promises he clung to even in the teeth of death, although she yearned for him to break that also, to find some value in his life and cling to that instead.

It could not last. A slip, a misstep, a jarring screech of steel sliding on steel – she waited for any one of those, knowing what must come after. Because they were not wooden poppets, those men he fought, they were not novices, although he made them seem so. They were masters, overmastered; but in the end he could not hold them all, unless he killed them. Which he would not do, and so in the end they would kill him, though they could never earn such a victory. It was written in his body, on his skin, in his determined will.

Except that what is written can be scratched out, or written over; and she was not alone in watching men by lamplight and seeing ghosts, shadows cast by future suns.

The Sultan stirred, and stood; his lords followed his lead, and guards stepped up from the divan's sides. He gestured them all back, and strode forward to loom above the mêlée. Elisande too had to scramble to her feet, to see around him;

but Julianne had done the same, and Rudel after. Only Redmond was left sitting now, and one kindly merchant prince was stooped above him, offering an arm to help.

Well, he wouldn't want to miss this, would he? Elisande thought bleakly that it was only the rush of idle scandal-seekers to an execution, wanting to be sure of a decent view. She hefted her knives again, and yearned to bring them out and use them, as she'd used one of them before. But the echoes of that one time were with them still, in Jemel's oath against Sieur Anton. She dared not imagine what vengeance might follow if she let fly at a Sand Dancer in the perfect moment of his vow, Ghost Walker at his scimitar's point . . .

The Sultan, it seemed, was less anxious about disturbing other men at their devotions – but then, the Sultan did not throw a knife. His heavy body was girdled round with a robe of dense embroidery, tied with a simple sash; as far as she could see, he did not have a knife to throw.

Instead, he seized a massive crystal vase of flowers from a pedestal at the divan's corner, and threw that.

He had a fine eye as well as great strength of arm and shoulder, or else it was a lucky cast: the vase tumbled as it flew, strewing blooms and water across the circle of the fighting men before it smashed to the floor in their midst, shattering into a thousand pieces.

Fragments skittered wildly across the tiles. Marron and his adversaries had been startled into stillness by the great falling shape of the thing and its glinting, spinning facets; now each of them jumped backward, skipping foolishly to avoid those vicious shards.

The near-formal symmetry of the dance had been destroyed; they seemed uncertain suddenly, lost in confusion. The Sultan clapped his hands twice for their attention, and stepped lightly down from the divan.

'Enough!' he cried. 'You have seen that you cannot slay him; you have seen that he could have slain you. All of you, and with some ease. Is that not enough?'

'We are men,' one man replied, the same man that Marron had spoken to, his blade still deliberately unsheathed and ready. 'Men may be slain by other men. Even Sand Dancers die. He handles his weapon with a rare touch, but it means nothing.'

'And his eyes?'

'There are herbs and powders, that can redden a man's eyes . . .'

'Not as his eyes are red, to the iris. You know that. But very well, for certainty's sake, let us test him here, under the eyes of all. If he is false, he dies.'

The Sultan stooped, and there was an unexpected grace even to his bending; he picked up a shining piece of crystal, delicately between finger and thumb, and beckoned to Marron.

'I regret this, lad – but for certainty's sake . . .?'

Marron stepped slowly towards him, taking his sword in his left hand and rolling back the sleeve from that arm. He was barely out of breath, though all his skin was flushed; Elisande saw that there was blood on his blade. Even his care hadn't saved his opponents from some harm, then. He was untouched, so far as she could see; hence the necessity of this.

The Sultan gripped his wrist, gazed for a moment at the

vivid red of the open wound on his forearm, and then pricked at it gently with the sharp edge of the crystal.

Blood oozed out and the Daughter with it, a red haze like smoke rising into the air. As it thickened, so Marron's colour faded.

'Now, is this enough?' the Sultan demanded.

'It is.' The Sand Dancers dropped swiftly to their knees and laid their weapons down, the hafts all toward Marron. The first among them went on, 'Ghost Walker, we have waited an age to serve you . . .'

'I do not want your service,' Marron said distantly, gazing into the swirling cloud of mist which had almost a shape to it now, was almost a creature with eyes and shell and claws. 'How if I had done this first, before we fought; if I had turned it against you, as I could. How then?'

'Then you would have died. Had you used it as a weapon, knowing what it is, you would have demeaned it and disgraced yourself; there would have been nothing we could teach you. And there are archers, in the gallery above. Even the Ghost Walker cannot stand against arrows.'

Chagrined, Elisande squinted up into the shadows under the doming roof. Yes, there they were, a man on either side though with their bows unstrung now, their hands clenched on the gallery rail as they stared down. She should have known, she should have thought to look; those perhaps she might have dealt with, if the need had come. She was good at throwing knives to a height . . .

'No. Though I knew they were there.' His thin voice drew her attention back to himself; with the Daughter released he was all Marron now but whittled, skimmed, shaved of any excess. No energy, no humour. Pain, she thought, a great deal of pain, and not only from his arm that never healed. And his eyes were natural now, their simple tender brown, and they looked as weary as the rest of him. 'I used it before, as a weapon,' he said, honest as he ever was. 'I killed dozens. If that offends so greatly, use your arrows; I'll abide their judgement.'

And be glad to do it, she thought angrily; she thought he'd welcome death, like a stranger's kiss that bespeaks a new friend. She tried to shoulder her way through to reach him, but Rudel was ahead of her, and so she checked.

Her father put an arm around Marron's shoulders and murmured, 'Take it back, lad, enough have seen it now.'

The nameless near-creature in the air there lost its form, flowing into smoke again; the smoke seeped into Marron's wounded arm, against the run of blood; the boy's eyes were red again and his skin was quickly pink, and no more blood dripped to the tiles at his feet.

Rudel hadn't shifted from Marron's side, nor his hand from Marron's shoulder; now he said, 'His Excellence the Sultan is quite right; you need not come with us now, all the way to Rhabat. What you need is here, with these.'

If you can endure it he did not add but should have; perhaps only Elisande heard what was not spoken. Almost sure that only she – or perhaps she and the Sultan both, but no more – heard something else, but for certain it was there: *if you cannot, if you die under their strictures, well, that may be for the best.*

'What he needs,' Elisande declared, pushing through to his side regardless of her hateful father, 'is peace, and rest.'

'That he may not have,' the Sand Dancer responded, the only one she'd heard or seen to speak yet. His face was a skull, bone-lean, desert-drawn: she'd known such men before, admired and detested them both at once. This one she thought she might simply detest. 'He is the Ghost Walker; it is not in his fate to know peace. Rest is waste, and we do not waste God's gifts. The bearded one speaks truly, though. We do not go to Rhabat.'

'And neither should you, Marron.' That was Redmond, joining them, leaning on the arm of an attendant. 'If counsel is being taken there, your presence would only throw it into confusion.'

Marron stood silent for a moment, before his bright, fiery eyes moved from Elisande's face to find Jemel's.

'I will go where my friends go,' he said calmly, irrevocably.

It was a visible shock to most of his listeners, almost a rebellion; and she loved him for it.

The older men – the Sultan, the Sand Dancers, Rudel and Redmond too – all wanted to argue with him, but he would not, he was implacable. Elisande seized the opportunity gifted to her by his stubbornness, to break up this difficult gathering. Julianne was all but falling asleep on her feet; it was no effort to take her arm and guide her towards the door. On the way, she could conveniently pause for a word with the slave who supported Redmond, to suggest that that old man needed his bed more than a wakeful night of talking, talking. And Jemel needed less of a hint than that, only a glance and a jerk of her head, *bring him too, before they back him into a corner and bully him into following their will rather than his own.*

The Sharai nodded, and moved to Marron's side. His devotion she could trust, though she was still not sure she understood it; she slipped her arm around Julianne's waist and urged that tall, sagging girl forward, towards their quarters.

The Sultan's information had been excellent: there were three bedchambers in the suite, with two beds set in each. Whether Redmond would claim his, Elisande was uncertain; she thought the slave would take him to the doctors first, and they might choose to keep him under their watch tonight. His hands and feet all had healed crooked – *lucky to have healed at all*, she thought, thinking of Marron, and suppressed the thought bitterly – and they hurt him constantly, that much she was sure of. There must be drugs, to ease the pain and help him sleep; she hoped that the doctors would have wisdom also, to see what other harm had been done him that he didn't talk about.

She guided Julianne to the furthest chamber, next to the hammam. No steam now, the fires had been let die; come the morning, though, she dreamed of another bath. Likely it would be her last, until they reached Rhabat. No more luxurious guesting: only the desert now lay between them and journey's end. If Rhabat should prove to be any kind of ending, and not just a place to pause in a longer journey. *Go back to the Sharai, Lisan of the Dead Waters. They will bring you a gift of questions.* But she was not going to think about the djinni's sending now, she was not . . .

Thinking of Rhabat instead, remembering the last time she'd guested there – though it was hard to think of Rhabat and not of the Dead Waters – she stripped Julianne ruthlessly and bundled her into one of the beds. Covered her over with a light cotton sheet, blew out the lamps, turned

yearningly to her own bed – and allowed herself to do no
more than sit on its foot, still fully clothed, and waiting.

Blessedly, it was not a long wait. She gazed around the
darkened chamber, seeing how starlight glimmered through
the traceries of a high shuttered window; then she heard
footsteps, the sound of male voices murmuring. Young
voices: not Redmond, then. Jemel had done what she'd
hoped for, had fed Marron's mulishness with an excuse to
escape the browbeating of his elders.

She didn't go to them, there was no point. She only sat
and listened as they took possession of the next chamber,
sat and watched as the light died in the doorway; sat and
held her breath and listened to the silence that followed,
and prayed that both boys might be sleeping.

Then she undressed, as quietly as she could manage,
and slipped into the bed. Closed her eyes, and felt weariness
engulf her.

And did not sleep, she could not; but lay and listened to the
slow rhythms of Julianne's breathing, and tried resentfully
to match it with her own, in case there should be some
sympathetic magic in the beat.

There was none. She gazed at the ceiling, where the
window had laid a pretty pattern of light; she thought it
ought to move as the moon moved, but it did not. That puzzled her, until she saw another pattern on the floor, that did
creep slowly across the tiles. Of course, moonlight would
not shine up onto the ceiling; there must be some other
source out there, fixed low, like the globe in the garden.

She tried to focus her mind on that, but it was all distraction. At last she allowed her true concern to take

command, to lift her out of her bed. She checked on Julianne, one last needless delay, and then padded barefoot and naked as she was through the connecting doorway into the boys' chamber.

There was more light in here. Jemel – it must have been Jemel – had put out most of the lamps all through the suite, but he'd left one burning in the furthest chamber, for Rudel's sake if he should return before dawn. Not yet: that light made a pale glow to show the way through, should she wish to venture further.

She did not. Jemel, again Jemel must have opened the screens across the window; a soft light fell in to show her Marron's head on a bright silken cushion, where he lay deeply asleep.

He was all her anxiety, tonight more than ever before. She went to stand beside him, gazing down almost in wonder to see his face so relaxed, his native beauty breaking through the strains that rived him moment by moment when he was awake.

How long she stood there rapt, she couldn't have said: only that the spell was broken by the sudden glimmer of a reflection on the wall behind his bed. She glanced round, startled – and saw Jemel sitting up with a drawn blade in his hand and his arm cocked, poised to throw.

She lifted her face full into view, and spread her hands slowly wide; he nodded, and slid the knife out of sight beneath a pillow.

And stood up quietly, throwing his coverlet aside, unconscious of his nakedness or as unconcerned as she was; that was Sharai custom, natural to him and taught to her. He gestured and she followed him to the window, then up onto the ledge and through to a place where they could talk without either disturbing the sleepers or being disturbed themselves.

It was a courtyard, closed in by palace buildings on all sides; but it was another garden also, dense with growth and harbouring a tiny pool at its centre where another of those globe-lamps glowed to light their way. The air was heavy with perfume, cool and damp and pleasant against her skin. She saw a door in one of the walls, but that was closed; all the windows that overlooked the court were shuttered, bar the one they'd climbed through.

Jemel's eyes too were shuttered and secretive, as ever. She meant to unlock that reserve, she was determined to do it; tonight could make a start, and she had the key, she thought. She gazed at his lean body, seeing white scars against dark skin, and asked, 'How did you get him to sleep so, did you beg a potion from the Sultan's doctors?'

Jemel smiled faintly. 'No. That would not work; what he carries in his blood would not allow it. But even the Ghost Walker is not immune to others' skills. He needs to rest, to dream a little; I led him there, with the *sodar* my father taught me. Do you know the *sodar*?'

Elisande nodded slowly. The *sodar* was almost magic, she thought, though everyone who used it swore that it was not. It varied from tribe to tribe, from family to family within each tribe; sometimes it was song, sometimes a chant, sometimes simple speaking but always touching too, a gentle massage to the rhythm of words. She could use it herself in a clumsy way, all but untaught. She had experienced it many times from her childhood on, from the days when she would allow her father to touch her; it had always seemed like magic, that easy drifting into sleep, guided by a loving voice . . .

She thought of Jemel's fingers on Marron's skin, the murmur of his voice insinuating into Marron's muddled mind, and tried to feel nothing but grateful that the Sharai had achieved what she could not. The result was all that mattered, she told herself firmly, Marron's peaceful sleeping; she struggled hard to believe it.

'Thank you, Jemel. That was a kind touch.' *To us both*, she meant, and he seemed to understand. At any rate he nodded, as though accepting that she had the right to thank him for a gift given to Marron.

She crouched down beside the pool, and dabbled her hand in the near-luminous water; a shift of shadows, and an invisible fish rose to nibble at her fingers. She smiled, and lifted a palmful of water towards the stars, and let it trickle teasingly down her arm

Above her, Jemel said, 'I have learned why the city is so quiet after dark.'

Bar'ath Tazore was hardly a city, she thought, hiding her smile; except to a Sharai boy, clearly, for whom three tents would make a town. What on earth had he made of Rhabat?

'Why's that, Jemel? And how did you learn it?'

'I spoke to the Sultan's slaves. They said there is a curfew now, from dusk till dawn. It was the sickness, it brought such fear with it; and the miracles that followed, they were fearful also. Most people kept their houses when night fell; but others went out in bands, and slew those they blamed for the evil, or burned them in their homes with families and servants and all.'

'Don't tell Marron that,' Elisande murmured. He was so tender still, about his stable-boy friend who had been put to death by fire at the castle.

'No. I would not.' They shared a glance of mutual understanding; she thought perhaps they were the only two who could.

'Go on, then. What else did the slaves tell you?'

'The Sultan called a curfew, to stop those killings. He said that they had more to do with blood-feuds than diseases, which was true. He said that the sickness was not the work of men, but of demons; and the healings too, he said, they were not miracles but curses. Those who had followed the holy man had been deluded, and were outcast for abandoning their people.

'There were some who disputed that; there are some still, though mostly they keep quiet now. One did not, a Patric priest who had been let live here for generations, to minister to those of your people who come to trade. He preached against the Sultan's ruling: he said that he had seen what he had seen. The Sultan put his eyes out this afternoon, that they might not confuse the man further. That is what Marron smelled on his hands.'

Julianne shuddered; the night seemed suddenly colder, and less welcoming.

'You should go back to bed,' Jemel said, surprising her.

'Yes. I will. But—' But sleep felt as far away as ever, or further; she had more to worry over now. 'Jemel, will you, would you perform the *sodar* for me too?'

'I would, and I will,' he said; and surprised her again by taking her hand, to lead her back to the window. Her feet stumbled a little, in the long grasses underfoot; she clung to his strength, and thought that his public oath had somehow mellowed him, that he could be kinder now that they were all witnesses to his sworn revenge.

Back to the chamber, with his hands to help her in through the high window; she fell gladly onto her bed, lay on her belly and felt his firm touch on her tangled hair.

He came from a people who whispered their *sodar*, it seemed; his voice was a soft sibilance, a flow like running water, like his fingers that flowed all down the run of her spine. She couldn't catch the words, they were too liquid, a quicksilver chorus, fish in a river, not to be distinguished one from another or any from the water that they swam in, his hands against her skin; she thought she heard more voices than his one, as her mind submerged.

She woke to laughter, and the tickle of cool fingers on her neck. Emphatically, that was not Jemel.

'Wake, laze! The men want to bathe before breakfast, as we do; but they will not share with us, so we must hurry . . .'

And Julianne snatched back the sheet that covered her, that emphatically she had not used to cover herself last night.

Obediently Elisande rose, and walked towards the hammam. Julianne shrieked, and threw the sheet hurriedly around her.

'Grief, girl, there are no doors to close here! Or hadn't you noticed?'

Marasson manners: Elisande knotted the sheet complaisantly about her body, and gave her friend a smile.

Julianne wore a white robe, simple but decent dress for men to see her in.

'It'll come off in a minute, love.'

'Even so. Do you want Jemel to blush for you?'

That was clever, that she'd noticed enough not to say *Marron*, as she would have done before. Still, Elisande hid another smile. Julianne had a deal to learn, before she left the desert. Elisande only hoped that Sharai ease with nakedness would be the hardest lesson, though she doubted that.

Julianne was easy enough once they were within the privacy of the hammam, with none but female attendants to see them. Hard enough to see anything clearly, through the billowing steam: but Elisande saw her lolling on her back on a marble bench, hugging one knee to her chest while her hair hung down in damp tendrils.

'Oh, this feels so good . . . Will you rub me down, Lisan?'

'I will if you call me by my name. Not otherwise.'

'Elisande, Elisande my sweet . . . Mmm. Yes. Harder,' as Elisande took a rough towel to sweat-slick skin. 'If we are to believe the djinni, your name will be Lisan; I was only practising for the change.'

'The djinn are not famous for their invention, Julianne; I have been called Lisan before. It's the Sharai version of my name, easier to their tongue. But let's leave it to the Sharai, shall we?'

'Surely. Jemel doesn't call you Lisan.'

'Jemel doesn't call me anything.' Except friend, perhaps, after last night; though she wouldn't care to count on that.

'No. He's very sparing with names, isn't he? I suppose you'll tell me that's Sharai custom again.'

'Sharai manners, yes. Names are potent, you don't bandy them about unnecessarily. And Jemel is very much adrift still, one among strangers; regardless of his private troubles,' *his dead lover, his oath,* 'he doesn't have the knack of being friendly. Best thing is just to leave him be.'

'With Marron. Yes. I do. The djinn follow Sharai manners, though, you told me that; and the djinni named you. Lisan of the Dead Waters, it said . . .'

'And it said your name would be greater than your father's,' she countered.

'If I fail not. I know. We'll see, won't we? Perhaps I'll fail, whatever it wants me to do. I've done the getting married, and I seem to have failed at that,' mournfully, trying to hide her true mourning behind a joke, not well enough to carry it off, though Elisande applauded the ambition. 'So what are the Dead Waters, Elisande?'

'A lake, an inland sea beside Rhabat. The water is so salt you cannot drink it, nothing can live in it, it's dead. And more, inhabited by some evil, according to story. It stinks; I lay no claim to it. Roll over.'

'Ow! Don't pummel me – oh. Actually, that feels good. Don't stop . . . So what did the djinni mean?'

'I don't know.'

'Shouldn't we try to find out? Before we get there?'

'Julianne, you can't interrogate a djinni! Besides, it's gone away.'

'I'm not so sure. And the Sharai are part of the story also, we can interrogate the Sharai . . .'

'Oh, yes? Which tribe, which family? Someone is to

bring me a gift of questions, whatever that means; but you ask the wrong questions of the wrong people, and the djinni can go play in the sand by itself, they'll slit your throat and mine besides for bringing you.'

'So what do we do, then? What can we do?'

'Nothing. Go to Rhabat, sit patient, wait. Patience is a virtue anywhere; in the desert, or among desert people, it's a necessity.'

'Tell me about the desert, then. How far is it to Rhabat from here?'

'Never ask how far something is, sweetheart. As well ask how far it is to the next new moon; nobody measures that way. They count journeys in days, not in miles.'

'Well, how many days is it?'

'I don't know.' She ducked, grinning, as Julianne threw a sponge at her. 'No, listen. For a pigeon carrying a message – and there will be birds with messages, don't doubt it – not long at all, a few days, no more. We're not birds, and cannot go their way nor at their speed. There is a slow road, a water-route that skirts the *mul'abarta* and meanders like a river from well to well. We might go that way, though it would not be safe. Your name and style will attract attention; if you have enemies, that road is where they'll look for you. Rudel certainly has enemies. And Marron is worse: half the Sharai in the wide desert would come to look on the Ghost Walker, if they knew where he might be found.'

'What else can we do, then?'

'We can travel quick and chancy, taking as straight a line as we can manage and keeping well away from the camel-trail. The desert is dangerous, though, and so are its people; that's why we need Jemel, for guide and guarantor among the tribes. He knows the ways of sand and rock better than we ever will, and he is at least Sharai. And tribeless now: that will help, although he did not mean it to. No one can claim a blood-feud with an outcast, though few will offer hospitality. The Patrics – that's you and me, love – are almost welcome here and tolerated on certain routes for certain purposes, but we are forbidden to wander at will in the *mul'abarta*. Even we from Surayon. Rudel has a reputation, and so does your father, but even so we need Jemel to make our excuses for us. And he still may not be enough.'

'And if he is not?'

'Why, then we have Marron. Trust me, love, Marron will always be enough.'

If they always had Marron, if the Sand Dancers didn't cut him out of the party, as was certainly their intent. Rudel and Redmond would put up no resistance, unless losing Marron meant losing Jemel also. Elisande thought it would; she thought one of the two older men should have realised that, at least. She was disappointed in Redmond, for being so obtuse.

They took their time in dressing while the men bathed, indulging the sheer pleasure of it, this one last chance of diaphanous silks, vivid embroideries, servants to help them with the intricate folds and veils.

When the men were decent they all ate together in the largest chamber, finding an array of food and drinks laid out that made Elisande wish they were true guests here, and for longer than just one morning. More practically, she wished for bags and flasks to take with them what they could not manage now.

'If this is breakfast,' Julianne said, slicing cheese cheerfully at her side, 'no wonder the Sultan is so portly. One such meal a day will do me . . .'

'Hush, and eat,' Rudel said repressively, with a glance at the silent attendants. 'Eat as much as you can; one meal a day may well be our lot, in a few days' time.'

Quite unsquashed, Julianne pulled a face at him, which made Elisande giggle around a mouthful of sweet fruit-bread.

They all took the wisdom of Rudel's injunction, though, and stuffed themselves to groaning. Even the boys ate well, Elisande was glad to see, without need of her nagging. Marron looked better than she had known him, she thought, fresh after his bath and well-rested, almost forgetful of his burden as he murmured quietly with Jemel. That would not last, it could not, but it was welcome none the less.

When they were done, the slaves began to clear the remnants of their meal; almost immediately, the Sultan's chamberlain appeared in the doorway.

After polite greetings and ritual questions as to their health and sleep and general contentment, which they answered equally ritually, he said, 'My lord has asked me to fetch you to the stables, if such a thing would please you. Will you come?'

Of course, they would come. They rose, brushing crumbs from their fine garments, and followed. Julianne took her usual duty at Redmond's elbow, though even that old man seemed fitter this morning, a tribute to the Sultan's doctors.

Elisande walked behind with the boys, as if only to avoid walking ahead with her father. She felt a great temptation to imitate her friend and tuck her arm through Marron's, but did not; instead she said, perhaps a little wickedly, 'Jemel, I have to thank you for your *sodar* last night.'

'You slept well?'

'I did. But you know that, you saw . . .'

She'd hoped to raise a question from Marron, that much at least; all she managed was a curious glance, though she thought he might ask the Sharai about it later. She gave him a bright smile to feed his piqued interest a little, and let be.

Ib' Taraffi led them through the palace complex, and out into a wide flagged court where they found the Sultan himself standing in the shade of a fringed parasol, held up by a gorgeously dressed black page. He greeted them magniloquently, asking the same questions as his chamberlain, but never taking his eyes from a string of half a dozen camels that were parading in a circle before him. They were fine bull beasts, decked out in jewelled golden harness that detracted not at all from their own quality; each was ridden by a small boy, no more than seven or eight years old by the look of them. They wore identical clothes, and all had a similar cast to their faces: fearful under their master's eye, Elisande thought, and hungry with it.

'You must forgive my passion,' the Sultan said, 'but this is the racing season, and these are my pride. All bred here, in my stables; I know the stars and lineage of each.'

And he proved it, stepping from one to the next as their riders drew them to a halt and greeting each beast by name, stretching up to stroke a high-arched nose or slap a tawny neck while the camels coughed or bellowed or stooped to snuffle at his robes. He beamed, clearly seeing each response as a gesture of recognition and affection. Elisande, who knew something of camel nature, was less than convinced. But at least none of them spat in his face, or tried to bite him; and they were exceptional animals, there was no disputing that.

'He breeds the camels,' Julianne muttered in an undertone, 'but where does he get the children, does he breed them too? They're tiny . . .'

'He'll buy them,' Redmond replied, equally quietly. 'Peasant children from their parents, nomads from raiders. There's perhaps more prestige in having a Sharai boy aback your camel, but not much. Being light and wiry is the only useful qualification; you don't need brute strength to sit a racing camel.'

'What happens when they grow too big?'

'There's always work. In the stables, the palace, the fields . . . The Sultan cares for his slaves, don't doubt it. He wouldn't cast them out, though they'll likely never know anything like these glory days again.'

'They don't look glorified, they look plain scared.'

'Only of falling or losing control, of disgracing themselves in front of him. Believe me, they're not frightened of the Sultan. They have no cause to be. We're the ones who should be nervous now.'

'Why so? He said he wouldn't delay us . . .'

'He's had a night to think about it, he's had a long night of talking with Rudel; and he has been known to change his mind. This isn't just a parade-ground, Julianne, it's an execution-ground as well. Ask Marron.'

Indeed, Marron's nostrils were flaring even where he stood right at the back of their group, and his face was tight with tension, losing half the advantage of his night of sleep. Elisande didn't know which she resented more, the effects of this place on the boy or those of Redmond's words on their friend. Unnecessary, she thought, to have brought them here; if the Sultan felt that he needed to make the point so crudely, he was less subtle than she believed. And stupid of Redmond, to spell it out for Julianne. Just healthy male detachment, no doubt, but that girl worried too much already. The last thing she needed was extra fuel for her anxieties.

He should have known that – no, he must have known that, he saw the world too clearly to miss what was so obvious to Elisande. Which meant that he'd said the thing deliberately, for deliberate effect, for purposes of his own . . .

Julianne could be detached too, though, or at least she could play that game. She didn't flinch; she smiled, indeed, and said, 'Perhaps we should sell ourselves into his service, if it means he'd treat us kinder. What would you say I was worth, Redmond?'

'Diamonds. Diamonds beyond number—'

'No,' and that was Rudel, interrupting. 'Not diamonds, old friend, your eyes are rheumy and play you false. Diamonds are for my daughter; she will have the hard heart of truth, and tell it too. Pearls for you, Julianne: pearls of every colour, pink and cream and black. Pearls are not so forthright, they're beautiful but subtle, disguising, deceptive. A many-layered thing, a pearl is, and you never can see to the heart of it. Tell me, do all girls resemble their fathers so much?'

At least half of that little speech was aimed at Elisande, if not directly said to her; she was ready to explode with indignant denial, except that Julianne spoke first and stole her air and her father's also.

'I think perhaps they do; though your daughter at least knows the colour of my heart, Rudel. Hush now, here comes the Sultan.'

Oddly, the Sultan came directly to Julianne. He took her hands and bowed above them, smiled down into her clear eyes and said, 'Forgive my lingering over an indulgent pleasure, my dear, but you I think will understand; I fancy you have your own similar attachment, is it not so? You will want to see how my people have acted, in your stead . . .'

Keeping a grip on one wrist, he led her a few paces forward and made a gesture with his free hand; across the court, one of three dozen stable doors swung wide, and there were figures moving in the shadows within.

Julianne's frown of puzzlement vanished in a moment; Elisande deliberately relaxed the tension in her muscles, and took her hands away from where she'd stowed her knives no more than half-hidden at her waist. She'd quite forgotten about their horses, what with all the turbulence of last night and her uncertainties about the road ahead. Julianne, of course, had not.

'Merissa!' In a moment of sheer childishness which she would undoubtedly blush for later, Julianne pulled free of the Sultan and fairly ran over the flags, skirts flapping and hair flying loose, veil coming awry.

Merissa it was, but not Merissa as she had been when last they'd seen her, her coat dull and gritty and her mane tangled for lack of proper grooming, her head hanging with weariness after the long trail. This was a proud, high-stepping aristocrat with two lads to attend her, as she deserved; sunlight gleamed gold on her russet flank, all her coat was bright with recent brushing. Jewels in her harness glinted as they caught the light.

The Sultan gave Julianne a minute to kiss the palfrey's soft nose, to hug her neck, to whisper endearments in her flicking ear; then he walked across the court to join her, his page scampering behind with the parasol. Elisande followed, her curiosity overriding manners; she wanted to hear what they said to each other.

'Excellence, this is, this is more than kind in you, to take such care of her . . .'

'Not at all. You are my guests; it was my duty to see to all your beasts, but my privilege in this case. It is not only camels that catch my eye. This little lady is a princess, she graces my stables as you grace my halls.' He reached out to stroke Merissa between the eyes, a tribute which she permitted; her blatant condescension made Elisande bite back a grin. 'If you will permit it, lady, I have a proposal to make. You cannot take your horses into the desert, which you know; let me hold them here for you, and I will provide you with camels in their stead. Under my eye they will be treated as they ought; my people know better than the market traders, what a princess requires for her comfort. These boys raced camels for me,' he added, his voice so neutral that for sure he had overheard Julianne's earlier hard questions, 'before they grew so large; they will give her the same attention they gave my beasts before.'

Julianne did blush at that, adjusting her veil too late to

hide it; but then she laughed, and said, 'I'm sure they will. May they ride Merissa, as well as pampering her? She's too feckless to race, I fear, but she likes a run; and they're light boys yet, they'll not be too heavy for her.'

The lads gawped at her, gawped hopefully at their master; all he said was, 'Someone must exercise her, certainly. Such a beauty must not stale in a stall. Will you trust her to me?'

'Gladly, excellence. It would be a great relief to me, to know her so well set up. I've been grieving over the loss of her; it must happen, but if I may give her to you, I can be much more easy in my mind . . .'

'Leave her; do not give her. She shall be another guest, until you can reclaim her. And the same for all your mounts,' the Sultan said, making a grand circle and bowing to the whole party; the men had come up quietly to join Elisande, Marron as ever hanging back, not to come too close to the animals. Jemel as ever was at his side. 'I have empty stalls, and lazy boys aplenty.'

Elisande caught Jemel's eye and flashed him a grin around her veil, delighted at the thought of his scruffy pony sharing the luxury of the Sultan's stables. He smiled back, which she counted a minor triumph.

'You are the soul of generosity, excellence,' Rudel said cautiously, 'but I am reluctant to dip so far into your debt. We do not know how affairs may fall out, at Rhabat; it may be a long time before we can come back. Nor do I think that racing bulls would make the ideal companions for a difficult journey.'

The Sultan snorted, and clapped his hands together; a boy ran to open a gate that led to another court. Another string of camels was brought through, each with a lad at its nose-rope. Females all, Elisande noted, and all mature beasts.

'This is Sildana,' the Sultan murmured, going to the first of them, whose coat was a shimmering white. 'She has been dam to three of my finest racers, and will breed again if you return her. If not – well, these things fall out as God orders them. You are here, and in need of good beasts; I need to see you gone. We will do this, Rudel. Here is Caret; she is full sister to my greatest hope this season . . .'

And so through all the string, each one named and flattered: a mount for everyone in the party – except for Marron, of course, no mount for him – and two besides to carry packs or riders if necessary.

'There is some food in your own luggage,' the Sultan added after each camel had been introduced, 'but I will give you more, plus whatever else is needful for the journey. Fresh clothes, at least, and a little gold to smooth your travel.'

'Excellence, this is far more than we had looked for—'

'I know it. You looked for me to forbid your going further, did you not, Rudel? And so I might have done, I would for almost any other of your kind; I do not love to see Patrics pass beyond my borders into the Sands. There is little trust between our peoples, and good cause for that. But the son and granddaughter of the Princip of Surayon make a special case, as does the daughter of the King's Shadow; and then there is Marron. For any one of you, I might have done as much; for all together, I dare not do otherwise. There is something momentous in your party, that lies beyond my judgement; this talk of the djinn makes me fearful, as does the sight of the Ghost Walker. Go to the council at Rhabat, and let the sheiks there make what decisions must be made. I cannot send my blessings with you, but I will do what I can to ease your journey. My concern is for my people here; they are restive since that cursed healer came. I keep them peaceable by day and penned in at night, but I want no further disturbance.'

'That is more than fair, excellence,' Rudel said quietly. 'We will take your gifts gladly, and go on today; we ask no more.'

'That is well. One thing further, though: go by the traders' route. It will take you longer, but the way will be easier; and the tribes too are restless. Hasan wants war with Outremer, and there are few who speak against him. They will look less kindly than I do on a party of Patrics, if they find you loose on their land.'

Rudel bowed, but said nothing; after a moment, the Sultan turned to Redmond.

'You, old man – you should not go with them. My doctors say so, and they are right. Stay with me until you are well, and then I will give you an escort to see you safe to the borders of Surayon.'

'Excellence, I agree with your doctors, and with you. I will go home happily, if I can persuade one other to come with me.' Redmond turned to Julianne and went on, 'Child, lady, heart's daughter: these others our friends have all some experience at least of the road to Rhabat, or else a pressing need to go there—'

'As does Julianne,' Elisande broke in, ready as ever to come to her friend's defence, needful or not. 'There was a bidding laid on her, we have told you of it,' *don't you remember, old man?* 'She's only fulfilled one half of the instructions, thus far.' *Go where you are sent, and marry where you must* – and she'd done the marrying because she had to, she'd been forced to it, and now she was running from her new-wed lord and looking for her father. Whom she would find in Rhabat, by the djinni's word. By her face, she had no plans to turn aside.

'That should not have been spoken of,' Rudel grated, ready as ever to stress his daughter's faults. There was none to hear but the Sultan and his page, though, and the Sultan had heard it all last night. Elisande glared, and was entirely ignored. 'Julianne, I would be glad to know Redmond in your company on his way to Surayon, and you would be very welcome there. Your father could find you as conveniently in that place as any other, once we tell him where to look . . .'

'I expect that's all very true,' Julianne said briskly, 'and all very wise to boot; but I was told to go to the Sharai, and I will go. Besides, I was also told that he would be in danger, and that I could save him. If I wait for him in Surayon, I think I might wait a long time, and waste it anyway.'

Rudel stiffened, and his eyes darted rage at Elisande. She moved not a muscle, gave him not so much as a twitch of the head that he might read as meaning *no, not me, a lucky hit, no more, a cruel chance; I have told her nothing.*

'A girl should go where she is told to go,' the Sultan said lightly; it was impossible to tell which way he intended them to understand that, whether he thought she should obey the djinni or these men.

'And so she will, excellence.' Elisande slipped her arm through Julianne's, deciding to claim his support whether he were offering it or no. 'We were both of us sent on this journey, and we two will see it to an end.'

'Or die trying.'

'Indeed, excellence. The one, or the other. We are quite determined.'

'Stubborn, I should have said. And wilful, and foolish, and—'

'—And so well supplied of your generosity that we have the finest chance of seeing Rhabat, girls and old men and all,' Julianne completed for him. There were famously risks in interrupting an arbitrary ruler, men had lost their tongues for doing so; but Julianne was a girl, and a guest, and the daughter of a powerful figure. Elisande didn't so much as nudge her in a belated warning to be careful, she only smiled and listened and thought she couldn't have played it better herself as Julianne went on, 'Redmond, I am sure that His Excellence is right, that you ought to stay and rest and then go home; but you know and I know that what is right is not always what is needful. If there is a council of the Sharai at Rhabat, and if there is a chance that the voice of Surayon will be given audience at such a council, then you know and I know that your wisdom should inform that voice. The Sultan has named me stubborn, and he is right in that also. I will go, for my father's sake. If it costs you pain, I am sorry; but I hope that my stubbornness and your understanding together will persuade you to travel with us, for the sake of all our peoples. With our companions to lead us and these magnificent beasts to carry us, I am sure we can come through safely.'

It was a clever speech precisely weighted, clear-sighted and politic, deferent both to Redmond and indirectly to

Rudel; it had what must have been its intended effect. Redmond sighed and bowed, while Rudel nodded his head.

'I am afraid I will slow you all,' the older man said, and little doubt of it, 'but that cannot be helped. If I can ride a horse, as I have, then I can ride a camel; and I can travel the traders' road. It may be true what you say, that there is need. And the Sultan's doctors have given me a measure of relief. So be it, then. You are a hard creature, Julianne; but these are hard times, and we must suffer them. I will come with you.'

Julianne kissed his cheek gently, in gratitude or apology, both; Elisande wanted to do the same, but instead looked around to follow the Sultan's sudden gaze, to see who or what had drawn his attention.

And saw, and recognised the inevitability of this even as her spine chilled at the sight, even as the Sultan spoke.

'Your party will be a little larger than you had anticipated, perhaps. I have no voice in this, they answer no command but their own. They will see you all safe to Rhabat, though, if the Ghost Walker goes so far.'

Everyone turned, at that; Elisande sensed their various puzzlement or doubt, quickly dispelled by understanding as they saw what she had seen, the Sand Dancers standing in a group in the shadow of the palace wall.

She watched Marron's face change, and Jemel's also; she watched how the Dancers moved forward with a slow dread grace, seeming to bring that shadow with them; and she swore a silent vow that whosever possession the boy might ultimately fall into, it should not be theirs.

4

Singing for a Stranger

At this distance she thought they looked like statues, mono-liths, black silhouettes that seemed to own more potency than their simple size would suggest. Hazed by the heat, they flickered and jerked in her sight like those deceptive, disturbing insects they were named after, unless the insects were named after them; sometimes she thought they'd van-ished altogether, only that they came back before her eyes had really registered their absence.

And yet she knew that they stood monolithically on the sand, still as statues, moving not a muscle. And among the Sand Dancers, at the focus of their little convocation, stood Marron: stiller than any except that the skin around his eyes would twitch with effort, that much he couldn't prevent.

Julianne knew all of that because the first day and the second day she had gone close to watch. No one had seemed to mind, and she'd been curious; bored too if she were honest, keen for any distraction to while away these noon-tide hours when it was too hot to ride and too hot to sleep.

After those first two days she'd kept her distance. Curiosity was sated, and she could only bear so much of watching a friend fail and fail at something that might matter beyond her ability to reckon its worth. Besides, this too was boring, though it was an agonising boredom. They would stand unmoving throughout the hours of rest, the Dancers in half a circle around Marron at its heart; only the one man would speak and perhaps Marron would reply, but only to say, 'I can't. I am trying, but I *can't* . . .'

He'd say it in Catari, but that much at least Julianne had learned.

That much and a deal more, actually, just as Marron had; though she thought he was the quicker pupil or had the better teacher or more application than she, unless having the Daughter in his blood somehow gave him an advantage in this too, as it seemingly did in swordplay. At any rate, he seemed fluent now when he spoke to Jemel, while she was still fumbling for the right words and her grammar made Elisande smile more often than Julianne quite liked.

Her friend was her back-rest just now, as she was Elisande's; but the other girl was restless, shifting and twisting to peer over Julianne's shoulder, to watch that same motionless group of men.

'Do you want to go and see?' Julianne asked at last, in careful Catari.

'Want to? No. But your back's too hot to lean on, so we might as well move; and there's nothing else to look at . . .'

Julianne understood more than the words, she understood her friend also, better perhaps than Elisande would want her to. The whole world was too hot, her back was not to blame; walking would be hotter than sitting still. But she stood, and waited for Elisande to do the same; and took her friend's hand in hers, and together they walked away from the roadside and across soft sand towards Marron and those unmoving Dancers.

Standing up, she could see now the one figure that had been missing before. There were the tall still figures, men and boy, who might have been statues; and there just a short distance off was the shorter, more squat shape of one young man sitting in the poor shade of a low dune, though he might have been a rock. He moved as little as the others, which meant not at all.

That was Jemel, of course, keeping as close to Marron as it was safe to come. It was towards him the girls chose to walk, not quite directly towards the group. He might not welcome their company, but they would welcome his.

Some days beyond the oasis, they had left the lava field behind at last, at a ridge of broken hills; there was gravel now beneath the hard-packed sand of the road. That was all the difference that Julianne could see, between this and their previous journey. The sun was hotter, or seemed so, but the Sharai robes they all wore were cooler than the clothes they'd had before. In truth she was disappointed, and a little angry. She'd expected real desert, high dunes and short water and only an intimation of a track to follow, no traffic. Instead they clung to this well-travelled route, met caravans coming and going, camped each night by a populous well. It was easier for Redmond, that was sure, and she supposed easier for her also; riding a camel was an uncomfortable art that she'd been slow to acquire. All her body ached, although Rudel had led them in steady stages and never pressed the pace.

What angered her, beyond her own weakness and inexperience, was that she saw no need for the camels, and felt cheated because of it. She could have brought Merissa after all, she thought, and so have had no need of sores or suffering. She felt that she'd been promised a hard road, and had not found it.

Not so for Marron, nor those who cared most for him. The Sand Dancers had claimed that boy, and he lacked the will or the knowledge to deny them. They walked with him while the others rode, and at times of rest they drew him away and tried to test or teach him. Jemel had been forced out, kept at a distance; the same was true, Julianne thought, of Elisande. At least she seemed as resentful, as jealous almost, as the Sharai lad so obviously was.

As now, when he could do no more than sit stone-still and bear witness, and neither did they dare go any closer. He greeted them, for a wonder, though only in a grunt and a Catari grunt at that; unfair to expect anything more, perhaps, when he was so visibly bound up in the show before him.

They settled down at his side, in what thin shade his little dune could offer, and gave their attention to what was gripping him.

Marron stood, and the Dancers stood about him; but only in half a circle or a little less than that, a few careful paces back.

Marron held his left arm stiffly, painfully out from his side, and bled slowly onto the sand.

In front of him, that thing that Julianne still thought of as the Daughter twisted slowly in the air. Trying to please him, Julianne thought, trying to be what he wanted. She'd have liked to dismiss that thought as fanciful, and could not. Certainly it was not shaped as she had seen it before, insectoid and deadly, a killing shadow; now it seemed more like a window or a looking-glass, she thought, its cloudy mass drawn out into a frame with only the faintest skein of red across the centre.

The man who was first among the Dancers, whose name she had learned – though not from him – was Morakh, that man was speaking softly. She couldn't hear what he said, only the murmur of his voice; Marron could hear, though, and his face was tight with strain. The Daughter shifted like smoke in a breeze, although the day was utterly still; for a moment a clear space seemed to open at its heart and a hard golden light shone through, almost tangible even under the sun's fierce glare.

Julianne's mind tripped, sending her back to a cave, an impossible brightness, dark terror that had snatched at her own stupidity. She jerked her head hard away from the memory, and was grateful to see distracting movement among the Dancers.

One of the men had reached into his robe and brought out something living, something that wriggled and squirmed in his hand.

'Sand-rat,' Elisande muttered at her side. It looked like a plain rat to Julianne, sand-brown perhaps but a rat none the less; squinting, she saw that its kicking back legs were longer than a rat's.

She heard its thin sharp squeal, saw it fly; saw it as a dot of darkness as the man tossed it carefully towards the gleaming light where the Daughter – or Marron, it was hard sometimes to distinguish between them – had opened a way into another world.

That way snapped shut, though, a moment before the tumbling creature reached it. There was a soft, implosive sound, and silence after; more blood than Marron's sprayed across the sand.

Marron cried out at that, and his voice carried his grief: 'How do I make it hold its shape?'

'Strength of will,' they heard Morakh reply, impatience sharpening his tone enough for it to reach them. 'It owns you, at least a little; you must make it serve you instead.'

To judge by Elisande's soft snort, that girl doubted Marron's strength of will as much as Julianne did. He had been owned entire by the Ransomers, and then by Sieur Anton; and then, yes, for a little time by the Daughter. Less so now, she thought, or wanted to think. Marron's life had become more complex, though not of his own desire; likely he still wanted to give his soul away, if he could only make the choice. Certainly the Dancers wanted to possess him, and believed they had the right, but there were others too who would make a claim. Jemel, for one; and Julianne thought that she could name another.

'Again,' Morakh said. 'You must learn to command it, as you command yourself.'

'He never has,' Elisande murmured distressfully, 'he doesn't know how.'

So it seemed, as they watched Marron fail, and fail again; as small creatures died to mark each failure, and each death upset him more. Elisande muttered, and fidgeted uselessly; it was Jemel at last who stood and walked boldly into that group of men, unslinging his water-skin as he went.

'Enough!' he cried. 'Marron, call it back now, and drink. We have a long road before nightfall, and Rudel will be eager to get on . . .'

Morakh moved scowlingly to block his way, to deny him; but Marron had already nodded and stretched his arm out, to take the Daughter back into his blood. He seemed grateful for the interruption, as Julianne was herself. There was no entertainment in this, only a brutal fascination.

'That's a brave boy,' Elisande said, her voice all regret, as though she blamed herself for lacking the necessary courage. 'Rudel would be pleased with him. If that meant anything to Jemel, though I'm glad to say it does not.'

Both halves of that were true. The Dancers worried Rudel, their influence over Marron worried him more; Jemel had his own reasons for everything he did, and they were none of them Rudel's.

'Come on,' Julianne said, rising and offering her arm to Elisande. 'Let's get back to those accursed camels. On the way, you can explain to me again how it's possible to sit in that saddle all day and not raise blisters . . .'

The camels were couched by the side of the road, high-necked and haughty with deceptive eyes, long-lashed and seductive. Julianne's own beast – or at least the one she rode, she would never claim possession, nor want to – was the white, Sildana, whose proud lineage the Sultan had first proclaimed. That pairing had been at his insistence, beauty to ride with beauty he had said, a compliment she couldn't refuse; she was sure now that a devil had inspired that choice, that this particular camel was the least-fleshed, the hardest-boned and the most wilful of them all.

They exchanged glares, she and Sildana, promises of later pain. Then men moved, rising from where they'd been resting in their camels' shade, Rudel and more slowly Redmond.

Rudel said, 'Where are the others? We should be moving on,' and as usual he spoke across his daughter and yet to her, implying that the delay was somehow her own fault and no one's else.

'Jemel is coming,' Elisande said shortly. Marron and the Dancers would follow in their own time, that was understood. The unspoken accusation was simply ignored; Elisande collected her riding-stick and went to the string of pack-animals, to begin the lengthy process of loading them up and persuading them to their feet.

Despite all these weeks of travelling together, despite the many hours of quiet and private talk, Julianne still hadn't discovered what it was that lay so bitterly between Elisande and her father. There had been chances aplenty, and many times she'd felt the question lie upon her tongue, but each time she'd put it aside unasked. She wasn't accustomed yet to having so close a friend; and even in the best of friendships, she thought, some secrets were too dangerous to share. She was frightened of making herself equally vulnerable, of hearing Elisande ask in return how she really felt about Imber, and about leaving Imber. It was a question she wasn't prepared to answer, for fear of discovering the truth within herself, whether she spoke that truth or no;

and so she did not ask, and Elisande did not tell her. She only showed her again and again how a warm and instinctive girl could be cold and hard and unforgiving, if she felt she had reason enough. Which was a useful lesson, Julianne thought, and one she might need later, though she dreaded the opportunity to apply it.

She helped Elisande lade the pack-beasts despite her aching muscles, heaving sacks of rice and flour with an ease that she certainly hadn't known before, and an economy of effort that she'd consciously acquired under the hot sun. Jemel came before they were finished, and lent his own hands to the task. Julianne could almost have resented that, except that she knew now that among his own people he wouldn't have done it, he'd have felt demeaned to work with women. More than her body was being changed by this trip, she thought.

All possible work done, even Elisande mounted now and Rudel manifestly impatient – manifesting it by pacing his camel in tighter and tighter circles on the road, while he glanced back and up at the sun and back again – she left the string of pack-beasts to Jemel and approached Sildana with a reluctance that was so passionate it was almost loathing.

There were minor skills to camel-riding, and those at least she had learned. She untied the hobble that bound foreleg to thigh with a single twitch of her wrist; she lifted her stick and settled into the saddle in a single movement before the animal realised its freedom; she tucked her right foot under her left thigh in that curious one-legged posture that was obligatory, it seemed, though whether for practical reasons or only for proper style she was still unconvinced.

Tap of stick on Sildana's flank and the camel rose, hindquarters first and already roaring. Julianne swayed back and then forward for balance, hoping for some grace, knowing that her companions were watching. All too soon, she knew – and her sore muscles and chafed skin were already reminding her, lest she forget – she'd have passed beyond all thoughts of grace or style: she'd be shifting her weight constantly from buttock to agonised buttock, she'd be changing her lead leg more often than her mount did and groaning more often also, though hopefully not so loudly.

If it weren't so constantly painful, she was sure there'd be pleasures in riding like this, so different from horseback. The slow rocking motion reminded her of boats, of her early adventures with sails and oars on the great river at Marasson. Elisande told warning stories of men being lulled into sleep on a long trek and falling from their mounts, being lost in the *mul'abarta*; those she could almost believe.

She looked about from the height of Sildana's back and spotted dark figures keeping pace across the sand, Marron and the Dancers taking up their usual station. Looking ahead was harder, Sildana's head got in the way; but there would be nothing interesting to be seen in any case, only the men on their camels and the endless hours of the unchanging road. She had Elisande at her side for company, teasing company for sure once she started to fidget. Julianne sighed and tried to settle grimly into her discomfort, knowing that there would be no break now until sunset.

And was proved suddenly, startlingly wrong, by the

sounds of running footsteps and jabbering voices just where
the road turned around a low hill. She glimpsed milling figures ahead, Rudel's camel twisting out of line as it met a
pack of men on foot. Elisande grunted and plied her stick,
to drive her own mount forward; Sildana followed without
Julianne's needing to lift a finger.

There were five or six of the men, camel-drovers by their
dress, and that they had abandoned their animals only
underscored the panic that was obvious in their gestures,
their high strained voices and their wild eyes.

They spoke Catari, too fast and shrill for her to follow
yet. Rudel was trying to calm them and his agitated beast
both at once, and succeeding at neither. It was Redmond
who produced an unexpected bellow, to still the scene; into
the quiet after, Elisande's voice fell like wisdom.

'Who is first among you? Let him alone speak, and tell
us what your trouble is.'

'He is dead,' three voices answered her, 'and a ghûl has
eaten him.'

No trouble understanding that, despite the chorus. The
words resounded in Julianne's head, dragging up echoes of
memory: another road, another delay, another encounter
with power freed from story. That too had left blood in the
dust; it had also and directly led this party here, and it led
them still. Briefly, she was afraid. If there was such potency
in these meetings, who could say in what direction she
might not be flung now, and for what purpose?

That was nonsense, of course. A ghûl was not a djinni.
And the djinni had waited especially for them, for her;
while the ghûl it seemed had killed and gone, and this
would not be in any sense a meeting or a confrontation

even if she were allowed to witness it, which likely she would not be. Rudel would forbid it . . .

But there again, here again came an echo of before, Elisande wickedly forestalling her father as she had previously forestalled Sergeant Blaise and all Julianne's retinue of guards on the road to the Roq.

Wicked it was, and consciously so, but not done out of mischief. Elisande's face was grim as she pulled a dagger from her sash and cried, 'A ghûl? Ride, Julianne – let's see if you can make that camel run . . .'

She could, though she hated the graceless jouncing of it and the insecurity, the constant fear of falling, almost the expectation. She bumped and gasped, clung to head-rope and saddle-horn, plied her stick determinedly in Elisande's wake and didn't look back even at Rudel's bellow, 'Wait! Both of you, wait till I . . .'

He would take a minute longer to be free of his beleaguers; Redmond would be slow to follow, as he was slow in everything except his mind; Jemel had the leading of the pack-string, and would be delayed by that.

Their road was clear, and Elisande for one must be rejoicing inside, however set her features. Even Marron and the Dancers were too far off to follow this tale or to interfere in its telling, her making. Any opportunity to defy her father was a godsend; this was defiance and action both, a hard ride under hot sun, burning fever below a burnished sky. This was how the Sharai lived, she'd said to Julianne with envy the salt on her tongue: slow days and sudden moments, idle as a big cat is idle, only ever a breath away from fury. It was how they lived and how they expected to live, how they loved, how they prayed, how they fought. The world was harsh and dull and repetitive, day on day and year on year, with no seasons to mark how the years passed. Pain and fear were events as much as joy or discovery; in that landscape they stood out just as boldly, and were welcomed just the same. The Sharai raided for the thrill of it more than for camels or honour; the death of their own was only a little less bright or less to be cherished than the death of an enemy. Anything, Elisande had said, to break the monotony.

They'd both had a taste of that monotony, on the road: protected, unchallenged, bored. Even Julianne's saddle-sores had at least provided distraction. Now she was tasting a little of the antidote, the sharp brassy tang of terror. There was a ghûl ahead, a killer that had killed already this day. By its reputation – her nurse in Marasson had told stories of ghûls and her friends had told others, cruel tales of blood and fell deeds and the victory of the dark – it would be glad to kill again, and yet again. And here they rode towards it, two girls with knives and nothing; and yes, she was terror-stricken and she thought her friend was mad and she was mad to follow; and yet her blood sang and her throat yearned to, and for that little time she could have been Sharai and glad of it, if truly their lives were lived like this.

But they came around the rise of the hill, she and Elisande, and neither of them Sharai; and there was no ghûl to meet them, no work for their blades or their working, cursing mouths.

Dry mouth, in Julianne's case: abruptly dry, and that

nothing to do with hard riding or the heat. Nor with the fear, released by the stillness of the road ahead, no sign of any fabled creature crouched snarling over its kill, no sign of anything that moved.

Rather it was that stillness that sucked her dry, certainty that followed doubt. She had not consciously doubted the drovers, perhaps, there hadn't been time; but men in a panic will run and not look back, will report their nightmares as truth observed. Men of the desert would see a ghûl's attack and flee, and say perhaps that it had eaten their master because that was what they knew of ghûls, what they had been told as she had. It didn't need to be true.

Men of the desert knew more than she did, though. What was true was what she saw, she'd been trained to believe her own eyes and none other; and what she saw now was the long run of the road, and a terrible stillness at the limit of her sight. She could see nothing clearly beyond the stretch of Sildana's neck, what with the jolting of the camel's speed and the dazzling glare of the sun, and Elisande ahead; but for sure there was some darkness that stained the pale road, a shadow of confusion, and for sure there was nothing there that showed any sign of life.

They came closer, too close; and still Elisande did not slow her mount, and so neither could Julianne. Not till the heavy smell of death rose to greet them, and then it was the camels' choice to slow, to halt, to stand and groan a few short paces from catastrophe.

Elisande slipped out of the saddle then, and so did Julianne; Elisande hobbled her beast quickly, and so did Julianne.

Elisande walked slowly, softly forward and so, reluctantly, did Julianne.

They walked among tumbled bales and bags; bright cloths and spilt foodstuffs were strewn across their path. On either side of them camels lay dead in their harness, slumped and vast and angular, their heads askew amid vivid pools of blood where their throats had been ripped out. The stench was vile, every breath was blood and she choked on it; but that was far, very far from the worst of this. Almost she turned her head to look more directly at the slaughter that surrounded her, only to avoid looking further, to where one more shape lay fallen in the road.

That shape had been a person once, so much was undeniable. Now, not. Now it was only rags and bones: rags of dark cloth that might once have been less dark, rags of flesh that must once have made a living, thinking man.

More recently, that flesh had made a meal for some ravening monster. A ghûl she'd been told, and so much she was prepared to believe, sight unseen. No mortal animal could have done this, could have killed and eaten such a weight of meat and then killed and killed again, and yet have vanished in the time those terrorised men had taken to run less than half a league . . .

She stretched up, glad of the excuse, and took a slow, measured look at the land around. Broken hills of rock and shale and shadow, ever-wider stretches of sand between; she could have seen further from Sildana's back but gazed more intently now, and found that she'd been wrong before, when she thought that nothing moved or lived. There were shadows that shifted, there were shapes, silhouettes against the sky. Lions, ghûls . . .?

She shuddered, and had to squint and shade her eyes to be sure. Only camels, broken away from the train and fled before the killer reached them. Of course, with that many drovers, there must have been many more camels than the half-dozen or so that lay dead here.

As she stared and stared, seeking more reassurance than her eyes or her logic could provide – or else only seeking comfort, looking away to prevent herself looking down and seeing again that mess of ruined meat almost at her feet – she heard the pounding hurry of riders at her back, which must be Rudel and Redmond following on. Jemel too, most probably, leaving the string behind. She heard them check some little distance off, she heard them dismount as she and Elisande had done, unwilling or unable to force their camels in among the dead; then she heard other, softer sounds, men running over sand.

She turned at that, to see Marron approaching fast, outsprinting the Dancers. They had their swords drawn, he did not. She saw him meet the invisible wall the camels had balked at, the stink of so much death; she saw how he balked also, how his blood rushed to the call of what was spilt here, suffusing all his skin. She saw how his right hand clutched at his left arm, as if to hold his own blood back within that ever-open gate.

The Dancers ran around him, and came on. Julianne's eyes remained fixed on Marron, where he stood transfixed. She waited for the inevitable, for someone to go to him; she wouldn't be the only one who'd seen.

A small figure rushed past her and scurried to his side,

and almost Julianne could smile at that, despite the devastation all around. Not a Dancer, and not Jemel; it was Elisande who took his arm and turned him, led him away, talking softly in his ear as they went.

'Well? Was it a ghûl?'

'Oh, yes. Did you doubt it?'

'I have never seen a ghûl-kill before.'

'Nor I, that I know of. A ghûl kills in the shape that it takes; it might be a woman, with a knife. This was not. But look here, the trail it left. See?'

'Are you sure those are ghûl-tracks? A man might ride an ass, on this road. Or there might be wild asses in these hills . . .'

'I have never seen an ass that went on two legs, Rudel.'

Julianne ducked her head quickly, to hide her sudden smile. She'd never suspected Morakh of possessing a sense of humour. Rudel snorted his self-disgust, and said, 'What should we do, hunt it down?'

'We will follow the trail,' Morakh said, with a subtle emphasis that clearly meant *we the Dancers* and no one else. 'I do not expect to meet the ghûl, but the effort must be made. You should stay, and help to clear the road. Bury that, with what rites you please; the men will return for the strayed camels, but they will not touch the kill. Wait for our return, when you are done. We must consider how best to go on from here.'

Julianne thought it would be best to go on quickly, and watchfully; it didn't seem to her to need discussion. She would have no voice in whatever decisions were made, though, she knew that. Rudel seemed a little startled, to have his own authority so ignored; just as well that Elisande hadn't overheard. There was no point adding further fuel to that particular fire.

The drovers did come back, slowly and warily, bringing the party's string of baggage-camels with them. They were willing enough to drag the dead animals off the road once packs and harness had been cut free, but as Morakh had predicted, they wouldn't even approach the body of their dead master.

Jemel took a short-handled spade from the baggage and went a little way into the sand, to dig the best grave that he could manage. Rudel was thoughtful and detached, Redmond too weak to help, Elisande still busy with Marron, two distant figures on a hilltop; Julianne appointed herself to assist. She gathered rocks to make a cairn, both to mark the grave and keep scavengers from digging up the bones. Building a heap close to where the young Sharai was digging, she said, 'Tell me about ghûls, Jemel. I only know what my old nurse told me, tales to scare a naughty child . . .'

'Ghûls can scare a grown man,' he grunted, flinging sand. 'And should do. They are deadly.'

'So are the djinn; but—' *But I have met a djinni and been more angry than scared, though Elisande tells me that was ignorance and not wisdom.*

'If a djinni were a man, a ghûl would be a jackal: mean and vicious, with no thought beyond its belly. But a jackal is a scavenger; ghûls kill. They can kill with terror, as today – I have not asked what shape it came in, but it was fearful. You have seen what its jaws did. They can kill with guile also. Sometimes they take the shape of a woman, to deceive a traveller. By God's grace they cannot change their feet; always they go on asses' hooves. That you should watch for, if you meet a woman alone on empty ground. They are fond of ruins, graveyards, places such as that. This one may haunt the road awhile, if the Dancers do not slay it or drive it off. Good hunting here, for a ghûl.'

That was evident, though it had killed the camels not for food, only for the joy of slaughter.

It was Jemel too who wrapped the body in its own torn cloak for decency, who carried it – alone, altogether too light a burden – to the narrow grave and laid it there. The others gathered then: Rudel and Redmond, even Elisande and Marron, to Julianne's surprise. The boy was again flushed with blood, though there'd been little enough left in the corpse for his own to react to. He came none the less, with Elisande gripping his hand in silent support. Not at all to Julianne's surprise, Jemel moved immediately to stand at Marron's other side.

Redmond spoke, from the head of the grave: chanted rather, and swayed slightly to the rhythm of his own beating words. A prayer it sounded like, in an old and formal style of Catari that Julianne could barely identify, let alone understand; but she could name it none the less. This was the *khalat*, the death-rite that would sing the slain to paradise; without it, his soul would haunt the ground he died upon. Julianne had heard the *khalat* whispered three times in Roq de Rançon, when Elisande had tried to free the spirits first of the man she'd helped to kill, then of all the Sharai who'd died that night, and then of the dozen boys

who'd died the night following, burned in the preceptor's
auto-da-fé.

Voices answered Redmond: Rudel's and Elisande's,
Jemel's, not Marron's and of course not hers.

The last part of the rite, though, that she could watch
and copy, understand and join in. They each took a handful of sand and sprinkled it over the covered body; and as
pale grains scattered over dark robe like salt over meat – but
no, she didn't want to think about meat, it was only sand
on sodden cloth and nothing more – each one nicked a
finger on a blade, gave a drop of blood to the dead and said
a few words, private thoughts for private sharing here under
the bright sun, under the shadow of a stranger's death.
They spoke in Catari still, to honour the departed, and
Julianne was pleased to find that she could follow it.

Redmond spoke of the Catari vision of paradise, a place
of soft air and sweet water, birdsong in gardens; she thought
of Bar'ath Tazore, an oasis in a desert, and thought that if
she had grown up Sharai in this harsh land – or simple
Catari, conquered under the harsh rule of her own people –
that would be her vision too, a place of pleasure after the
release of death.

Rudel spoke of journey's end, rest after hard travail;
Elisande of what was good in travelling, the lessons of experience, the getting of wisdom. Only Jemel spoke of the ghûl,
and even he managed to set shock and anger aside, to find
some good in a horrific death: 'He gave himself to the beast,
to save his men. They say he threw himself into its jaws. To
choose death for your friends' sake is high honour; to do so
for such as they, for servants and vassals, is beyond my praise.'

Julianne waited, but no one moved, though no one looked

at her. At last she drew her knife and touched point to fingertip, squeezed out a drop of blood and let it fall. She drew a breath to follow and said, 'I do not know what is common or right to say, at such a time; and we none of us knew him who is dead here,' indeed she didn't even know his name, and wasn't sure if anyone had heard it. 'But Jemel says he died bravely, and him I trust; Redmond says he is in paradise, and him I trust. Rudel and Elisande say that his journey was worthwhile, and his peace now well-deserved. The only sadness, then, is that his family is not here to see him buried and hear him praised; I will stand for them, if I may. I have nothing to say of a stranger, but I can grieve his death.'

Elisande kissed her. Still no one moved, they were only waiting; there was one more to speak.

Marron said, 'He is dead, and I, I did not kill him; that's all I can offer him. Not my blood.' *For the God's sake no*, Julianne thought, *not that!* – and thanked the God that Marron had that much sense, at least. 'This is dead ground we leave him in. Nor can I open any door to where his soul is now, if anywhere . . .'

And he turned and walked away, and there was a long moment's pause before Jemel and Elisande both hurried after.

Rudel lifted his head, to watch them go; he said, 'I hope that boy is right, that he did not kill this man. Myself, I'm not so certain.'

Julianne didn't understand that, but the grim expression on Rudel's face made her shiver none the less.

The Dancers returned before she'd finished shovelling sand and stacking rocks to build the cairn above the grave. Small help she'd had in that: Redmond had stayed but said little and did less, Rudel had taken a turn with the spade but then excused himself to go and speak with the drovers. Elisande and both the boys were distant figures, holding themselves apart.

She might have resented that – Marron was tireless, the other two were not saddle-sore as she was – but was surprised to find that she did not. Hard work, stretch and sweat was better than the cramping discomfort of her seat on Sildana's back; and it made her feel useful, which was rare on this journey. It also kept her from thinking too deeply, which was also rare, and equally welcome.

But the Dancers returned: a twist in the horizon's shimmer like a flaw in a glass, and then a single broken line of black that marched like killer ants, like the killers that the Dancers were. Rudel went to meet them. For a moment that vision of rapacity stayed with Julianne, so that she wanted to call out, to cry him back.

They brought nothing but their predicted failure with them, so far as she could see. Certainly none of them carried the head of a ghûl as trophy or reassurance, proof that they had slain the monster. When a ghûl died, did its corpse keep the shape it had died in? Might they have come swinging a woman's head by the hair, claiming that it had changed to deceive them – and would they have been believed, if they'd done so? Not by the drovers, she thought, who had seen the ghûl in some more dreadful shape. Rudel and the others would have wanted to see the asses' hooves, to be convinced. Herself, she simply felt glad that the ghûl's trail – or the Dancers' – had not crossed a solitary woman's path this afternoon. She thought those men might have swung the sword without looking for tracks in the sand, or the feet below the robe.

She watched them coming closer, the discipline of single file broken now by Rudel's walking beside Morakh. The discipline of single-mindedness might be broken too, she thought, seeing how those two argued. How Rudel gestured, at least, angry or emphatic or both; how Morakh only walked steadily with his hands hidden in his sleeves, but his head's jerk, his jutting beard's stiffness spoke more loudly than his voice.

As though the Dancers' arrival were a signal, a summoning – unless it was the argument that drew ever-eager Elisande, the hope of seeing her father worsted – that little group of Julianne's friends came down from the hill to join them. To join the debate, as well; as did Redmond, making only a perfunctory sign to her that must have been intended as a sketchy apology, *I'm sorry to leave you with your work unfinished, but . . .*

Seeing the conclave gather without her, now Julianne was resentful. She slammed rocks together, hoping that the noise she made would make her point also, refusing to look and see if it were noticed; she built the cairn as best she could, high enough and strong enough to withstand storms and digging animals, she thought; and then she walked across to where her companions were gathered. As she went, she ostentatiously slapped her hands together to shake off sand and rock-dust.

And went unnoticed or was deliberately ignored, one or the other; and realised that once again dispositions were being made, her future was being decided without reference to her. Now that she could and really did resent. That it was in part her own special friend who was doing it only fed her vexation further.

'Julianne and I,' Elisande was saying, 'will come with you, Morakh. Whatever others decide.' 'Others' in this context clearly meant her father; a disdainful twitch of the head in his direction underscored that. And no doubt that was the only reason Elisande was taking such a stance, to be in opposition to her father; and even so, Julianne had had more than enough of hearing what she would or would not do, of never being asked.

'Oh, will we?' she asked, in a voice that had lashed princes and earls before this. Elisande was a princip's grand-daughter; Julianne didn't expect the girl to flinch, exactly, but she meant to make her mark. On Elisande's hide, if necessary. 'And where is this, that we will go with Morakh? And why must we divide, what decision is it that will take others elsewhere? Why must our plans change at all? We are delayed, perhaps, but not by half a day . . .'

Morakh and the Dancers stared at her; more than one turned his head towards Rudel or Redmond, expecting to see them discipline her, teach her where her duty lay, in obedience to men. She snorted and turned the same way herself, expecting answers when Elisande gave her only a look that was half stubbornness and half appeal, *back me up in this . . .?*

'It is suggested,' Rudel said neutrally, 'that this road should no longer be considered safe: that we should there-fore leave it, and take the harder but more direct route across the Sands, across the *mul'abarta*. I say that this is an over-reaction, and that we are in any case safer on the road than away from it. My daughter is pleased to disagree with me.'

As ever, in every meaning of the phrase. Julianne nibbled at her lip where it was chafing in the heat, glanced at Elisande and then at Morakh. This must have come from him, so . . .

'Morakh? Why is the road unsafe? One has died here, but we are warned now, we can be watchful . . .'

'Can you watch against a creature that may shadow any living thing, that takes what image it desires? Can you distrust every man and every woman on the road? A ghûl will haunt a place where it can feed in safety; a road such as this, where people come and go but no one guards, it will haunt until it is killed or driven off. We could not find it, but it will be here. Also, it might not be accident that we so nearly met it first.'

'How not?'

'It might be hunting one of us,' and his mouth did not, but his eyes said *Marron*.

Rudel had said almost the same thing, by the grave. This time she asked, 'Why?'

'The Ghost Walker would draw such a thing from half the world away.'

Again, *why?* She saved her breath, though; he had clamped his lips together behind his beard and turned his back, a little disgusted with himself perhaps for having taken so much talk with a woman.

Redmond picked up the thread, and made an argument of it. 'If Marron draws the creature, he will draw it into the desert also, and we will be no safer. Less, perhaps.'

A dismissive gesture of the head, and, 'In the Sands we are alone; whomever we meet, man or woman, is an enemy until they prove themselves a friend. An animal is prey. In the Sands, simplicity is guard.'

And on the road not so: life was complex and unpredictable, everything was shaded, appearance deceived. It made sense, in a way.

But, 'I cannot cross the *mul'abarta*,' Redmond said.

'No.' No argument there, from the Dancer or from anyone. Julianne had not travelled in the true desert yet, but even she knew that much. 'You can go to Rhabat by the road,' Morakh went on, 'alone or you can take the women with you—'

'No,' instantly from Elisande, leaping in before Julianne could gather breath to get there. 'Where Marron goes, we go.'

Which was interesting, no part of the djinni's charge laid on them, but no surprise to Julianne. Nor to Morakh, though by the look on his face it was more than unwelcome. The Dancers were unfussy about veils, to the point where both girls had virtually discarded them, using them only as the men did, to mask their faces against the gritty wind; it was the entire presence of women that revolted the Dancers, against which their naked faces were no more than an irritant, a speck of dirt in an open and poisoned wound.

'I think it is foolhardy to leave the road,' Rudel said, glowering, 'but similarly, where Marron goes I will go. Perhaps Marron himself should say, where he will go . . .?'

At least that one was easy for the boy. He looked around at the Dancers, at Jemel, at Elisande, and said, 'I do not care much, where I go; but if we will be safer in the Sands, then perhaps it might be wise to take that route.'

'Marron, you betray your own ignorance with every word,' Rudel countered. 'No one is safe in the Sands. The

Great Waste, your people calls them, and with good reason.'

That was a mistake; Marron's face closed down. 'I have no people,' he said, his voice harsh and broken suddenly. 'Not there,' with a jerk of his head to the west, to Outremer, 'nor there,' to the south, to Rhabat. 'Nor these either,' the Dancers, 'and not you, Rudel. I go where my friends go; if they choose the Sands, then so do I.'

His friends only chose the Sands because he did, to go with him. Sometimes Julianne thought this whole mission was like that, a quest to nothing; it was hard these days to remember the djinni's warning, her father's peril. She was the one with the most need to reach Rhabat; the rest she thought followed each other, and it was only chance that took them all in the same direction. Chance and stubbornness. Elisande went to watch Marron and to spite her father, more than to support her friend or to obey the djinni; Rudel went to watch Marron and his daughter both, Jemel to watch Marron only, deferring even his vengeance to that end. Redmond – Redmond was old and hurt and should be going home. He was the only one of sense among them, she thought, ready to quit their company sooner than ride the *mul'abarta*, but still he was going to Rhabat. Not so much sense after all . . .

'So be it,' he said then, strength of will overriding the weakness of his body, or he wanted them to think so. 'You follow your paths, and be careful; I will take the slow road, and be patient. I will organise these frail folk,' the drovers, 'and bring their master's goods in with me. They will loot them all, else. I have played the merchant too often to see that with equanimity, it offends my soul.'

'Old rogue, you were a thief before ever you were a trader.'

'Even so. A thief reformed, which means the most rigid of men.' Redmond and Rudel grinned at each other; Elisande growled in her throat.

'Rigid as that one will be rigid soon,' she snapped, jerking her head back towards the fresh cairn, 'if you travel alone. Those frail folk will slit your frail throat, Redmond, and take their loot regardless of your corpse.'

'Not they. They'd be afraid of my ghost.'

'And might meet it even if they do nothing. You need more than a companion to watch your back; you need a healer to keep you upright through the day. Do you think I don't know how much strength you've been taking from Rudel? How do you imagine you're going to manage without it?'

'Poorly, I confess. So come with me, Elisande: you and Julianne both. She can watch my back while you stand in for your father, lend me your youth and resilience . . .'

'I do not have the skill,' she replied tartly, without a hint of regret. 'You know that. Take Rudel. Neither of you is needed, in the Sands.'

'None of you is needed in the Sands,' said Morakh, with simple blinding truth. 'For the sake of the Ghost Walker, because we are his servants, we will take those he names to come; but none other. Fetch up the camels now, it is time to prepare. If ghûls sleep, I have never heard it. We should be far from this road by nightfall.'

If Julianne had thought that leaving the road would be a simple matter and leaving Redmond the only difficult part of it, she was swiftly disabused. Two of the Dancers walked back along the road, searching it seemed among the baggage discarded in the panic of the ghûl's attack; the others unloaded everything from the pack-camels, and began to slash open the cords that tied the food-sacks.

'What are they doing?' she demanded of Elisande. 'Surely we're going to need that, more than ever?'

'Of course. We'll eat nothing in the Sands, bar what we can hunt or glean or carry. But can you carry one of those flour-sacks?'

'No, but the camels . . . Aren't we taking the camels?'

'Yes, we're taking the camels. Camels die, though, sweetheart; sometimes you have to let the camels die. Sometimes you have to kill them, or else die yourself. Never take anything into the desert that you need but can't carry on your own back, because you may well have to do that.'

'Elisande – just how dangerous is this journey now?' Not a stroll, of course, not a pleasure-trip: but if those dour Dancers judged it safer than keeping to the road, then it couldn't be so very bad. Could it?

'Julianne, my love, this is the most dangerous journey of your life, the most dangerous adventure you've ever undertaken. Believe that. You must believe it, or you will endanger us all, even more than we are endangered already.'

No. She would believe many things, she would believe everything that Elisande had ever told her, but not that. She closed her eyes and remembered falling, *falling and falling, and in the dark too* – her life had hung by a stretching thread during that endless fall. Nothing here could push her close to such an edge again . . .

And yet, when she opened her eyes, she saw not her friend's determined face urgent with its message, nor the busyness about her on the road: only the desert, the *mul'abarta*, the Sands. Grey dust and gravel underfoot, golden dunes building just a little walk away; building and building, a rolling sea of sand broken only by hills like rocks and darkening with distance so that what was far away – what she looked at now, what held her eye – was red under the burning sun and shimmered like a dreamscape, moved momentously towards her like the sea . . .

'Hush now and watch,' Elisande said. 'These men know more than I ever will; we can both of us learn by watching . . .'

Each of the Dancers carried water and flour in evil-smelling goatskins, pressed dates in a wrap of rags. Julianne had noticed that already, though they'd been using the company's general store of food and not their own. Necessarily, she supposed, each man's rations must be enough to see him through the desert, at least from one well or one oasis to the next, as they had no beasts to carry more. Unless they did use pack-camels on a long march, they might be forced to do that, although they would not ride. She knew so little about how the Dancers lived . . .

She would learn more in these next days, that much was clear. Obedient to Elisande's command, she watched them now as they transferred flour and dried fish from sacks into scavenged skins.

'Why not the rice?' she asked, seeing how they left some sacks untouched.

'It takes too much water to cook. It's water that matters now, Julianne. We can live hungry, on a handful of flour a day – and wait till you've eaten desert bread, it's a revelation – but thirst is the killer.'

'Dried fish will make us thirsty . . .'

'The fish is for the camels. We'll find little forage for them; it may be that they have to eat before we do.'

Indeed they fed the camels with all they had of greenstuff, before they left the road. Redmond had taken brisk charge of the drovers, as they returned one by one with their strayed camels; those beasts were laden high now and tied nose to tail, a caravan ready to march.

He was satisfied but sombre, anxious about his friends' more perilous journey; he tried once again to persuade the Dancers that there would be less danger on the road. Safety in numbers, he pleaded, now they were alert against the ghûl; so much greater risk their way, not the ghûl alone but all the possible mischances of the desert too, especially with those who were strangers to it . . .

'We will watch them,' Morakh said. 'The Sands are ours; we know where evil lurks, and can avoid it. The ghûl will haunt the road – they do not love the desert, nor the Dancers. I have killed a ghûl before this. You stand at greater risk than we do; be prepared.'

Redmond sighed, and conceded. Then he said a slow and private farewell to each of the companions. Julianne couldn't hear what more than farewell he said to any of the others, but to her he murmured, 'This is an adventure more than your father or any of us had hoped for you, child. Enjoy it when you can, learn from it whatever you can; but above all come safe through it to Rhabat, and bring your sister with you . . .'

Soul-sister he meant, she understood him perfectly; and kissed him before he could her, and gave her promise to hold fast to Elisande.

She watched him give messages – the same or similar, surely, what else could he say? - to Marron and to Jemel, though both boys flinched a little from his words. Then Redmond mounted his camel, threw his arm in a wide gesture that ended with his riding stick pointed firmly to the south, and called much the same thing to them all: 'Go straight and safely to Rhabat, and meet me there!'

Julianne twisted her head aside, wrenched suddenly by the loss of him when she thought she'd been managing so well; and so she happened to see Morakh's face before he could control it, and she had a moment to wonder why mention of Rhabat should make him smile so when he was not a man who smiled, when he himself had said that the Dancers did not go to Rhabat . . .

Then he caught her gaze, and turned away; and the blaze of the sun stung her eyes where she'd stood in his shadow and not realised it.

5

The Pillar of Lives

Marron felt that he had been remade for this exactly: the heat underfoot and in the air to match the heat in his blood that surged and pulsed in sunlight, that was very much a creature of the Sands and nothing at all of what had once been his; the slow endurance of the days to match the slow endurance of his body, that could run grimly all day and all night too if he willed it so, and there seemed so much to run from; the dark robe that cloaked him, the dark figures that surrounded him to match the shadows that swathed his heart, the dead and the betrayed he'd left behind him.

He had been remade, he thought, to be the Daughter's host and nothing more, no vestige of himself.

He thought he should resist that, but it was hard to do. The sun drained him, the stars sucked at his soul, the desert was alien and endless so that he felt utterly lost within it; the Dancers were with him constantly, allowing him no privacy. This was how they wanted him, only a vessel, a doorway to open at their word. It was his abiding failure to do that which served as a reminder that he was still Marron after all, still a boy with a history and sometimes a touch of hope.

Elisande knew something at least of what was happening to him, and tried to help. Whenever they paused to rest, at the sun's height and at night, she brought him food and sat with him while he ate it, talking of the world they'd left, of Outremer, or else of Rhabat where they were headed; she asked him questions too about his childhood, though he was finding it increasingly difficult to remember that. And the Dancers were always there, always listening as they plucked at bread with their maimed hands, condemning her with their silence.

Jemel sought Marron's company less often now, or less obviously. He had taken the string of pack-animals as his duty, which kept him at the tail of the line of riders and kept him busy at the halts. When he did try to come closer, he couldn't breach the wall of Dancers that enclosed Marron. They had rejected him, and the bruise was sore yet.

It had been their first night in the Sands, that Jemel had made his declaration. He'd left Marron's side without a word, and had taken a flat stone to the Dancers' fire; had sat in their circle without invitation, and laid the stone on the sand before them like an offering.

Confused, intrigued, Marron had followed him a little way over, just close enough to see and hear what had passed.

Jemel had spoken to Morakh, as the leader of the band; had said, 'You serve the Ghost Walker; so do I. I would like to swear myself to your brotherhood, to be as you are, wholly committed. Give me grace to join you in your service . . .'

And he had laid his left hand out on the stone, with the fingers spread; had taken his knife from his sash and set the edge against the lowest joint of his smallest finger; had looked to Morakh for the nod of permission.

And Morakh had said no.

Had said, 'No, you may not. I know you, tribeless; I know that you have sworn another oath, which touches on another life. This corrupts you. And I also doubt your desire for the Ghost Walker's eye; your intent is not pure, it defiles him and you. We will have none of you.'

Jemel had hesitated, and Marron had thought for a moment that he might have cut anyway, regardless. But the young Sharai had sheathed his knife and nodded, had risen and walked away without another word.

He had walked away from the fires then, out under the blazing stars, alone; and when Marron had followed, Jemel had sworn at him spittingly and turned his back.

He didn't turn his back now, but neither did he come close; only lurked, gazed from a distance and tended his animals obsessively to keep himself from gazing longer. Even Elisande could find no way to reach him. That was one tool, one weapon she used to keep some kind of grip on Marron, feather-light and failing though it was: Jemel's detachment made it easier for Marron to slip into numb acceptance of the Dancers' will, but Elisande's anxiety about the Sharai could pull him back where his own could not. Pull him back a little, at least, though not far and less far every day . . .

The desert made strong things weak, he thought, and not only bodies. He could watch the bonds between people fraying as the Dancers' robes frayed at the hem, where they pulled threads loose to make tinder; some he thought might flame suddenly and shrivel as those threads did, when a spark caught them.

Rudel, he thought, might scorch every hand that reached to touch him. The older man rode with a constant glower, making plain his distrust of the Dancers and his disavowal of every decision made since they'd left the road. He argued as always with his daughter, but now also with everyone else. If there'd been another Patric man in the party – well, any Patric man bar Redmond, who was so much missed – they'd have come to blows by now. More than once, he'd nearly come to knives with one Sharai or another.

It was the desert doing this, Marron thought, remembering the wise and witty jongleur whom Rudel had been in the castle, courteous and diplomatic and endlessly patient. The sands blew in, and made gritty what had once been smooth; clean and solid structures deformed in the heat. The desert separated people from themselves. He'd have been more frantic than fretful, bitterly concerned, if only it hadn't separated him so far from what was Marron, what was capable of concern . . .

Instead he only watched and saw it happen, and wondered what would happen next. He felt himself some kind of witness on this journey, observing and remembering, all but untouched by the pain and the anger, the fear and the scorn the others bartered between them. As he was by the journey itself, the long toiling miles of it, as they were not.

Since he could not do what he was meant to do, he was as useless to the Dancers as he was to his friends. They guarded him not for his own sake, but for what he carried. He was their talisman; they meant him to be their tool. He watched them also, and listened where he could, though they used a private language between themselves that he couldn't quite follow. It seemed somehow to snag at his understanding, teasing him like a face behind a veil, allowing him glimpses that always fell just short of recognition. He thought perhaps the Daughter could understand it; a man who could use the Daughter as it was meant to be used could perhaps use it for this also, to open a doorway into comprehension. All he could do was mark it up as another minor failure, of a piece with what was greater.

When the Dancers spoke with his own people, though, he needed no translator. Even when they spoke Catari: he was as fluent in that now as in his own tongue. He thought again that that was the Daughter's doing, mostly, although Jemel's had been the hand that drew the veil back.

He had overheard – from a distance, the Daughter's gift, sharpening his ears as all his senses – the first time that Rudel had questioned the route they followed, more west than south; he had heard Morakh's reply, that the tribe holding the land to the south was no friend to the Patric. Dancers could travel freely anywhere among the Sharai, and Jemel perhaps, now that he had forsworn his allegiance. For their own safety, though, Rudel and his party must skirt this territory . . .

'We of Surayon have a special dispensation,' Rudel had growled in response. 'I have never been other than welcome, to any tribe.'

'Times are changing,' Morakh had said. 'Even Surayon is in Outremer, and so accursed. Hasan has drawn the tribes together in this, and word of the Ghost Walker will be spreading also; our people will see that as a sign. You would find yourself less than welcome now. You can go your own way, if you choose; but if you go with us, you must trust our choices.'

Rudel trusted nothing about the Dancers, that much was clear, but he had said no more that day.

This day, though, they'd climbed a rocky bluff above a wadi, and now their only course was west and nothing but west; the steep fall down to the wadi was overmatched by cliffs to the south. They walked atop a wall, leading the slow camels; by the midday halt, Rudel's doubts had mounted into fury.

'This is useless to us!' he stormed, in full hearing of the whole party. 'There's no break to these cliffs, where we might take the camels down. We should go back, and strike south straight away. I'll risk the Ashti or any tribe else, sooner than wander like some lost soul in the *mul'abarta* till our food runs out and we lose all trace of water. Our mission is urgent, Morakh, and imperative.'

'You will risk the tribes, even when they are risen against you? Good. Will you also risk the ghûl?'

'The ghûl? What ghûl? We left that days ago, by the road. That's why we came this way, at your insistence . . .'

'I was wrong,' Morakh said simply. 'I had misunderstood it, perhaps – though it behaves like no ghûl I have heard of. Something drives it, more than hunger; it may have smelled out the Ghost Walker, and be drawn to him. It has followed us, at least, since we left the road. We have found tracks; last night I saw a shadow skirt our camp.'

'Why have you not said, before this?'

'What point? We know the danger, and we guard against it. So long as you trust no strangers and keep your swords to hand, you will be as safe as you can be. It will not attack a group alert, as we are. This is neutral ground we stand on, sacred, forbidden to the tribes; if the tribeless one were still Saren, we could not have brought you here. The ghûl may be afraid to follow, where God has walked; I do not know. But if you go down, how will you know what chance encounter is a woman drawing water on her own land, and what is a ghûl eager for your blood?'

It seemed a fair question, though Rudel gave no fair answer, only a snort and a dubious glare. 'Next time you see a monster's tracks, I would appreciate it if you showed them to me.'

'As you wish.'

'In the meantime, can you say how we will find our way to Rhabat? This sacred crag of yours is leading us far astray . . .'

Morakh's face darkened at what might have been a blasphemy of tone, what might be a case of knives against this rud-skinned Patric; but there was perhaps a law against the spilling of blood in high and holy places, or else he was uncertain of his ground, or more peaceable than he appeared. 'Be easy,' he said shortly. 'The ridge rises to a flank of hills tomorrow, where a track comes down to the open sands again. From there, due south and perhaps a week's travel lie the Dead Waters, and so Rhabat. Are you content?'

'When we stand in that place, I will be content.'

'Even so.'

A gesture that was not the graceful bow of Sharai convention but a deliberate mockery of it, and so an insult; Rudel's turn to flush. But he said nothing, and he kept his hand far from the haft of his dagger. Marron felt that he should be grateful for so much self-control; only that the Daughter was singing high and pure in his ears and had been all day, louder and more strident every hour, and tugging his mind further still from any human sympathy. He rather thought the Daughter might have liked a little blood. Perhaps this place really was holy, and that was what it responded to; perhaps it only felt its power more, its slow victory over what had been Marron, and so exulted.

Marron felt its power more, that much was certain. The higher they climbed this ridge, the clearer the air, the further he could see across the Sands; and all he saw was sand and rock and shadow, and all of it reddened by the Daughter's bloodied eye, and that he thought was his life now, what was left that he could call his own: barren and dry and overcast by an eye and a will that was not his own at all.

Swept by the wind of centuries and scoured by what sand the wind could lift up from the plain below, the bare rock was smooth beneath their feet, even the bare feet of the Sharai. Marron was forbidden to go shoeless, for fear of a cut; the girls chose not to. Elisande had said, 'I have done that, when I was a hoyden; it took years to be rid of the skin I was left with, like dried leather, I could strop my knives on it. I did. Now I am a lady, I prefer to keep my feet soft and pink and sweet of my perfume . . .'

Even Jemel had smiled. Julianne had collapsed in giggles; only Rudel had schooled his face to stillness, and even he had seemed to take a little effort over it.

Rudel also wore his boots beneath his robe; Marron thought he kept spare knives sheathed in them. But then he thought so did Elisande, now she was a lady . . .

The rock was smooth but awkward; that same wind that had abraded its harsh edges had cut it also into uneven steps, up and down. Where the camels could be ridden, progress was still slow. Marron ranged ahead, with his constant companions the Dancers; a couple of them had gone further still, scouting or hunting, though he thought their bows would find little meat on this denuded height.

Morakh walked beside him, but for once was not speaking of the Daughter and how to control it. Neither had he forced Marron to the test, to yet another failure at the noon break. That was the first time in days. He had perhaps been distracted by the argument with Rudel; that was perhaps unfortunate for him, for his cause, with the Daughter seeming so alive in Marron's blood this day, its shrill song jagged in his ears. Himself, he was only glad of the respite.

Gazing ahead, he saw the two Dancers as dim dark shadows in the eternal red, tiny shadows, too far away for normal sight to find. He watched them moving, and then he saw them standing still, waiting as it seemed.

He walked on with the others, and they waited. After a while, when they were sharp and clear to his adapted eyes, he saw one of them stand tall and gesture stiffly, his arms making signs in bright light.

Marron pointed, needlessly; Morakh had seen already. He stepped up onto a high rock, wind whipping his robe as his arms whipped the air, stabbing forcefully. The distant Dancer shaped a sign in response, and then stood still.

He has found something . . . He wants to show it to us . . .

Possibly anyone with clear sight and an abstracted mind could have understood such basic signs; possibly that touch of familiarity, that sense of a veil lifting in the wind to show the face beneath was no more real than a mirage. Possibly. But Marron felt the Daughter fizzing throughout his body, and couldn't truly doubt it. The Dancers' spoken language might still be shadowed even up here, he wasn't sure, but their language of signs was open and accessible for him to read.

He said nothing, though, he only followed as Morakh hurried forward.

That narrow wall of rock had widened into a broad shelf, by the time they reached the waiting Dancers. Ahead, at the furthest limit of Marron's sight, a line of shadow lay across the horizon, first glimpse of those hills that Morakh had promised.

A dusting of sand gritted underfoot; in places here it had pooled like water in dips and crevices too deep for the wind to rake clear. The Dancers were standing by one such dip, where level stone was interrupted by a run of sand before the stone thrust up again.

The sand had been smooth, and would be smooth again; already particles were flying in the wind, whipped away, the sharp edges of the tracks eroding as Marron watched.

The tracks of an ass's hooves, except that there were only two, spaced as a small man might space his feet if he were hurrying, a small man or a woman . . .

'Shield those from the wind,' Morakh snapped. 'Rudel will like to see them.'

Marron couldn't wait for the riders to come up; this shelf might be broader now, but it was still no place to terrify an animal. He withdrew to a prudent distance, and sat with his back against a rounded pinnacle of rock. He could see well enough, and hear too; he heard the whisper of the camels' feet on sand and rock as they approached, he heard the questions passed from rider to rider, the silence that fell after as they saw their answer.

He heard the thud of Rudel's boots hitting ground, his stomping paces forward. In the next moment of silence, that moment where Morakh might perhaps have spoken – *see, unbeliever?* – and did not, he thought he even heard the insuck of Rudel's breath as that man stood and gazed down at the ghûl's prints in the sand.

'What, even here? I thought you said that it followed us?'

'So it did.'

'And now it is ahead. How did it come here? Nothing has passed us, and we were camped at the foot of the climb all night. You watched, and so did I. Did it fly up, is it a harpy now?'

'What is a harpy?'

'Part woman, part bird. A woman with wings.'

'And claws,' from Elisande, never content to hold back at any meeting where her father had a voice. 'Harpies snatch.'

'A harpy now, why not?' Morakh said, with an exaggerated shrug. 'A woman with wings, it can be that if it chooses. If it has the idea in its head. They are stupid creatures, but they can take an idea and hoard it like a treasure . . .'

'Harpies come from stories,' Elisande objected, 'not from truth.'

'So. The ghûls listen to stories when they can, or so the stories say.'

'I meant I don't believe in your harpy.' Her father's harpy, rather. He had blatantly not meant it as a serious proposal, but it had come from him, and so she must reject it. 'It must have come some other way, got ahead of us in yesterday's travel. Or there are two of them, why not? There could be two?'

Again, Morakh shrugged. 'There could be two, there could be many. We could be hunted by ghûls, though I have never heard that they hunted in a pack before. It could have taken goat-shape and climbed up from the wadi, perhaps . . .'

He gestured north, but that bluff was too far now, they couldn't see how steep it fell away. No one volunteered to ride across and look; some at least were thinking of a ghûl, crouched out of sight and waiting . . .

'It is here,' Morakh went on. 'That matters. Not how it came.'

'So what do we do,' Julianne asked, exposed by her nervousness, 'go back?'

'No. If it hunts us, it would follow; if there is another we would meet it, perhaps where we could not fight. This is better ground than this morning. We will go on; we know it is ahead, we can be watchful. And we, we Dancers know this way, as the ghûl may not. We will lead you in the dark, and so deceive it.'

'And if it takes some form of life, something monstrous that can see in the dark?' Rudel demanded.

'Then it will not be deceived. It hunts us anyway; we lose nothing. And if it sought to attack, there is nothing that can see in the dark, in the Sands, better than the Ghost Walker. We would have warning.'

'Marron can neither walk nor watch all night.' Jemel, objecting fiercely, where Marron might have expected Elisande.

'Do not be foolish, boy. He can, and so can we. Even the women can at need, though we will not push them so far. If the ghûl come, it dies; if not, we have a better chance to evade it, if we keep moving at least some hours of the night. At moonrise, there will be light enough to cast strong shadow. You know this, you have seen. We do not truly need the eyes of the Ghost Walker, our own are good enough.'

Then how will you evade the eyes of what tracks us? He was too far away to ask, and too little interested; a night march would be welcome, a welcome change from common nights. He needed little sleep now, and the Dancers spoke to him in shifts while he was wakeful. Sometimes he lay down and pretended to sleep, only to escape their whispers, but that was small improvement. Hours of tedious discomfort on hard and stony ground were as nothing to the timeless, endless parade behind his eyes: what he had done, what he had not done, what he would doubtless do and not do in the long ache of shame and sorrow and self-disgust that would be his life to come, however it come out . . .

They rode on, leaving the ghûl-sign in the sand for any later traveller to read, if travellers came before the wind had finished its deletion. Marron strode on, no need to run; he could lead the camels and outpace them walking, where they were so cautious. He'd like to outpace the Dancers too, but they were constant as his shadow, and as fast. If he chose to run, they'd match him up here as they had on the sands below. He might outrun them on a road – he didn't know how fast he could run now: faster than before, though, that much he could count on, as well as very much further – but not on uncertain ground which they knew and he did not.

One thing he did know, though, or seemed to: he knew where they were going, although what waited there was a mystery to him as all this land was. Or perhaps not where they were going, but where the Daughter wanted to go, at least – he could feel it, no longer a passenger but something stronger, more demanding, impelling his feet forward. The wadi had turned away to the north, so that this was a high plateau that they walked on now; there was no visible path, nothing to hold him to the line of the southern cliffs except Morakh's promise of an eventual way down, and the knowledge of Rudel's intent to take that way. Whenever he tried to wander, though – and he did try, if only to test himself or the Daughter, to challenge this compulsion – the song in his ears grew harsh and discordant, his arm throbbed and threatened worse, his legs grew heavy as though he waded through water that flowed against him. If he only paused to look back at the following riders, even so small a resistance was difficult, almost painful.

Soon he abandoned any rebellion, and simply set his eyes and his will directly ahead. That was easy; for a wonder even the Dancers fell back, or rather allowed him to forge on alone. The wind was dry and clean, the heat lifted as the sun lowered, he could walk and walk and never tire of walking.

Due west he went, leading or being led, both; the range of hills on the horizon grew slowly, marking an end that they would not reach on this march. He wondered what would happen tomorrow, if the route to the south opened before the Daughter was done with calling or driving him west. He must betray one or the other, and he had betrayed so much already . . .

He thought it likely that he would leave his friends, or force them to follow him; he could neither leave nor deny the Daughter. But that was for tomorrow to resolve. Today, tonight he had nothing to do but walk.

Briefly, as the sun set directly in his sight, he thought he saw the shadow of something tall against its brilliance, a tower or a pinnacle of rock; momentarily he thought it was a needle, seeing a flash of fire through its rooted eye.

Morakh hailed him then, from some distance back. Marron turned, and saw the Dancer's arm move in a gesture that anyone could have read, *wait there, until we come*. That made sense; even the Ghost Walker should not walk alone in the dark, however certain he felt his path to be. Not where a ghûl might be lurking behind any rock. He was surprised they'd let him come so far on his own, even in daylight. Would the Daughter be a match for a ghûl? He didn't know, and didn't want to discover.

He might have asked Morakh when the Dancers caught up, but did not. Neither did he ask about that needle of rock, though its image still burned behind his eye. His curiosity was a small thing, all but smothered under weightier concerns. Nor was Morakh an easy man to question, or a natural confidant. If he could have walked with Jemel or Elisande, he might have tried their knowledge, but that was impossible while they rode.

The party closed up with the sudden fall of night, the riders coming as close to Marron and the Dancers as their animals could bear. For an hour they went by starlight, and slowly; desert stars threw strange shadows underfoot, though they were bright enough even for mortal eyes. To Marron's they were a gorgeous blaze, a veil of scarlet fire thrown across the sky.

When the moon rose they could make a faster way across the uneven rock, and did for several hours, until Rudel called out that the girls were swaying in their saddles. A snort from Elisande might have disputed that, but Julianne at least confessed it. So they made camp in a bowl they found, a little dell of rock where the low walls offered at least some shelter from the wind and gathered sand offered a softer bed than stone, if not much softer. They made no fire that night, despite the chill of air and ground; they must harbour what fuel they had, Rudel said. Morakh said nothing to that, but agreed that it would be foolish to set a light that might attract any eye that sought them.

They organised watches in stints for what remained of the night: Rudel and Jemel, and then the Dancers, two by two. No one suggested including Marron, though he didn't expect to sleep. The Dancers of course would watch for his protection, which was perhaps some hint how he might – or might not – survive an encounter with a ghûl; Rudel and Jemel both he thought would watch him, as much as they watched the rocks and the shadows and the sands below the cliffs. Both would have their reasons.

And both, all of them might be right, he thought, to keep more than half an eye on him, if only to cry the alert if he tried to slip away while others slept. His feet might take him, he thought, even against the wishes or the instinct of his mind. His feet, he thought, were barely under his command now; if his attention wandered, if his thoughts did drift into the margins of sleep . . .

Even now, wide-eyed and focused as he was, his feet had brought him to the far western lip of the hollow where they camped. Nor was it his feet alone that were drawn so, to the edge of rebellion; his eyes strained westward, seeking he knew not what, but finding – or so he imagined – a thread of dark caught between land and sky, crimson thread against scarlet cloth, a night thread that might well be a needle by day, tall enough now that it didn't need a red-ochre sun behind to make it show.

When he looked back to call or gesture one of his friends up to say if they could see it too with human eyes unfiltered, it cost him an effort to turn his head even so much, so little from their westerly path; it cost his eyes a genuine pain, a stabbing hurt that was worse for being so unexpected. He'd thought himself immune to pain now, he thought the Daughter drank it, except when he opened his arm to let that creature out and pain flowed back to fill the space where it had been.

Besides, they were busy down there, making camp and setting watches, feeding the animals, feeding themselves. Soon no doubt Elisande would come to feed him, and he could ask her then.

So he stayed where he was and as he was, eyes and thoughts all bent to the horizon and more interested now in that needle, that stood so exactly in their line of travel. It could be coincidence, he supposed, a way-marker and nothing more; but this hunger in the Daughter was nothing random. There was an object, a place it yearned for, to which it meant to drag his body whether he would or no. And that hunger had grown so quickly through this day, surely it meant that they were coming close . . .

Elisande did bring him food, cold and leathery bread from that morning's bake. He tore at it to soothe her, and asked to test her eyes for his reward. She frowned, squinted, stared; said, 'I'm not sure. Perhaps, I think I do see something, like a pillar, a pinnacle . . .? Silver in the moonlight, but what isn't . . .?'

Which, as he had not said what he would have her see, was satisfaction and answer enough.

'Why don't you ask the Dancers?' she asked, glancing round her suddenly, registering his solitude and seeming as surprised as he was. 'If there's anything there, they'd know it.'

'That's why I don't ask them – because if there's anything there, they must be prepared for us to ask, and would you trust what they told you?'

She tilted her head and gazed at him thoughtfully, a little sadly. 'We've all changed, and are changing,' she said. 'Except Rudel, obviously. But you – ah, you're not the same boy at all, and I do miss that Marron. Too much wisdom isn't good for you. You're young yet, Marron, despite the age of that thing in your bones; can't you be a little foolish sometimes? Just for me?'

He opened his mouth to say that he was, that he had been, and recently so – but remembered just in time that he'd been with Jemel then, which he thought wasn't what she meant at all.

And here was Jemel, coming up with the smell of camels hot and heavy on his clothes and skin, though the smell of boy was stronger. Marron hoped he'd adjust soon to such intensity; he didn't think he could live for long in so enriched a world. Perhaps that was why the Daughter made him feel so detached from it, so uncommitted. It was only his friends who caught him, held him back.

Jemel came, and Elisande left; Marron chewed bread in silence, then pointed to the horizon when Jemel was equally silent and asked what the young Sharai could see.

'A tower, or a pillar of rock,' was the immediate answer. 'A tower, with light at its door?' To be sure, a star's gleam showed through the eye of the needle; even to the sharp eyes of a Sharai, it could look like a lamp at a doorway. 'But I have never heard of anything such, in the Sands. The hermits are all dead or fled, and none of them built so high. If some madman had made himself a desert hold, we should have heard, the Dancers should have told us . . .'

'So they should,' Marron agreed. 'Perhaps they don't know of it. Don't mention it to them, Jemel, not tonight.' If it were new, they would be shamed by their ignorance, and doubly so by his finding it out; they were his guides in this their world, and even the Ghost Walker should not lead here. But he did not believe that it was new. He thought that they knew it, whatever it was; and whatever it was, they chose to march towards it through the dark. He thought that might be no accident.

His feet burned to be moving, to get on. Due west, and directly toward the needle. He thought that might be no accident either.

Even the little distance down from the lip of the bowl and towards where his friends sat in a chilly huddle, where the Dancers sat in another, where Jemel stood uncertainly between – even those few short paces were next to impossible. He walked or tried to walk against a fierce will, against the solidity of air, as though a gale blew directly against him although the night was still. Standing had been hard, like standing in a tugging stream, a torrent; it hadn't hurt. This hurt.

A few grim, determined, stumbling steps were all that he could manage by himself, and all that he was allowed to try. Jemel came back to him, almost at a run; Elisande started up with a soft cry, gazed at him – at them – and subsided slowly.

'What is it?'

'Me. It's just me,' *as it always has been.* 'Best if I sleep apart tonight,' as he always did only higher, further and the only way that he could go. The camels agreed with him; although they had been couched on the far side of the hollow, it was none the less too close for them, they were grunting and restless, lying still only because they were hobbled too tight to stand.

'Best you sleep,' Jemel said sourly, 'I care not where. And I with you; you must not be alone tonight.'

Marron didn't argue. He turned and floated back up to the ridge, feeling that he hardly need set foot on the earth; the absent wind would carry him west, the wind that blew in his mind and only there, unless some shred of it whispered also among the Dancers.

Stopping was not easy, but he did stop; he had Jemel at his side and could grip his arm for steadiness, for the little time it took to take control again of his feet.

In order to tempt them no further, he sat down, setting his back against an outcrop and gazing, gazing west, gazing at the needle.

'This will do,' he said, drawing his robe about him as though he meant to sleep. 'How long do we rest?'

'Until dawn, you. I have the last watch, before.'

'Then lie down, and sleep.'

Jemel did, like a servant at his master's feet. Marron scowled, and shifted a little further off. And turned his eyes and his mind to the needle, squinting through the red-hazed night, trying to see what he could not quite make out, trying to understand what he could not grasp either out there or within himself.

Closing his eyes was useless, turning his head or his thoughts aside was impossible. He thought it would be a long night, although they'd marched through half of it already.

He thought so, and was wrong. Barely two hours had passed before there was a cry in the night, and the grate of steel; Marron heard nothing more than that, until he heard the sleepers waking, calling to each other and to the watch, running to see.

Running east; Marron stayed where he was. Jemel started to go, then checked and came back.

'What has happened?'

'Hush . . .'

Distantly he could hear Rudel and Morakh questioning one of the Dancers, who had stood on watch; who had seen a moving shadow in the moonlight, as it might have been a woman slipping from rock to rock and stealing closer. He'd thought it best to cry out, to wake the camp; he'd known it best to draw his scimitar. A man only ever had one chance to slay a ghûl . . .

Marron relayed that, and Jemel's own scimitar hissed from its scabbard. 'Indeed; and the dark is no time for an arrow. Shall we move?'

Marron nodded, but his feet stayed rooted. He was fairly sure they'd move, yes – but not to hunt the ghûl. Jemel perforce stayed with him, as self-appointed companion and protector only ever reluctantly relieved by Dancers; when Morakh came to do that duty, Jemel at last found cause and courage to challenge him.

'Well? Did your man see true, is there a ghûl in the rocks?'

'We found tracks that were not ours, nor yet a goat's: something two-legged and hoofed, it seems to be. We would see better in daylight.'

'Undoubtedly. And it would seem we must wait till daylight, before you go to follow those tracks.'

'By daylight,' Morakh said after one slow, controlling breath, 'we hope to be far from here. No one can sleep now, and we will be safer moving; let the ghûl follow us. We can rest in the day, when we can see what moves around us. Do you see to your camel now, boy. I will watch the Ghost Walker.'

Jemel snarled, but that was sheer temper. He slammed

his weapon back into its sheath and ran off, to where other members of the party were indeed busy around the camels.

Marron turned his back to the scene, standing fully exposed on the lip of the hollow, his eyes once more drawn to the needle that he saw as darkness, that others saw as light. He didn't think he stood in any danger now. Indeed, Morakh made no move even to touch hand to sword's hilt, to be ready to draw. He stood with arms folded, watching Marron, watching his stance, watching the direction of his eyes.

'How far is it?' Marron asked.

'Not far. Not far at all.'

They might both have been speaking of something else, or else of different things entirely. Somehow, he didn't think so.

Not far at all: he'd known that in any case, he'd have known it blindfold or blind. His eyes were his least informant. Every beat of his heart, every yearning muscle in his body, every bone, every hair on his twitching skin told him that it was not far, it couldn't be. There was no pain now that they were moving, but the compulsion was momentous. He felt more than inhabited, he felt possessed; the Daughter sang in his ears like the demon it was to his old masters, Church and knight. It was a tide and not his feet that carried him forward, once more leading alone. He didn't watch where he walked, he didn't need to, though the ground was treacherously uneven; he wouldn't be allowed to fall. Neither did he so much as glance back. Again, there was no need. He could see them, almost, without looking, they were shadows in his mind: the Dancers arrayed like a wall at his back, the riders on their beasts in line behind. Rudel had stood the first watch, had had no sleep at all; Marron could sense how he dozed on his swaying camel, how his head sagged and his thoughts drifted. He was the only one, Marron thought, whose eyes had not yet found the needle. The Dancers knew of it already, had been looking for it, surely; he had himself shown it to Jemel and Elisande; she would have warned Julianne, but surely not her father. Whatever it meant, if it had meant lethal danger she still would not have told her father.

The plateau dipped, or the hills rose ahead of them, both; whichever, the needle was lost behind a slope that intervened. Their way still led directly toward it, though. Marron had no doubt of that. He reached the foot of that slope, and started up; as the camels' stride altered to meet the climb, he felt Rudel rouse and stir. He would see nothing but the hill now, until they breasted it. Marron could do nothing to alert him, even if he'd been certain of the need. His body was no longer his own; he was no more than a passenger now, borne along by another's will, as the Daughter had been all these weeks. He thought perhaps he ought to be frightened, but was not. He seemed to have lost that ability too, to have lost everything that had made him Marron. Elisande had said that or something like it, more than once. Now, suddenly, tonight he seemed to have lost all that had made him the Ghost Dancer also. There was so little left of him, only a bare thread of awareness swamped by haste and thirst for something that was not water, and he couldn't even fear the finding of it . . .

*

Haste indeed up the flank of the hill: he was running now, running to beat the sun; he didn't look back to see, but knew that all the sky behind him was paling, from rich indigo above through lilac to a shimmering pink. Ahead it was dark yet, but the needle not; he could see the tip of it suddenly, touched with early light. Not so sharp now, not this close: it was broad and textured, built of dusty stone. And it rose as he climbed, it towered over his head and he still couldn't see the eye of it, only more and more of the shaft, so that it seemed to stab higher and higher into the sky.

Again he thought he should feel frightened, and could not. All he could do was run; and did run, and so came at last to the crest of the hill, just as the sun rose at his back so that his own shadow ran ahead to find and strike, pure through the eye of the needle.

A great arch that eye was, three times his height and half of that in width, cutting clean through the massive base of the needle where it stood on this high promontory. His feet faltered, the singing in his ears died to a murmur, all rush was gone and his body was his own again, now that he was here. He could tip his head back and gape, and wonder why; and now, yes, at last he could be afraid.

The needle was not a tower, it had no doors or windows. He had known another tower like that, but this was different; there was no hollow space inside, he could sense that, he could feel the incredible mass of rock that made it. Small rocks it was built from, no single piece greater than a strong man could carry; he thought that might be important. Many, many rocks, each crudely shaped and precisely placed: there was no mortar to bind them together, each was gripped only by the solidity of those around and the weight of those above. The wall of it was rougher than any masonry he'd seen; he thought he could climb right to the top, to the tip, there were cracks enough for hands and feet to find, if only he dared to touch it . . .

He did not dare, he wouldn't even go closer than this, still its own height's distance; this hilltop was broad and flat, and the needle – pillar? monument? – stood at its centre, set back from all sides.

Marron heard the Dancers come up and stand about him, like a wall still, to divide him from his friends. Like a curving wall that embraced him, almost, that gave him no more choices than the Daughter had before: he could stand where he was and look at the needle, or he could walk towards the needle. Bodies blocked him at either side and behind, left him no route else.

He stood still, and went on gaping.

Soon the camels came, snorting and blowing and keeping their distance, from him and the needle both. Even before they breasted the hill – and even shielded as he was from the sight of them, by the Dancers and his own back turned – Marron felt that same awareness of the pattern of their thoughts. It wasn't much that he could glean, but he knew some seconds early that Rudel was furious, and frightened too. Frightened for him, he thought – or frightened of what this place might mean or do to him, that was more than what he might mean or do on his own.

Some seconds early he was with that knowledge, but not many, and nowhere near enough to be useful. The camels came, and Rudel's was the first among them now, and breathing the hardest. It sidled unhappily across the

rocky ground; its rider slid down unheeding, left it unhob-
bled as he stormed across to the Dancers where they
guarded Marron, seemingly from him.

His riding-stick flailed the sand and stone at his feet;
even in his anger, though, he was giving sidelong glances to
the needle. Marron could feel that too, without being able
to see past the bulk of the Dancers' bodies. He thought it
was a mistake, to show fear or weakness to these men. They
would be merciless.

'This . . .' Rudel began – and stopped, spat over the hill's
edge, drew a breath and began again, more temperately.
'This is the Pillar of Lives.' A statement, no question about
it.

'It is.'

Marron still thought it was a needle and he the thread,
plucked and drawn.

'If I had known your path would lead us here, I would
have forbidden it.'

'It is not yours to forbid. We go where the Ghost Walker
goes.'

'And the Ghost Walker goes where you lead him. Well,
we are here – but we do not stay, do you hear me? I lead the
Ghost Walker now, and we return to the cliff-edge and
seek a way down to the Sands. You can follow or not, as
you choose.'

'It is not ours to choose, nor yours to lead. The Ghost
Walker goes where he will . . .'

'The Ghost Walker goes nowhere,' Elisande's voice,
sharply cutting across, 'until he has eaten, and rested. This
seems no bad place,' though her voice seemed to hesitate
and lost its certainty for a moment, and Marron thought

that her eye too had been snared by the needle then. 'We can stay here and watch all sides for any sign of the ghûl. I will make a fire; its smoke will announce us, but . . .'

'You will make no fire here,' Morakh interrupted brutally. 'Do you think this is a jaunting-spot? You stand on holy ground, girl, and you will respect it.' And his hand was on the hilt of his scimitar, as though to enforce that respect.

'What is this place?' Marron asked quietly. 'It sucks at my soul . . .'

'You are the Ghost Walker; this is your place of power. That is what you feel. What you carry was created here, given its life and purpose; you have brought it home.'

'And that . . .?'

'That is the Pillar of Lives. We made it, we the Sand Dancers, through all the generations we have waited; it is the rite of acceptance to our brotherhood, that each new postulant bring a stone from elsewhere, climb up and place it in the Pillar. We build slowly, but what we have built endures.'

So many stones, so many thousand stones; so many lives, and how long had this thing been a-building?

'Is it finished?' he asked, in a whisper. Morakh only smiled. Of course, it was not finished. The Ghost Walker was here, to be sure, the Daughter had returned from its exile of centuries – but for how long? He might be hard to kill, but he would die regardless. No one could say what would happen then. Or before then. The Ghost Walker was an infidel to these men; they might have refused Jemel the chance to join them, but Marron thought they would still go on recruiting. Or accepting postulants, that seemed a closer way to say it.

'Tell him about the oaths you swear,' Rudel urged, not pleasantly, 'as the other part of the rite. When you cut your finger off, in witness of your earnest.'

'Those oaths are none of his concern. Nor yours.'

'Oh, I have heard them; and they concern me greatly. As they should him; and how can they not be his concern? He is the Ghost Walker.'

But he is infidel, Morakh's face said; his lips said nothing. Rudel it was who said, 'He said before the Sultan that they were sworn to your service, did he not, Marron? That is true, but it is not the whole truth. The Sand Dancers are sworn to serve you by sword and fire, till all unbelievers are harried from the land of God. You are meant to lead them in this venture. That is so, is it not, Morakh?'

'So it is foretold.'

'You see what this means, Marron? They are your private army, and your bodyguard – but only so long as you will lead them against Outremer. Against your own people, Marron . . .'

'Are they my people? They cast me out, and I fled them . . .' That wasn't quite right. *They cast me out, and I fled him . . .* But the truth was still there, a kernel to the words. Words were only a dressing, and could not numb the pain of what was true. Whether he was traitor or betrayed, no matter; treachery, two or more, several treacheries lay between him and his people now.

'You are the Ghost Walker,' Morakh said and suddenly, rarely touched him, gripping his wrist in a hand that was hot and hard despite the dawn chill in the air. 'You have no people but ourselves.'

Themselves or his friends, perhaps. Not both. And one

of his friends was Sharai and one was Patric, and who could choose between them?

'You are a small army,' he said, 'to set against Outremer.'

'There are more of us. Not enough, for that battle; but you need not lead the war, you need only fight within it. The prophecy speaks of a gathering of all the peoples of the Sharai, and it says the Ghost Walker shall be one among them.'

'And if I say no?'

'Then you are not the one foretold, or now is not the time. But there is a gathering of the tribes at Rhabat, Hasan has called the leaders there; and you go to Rhabat, you said, though we do not. We will wait, we will gather also; and after the conclave we shall hear what has been said, and what you have chosen.'

And if he had chosen wrongly, they would perhaps decide that the Daughter rested in the wrong body; and so he would die, beneath their arrows if they could not kill him with their swords . . .

Well, so be it. If they offered him the choice today, now, one path with his friends or another with the Dancers, he knew which way he would go: neither to the left nor to the right, but straight ahead and alone, through the arch in the Pillar of Lives, the eye of the needle . . .

His own eye still hadn't strayed from that massive monument to patience and belief. So many lives lived out, first to last, in waiting for what had not come; he marvelled that Morakh and his brethren could be as calm as they were, discovering their miracle in their own generation.

Morakh's hand was still about his wrist; now the Dancer lifted and turned it, so that Marron's sleeve fell back and the ever-open wound was revealed. A blade appeared in Morakh's other hand, a long fine poniard that Marron had come to know well.

'Now,' Morakh hissed, 'now you will learn, boy. You have been slow, and stupid; here, it cannot be denied . . .'

'No!' Rudel tried to push his way through to them, but two of the Dancers gripped his arms and held him fast. His voice rose, almost a gabble: 'Marron, listen to me! Whatever you see happen, remember that this thing leads to death, to uncountable deaths if you let them take you down their road. Remember the stables, at the Roq . . .'

Marron had not forgotten the stables; he carried Aldo with him always, a terrible pain in his heart, and the guilt of what had come after. But Morakh's blade slid neatly between two of the leather stitches, a sharp prick of pain; his blood rose to meet it, and the Daughter followed.

This time it did not float in the air before him, waiting for his inadequate control. This time it flowed, it ran like water, much as he had run to fetch it here. It ran straight to the arch in the pillar, and there it spread itself like a veil, like a curtain between stone and stone, between sky and sky.

It clung to the rocks above, the rocks on either side, the rock below; and then, like a curtain rent asunder, it rippled and tore from the centre, from top to bottom it spread itself apart, it opened like an eye.

Through the needle's eye, Marron found himself staring at a golden country, under a golden sky. The same landscape he saw, or thought he saw, only that now it glimmered and shone.

He took one slow pace forward, and then another; and

heard Morakh's soft approval. 'Good. Will you go, boy, will you lead us through?'

His arm hurt unbearably; he gripped it in his free hand, pressed it to his chest despite the stickiness of blood, and felt no relief. Would he go? He had no answer, except his eyes' focus and his feet's slow shuffle.

Suddenly, though, there was something more to look at, between himself and bright gold. It was a shadow, a figure, a man: a young man, much like himself.

And that was Jemel, who had his own answer for Morakh. Before Marron could stay him, he strode ahead, all purpose. When he came to the open iris that was the Daughter, he barely hesitated, taking just time enough to glance back once and meet Marron's gaze; there was a message in his eyes, perhaps, except that Marron could not read it.

And then Jemel stepped through.

6

With and Without Him

Jemel stepped through, and stood for a moment in two worlds, one bare foot grounded in each.

The one foot stood in shadow, the accustomed chill of desert stone at dawn, unwarmed as yet by desert sun; the other reached over the eddying red line that marked the doorway – careful, careful! – to touch gold and feel the instant strike of warmth through leathered sole and numbed bone, as though he trod on hearthstones or the slab floor of a hammam. Except that the floor of a hammam is damp always when the fires are lit, and the air is damper; and here the golden rock was as dry and dusty as the grey, and the air was dry too when he gasped it in at the shock of that warm touch.

The two airs mingled in his throat, the bitter cold and the bitter warm, and he might have gasped again if he weren't coughing.

And then momentum had carried him through, and he stood entire within the golden light of that other world.

No glancing back, not now, although he yearned to; they must not think him fearful of this, those men who had refused his brotherhood. He lifted his eyes and his head, straightened his back and walked forward, through the arch and out under an opalescent sky, and even that had a shimmer of gold to it.

Only then, as he stood looking at a landscape that was not his own, as he struggled to build walls in his mind against the sudden press of fear that he was still determined not to show, only then did he think how strange it was, that there'd been an arch on this side to walk through. The Pillar of Lives was a work of man, which inhabited man's world; those who had built it had had their reasons. What reason could there be for anyone – anything – to erect its like here? Unless there were a law of symmetry between the worlds, and whatever was done in one must be mirrored in the other. But men were busy, always busy, and it would so debase those who lived here, to copy mortal labour to no purpose . . .

So he turned although he had sworn not to, not to let those watching think him frightened; he turned to see what point there was to a pillar here, and what he saw threw a shadow over his eyes, although there was no sun to cast it.

He saw that it was men who copied, who struggled vainly to imitate their masters. He wondered if any Dancer, if any one among the early Dancers had stood here and seen as he did, or if it had only been some dim-heard echo, a sense toward a greater truth that had driven them to raise their Pillar. Or if they'd been instructed to, perhaps . . .?

He stood beneath a God-sign, he thought, a testament to power and a call to worship. Almost, he fell on his knees.

Certainly no man had made this thing; that was inherent, there were no men here, save him. But it seemed to him also that whoever had made it, they'd done so in praise or promise; not for themselves, surely no creature could think itself so mighty . . .

It was a pillar, as the Dancers' was; but theirs was rough, blunt, unfinished in every sense. This was a leaping spire, smooth and slender, a blade of golden stone thrusting at the pearl-gold sky. It towered higher far than ever man could build; Jemel didn't want to guess how tall it was, nor did he ever want to see anything taller.

He looked back at the archway, and perhaps that shadow hung still across his eyes, because it was hard to see through to the land, the world that he had come from. He saw the red shimmering outline of the way from there to here, but beyond what he saw was grey and dim. There was ground and sky, a bare line of hilltop to distinguish them; a ball, a dull globe hanging, and that must be the sun; between that and this a shadow, moving . . .

A faceless shadow, a figure closing, looming; Jemel's hand touched the hilt of his weapon. The Dancers might hold this as sacred ground, forbidden to those not sworn to the Ghost Walker; they would not recognise his oaths, nor share theirs. They had said he was defiled. They might be right, he had no eye to judge himself; but he would fight for his life, if they sought to take it . . .

The figure blurred momentarily, becoming more vague than a shadow, even; and then it was through, and there were no shadows even under the arch, and it was no Dancer who had followed him.

He breathed out explosively, a moment of relief chased

hard by wondering. He took his hand away from his scimitar, but stood still, only watching as Marron turned to face back the way that he had come. He made no gesture, but there was suddenly a veil of red across the arch, no way through for the Dancers or anyone else.

Jemel waited, frowning as he saw how slowly Marron moved, how he hugged his wounded arm to his chest, how his face was twisted with pain. It was an effort not to go to him, not to offer strength against his weakness; but even an ordinary man must be allowed his pride, and Marron was the Ghost Walker, and Jemel could still find it in himself to fear that name.

So Jemel waited, until Marron had come to stand beside him; then, 'You could have taken it back inside yourself,' he said quietly. 'That would have eased the pain.'

Marron smiled tightly. 'I was afraid it might not come,' he confessed. 'It fought so hard to be there, to do this . . .'

'And yet you could make it close, to be a barrier and not a door.'

'Yes. It seemed easy, now. I can understand it; but can I command? I don't know.'

'You are the Ghost Walker. There is more than that, which you may command.'

'Perhaps. The Dancers serve me, they say – but will they obey me, even as much as the Daughter does? Again, I don't know. Nor if I want them to. I never sought servants, Jemel . . .'

'This I know.' His own smile was as thin as Marron's had been, and as hard to make, and perhaps as full of meaning. Of course he knew. Marron had been a servant himself, to his Church first and then to a man, his knight, Sieur

Anton. Given his will, Jemel thought, he'd be doing that service yet. His soul craved to follow, not to lead. There was no dishonour in that; proud as they were, quarrelsome as they were, the Sharai understood rank and duty, none better. Marron's choice of master was another matter, and an issue between them, one they could not speak of. *Not yet* – but soon, he promised himself. Soon, they must. *For Jazra* – and for himself too, Jemel couldn't deny so much. His future perhaps hung on that conversation; aye, and perhaps Marron's too, Ghost Walker though he be.

And, of course, Sieur Anton's future also . . .

But not yet, not now. Now, at last, the place where they stood was having its effect on Marron, as it had already on Jemel. He was all young man suddenly, and all Patric, no hint of the Ghost Walker about him; he seemed misdressed in Sharai robes as he stood and stared about him. At the glittering golden ground they stood on, the great stretch of hills before them, the paler sky that was yet shot through with hints of gold like a dim reflection of the land below.

'Look back,' Jemel murmured, 'look up and see what the Dancers seek to build, how short they fall . . .'

Marron did look back and up, at his injunction; and gasped, and staggered perilously close to the steep fall of the slope. Jemel flung an arm around his shoulders, and held him firmly until he was sure of the other's balance against his wound and weakness; and kept his grip even after he was sure, reaching with his other hand to take Marron's wrist and turn it into the light. There was a heavy wet stain on the dark robe, and all the skin of the arm was streaked red.

Jemel watched the wound pulse, and said, 'This bleeds

more than usual, far more than a dagger's prick should cause. It hurts more, also. Yes?'

'Oh, yes. Since I came through.' Marron's voice was vague, detached; his eyes were still on that towering monument, gazing up and up. 'What is that thing?'

'Some work of the djinn, or their servants. I do not know. Only that the Dancers would like to make their own, and cannot.'

'No. No man could . . . Jemel, where are we?'

'In the land of the djinn. It is said to be the source, the true land, and ours only a crude clay shadow. I do not know. At least ours is alive. Even in the heart of the Sands, there is life.'

'And is there none here? Someone made this,' with a gesture up at the great spire.

'The djinn, or something lesser of their kind. The Sharai say that if you do not die, you cannot live.'

'The djinn die.'

Jemel laughed, surprising himself. 'They don't expect to.'

'But they do, they can be slain. And their kind. I heard that you killed an 'ifrit . . .'

'Yes.' With an arrow blessed to the task; he and Jazra both had carried one, a rare gift from a rare imam. Now Jazra's was lost, and his he thought might find a baser purpose, if ever he saw a certain white-clad knight and could not come close enough for sword-work . . .

A knight whom Marron had served, before he was the Ghost Walker. And if Jemel had not slain the 'ifrit, if he had left it to kill Julianne, then so much would have fallen out differently. Certainly he would not be here now; he would neither know the knight's name nor be bound to his former squire, as he was bound, though Marron seemed not to know it and the Sand Dancers had forbidden him to take their oaths and make it public.

He crouched, and sifted golden dust between his fingers. It was warm to the touch, as the air was warm, though there was no sun to heat it. If the Sands had been made in imitation of this, he thought, that was a great making, and yet it had failed. Their yellow could not match this gold, nor their coarse grains its silky texture; they were hot only by day, and brutally cold by night. And yet men could live in the Sands, if they only knew the way of it . . .

'Men cannot live here,' he said, continuing both thought and conversation. 'Nor anything that has flesh, or needs water.' He could not pray here either, though it was dawn in his own world and he owed that duty to his God. He thought perhaps that God needed men, a world of men; this bitter, beautiful landscape held no mystery except its own creation. There was no place for worship here.

'We are here, and alive.'

'For how long? We should go back.'

Before we are noticed, by something that even my blessed arrow cannot slay was all he meant, but Marron cast a glance at the archway and the shimmering red curtain that blocked it and said, 'Yes. Before there's trouble, between Morakh and Rudel . . .'

There would always be trouble, Jemel thought, between Morakh and Rudel. Trouble between Morakh and Marron might be harder to allay. It must come, though. The Sand Dancer had seen his dream turn real – and his dream had turned out to be a Patric boy who would not kill. Trouble

must surely come of that; and when it did, Jemel meant to
be there, to set his scimitar and his body too between them.
Marron was more than one man's dream made flesh, and
Jemel would not see his own dream perish on a fanatic's
blade.

Marron walked back towards the arch, leaving a trail of
blood in the sterile dust to mark where he had been. Jemel
went to follow – and hesitated, and turned back. He
scanned the ground quickly, saw what he was seeking and
hurried to gather it up. It was hot against his skin, though
not too hot to handle; and heavy, heavier than he'd
expected by its size, though not too heavy to carry. He held
it two-handed against his chest, and took one last look
around at this empty, wondrous land before going over to
where Marron stood watching, waiting, wondering.

'Why do you want that? And should you take it?'

Jemel shook his head, to both questions. The one was
easily answered, Marron should know, and if he did not he
would see soon enough; the other was impossible to answer.
What did Jemel know, what did any of them know about
the rules that governed the two worlds, this and their own?
If the djinn were jealous, possessive – well, no doubt they
would make that known. Again, soon enough . . .

This time Marron made no gesture that Jemel could
see, but the red haze that blocked the arch drew itself apart,
like diaphanous curtains opening to an unfelt breeze.
Marron stepped through and Jemel followed, stumbling
unexpectedly, almost brushing against the lethal scarlet
border that shaped that gateway; what he carried felt suddenly hotter and heavier, a burden greater and more
perilous than it had seemed in its own country.

He bore it through, though, hugging it to him, masking it almost with his loose sleeves; and paid little attention to what Marron was doing, drawing up his own damp and bloodstained sleeve to take back his draught of smoke and danger, what he called the Daughter. That was unexpected, deliberately defiant, denying the Dancers any access to the land of gold; but Jemel had his own concerns, and for once Marron was not the most urgent of them.

He stepped out from under the arch, and turned his eyes to the rough stone wall of the Pillar of Lives. Eyes and touch: he could – just – grip his burden one-handed, freeing the other to test the solidity of that wall. He tugged at several of the stones; none moved, although there was no mortar to bind them together. Good.

At his back he could hear loud voices, Rudel's and Morakh's, an argument. He ignored it, slipping what he carried inside his robe and drawing his rope girdle tighter to hold it. It burned against his skin, but not enough to blister. This deed of his must have consequences, he was sure of that; what they would be, he could not predict. It was necessary, though, a private avowal and an act of independence, perhaps of rebellion, as his oath before the Sultan had been.

He set both hands to the wall, lifted one bare foot and worked it into an open crack, began to climb.

He was some way up before he heard a voice, a girl's voice call his name. He didn't look down, even when Morakh hailed him in fury; he just kept his eyes focused on his next handhold, his mind fixed on climbing. He had spent half his childhood clambering up and down cliffs as steep as this; his only concern was the awkward weight against his stomach, the urgent need not to let that either pull him off-balance or – worse – slip free and fall to ground, and make a nonsense of his ascent.

Higher and higher: there was a breeze up here but not strong enough to worry him, warmed already by the sun but not enough to challenge the heat of the thing within his robe. He'd thought that might cool after its transition from world to world, but he'd been wrong; if anything it was growing hotter yet. He dug his feet deep into a crevice, detached one careful hand to touch and felt its energy even through the wool of his robe. No time to rest: he'd best get on, he thought, before it burned for true. Before it scorched the robe to flame, and himself also . . .

And so up, and further up. Spot a hold, reach and grip; he watched his hands and let his long toes find their own anchorage, never looking down. So it had been the night they had attacked the Roq; so it had always been. It was unusual, to say the least, such a talent among the Sharai; the tribes generally avoided the heights, or any fixed settlement. But then he was – no, he had been Saren, and the Saren were an unusual tribe.

At last even his muscles were aching, and his arms were trembling through to his shoulders. He'd travelled far since the cliffs of his childhood, and he was out of practice for such a climb – except for that one terrible night at the Roq, and then he'd had Jazra at his side and Hasan to lead, the promise of glory and the dread of shame uniting to overcome any weakness in his body. No longer. He would never see Jazra again this side of death, he would never follow Hasan again; today there was only his own fierce will to drive him on.

Drive him it did, until one hand and then the other found the topmost edge, and clung. One final effort, and he hauled himself up and over.

Briefly he lay flat on his back, breathing hard, his skin slick with rare sweat and his burden a searing weight below his ribs. He felt unmanned, all but overmastered, and was glad that none below could see him like this. Especially, that one below could not see him so . . .

Soon, though, that same implacable determination that had brought him this far drew him to his feet, although his legs shook and he felt dizzy and unbalanced. He still didn't look down, nor around at the wide country of the Sands; he kept his head down and fixed his eyes firmly where he stood, on the summit of the Pillar of Lives.

This was a place of myth among his people, almost as much so as the land of the djinn, where he had stood only a few minutes previously. It lacked any of the wonder of that place, though: only a crude circle of stones, with a long drop below its rim. As with the walls, there had been no attempt to level off the summit; indeed, the Pillar had not yet reached its final height. The centre stood two or three courses higher than the edge, where the last few dozen men to join the fraternity of Sand Dancers had laid their individual rocks.

Which was why he had come this far, why he had made that climb. Denied the chance to share their vows and their brotherhood, he had brought a rock of his own regardless. Theirs had been gleaned from the desert; his he had fetched from the land of their aspiration, where he and none of them had walked.

He reached into his robe and drew it out, cruelly hot

now and shining more brightly here than it had in its own country. For a moment he stood right on the rim where his friends – and his unfriends – could see him, held it high to show them what bright thing he carried; if any were uncertain, Marron could tell them. Then he stalked proudly, defiantly to that raised centre and treated it like a pedestal, like an altar almost, setting his rock to stand higher than all the others, in the place of pride and honour.

It was a statement at the least, perhaps another oath, though even he was beginning to doubt quite what he was swearing to. He stood and gazed at it a little while, feeling more muddled than he had expected, less triumphant; then at last he raised his eyes and gazed about him.

And he who had grown up with far views was transfixed again by a view, the second time this morning. This was a place of wonder after all, only that the wonder lay not in itself, but in what it commanded.

He could see for days, by the Sharai way of measuring. Not so far to the east, where the low strong sun defeated his eyes; but eastward lay no lands that mattered, only the margins of the Sands where they were claimed by tame tribes, peoples who would allow a merchants' road and the passage of unchallenged strangers. To the north and the west were lost lands, where once the word of the Sharai had been the word of law – and would be again, that at least he was certain of, that was inherent in any vow he made – and he thought he could see them all. That purple haze which made the far horizon, he thought that was Outremer as the Patrics called it, as he was learning to. All the wide country between there and here he could see, and he thought he could overleap it in a bound.

Hasan had thought so, and had tried to make it true, with his doomed, disastrous expedition against the Roq. Jemel wondered if ever Hasan had stood here, if this was where the idea had been born; or did Hasan see the world always from such a height, in such breadth and detail? Did he perhaps have a Pillar of Lives in his head – and did he count the lives that fell from it, as he reached and over-reached?

Thinking of Hasan, Jemel turned to face the south, where the true Sands lay and Rhabat at the heart of them.

He saw ochre instead of gold, and thought he would never see true gold again unless he walked again in the land of the djinn; but ochre was enough, he thought, where it meant the rolling dunes and sweeping plains of his own dry country. From here he could see how broken that country was, the grey of rock upthrusting and the black shadows of sudden scarps; distantly he thought he could see a gleam of water. If true, that must be the salt sea, the Dead Waters that were once more a place of myth and legend; if so, then there lay Rhabat also, where Hasan was or was headed, and so was he if Marron's intent held good. So were they all, except that the Dancers did not go to Rhabat . . .

Thinking of Marron and the Dancers, he strode confidently back to the summit's eastern rim and looked down. He didn't mean to wave, exactly, nothing so childish, but he would like to be seen as himself and for his own sake, not as the answer to a question, what he carried. Also, he wanted to see. Morakh and Rudel had been arguing; that was no surprise, but he'd like to see how that had fallen out, who stood with whom, whether Marron had been drawn in or had become the cause of another argument, perhaps.

Maybe so. It was hard to be sure from so high above, when so many of the party wore the same dress; but the air was clear and his eyes were sharp, and he thought he would know Marron at any distance, from the way that boy moved, the way he held himself. He thought that was Marron, the small figure moving swiftly away from the Pillar and down the hill, as swiftly almost as he had climbed it as the dawn came up. He might well be taking himself away from an argument, whether or not he was the cause of it.

If so, then that was very likely Elisande who followed him, scrambling down the slope with bags swinging loosely from her shoulders: empty water-skins, Jemel thought, a reason or probably an excuse. They'd be more than lucky to find water anywhere up here, but they could spend a long time searching, or claiming to search . . .

Certainly those were the Dancers, that small huddle of black-robed men directly below, where he could spit on them if he had not been too careful of his body's water, if he had not done more than that already. That was equally certainly Rudel, the broad-shouldered man who stood apart from them; which left only Julianne, and it took only a moment for him to find her among the camels, keeping her distance from all arguments.

Satisfied, he sought Marron once more. Elisande had all but caught him up; indeed he paused and waited for her, probably at some screech that Jemel couldn't hear. She flapped her bags at him, and gestured: *Morakh says there's water over there, we may as well fetch it, rather than just storming off in a rage*, or else *Look, I brought these, I said we'd look for water, there's a path down there looks as likely as anything and they won't expect us back for an hour . . .*

There was a path, of sorts: a goat-path perhaps, though Jemel had seen no other sign of goat or any game since they'd climbed above the level of the Sands. The Dancers surely didn't come here often enough in their separate troops to wear a path across the rock; and if it were only beaten sand that marked it out, then a week's winds would shift or bury it for ever . . .

Slightly puzzled, rather more curious and almost alarmed already – Jemel was of the desert, and what was unusual in the desert was always a caution to the wary – he looked ahead of them, further down the path than they could see.

And saw movement, and saw too what it was that moved, or thought he did.

And was bellowing a warning that same instant, lifting his hands to make a trumpet-mouth to carry the sound far; and whistling and waving, and dancing almost on that great height, doing anything he could think of to attract the attention of either one of them.

Marron heard, of course he did, nothing happened that Marron could not hear with his alien ears. His head turned and tilted, Jemel could see a pale blur beneath the hood that was his face; Marron no doubt could see a great deal more.

But all Marron saw, it seemed, was his friend capering on the Pillar's tip, solemn gesture over and *look at me!* He lifted an arm, to say that he had looked and seen; Elisande waved both arms extravagantly.

Jemel cursed, tried to shout words and knew they were not reaching even Marron across the breeze and distance. The Dancers had a code of signs, of gestures; but Jemel did not know it, and couldn't think how to sign *danger!* in any common way that would be understood.

Those below were all staring up at him with no more understanding, making no more effort to understand.

He saw the two Patrics turn away, and go blindly on; and gave up his wild shouting and crouched, took his weight on his hands on that extreme edge, lowered his legs over and began to climb down.

If you chose to call it climbing. Even in his wildest days, he'd never made such a descent: skidding and sliding, barely holding on, letting his weight as much as his skill carry him down the near-vertical face of the wall. They'd called him 'Spider' as a boy, before he'd earned his name, but spiders were more careful. And spiders had rope, which he did not.

He might have died a dozen times or more, when his fingers missed their grip or his foot failed to find a ledge to lodge on. He had no balance and no sense, only desperation in head and hands and heart as he went slipping catastrophically from one juddering moment's halt to the next, with a long slither in between. He should have died, it was impertinent to God that he survived, he thought after.

Survive he did, though, even the last uncontrolled tumble that had him sprawling at Morakh's feet with all the breath knocked out of him, his palms skinned and hurting now as his toes were also, which he hadn't felt before. There was blood on his face too, sticky and stinging, and he had no idea what had happened there.

'You have profaned what is holy to us, tribeless. I forbade you—'

'Morakh, listen! Ghûl . . .'

'Ghûl? What do you mean, ghûl? There is no ghûl.'

He seemed very sure, for someone who had seen and shown footprints of the ghûl only yesterday, whose man had heard and seen it just last night.

But Jemel's sighting was more fresh, and urgent. 'Where they are gone, the Ghost Walker and Elisande. I saw it, waiting for them . . .'

'What did you see?' Rudel demanded, gripping his elbow and drawing him ruthlessly to his feet.

'A ghûl. No. A woman. Perhaps. Something in women's dress, but its shape seemed wrong, and the way it moved was not human . . . Oh, go! Run! They have not met it yet . . .'

'The boy is dreaming,' Morakh said. 'Or seeking to distract from his offence. It cannot be . . .'

'Why not?' Rudel snapped. 'We have been plagued for days with ghûls and rumours of ghûls . . .'

'Well, perhaps so. But if there is a ghûl, the Ghost Walker will destroy it.'

'Has anyone told Marron how to destroy a ghûl?'

There was a silence; then, 'He does not know?'

'How should he? This is not his country . . .'

'We will go. Immediately . . .' And now suddenly there was almost fear in Morakh's voice: fear of Marron's dying, Jemel thought, and he not being there to receive what he most desired. That man might have sworn to serve the Ghost Walker, but he was not content with his service.

The men left at a sprint. Jemel tried to follow, but all his body was sore and bruised, and his legs would not hold him. When Julianne came hurrying over she stayed him with ease, her woman's body a support he clutched at shamefully.

'What is it? I could not hear . . .'

'There is a ghûl, they are walking straight towards it . . .'

She gasped, but still did not release him, though he struggled against her grip.

'You cannot follow, you are hurt. And bleeding . . .' Her hand touched his forehead, and came away stained. 'The camels . . .?'

'Yes! The camels, quickly . . .'

She had to help him, even over that little distance. The beasts were couched and hobbled, but this at least he could manage, tugging at the tie and dropping into the saddle, plying his riding-stick furiously until his mount was on its feet and running, though it roared its displeasure.

With Julianne at his back, he drove the camel downslope to where that path began, winding away north between buttresses of rock high enough to block their view. They could hear the men ahead, calling loudly; no answering shouts came back. Jemel beat his mount to greater speed, bending low over its neck to watch the path; there was a clear track in the sand, marked by nothing but the booted and bare feet of his companions. He thought how a wily ghûl might have laid just such a trail for temptation's sake, trusting its disguising robes to sweep away the signs of its own hoofed feet. Were ghûls that wily, that intelligent? Not of their own nature, by all the stories that he had heard, but there was something more than natural in the way that their party seemed to have been hunted by these creatures . . .

They caught up with Rudel and the Dancers, sweeping

past to round another high outcrop. Now at last they had free running for a distance, and a glimpse of two small figures a long way ahead. Too far: Marron and Elisande had almost reached the jutting rocks where he had seen the lurking thing that had alarmed him. He yelled, a high whooping call that made them stop, and turn. He waved his stick wildly, and called again; they hesitated, and began to make their way back towards him.

His cries had alerted the ghûl also, if ghûl it were. Something emerged from those rocks, only a few paces from his friends. It still looked a little like a woman, but that was its clothing only; even from so far higher up and further away he hadn't been deceived, and was not now. He had thought ghûls better at disguise than this. Perhaps they were, when it was needful; it could have nothing on its mind now except attack.

Attack it did, in a great leap that had its hood falling back from its head, revealing a long head like a horse's, except that no horse had ever had such a mouth, gaping wide and toothed like a lion. Nor such arms, long and clawed and reaching, flailing toward Marron . . .

He heard its coming, of course, and twisted round to face it; and had his sword out to meet it, barely in time. A low slashing cut made it jerk back; it seemed to grow taller, letting its last pretence fall away.

Jemel heard Julianne's gasp of relief behind him, and realised that she was confident of Marron's swordsmanship, even against such a nightmare creature as this. Well she might be; but no more than Marron, he guessed, did she know how a ghûl might be killed. Or not killed, which was what mattered more.

If he could only hold it off, though, until Jemel arrived . . .

Jemel shifted his riding-stick to his left hand, drew his scimitar and wished for a horse, and spurs. A horse can be brutalised into a sudden burst of effort, though it may die as a result; a camel, not. A camel treated too harshly will slow rather than speed up, may balk altogether, and he'd already belaboured this one to the point of risk. He fixed his eyes on the conflict ahead, and prayed.

The ghûl was all demon now, the robe ripping asunder as its back swelled into monstrosity. Elisande screamed; when the creature's head turned towards her, she flung one of her knives. Jemel saw it glitter in the sunlight, saw it embedded deep in the ghûl's throat. A clever play, and one that might prove enough, if they would only back off now, if she would only cry a warning to Marron, call him away . . .

But Marron saw the creature stagger towards Elisande, its long arms reaching. She tried to run backwards, her heel caught a jut of rock and she fell sprawling in its path. Marron leaped to straddle her body, and showed his reluctance in only a moment's hesitation before he drove his sword hard through the ribbons of cloth that still clung to the ghûl's chest. It should have been a lethal stroke; Jemel groaned.

The ghûl recovered in an instant. Its one arm swiped across its own neck, knocking the dagger out; its other slashed at the stunned Marron, tearing through cloth and flesh alike, opening his shoulder to the bone.

It was unlucky, matching mistake with mistake. More than blood ran from the wound; a soft smoky shadow formed between man and monster. Marron could slay it now, with a thought; or Jemel was closing fast, Marron must have heard his approach. If he would only hold still and wait, all would be well now . . .

Marron did neither. He had only a moment to choose, and he chose a third way. The dim scarlet shadow stretched itself into a frame, a doorway with a shimmer of gold at its heart; and Marron bent, scooped Elisande up in his one good arm and stumbled through that door.

Jemel screamed his name, too late; and cursed, and tried to ride his camel in a hectic plunge through at his back, and was too late again. The frame shrank and disappeared, seemed to be sucked into a vanishing point of gold, and Jemel was left facing the bewildered ghûl.

Well, this at least he could do as it should be done. He swung his blade once, ferociously, hewing clean through the creature's neck. The head fell and rolled, the body slumped; this time it was truly dead, and Jemel's camel danced away from its corpse.

He slipped to ground, letting the beast wander as it would, till Julianne collected it; he stood gasping, sobbing almost, staring not at the awful remains of the ghûl but at the bare patch of sand and rock where Marron had been, and Elisande.

Rudel reached him first. The older man took his blade gently from nerveless fingers, wiped it fastidiously on a rag of the creature's robe and returned it to him with a gesture that was almost a salute.

'That was well done, Jemel.'

'It was useless, I came too slowly. Any of you could have

done as much, anyone who knows. They are guileful, but not great fighters. Will he come back?'

'The ghûl? Not now.'

'Not the ghûl.'

Rudel sighed, as though he'd known exactly what Jemel had meant, and said, 'I do not know. He was hurt, yes?'

'Yes. Badly hurt, perhaps.'

'Then not soon, perhaps. Not here. Would you? Not knowing what had fallen out, with the ghûl? He has Elisande with him, she will tend the wound. When he is fit, they will likely travel a little before they chance returning. If nothing disturbs them, where they are . . .'

'Travel? Travel where, where will they go?'

'South, I would guess. If they can find the south, without sun or stars to guide them. They know we are headed for Rhabat; they should go in the same direction, and cross back into this world when and where they think it safe . . .' Though his voice betrayed a little doubt, as though whatever he thought they should do, his daughter would be sure to do something other.

'He was safe. With me. I would have killed it for him, or he could have destroyed it himself . . .'

'He doesn't like to kill,' Julianne said wearily. She'd hobbled the camels, and came now to join them. 'Didn't you see what it cost him, to try? When Elisande fell? And then, when that didn't work, of course he wouldn't use the Daughter, except to escape. He wouldn't have used it in any case. Why didn't his sword kill the thing, though, Jemel? When yours did?'

'It was a ghûl.'

'I know that.'

'Then know this, it's important. You have to kill a ghûl with a single stroke; a second only restores it to life again.'

'*What?* That's ridiculous . . .'

'It's true, Julianne,' Rudel confirmed. 'Well, you saw. Elisande's knife wounded it badly, might have killed it, given a little time; but Marron struck again, and it was as though the creature had never been touched by either blade.'

'I confess, I saw it. But how . . .?'

'Magic,' from Rudel and 'God's will,' from Jemel, both speaking together. They glanced at each other, but neither so much as smiled. Jemel made a small, polite gesture; Rudel bowed, before continuing.

'God's will, the Sharai say; they are a fatalistic people, they tend not to ask why or how such things happen. That is the way of the world, and they live within it; that is enough. Those of a more enquiring disposition say that creatures of spirit bend themselves only reluctantly to the limitations of flesh, and will stretch those limits in every way they can. Even to the point of a joke, "slay me once, I'm dead; but do it twice and back I come again . . ." Myself, I do not believe that ghûls have a sense of humour. Remember that they are shapeshifters, like all the spirit-creatures; again, you have seen. If they can do that, if they can change the body they inhabit, they can heal it also; so you must slay them instantly, and give them no chance to recover. As Jemel did. By the time a second stroke falls, they're already altering, shifting, flowing to meet the effects of the first; and so the second is useless, and seems almost to heal the damage dealt by the first. That's my belief, at least . . .'

Jemel frowned, shook his head, would have argued; that was not what he'd been taught, nor what he had seen. But Julianne got in ahead of him, with another puzzled question.

'Creatures of spirit, you said. But the 'ifrit was a creature of spirit, and its body melted into smoke or dust, when Jemel killed it. This does not . . .?'

'Never confuse ghûls with 'ifrit, child. The 'ifrit are closer to the djinn, they do not inhabit this world naturally; when they come, they take what form they like, and when they die they dissipate, as you have seen. Ghûls are bound to this world; they can shift their shape, but what spirit they have is yet contained within a vessel of flesh and blood. That remains, when they are slain. You could say that they are servants to the 'ifrit; they share at least the same evil nature, though they follow their own desires and none other, but they are by far a lesser order . . .'

His voice trailed off, as he turned to watch what Morakh was doing behind him. The Dancer was bent over the ghûl's severed head and busy with his knife, cutting something out of the creature's mouth. When he straightened, he showed it silently to his companions, and then came across and thrust himself in between the two Patrics.

'This one at least was true servant to the 'ifrit,' he said, and held out his hand for evidence.

In his palm Jemel saw a pebble, slimed with the ghûl's thick blood but gleaming gold beneath the stain. It should be hot, to judge by the way Morakh shuffled it around with his fingers.

He and Rudel only stared at it; it was Julianne who asked, 'What is that?'

'It is a stone from the land of the djinn,' Jemel said when neither of the older men replied; it was small cousin to the rock that he had brought through the arch himself, though he said nothing of that. 'I do not understand what it was doing in the ghûl's mouth?'

'It was embedded in its tongue,' Morakh told them shortly.

Julianne frowned, and shook her head. 'I still don't understand . . .'

'Such things are potent in this world,' Rudel said, barely glancing at Jemel. 'Among the spirit-kind, they can be over-mastering. The 'ifrit are said sometimes to use a ghûl this way, to set a token from the other world within its body; then its will is subordinate to that of the 'ifrit and it is forced into service, to do its master's bidding. I have heard tales that tell of this, though I have never seen it before, nor ever heard that the tales were true. I would never have thought to look for such a thing . . .'

Jemel grunted his agreement; he too had heard the tales, and had thought them only storytelling. He faced Morakh and said, 'You cannot have seen that; I did not, and it was I who slew the creature. How did you know to look for it?'

'The creature's behaviour seemed strange; this is no normal hunting-ground for a ghûl, so far from any road or village. Only we Sand Dancers come to this place, and we are no meat for their tasting. Nor are they ordinarily crafty enough to lay a false trail. So I thought to look for this, and so I found it. This is my country; I at least can tell fable from truth.'

Jemel bridled; this was his country too, and he would not be scorned. Especially by such a one, at such a time:

after he had lost Marron and slain his first ghûl, he deserved better on both counts . . .

Before his hot tongue could say so, though, or say anything, Morakh had said something more.

'Besides,' the Dancer said, 'I have seen this before. And the ghûl was silent in its attack, where normally it would have been screaming; so that I knew where to look for the stone.'

'Seen it before?' Rudel challenged. 'Seen it where, and when?'

'This is not my first ghûl,' was all that Morakh said, as though he had read some or all of Jemel's thought upon his face. He said it near-contemptuously, as though putting down a boy who had thought to claim some honour. Jemel's scimitar twitched in his hand, but Morakh had already turned his back and was speaking to his younger brothers in their own coded tongue.

Jemel burned for a fight, a true fight, to assuage the ache of loss in his heart. Marron had been his talisman, no substitute for Jazra – never that! – but a powerful charm, a lodestone on his own account. In his sudden absence, Jemel was struggling under a double grief, the old and the new; and he had seen Marron hurt, which felt like his failure. He needed action, to blunt the pain of it. Killing the ghûl had not been enough, too easy and too soon over; Rudel's praise had been a sop, no more, and all this talk was nothing but distraction. He would have loved to set himself against Morakh, blade to blade, for the implied insult. But even a tribeless man sworn to a Patric's protection has his honour, and he would not attack even his greatest enemy from behind. Besides, Rudel's hand was clenched now around his wrist, to hold his sword-arm down. The older man's eyes carried a message, *we are one party yet, and have no time for petty quarrels*. Jemel gritted his teeth, nodded a reluctant acceptance of that wisdom, and forced his muscles to relax.

When Morakh turned back to face them, though, he did so swiftly, and his own scimitar came hissing from its sheath in the same movement. Jemel cried out, startled, and flung up his left hand, his only hand that was free; he felt the bite of steel in his fingers, and the sharp shock of pain that followed after.

Rudel bellowed, drew his long sword and closed with Morakh. That was a private combat that swirled away across the sand, too fast and too far for Jemel to follow. He shook his head against a sudden dizziness, and looked to find the other Dancers.

They were five men, swordsmen all, and they faced one girl. Julianne had a knife in each hand now, but little good those would do her. She knew it, too; she was backing already, against their inexorable advance.

Jemel thrust himself forward, exulting almost despite the odds; this was what he'd wanted, what his soul had been crying for, the chance of battle to allay his guilt and all else that he was burdened with. Never mind that it came from among their own number and inexplicably, without warning; never mind the deadly reputation of Sand Dancers. Now he could fight, he could kill or die or both. If he killed and killed well, he might with luck see Marron again, if Marron lived; if he died and died well, he should with luck see Jazra. That was enough.

A blade came at him from the right; he met that edge to edge and felt it skitter off, turned quickly to beat back another from the left, and still found time to wish that he had said his prayers today, that he stood in good grace with God. Gambling was forbidden, but he had seen men gamble, he understood about odds. He did not think that Rudel would defeat Morakh, and come to help him here. One wounded boy – his long sleeve covered his left hand and he'd had no chance to look at it, but it hurt terribly and he could feel blood running – and one girl, against five Sand Dancers? He thought this was his death-hour, his and Rudel's and Julianne's also; he didn't understand it, but he thought his bones would lie here to bleach in the sun, and only hoped that one at least among the Dancers would have the kindness to say the *khalat* for him, if not for the Patrics.

Gambling was forbidden, but he thought that all men gambled, with every choice they made that changed their life or others'. He had gambled on Jazra, and had won and won until he lost him; they had both gambled on Hasan, and had lost the world in each other. He had gambled again on Marron, and seemed likely to have lost him too, to death or Elisande. Now he flung his life down as men fling dice, to chance or God's decision. Not to skill: if skill alone decided this, then there was no breath of hope, fight as he might.

A blade to the left, a blade to the right; he parried them both, glitter and kiss and the grating hiss of steel on steel. Still only the two, though: they were playing with him, he thought, and not for honour's sake. The Dancers were Sharai, but they kept only those customs that were useful to them. When they chose to kill, they would ordinarily kill without honour or mercy, in defiance of all teaching; and two of these men had bows. He and Julianne should both be dead already. They had chosen swords, though, and three were hanging back. Jemel thought perhaps that they remembered the humiliation of their bout with Marron in the Sultan's palace, when he could have slain them all and did not, time and again did not. This was perhaps their revenge for that, to slay the Ghost Walker's chosen companion but to do it slowly, to take turns to nick and wound until the sand was sodden with his blood and he was emptied of it . . .

Determined at least to nick them back, not to die with his blade clean, he closed with one; battered his scimitar aside, saw what seemed to be an opening, and thrust – into empty air. A moment before his point must have met and cut cloth and flesh and bone beneath, the man was simply not there.

Briefly, Jemel was shaken to his roots, all his certainties trembling on the point of collapse. Then there was a guttural laugh at his back, he twisted round – and saw two Sand Dancers where there had been one, and both of them were grinning coldly.

And that was right, of course, that was why they were so deadly. One reason why. They were masters of their weapons also, no one could dispute that; if they served the Ghost Walker, they meant to do so with war and slaughter. But they had this talent, this magic, this gift of God they called it, to be in one place and then suddenly in another, without seeming to move between the two. And so they were named Sand Dancers, after the little insects that seemed to do the same – unless the insects had been named after them, he wasn't sure – and so Jemel thought that he would certainly die today, when they were tired of their gaming with him.

Well, he would play along; there was nothing else he could do, and besides, his blood was raging. He felt mocked, degraded as a man and a fighter; and worse, when they made no effort to raise their weapons against him. He slashed at one in a tricky feint, lunged at the other; the one merely laughed at him, the other was not there when the scimitar sought him.

Cold steel touched Jemel's neck and withdrew, leaving blood to trickle warmly down his back.

And so the fight went, if fight you could call it. Jemel spun and leaped and sweated, focused his fury, used all his knowledge and training and a lifetime's guile, and still could not lay edge or point on either man. They danced about him, here and there and further off, and never moved their feet. Only their swords moved, and only to prick and prick again.

Beyond them, beyond this circle of his rage and frustration, Jemel caught glimpses of Rudel and Morakh still fencing, though Rudel had blood in his beard now and seemed to be weakening, only warding off the other with slow, heavy strokes. Those would grow heavier and slower yet, Jemel knew, as the sword's weight grew in his exhaustion, until at last he could not raise the blade at all. Then Morakh would have him – but again, Morakh should have had him ere this. Rudel too was being toyed with, Jemel thought.

Fuel to his fire, though that burned hot enough already and was pointless. He could not kill what he could not touch; and he could feel the weight of his own weapon now, which he had not earlier. Oh, he was bitter, and would die so, no doubt; but not give up, not that. So long as he had the strength to swing his sword, swing he would. They must tire of sporting in the end; he only hoped that would be before he was too tired to fight.

He had all but forgotten Julianne, forgot certainly to keep himself between her and the Dancers. So it seemed had they forgotten her, or else discounted her; one of them worked his vanishing trick once too often or too carelessly, appearing again right in front of her, but still facing Jemel.

When Jemel turned to close with him, half minded to shriek at her, to tell her to run to the camels and flee, he saw that man crumple suddenly, and fall. For a moment he was nothing but confused, until he saw the knife-haft that jutted from the Dancer's spine. He yelled his joy instead, and wheeled round to fall upon the other.

His brother's death seemed to enrage that man, so that he would play no longer. Sword met sword's edge, and now Jemel could fight at last; and never mind that he had more than one to fight, as those who had been standing back came running forward. He blocked and parried and stabbed, exulting; his turn to dance, to shimmer and twist across the sand, to be somewhere else than at their swords' points. Even the pain in his hand was a blessing suddenly, a burning-point that helped him to focus. He still thought he could not win, but there was honour in his imminent death now, it would be no mocking jest. If he could make one kill before he died, he would go to paradise rejoicing . . .

The chance came sooner than he'd dared to hope. He faced three Dancers side by side, and had to fall back from their probing blades; but something ripped through the air, glittering, light made solid. One of the three checked suddenly, the one in the centre, and Jemel saw a strange growth jutting from the shadow of the man's hood. He fell, his hood slipped from his head; there was a knife sunk deep into his eye.

The other two Dancers were more startled even than Jemel, or took a moment longer to recover. A moment was enough. He leaped and slashed, and opened one from throat to belly before he could even see the blade's approach, let alone gather his thoughts to work that vanishing-trick.

The other did flick out of sight a moment before Jemel's scimitar found him too; but when he reappeared he was some little distance off, beside his remaining brother. That one was stringing his bow; Jemel turned his head to find Julianne, and saw her tugging her first knife free of the Dancer she'd stabbed. He snapped, 'Help Rudel! These are mine,' and plunged towards the archer.

Arrived in time, if only just; the man was pulling an arrow from his quiver. Jemel's sword harried him into dropping his bow; defenceless, he was gone, but his bow was left behind. Jemel faced the other, who had no stomach it seemed for single combat; he too disappeared.

Jemel scanned the ground around and saw them both, standing on an outcrop: not far, but no danger either at that distance. If they came back with swords, then he'd be ready; meantime he looked urgently for his companions.

Rudel seemed all but finished, using his sword two-handed now, only blocking Morakh's thrusts and backing, always backing. But there was Julianne, knife in hand, arm cocked to throw; Jemel saw her cast, and watched the weapon spin through the air. Her aim was good, only that the distance was too great for her skill; it was the haft and not the blade that struck Morakh clean in the head. The blow seemed to stun him, though, so that he staggered; now Rudel could step forward, and swing with a tremendous effort.

Morakh recovered his wits a moment too soon. He had no time to bring his blade up in a parry; like his brothers before him, he melted out of sight and Rudel's blade met only air.

And then there were three on the outcrop, and three on the sands below. Jemel made his way warily towards his companions, more watchful still after there were suddenly none on the outcrop. If the Dancers came again, they could come without warning, and from any side . . .

Only the breeze stirred the sand, and Rudel's heavy breathing was the only sound he could hear until Julianne broke her stillness, hurrying to the older man's side. Her arm supported him, until he could sink onto a low rock; but it was to Jemel that she addressed her question, 'Have they gone . . .?'

'Who can tell? You tend him, I will stand guard. Or perhaps you should guard us, you killed most . . .'

'Did she?' Weakly, from Rudel.

'Two. And you she saved.'

'I know it. Thank you, Julianne. And well done.'

She made a face, reluctance warring with modesty; it became her well, Jemel thought, that moment before she busied herself with stripping back Rudel's robe to see how badly he was hurt.

'You did well yourself,' she said, grunting with relief; he

was marked many times, but they were all small cuts, few deeper than a finger's width.

'He was biding his time. And making sure that I knew it.'

'Why did they attack us? And that, that thing they did, that disappearing act – how . . .?'

'One at a time, child. There is water in my bag, here; tear strips from the hem of my robe, if you need cloth. I think they attacked us because we were unnecessary, with Marron gone; they had only endured us this long on sufferance, for his sake. And we had seen their holiest site, perhaps profaned it.'

'They are Sand Dancers,' Jemel added. 'They live to follow the Ghost Walker, and kill Patrics.' *And renegade Sharai*, but he did not say that aloud. Perhaps he did not need to.

'As to the vanishing – ouch! – there is more than one magic in this land, and the Sharai have their fair share of it. You have seen a little of what your people can do, at your wedding in the Roq; I have seen more than that. I have seen a great deal more, among both peoples, and learned from both. In Surayon, we use what we can find; we have to. I had never seen quite this before, but I knew of it. The Dancers have spent decades, centuries, developing the arts of combat; what more useful than to fold space together, to be here one moment and there the next? It's all knowledge, all depends on understanding how the world is made. Also, it is a fragmentary imitation of what the Ghost Walker can do, walking between worlds; they think it honours him, or them . . .'

Julianne would be some minutes, Jemel saw, washing

Rudel's wounds and binding up the worst of them. His hand hurt him; to distract himself, he wandered off to where the bodies of the Dancers lay. They would each of them have been carrying water, flour, dates; those would be useful.

Rummaging one-handed among the robes of the fallen, he found a bag that puzzled him, that seemed to contain two short, fat sticks. He worked the mouth open, and tipped the contents out; stared for a moment, then slowly understood. Scooped them up and carried them back, to lay in the sand before Rudel's feet.

He straightened, saying nothing. The bearded man gazed, and nodded.

'Morakh said he had seen such a thing before, that stone in the ghûl's tongue. He did not say when; a few short days ago, I guess to be the answer. This needs thinking on . . .'

'I don't understand?'

'Julianne, these are the feet of a ghûl. See the ass's hooves? Those are no ankles of an ass, above. That one that killed the merchant on the road, they lied to us, when they said they could not find it; they must have tracked it down and killed it. And kept the feet, and made those tracks they showed us, to force us on last night and bring us here, to where they thought that they could control Marron. They were wrong; that boy answers only to himself. Leave me now, and see to Jemel. He is more pale than you are, and hurt worse than me. I don't think he can stand much longer . . .'

He could not; he was sinking already, under a sudden dizziness. He barely felt Julianne's hands on his sleeve, drawing it back to expose the hidden hand; he could hardly force his eyes to focus, to see how bad the damage was.

Still, blurred sight was enough to show him the joke of it, sweet irony that forced a painful laugh from his throat.

Morakh's scimitar had sliced clean through his smallest finger, so that it hung now by only a sliver of skin. The other fingers were cut, but none so deeply. Those he would keep.

It was Morakh who had forbidden him the Dancers' vows, the sacrifice of a finger and a stone set on the Pillar; Morakh who had brought them here and shown Marron how to open the gate between the worlds, so that Jemel had set a stone – and a potent stone – on the Pillar regardless; Morakh now who had completed the ritual.

Jemel smiled, against the swirling darkness of the world. God worked in His own way on His people. The oath was made, and witnessed; Marron would come back, and Jemel would follow him. It was written, in blood and deed. There were no choices now, for either of them.

7

Days of Gold and Thunder

Elisande thought that terror was an oil, which meant that time simply couldn't get a grip on her.

When the ghûl had sprung out at them, after the first heart-stopping moment it had seemed to move so slowly, they should have had all the time they needed to fight or flee. And yet for her it had been like moving through oil, instead of air; her thoughts raced, but her body was left behind.

When she had screamed and flung her knife, it had seemed to drift, to hang almost like a banner on the breeze, it took so long to strike home. When she'd fallen, she'd thought that she was floating; when Marron had overstood her with his blade in hand, her tongue had been too thick and heavy to shape the words she needed until it was too late, creeping sword had pierced crawling monster and the thing was made well instead of slain.

If they'd had time, she could have warned him – but however slow their bodies were, words had been slower still to come.

The Daughter had risen out of Marron's ruined shoulder, and even that had seemed leisurely to her; and Marron's hesitation had taken an age, long enough she'd thought for the ghûl to devour them both, though not long enough for her to drag herself to her feet.

Then he'd shaped the Daughter into a door, and hauled her through; and thank the God her mind had still been running fast, not numbed into stupor by her first sight of the place he'd brought her to.

Because Marron at least was not thinking now, he'd done that; boy-like, all he was doing now was react. The first thing he did, of course he did, was to close the door that he'd made, to keep the ghûl – and others too, maybe – on the other side of it. He let that near-solid frame fold in on itself till it was only a heavy, shapeless waft of smoke. It looked thicker, stronger here than it ever had before; and that was perhaps a blessing, it might have given him a moment's pause.

At any rate, the second thing he did was to set her on her feet and hold her so, until she found her own balance; which gave her just time enough to realise what he intended next, and to prevent him.

She clapped her hands over the bloody ruin of his shoulder, where the ghûl had gored it, just a moment before that dense streak of smoke could reach it.

Marron screamed and jerked away, but just had wit enough to jerk the Daughter too, so that it rose high in the air above them. Then he stared at her, and said, 'If that had touched your skin . . .'

'I know.' She would have died, he couldn't have prevented it. Perhaps she too had only been reacting – *girl-like*, she thought, with a touch of grim humour that she didn't share with him – though she'd rather think that it had been a gesture of absolute trust, that she'd been certain of his quick response. 'But, Marron, you can't take it back through this,' lifting one hand towards his shoulder again but not touching this time, not to hurt him further.

'It would stop the bleeding . . .'

'Yes; but it would stop its healing too. You know that. It'd be like your arm, you'd have two open wounds that would never close again.'

He shrugged, one-shouldered, and gazed at her, huge brown eyes in a face that was white with pain. 'I could live with that.' *As it is, it may kill me, soon or later* . . . He didn't need to say that aloud. And he could be right; it was a dreadful wound, she could see white bone beneath the torn flesh and the pumping blood. He could bleed to death quite quickly, or else it could fester and poison slowly; she'd known a man die from the simple prick of a thorn.

But that man hadn't had Marron's advantages, nor Elisande at hand when he needed her; she had come to his bedside too late, when his whole arm had been putrid and her skills too little to save him.

'You'll have to endure the pain a little longer,' she said softly, 'you can't take the Daughter back till the blood stops flowing. But that at least I can do for you.' That and more, if she could work at all in this strangest of landscapes, where all her talents and knowledge might come to nothing.

That she didn't believe, though; she felt herself strong and potent, more so than usual, just as the Daughter itself seemed to be more potent here. She tucked her shoulder under Marron's good arm and guided, half-carried him to a rock that was warm to the touch, as the air was warm, and the ground beneath her booted feet. He could at least sit down; she didn't think he could stand much longer. All his skin was slick with a chill sweat; pain and blood-loss between them were draining him faster than she cared to think about.

She still had one knife remaining to her; working quickly, she used that to cut away the ripped shoulder and drenched sleeve of Marron's robe, peeling them carefully back from ruined flesh. For all her care and his courage, still he gasped; she took a moment to touch his cheek with tender fingers, leaving it printed with his own blood, the marks of her concern. Then she slashed a swathe of cloth from the hem of her own robe and shrugged off the empty water-skins she'd been carrying till she found the one that was hers beneath, husbanded through the long night-ride and still full.

She soaked the rough dark cloth, and swabbed at Marron's wound. Here she had to be unkind, ungentle; he sobbed under her touch, but who knew what filth a ghûl might carry on its claws? Not she; and though the Daughter was said to be sovereign against poisons, she wouldn't trust what she didn't fully understand. Better to be certain, to do the work herself.

When she was sure as she could be that the wound was clean, that water and blood between them had carried off all dirt, she threw the cloth aside and laid both hands against the wound. She closed her eyes and concentrated her mind, shutting out all thoughts else and drawing on everything she knew, every power that she possessed; then she pressed hard, pulling rags of flesh together as best she could, forcing the wrenched and twisted joint back into shape.

This should have been cruel, but was not. She heard Marron gasp again, but only in surprise; she felt the cold flesh warm beneath her tingling fingers, as she channelled healing strength through them and into him.

At times like this, when she was so focused on another's body and wellbeing, it had often seemed to her as though her thoughts followed that flow of power, out through her fingers and under alien skin. Today that effect was amplified beyond measure; she felt almost like another Daughter herself – though she flinched from the word, she hated to think of herself as anyone's daughter – as her awareness seemed to leave her own body and slip into Marron's. She could sense, almost see the damage that the ghûl had done, although her eyes were shut; she could feel how torn vessels closed beneath her touch, how stretched tendons drew tight and firm again, how shattered bone itself started to rebuild. Above all, she bathed in the glow of healing well begun. Almost she wanted to pass out of her body altogether, to leap that extra little distance and flow entire into Marron, to visit his heart and all his other organs, to sidle into his head and try to read his thoughts as well as she could read the processes of his flesh and blood . . .

Almost, but not quite. She retained so much sense, at least, to resist that call at the last and draw back instead, forcing her eyes to open and her hands to fall away. Staggering, gasping, she needed suddenly to sit herself, and did so at his side. Her turn to sweat, she found, pushing her fingers through tangled, sodden hair.

When she lifted her head, she found him looking at her;

but she'd known that already, she had felt it even through that enveloping exhaustion.

'How is it now?' she asked, only to have some passage of words between them; she knew how it was, she had seen it from the inside.

'Better. So much better, I can't believe . . .' He tried to swing the arm to prove it, and yelped instead. She amazed herself by laughing at him, though it was a hoarse, hard little bubble of a chuckle that hurt her throat in its rising.

'Steady. It's not mended yet, only started. It'll be a long journey.'

'Even so. I didn't know that you could do such things . . .'

'Neither did I,' she confessed. 'It wasn't me – or only partly me. Partly it's this place, there's a power here . . .' More powers than one, she remembered; she glanced upward, to see where the Daughter still hung above them in the sky. 'You should take that back now, it'll kill any pain you feel and maybe help the healing, I don't know . . .'

She didn't know either if she could work even here on a body that contained such a creature; she'd had no success before, on Marron's arm. But if need be he could release it again, and let her work on him while his blood was pure, untainted. While his eyes were brown . . .

When he didn't move, she reached to do it for him: lifting Marron's bare arm – just a little, not enough to make him cry out with the pressure on his shoulder – and taking her dagger again, pricking lightly between the stitches of his old wound and squeezing until the first drop of blood appeared. There should have been no more than that, he had lost too much already. A drop would have been enough, a pin-hole sufficed. But it spurted, even through the tiny cut she'd made, and she felt Marron jerk with an unexpected pain.

He looked up and the Daughter flowed down like a scarlet thread, insinuating itself into his body. The run of blood died as swiftly as it had begun; his terrible paleness receded, and so clearly did his discomfort, as he gazed with an oddly detached interest at the results of her work on his shoulder.

As did she. There was a great ragged gash, and the edges were open still; no miracles, even here. But the blood had stopped running, there was no open gateway now out of which the Daughter might have slipped uncalled-for. And the flesh was pink, the bones she knew were rightly set, and knitting . . .

'I must bind it up,' she said, 'to keep this out,' this fine warm golden dust that covered the rock they sat on and the ground below. What that might do in a wound, inside a body, she couldn't begin to guess. 'And we'll make a sling to hold it, you mustn't use it yet or you could tear apart what's just begun to mend . . .'

His face twisted, at a memory she couldn't share; she could guess at it, though, and hurried on.

'I'd like to know what's happening back, back in my world,' – she couldn't say 'our world', not quite; with the Daughter in his blood Marron was a bridge between that and this, and seemed to belong in neither – 'but . . .'

'No,' Marron said, decisive for once. 'You need not worry for the others; Jemel will kill the ghûl.'

'Will he?'

'Oh, yes.' Utter certainty in his tone, and almost a hint

of pride. 'He was behind us, when we came through. He will do that.'

'Well, he should know how, at least. I'd like to be sure,' *as sure as you are*, 'but we can't tell what we'd be going back to. I don't think you should let the Daughter out again, anyway, not for a while. What I've done felt good, better than I'd expected; your body needs a chance to heal properly, though, and it'll do that best if you're free from pain. The Daughter can do that for you, at least . . .'

It could give him the strength to travel in this country, too; and that was what she wanted most, now that they were here. She was concerned for their companions – well, for Julianne, at least, and of course for Jemel – but after being flung so abruptly away from them, and so far, it was hard to feel involved in that small struggle. What she felt rather was enchanted; as though she'd been gifted a glimpse of wonder. It would be cruel to wrench her back into that company of secrets and doubts and mistrust, when she was suddenly here in this place of mystery and myth. And with Marron, the two of them together and alone, as they had never been before . . .

She pushed herself to her feet, looked around and saw a low scarp of rock just a little distance off. She left Marron – and marvelled that she could do that, even for a minute, but did it none the less – and walked over to the foot of the scarp. Set her hands on it, and found that it too was warm, as all this world was warm; lifted her eyes to the peak, and began to climb.

She was still weary in mind and body both; this was no great ascent, but still it was an effort to push and drag even her light weight up to the summit. She wanted to see, though, more even than she wanted to rest. She knew where they were, in the land of fable, but she needed her eyes to confirm it. Knowing wasn't enough. Neither was touch, that warmth that pervaded everything; nor taste and smell, though the air both smelled and tasted uniquely different, rich and flat at the same time. *Unbreathed,* she thought, and smiled at herself for thinking it.

There was hearing too, of course, and she could hear nothing but her own hard breathing; she'd heard silence before, though, the deep silence of the Sands at midday when nothing moved, when even the air was still. It was strange, but not strange enough. She burned for a long sight of this mystical country, and all she'd seen thus far was a close view of dust and rocks. Golden rocks, to be sure – but still, not enough.

And so she hauled herself to a height, not a tremendous height but the best that she could manage just now; and when she got there, sweat stung her eyes so that for a little while she could see nothing but a blur. She rubbed at them, and staggered where she stood; caught her balance with a wild swing of her arms, and looked about her.

Now she could see for miles, for days; days of hard travel they would be, too, but she yearned to make them. Softly gold under the soft light, the land stretched before and below her like a glimmering image of the Sands, except that she thought that the Sands were an image of this. A crude image too, more coarsely made of ruder stuff and patched by shadow, which this land was not . . .

Puzzling over that, she glanced upward, and realised suddenly that there was no sun in the sky. How could that be? And would there be a soft and starless night to follow day, or was this land unchanging even in its light?

Well, an answer to that would come in time. For now she turned in a slow circle, feasting her eyes; or turned half a circle, rather, and came to a dead stop. Where in their world the Dancer's Pillar had been raised on its high hill, here a gleaming blade of stone leaped up, too high almost for her mind to fathom.

She gaped, recognised that she was gaping, and closed her mouth with a conscious effort. Completed her circle quickly, wanting no more wonders and glad to see none; and dragged her eyes down to find Marron where she had left him, sitting on his rock. With his head lifted, she saw, watching her . . .

That was enough, and more than enough. She scrambled back down the scarp in what came close to a headlong tumble, was almost indeed a fall; arrived at the bottom with sore fingers and scuffed boots, dust in her hair and hurry in her feet.

She ran over to him, running into his gaze all the way like a girl who ran into a hard, hot wind for the sake of something precious at its back. When she reached him, she sank breathless to the ground just a little touch away from him, the distance that red eyes could keep a girl; and she said, 'Have you seen it? That, that . . .'

She didn't have a word, but she could point: *that* way, what should be north by her memory of where they'd been in the other world. She'd always had a strong sense of direction, and she was relieved to find that it felt like north here too, though there was no sun to confirm it. At least the two worlds seemed to map each other.

Marron nodded, more distracted she thought than wordless from amazement, as she was. It couldn't be seen from here, the scarp was in the way, but of course he'd seen it. That had to be where he and Jemel had come through before. She wanted to ask what it was, what on earth it might mean; but how would he know?

Instead she busied herself with making bandages, improvising a sling to hold his arm. He'd have to go bare-chested, but that should be no hardship, even for a pale-skinned Patric; the warmth was better than pleasant, it was delightful, and he couldn't burn where there was no sun.

That was another reason, she thought, why they should stay and journey in this world and not their own. The others of their party would move on, south to Rhabat; if she and Marron tried to follow over the Sands, he would blister and sicken of sunstroke without a robe to cover his head and back. Here they could do it safely, if they could find their way . . .

Except that here there was nothing of this world that they could eat, and no water they could drink. If there were water at all, she wouldn't risk it; nor allow him to do so, despite the Daughter's internal watchfulness. Perhaps they should hasten back after all, hope to catch the others before the party abandoned them and moved on. She was only looking for excuses to stay, after all, and here was a better reason to leave . . .

'Marron? Would you like to go back? It would mean more blood for you, a little, and more pain' – *a lot*, she thought, and perhaps more blood than she was saying, per-haps more than he could afford – 'and we don't know what we'd be going back to; but you could, you could check on Jemel,' a low stroke, she knew, but refused to blush for it, 'and we'd have supplies and company. And a known route to follow, though there may be trouble on the way. We wouldn't just be striking out in the dark . . .' Or *in the light*, if this place knew no darkness.

She knew what she wanted, but she didn't know what was best; it was a genuine choice she offered him, and if he'd said *go back* she would have gone, and never challenged the decision.

But he gazed at her with those strange, inhuman eyes she could not read, and said, 'We'll do what you want, Elisande. If it's safe for you. What supplies do you need, that you have not got?'

'We both need food and water,' she said, trying to obliterate the difference between them, and only seeing him smile at the attempt. 'I have one skin that is full, these others that are empty, except for what drops we can squeeze from them. I also have a bag of flour' – Dancer-like, in the desert she carried her survival on her back always, even where there were wells and pack-camels and friends and all – 'and flint and tinder, but no firewood. We will need a fire, to cook the bread; I don't think we'll find anything that we can burn.' It seemed to her that except for what came up out of the earth, oil and tar and coal, anything that burned must once have lived; she thought that nothing lived here. Except the djinn, of course, and the 'ifrit. Neither of those, she thought, would feed a fire.

She seemed to have persuaded herself, against her own intent; when he said nothing, she sighed and said, 'We'd better go back, I suppose.' And once gone, they were gone for good, most likely; she didn't expect to have this chance again. She couldn't ask Marron to bring her through on a pleasure-jaunt, it cost him far too severely.

But Marron surprised her with a smile; he said, 'How far do you think we have to go?'

'I'm not sure. They said Rhabat was a week's journey; but that was on camelback, and through the Sands. I don't know how fast we can travel here, on foot . . .' They could go as directly south as the land would allow, no need to seek for wells when they couldn't drink the water; she felt a flicker of hope which blossomed into flame, a burning desire when he reached down with his good hand to lift a large rock that lay on the ground beside her, that she'd been resting her elbow on.

Marron turned it over with an easy flick of his wrist, and said, 'I don't think we need fire, Elisande. I doubt it ever gets cold in this land; and as for cooking bread — well, touch. Touch lightly . . .'

She did, the swiftest brush of her fingers; and still she had to snatch them back and suck at them. Warm like everything on its upper surface, it was scorching hot on its underside; lay a dough on that and he was right, it would bake through in minutes.

'We still don't have much, either flour or water . . .'

'Not much, no — but enough, perhaps. I don't need much, and nor perhaps will you. Less than you would in the Sands, in any case, with no sun to roast you. And this country lends me strength, as the Daughter does too; it may do the same for you, when you are not so tired.'

Indeed, she felt stronger already, stronger far than she'd expected after the exhaustion of healing him. They shouldn't take the risk, even now her good sense told her to go back and join the others; but he was offering her the chance to stay, and she lacked the will to resist him.

She lifted her head and gazed into those fierce eyes, seeking the gentle soul behind and not finding it, as ever. Sure of it none the less, she laid a hand on his knee and said, 'There must be dangers here, that we can't foresee . . .'

'Yes. But we can flee them, if we must, as we did the ghûl. You want to stay, Elisande; don't work against yourself.'

She sighed, for pure contentment. Adventure, exploration, new wonders to discover, and all of it in his company, which was adventure and exploration in itself; there was risk, of course, but that only spoke to her soul the louder. Hunger and thirst she'd met before, and survived them. If they met worse, or stranger – well, that was the quality of the world, and some part of what she sought.

Was she too tired to begin now, as she ought? Perhaps she was only too happy to move; she could begin in any case, or rather take another step on a journey already begun. She sat entirely still and said, 'Marron, you've changed so much, so quickly. You used to be simple, but these days I can't predict you at all. There's the Daughter, of course, but it's more than that. What's happened to you?'

'I killed my friend,' he said, his voice flat with honesty, 'and left my master; I betrayed my people and my God. I killed more than one friend, I killed many. With a monster that I took into my body. How could I not be changed by that, by all of that?'

Elisande sighed again, for the opposite of contentment, for him; and laid her head against his leg, and waited to feel his hand touch her hair. Waited in vain and ached for him, that he could not make so easy, so human a gesture, and was content none the less, although she understood herself little better than she did him.

Time passed, though she had no way to count it unless she'd counted the beats of her heart, which she had not. At last, because he would not stir, she had to. She pulled herself reluctantly to her feet, and allowed herself one swallow of their precious water; offered the skin to him, and felt some relief when he only shook his head. His abstinence had distressed her for weeks; now it was a blessing.

'We should start out,' she said. 'There's a long way to go.' And she'd never been less prepared for a journey, nor looked forward to it more.

He nodded, and rose; glanced about him and turned unerringly towards the south, or so her own senses told her.

'You must say,' he said, 'when you need to rest. I think I could go for ever.'

That was a glimpse of the old Marron, almost, the boy who would exhaust himself without knowing it; only that the old Marron would never have thought to say so. Elisande hid a wry smile inside her hood, and waved him on.

The healing had drained her, a short climb too soon after had exhausted her; it seemed though that there was something restorative about unbreathed air, or adventure, or shadowed but much-desired company. Once started, she felt like Marron that she could walk for ever.

Unlike Marron – perhaps – she wasn't fool enough to

believe it; but there was enchantment enough in the simple act of walking here to bury all her doubts. Unless it was simply the fact of being here, or the fact of being with him . . .

Certainly it wasn't the landscape itself that struck her so with rapture. She had been in many places, both natural and man-made, that were more beautiful to the eye, once that eye had grown accustomed to the golden sheen that overlay everything here. She had walked in lands that were wilder, and far more dramatic. This was dead country, or seemed so. There was only the absence of any sun in the sky or any shadow under their feet to speak of the strangeness of where they were; only that towering monument, that blade or needle or pillar of stone, to speak of the powers that dwelt here, and that was behind them. A glance back could find it at any time during that first day, like a finger to mark where they had started their trek, but she glanced back seldom. It wasn't even useful as a guide, to say how far they had walked; it was too big, she couldn't read the scale.

Besides, that first day, she didn't care how far they'd come nor how far they had yet to go. She was entranced only by the journey, by each separate moment of it. To step where perhaps no human had stepped before – and she walked at Marron's side to be sure of that, or as sure as she could be, not to walk in his footsteps – and to see what perhaps no human had seen before: that was enough, or nearly so. To share that walk and those sights with this damaged, dangerous, delightful boy: that was plenty for Elisande, it was all the thrill she craved and more. She didn't need towering cliffs and thundering falls, nor yet gardens with gorgeous blossoms and overpowering scents. She had known those and loved them, drawing them soul-deep with every sense she had; but she loved this better.

There was no path, there couldn't be, where no creature lived to make one; neither djinni nor 'ifrit would leave a track where it passed. Unless it chose to, she supposed – and then only if it could form a physical body in this world, as it could in the other. She remembered the djinni she and Julianne had met, how it had avoided any contact with ground, the touch of anything more solid than the dust of the road – and the flesh of a boy's arm, that too, but that not by its choice – and decided not to expect djinni-tracks here.

There was no path, but a way was easy to find. It must have matched the way their friends would be going, she thought, down from the heights of the Dancers' Pillar to the great Sands below; except that here the pillar they left behind was so much greater, and what they came down to was softer, kinder country, and so much less than the Sands.

The way they went pitched steeply downward, but the dust was firmly packed, and where the slope fell sharply there was rock aplenty jutting through, to give good footing beneath their boots. She worried a little for Marron at first, for fear that his strapped arm would upset his balance; it was wasted worry, though, she saw that soon enough. He went down the incline like a mountain goat, taking it almost at a run, leaping sometimes from ledge to narrow ledge. She followed more cautiously, watching his progress always with one eye and hoping that he laughed as he leaped, that he could find some fun in his wild descent. He was too far ahead too quickly for her to be sure, but she did hope.

Reaching the foot of the drop at last, she found him waiting for her, a kindness she had almost not dared to hope for. For Julianne and the others, this would be burning sand and a long hard road ahead, veering constantly off their true direction from well to necessary well, each one claimed by jealous and likely hostile tribes. For her and Marron, not so. There was only that hard-settled dust stretching before them in rolling dunes which were broken rarely by an upthrust of the rock beneath. Their way lay straight before them, due south. The dangers of the Sands, both human and natural, she knew; the dangers of this place she could only guess at, and she would not trust her guesses. No point in anticipating them, then. She set herself at Marron's side and strode forward, eager to leave her light prints beside his, and never mind if no one ever saw them, she knew they were there . . .

They walked and walked, and saw nothing that moved except each other, bar an occasional light rippling in the dust under a vagrant breeze. Mostly, even the air didn't move. Nor did the landscape change except in detail, the shapes and numbers of the rocky scarps that lifted above the level of the dust. Elisande had seen the Sands in many different faces, dune and gorge and gravel plain; she never had seen such a view as this. As the stories said, though, she did think that this was the original; that the desert she knew had been hacked out of coarse clay and rubbed into rough shape by a clumsy thumb, in brute imitation of what was here.

What was here and endless, or so it seemed. Sometimes she thought that they were not moving at all, or that the land carried them backwards at the same speed that they progressed; that was when she counted rocks, or took a rare glance behind her. In fact, by worldly standards, they were moving fast; those hills they'd come down from were a ridge of dusky gold on the horizon, that monument that had looked for a while so like a pillar holding up the sky – unless it was a blade that threatened it – had fallen to a line, an ink-stroke on parchment, its impression lost with distance. This far away, her eye could pretend that it was closer, not so big . . .

They were moving fast, they had come far: too far, too fast on just a mouthful of water. And yet she wanted no more; she wasn't thirsty at all, wasn't hungry, nor tired now. She swung along easily beside Marron, aware that he was holding himself back to her pace, that left alone he would have run and run; and into the silence that had held them both for a long time now, she said, 'Is this how it's been for you, all these weeks? While I bullied you to eat and drink, and rest?'

'Yes,' he said, 'except it's stronger here. I think I really could go for ever . . .'

Well, and so he might; she could not, though she felt it. She would be sensible, she would call breaks and longer halts – but not yet, not with this next dune to mount. The landscape could and should grow dull, she thought, and yet it had not; every dune-top gave a slightly different view, even if it was a view of the same thing.

It was Marron in the end who pointed out the changes that were coming. She could almost have been resentful, except that change was wonder too. Everything in this world was new, untried, intriguing . . .

'Look,' he said, 'those must be hills ahead. And the sky is growing darker.'

True, and true. At least those must be hills if they were as like as they seemed to what lay behind the travellers now, a narrow ribbon of darker shade set between ground and sky. Not the hills that guarded Rhabat or their equivalent, not yet and not for a while yet; but there were ranges throughout the Sands where the land lay in folds and creases, and in those more primitive structures the two worlds seemed to match each other.

Also, the sky was undeniably growing darker; though she was glad that he had said it that way, not *night is falling*. This was no night as she understood it, the sun setting to the west and darkness rising in its absence in the east. All around the wide horizon – and she turned in a slow circle to be sure, to confirm its strangeness – there was a subtle change of colour, as though the sky were an inverted bowl with a rim of glaze darker than its body.

They walked on and watched it deepen further, watched it rise until the sky was altogether black on the horizon, fading through grey and still gleaming golden-white only at the apex, directly above their heads.

Marron stopped abruptly, atop yet another in the long march of low dunes. 'We should find a place to rest,' he said, 'before the light has gone completely.'

'I don't need to rest.' Which might or might not be true, she might only have inherited his foolish mantle, along with some at least of his restless energy; what was true was that she simply didn't want an end to this steady walking. There was some magic in it, more than the abiding strength of her legs and the fascination of the place; she felt as though she'd left all anxieties back in the other world, and she could stay free of them so long as she kept moving. A long night's lying still – and she was sure that she would not sleep, she could find no trace of quiet in her – could bring them back, could send her thoughts probing relentlessly across the gulf to seek what she could not find; or worse, just have them spinning hectically around and around, tangling in the mess of her own desires and doubts . . .

Marron smiled. 'We would lose each other in the dark,' he said. 'There'll be no moon to find each other by. Besides, we both should eat, hungry or not. And rest too, weary or not.'

She didn't believe that he would lose her, his eyes and hearing were both so unnaturally sharp now. Nevertheless he was right and she was wrong, twice over; she was not used to that, and didn't like it. Sourly, she grunted her agreement and followed as for the first time he led away from their straight path south, off to the shelter of one of those sudden islands of rock among the dust. Not that they needed shelter, or not from wind or weather; there had been none of either, bar those occasional light zephyrs that stirred the air a little but had no presence else.

Shelter from watching eyes, perhaps, but there'd been none of those either, or none that either one of them had seen or sensed. Still, there was comfort in walls, even if it was only a single wall of rock at their back; better that than camping entirely in the open. And in fact Marron found a shallow gully in the twilight, a slot where they could lie sheltered on two sides and exposed only on one. Less light in there, only a notch open to the opal sky, and that was dimming; light enough, though, to show her a number of rocks fallen loose. Warm seats they would make until it was time to lie down, if time had any meaning here that she could judge. It didn't seem to; night — if this was night — had come before she was ready for it, after she'd trekked so far that she should have been worn out long since. And dry, and starving hungry, and she was none of those, she felt fresh as morning.

And was probably deceived, or so she told herself. Firmly. Marron turned a large rock over with his casual strength, and she burned her fingers brushing off the dust to find where it was flat; there was already too little light to see well. She tipped a measure of flour out of her bag, too little it should be for two young appetites at the end of such a day, though it seemed too much to her. She added a little water and this time used her knife to mix them quickly into a dough before the flour scorched.

When she smelled smoke, she flicked the dough-cake over with the point of the knife; when again her nose told her that it was starting to burn, she lifted it off and tore it gingerly in two. It was almost too hot to handle, though Marron seemed not to notice as she handed him his share.

'I'll eat if you will,' she said gruffly.

'Oh, I'll eat.'

And he did, and so she had to, although the crust of the loaf tasted like cinders in her mouth and the inside was still wet and somehow rancid. She choked it down, necessary fuel, and unslung her water-skin to rinse her palate; the water was blood-warm and rank, tasting of ill-cured leather. She took less than she'd meant to but still more than she wanted, and passed the skin to Marron. He drank even more sparingly than she had.

There was nothing to do then except sit on her chosen rock and lean her spine and shoulders against the towering wall behind her, regretting just a little that he had chosen a separate rock from her. She tilted back her head and watched as that little notch of sky darkened overhead, till it was as black as the rim had been earlier. No moon, as Marron had predicted, and no stars either; only an all-encompassing darkness. It wasn't quite a dead black, though, just as the white of the day-sky had not been a pure white; this like that had a pearly sheen to it – she had seen black pearls as a child, and had yearned to possess their beauty – and was shot through with glimmers of gold.

Still, it was black enough, it sufficed. She could see nothing. She held her hand a short inch from her face and could not make out a single finger. Marron was a sound of breathing in the stillness, nothing more. This was just what she'd been dreading, an engulfing shadow that would let her mind slip free and so torment her; she didn't think she could endure hours of it, even assuming that it lasted only hours. She had no real reason to suppose that light and dark followed the same rhythms here that they did in her own world, only a desperate hope; and that hope itself still left her facing a nightmare time, without even the benefit of waking.

She did what she could to meet it. She lay down on the dust of the gully's floor, which should make a warmer and a softer bed than she'd known for a while; it showed no hint of cooling. She settled herself as best she could, closed her eyes like an obedient child at bedtime and waited, hoping, praying almost that her body had deceived her, that in truth it was as weary as it ought to be, and so would slide gently into sleep and take her with it . . .

*

Which it did not, and she was not in the least surprised. She lay striving after sleep, and could not achieve it. After a while her eyes opened of their own accord, and she stared upwards until she could just barely distinguish the black of the rock from the iridescent black cleft of the sky. That seemed to ripple with faint light for a moment, as though a golden twist of air had passed across it. She sighed, hoping that weary eyes were playing tricks on her; and forced them closed again, tried to squirm more deeply into the soft dust, and went chasing once more after an oblivion she could not find.

In such a darkness, she didn't need to lift or turn her head to know that she had no chance of seeing Marron; equally surely, she knew that he was not sleeping, nor trying to sleep. His breathing betrayed him, as did every slightest movement of his body where he sat yet on his rock, just a few short paces from her. Cruelly alert to him, she lay and listened to his wakefulness, as she was certain that he was listening to hers. She raged against the stupidity, until his patience had outwaited hers; then, fighting against honesty with all the guile she could find in herself, she called to him softly.

'Marron?'

'Yes, Elisande?'

'Please, I can't, I can't sleep. I love this country by daylight, but in the dark it frightens me. It's so strange, and we know so little about it; I keep imagining monstrous things. And thinking we deserve them, we shouldn't be here, we don't have the right. Even you, you don't possess what you carry, you don't have any claim over it. The djinn would be so angry, if they found us. Or 'ifrit might come, and they are terrible . . .'

'Do you want to go back?'

'Into the Sands, blindly, at night?' If it was night in the Sands — but never mind that doubt, it was no use to her now. 'No, that would be foolhardy. I just want company, that's all, and I can't see you. I hate being this helpless,' and that at least was true; she was no Julianne, trained to rely on wits and tongue. 'Would you come and lie beside me? Just where I can touch you? You should lie down in any case, you need rest as much as I do, even if neither one of us is sleeping . . .'

There was a moment's pause, she heard the silence of his breath and doubted her own wisdom mightily. Then he answered her without speaking. She didn't know if even his eyes could find her in this blackness, but his ears were sharper than hers; he walked swift and sure-footed to her side, and lay down to share her dust.

Almost to share. He lay close, but not close enough: an arm's reach away, and an arm was all that he offered her, reaching across the space between them to lay his hand on her wrist. She wasn't having that. She rolled over and nestled against him, her head on his good shoulder and all her short body pressed against his.

He stiffened; she flinched inwardly, but wouldn't pull away. Again she had no resources but her voice, and used it as best she could.

'How's your hurt, are you in any pain?'

'No. I don't know how it is, I don't feel it. I expect it's healing.'

'I should have worked on it a little more, maybe; but

that would hurt you, because I don't think I could do it unless you let the Daughter out. That thing overmasters me . . .'

'I wouldn't let you,' he said, surprising her one more time with his firmness, so far from the biddable boy he had been. 'It exhausts you, to do that; you must husband your strength.'

'At least I might have slept,' and she forced out a chuckle through a tight throat. 'You're not comfortable, though,' and now perhaps was the time for honesty, now that he'd come this far; at least, she hoped so. She was all out of guile. 'Why not, if you're not in pain? You're very tense . . .'

'I'm – not accustomed to this,' he whispered, 'to lying with a girl.'

Neither lying to a girl, seemingly; she was grateful that he hadn't done that. Once she'd thought that he wouldn't know how to lie, but he'd had to at the castle, again and again. Maybe all boys had the talent, even those who'd never used it. Girls, she was sure of. But no need now, he'd matched her honesty with his and she felt on safe ground suddenly.

'I know that, Marron. Don't worry about it, just relax. Forget that I'm a girl; I'm your companion, that's all, and it's good to stay close. There must be danger here, although we have not met it yet; we depend on each other, we have to learn to trust. With our bodies, too. The Sharai don't worry about bodies, and neither should we . . .'

And as she spoke she rolled again, she straddled him and sat back on her heels; and laid her hands on his neck and pushed him down when he tried to rise, left her fingers on the pulses of his throat and began to hum.

'What is this?'

'The *sodar*. Be easy. You met Jemel's, in the Sultan's palace; now meet mine. It will guide you into sleep.'

'It was you said you could not sleep . . .'

'Because you would not, fool,' she whispered. 'Be still, be easy . . .'

She slid her fingers through his hair and over his bare skin, she sang low and husky as her father used to do, she worked this little magic and barely dared to think that it might work. Likely the Daughter would work against her, here as elsewhere. But here all their little magics seemed to work, faster and stronger than in their own world; it took only a brief time before she felt the tension flee his body, heard his breathing slow, felt his head topple gently to the side.

And she stayed where she was a little longer, not singing now but touching, her hands falling still on his chest; and she sighed one last time that night and lay down close beside him, wishing almost – almost! – that Jemel was there, to say the *sodar* for her in her turn.

But maybe what she had said to Marron was truer than she'd meant, because his sleeping lulled and contented her, and it was not so very long before she slept herself.

Nor so very long before she woke, or so it seemed; only that there was a line of light all around the bowl of sky, and it was starting to creep upward into the lustrous black.

She turned her head, and saw that Marron was still well asleep; and smiled with a wicked cheerfulness, no doubts in her head this morning as she reached for her knife.

Its prick woke him, as it must: too late. He gasped at the pain that followed, and she bit her lip hard; but she kept her hand steady on his chest and her eyes on his, seeing how they faded from fiery red to puzzled brown as the blood flowed out of his arm, and the Daughter too.

'Why . . .?'

'Because I must see to your shoulder, I don't trust your reports; and that only gets in my way. I know it hurts, and I'm sorry. Now keep that thing out of my way, and lie still . . .'

She was all brisk efficiency this morning, and – without the Daughter to give him confidence, perhaps? – he was all compliance. She set her hands on either side of his half-healed wound, and closed her eyes to see the better.

Good. Better than she'd hoped; healing was well begun. If the Daughter didn't help, at least it didn't interfere. She had no need to waste her strength on him today; just a little warmth, a little gentle encouragement, and she withdrew.

'Take it back, then. Quickly: the less blood you lose here, the happier I'll be. And it might attract attention, it is half of this world, as we are not . . .'

Again he obeyed her, and she saw his eyes flood with scarlet. Before he lost the habit or the Daughter stole it from him, she said, 'Breakfast, before we go on. Turn that rock again, would you?'

He did, and she found the upturned surface hot: hotter than it had been the night before when it had been upper-most and nothing more than warm, but not so hot as the underside when Marron had first lifted it. This heat wasn't inherent, then; it welled up quite slowly from below, and dissipated into the air. She wondered how hot a cave would be, a mine, a sink-hole . . .

She baked bread again, and this time – by virtue of

slower cooking, and also of her being able to see – managed to produce a loaf that was baked through and hardly burned at all. Eating was still an effort, she had no appetite and didn't see the point, and besides the taste was no better than it had been the previous night; but she'd eaten worse bread in the desert, and forced herself to it for Marron's sake, because he would not without her lead. Sleeping against his unprotected bones last night had impressed upon her just how skeleton-thin he was. He'd lost weight, she thought, since they left the Roq; and he'd been skinny enough before, a carcase entirely without meat . . .

A mouthful of water each, and at this rate their supplies would last them to Rhabat and beyond; and so they set out walking.

That second day they came surprisingly soon to the range of hills they'd seen the previous evening, and climbed without effort. The rise was steep, but nothing like the savage heights she'd met in the Sands, where a difficult scramble up might lead only to an impossible crevasse, forcing a harder retreat and perhaps a day's detour. Admittedly she'd generally been encumbered with camels then, who were not made for mountains; but even so the land here was far less brutally torn, and offered little resistance to their passage.

The only trouble they encountered was one low cliff that lay directly in their way. They might have gone around, at the cost of an hour or two; but the rock offered plenty of handholds, and Marron said, 'I can climb this, if you can.'

'Easily. But should you, with your arm . . .?'

'I will not need it. One hand is enough.'

He proved that, all but skimming up the face of the cliff, barely seeming to grip even with the one hand. She waited below until he was safely over the top, envying him his confidence but still slightly regretting the doubtful boy he used to be; then she made shift to follow.

She'd taken on harder climbs in Surayon for sheer pleasure, learning in the company of friends and later going alone, driven to it, wild child pitting herself against the rock. No one climbed for pleasure in the Sands, but even there she'd felt a grim determination sometimes that had forced her higher than she'd needed to go, and a sense of triumph after at having overcome.

Here she hoped for pleasure and was well on the way to finding it, halfway up the cliff and already anticipating the top, intent on climbing as smoothly as Marron had if not so fast when she was stayed, frozen almost by a sudden touch of wind against her face, and a voice that was not Marron's.

A voice that offered no greeting and no warmth, no hint of humanity; a voice that chimed instantly in her memory, *djinni*, and had her clutching hard at holds that seemed abruptly perilous, as this land was perilous, which she had almost managed to forget.

'It is unusual,' it said, 'to find a child of the earth within our lands. To find two is not unprecedented, but it is perhaps worth a remark.'

It sounded to be close by her ear, and yet a startled glance in that direction showed her nothing, unless there was perhaps a light disturbance of the air. Nothing more, nothing to give her eyes a focus. She hung on, both to the rock and to her reeling thoughts; drew a breath and held it, thinking hard, before she spoke in reply.

'Spirit,' she said, fighting to sound calm when she was not, when she was anything but, 'believe me, the circumstances that brought us here were no less unusual. We would not have ventured here from mere curiosity,' which was a lie direct, but hopefully the creature that addressed her would not detect that. 'We fled a ghûl, that might otherwise have killed us both . . .'

She hoped, she prayed almost that it was a djinni she spoke to, and not an 'ifrit. She had no way of telling, except that it had said 'our lands', and this country was always said in stories to be the land of the djinn. All she was certain of was that this was not the djinni she had met and spoken with on the road to the Roq, and later at the castle; the voice was indistinguishable, high and sexless, but that other would surely have called her by her name if it had found her thus, and perhaps have made some reference to their previous encounter, or else to Julianne. It had betrayed a rare interest in their doings; this one, not.

'Indeed,' it said, not even rising to the bait she'd laid, that mention of the ghûl. 'It will have been your companion who brought you here; I sense a power in him, that you lack.'

'Yes. The Sharai name him the Ghost Walker; he has that within him,' and never mind how he'd come by it, or how he made it work, 'which can open a gateway between the worlds. But he has been hurt, and so I thought it better to journey here awhile, before we venture back.'

That was an apology, as best as she could frame it, and also a plea for permission to go on. She dared not ask directly; the djinn were quick to assume a debt, and to demand payment. Why else was Julianne headed for Rhabat?

'I am unconcerned with his hurts, or with yours. Nor does your presence disturb me, as it will not endure. You will find, though, that the 'ifrit are very much concerned.'

'We had hoped to avoid the 'ifrit, spirit.'

'No doubt you had. Human.'

Was that a warning, was it telling her to beware the 'ifrit? She couldn't ask; even in this precarious position, her fingers aching and ready to slip and her feet none too secure, she had enough presence of mind to avoid the question. If it were a warning, though, it was unnecessary; of course she would beware the 'ifrit. At her first sight of one, however distant, she'd have her knife into Marron's arm whether he was ready for it or not. That assumed, of course, that she would see an 'ifrit and know it for what it was. She couldn't see the djinni . . .

On the other hand, the djinn were said to have an inner eye that could read something of the future; perhaps it meant that they would meet 'ifrit, however prepared she liked to think herself.

It was possible to be too clever, even when exchanging dubious compliments with a djinni. Her fingers did slip suddenly, so that she had to make a wild grab at the rockface and barely managed to hold on.

'Forgive me, spirit,' she gasped, 'but I'm going to fall . . .'

'My forgiveness would not seem to be necessary,' it replied. 'You cannot injure me, by falling.'

She gritted her teeth, held back a sharp retort, and began to climb again, with cramped muscles and a deal more care than she'd used earlier. She thought the djinni had gone, hoped that was true; persuaded herself definitely that it was, before her hands at last closed on the lip of the cliff and Marron was there, stooping to grip her wrist and haul her up with one swift tug.

For a moment she only sat at his feet, breathing hard; then she said, 'Did you see it?'

'See it? Perhaps. I heard it come; a noise like rushing wind, but small. Not quiet, only small. I saw a zephyr, that hovered by your head. And I heard your conversation. You shouldn't fear the 'ifrit.'

'Marron, it makes good sense to fear the 'ifrit. Sit down, we're not moving on for a little while. I'm blown.' The truth was, she was trembling so hard she thought her legs might not hold her if she tried to walk. It made good sense to fear the djinn also, especially so here in their own land, and she strove always to be sensible . . .

'I do not think they would be let harm me,' he said, settling down beside her, 'and that protection is yours too, you know that.'

'The ghûl harmed you, remember? Oh, not to death, and you recover fast,' *with my help*, 'but if that claw had found your neck, nothing could have saved you. And that was just a ghûl. How will you stop an 'ifrit, if it has no solid body here? How would you have stopped the djinni, if it had sought to kill me? Just a breath of wind, how can you cage that?'

She might be wrong about the 'ifrit, she very likely was. They were subservient to the djinn, a lower order — surely there must be some distinction between them that would be clear even to human eyes? Marron knew less than she did, though, and she had to persuade him somehow out of that dangerous confidence. The Ghost Walker was tradionally very hard to kill; but not immortal, never that. Even the djinn were not immortal . . .

'Mind,' she went on slowly, following that thought, 'what it said at the end there, "you cannot injure me, by falling" – do you think it meant there was some other way I could injure it, or we could? I'm sure it meant more than the joke. Khaldor laughed at us more than once, but I don't think this one had a sense of humour.'

'I don't know what it meant,' Marron said. 'After all you've said about the djinn, what's the point in trying to outguess it?'

'Because it's easier than trying to outguess a boy,' she muttered darkly, gazing at him through narrowed eyes. 'And it might be important.'

'Anything might be important. Or nothing might. Come on,' and he rose smoothly to his feet, bent and pulled her up after him, 'let's at least finish the climb and see what's to see from the top. You can rest there, if you need to.'

She didn't need to rest, or not from her exertions; but she looked at the slope that still rose for some distance above them, she gazed pointlessly at the sky to try and guess the time when there were no signs to show her, and she tucked a hand under Marron's girdle at the back.

'You'll have to pull me,' she said; and felt his laugh more than heard it, a chuckle that twitched at his spine, followed by a shiver that was entirely silent.

Anything might be important; they came at last to the high point of this ridge of hills, and found that of course it was the highest that they'd climbed, they could look down on the peaks of all the others.

At first, though, they looked further down; even before they looked at the view, they looked at their boots and what they stood on.

The hill must have been higher yet at one time, it couldn't have been made this way; but the whole of its summit had been flattened, levelled, cut off perhaps by a shearing blade, and the exposed rock polished to a mirror's shine. In the gloss of that polish they could see faint images of themselves, reflected above the rock's gold.

If there were a purpose to it, they could neither see one nor divine it; but the work was on such a tremendous scale, so much more than men could achieve, it rang a bell of memory in both of them.

They turned to face the way they had come, and squinted against the pearl-white gleam of the sky, which seemed brighter or more concentrated at the horizons; Elisande thought that she could just make out a faint hairline, like a crack in the rim of the bowl. Marron said that he could see the needle clearly.

There was that, and there was this; both were vast, majestic, incomprehensible. They turned again, and walked almost reluctantly across the great floor they stood on. Something perhaps should be dancing here, but not they.

'It's stupid,' Elisande murmured, 'but I feel so exposed here, as if we never were before. Which is ridiculous. Do you think all those little winds that blew the dust about yesterday were djinn?'

'Yes,' he said.

'Me too. But even so. I feel like we ought to skirt around the edge, like servants . . .'

'Do you want to?'

'No.'

And so they did not; but she did take Marron's hand as they crossed the centre of this place, whatever it might be, and she thought the tightness of his grip was not entirely for her comfort.

They came to the further side, and stood looking. If anything, the southern face of the hills was gentler than the northern; they could walk down with relative ease, she thought. And then the long sweep of a plain, simple going again; and beyond that, dusky with distance, hills again. But running from the hills, absolutely at the limit of her sight even from this high aspect, she thought there was a line of cloudy light that shone back dimly what the sky had given it.

'Marron, what's that there, can you see? It's not the horizon, it's like a hazy bar of light beneath, but I can't make it out . . .'

'It's a bar of light,' he said, and almost earned himself a fist in the ribs before he went on. 'There's no more detail than that, that I can see. As you said, it's hazy. But I saw something like such a thing before, once. When Aldo and I took our Ransomer vows and travelled from the monastery with Fra' Piet, to take ship to come to Outremer.'

'Well? What was it?'

'It was the sea,' he said simply. 'I'd never seen it before, I hadn't thought that anything could be so big. But we first sighted it at dawn, from a height, from a great distance; and it was a gleam that ran the sun's light along all the horizon, and nothing more than that. It terrified me; for a moment I thought it was the God, sending fire to bar our way. Perhaps I should have listened to myself . . .'

'No. Oh, no. You shouldn't be frightened of a lie, even one you tell yourself.' She gripped his good arm with both hands and hugged herself against it, for what comfort she could give, if it could reach him.

'The sea was bigger,' he said, his face still fixed to the south though his eyes had lost their focus, 'but it looks the same. Can there be a sea in the desert?'

There could; there was. And here too, apparently, and close enough to be in sight already . . .

'The Dead Waters, the Sharai call it. That's journey's end, Marron. We'll go back to our world there, and try to find the others before we all go on to find Rhabat.'

8

Blood Heat

Julianne slipped as her feet broke through the crust of hard-baked sand to the soft, sliding stuff beneath. She fell flat on her back, and was dragged a little distance across the scorching, gritty surface; she rolled effortfully onto her stomach, and lost a little more skin off her elbows before she managed to haul Sildana to a halt. She'd learned to knot the rein around her wrist, for just these occasions; she tried to be grateful for the lesson, as she struggled to her knees and saw fresh blood on the leather. Better to bleed, she told herself forcefully, than to watch her camel race away along the dune one more time, and have to sit in an embarrassed huddle on the sand while Jemel fetched the beast back.

He was below her now, still in his saddle, holding back the baggage-string with every appearance of patience while he waited for her to regain her feet. She did so, furiously, and began the slow trudge up again, hauling Sildana in her wake. She thought there was some witchery in the

Sharai, that he could ride these slopes even with three spare camels tied to his saddle-horn. She wasn't alone in her failure there; Rudel also had to dismount and drag his mount after him.

If there were witchery in the Sharai, though, there was sheer devilry in their camels; unless it was some great joke of the God – or their God, perhaps – that had made the only animal that could bear burdens in the desert so ill-designed for the work. Camels had great strength and great stamina, they could go for days on a mouthful of food and no water, as these had had to do; but they were precious poor on slopes. And the Sands, of course, were full of slopes: where there weren't hills or crags, there were always dunes.

These dunes, though – these were evil. Even Jemel had looked anxious, faced with the massive reality of them: dunes like hills themselves, lying east to west and so cutting straight across their path. They had too little spare water, too little time to make a detour that would run to days; nor was thirst the only danger, though it was perhaps the most immediate. There had been signs of recent usage at the last well they'd found, two days ago: fresh tracks, and camel-dung not dry yet. They'd been lucky thus far, Jemel said, but the borders between one tribe's lands and the next were always closely watched. If they crossed too many, they couldn't hope to hold their luck. Detours, by their nature, would have them crossing borders . . .

And besides the tribes, hostile or otherwise, there were also the Dancers. Morakh and his surviving companions, perhaps others also. Their absence was a constant threat, weighing on everyone's minds. There had been no sign of them since the fight below the Pillar, which lay days behind them now, but that meant nothing. Rudel said that their vanishing-trick and its reverse, their sudden appearance from empty air worked at close quarters only, they couldn't cover any great distance that way; he said also that they were masters of the desert, which she knew already. Jemel said that they could follow a trail that the wind had buried a week before, that they could walk into a guarded camp by daylight and be seen by none. She hoped that was legend more than truth, but knew that it would be wiser to believe him.

Not tribes nor Dancers nor water were her immediate concern, however. She drove herself onward, up this endless dune, cursing sand and camels and their journey indiscriminately. She had learned in recent days to swear fluently in Catari, but now was not the moment; she stuck to her own tongue, as though to stress to Sildana, her other companions and the listening Sands that she was alien here, no part of this their world. And that they were all equally at fault, equally guilty that she was here, and driven to such profane cursing . . .

Rudel, she knew, had been startled by her coarseness the first time he'd heard it; she'd been a little surprised herself, in all honesty. She hadn't realised how much of the waterfront had sunk into the diplomat's pampered daughter, during her more wild adventures in Marasson.

Step by slow step, she fought grimly against the clinging sand, the struggling camel, the bone-ache in her exhausted legs and the roiling, miserable fury in her head. Step by barefoot step, or as good as, only rags wound around her feet now to save them from the worst of the blistering heat that the sand soaked up by day. She'd abandoned her boots when Rudel did, when there seemed to be more desert than foot inside them, and that grating cruelly on already-sore flesh. Her soles weren't ready for this, they weren't tanned hide like Jemel's; but neither were Rudel's. The two of them doctored each other at every halt, working with a barely moistened cloth – spit-moistened at first, only that now neither one of them could raise the spit – and then rubbing in a meagre allowance of camel-grease, that Jemel swore would help to toughen them.

Privately, Julianne suspected that of being a Sharai joke. The grease stank abominably rancid, as Jemel had sworn their feet did while they still wore their boots, when they tugged them off at each day's close. Sharai humour, she thought, was like that; and certainly Jemel flashed her a brief grin as he played baggage-master each time, producing the pot and watching – from a cautious distance – while the two Patrics worked it in with careful fingers.

On the other hand, it might be desert-wisdom and no joke at all. There was little laughter to be had on this trip, and Jemel was least likely of the three of them to waste precious supplies; even rancid camel-grease must have its uses, she supposed, and wasn't to be frittered away in foolish mockery. So she decided to believe that this was one of those uses, and hoped each night that the following day would prove it, that what skin was left to her feet would have become miraculously harder. She didn't want Sharai horn soles, only a polite gesture towards that, a diplomat's imitation . . .

And didn't have it yet, and so suffered in her feet as elsewhere; but slogged on, hissed abuse at Sildana and jerked cruel-hard on the headrope when the camel balked, and so came at last to the summit of the dune.

Found Rudel resting on his haunches, offering an excuse she would gladly use but did not need; had he been halfway down the opposite slope, still she would have stopped here. If it had meant Jemel's riding by and her being left completely alone, still she would have stopped, she had to.

She couched Sildana – and even that took effort and use of her riding-stick, just to force the contrary animal to rest – and dropped into her shadow, resting her back against the camel's flank. Sildana turned her head and hissed at the liberty, another failing of the breed, that they had no idea of teamwork. Julianne ignored her. Never mind that the sparse white coat was hot and rank and full of sand and grit, badly in need of a grooming; still it made a cushion for her head, a support for weary bones.

Rudel made a sympathetic gesture towards her, and tugged his own camel down in imitation. He stayed where he was, though, some little distance off in his body and a great deal further in his mind. In another world, perhaps, Julianne thought. She'd foolishly imagined that he might make an easier travelling-companion, with his daughter gone; instead he had become withdrawn, morose and snappish, the last thing they needed at such a time.

Jemel rode up between the two of them, leading the spare camels and gazing down with that air of forced patience which he wore so superciliously that she wanted to throw something at him. Nothing to hand, though, except a knife – which was extreme – or else a handful of sand, which was pointless. The sand was everywhere already: in the food, in the water, in their clothes, in their mouths and on their skins. Under her skin, she thought sometimes, and working its way in deeper, till it would clog and saturate every organ of her body. Certainly she had sand in her mind already, causing her thoughts to stick and tangle instead of flowing smoothly. It had even invaded memory and dream, and that she resented most of all . . .

Jemel would dismount in a minute, she knew, with an expressive sigh at being cursed with two such feeble cohorts. He would sit his camel for a while first, though, just to emphasise the point, young man's arrogance and his people's arrogance commingling; also, though, he would use its height to advantage, to survey the surrounding terrain.

What point? she wondered dismally. She knew what he would see: dunes. Dunes behind them, two of these monsters marked already with their trail; and more dunes ahead of them, only ripples on the surface of the Sands perhaps but a terrible time foretold. A girl could drown, she thought, among such ripples . . .

'Tell me how many more to come?' she called, in the husky shadow that she was learning to recognise as her own voice. 'If there are more than two, give thought to my shroud. Another three would kill me.'

'No,' he said. 'Another day would kill you, I think – but perhaps you need not worry about that.'

Puzzled, she squinted her eyes to try to read him against the sky's glare. He was sitting fixedly, gazing to the west, along the line of this dune-top . . .

'What is it?' Rudel demanded, rising swiftly to his feet. 'Company?'

'Yes. Five riders.'

'Sharai?'

'Of course.'

Of course, indeed. Who else?

'Can you tell their tribe?'

'From here? No. They should be Tel Eferi. The Tel Eferi do not tolerate strangers on their lands. So it is said, at least. I do not know, I have never met one. There were none among the party that Hasan led against the Roq . . .'

And that was telling, Julianne knew. That war-party had been as much symbol as invasion-force, designed to teach the Sharai that they could fight shoulder to shoulder with sworn enemies, blood-feuds set aside in pursuit of a greater goal. It had failed against the castle; whether it had failed in that other aim also, whether more had been broken against the hard walls of Roq de Rançon was yet to tell, or to be told.

'Must we fight again?' Julianne asked, more in resignation than in terror. They had fought six Sand Dancers, and won; perhaps they could repeat the miracle.

It seemed that they would have to try. Jemel said nothing, but his hand went to the haft of his scimitar, and his face was tight and grim and saying much.

Foolishness, to suppose they could win such another fight. Oh, he would fight, his face said, and be confident of her and Rudel at his back; confident too of their deaths, all three of them. It would be waste and nothing but waste, his face said, no honour in it for either side, but it would happen none the less.

Now, she thought, they needed Marron, they needed the Daughter; and why hadn't he and Elisande come back to them, after escaping the ghûl? She'd asked herself the question repeatedly, and her companions too; but all their answers were guesswork. She could guess privately at her friend's desires, and wonder if those would outweigh the calls of friendship, the needs of the group; but the decision had surely been Marron's, and he was a mystery to them all.

Lacking him and the quick evasion that he could offer them, she turned instead to his less potent substitute, their only other magic-worker. 'Rudel? The people of Surayon are skilled at hiding, you have hidden your entire country; can you not . . .?'

'Hide us?' he finished for her. 'No. I have not the Dancers' skill, alas,' and he was always secretive even among his friends, about how Surayon had been folded out of sight or finding. So was Elisande, and no blame to either one of them for that; even friends could betray, without meaning to. 'Neither, of course, have you; nor the camels, and we could not abandon them. No, we have been spotted, and must face the consequences. There is perhaps something I can do, though, to avoid a fight we cannot win. Do what I tell you without question, without pause; in the meantime be calm, be patient . . .'

Well, that she could manage. She rose to her feet, and was glad to see Jemel slide down from his camel, at Rudel's urgent gesture. At least they would look peaceable, unchallenging; though how much good that would do them was questionable. By reputation, the Sharai could be generous and welcoming to strangers discovered on their lands; they could also be swift and brutal. Jemel was clearly expecting no generosity, and she had no reason to doubt his assessment.

They were in Rudel's hands, then; and Rudel had been distracted for days, and had shown no gift of magic when they had needed it most, in the fight with the Dancers. A gift for swordplay he had, undoubtedly, but he himself gave that no credence now. She touched the handles of her knives where they were thrust into her girdle, and prayed that they might stay there, though she had small hope of that.

Small hope of anything, in truth, as she watched Rudel rummage in a saddlebag and pull out a gaudy but battered leather scrip, part of his jongleur's equipage. He slung that over his shoulder, and she thought it inappropriate and deadly against the midnight blue of his robes; what better way to declare himself a stranger, mocked up as a Sharai?

She thought she might never see his living face again as he turned his back and walked away from her, from them, towards the approaching tribesmen. Julianne could see them now, five dark lines they seemed to be in the heat, swaying gently as they grew; and against them one tired man with white in his beard. With talents too, true; but those talents she'd seen and most applauded had been with voice and mandora, in his guise as a jongleur. His wonderworkings had been less impressive. He hadn't been able to lead them either into or out of the Tower of the King's Daughter in the ways that he'd intended. True, both Marron and Redmond, even – reluctantly – Elisande had said that he had great strength as a healer; but he hadn't been able to heal Marron. He hadn't tried to heal her feet, except with water and grease. He said they must toughen naturally, that his interference would only prolong her pain as he made them soft again; of course she believed him, but even so . . .

When he had left companions and camels both some distance behind him, Rudel stood still and lifted one hand to his face. She couldn't see, but she thought he would be scratching at his beard as he did when he was thinking hard, when he was uncertain. Then he flung both hands high, in what might be seen by peaceful folk as a gesture of peace and greeting; others might read it as a prohibition, a forbiddal, *come no nearer.* Julianne held her breath, wondering desperately what he intended to do.

Jemel grunted at her side, and said, 'At least he has a beard.'

So did Jemel now, or at least a dark growth of stubble on chin and cheeks; they had no water spare for shaving. She didn't see the point. 'What, will they respect his age?' It didn't seem likely.

'No, but he has a wild look about him, and all the Sharai respect a shaman.'

That assumed that he could demonstrate the abilities of a shaman; anyone could grow a beard. Even Marron had shown a scattering of fluff before he left them so precipitately; she'd meant to tease him about that, and hadn't found the opportunity. Julianne chewed her lip, and waited.

Five shimmering shadows resolved themselves into five men on camelback, riding in line abreast. At first she thought that they wouldn't even pause when they met Rudel, that one of them would dispatch him with a single swing of a blade, without a word exchanged between them. By the way he sucked air through his teeth, Jemel expected much the same.

But they drew rein together and halted neatly, as though one man, one thought commanded all. Excellent discipline; she thought Rudel would approve. For herself she was surprised, she'd thought the Sharai more individual.

Perhaps they kept a harsher discipline here, in the harshness of the Sands. One man spoke, and Rudel answered; too far away for her to hear what was said, but the tone of their voices carried. The Sharai had challenged, Rudel had snapped a response.

Oh, let him keep his temper, now if never again . . .

It seemed that he had, it seemed that he was in doubt, though his voice surely would deny it; he appeared to be chanting now, to judge by what sound came back to her, but that betraying hand had lifted to his beard again, to tell her that he was in doubt.

No – the other hand, she realised suddenly, the left. It looked wrong, even from a distance, from the back; men have their unconscious habits, and never break them. She'd never seen him scratch his beard left-handed.

She'd never seen smoke rise up to wreathe his head either, thin grey wisps that tangled like rising, writhing serpents in the air above and drifted slowly, slowly into fragments and nothing on the breeze.

A sudden silence, as Rudel ceased his chanting; it lasted as long as the Sharai's startlement, was cut by the sudden sharp edge of their fear. One man cried out, another hissed what might have been a prayer for protection. All twitched at their camels' reins, caught between backing and wheeling, creeping and charging away. Nothing else, clearly, was on their minds, confronted as they were by a man whose head was smoking.

'A juggler's trick,' Jemel muttered.

'Yes – but think, Jemel. If these people are as isolated as you say, if they don't even mix with their own kind, if they forbid strangers on their land — when will they have ever seen a juggler?'

Rudel brought his hands together in a sharp clap, high above his head. Julianne saw, but didn't hear; the sound of it was lost in a fierce crackling noise like dry timber burning, as smoke poured out between his fingers. Briefly, she thought she saw bright sparks between his palms, contained lightning.

Two of the tribesmen's camels shied, and bolted downslope; one rider fell, the other clung to his mount's neck and barely kept his seat. The other three, she thought, were only in control still because their own instincts matched their beasts'; all had twisted around and were galloping now, back along the dune-top as they had come except much faster now, and crying to each other as they went in high, hoarse voices, men and camels both.

Julianne wanted to laugh, but dared not. It wasn't truly funny, danger and likely death averted by a simple trick. Rudel came storming back to join them — smelling strangely acrid, but quite unscorched in beard or hands — and his scowl was warning her, she thought, *no reaction, not a sound*; camels could not or would not run too far downhill, on slipping sand.

Those who had fled that way were still in hearing. Indeed, the unmounted one was dangerously close. His tracks showed that he had run a little, or tried to; she knew how impossible that was. He was not trying now. He was standing still, watching them; waiting, as it seemed.

Waiting for his brothers, of course. They were of one tribe, and would not leave him now. One — back in control

already, of his mount and of himself: she was impressed –
was going after the strayed camel, which had not bolted far;
the others were leaving the dune-crest and riding down in
single file to join their fallen man.

Which meant that they were riding back towards
Julianne and her companions, or nearly so. They *were* impressive, she decided. One moment of superstitious panic,
anyone could be allowed that; but they had mastered it so
quickly. Too quickly: they were too soon themselves again,
and deadly still . . .

Deadly still was how they stood, she thought, and how
their camels stood beneath them, when they were together
and the fallen one remounted; deathly still was how she
stood herself, and those about her. Even their camels were
quiet for a change, long heads on long necks turned to
stare where they themselves were staring.

So much stillness, so much silent watchfulness on both
sides, it was unbearable; someone had to break it soon, or
she would. She would break altogether, she thought, and
run screaming, the worst thing . . .

Well, no, she wouldn't. She wasn't even tempted, not
seriously. She just wanted something to happen; what was
hardest for her was being able to do nothing herself, being
dependent on others.

At last something did happen, inevitably, it had to; and
it was of course the worst thing that could happen in such
a case, given that she wasn't going to run screaming.

One of the tribesmen touched his camel into slow movement and came riding up towards them, with the others
following in his train.

'Well,' Rudel murmured, 'a little conjuring was never

likely to be enough, once they rediscovered their courage. It should buy us some talking-time, though. Jemel, you stand quiet, whatever they say; their pride drives them, so you must sacrifice yours. Julianne, be ready. Whatever I ask of you, be ready . . .'

One by one, the Sharai came up the slope at an angle that brought them to the crest of the dune just a little beyond fighting-distance. That had to be deliberate; Julianne tried to be grateful.

The one who had led them back was an elderly man, with more white in his beard than Rudel had. He had scars too, though, to remind her not to make assumptions. His body under his robe looked as lean as whipcord, and as tough.

Rudel stepped forward alone, as he had before; when he lifted his hands, all the Sharai flinched. This time, though, he only spread them wide, in a gesture that could surely only be read as peaceful. Except that such a warlike people might have read it as weakness, Julianne thought, first time around; now, though, after Rudel's display of seemingly mystical potency . . .

Now that elderly Sharai spoke almost deferentially to him, certainly without any hint of aggression in his voice, though his words were still a challenge.

'We of the Tel Eferi do not welcome strangers on our lands; we guard our borders even against those of our own faith. You seem to have one such with you, though his dress declares him tribeless. Very well; he is of no account. Neither is the Patric girl. You, however – you are a shaman, and a Patric also. That is strange to us. It is death to trespass, and we are not afraid of your magic; but we would know why you have come, and where you are bound.'

'I am not afraid of your death, Tel Eferi,' Rudel replied – *and let him interpret that as he will,* Julianne thought, silently applauding. 'My purposes are my own, and I will pursue them, whether I trespass or no. I will tell you this, though, that we are bound for Rhabat, for the council of tribal leaders that has been called there. Your own sheikhs may have chosen to answer that summons, or to ignore it; I neither know nor care. If you seek to stay us, though, you will suffer for it. Let us pass unhindered, and your rewards may be as great.'

'I have heard tell of this council – but not that any of your kind have been summoned to it. Who are you, Patric?'

'My name is Rudel, and I am a prince of Surayon; but that is unimportant,' though it had some effect, to judge by the way the Sharai muttered together. 'What matters more is that I and my companions were leading another there, who is of great importance. We have been separated, but I hope still to find him before we arrive.'

'This other, who is he? And why should he need your guidance?'

'He is a boy, a Patric like myself, who could not find his way unaided; though he has found his way into another land entirely, and chooses to stay there awhile. Do not you stay us, Tel Eferi. We are the chosen companions of the Ghost Walker, and he is one of us.'

Again that hissing mutter among the tribesmen, this time accompanied by snorts of contemptuous laughter; their leader said, 'I do not believe you,' and his hand strayed to the scimitar in his belt.

'I can show him to you,' said Rudel. 'Will you believe your eyes?'

'Perhaps not, if they try to tell me what cannot be true. Who knows what lies a sorcerer may not tell? Your arts are demon-born, and there is no truth in them.'

'What does a Tel Eferi know of truth?' Another voice, sudden and harsh; and that was Jemel, striding forward in fury. 'No more than a scorpion, who lurks beneath his stone and stings any hand that touches it! The Ghost Walker is among us, this man has seen and known him; so has this girl, who is like him a prince among her people; and so have I.'

'Well. It has a tongue after all, if no tribe. Or none that it will admit to, at least; and perhaps it is wise in that . . .?'

Julianne thought, dreaded rather that Jemel would draw his scimitar in reply to the insult, and so doom them all; instead, startlingly, he laughed.

'Tel Eferi, I have a name, that I am not afraid to share even outside my friends. I am called Jemel, and I was of the Saren; but I have been called to a greater service since. Even you may perhaps have heard of the brotherhood of Sand Dancers; even you may know that they forswear tribal allegiance, and follow only the Ghost Walker wherever he may lead. I have not had time or chance to change my dress for theirs; but I have laid a stone on the Pillar of Lives, I have sworn my oath on its summit, and—'

And he lifted his hand, his left hand; and his sleeve fell back, to show the crusted stump where his finger had been cut away. Only that morning Julianne had removed the dressing she'd bound it with, to let it heal cleanly in the air.

There was a moment's silence, before the Tel Eferi said,

'My name is Wali Ras, and I am familiar with Sand Dancers.'

'Then you know that on this matter, I would not lie to you. What this man has said to you is true.'

'He said that he could show me the truth of it; yet he said also that the Ghost Walker walks in another world . . .'

'That is so. He chooses to walk with the djinn at this time. What this man can show you by his skills, I do not know; but it will be no demon-picture, that I swear to you. If it be the Ghost Walker, you will have my word that he shows you true.'

'So be it, Dancer.' The old man couched his camel, and stepped free; at his back the other tribesmen stayed silent, mounted, even now a guard against treachery and an unspoken threat.

'Jemel, that was very well done, though you had me frightened for a moment there. Julianne,' Rudel was speaking rapidly in her own tongue, 'I regret this, but you must act my serving-girl, and the work will not be pretty. Fetch me the brass pot from the baggage, and be quick.'

It was more a ewer than a pot, an ornate rice-bowl although they had no rice; Rudel had meant it for a gift, to any sheikh who offered hospitality. Now he had another, she guessed a darker purpose to confront these men who had offered nothing so courteous.

She fetched it as she'd been bidden, with speed and silence and the best air of servility that she could manage.

'Good. Now, we must lose one of the camels; it would be well to choose the weakest. Jemel will hold its head for you; I will hold the bowl.'

It would be well to choose the weakest, but he was leaving the choice to her. Her eyes strayed to Sildana, and she was sorely tempted; they would be more impressed, surely, by the sacrifice of a white beast, and such a fine one . . .?

Good sense overruled vengeance, though. She hesitated only a moment, before walking to what had been Elisande's mount and quickly unstrapping its burdens. That animal had an ulcerating sore on one leg, and was suffering in this hard scramble over the dunes. Jemel came after her, grunting his approval; she whispered quickly, 'Is this wisdom?'

'No,' he murmured, straddling the beast's neck and gripping its chin, forcing its head back against its struggles, 'it is the act of a madman, and so may save us all. All shamans are mad, they know that . . .'

Rudel took the bowl from her, and held it poised below the camel's throat; Julianne pulled out one of her knives, glad of the edge on it and only praying that it would have no worse use than this today.

She laid the blade against taut flesh, gripped her wrist with her other hand for support and drew it back in a single stroke as she had seen the butchers do in the market at Marasson, using all her strength to slice as deeply as she could.

Hot blood gushed and Rudel caught it – most of it – in the bowl, though they were all splashed as Jemel wrestled with the bucking camel's body.

At last it slumped, and lay still. They stepped away; Rudel carried the brimming bowl over to where the old man stood impassively watching, and set it carefully on the sand.

'Wait till the surface is still,' he said, his voice soft and authoritative, 'and then look. Look carefully, and with honesty.' Then, changing tongues again, he went on, 'Jemel, you must look too, to confirm what he sees; but turn your head away when he is done. Julianne, it would be best if you did not look at all.'

Perhaps it would, though she didn't understand why; but she made no promise. She had promised herself to her young Baron Imber, and had torn herself away from him next day; she meant to make no more promises that she might not be able to keep.

Rudel knelt beside the bowl, murmuring softly in a new tongue, a third tongue, one she could not follow although the sound of it struck resonance in her mind and heart. He stretched both hands over the dark, reflective surface of the blood, then lowered them till his fingers touched it.

When he took them away, there were no ripples; the liquid seemed suddenly solid as glass. Glass coloured blood-red, ruby-red – but with a golden gleam at its core, she saw, as Rudel breathed on it. A gleam that grew, she saw, that seemed to pour up from the base of the bowl until the red was washed away by fierce-glowing gold.

It was like staring at the sun, she thought, blinking and turning her head away. The old man's gasp pulled it back, though, and she was suddenly glad she had not made that promise.

The bright glow had died within the bowl, although the image there was still golden. She gasped herself, seeing the image move: or seeing the people move within the image, rather. Two people, and she knew them both . . .

Marron and Elisande she saw, walking together in a land-scape of gold: for a moment she almost thought they walked hand in hand, and her heart twisted for her friend's sake. But no, they were only side by side; though that was wonder enough, to see them like this. She wanted to apologise to

Rudel for ever doubting his power, and of course could not. It was not the place of a servant girl to speak first to her master. Besides, he would not know of her offence, unless she first confessed it.

Though he might have guessed, she thought, seeing how he looked up briefly from the bowl to frown at her – but no, he had told her not to look and caught her staring, that was all. She turned her head ostentatiously to the side, saw how all the tribesmen were gaping at the bowl, and felt excluded, resentful. Why should all these men have licence to view his magic, and she not?

'Is that he?' the elder tribesman asked, stooping low over the bowl as if to imprint the scene on his mind, his voice breathless with wonder at more than the miracle of Rudel's showing it to him.

'It is.' Rudel confirmed it, and Jemel also.

'How is it possible? A Patric boy . . . This is not the prophecy.'

'Even prophets cannot see the whole of the truth; not even the djinn can know exactly what the future holds. It is a mystery to us all, why Marron has been chosen to bear this burden, or what will come of it or him. If he were chosen. It might be sheerest luck. For good or ill, though, that boy has that gift in his possession, in his blood . . .'

If it were a gift. Julianne thought it was a poison, or a curse.

'And see,' the Tel Eferi whispered, 'see where he walks . . . You show us marvels, shaman,' though there seemed little to her that was marvellous about that golden landscape, bar its colour. 'But enough; I will look no more.

Such sights are not meant for mortal eyes. Who is that who walks beside him?'

'She is my daughter,' Rudel said flatly.

There was bewilderment on the old man's face: was she perhaps another wonder-worker, a Patric girl-shaman and hence fit companion – perhaps – for a Patric Ghost Walker? He didn't ask; Rudel's tone had forbidden the question, and he seemed to have enough respect – or fear might be a better word than Jemel's, Julianne thought – not to force the issue.

This was still his tribe's territory, though, and his own people stood witness to his words; his pride required him not to show fear, even of a fearful man. He drew himself up and said, 'You hope to find him again, you have said, this side of Rhabat. How will you achieve that, shaman? Can you too open a way between the worlds?' *Are the laws and prophecies so debased, that a Patric magician can do what we cannot, when what we have waited for so long comes not to us but to a Patric boy . . .?*

Rudel laughed shortly. 'Not I. I should have said, I hope that he will find us. Or perhaps the hope is mutual; it is certainly no stronger than a hope. We were parted suddenly, without the chance to make plans. But he knows our route, south to the shores of the Dead Waters and so down, and over the hills to Rhabat. A boat would be easier, but there are no boats that I know of . . .'

'No man sails the Dead Waters, shaman. No living man,' and the Tel Eferi chuckled dryly, unpleasantly. 'So. He knows your route, you say; do you?'

'South,' Rudel repeated. 'I have not travelled these lands, but a true line south must bring us to the Waters.'

'A true line south will bring you to a crevasse you cannot cross, unless your powers allow you to fly its span. You and your camels. Come. I will allow you through our lands, for the sake of the news you have brought us; but I will show you the shortest way that is safe. Do not stray from it.'

'We need water,' Rudel said mildly.

'Then you will travel the speedier, to find it beyond our borders. Our wells are our own. Take a line east of south; there are crags beyond these dunes, and you must climb where they are kindest . . .'

The old man stumped across the sand, pointing with his riding-stick; Rudel followed him, and Jemel also. The tribesmen's camels paced behind them; Julianne was left alone, abandoned. *Just a servant girl,* she reminded herself sourly.

Well, servant girls didn't have to be responsible; and no one was looking, so she could . . .

She turned her eyes back to the bowl, wanting only to watch her friends wander in the wonder of that other world, no more than that, and not at all seeing why she shouldn't.

The image was gone, though; there was no gold now, only darkness. She bent low above it, trying to see if the blood had turned liquid again, with Rudel's power gone from it; she saw only her own reflection, and sighed mightily for the loss of magic.

Her breath misted the surface, and that glow came again, starting as a spark deep down. She gasped and drew back, too late; the spark blossomed like fire, driving out the dark. It was a gentler glow this time, softly golden, with no hint of dazzle to it; Julianne dropped to her knees, entranced.

When the bowl was filled with light, she saw a picture forming. Three figures, standing: the central one was a girl, long dark hair and a deep green robe. Julianne recognised the dress a moment before she knew the face; it was herself, and that was the robe she'd worn to marry Imber . . .

There was a man standing on either side of her, and she was holding a hand of each; they were both standing with their backs to her, but she still knew one of them. That tall figure with the blond hair that shone so, the youth of him clear even from a rear view: she didn't need to remember the green velvet that he wore – though she did, it was branded deep in her memory, never to be forgotten – to know her husband.

The other man was a mystery, shorter and black-haired, dressed much as she was now, in the midnight blue of the Sharai.

There was movement in the image suddenly, that picture of Imber turning and bending, and herself turning to meet him, stretching up; she caught a glimpse of his soft short beard, and saw herself kiss him deeply.

Felt it too, a tingle of memory on her lips, though he'd never kissed her as his image did. Only a dry and fleeting touch of his mouth against hers, with all the complement of the Roq as witness; but that again was a brand she bore, ever fresh and hurting.

She saw him straighten and turn his back again; saw herself turn the other way, towards the other man; saw him too meet her mouth to mouth in a passionate kiss.

This time the beard was black, though equally close-cropped. She could see no more of his face than that, bend and stare as she might, as she did.

And then startlingly, shockingly, there was a hand swooping down from the periphery of her vision, scooping up the bowl and lifting it, hurling it, sending it rolling far away down the slope of the dune. The blood poured out of it in a great wave – and it was only blood, no more than that, a dark liquid stain that soaked quickly into the sand.

She stared up at Rudel where he stood looming over her, his face set tight. For a moment she thought he was raging, and she almost quailed where she knelt before the force of him – but no, it wasn't anger that gripped him so, not fury that had drawn such violence from him. Perhaps he wanted those watching tribesmen to think so, that he was only livid at his servant for meddling where she should not; in truth, she thought, he was afraid. Afraid for her, for consequences . . .

Well, he wasn't the first to fear so, and nothing dreadful had come to her yet. There had been strange outcomes to her wilfulness, unexpected outcomes, this journey was one and her hurried marriage she supposed was another; she remained whole and healthy – in her body, at least: heart-whole she was not – and it seemed she remained wilful also. None of her adventures had proved a lesson in obedience. Not even that one in childhood that had broken bones and courage both, had left her terrified of heights . . .

She rose to her feet as gracefully as she could manage. She would have faced Rudel eye to eye, but for her knowledge that they were observed; she kept her head submissively low, spoke softly, and only her words were firm.

'I know, you told me not to look – but how could I not? As well tell me not to listen when you're shouting, or not to think . . .'

'What did you see? When I was gone? I know what was there before.'

'I'll tell you – but not now. Later. When we're alone.' The Tel Eferi showed no signs of understanding them, but ignorance was easy to pretend to.

'Very well. You should not have looked, though, child. I had my reasons to say so.'

'Which you did not explain to me.' Indeed he still hadn't, though she had a feeling for them now, perhaps; she thought she would rather not have seen herself so brazen. Or so torn . . .?

'There was no time; there still is none. Later, we'll talk.' And he turned a contemptuous shoulder to her, for all the world like a man who has not chastised his servant as much as she deserves, but will not do more in front of strangers.

And so she was left with her head aspin, wrenched away from a vision that she didn't understand. Ordinarily she'd have told Elisande, they'd have talked it through together; though ordinarily she wouldn't have needed to tell Elisande, because the wretched girl would have been right there pushing her face in beside Julianne's, in the flesh if not in the picture.

But Elisande had been in the picture already, pictured in another world entirely and in other company, very much not here to talk to. There was Jemel, but he was no real confidant of hers at the best of times, which these were not; the sight of his precious Ghost Walker ghosted off to walk in someone else's company had flung him into a fit of the sullens, and he would willingly talk to neither of them.

And then there was Rudel. Who had promised her a

talk, but not yet; who was wise in his experience, and remarkable in his talents; who was her friend's father, and also to Elisande the most despised of men, for reasons that Julianne had still not contrived to learn. She could not confide in him, until she knew the truth of what lay between them. She would feel treacherous to her friend to do so; besides, it might simply be unwise. Despite all appearance, he might not be a man to whom it was safe to unburden her soul . . .

Not for the first time, she wished fervently for her father's company, almost more than she wished for Elisande's, or for Imber's. And could have none of them, or not yet; and so set her eyes and mind grimly to the journey, at the end of which she could at least hope for two out of the three.

Down the steep dune, alternately coaxing and yanking the splay-legged and stubborn Sildana; up the next, at an angle now that made the slope a little easier, though not much. All the way, she was conscious that they had acquired a shadow, a black smudge on the skyline, following their slow progress at a cautious distance. Being sure that they knew he was there, she thought; and riding these impossible dunes as easily as Jemel did, which only added injury to the insult of his so-obvious presence.

The dunes broke at last, as they had been promised, like waves against a rocky shore. A band of ink rough-washed on the horizon resolved into high basalt cliffs; they had again been promised a way through, though, and found it swiftly. A break among the crags became a path, the first sign of human use they'd seen on the land for days. Here she could ride, thank the God. Sildana tried to knock her off a time or two, lurching suddenly against the rock walls that squeezed close on either side; but Julianne had ridden difficult horses all her life, she was well-versed in countering such tricks and plied her stick with cheerful abandon to drive the camel on. There were tufts of sandy hair, she noticed, caught in snags of rock along the way; Sildana wasn't the first to try this. At one tight angle where the path turned sharply, where no one could blame a camel for rubbing against the rock, she saw how the basalt had been worn away to a smooth curve, though it was knife-sharp above. How many years, how many centuries of traffic would it take, she wondered, to erode the rock so far?

That narrow and twisting path, shadowed even under the high desert sun, debouched eventually onto a high shelf, a sweep of sand-dusted rock that offered a long view to the long-sighted. Julianne squinted, and thought she saw a glint of light on the far horizon. Jemel shaded his eyes with his hand, looked long and steadily, and finally gave them a promise not of journey's end, but at least of the final push towards that end.

'I can see water,' he said, 'a desert plain of water . . .' There was awe in his voice, even though he must have seen it before; this was not his first time coming to Rhabat. Likely – no, certainly – it was the greatest body of water he'd ever seen or dreamed of in his life. The sea would be a myth to Jemel, a myth misunderstood, mispictured in his mind. This little lake, this pond was more than enough to outmatch it.

This little lake, this pond was what they called the Dead

Waters, and Julianne wished she had another name for it. That title resonated too strongly with the djinni's high voice, Elisande's mysterious future. Though she was glad to see it, none the less. It gave hope of Marron's returning, and Elisande's beside him; it gave hope also of her father. Or at least it brought the djinni's prediction closer, that time when she could save her father from great danger. *Though it might be better if you did not* – she remembered the djinni's words exactly, and shrugged them from her. Whatever its intent, whatever its doubts, it had gifted her this chance, and she would take it. If she were able . . .

They paused to drink, though the water in their skins was foul now, and to chew a little on what was left of that morning's bake of bread. The water might be foul, but the bread was almost worse; she pined for proper food, and found herself yearning for the evening. Jemel had butchered the dead camel, before leaving its corpse to wither in the sun; he had left most of the flesh also for the Tel Eferi to take it if they would, but he'd brought enough that they were sure of meat tonight and every night until they reached Rhabat.

'We might have rested,' Rudel said, 'until the sun was lower; but—'

He signed to the rear, with a jerk of his head. When she looked around, Julianne saw a shadow at the path's mouth, their Tel Eferi tracker silent on his camel.

'Julianne, can you ride in the heat, this once? It would be wiser in any case, we should press on until we can find water . . .'

Oh, she could ride in the heat, if they could; the sun was not her concern. She nodded firmly, and then spoiled that decisiveness with a question that would have betrayed her to these two, even if her voice hadn't quavered in asking it.

'How do we get down?'

Jemel had ridden forward, right to the shelf's edge; he called back, 'There is a path. Not difficult, it cuts to and fro across the cliff-face . . .'

Not difficult for him, perhaps. She dreaded it already, from his report. But she must go down, she must go on; even if they'd been allowed to rest here, it would have been only a temporary respite. And as she must do it, she might as well do it now.

'Jemel, you lead,' Rudel ordered, 'with Julianne behind you. I will bring up the rear. I would guess this to be the Tel Eferi border, I don't think we'll be followed further, but if I'm wrong he still won't press me too closely.'

That was neat; it set her where she could feel safest, if not safe. She said no more, but touched Sildana on to follow Jemel. He seemed to ride his camel straight over the cliff; only his bobbing head beyond assured her that there was indeed a path.

It seemed more like a goat-track when she found it, plunging suddenly downward. He was already at the corner where it turned back on itself for the first time, the first of many; she saw its zigzag progress dimly, swimmingly, already dizzy from the great fall before her, hundreds of feet it seemed before the path came down to solid ground. She swallowed hard and nudged her mount forward, hoping that Sildana would have a head for heights, and praying that she'd have the good sense not to act stubborn or wilful until they reached bottom.

*

Seemingly, she did. She picked her way as delicately as any nice-mannered pony might, as sensibly as the most candidly frightened girl could wish. Even if she were being candid only with herself: if she were riding with her back straight and her head up, arms high in classic style, headrope in one hand and stick in the other. She was, she knew, fooling no one – not herself, not Jemel before her or Rudel behind, and certainly not Sildana. That beast could smell her terror, she was sure, she could see the wide nostrils flare to seek it out; and smelling, knowing, the creature had made the decision and walked as if on eggshells, making almost a show of how she placed each foot with pretty care.

During those long, long minutes, Julianne fell entirely in love with Sildana.

Abject fear has a cold hand that grips internally, that squeezes a chill sweat from the bone's marrow, then chases it through frozen muscles and out onto shivering skin. This was nothing new to Julianne; she was barely conscious of the waste of her body's water, it was so familiar. And it meant so little to her. She didn't look down, not once, leaving Sildana to find her own way, or to follow Jemel; but still that dreadful drop hung in her mind's eye, sucking at her. She had no thought to spare for how she was sweating.

Until she reached the foot of the cliff and let Sildana amble to a standstill while she shuddered, while her companions waited patiently a little apart from her, giving her decent space to recover herself.

When she had done that, when she could be aware of herself again, she became aware of how she was suddenly and strangely dry: dry of mouth, which was not unusual, but quite dry of skin also, where she had been, must have been, remembered being clammy such a little time ago.

She took a deliberate breath, and tasted heat at the back of her throat. She'd thought she'd been hot before, when she rode out of the path's shade onto the shelf above and into the full glare of the light; she'd thought that fierce, until the first sight of the way down had chilled her.

Now, though, she felt the sun's weight on the back of her neck, and all but buckled under it. This was the true Sands, the Sands that Jemel had promised her, and Elisande also; the heat lay on the land as fire lies on coals, a thing in itself and almost tangible.

Absurdly she shivered, one more time, though this at least she was not afraid of. She ought to be, she knew, it could kill her as surely as a fall; she'd be wise to find some fear in herself, but could not. She'd trust her life to either one of her companions, anywhere in any desert that the Sharai claimed as their own; here, with both together, she felt entirely safe.

Safe and exhilarated, briefly; she grinned widely and wordlessly at Jemel, as he came riding over.

Did he smile back, did he understand? She couldn't tell; he wore his hood low and a veil across his face.

'Here,' he said, his voice muffled by the cloth. 'Put up your hood, so,' and he reached to do it for her. 'And you must adjust your robe also, or you will lose too much water to the air. Like this,' and he gestured at his own dress.

She looked, tried to imitate how he had adjusted the robe, and could not; her fingers felt light and awkward, barely attached. She fumbled with the ties, tugged at the hems and only made matters worse. In the end he had to lean across from his saddle and do it for her. However bronzed his skin and however shadowed, she was still certain that he blushed as he did it, fumble-fingered himself when they touched her bare skin beneath the robe.

'You have seen the high dunes, and crossed them,' he said, as though it were a rite of passage; perhaps it was. 'You have seen the crags, and passed through them. Now you meet the plain, and the heat of the plain. Now we ride.'

'What about water?'

'You ride, Julianne. Leave us to worry about the water.'

So she rode. She felt their worry – the heat stole in like a thief to lay itself against her like a lover, a thief of love; and like a thief it stole all the moisture she had in her, drying her like a husk so that she had to keep sipping and sipping at the skin she carried, although she could barely swallow the foul liquid – but she could not share it. She'd been told not to, indeed, and for once she practised obedience, if only because she had no choice. It was enough simply to ride, to breathe; thinking was too much to ask in that draining, enervating heat. Worrying lay far beyond her reach. She couldn't even worry about Elisande and Marron. Like these that she rode with, those two were survivors; they'd all meet again. By the Dead Waters, or else at Rhabat . . .

The Dead Waters were far away, though, and Rhabat was further. Between lay this endless plain, this air that stifled, was almost too hot and dry to breathe. A fine sand drifted through her veil, gummed her eyes and choked her throat; again she was driven to her water-skin and forced to swill her mouth around before she swallowed, tasting every last nuance of the rank water. She'd have preferred to spit, but she had – barely – enough desert-wisdom to resist that, though her face twisted with the effort, cracking the mask of sand that had accrued like a second veil across her skin. She would even have preferred to ride without drinking at all, to endure the shrivelling thirst that puckered her lips and seared her tongue and throat; she had to breathe, though, and so she had to rinse and swallow, making a meal of the sand that threatened to clog her airway.

The sun burned her eyes whenever she cracked them open against the sand's seal, but they were too dry, she was too dry altogether to allow them to water. She longed to bathe her face; she did surreptitiously moisten a corner of her veil and use it to wipe the worst of the crust away, but it was dry a minute later when she reached to do the same again.

So she rode blind, often with her eyes closed, gratefully learning once again to trust Sildana. Here on the open desert the camel's behaviour was impeccable, as though all her earlier stubbornness and aggression had been protest at that demeaning, easy country she'd been forced to endure. Here she carried her head high, alert to every breeze and whisper, every change of light; her long, long lashes shielded her big eyes from sun and sand, her body rocked from side to side in a gentle, lulling motion as she paced steadily behind Rudel's mount, as the hours passed and she never broke stride, never jolted her nodding, drifting rider . . .

Jemel's stick cracked across Julianne's shoulders suddenly, not hard but stinging, jerking her out of her dreams. She glowered at him where he loomed beside her, a black silhouette blocking the sun; he said, 'Do *not* sleep in the saddle. Look about you.'

She looked, and cried a protest, almost reeling from the sheer force of the light that struck up at her from all sides, glaring, blinding white.

'Salt-pans,' he said shortly. 'If you sleep, you may fall; I may not see. By the time you recovered your wits enough to stand and look for us, you would not find us. Better to stay awake, and live.'

She nodded her understanding; she couldn't speak, and wondered that he could. A leather throat, or some Sharai trick of folding the veil, something he hadn't thought to show her, that could keep out this insidious sand? She must ask, when she had a voice for it.

Meantime, he was right. She worked her sore shoulders against the roughness of her robe, as a reminder. Even if Sildana felt her fall and stopped to find her, to allow her to remount – she would do that, Julianne was convinced, carried away by this new mood of affection and trust – Jemel was still right. In such a dazzle, she'd be disoriented from the moment of her falling; Sildana was no bloodhound, she needed sight and sound of her companions. Between them they could lose both men in a minute, and never find their trail.

So she fought the doziness that came with heat and inaction and the steady sway of the miles passing underfoot; unable to distract herself with views and still too numbed to think straight, she rode side by side with Jemel, forced a thin voice from her throat and set about extracting his life story. She gathered quickly that this was a terrible breach of good manners, as well as of desert convention: he muttered sullenly that a small party in unknown and possibly hostile territory should always ride in line and apart, to allow a better watch. She persisted, though; for her it served several purposes, not only focusing her mind but strengthening her newly fluent Catari and also satisfying her perennial curiosity. For him, her probing seemed as uncomfortable as her abandonment of good practice, or more so. He wriggled physically under her questioning, and his answers were as evasive as he could make them. She thought perhaps he was unused to being interrogated by a girl, as much as he was clearly unused to touching one.

Still, she learned more than she had known before, and more certainly than he had wanted her to know. And she came through the salt-pans and the gruelling heat of the day, albeit with a fried brain and a water-skin that was slack and nearly empty. When Jemel abruptly reined in his camel, yelled ahead to Rudel and pointed with his riding-stick to where a long tangled shadow lay across a low dune, she even managed a smile at the patent relief in his voice, in every line of his body.

They all three turned aside from their steady southward progress, to investigate the source of the shadow. It turned out to be what Jemel had clearly been certain of, a small patch of thorny scrub, pale and dry but forage for the camels none the less. And more: Jemel crouched and began to dig among the roots of the scrawny plants, digging like a dog, hurling back double handfuls of sand.

When he'd burrowed down the full length of his arm, he sat back with a grunt of satisfaction; Julianne saw damp sand clinging to his fingers. Disbelievingly, she peered into the pit. Slowly, sluggishly, dark and dirty water was welling up around the exposed root-system.

They took turns to lie on their bellies and scoop up sparse and precious handfuls, sucking the warm and gritty liquid from their fingers as though it were finest sherbet. While her hands were still damp, Julianne scoured her face with them, for what little relief that could bring to skin that was chapped and sore beneath its crust of sand.

'We'll go no further today,' Rudel declared. 'There's another hour's riding by the sun, but we could ride half the night and find nowhere better to halt. Come the morning, that hole will be half full of water, enough to see us through tomorrow.'

'And the camels?' she asked, urgent with her new concern.

'Will have eaten this back to the sand, and be fine. They won't need water for a day or two yet. Though we'd be wise to cover it over, or they'll drink it regardless.'

Indeed, they were already questing towards the pit, scenting moisture; Jemel drove his back with a hard heel to the nose. Julianne tried to be gentle with Sildana, to guide her away with voice and touch; Sildana's response would have left her face a scarred ruin, if the bite had been just a little quicker.

It took two, they found, to guard the water. The camels couldn't be hobbled safely away from it until they'd finished grazing, and they were slow eaters in any case and worse today, taking a dry and thorny mouthful, chewing stolidly and turning towards that scent of water as they chewed, having to be beaten back to their meal.

'Where does the water come from?' Julianne asked, as

she shared that duty with Rudel. 'You couldn't dig such a hole anywhere else in the Sands, and hope to find water . . .'

'No – though there is water, often, where you would not think to look for it. These plants look like shallow-rooting scrub; they are not. They reach deep under the sand, and when they find water – after a rain, say, or if they chance on some hidden source in the bedrock – they draw it up while they can. They need little day by day, though, and when they find it, they find plenty; so they have learned to store. They spread it through the sand around their roots, low enough that the sun won't burn it off; and so they sip it as they need it, and never go thirsty.'

'Until we come, and steal it.'

'Ah, but the camels are cropping them back to the stalks, so they'll not need the water. They'll live, and grow again. We have not harmed the roots . . .'

'Rudel?'

'Yes?'

'What harmed you?' Whatever it was, it must be deep-rooted; and she'd never have a better chance to ask. 'You and Elisande, I mean? You're her father, but you're so cold towards her; and she, she seems to hate you . . .'

'Hate me? No. She thinks it hate, perhaps, she calls it so, but she's wrong. It's not hatred, it's blame. Though as Elisande practises it, I grant the two are easily confused.'

Half an answer was more than she'd ever got from the girl; Rudel had turned his back, a sign perhaps that the conversation was over, but Julianne decided to press her luck regardless. 'She blames you for what?'

'For her mother's death. You know how hard that is for

a girl, Julianne, how deep it cuts. Elisande finds it useful, I think, to have someone to accuse.'

'I never knew my mother. She died when I was born.'

'Ah, that's right, of course. I had forgotten. Perhaps you never felt the lack of her, in that case? Elisande was less fortunate.'

Julianne hadn't ever seen herself as fortunate, growing up with a succession of nursemaids and chaperones; but now was not the time to argue. She bit back a sharp retort and said simply, 'Tell me.'

He sighed softly, and for a while she thought she might get no more answer than that. Then his slow voice began, 'Cireille was young, and bright, and beautiful of course; one of that rare kind, a laughing spirit who sees no evil in the world until she meets it. Then it can destroy her . . .

'Cireille loved me, past hope or reason; and I her. I wanted only to protect her – to protect them both, after our child was born, our daughter. I was thankful that they were in Surayon and so well hidden, safe from all the world outside.

'At the same time, though, the same knowledge terrified me. Surayon is everyone's enemy. The other states of Outremer work against us all the time, testing our defences, seeking a way inside. They would destroy us if they could, the men who lead them would burn every living creature they found within our borders. And the Sharai – well, we have friends among the Sharai, but they too have their fanatics. Those would burn the Outremer entire, and us with all the rest.

'So I sought to keep my country and my family secure. I spent more and more time beyond our borders, travelling in Outremer and among the Sharai. You have met me as a jongleur; I have had other faces at other times. Always, though, I was a spy. Sometimes more than that, a secret diplomat: the Church denounces us, and so the princes must, their power is shored up by the Church, but Surayon has yet a few friends who see the benefits of our ways and do not believe the slanders.'

He fell silent briefly, and Julianne wondered if there were more to his journeys, that he was not telling: if he had not perhaps been an assassin also at need, or something other that he was ashamed to say.

He shook his head, though, as if in answer to a question that she had not asked; and went on, 'Cireille mourned, when I was gone. She worried incessantly for me, but it was more than that. She was a simple soul, and her life was entirely bound up in us, in me and Elisande; she felt herself incomplete in my absence. I was her criterion, or half of it. She loved our daughter too, but not enough; she needed both of us, to thrive. And I knew that, though I tried hard to deny it. I tried too hard, and too successfully. We were both of us obsessive, in our way: she for me, and I for her protection.

'And so I left, and left again; and managed somehow not to see the damage that my leaving did. Every time I returned she was thinner and more pale, and that much more joyful to have me back. I focused on the joy, and ignored what else was plain to see.

'Each time I left she plagued me with questions, how long I would be gone, when she should look to find me coming home. She demanded promises; I made them lightly, as any lover does.

'But then of course there came a time when I broke my vows to her, when it seemed more important to me to stay away. I was gone a year or more, serving the Duke of Less Arvon in his court and watching his army build. He wanted Surayon, not us but the land; he had a quarrel with the King's son who was Duke in Ascariel and did not like the weakness of his border, where we were. The shadow you cannot see is always more frightening than the one you can. It preyed on his mind, that we were there but hidden; he feared that we might make compact with the Ascari Duke and pass his armies through, to fall on Arvon all unseen and unexpected.

'So I played courtier longer than I should have, longer than I'd promised. I made a quiet peace between the two states, without either duke realising what I was about till after they were friends again; and I confess, I enjoyed it. I missed my wife, my daughter, of course I did; no news could reach me, and I dared not take the time or the risk to visit home. No – I did not take the time. Let me be honest now, as I was not then. It was no great risk, and no great distance either; I could have afforded both. But I did not, until my task was done.

'My task as I saw it, then. I was self-appointed; I had gone to scout, with my father's blessing but not his instruction. I stayed by my own choice, judging it more important than to spend time happy and idle with my family.

'When at last I did ride home, I went expecting another merry reunion, no more than that. Oh, perhaps a little scolding, that I had stayed so long; but Cireille would understand, I was sure, when I explained the importance of what I had achieved.

'But I came back to a house in mourning. Cireille had pined in my absence, and died for lack of me. They tried to tell me she'd died of sickness, a wasting disease that none could cure; but I pressed the doctors and the servants both, and learned the truth of it. The longer I stayed away, the more heartsick she'd become; she believed alternately in my death and then in my betrayal of her, when she heard through others that I was still at the Arvonian court and playing the Duke's fool. She thought I had some reason to stay, some pretty lady who had won my favour. And so she faded, and so died the month before my return.

'Elisande was eight years old, and had endured every moment of her mother's suffering. She had endured her mother's fantasies too, and believed them, as she must. No child can see true, at such a time. Besides, they were true, in all but detail; the court's intrigue was my mistress then, and sang closer and louder than my wife.

'Ever since, she has held me to blame for that loss; and she is right. She uses it as an excuse to behave foolishly. There is more at peril here than an inexperienced girl's shoulders can bear; she acts like a child, always, and so I treat her like a child still. Again, no doubt I can be blamed for that. I know it makes her worse. I have made peace between nations, but I cannot make my own peace with my own daughter; it reflects poorly on my skill and my judgement both. I know all of this, you need not say it. But I will not have her acting as my conscience and my constant critic, thrusting my guilt at me at every turn; and I will not willingly see her destroy the security of my country, by her wilful adventures. She is neither as wise nor as strong as she believes herself to be. Enough now, Julianne. She is your friend, I know, but so I hope am I. Do me a friend's kindness, and question me no further.'

And yet you love her, Julianne thought, watching how he reached out to strike a camel's probing head away, harder than he needed, *and so you follow her, when she strikes out wild; and so you keep her by you when you can, despite the pain she brings you. And so you worry about her when she slips your guard, as now, when she is away in a perilous land with a perilous companion . . .*

How much had it cost him, she wondered, to slay that camel and seek her image in its blood, when he could not know if she were living or dead? It must be better sometimes not to know, to have the freedom to hope; he knew that better than her, he must carry the memory of it with him always, all that time his wife was failing in his absence, in his ignorance . . .

She had a better understanding of him now, and of her friend also. She wondered if Elisande had more reasons than one to keep her hair cropped as she did, boy-short. To be sure, it had helped her in her travels, to pass as a lad at a distance; but what was also sure, she did not favour her father in looks. Perhaps when she grew it long, she had some look of her mother. If so, it could be an unexpected kindness in her to wear it short, not to remind him too closely of lost Cireille; or it could be another punishment, more subtle and more cruel, *you killed her for me, and so I will not carry her likeness in the world, I will not give you even so much satisfaction . . .*

She sighed and pushed Sildana back from their precious ooze of water, barely remembering to duck in time as long and yellowed teeth snapped back, in a miasma of foul breath.

9

Water of Life

Stupidly, Elisande had begun to think that this country could hold no more surprises.

She barely saw any more the golden, shimmering sheen that overlay everything from the sky above to the dust underfoot; her eyes had adjusted so far that it seemed nothing but normal now. Likewise the constant warmth in the air, the dust, the stone – she'd ceased to notice that at all except when she cooked bread, morning and evening, and even then she took it quite for granted.

And so as they came closer and closer to the reflection or the source of what in her world was called the Dead Waters, she thought of it only in terms of those Waters that she knew, close by Rhabat. If she'd been asked the question, if she'd been forced to think, she would perhaps have said that the water here would be golden, yes, of course, as it all was, all this world; also that it would be warm, hotter than body-warm, pleasant perhaps to bathe in but dangerous to drink.

Chased even further, she might possibly have added 'dead' to that list. Golden, warm and dead as all this land was. If the Dead Waters were well named – and they were: she had stood boldly at their margin, had dabbled her fingers in the blood-warm shallows and sucked them after, had tasted bitter salt and darkness, which was entirely her idea of death – then here where nothing lived that grew or ate or had a body to it, here assuredly the waters would be dead . . .

She'd never thought to see them steam, to see them seethe and hiss and bubble like something that lived in itself, even if it could not harbour life.

She stood atop the low rise that had hidden the sea till now, all but the cloud of steam that rose above; she had to struggle to find her voice at all, and then again to keep it light and jocular.

'Well,' she said at last, 'I don't think we can call them the Dead Waters here, do you?'

'Do you think you would live, in such water?' Marron countered quietly.

'Not me, no,' *and maybe not even you,* 'but something should, surely? Something must. Unless it's the water itself that lives,' giving voice to the thought that most disturbed her.

'No,' he said, and she thought she was almost being laughed at. 'It's hot, that's all. As the rocks are, heated from below. I expect all open water steams, here. This goes deep, though, and so it boils. Nothing more than that.'

She gazed across the vast sea that had no horizon that she could see in any direction, no further shore; she tried to imagine how hot it must be, how far beneath the ever-moving surface, to keep such a weight of water at the boil. And could not, would not believe it: she'd rather believe her own idea, that something vital and monstrous lurked beneath the steam. She knew the myths of the Dead Waters, as he did not; surely they must have their own counterpart in this mirror-world? Unless the reflection did indeed go the other way, and what was myth in her world had its truth here . . .

Lisan of the Dead Waters, the djinni had called her. Now she really yearned to deny the title; she wanted no part of this.

'Do you think perhaps we ought to go back now?' she asked, and heard the pleading in it and was disgusted by herself. But she'd had enough, truly; the wonder of being here had grown a little stale at last – even the wonder of being alone with Marron, of having his body to hold to every night, when she could do no more than cling like some parasite with secrets – and this last shock was too sinister to refresh it.

'Probably,' Marron said. His gaze turned bleak, though, and she thought he was less keen to leave than she was to stay. Which seemed to sum up everything that lay between them, and quite decided her.

'We should find Jemel, and the others,' she said, trailing a little temptation in his path, thinking he'd snap at it.

'We'd need to be lucky,' he replied. 'So many days apart, and so much distance – we must have been faster than them, to reach this place.'

'Perhaps. Unless our days are longer.' Only three nights they'd had here, when Morakh had promised a week's journey; but she'd lost all track of familiar time. 'We won't know, unless we go to see.'

'And if we go, and do not find them – what then?'

'We can wait. They will come.'

'We don't have enough food. Or water. It would be wiser to go on here, where we don't need it. We could go all the way to Rhabat, and wait for them there . . .'

He was right, of course; but, 'Marron, I don't want to walk into Rhabat with you, and without them.' Truly, she did not. Hasan had called a council at Rhabat, to urge the tribes of the Sharai into full war with Outremer. If she brought them the Ghost Walker and no temporising voice that they would listen to, for they surely would not listen to hers, she dreaded to think what might result. Marron was the weapon of their prophecy, that they'd waited for so long; and he had small loyalty left to his own people. He might refuse to kill, but that would make little difference. He was still a symbol, who could hold the tribes together more strongly even than Hasan . . .

He looked at her as though he could read all of that in her face and perhaps more too, that she would have preferred to keep private; and he said, 'You may be right. I don't want that either. But we could wait here, another day or two. Let's rest a little, at any rate, and think about it.'

That was delay, and nothing more; she didn't want to rest, and certainly he had no need to. Nor did she want to spend any longer than she must, beside that writhing water. She nodded her acquiescence, though, thinking that she'd pushed him as far as she could, for now.

'I could bake some bread . . .'

'No. Let's save what we have. Unless you're hungry?'

She was not, and knew he wouldn't be. She only wanted to be busy, not to have to sit and stare at the surging sea.

Instead she turned to look back at how far they'd come across that endless dust that carried no footprints but their own, two tracks that made the faintest of paths between them, perhaps the first this land had ever known. She wondered how long those marks might last: millennia, maybe, in a country without wind or weather. Long after she was dead, at least. She could almost be content with that, she thought, to have left so enduring a memory of her passage through life, of her presence here with Marron these few days.

Almost . . .

Something snagged at her eye, just a moment before she could lose herself entirely in melancholy. Something like an insect in the air, only that there were no insects . . .

She tried to find it again and could not, but there was another suddenly; and no, it was not an insect. It was a hair of darkness, hanging almost at the level of her eyes and twisting like a thread on a spindle: twisting and growing thicker as she watched, a string of smoke, and there was another behind it, and another over there . . .

'Marron,' she called softly, urgently. 'I do not think we should wait a moment here. Do you see?'

She didn't take her eyes from what she was watching, but she heard his turning, heard his sharp insuck of breath, anticipated his question before he asked it.

'What are they?'

'I think they are 'ifrit. Find your knife, Marron, and let us go.'

If the djinn were threads of light and air, all but impossible to see except in darkness – she remembered that flicker of gold that had distorted the sky on their first night here, and thought it must have been a djinni – then it seemed likely to her that 'ifrit would be the opposite of that. She thought she was gazing now at a swarm of them, and far too close.

She heard the hiss of Marron's dagger drawn, heard his gasp of pain as he cut open his arm. Then there was a red blur beside her, the Daughter spreading itself into a welcome gateway.

Her feet itched to make a leap through, but she held back, waiting for Marron; she meant to see him safe first, before she saved herself.

He was slow too, though, seemingly for her sake. Between them, they were both too slow.

The 'ifrit stretched themselves out, longer and longer; like black ropes drawn to an unseen windlass they ran, and that windlass on the further side of the Daughter's portal. Too late to make that leap: she clutched at Marron's arm to hold him back, and only realised when he cried aloud that it was his left arm she was grabbing.

There was a mass of those smoky ropes pouring through the Daughter now, flooding from this world into theirs. She tried to count them, and could not; they writhed as they flowed, but there were certainly dozens. As one tail flicked through and vanished beyond the blur, another head would follow. By the time she thought of how to stop them, shouting to Marron to call the Daughter back and never mind that they'd be stranded here to face however many remained, it was too late even for that. They were gone, they were all gone through.

She stared at Marron, aghast. 'That, that was what they wanted. It wasn't us at all, they only wanted a way into our world, and we gave it to them . . .'

'Not us,' he said bleakly. 'Me. I did it. Even when I don't mean to, I still betray. This time my whole world . . .'

'Our world,' she replied fiercely. 'And it was my idea, I called you to it. You can't take this on yourself. But – oh, Marron! Julianne, Jemel . . .'

'They may not be there. We said that, remember? They should not be there yet.'

Perhaps not. But still there was a plague of evil passed through, and by their hands. With what intent, she couldn't imagine and didn't want to try. She remembered the one 'ifrit that Julianne had brought through by chance – perhaps by chance: she doubted that, suddenly – and how deadly it had been, how it had taken an arrow specially blessed to kill the thing.

'We have to follow,' she said numbly. If only to be there, to fall alone or with their friends; likely the first of many, perhaps very many indeed . . .

'Yes,' he said; and drew his sword and stepped through that blurring gateway, and was gone.

She hurried to go after him, fearful that he might find himself in battle immediately and close the gate behind him, leave her stranded rather than let her die.

It was like running into a wall, a fiery wall: she thought for a moment that he had started to close the gate and she'd met the Daughter half-withdrawn and she'd be dead indeed, it would slay her here or suck her through and slay her there or maybe leave her between two worlds, nowhere at all. When flesh met Daughter, flesh ruptured, it blew apart, as though every smallest fragment of it were ripped between irresistible forces . . .

But if she could think so clearly, she couldn't be dying, surely?

Nor was she. She hadn't been splattered, at least, as she had seen men splattered by the Daughter's kiss. That fire-heat had encompassed her entirely – as she had seen the Daughter do, wickedly, to its victims, before it disassembled them – but she knew it now, by its touch inside and out. She'd forgotten its thunderstrike effect, that was all, on stepping from caveshadow or cool pool – or even from golden-warm air beside a boiling sea – into the sudden full heat of the Sands.

She opened her eyes, only realising as she did so that she must have closed them when she made that hectic plunge through in Marron's wake. So much for the clear-eyed heroine, walking boldly to meet her fate at her man's side . . .

But he was not her man in any case; and he stood some paces from her, and seemed to be staring in fascination at his feet while his sword Dard hung slack and disregarded in his hand.

She had her remaining knife in hand, though she couldn't remember drawing it; she hurried to stand at his unprotected back, to watch over him as he would not watch over himself.

There seemed no immediate sign of the 'ifrit, but they could come from any side, or all at once. She said, 'Marron, did you see which way they went?'

'Mmm? Oh. Yes. At least, I didn't see, but look . . .'

She risked a quick glance down, where he was pointing; and then a longer stare, as every horizon was still clear of any ink-black shadow that moved. Marron stepped a little way away, and took the Daughter back into his blood. She made no protest.

Here, as in that other country they had so abruptly fled, the ground fell in a smooth and shallow bank down to the lapping waters of this desert shore. Here the sand was coarse and tawny, seeming tarnished after the glitter and glow of what they'd left; here the water was dark and dirty, and blessedly still . . .

Almost still, she corrected herself, seeing a patch of bubbling disturbance some distance out and moving further. As though a shoal of fish were fighting just under the surface, she thought – except that there were no fish in the Dead Waters, nor anything that lived, except perhaps a monster.

From that point where the Daughter had stood, opening a way between the worlds, the wind-smoothed sand was disrupted, churned into a cattle-track, it seemed; and that track led straight down to the water's edge, and the same line followed underwater would run precisely to that roiling agitation, except that as she watched it settled slowly into nothing more than a shimmer under the sun, and then into nothing at all.

She turned her eyes back to the sand, and crouched to check. No tracks led in any other direction – though 'ifrit might fly in this world as in their own, if they took a shape with wings – and what individual marks she could read were pockmarks rather than prints, little pits that seemed to have been made by spikes or needles . . .

Well, an 'ifrit could take what shape it chose, in this world; by all that she'd heard they favoured monstrous forms. That one that Julianne pulled through and Jemel stepped in to kill, that one had shaped itself into a giant beetle with a demon's head.

She glanced up at Marron and said, 'Crabs?'

'Something crab-like,' he confirmed. 'Something with many legs, sharp little legs that can run on sand and underwater too.'

'I wonder why?'

'A good shape to use under the water, I suppose.'

'Yes, but why come through here, only to go deep into the Dead Waters?' It must have been planned, so much was obvious. Likely the 'ifrit had shadowed them a great part of their journey, waiting for this place, this time to show themselves and so force open a door that the creatures couldn't open on their own account – but why? What lay under the water here, that they could possibly want?

'Safety, perhaps?' Marron was answering her spoken question, but his answer fitted the unspoken as well. 'They are not immune to the weapons of men. The Sharai would hunt and kill them gladly, however many lives they lost in that hunt; but not even the Sharai can come at them while they lurk down there. And with the shell and claws of a crab, they can defend themselves against whatever might come at them in the water . . .'

'Nothing will. Hadn't you heard? The waters are dead here, there's nothing living to disturb them.' Only ghosts, and she didn't suppose the 'ifrit were susceptible to haunting. But she glowered at the murky surface, blinked away the sun-dazzle that bit back at her eyes, and said, 'I don't believe it. Why take so much trouble, only to hide in the end?'

'I didn't say only to hide. They must have some other

purpose. But in the meantime, until they are ready, they are very safe.'

'Well, perhaps. Perhaps. Perhaps. Are we safe?'

He smiled. 'No, of course not. They could come back; if they came slow and quiet, or in another shape, we would not even see the water ruffle.'

She eyed the water's edge a little nervously, and skittered to the other side of Marron. Which made him smile, which had been her intent. She tucked her arm through his, and smiled back. 'You're not worried, though. Not about them. Are you?'

'No. At the moment, no. If they had meant to kill us, they would have waited for us and done it quickly, before I took the Daughter back. It would be harder for them now, whatever shape they came in. Perhaps they think their way home will be easier, if I am still alive; perhaps I can still surprise them.'

'We,' she said, 'we'll surprise them together. They surprised us, both of us. We owe them, and I always pay my debts.'

Not a smile this time, a real grin on his face, and she hadn't seen that for so long. 'We, then,' he said, 'if you can get that dagger blessed. What prayers do the imams put on weapons, do you know?'

'I'll ask, if we ever see an imam. They are rare in the desert, the Sharai have little time for them; that's why blessed weapons are so precious.'

'Good enough.' He looked about him then, and walked a little way away from her, to the top of the rise, to see better; she followed his every step like a well-trained servant or a well-trained dog, and couldn't even resent herself for doing it.

There was no sign of the rest of their party, no sign of anyone; not even a track to show where people had passed on these dull, dun sands. She remembered that no roads ran close to the Dead Waters. Rhabat was well protected, sheltered both by its towering hills and by age-old custom; either superstition or true caution kept the tribes away from its open waterfront.

'Well, we are here,' Marron said, 'and so are the 'ifrit; and I'm more worried about us for now. We need food and shelter, and particularly water. Water we can drink,' with a scathing glance at the lapping sea behind them. 'And for that, I have to depend on you. I don't know the ways of the Sands, where to look or how to find it . . .'

I'm more worried about you, was what he was saying; she understood him perfectly, and her heart thundered in response. He might survive the long trek along the shore-line to the safety of Rhabat, but she could not . . .

'I'll find water,' she said confidently. 'Food, too. We can hunt; there's always life in the Sands, if you're alert to see it.'

The search might lead them far from any hope of meeting their friends, but that she did not need to say; he knew it already.

'And shelter? This sun will scorch you . . .'

Marron, it will scorch us both. He was bare-chested and bare-backed; the Daughter would not shield him from the sun, only stop him feeling how it burned. He was stupid about his body, he always had been and now he was worse; he'd neglect it altogether, if she allowed him to. But she loved his care of her, and the chance to return it.

'No shelter here,' she said, stating what was obvious, 'except what we make for ourselves. We can dig a little into the side of a dune, and find cooler sand to hide in; there are lizards that bury themselves completely, they make good examples. We'll move by night, lie up through the day and hope to meet our friends quickly. That wound's all but healed now, but you can't walk through the Sands like that, no one could . . .'

Her fingers trembled just a little where she touched his deep-scarred shoulder, which was foolish; hadn't they slept close-wrapped together last night, and several nights before? But that was in another country, in their solitude, quite unobserved except by passing spirits who would give no weight to such an act, as neither perhaps had he. Here Jemel was close, and Julianne, and others; the clasp of a hand carried portents that even he might not manage to misinterpret.

She took her hand away and used it to shield her eyes as she scanned the far and flat horizons, trying to look wise in the ways of the desert. In truth it mattered little which way she led him; or rather it mattered enormously, but that she saw no signs to say where water might be found, and so she had to guess. What roads she knew of were too far to seek, where they might have found wells in common use.

'We'll go west,' she decided. 'The others must come that way, once they reach the Waters; Rhabat lies on the southern shore, and the other way around is too mountainous. I don't say that we should wait for them, unless we find water and better shelter than I can see from here, but we can leave signs that they may find and follow . . .'

There were many such signs, that could be carved in rock or set out in smaller stones, even trampled into sand where no other means afforded. Each tribe had its own, but some at least were understood by all: *you may drink from this well* or *you may not, good hunting here, beware of quicksands ahead* . . .

Here on the rise was good; she gathered pebbles and laid them out in pattern, to say nothing more complex than *we were here, and have gone west.* Even so much was probably not necessary; Jemel or the Dancers would see their tracks, come from nowhere, and know who had made them and where they were headed. The tracks of the 'ifrit might puzzle even Dancers, though; she thought a moment, and added a sigil that meant *beware the water.* It was more usually used to warn travellers of a well that harboured disease, but she could think of nothing better on the spur of the moment. There were those among the party who might make a sound guess as to her meaning, when they had seen those tracks.

Or they might not find this spot at all, of course. She'd done all she could, though; she straightened up and scanned the horizon one more time, against the small chance of seeing a shadow rise. And did not, and so led Marron away on a line a little north of the sun's path west, to give them some distance from the Waters.

And so she found what she had least expected, tracks that she could read herself, although she did not understand them.

They came from the north, the way her friends must have come; and they were camel-tracks and bare feet to speak of that party, riders and Dancers. The camel-tracks were fresh, made perhaps that morning, there was only a little wind-scuff blurring them; but the feet had come later.

Their marks were sharp and clear, a couple of hours old perhaps, no more.

By her count, there were five camels and three men afoot. Which was not enough of either, if this were truly what she hoped against all reason.

'They can't be ahead of us,' she said, 'how can they?'

Marron shook his head. 'Either the Dancers were wrong about how long the journey would take, and I don't believe that—'

'No,' she said positively. 'I saw it, some of it, before we left them. Easily a week across that ground, and I couldn't see the Waters.'

'—Or we were right, that time moves differently in the other world. Why not? The djinn have no need to count the hours. But are you sure that these are our camels?'

'I can't see mine. She had a scar on one pad, and I don't think she's here. But Julianne's white, she's so proud, that one, she throws her feet out as she walks. Look, here . . . I'm not positive, no – but as near as I can be. Though there aren't enough Dancers, either. Only three, and they're hours behind. I don't understand it.'

'Perhaps they were delayed, while the riders went ahead; perhaps they met trouble on the way, or they just met news, and have divided. We'll find no answers here. What should we do, follow the tracks? Or go on looking for water?'

'Whoever made these tracks, whether they're our people or not, they've come across the Sands; they'll be looking for water too. Let's follow. We won't catch up with the camels before dark, unless they found a well and chose to rest out the day; but if they found a well and moved on after, their tracks will lead us to it. With luck we'll find the walkers, at least. Come on . . .'

She was more worried than she cared to admit; if the camel-tracks were from their party and the feet did not belong to Dancers, then their friends were being stalked, and probably not by anyone with peaceful intent. She couldn't remember which tribe laid claim to the lands around the northern end of the Dead Waters, but this was a deadly time; few of the Sharai would welcome strangers. In isolated areas where no roads ran, at high summer when water was short and precious, few indeed . . .

She was anxious not to alarm Marron, he was so reluctant to fight, and so adamant in his refusal to kill any more. She didn't know what he might do if he thought they were headed for a battle. Wake the Daughter, perhaps, and go back to the land of the djinn? Take her with him, perhaps, or else leave her to face whatever trouble she found, quite alone? Every option made her more unquiet, and so she held her tongue and could only hope that his thoughts were following a different, more hopeful track than hers.

The land was rugged here, gravel plain with scattered dunes rising unpredictably; impossible to see much in any direction, each dune-top gave a view only as far as the next. The tracks were easy to follow, though, human toes breaking camel-pads all the way. Their depth and clarity renewed her unease; perhaps she was a victim of their legend, but she was surprised to find Dancers leaving so obvious a trail. She'd thought they would walk across dust and not leave a mark. So perhaps these were not Dancers, these three men. But if so, where were the Dancers? Left the group after

Marron did, for lack of their Ghost Walker? That was certainly possible; on the other hand, if they wanted to find him again, their best choice was to stay.

To stay, or to follow. That might be it, that they had detached themselves completely but still kept the same route, holding themselves aloof and apart. That fitted; but if so, why were they hurrying? No one hurried in the desert, but these men did. Toes and balls of the feet she saw, rarely a heel. Their strides were short, so they weren't running full out, but trotting certainly. Had they simply let the group get too far ahead for their comfort? Or was it that they had some insight, perhaps foresight: did they expect Marron to return tonight, and so they closed the distance quickly?

Questions, questions. She struggled to believe the best, and rarely managed it; so that when at last Marron did spot dark figures against the sand, she was hardly surprised to see him gesture her to stillness as he crouched low beside her.

She shaded her eyes against the glare of the lowering sun, and strained to see. There they were, she had them now, three men lying prone in the lee of a dune that ran due west ahead, so that not even their shadows broke the crest.

As she watched, one of them snaked backwards down the slope, not standing until he was sure of avoiding any wary eyes on the further side of the dune. He ran off westward, and she thought she saw a bow in his hand; certainly it was too long and thick to be a riding-stick, and in any case these men had no camels.

Who but the Dancers would venture the Sands without camels? None, that she had ever heard of. She couldn't see whether their robes were blue or black, but she was sure none the less, although she didn't understand it.

'Marron? Can you see more than I can?'

'One of the men is Morakh; the other two were also with us, although I never learned their names.'

No, neither had she. Morakh did all the talking, always. 'They, uh, they don't look very friendly, do they?'

'No.'

'And it must be our friends, beyond that dune . . .'

'It is. I can hear their voices, and the camels. They have found water, I think.'

She could hear nothing, but she was growing accustomed by now to how Marron's abilities far overreached her own.

'What did the Dancers say to each other, when that one left? Could you hear that?'

'They didn't speak. I think they used signs, not to be overheard, but I couldn't see their hands. What should we do?'

'You could call to them, call them off, whatever it is they're doing . . .'

'One has gone, beyond the sound of my voice; the others – well, do you think Morakh would set his plans aside because I bade him? Ordered him, even? They are sworn to serve me; I don't believe that his idea of service includes obedience to any will other than his own.'

It was a fault he was familiar with, to judge by his bleak tone and bleaker look; she remembered Marron and his master, Sieur Anton, how hard it had been for the boy to leave the man. And how he had left regardless, she remembered that too. No, oaths bent or broken were nothing new to Marron.

'It would warn Julianne and the others, though. Warn Jemel. If you shouted . . .'

'And perhaps push the Dancers into violence that we might otherwise avoid. A hasty enemy is a dangerous enemy, Elisande; he will kill for convenience.'

'A friend alerted is as good as an enemy surprised,' she countered, her overheard wisdom for his. Neither one of them knew so much from practice. 'And why are they enemies, anyway? They were companions when we left, if not exactly friends . . .'

'A long way from being friends. And we left. They were there for my sake, and I left. With you, without them. What happened after we were gone — well, we can learn that later.'

'What do you want to do, then?'

'For the moment, nothing. Watch, and wait. It'll be dark in an hour. If the Dancers move before nightfall, then yes, perhaps I must distract them; but I guess they're waiting for the dark. So can we.'

'Marron, that one who slipped away, he was an archer, he had a bow . . .'

'I saw it. So?'

'So what if he shoots Julianne? Jemel? Now, while the sun's behind him and the light's still good? We can't even see him from here, we won't have time to interfere . . .'

'If he stands to use his bow,' Marron said slowly, deliberately, maddeningly, 'then he makes a target of himself; the sun won't hide him, it'll mark him out. His shadow will cover all the land between, faster than any arrow he can draw and shoot. Even if that's what they intend, they'll wait till dark.'

'And how will he see to shoot then?'

'Jemel will light a fire. That's one reason why they stopped, perhaps: not only for the water, but to gather fuel too. There's driftwood along the shore. Jemel will light a fire, and the bowman will see them outlined against the flames, and they won't see him at all . . .'

'No. So how do we prevent it, pray for rain?'

'As soon as it's dark, I can take you to the well. I could do it now, but Morakh would see.'

'He'll see after dark, too. He doesn't need firelight, he has owl's eyes. Like yours.'

'No, not like mine. If he sees us at the fire, that's too late for him. And he won't see us crossing the sand; we'll go the other way.'

'What other way?' she demanded; and felt stupid immediately the words were out of her mouth, didn't need to see him tap his arm to tell her.

So they waited and watched; and as he had predicted, the Dancers did the same. The sun set in a riot of reds and purples, that still seemed tawdry to her gold-adapted eyes; she said, 'Now?'

'Wait,' he said, 'you know Jemel's fires. It'll be a smoky smudge for the next hour, he won't build it up till the heat goes from the sand. They won't move yet, so we don't need to. Not till it's full dark.'

True enough, but she was restless with impatience and anxiety, desperate to carry the warning to their friends. Darkness swept up from behind them as the sun disappeared ahead; she wanted to go immediately, and thought she had her wish when Marron sat up beside her, suddenly alert. She touched his shoulder enquiringly, but he shook his head and gestured her to be still. He seemed to be listening, to something far beyond her hearing; strain though she might, though she did, she could hear nothing but distant sounds of the sea's stirring.

She fidgeted at Marron's side while he listened, turned his head and listened again. At last he reached to take her wrist and tug her gently back into the star-shadow of a dune, safely away from the skyline. She wanted to ask him what he'd been so attentive towards, but he gave her no opportunity; his knife nicked his arm, and the Daughter flowed.

It was only dimly red in the darkness, but when it shaped itself into a doorway, the heart of it glowed brightly; when they stepped through, it was more shocking than the plunge from the steamy heat of the hammam into an ice-cold pool.

They stepped from night into day, from darkness into pearly light that didn't even have that border of gloom on the horizon to say that night was coming. Proof positive that the days of the djinn were longer, or else that time here followed other patterns entirely; she only hoped that none of the Dancers had noticed any flare of light leak from the Daughter as they'd passed through.

Marron might have had the same concern; he closed that doorway behind them, even as his blood ran into the sand, as he staggered from the pain.

'Take it back,' she urged him, slipping her shoulder under his arm for support, wrapping her own arm tight around his waist.

'What, for a walk of a hundred paces and then scratch at the door to let it out again?'

'Marron, please . . . For my sake, if not your own? I can't, I can't carry you that far . . .'

She was lying, of course; she could carry him to the moon if she had to. He believed her, though, or let her believe that he did; either way, the Daughter sucked itself back under his skin, the bloodflow stopped and his weight lifted from her body.

A long moment later, she uncoiled her arm and stepped away.

'At least it should be easier to find the place in the light,' she said determinedly, 'even though the land's so different. Which direction?'

'Over there.' They were standing among dunes again, but dunes of dust that were shaped quite differently from the sand they'd come from; his pointing finger betrayed no doubts, though, and she agreed with him. They had no sun to guide them, nor any sight of the sea, but still that felt westerly and a little south, it felt absolutely right.

And was right; they were sure when they saw steam rising from a little dip in the dust. As they came closer, they saw a pool of gently bubbling water at the bottom of the dip.

'Not too close,' he said, leading her away to the south. 'I don't want to risk touching anyone. Not even one of the camels . . .'

Touching them with the Daughter, he meant; she shuddered at the memory of another night, when he had slain and slain in the stables of the Roq.

Where he judged it safe, he cut his arm once more. Elisande thought that even the colour of the Daughter was stronger here, richer and less smoky, though it still behaved like smoke, pouring heavily through the air. Smoke with a will, she thought, that was in some part its own, only directed by Marron; here was something at least that did practise obedience. It would be a day of terror, she thought, the day that it did not . . .

She stepped forward and through the portal that it made, back into sudden dark; as she went she heard Marron murmur, 'Elisande, beware the south, beware what comes from the water.'

She didn't reply immediately; blind eyes overruled and she had to stand blinking, lost in utter darkness until her sight came back to her a little. Then she saw the soft glow that was Jemel's fire, the shadows of her friends and their mounts around.

A voice cried a warning, weapons scraped from their sheaths, and she had no time to question Marron; she stumbled forward, and another voice called her name.

'Shush, Julianne!' she hissed frantically. 'All of you, listen to me! You're being watched, Morakh's behind that dune,' with a jerk of her head northerly, 'and he's been tracking you all day. We tracked him. He's got other Dancers with him. Only three of them altogether, though, I don't know where the others went, they might have circled round to get ahead . . .'

'They're dead,' Rudel said shortly. 'What more?'

'One of the Dancers has a bow and he went west, along behind that ridge there. I thought he was looking to catch you in the sun but Marron said not, he said he'd take you by the firelight and he was right, so put it out, Jemel . . .'

A sudden barefoot kick, a yelp as the smouldering fire

bit even through leathery Sharai soles, a scatter of sand and that little glow was gone.

'Where is Marron?' her father demanded, just a voice in darkness.

'Why, here—'

But she turned as she spoke, sensing at last the absence behind her, where there should have been another human body.

There was nothing: no Marron and no sign of the Daughter, no gateway open or closed . . .

'Didn't he come through?'

'No,' Julianne said softly, slipping an arm around her shoulders. 'Just you. And barely even you, girl. What have you been doing to yourself? You're so thin . . .'

Was she? She was hungry, she was suddenly, inappropriately aware of that; no, more, she was ravenous, as she had not been for days. Djinn-length days . . .

'Short commons,' she said briefly. There would be time later, to eat and talk both; or there would be no chance for either. Even so, even in her urgency, she found just time enough to feel a pang of betrayal. He had gone back – stayed, rather, let her come through alone – to avoid the fight he foresaw, the possibility of his having to kill. He'd abandoned her and all of them to fate or chance, for the sake of his own heavy conscience; and oh, that was bitter to her. He'd said it himself, that he betrayed wherever he touched. She should have trusted his judgement on that, and had not.

'We can move now,' Jemel said. 'It will be hard to rouse the camels silently, but we can bind their jaws. Where we go may not be seen, if we avoid the skyline . . .'

But there was doubt in his own voice, and she knew it was the wrong choice. There was no moon, but stars blazed overhead; it was not so dark at all, now that her eyes were accustomed. The Dancers would need no more light than that to see them leave, nor to follow them. Perhaps the archer could even shoot in such a light, though she could not; she might risk a knife, but not with any confidence.

'No,' firmly, from Rudel. 'Safer to stay where we are; a party on the move is always vulnerable. We can use the camels as shelter against arrows. At close quarters, we have a chance; we have beaten the Dancers before, when there were more of them and we were unprepared. Quickly, come . . .'

'We need the camels,' Jemel objected.

'Jemel, we need to live. If the camels die, so may we, granted; but if they die in our stead, their deaths may at least give us the chance of life. We have no other.'

No further argument; they huddled close against the sandy bodies of the beasts. Five camels, and four of them: one short, on each count. To save thinking of Marron, Elisande whispered, 'Julianne, where's my camel?'

'Oh. Unh, I'll tell you later, I can't think about that now . . .'

Dead, then, somewhere in the Sands; she was sorry. So would the Sultan be. Julianne was right, though, this was not the time. Elisande lifted her head cautiously, and peered over her warm, protective bulwark.

What had been an open pool in the land of the djinn was a well here, or at least a stone-rimmed pit that ought to signify a well, with a leather rope coiled beside. There was no gleam of light reflecting up from that black hole; the water would lie deep, in such country. If there were water, if it weren't dry and her friends' dipped skins had brought up nothing but dust . . .

The dunes held the well closely; too close, she thought. This was poor ground to defend, as any such isolated well would be. Rudel should have known that. Desert wisdom decreed that camp should always be made a little distance off, on a dune-crest where one could both see and be seen; it was less aggressive, and tactically far safer. With such a well, the wind blew sand against the stones that covered it, and every passing party dug it clear; and so a rampart of dug and discarded sand would build up through the years, all around the well-head. More wind, more nomads, much more time and this was the result, a well at the bottom of a wide, high bowl. Too wide for a small party to protect, and too near a horizon: she could see little further than she could throw a knife. She'd be lucky to have time to make the throw; a man appearing on that short horizon, a running man would be down and among them before she'd done more than yell a warning.

Blade in hand, she scanned her quarter of the skyline grimly, determined to throw before she yelled.

When the man appeared, he was not running; neither was he in her range. He caught just the corner of her eye, a shadow rimmed by starlight, rising to his feet in her father's quarter. She should watch her own horizon, and not his; but that was the archer, his bow was too fine a line but she could read his stance. And her father juggled knives with breathtaking skill until he tried too many, but she'd never seen him throw one. It wasn't he who'd taught her.

Had she doubted that the archer could shoot by night?

At this distance, he could shoot blindfold and not miss. She crouched lower behind the camel's bulk, and thought they should have run after all; they had no chance here, none. Fish in a pond, a child could pick them off . . .

A hiss and a thud, a camel's shriek of pain; the beast that sheltered her father staggered half to its feet and fell back grunting. Dead, it would make as good shelter – but Rudel was standing suddenly, a clear target for the next arrow.

She opened her mouth to shriek at him, *stupid! get down!* – and bit the words back unformed, as she saw his arm cock and hurl. She looked for the glint of a knife in transit, and didn't see it; he seemed to have thrown a ball instead, in a high slow lob.

She didn't understand, and wasn't granted the time to puzzle over it. The archer drew and shot; she saw her father fall.

And did shriek then, wordlessly, and leaped to her feet, as stupid as he'd been; and so made a target of herself, a brighter target by far as the well, the camels, her friends, her father's body and all that lay within that broad bowl shone suddenly in a flaring light. Harsh sharp shadows moved and ran into the night beyond the walls of sand.

Startled, she flung herself around – not down, not clever even now, exposed and helpless – to see that ball of stuff her father had flung up, now falling fast. Falling and burning, blazing, trailing a fierce guttering flame of blue and green, while the core was white as a streaking star.

Down it plummeted, too fast almost for her eyes to follow; too fast surely for a human body to avoid. The archer seemed not even to try. She saw him standing rooted, gaping as that fireball plunged towards him.

Flame and body met and merged. The ball lost its solidity and seemed to flow, to melt not over the man's body and robes but into him, into soft flesh and running blood. He didn't catch fire as a man ought, hair and clothes aflare and his hands beating, flailing uselessly, his voice a scream of horror; he burned from the inside and glowed like a lamp, as though his bones were blazing.

When he flung his head back and his mouth gaped, no scream came out of it: no voice at all but only a leap, a vivid flare of light.

Elisande had seen fire-eaters many times; she'd heard boys being burned to death. One was a fairground trick, the other a truth, a memory seared deep. She'd never seen a man eaten by fire, consumed from within; she'd heard such things in stories, and never believed them true. Tricks of the tongue, no more . . .

But that man burned and his tongue was tricked with flame, and shadows danced; and the Sand Dancers added their shadows to the dance, she saw them, two men rising up and running down through that shimmering light.

She was offered horror on the one hand and danger on the other, and she rejected them both. For the moment, while that dread light lasted, she turned her back on her friends in their peril and ran to her father, with never a thought for the strangeness of that choice.

Rudel lay on his back, with the arrow jutting from his chest. She dropped to her knees beside him and reached to lay her hands on his body, one beside that arrow and the other on his head. He was not dead, she could feel his breathing, hard and shallow; her own breath choked her briefly, one quick sob of relief.

His eyes were open, staring up at her; his mouth worked, but only to splutter a thick dark liquid into his beard. He was drowning, she thought, as his lungs and airways filled with blood. She closed her eyes against the desperate sight of him, tried to close ears and mind both to the sounds around, harsh grunts and the clash of steel, the bellows of terrified camels struggling against their hobbles. Never mind that he was her father, with all that meant to her; never mind that her friends were fighting for their own lives and hers also. She distanced herself from all that was happening around her and within her, struggling to focus only on this broken body, seeking as she'd been taught to with her inner eye.

She felt her fingers tingle as she drew on her own strength and gave it up to him. After a little, his breathing seemed to ease; that was a distraction, though, not enough. Far short of what he needed. Her thoughts seemed to slide down her arms, down through her hands, her skin and his; her mind seemed to wander in the pathways of his body, till she found what was ripped and torn, where metal head and wooden shaft had invaded.

Nothing she could do about the arrow now, but she could stop the blood from flowing out so fast, close up minor vessels, clot the major. It was patching only, but it would serve. Time enough later for the slow arts of true healing. If they were granted time, and the opportunity to use it . . .

Whether what she saw was real, whether she actually reached inside his body and touched her thoughts to his flesh, she couldn't say. It might be only imagination and knowledge working together, while the undoubted power that she had found its own way to where it was needed. But it seemed to her that she did see and touch, as she had with Marron also, in the land of the djinn; she thought she saw her father's blood clotting around that brutal arrow, to stem the leaks that would kill him else.

At last she lifted her hands away, and turned him quickly onto his side. A little more blood flowed from his mouth; she watched anxiously in the fading light – fading as the fire must be dying in the dead Dancer's body, but she didn't turn her head to see that – until she saw that he could breathe and not choke now, until she was sure that it was safe to leave him for a while.

Then she stood and looked around, though it took an effort to do so. Jemel was fighting blade to blade with Morakh; he was hard-pressed, but holding. Julianne was facing the other Dancer, across the struggling body of a couched and hobbled camel; she had her knives in hand, but his scimitar slashed and lunged at her above the animal's back and all she could do was dodge. Elisande pulled a knife from her father's belt and cocked her arm to throw, but in that instant the light was lost to her, as the last lingering flames lost their hold on shrivelled flesh, and darkness fell.

It would take time, too much time for her eyes to find enough light by the stars. Drained though she was she ran instead, a knife in each hand now. She saw one shifting shadow, two, and a third on the ground between them: that was Julianne, that was the camel, this must be the Dancer. She hurled herself at him, blades outstretched, wanting only to wrestle and slash, too close for his sword to find her.

The moment before her body must have plunged into his, he was suddenly not there. She hit only empty air and staggered, fell, fetched up against the surging weight of the camel. Struggled back to her feet, bewildered; and saw him now on the other side of the beast, face to face with Julianne.

Her friend took the same desperate chance that Elisande had, hurling herself across the space between them, a beat ahead of his swinging sword; the blade missed her back by a finger's width. Julianne thudded up against the Dancer, with force enough to send him staggering; but she'd flung her arms wide as she leaped, and now she had no weight behind her knives. She slashed wildly at his face, not even trying for his eyes, as Elisande would have done. He flinched back from the flashing, biting blades, but then rooted his feet and flung her off.

Julianne lost her footing, and fell sprawling. And would have died, as the Dancer at last had room to skewer her; but Elisande threw a blade in that moment, and the next vaulted over the camel with one hand on its back, lashing her feet around to catch the man behind his knees and bring him down.

She landed in a tumble on top of him. Her one knife had taken him in the shoulder; her other she slammed into his side, yanked it out and thrust again. He was still struggling, still strong, writhing beneath her; but then there was another body falling onto him beside her, and more blades flashing, sinking deep.

Elisande felt his final shudder, felt him relax into death. She breathed deeply, once, and lifted her head to find herself eye to eye with Julianne. There was a spray of blood across her friend's face and a frenzied look to her, her eyes wide and white behind her tangled hair; absurdly, Elisande wanted to wipe her clean and tidy her, to bring back the calm and courtly maiden. Julianne had been made for another kind of warfare altogether, not this desperate brawling in the dark . . .

But sounds of grating steel and gasping breath pulled her back to where they were, in deadly danger still. She jerked upright and saw Jemel blundering backwards, swinging his scimitar two-handed now and with no art or skill, battering his opponent's blade aside and barely recovering in time to do the same again. It couldn't last; Morakh stalked him across the sand, merciless and deadly. Feint and thrust, feint and cut: soon one of those strokes would tell, it must do. And then he would have the girls to kill, and that he could do, though he was alone to do it now; in such a fight victory lay in the head as much as the hands, and he was their master in both. He knew it, so did they. So did Jemel.

But Jemel had held him already for longer, far longer than Elisande would have believed possible; and thanks to that heroic effort there were still three of them, and so they might yet have a chance . . .

She scrabbled for her knives, and found one; pushed herself to her feet and found Julianne at her side, again with only the one blade in her hand.

'Jump, or throw?' she gasped.

'I throw,' Elisande said, *and then I take your knife and jump, my sweet, you weren't bred for this* . . .

So she poised herself to throw, and almost as if to oblige her the duelling men shifted, so that Morakh's broad back was before her. She couldn't miss . . .

Even as her arm began to move, though, a monstrous shadow blotted out the stars above Jemel's head, as something rose up from behind the crest of the dune. She could see only the creature's silhouette and a glimpse of claws, of a fearsome tossing head; but that was enough to say *ghûl* to her, and just enough to shift her aim. Morakh might kill Jemel with his next lunge, or the one following; the ghûl would do it from behind, immediately and certainly.

She couldn't hope to be accurate, changing her cast so suddenly. Nor was she. Her only chance to kill the ghûl with such a small blade at such a distance was to take it in the throat; she saw the knife sink home into its chest, an arm's length below her mark.

It hissed and roared, louder than Julianne's cry of warning. Jemel perhaps heard both, though he couldn't have understood either. He understood his peril, though, and dived rolling down the dune, beneath Morakh's killing-stroke.

The Dancer wasn't fool enough to turn his back on a wounded ghûl; nor alas was he fool enough to strike at it. Instead he simply flickered out of sight, that legendary ability of his kind. Elisande had heard it told in stories, had seen it once before tonight. She spared time for one quick glance round, but couldn't see him anywhere within the bowl. She ran instead to Jemel's side, with Julianne not slow to follow; the three of them faced the ghûl as it came slowly down towards them.

Behind it, two more appeared above the dune.

Beware the south, Marron had said, *beware what comes from the water*. He had known, somehow – had heard them, perhaps, or understood better what they'd both heard, the sounds of heavy bodies rising from the sea. Certainly he'd been listening to something. And still he'd left . . .

'What should we do?' Julianne whispered.

With a heavy heart, Elisande made swift plans that any swift mind would dismiss as nonsense, as the dreaming of a stupid and frightened girl. 'This one's wounded; a second blow will heal it. We must be quick, then. Give me your knife, Julianne. I'll throw. It'll recover; but then you can slay it, Jemel. After that we're in your hands, you must kill the others yourself, or at least delay them till Julianne and I can gather swords from the fallen . . .'

It wouldn't work, it couldn't work; already the first ghûl loomed above them. A foul smell was its herald, salt and filth on damp rank fur. Julianne breathed at her, 'Throw, for pity's sake . . .!' But it had to be close, to give Jemel a chance to slay it in the instant of its recovery. She waited, waited—

—and didn't throw at all, she didn't need to. The air thrummed with a bass note, they heard the thud of an arrow striking home. Next moment the ghûl had reared up, its dreadful claws raised high; and in that moment a second arrow shattered its skull, and so it died.

And then they heard men's voices yelling, over the softer sounds of camels ridden hard, ridden at the gallop. Staring, they saw a squadron of Sharai come pouring into the bowl, scimitars drawn.

They could finish the ghûls, however many there might be lurking beyond the dune. Elisande sank down onto one knee, abruptly drained; and then rose up again, as quickly energised, when one boy on foot came running after the riders, skirting round the couched camels by the well, trotting over to join them.

'Marron . . . I thought, I thought you'd left us, for fear of the killing . . .'

'I will not kill again, unless I must,' he confirmed softly. 'But I heard the ghûls in the water, and I heard riders further off; so I went to fetch the riders, to face the ghûls. I thought you could outface Morakh,' he added.

And she thought he was teasing, almost joking, which he never did; and she surprised herself and all of them by bursting into tears, and burying her face in his shoulder as she hugged him.

Easy to begin, but hard, very hard to stop; harder still to look her friends in the eye, immediately after. Jemel's expression . . .

But there was her father, lying sick and needful. Another surprise, that she'd be so glad to push Marron away – though by the look of him he was never so glad of anything, which was no surprise at all – and hurry to Rudel.

He was no better, though he seemed no worse; that was as much as she could expect, and perhaps more. She didn't think she could have treated a death-wound at all, a week ago. Something she'd gained, from the land of the djinn: something she'd brought back, perhaps, a little of the strength she'd felt there, or just a little more understanding.

He was conscious, she saw. He didn't speak, but his eyes glittered at her.

'Well, what?' she mumbled crossly. 'Should I have left you to die, is that it? Well, perhaps I should. But I thought Outremer might need you. To speak for it, if Redmond doesn't get to Rhabat. Though why you'd want to, I don't know. Save Surayon and let the rest go burn, it isn't worth the saving . . .'

As she talked she laid a hand against his brow, feeling for the chill sweat of fever or that simple chilling that can follow a severe wound, that can kill the patient though the wound recovers. She found neither; he was cool of skin, yes, but the night had swallowed the day's heat already and was turning sharp now, she was starting to shiver herself . . .

'Jemel!' she called. 'Get that fire going again – and build it up, Rudel needs warmth . . .'

'I think we all do,' Julianne said, rubbing her arms as she came running in response. Marron could not, of course, with the camels there; and so Jemel had not either. The two boys were standing together on a dune-top, watching the ghûls being hunted down, she thought. Perhaps that was why she'd called Jemel, because they were together, and she could not leave her father. She hoped not, but perhaps . . .

Perhaps Julianne would fail with the fire, and have to fetch Jemel; burning dung-cakes was an art she might not have.

Perhaps Elisande would grow into a crabbed and bitter soul, jealous to the core of her. Perhaps she had already.

'Talk to me,' she said hastily. 'Tell me what's been happening to you, why Morakh wants us all dead . . .'

Julianne did that as she built her fire, finding some wood from somewhere to make it blaze, no help needed; and then asked simply, 'How is Rudel?'

'He'll live.' He was sleeping now, but it was a real sleep, a healing sleep she thought. Thanks to her, he would live. That was something to be considered later, to be made to fit with her conscience, and her ever-burning rage against him. She'd never truly wished him dead, even in her most anger; he was too necessary, too valuable to her beloved land and her people. But still, she'd never thought that she might save his life.

There were more figures on the dune-top at last, the Sharai riders; they paused to speak to Jemel as Marron backed away, and then came slowly down towards the well. A dozen of them, and half had ghûl-heads swinging from their saddles.

The man who led them bore no trophies; he needed none, Elisande thought, seeing the easy confidence in him as he couched his mount and stepped to ground.

He threw his hood back to show himself clearly by the firelight: a man in his early thirties, perhaps, hawk-nosed and trimly bearded. Then he bowed to them Sharai-fashion, a grave inclination of the head and a complex gesture of the hands.

'Lady Elisande d'Albéry, I believe, and Lady Julianne de Rance?' He had them right; Elisande bowed as gracefully as she could manage, squatting as she was beside her father; Julianne rose only in order to make a full courtly curtsey, meeting manners with formal manners. 'I am called Hasan, of the Beni Rus,' he went on, his voice soft and mellifluous, his accent an ornament to their tongue. 'And this is Rudel?'

It was a moment before either of them could reply, so startled they were; then Elisande stammered, 'It, it is . . .' She should perhaps give him a title, but wasn't sure if he wore one. For sure he needed none; Hasan was Hasan, all the tribes would know that name quite unadorned.

'Your father, and he is hurt? How badly?'

He stepped forward to see for himself, and checked suddenly at sight of the arrow still jutting from Rudel's chest. It was the first ungraceful movement that he'd made; Elisande was quite glad to see him human, susceptible to shock.

'He should be dead,' Hasan said simply. 'With such a wound, we would have left him to the vultures.'

'He needs to live,' Elisande replied, equally simply.

'Perhaps so. I would not have thought God meant him to; but you are from Surayon, of course.'

'I am. Though much of what we know, we learned from your people, prince.' No harm in flattery, of him or of his people. Besides, she told nothing but truth, in both cases. Without the Sharai, her country would be near as ignorant as its neighbours; and in a land without titles – which this was not – he would still be a prince among men.

'Not this,' he said absently. 'Not to keep a man alive and without pain, when he should have gone to paradise in minutes.'

Well, no – but I am Surayonnaise, and so a witch. Will you burn me for it?

No, of course he would not. It was her own people who kept fires for the likes of her.

'The arrow must still be removed,' she said quietly.

'My men can do that, if you are not able . . .?'

'Thank you, prince. I'd be glad if they would.' She was able, but not particularly willing, now that the need was gone. If ever a man deserved to carry a blade in his heart, that man was Rudel; far be it from her to remove it. Though this was not a blade and not in his heart, the symbolism still mattered to her. 'The sooner the better, if you please. I can hold him asleep, to make it easier for all.'

He nodded, beckoning some of his men forward and speaking to them in rapid Catari: the man lived by the lady's skill, but the arrow must be drawn, and swiftly . . .

It took little effort on her part to keep Rudel unconscious through their knifework; she cradled his head in her lap and stroked his temples gently, whispering under her breath. This was only a subtle variation on the *sodar*, a tendril of her mind whispering to a tendril of his. Just as well: she'd all but drained herself with that first hurried healing, and then she'd had to fight after. She was exhausted now, almost slipping into sleep herself despite her rabid hunger as she lulled her father's mind and numbed his body to any pain.

Almost – but not quite. Exhaustion never touched her curiosity. Hasan was speaking with Julianne behind her, and she could listen while she lulled, while she lolled.

'Lady, it was a great surprise to me when your companion gave me your name. I think I was only ever once more startled in my life.'

'Oh? And when was that, ah, prince?'

'You need not call me so,' with a chuckle. 'It is a politeness of the Lady Elisande, but I am not a prince. My name is Hasan, that only. When was it? A short time ago, when the Ghost Walker came running half-naked out of tales and terrified my camel.'

'Ah. Yes, he would do that. I hope the surprise of finding me was not so terrifying? To you or to your camel?'

'Not at all. She is a placid beast ordinarily, she takes what comes, as a servant of God should do. Alas, I cannot be so stolid, faced with such beauty. The surprise is as pleasant as it is remarkable. That your father came to my council was unforeseen, but not in truth unaccountable; he has done such things before. That you should choose to do the same is a grace quite unlooked-for.'

'My father, Hasan?'

'Yes. Did you not know?'

'I, ah, had been told. How is he, is he well?'

'Quite well, I believe. He seemed so this morning, at least. If he was expecting you, he did not mention it.'

'No. I think I will surprise him also, if we come safely to Rhabat.'

'Lady, trust me; I will bring you there.'

'My name is Julianne. Prince. But there are dangers you may not be aware of . . .'

'Not in these lands, Julianne. You are on my territory here; I know every rock, and every insect that inhabits them.'

'Oh? How many ghûls have you killed tonight – and how many before tonight?'

'A few, before – but never in a pack, as they were tonight. That I confess.'

'Cut into their tongues, Hasan, and see what you find there.'

He gave the order, and waited in silence until the thing was done, and the results shown him; then, 'What are these? And how did you know . . .?'

'They are a device the 'ifrit use, that give them power over ghûls. I am told that they are stones from the land of the djinn; I have not seen that country for myself, but I believe it.'

'As do I; their warmth confirms the story. You continue to surprise me, Julianne – though the greater surprise is that there is something you do not know for yourself.'

'Oh, many things. I'm only a girl yet . . .'

'Then I would like to see you grow into a woman. Would you marry me, Julianne? If your father consented to the match?'

A pause, and then a laugh, more breathless than amused: 'Alas, Hasan, I am married already.'

'What of that? So am I, several times. But of course, your customs are different; and you are not a man. Tell me his name, then, that I may kill him.'

'Oh, no. Would you make me a widow before I have been made a woman?'

His turn to pause, and the lightness was gone from his voice when he spoke again. 'No, Julianne, I would not do that. Perhaps I will not need to. I will speak to your father on the subject. But for now, it is time to rest. You have the well; we will make camp beyond the ridge there.'

'Keep a good watch overnight, Hasan. There is a Sand Dancer unaccounted for, with brethren to avenge; he sought our blood, he may seek yours also, whether you have a quarrel with him or no. I think he is mad, myself.'

'All Sand Dancers are mad; but your Ghost Walker may have given them reason. That one makes me anxious myself. My thanks for the warning; we will guard your camp as well as our own. Sleep easy, lady.'

'I will, prince . . .'

She didn't, though. Elisande set herself to wake several times during the night, to check on her father and keep him deep asleep. Each time she was aware of Julianne's restlessness, each time she expected her friend to sit up when she did, and share whatever was disturbing her; each time she was disappointed.

In the morning, as they broke camp, Elisande surprised Hasan on her own account, telling him of the 'ifrit in the Dead Waters. She took him to see the tracks, at his insistence. They found hoofprints also, where the ghûls had come up out of the sea; and they found one thing more, the prints of a barefoot man that overlay the ghûls'. Elisande couldn't identify them with certainty, but Jemel could. He said they were Morakh's.

PART TWO

The Road to Release

10

A Dark Way to Glory

'There's only one way to see Rhabat for the first time,' Elisande muttered, 'and this is emphatically not it.'

'No?' Julianne countered, sweet as a nutmeat, hard as the shell around it. 'What shall we do, ride down with our eyes closed until you say we can open them?'

Elisande just snorted; Jemel said nothing at all, either to the girls or to Marron on his other side.

Marron himself could find nothing to say. Which he knew was not unusual, was indeed what they would expect. What they couldn't know was that his silence this evening had little to do with the Daughter in his blood, or with his own internal conflicts. He was simply overwhelmed by what he was seeing, as Jemel had meant them all to be, as Elisande was so perversely determined not to be.

It was two days since he'd fetched Hasan to the battle by the well: two days of travel, his friends riding with the Sharai and he walking easily before or behind them, keeping his distance both for the camels' sake and to avoid the stares and whispers of the tribesmen. The staring and the whispering had gone on regardless, he knew that, though he hid his eyes beneath the hood of a new robe; he knew also that there would be a great deal more of it in days to come, and that he couldn't avoid it all. For these two days, though, he had clung to what separation he could. He'd led when the trail was obvious, followed when it was doubtful; when they had camped last night he'd held himself apart, with only Jemel for company.

The party had kept its own distance from the Dead Waters, following the line of the shore but staying always some little way inland, where the sea was just a glimmer of light on their left and the wide and trackless Sands stretched to the horizon on their right to blend at last invisibly with the pale rim of the sky. This was Beni Rus land and they patrolled regularly, Hasan had said, to know who moved at Rhabat's back, and also to watch that no evil arose from the Waters. The duty was shared, between the tribe's commanders; he had refused to discount himself, despite his council's slow assembly and the urgency of the times. And so he had led the squadron out, and so Marron had found him . . .

Though she seemed to hate to touch her father, Elisande's magic touch worked as well on Rudel as it had on Marron; he was riding with the others, when he truly ought not to have been breathing any more. The healing had brought no sign of reconciliation between father and daughter, though; if anything it had aggravated the tensions they felt around each other, that they had been forced to come so close.

Around noon today the ground had begun to rise

steeply, as the party approached a ridge of high hills, almost mountains; they'd found a path then, a narrow way that wound to and fro across the face of the climb until it disappeared into a cleft in a sheer escarpment that showed rose-red to other eyes than Marron's, so that he knew the colour was true.

They'd passed from fierce light into black shadow, and then out into light again as the path brought them ever higher. That had set the pattern for the afternoon; the hills had risen in a series of steps which the path alternately ran over and cut through, always seeking a way that was gentle enough for the camels. Some of the gorges were smooth-walled to a point higher than Marron could reach, as though worn by torrents of water; others seemed freshly torn in the living rock, so sharp and harsh the walls were, though the path under his feet told of the traffic of ages.

At last there had been one easy stretch, out in the open once again, and nothing but sky to be seen beyond, all the great desert behind and below. Marron had heard a boy's shout at his back, and the sounds of a galloping camel; he'd trotted quickly off the path, to let Jemel pass without panicking his mount.

Jemel had ridden to the top of the rise, hobbled his camel and walked off to the north, where the slope was cut away in a sharp cliff-edge. He'd beckoned urgently to Marron, and to the girls behind him.

The other Sharai must have seen this before, many times; they stayed by the path, waiting in a tolerant group while their guests were given this first sight of Rhabat.

*

An extraordinary sight it was, though Elisande disparaged it. Marron thought she might be doing that for a purpose: to give herself an excuse to stand a little way back from the drop where Julianne could stand with her, hand in hand and unexposed to shame, here where courage counted above all.

Certainly the view did not deserve the girl's scorn. The desert lay spread out below them like a wrinkled sheet of linen, yellow and dun with age; far to the west was the ridge of mountains that closed off Outremer. To the north, Marron thought that he could just make out a jutting nail on the skyline that might be the Dancers' Pillar of Lives. By their feet, the cliff dropped sheer to cast its shadow like a mantle of mourning black across the Dead Waters far below. And, here, across more than water: for the cliff was bitten back into a wide bay, and where the sea lapped at the back wall of the bay it lapped at rock that had been shaped by more than its own tongue's lapping.

Still daylight up here, with perhaps another hour's company to be kept with the sun before it left them; down there it was dusk already, the last of the sunlight gone some time ago, though the sky would still show blue overhead and beyond the mouth of the bay.

Deep shadow couldn't deceive Marron's alien eyes. He saw how that back cliff had been worked for perhaps half its height, how natural caves had been widened and new ones cut, how steps had been carved in the cliff-face leading down to what was almost a wharf, a man-made pavement of stone to hold the waters back a little from those open caves.

It should have been a wharf, he thought, a quayside; there should have been boats tied up, ships perhaps moored out in the bay. Ropes and barrels and all the noise and chaos of a port, and those caves used for storage, for chandlery, for drinking-dens and worse . . .

But the Sharai did not drink, of course, or not in dens; and it seemed they did not sail either, or not this sea. There were no boats on the water, not a skiff, not a raft; nor was there any sign of habitation in those caves. No hint of lamplight in the darkest recesses, no whisper of sound beyond the whisper of the water on the stone.

There was a breach in the face of the cliff, though, a steep-walled gully where once a river might have run if ever there were rivers here, if ever they'd been needed to feed the sea. That would get little enough light at midday; even Marron could make nothing out within its cleft. He imagined shadows growing there like creepers, utterly undisturbed, feeding on the night-dark and blossoming by day, tangling together into dense mats of black that even his eyes couldn't pick apart . . .

Neither could he hear anything from the gully, this high up and far away. And yet this was Rhabat. Elisande had said so, and Hasan had promised they would reach it today. It took small intelligence to determine that there must be life below them somewhere, or that it must lie along that gully.

Footfalls from behind, one of the riders walking over. Hasan: Marron knew him by his breathing as much as by his step, as by Jemel's sudden stiffening beside him.

'Well, Julianne? This is the back gate into a place of splendour, and I suppose I should apologise for its shabbiness; but I never have, and by your grace I'll not do so now. God has lent it ornament enough, by laying out the whole world as a doorstep.'

'It is a very far view,' Julianne replied gravely, if a little faintly, 'though not perhaps the whole of the world. I cannot see back all the way to Marasson.'

'This is all the world that matters,' Hasan said, 'at least to me. Perhaps I will persuade you that you need no more. For now, though, we must go down; which I regret means that you must turn your back on distant hopes and ride in shadow for a while. I hope you do not mind enclosed spaces?'

For a moment, Marron thought she was going to laugh aloud. Her mouth did twitch, he thought, behind her veil, before she had control of it; and her voice bubbled a little as she said, 'No, Hasan, I do not mind enclosed spaces. Not at all. Though if you mean to shut me in a box and lower me on ropes, then . . .'

'No, lady; I said you would ride, and you shall. The way is hidden, though, and long, and the roof is low; some find it disturbing.'

'I think I can promise not to be disturbed by a low roof. I can't speak for my camel, mind . . .'

'Not many can. If she objects, we will blindfold her and I shall lead her down myself. I will not be forsworn in this, Julianne; you will ride into Rhabat as befits you, even if you must come by a tiresome road.'

'Yes – will you tell us more of this road? I had heard that there was only one way in or out of Rhabat.'

'Many people have heard that,' he said, smiling. 'Just as I have heard that there is only one way in or out of the Roq.'

'That at least is true, or would seem to be. For the moment. We left that castle as we arrived, through the main gate.' Not for want of trying another exit, Marron remembered, with a touch of chill. They should have gone through the Tower of the King's Daughter and into the land of the djinn; the way had been blocked, and all Rudel's art and understanding had not been enough to open it. Indeed, the man hadn't even tried. A minute's thought, and he had turned back. To lead them instead to the stables where he had killed Fra' Piet, where Marron had killed Aldo and others, so many others . . .

Marron remembered little of their time in the Tower, he had been in too much pain; but he did remember a great wall of blackness, barring their path through.

'Mmm. I cannot say how you will leave Rhabat, Julianne: no doubt in your own way and unannounced, as you have arrived. But when next you come, send me due word and I will meet you before the siq and lead you through, while my people throw palms before your camel's feet . . .'

'I think Sildana would like that,' she said lightly. 'For now, though, you say we must go another way. For the second time, will you tell us more?'

'Better; I will show you. Come back and mount. Sildana is her name? She is a majestic beast; white camels are said to be lucky, though I should say that it is she who has the luck, to carry you . . .'

'Would you speak to her, on that? I don't believe she sees it your way . . .'

They moved off, with Elisande behind; Marron watched them go, then glanced questioningly at Jemel, who had made no move to follow.

'I will walk down, with you. Someone will lead my camel.'

'There's no need, Jemel. Ride with your brothers.'

'I have no brothers here; I am tribeless now, and they would not acknowledge me. Besides, I am a Dancer, in my fashion,' and he showed his maimed hand, which Marron ached for.

'So?'

'So I ought not to ride.'

'You've been riding all day. You've been riding every day since you lost your finger. Haven't you?'

'Yes, of course,' smiling. 'I am not a Dancer like Morakh; where it is useful or convenient, I will ride. But you heard him,' Hasan he meant, but would not speak his name, 'the ceilings are low. Better to walk.'

'Jemel . . .'

'Marron, I am sworn to your service, and should attend you. You are the Ghost Walker, and you will not walk into Rhabat alone.'

And so he did not. He and Jemel followed the camels at a distance, over the brow of the hill. Nestled on a shelf just below they found a small temple with a domed roof, hewn crudely as it seemed from the living rock; in the cliff-face behind it was a crack, barely wide enough for a laden camel to pass through.

A Sharai in the robes of an imam was waiting for them there, with a lit torch in his hand. He gave that to Jemel, though it was Marron he was staring at; then he waved them through.

They'd gone barely a dozen paces inside before the dim daylight was cut off, with a soft thud as though a door had closed at their back.

Marron paused, and glanced behind him. The torchlight showed only bare rock closing the passage, with no sign of a doorway. Neither any sign of the Sharai; he must be the keeper of the temple, as well as of Rhabat's secret gateway.

The tunnel they stood in was wider than its entrance had been, though not by much. The ceiling was low indeed, and more roughly cut even than the walls. The camel-party had already disappeared around a bend ahead, but the sounds of its passage came back clearly; Marron heard Julianne's soft curse, and guessed that she had just learned to stoop in the saddle.

The tunnel sloped steeply downward and turned constantly as it fell within the massive escarpment, like a long and coiling hair caught within a crystal. Jemel held the torch at Marron's side, and said nothing; Marron looked about him, and found nothing to say. Walls, ceiling, floor all the same, endlessly curving, and themselves endlessly pacing with a steady, unchanging rhythm; it felt almost as though they were motionless, walking in place while the tunnel wound itself up around them.

The only relief was the girls' conversation ahead, rising to meet them:

'Elisande, how long have the Sharai been here? It must have taken decades to cut such a passage; and if what I have heard of Rhabat is true, this would have been the least of their work . . .'

'Nothing you have heard could come near the truth of Rhabat, sweet – but the Sharai did not make the least little fragment of it. The Sharai do not build. They found it, stole it, were given it.'

'Well, which?'

'All three.'

'I hope you're going to explain that.'

'No one knows truly who made it. The Sharai discovered it, centuries ago; but it wasn't empty at the time, there were people living here, occupying a little of its immensity. They might have been descendants of the original builders; some of the stories claim as much. The Sharai drove them out, and took possession.'

'As we were meant to,' Hasan's voice cut in abruptly. 'It was a gift from God, provided at a crucial time. Our tribes are disputatious, Julianne; we needed a place that belonged to none and would be accessible to all, where our leaders could meet in peace and speak to all our peoples with one voice. Rhabat is a symbol, and more. Elisande says that the Sharai do not build, and that is true; but I mean to build a nation of the Sharai, and Rhabat will be the focus of it.'

'You see?' Elisande again, cheerfully, almost laughing. 'I said, all three . . .'

At length, they heard the party ahead stop to light fresh torches. Jemel glanced uncertainly up at his own, where the flame was guttering and weakening; he said, 'I could run ahead and fetch another, bring it back . . .'

'No need,' Marron said. 'So long as there's an ember's glow to that, I can see well enough for the pair of us. Take my sleeve, if you think you'll lose me . . .'

Jemel snorted, as though there were no chance of his losing Marron, even in the uttermost dark; but he took a grip on the offered sleeve regardless.

Their light faded quickly, and even the embers died before that long march was over. But Marron could see the faintest reflection on the walls, coming back from their companions' torches, though Jemel swore that they were walking in total darkness; and he could feel the movement of the air around him, he thought he could hear its touch on the enclosing rock. He thought he could find his way down now with his eyes closed, and still hold constantly to the centre of the passage.

He told Jemel to discard the dead torch and walk with one hand brushing the wall, if he were unnerved by the dark. His friend laughed harshly and said that there were stories to frighten children, that might also frighten men of other tribes, of any tribe; the Sharai were not used to night without stars, and did not like it even in legend. But he, Jemel, would not be made afraid by a simple lack of light . . .

His other hand, though, the one that had taken a tuck of Marron's sleeve: already that hand had slipped down to fold itself around Marron's fingers. The skin was cold, but the hand was slick with sweat. Marron allowed himself a smile that Jemel would never see, and gripped tightly.

That weary walk went on and on, but had to end at last. The first sign of its ending was when the quality of the light changed, that faintest hint that Marron's eyes had been following so long. It seemed to lose colour, to become not brighter but more grey than yellow against the rose-red walls.

Then he heard the girls' voices again, which had fallen silent some time since, oppressed by all that weight of rock above and the dreary monotony of their turning path.

Julianne said, 'Is that . . .?'

'I think it is,' Elisande replied. 'I'll race you to it.'

'Do not,' Hasan said swiftly. 'That is the end of this road; but where it comes out is no place for foolishness, and you have another road to ride before your beasts can rest.'

Julianne groaned slightly, but offered no protest; to Elisande, it seemed, this was not news.

Neither to Jemel: he clearly knew exactly where they were, and what they were coming to.

Marron murmured, 'Do all the Sharai know of this way, and where it leads?'

'Not all; few. Very few, I think, beyond those few who live here. The tribes seldom come to Rhabat; and when they do, only their leaders venture far within its walls. It is said in the Sands that there is only the one way, in or out, that the Dead Waters guard where the mountains don't. Most believe that; why would they not? I know I did, until I came. We were privileged, we who rode with Hasan against the Roq; we gathered here for the blessing of an imam that he had sent for, and it was weeks before that man arrived. Weeks to wait, and a legend to explore – we went everywhere, Jazra and I, of course we did, how not?

'A child of the city showed us this, though he took us only a little way up. If the children know, then so must everyone who lives here, or who stays for any time. But it is a secret, it's hidden, that much is clear. I would not have spoken of it, outside the city.'

The light grew slowly, dimly: better than walking suddenly into hard sun, Marron thought, for Jemel's eyes that had been bathing in darkness for so long. His own eyes he thought could take any change, from black to furnace-bright, and not blink now.

The light grew, and the path turned – and stopped turning, stopped altogether at a simple square doorway that must have had the party ahead ducking low indeed. If this road had been meant for camels and their riders, then those who built it must have smiled as they worked . . .

No priest to watch over this door: one of the mounted Sharai did that duty here. Marron wondered how much of an imam he was, the man above, and how much of a guardian; Hasan had wanted another, to bless his adventure.

Jemel slid his hand free, a moment too late, perhaps, and walked out into the open. Marron followed, stepping wide to avoid the restless camel and breathing deeply to rid his lungs of the dry musty feel of the tunnel – and almost choked as they filled instead with warm wet sour air. He tasted salty bitterness on his tongue and wanted to spit, barely restrained the impulse; and so forgot to look behind him until it was too late, until he'd heard again the quiet, firm sound of a door being closed. He glanced back anyway, and saw only the Sharai on his camel sidling sideways along a wall of what seemed virgin rock, that held no sign of any doorway.

Pointless to stare, or to go closer and search: Jemel knew the secret, and so did the children here. Marron could learn it, if he were here long enough. He'd have liked to know now, to have the opportunity to slip away quietly and alone if ever he needed to, but he'd missed the chance. Instead he turned again and looked about him, and saw immediately why the air was so rank here.

He was standing on that broad flat area of pavement

they'd seen from above, between the cliff-face with its workings, its natural and man-made caves and steps, and the sea. The water lapped the rock only ten or a dozen paces from him. In this enclosed bay, it tainted the atmosphere as it had not in the open Sands. There he had smelled the salt and the stagnation of it; here its nature was tangible, and there was more to it than simple sterility. There was a foulness that caught at his throat, a threat inherent, as though something utterly evil dwelt there and permeated all its breadth and depth; he understood now why the Sharai watched it so closely, why they were so reluctant to approach it too nearly.

Why these caves were empty, uninhabited, unused; why there were no boats, although this surely must have been meant once as a quayside. There were steps along the rim of the ledge, leading down into the water; but they were deeply, darkly stained, as though that evil he could sense had saturated the pale rock they were cut from and was rising still higher, seeking slowly to invade the land.

Even now the Sharai and their camels both were visibly uneasy, shifting restlessly and casting sidelong glances at the water. Hasan was less nervous or simply more in control of himself, as befitted his rank and reputation; he was sweating, though, Marron could see and smell it on him, and there was an urgency in more than his words as he said, 'We should move on, quickly, before we lose the light here. We have no more torches . . .'

The sun was setting invisibly, behind the cliffs; far out beyond the bay, the waters were tinged with red to mark it. Where they stood was deep in shadow, must be all but dark already to those with merely mortal eyes. Hasan waited, though, for Julianne to sign that she was ready, before he led the party off.

Their route lay along the gully that Marron had noted from on high; there it would be dark indeed, and the riders must trust to their knowledge and their camels' better sight. Even the girls seemed to prefer that, though, to the water's edge; Marron heard Elisande's voice, straining to be cheerful, 'Not far now, Julianne, and just wait till you see . . .'

Jemel still chose to walk, at Marron's side. He too was full of promise, for the wonders to come. He said, 'This is not what they meant, perhaps, but the imams have always taught that the Sharai must walk in darkness for a while, for a little way, before they can come to light and joy. The Dancers say the same – we Dancers do – though we surely do not mean Rhabat.'

'Jemel,' Marron said carefully, 'you are not a Dancer.'

'Why not?' He was laughing suddenly, light-headed, bouncing on his feet as they entered the cleft and the dark of it folded itself around them. 'I have placed a stone on the Pillar, and made my oath to serve you; I have given my finger for you, in witness. How am I not a Dancer?'

You are not like Morakh, who would kill me if he could; but that was not an answer. 'I do not want your service. Only your friendship.'

'You will have to endure both. I would kill for you, Marron; I will kill, for you.'

Which was the closest he had ever come, and likely the closest he ever would, to saying that he had more reasons than the one for that public oath he had sworn, against the life of Sieur Anton. His hand said the rest, coming back to seek Marron's again and touching fingers to wrist, then knuckles to knuckles in a gesture that was both cryptic and immediate.

Marron renewed his own private oath, that he would not permit Jemel to harm Sieur Anton, nor the knight to harm the Sharai. Jemel thought that Marron would bring the two men together eventually, face to face; Marron meant never to do that, never to risk the chance. If it meant losing the one as he had lost the other already, if it meant that he must run from both, so be it. Again he regretted the loss of knowledge, that hidden gateway by the water; but drew comfort from what was certain, that Sieur Anton was a month's travel, a whole desert's width from Jemel's eager sword. The chance of war, what they both sought so keenly might yet act against him; but for now, both were safe from each other. He could only live each day, each night as it came . . .

This night came in a hurry, in a cloud of stars like a banner flung across the narrow strip of sky above the gorge; he glanced up and laughed at them, snatched for Jemel's hand and held it tight. If his friend must walk in darkness for a while, at least Marron could be his guide, though Jemel knew better than he what waited for them on the further side.

What waited was more and greater than he had imagined, almost greater than he would have believed possible, though he had seen extraordinary things.

It began quietly, unexpectedly, with trees and water: gentle water, fresh and clear and still as a glass, reflecting the night and the blaze of stars overhead. The gorge had widened abruptly, as though to make room for this long, narrow pool and its attendant trees, tall palms whose giant fronds drooped over the water's margin like hands stretching down for some touch of its purity.

There was a clear path now, more worn by use than laid out by design, though the imprint of the camels' pads suggested that it was little used these days. Marron could see barefoot tracks but few of them, and those small, to suggest that it was bold children mostly who came this far, this close to danger.

The path led between the trees and the water, to the pool's end. There the walls of the gully closed in briefly, before they opened like a tremendous gateway onto a broad valley. Here again there was water, wide and shallow, studded with boulders; to one side the land was terraced and farmed, all the way back to the louring shadow of a tremendous scarp.

Marron spared that barely a look, only to assure himself that the wonder of this place was not reflected both sides of the water. On its nearer bank, the pool pressed hard against the cliffs that hid this valley from the world around; there was a ledge of rock wide enough perhaps for five to walk abreast, no more, before the wall rose sheer.

This wall was no cliff-face, though – or no longer. As down at the abandoned waterfront, the rock had been worked by industrious hands, so long ago that even here, protected against sandstorms and rarely seeing rain, that work was so weathered that it seemed almost natural. But what had been done at the waterfront had been simple, practical; what had been done here was grandiose, extravagant, exultant almost.

See what we can do, Marron thought briefly, *we can rival the gods . . .*

Then his cynicism was overwhelmed, crushed by the brutal scale of what he was looking at; for a while he stopped thinking at all, he only stood and gaped.

From base to high crest, this entire wall of rock had been carved and hollowed into the semblance of a city. It might almost have been the work of a god, the original that man's buildings merely mocked. Unless this had been meant itself to mock those who built with common stuff, stone and brick and wood. There were separate faces here, divided by deep recesses, as though it were a street of separate houses; each had its arches, windows, pediments and pillars, all manner of decoration and ornament.

There were lights, too: great torches and braziers burned beside open doorways, lamplight showed in many of the windows.

There were people, too. Shadows moving in the lit windows, men on guard beside the braziers; men bringing more torches now, and boys running to the camels' heads, waiting while their riders dismounted and then leading the beasts away through an ornate archway. Lights there, too, and beyond it, but Marron didn't need light to tell him that the city's stables lay that way; his nose picked out the odours of stall and manger and dung-heap, his ears the sounds of restive animals.

He felt a pang for other stable-lads, one he could name and had named a friend, dead now in pain and terror; but shook it off with an effort in response to Jemel's gentle nudge.

'You should hide your eyes, perhaps . . .?'

Perhaps he should. His coming would be common knowledge soon enough, but the news should reach the tribal leaders first. He flung up his hood and lowered his head, then let Jemel draw him forward to join the rest of their party.

Elisande appeared quickly at his other side, slipping her arm through his. He might have been surprised that she'd left Julianne at such a time, at the fulfilment of her promise; he'd have expected her to be basking in it. But he stole a glimpse ahead and saw the other girl walking with Hasan, the Sharai's head almost on a level with hers while his arm gestured high and wide, pointing out this decoration or that.

'Isn't it wonderful?' Elisande breathed, for all the world as if he were not second-best. 'I spent the best part of a year here, and thought I was living in a dream the whole time. Wait till daylight, when you can see it properly, all the colours . . .'

Marron could see colours enough already, a red stain to everything, like an omen of blood to come; but he didn't want to taint her enthusiasm, or Jemel's. He tried again to dispel that sense of sorrow for what had gone, of foreboding for what was yet to be; and failed, and held instead to silence, hoping that they would think only that he was awestruck. As he was: but his awe had turned inward, now that they were here at last. He knew himself to be crucial, potentially a pivot to the world; and he felt himself to be weak, impotent almost, only a weapon for someone else's use. Even these two, gripping either arm – they would tug him this way and that, each trying to draw or persuade or force him in opposite directions. And he would inevitably go one way or the other, he would have to; and whichever way he turned there would be war and death. War would come in any case, with or without him, but he had the power to make it so much worse. And he had no power for peace, that he could see. Even his friends contended for him; they would wrestle over his bones, he thought, and over his memory when his bones were dust.

The one among his companions whom he still thought would welcome such a sight, Marron dead and a danger taken from the world, Rudel should have been walking alone – rejected by his daughter, abandoned by Julianne and discounted by Jemel. Typically, though, he wouldn't allow them to put him in that position; instead he'd made himself one among Hasan's tribesmen, laughing raucously with them, telling jokes in a Catari that matched their own for idiom and accent. Well, if his daughter had spent time here, so no doubt had he, though doubtless not the same time. Rudel had shown no signs of building bridges to the Sharai on the journey here, indeed he'd held himself quiet and apart, much like Marron, though for different reasons. He had his recovering wound to excuse himself for that, though; and now he was using all his jongleur's skills to win himself a welcome. That it was a lesson to Elisande was certain; Marron hoped it would prove to be more. Rudel had skills that Marron lacked, and for sure he had reasons to use them: a land and a people that he loved, an inheritance, a family and a position in the world. All of which Marron lacked.

That rowdy group that Rudel was so much a part of moved on along this spectacular frontage, passing the guards at some doorways with ribald jests, others in ostentatious silence. Hasan followed with Julianne, and so perforce did Marron with his two companions. He noticed that Hasan had quiet words for all the guards, and more perhaps for those whom his fellow tribesmen had ignored.

Hasan drew Julianne to a halt, though, before one particular doorway that was not only guarded but screened with an intricate lattice of wood, as were the windows above. Elisande pulled a face, and sighed loudly.

'Women's quarters,' she said. 'It's the only drawback to this place: we're supposed to know our place, and keep to it. I was young enough to get away with a lot before, but probably not now. Especially keeping company with a married woman . . .'

That was aimed at Julianne, and sharper perhaps than it was meant; she flinched, at any rate. And glanced at Hasan, and said, 'Well, if we must, we must.'

'I regret that you must,' he said. 'There are compensations, though.'

'Oh? How would you know? Prince?'

He smiled. 'I am not without women in my life, lady. I have told you that; and they tell me that there are indeed compensations. You will be well cared for.'

'To be sure,' Elisande grumbled, though without a great deal of heart to it. 'We will be fed and groomed, and cosseted even better than the camels are, though not perhaps the horses.'

'Are there horses?' Julianne demanded, so eagerly that even Elisande had to laugh at her.

'There are indeed, sweet – and yes, I'm sure that you may ride them. With a suitable escort, of course.'

'Of course.' Again, she looked to Hasan; he bowed.

'It would be a pleasure, lady. Tomorrow?'

'If you may. If you are at liberty, I would like that exceedingly. I have learned to love Sildana, but a camel is still a camel; a horse is . . .' Words seemed to fail her.

'A horse?' Hasan suggested.

'Exactly so. There is a difference.'

'Indeed there is. Hooves, a mane, no hump . . .'

'And a temperament, rather than a temper. Prince, you're mocking me, but I can endure it, if I am promised two things. No, three.'

'And they are—?'

'A ride with you in the morning, early, for which I already have your word; a meeting with my father tonight, if he can be found; and a bath. Immediately. Please?'

'The first I am sworn to, as you say. The second – well, I would never like to speak for the movements or choices of the King's Shadow, but I will move the stars in their courses to discover him, if I must. The third, though, that is beyond my powers. Alas, I dare not cross this threshold; and if I did, my orders would be so much wasted air. I have no authority among the women.'

'Julianne, he's teasing you. There will be a bath, I promise.'

'Oh, bless you. I haven't felt clean since we left Bar'ath Tazore.'

'Sweet, you haven't *been* clean since we left Bar'ath Tazore. But the Sultan's hammam is a bowl of cold water and no tent for shelter, next to the baths of Rhabat. Come on, if you're so urgent. Can't you smell the steam?'

Marron could; there was warmth and fragrance waiting in the shadows beyond the screen, aromatics and unguents and oils. Food, too, a great deal of food, and cooling drinks. It was the bath he envied, though. His own skin was parched and roughened by too many days of sand and wind. He could smell himself and the others of his party, more strongly even than the sweet and spicy remedies that awaited the girls.

A shadow moved behind the screen, a woman appeared, robed and veiled as the girls were; she beckoned, and as they went to her Hasan called after them, 'Tell Sherett that I send you to her with a strict command from her lord, that she take particular care of you . . .'

'Prince,' Julianne returned smartly, 'I thought that you had no authority among the women?'

'Lady, I do not. She will snort at it, and bring you thorns to scrub your backs . . .'

Still laughing to himself, Hasan beckoned the others on. He brought them past one doorway, past another and to a third, where the fat pillars that held up an elaborate pediment were only half-cut from the rock behind, and that had been left natural and rough. Unless it had been deliberately roughened, the art of looking natural . . .

'You read the message, Rudel?' Hasan said, suddenly sober. 'Unfinished, but yet strong.'

'I have read it before, Hasan. Believe me, I never doubted it.'

'You are a wise man. And my guest, for tonight at least. As are you all,' and he turned to face Marron and Jemel, throwing his arms wide. 'This is our house, the house of my tribe, when we are here; and you are welcome to it. I must apologise, that we do not pamper ourselves as the women do; we keep desert customs, and live simply. But what we have is yours to share. Come in and wash, and eat . . .'

Rudel bowed, and led the way inside. Marron moved to follow, but checked himself when Jemel paused.

'Will you welcome a tribeless man?' his friend asked stiffly.

'Of course – if that man will accept my welcome.' There was a moment where they simply gazed at each other, where Marron could not read the expression of either one. Then Hasan added in a softer voice, 'Such a thing could happen to any of us, Jemel. As other things can happen: the death of a friend, a strong man's arm to keep you from dying at his side. Enter. I cannot give you peace, but the peace of my roof I can; I know you will not violate it. Besides, how could I refuse hospitality to the chosen companion of the Ghost Walker? You do me honour.'

Oh, it was complex, the look on Jemel's face as he nodded and stepped forward. Marron went with him, wondering more simply whether there had ever been a choice, and if so, whether it had been he who had made it.

A bath would have been welcome, but a ewer of cool water in a warm room was plenty enough for Marron; it was what he'd been accustomed to, life-long. Even the Ransomers' cold plunges had seemed a luxury.

He stripped and splashed, dunked his whole head in the ewer and came up gasping, pushed away Jemel's fussing over the savage scar on his shoulder – and was startled to be pushed back in his turn.

The shock of a wet head seemed to have numbed his

earlier depression, if not washed it away entirely. He reacted forcefully, wrestling the spare, lithe Sharai back into a corner. It was hard to use only his own strength, and not the Daughter's; but he made the effort, straining against his squirming friend and laughing with him, until Rudel's voice called them sternly to order.

'Boys, this again is neither the time nor the place for horseplay. If you don't understand that, be still, and listen to those who do . . .'

Jemel pulled a face, and straightened slowly. The arm that had been tight around Marron's throat relaxed, but stayed hanging loosely around his shoulders; when he made to move away, it tightened just a little, just enough to hold him.

Marron turned to face Rudel, who was washing himself briskly; the older man went on, 'There is a council of grave importance met here; this you know. It could mean full war between our peoples, Jemel, yours and mine.' His eyes and voice and meaning all slid over Marron, awarding him no place, no loyalty. 'It likely will, though I will do my utmost to prevent it. Hasan knows why I am come; that is important to the council, and they will send for me soon, if only to welcome me here. They can do no less, when he of all men has already given me guest-rights. It was a lucky chance that had you finding him, Marron; other captains might have been less accommodating. However, Hasan will also have told the council of you. That is more important yet. They might simply have tolerated my presence here, allowed me my say and ignored it. They cannot do that with you. They will want to see you, immediately by my guess; which means that you

must be ready. Calm, and controlled – Sharai elders give
no respect to wild youth. You are a changeling, your very
existence defies their prophets; they will want to ask you
where you stand in this conflict, and you must have an
answer prepared.'

'I stand with my friends,' Marron said simply.

'That is good – but not good enough. You have friends
in both camps, and—'

What more he would have said was interrupted, as
Hasan came into the room. He had washed elsewhere,
there was still water in his beard; he had also changed into
clean robes, and he carried three more across his arm.

'We can offer you no softness,' he said, 'but comfort at
least lies in our gift. Comfort against the skin,' and his eyes
barely touched on Marron, on his two visible wounds, the
one well healed and the other never to be let heal, 'and
comfort within it too. If you are ready, will you come to
meat?'

Jemel seemed to startle for an instant; Rudel ignored
him, somehow assuming a dignity that belied his nakedness. 'Our thanks, Hasan. We are quite ready, and will be
with you immediately.'

He took the robes, and distributed them; as soon as
Hasan was gone, he added, 'I *told* you, Jemel – the situation
here overrides all common custom. Hurrying a guest is
nothing; be grateful that the council is granting us time to
eat. Though that is a double-edged gift. They will be using
the time to debate between themselves, which we cannot.
Come, dress yourselves; and remember that you will be the
focus of all eyes tonight, Marron. You wear their clothes,
you carry their prophecy in your blood, but you are not one

of them; they will be confused, and tense. Jemel will not mind it, if I say that the Sharai are a hot-headed people, and quick to take offence. Some will find you an offence however you act, but do your best. Above all, eat, even if you have no appetite for it; to refuse, or just to make a pretence at eating, would insult Hasan and all his tribe. That we cannot afford.'

Marron might have taken offence himself, at being addressed as though he were a child; he decided it was too much trouble. Instead, he simply made a point of allowing Jemel to act the servant for once: to help him into a robe and tie it properly, to ensure that he wore sword and knife as he ought, even to push his fingers through Marron's wet and tangled hair in an effort to persuade it into some semblance of neatness. They had been given no time to shave, but among these people beards were commonplace, a sign of manhood; the soft stubble on his chin would be if anything a point in his favour.

Jemel himself took a little extra time over his own robe, cutting off those small knots and tassles that bespoke Hasan's tribe. 'It is a compliment for you, for both of you, to wear their dress; from me, it would be an insult.'

Rudel didn't dispute that. Indeed, his patient waiting seemed to applaud Jemel's caution, if caution it were. Marron thought that actually, it was pride; he might be Saren no longer, but he would still not appear by choice in the insignia of any other tribe.

He was ready, though, as swiftly as he might be. Rudel gathered them together with his eyes, nodded once with a wary satisfaction that was yet a reminder and a warning, repeated it unnecessarily in words, 'Be very careful tonight,

in words and manners; more than your own lives hang on
this,' and led them out.

The outer walls were bare rock that bore the illusion of a
palace; inside it was plain that the Sharai at least did not
deal in illusion, even if their predecessors did. The rooms
were high and square, the doorways arched and graceful,
but the occupants truly did inhabit them as though they
were deep in the Sands, and in their tents.

There was no decoration on the walls, only rough
patches and signs of breakage to show where there might
have been once, before the imams came to purify the place.
Marron and his companions walked barefoot as their hosts
did, on sandy stone; they followed a lad with a lamp across
a broad hall and up a turning flight of stairs, into a long
room with windows looking out across the valley.

In the centre of the room the floor at least was covered,
in layers of patterned rugs. There sat Hasan, the men of his
patrol and perhaps a dozen more; they were grouped in a
circle around bowls of boiled meat and platters of bread,
but none of them was eating. Jemel sucked air through his
teeth, as though to say that things were not done such a
way among the Saren, that no guest should be made to feel
his hosts were waiting for him.

Space was made for them, to Hasan's either side; the
place of honour, on his right, he might perhaps have meant
for Marron by his smile, but Rudel took it. Hasan's face
didn't twitch; Rudel was the elder, after all, and should
ordinarily take precedence. A hand beckoned Marron to
the left instead. As he settled himself on soft wool over
hard rock, Jemel slid in between him and the next

tribesman, another kind of padding altogether: even more kindly meant, just as unnecessary. Marron could have sat on stone all day and all night, and never felt a moment's cramp; he could have sat all day and all night next that man and never had a word of speech from him, desert manners and a guest's welcome notwithstanding. Hasan was still the only one of these who'd broken his silence with Marron, or Marron's with him. Deliberate isolation had played a part in that, but only a part; the tribesmen were equally complicit. Marron supposed that in his days as a Ransomer, he might have felt as tongue-tied or simply as wary in the presence of a Church Father, or perhaps of a saint. It was hard to picture himself as either one, but the comparison came close: a saint reborn, perhaps, might be closer yet. A Patric saint in a Catari body, now that was almost exact, except that no saint he'd ever heard of had had anything like the powers that he possessed . . .

Hasan made an open-handed gesture, politely to his right and then to his left; Rudel reached for a piece of meat, and Marron copied him.

They might keep desert customs in this house, but it was no stringy desert goat that they were served. It was mutton, pink and tender and flavoured with the salty herbs the sheep had fed on. The bread was soft and fresh, the water that was passed around had a pleasant mineral tang to it; for a wonder, eating was no effort. Even Jemel stopped watching him, after a minute or two.

Chewed bones were flung onto a platter that had held bread; the meat-bowl emptied quickly, and was not refilled. Even Hasan seemed a little embarrassed about that, breaking off his easy talk of life in Rhabat and life in the Sands to dip crusts into the juices that remained and pass them to his guests, right and left and further left. Jemel hesitated only a moment, before he took his portion.

Rudel was first to sit back, to wipe his fingers and beard on a linen napkin that Hasan handed to him; then he gave that across to Marron, a clear signal, not to be declined. The meal was over, and Marron could almost regret it for its own sake, let alone his dread of what would follow.

Jemel took the napkin from him, cleaned hands and mouth and passed it on around the circle. Hasan used it last, tossed it into the empty bowl and stood up.

'If you will come,' he said, again to all three of them, 'there are sheikhs and elders here who would be glad to meet with you. This haste is not of my choosing, believe me, but . . .'

'The time dictates its own urgency,' Rudel replied. 'If there were never any other lesson to be learned in the Sands, they would teach us that. And I too am impatient to speak with your council.'

'Ah, Rudel, you are too late to deflect my disgrace; I will not blame my guests for my own discourtesy. But thank you for the attempt. This way, then. They are waiting in the Chamber of Audience . . .'

Out into the night again, and along to another guarded doorway. That brought them directly into a vast hall, lit only at its further end, where perhaps two dozen men were sitting on a carpeted divan.

This place was well named, Marron thought; it wasn't only his unnaturally sharp ears that caught the murmur of those men's voices as they entered, to judge by the way Jemel stiffened suddenly, the way he stalked at Marron's side. Rudel was too well schooled to show any reaction, but Marron thought that he too was listening intently to the muttered words that reached them. Something about the intricate way the chamber's roof was carved meant that the slightest whisper was channelled and amplified, to reach even the furthest corner of that tremendous space. He reminded himself to speak no secrets here, and only wished that he need not speak at all.

No chance of that: it was of him that the waiting men were speaking already, and in no terms of welcome.

'He is an abomination, we cannot permit . . .'

'He exists; we have to deal with what is.'

'He could cease to exist. This should never have happened, but it is not too late to correct.'

Small wonder that Jemel was so tense, walking with his hand on his sword-hilt now. Marron touched his elbow; when that had no effect, he took Jemel's wrist and drew it forcibly away, held it tightly. Let them see that, as he walked into the lamplight. Perhaps it would help; it could at least do little harm in such company, in such a mood.

They were lords of many different tribes, these men. He could read that much by their subtleties of dress, without knowing what each fold or adornment signified. Such a meeting would always be angry, he thought, each man would bring generations of wrongs and slights to it. Perhaps he should be glad to give a focus to that smouldering heat. Marron was incidental here, though they would not and could not see him that way. Rudel's mission was what mattered, the chance to talk peace instead of war;

they might hear him the clearer, if they had burned out their resentments on another target first.

He set himself beside Rudel, on the floor before the divan, and drew Jemel up close. Hasan said simply, 'Lords, here are the guests of my house, to hear your joint welcome to our place of council.' Then he stepped to one side. There were messages here, more than the obvious. He was of course telling the council that these newcomers all stood under his protection, which was or should be potent; at the same time, he was telling the companions that although he might have summoned the council, he was not a part of it. He had said before that he was no prince among his people; he could be no more than a supplicant, as they were.

When the council spoke, whosoever voice it spoke through – and that would have been a debate worth hearing, Marron guessed, with no one tribe willing to accede priority to another – it should speak first to Rudel, as being so obviously the eldest and already known here. But the talk had all been of Marron, of the Ghost Walker; perhaps it would be he who attracted first attention . . .

He scanned the faces before him – old men and younger men, though none so young as Hasan; bearded and clean-shaven, scarred by war and blemished by old sickness – and saw no hint of welcome anywhere among them, only hard dark eyes and grim expressions.

Even so, he was startled when the first reaction to their arrival was no word at all, but a dagger thrown.

A dagger casually tossed, rather, to skitter towards them across the rock of the floor, spinning as it came.

It was a gesture of utmost contempt, as he read it; and he

was doubly startled when it stopped not at Rudel's feet and not at his, but at Jemel's.

That was no accident, no miscast; so much was clear in his friend's reaction. The proud toss of his head, the glare, the instant tightening of every muscle and the leap of hand towards sword-hilt, that Marron fought to restrain: another message had been sent and received, though it bewildered him.

'We did not send for the renegade,' a slow voice said. One man moved: a swarthy man in his middle years, burly in his body, one of the few who were beardless. He rose to his feet and went on, 'He ventures where he was not invited; let him pay the price of it.'

Hasan strode quickly back, to stand at Jemel's other side. 'My lords, Jemel takes his rice with me tonight. I understood that you wished to meet all my new-come guests; if I have misunderstood, the fault is mine and not Jemel's. You will not dishonour me, I know, by offering offence to one of mine . . .'

'Is he yours, Hasan? Well, perhaps — though his robe does not say so. I say that he was ours, he was of the Saren, but he has turned from us. If the Beni Rus have taken to welcoming the tribeless, that of course is their affair; but in that case he should keep to your kitchens. He disgraces this assembly; he disgraces me. If he denies that, let him return my blade.'

That was a challenge, plain and simple; Marron had to call on the strength of the Daughter to hold Jemel still, to save him answering it. Swiftly, before that silent struggle became too obvious, he said, 'My lord, Jemel has turned from his tribe, so much is true; he has done so on my account,' which was almost true, he hoped true enough to pass, 'and stands here with me, as my man.'

'Does he so? Hasan, show his left hand.'

Before Hasan could move, Jemel jerked back his sleeve and held his hand up high, to show them all where his smallest finger was missing.

There was a hiss of talk on the divan, too many voices speaking at once to be clear even in this space; the words 'Sand Dancer' came down, though, from several throats. More than one dagger was drawn.

Eventually, one strong voice cut across the whispers.

'The Sand Dancers are outcasts, of their own choice. They are forbidden Rhabat, with good reason; they bring nothing but strife, here where we strive for peace between our peoples. The penalty is death, for those who break this law.'

'My lords,' Rudel, speaking at last and too late, 'this boy is not a Sand Dancer. He lost his finger in a fight we had with them; a coincidence, nothing more.'

'Let him speak for himself.' That was the Saren sheikh again. 'He has a tongue, I presume – or did he lose that too? Or perhaps the courage to use it?'

'I have a tongue,' Jemel said softly, against the sudden silence. 'I have used it to forswear my tribe and my allegiance; I have used it again, to make new oaths. I have stood atop the Pillar of Lives and set a stone there, where I swore my life to the Ghost Walker. My finger was given in support of that oath; if Rudel says otherwise, he lies. Make of it what you will.'

'Out of his own mouth,' a grunt of satisfaction from the sheikh. 'Shall it be my sword that takes him here, or shall we send him to die out of our sight and cognisance, as he deserves?'

'Neither one,' Marron said hotly, choking almost on a flare of anger. 'You know what I am; I have said he is mine, and he confirms it. I will not give him to you, for this nonsense nor for any true offence. If you try to take him from me, beware.'

That brought all the council to its feet. Scimitars scraped from their sheaths; Rudel groaned audibly. Marron stooped, to scoop up the dagger from where it still lay at Jemel's feet. Another moment and he would have used it, he would have cut his arm and opened a portal, dragged Jemel through by force if need be to avoid his friend's death or his own, or anyone's.

But in that moment of delay, there was a ripple of new light at his back that threw his shadow forward; and a new voice yet, a clarion voice that stilled every other in the chamber, that needed none of the arts of that place to make itself heard.

'What is the trouble here, my lords? I came to seek my daughter; and I find you all in uproar, which is nothing unusual when Julianne is about, but I do not see her here . . .'

Marron dared not leave hold of Jemel, but he risked one quick glance over his shoulder. He saw a single man, a small man in a green robe with his white hair ruffled around his balding crown, as though he had been disturbed from sleep. He held an oil-lamp in his hand, and looked almost foolish as he blinked about the hall.

11

The Unexpectedness of Men

Julianne had bathed slowly, had eaten quickly – with the promise that there would be more food later should she want it, that there was and always would be more food, more water or else fruit-juice or sherbet if she preferred it, more of anything and everything she wanted – and now she was exploring, while Elisande laughed at her heels.

'Oh, be quiet,' she grumbled, 'it's not funny. You've been here before; I haven't. I didn't dog you while you were crawling into every corner of the Roq, did I?'

'Only because you were too prim to leave your room without a man's permission.'

'Nothing to do with being prim!' It was too true for comfort, all the same; and there was nothing conveniently to hand to throw at Elisande, in lieu of a rebuttal.

In fact it was still true, that she was always ready – perhaps too ready – to conform to local custom, however much it irked her; she was always reluctant – and her friend would certainly say too reluctant – to challenge convention without cause. Like everything that had gone to make her what she was, it came down in the end to her father's training. *Work within the system, child, don't work against it; you'll get a lot further, and achieve a lot more along the way.* That had been after an argument over a new harness for her pony, she remembered, when she was very small. All the boys were using them, so she'd demanded one to match; her father had flatly refused. And had gone on refusing, despite tears and tantrums and monumental sulks. In the end she'd thought it through, washed her face and changed her dress and gone in frills and flounces to sit on the knee of her favourite adoptive uncle. She'd wheedled, little-girl style, and the harness had been delivered the next morning.

She'd thought her father would be angry; instead he had applauded, added a new saddle that he'd had waiting, and turned the whole affair into a lesson for life.

Her father's lessons clung. Even now: she was exploring, yes, and unchaperoned, yes (except by Elisande, who most emphatically did not count) – but only within the bounds of the women's quarters, and she had been careful to ask licence even for so much unchecked wandering.

Whether she'd heard Hasan's crying her name, or whether she took it on herself to welcome all the new arrivals to her domain, Julianne hadn't asked and had no way to guess; but they'd got no further than the hallway behind the screen before another woman had come lightly down a curving flight of stairs to greet them.

'Thank you, Tourenne,' she'd said in brisk dismissal to the girl who'd brought them this far, 'I will see to our guests' comfort now.'

The girl had dipped her head submissively – in

Marasson she would have curtsied, Julianne had thought —
and whisked herself away without a word.

'I am called Sherett,' which had been no surprise at all,
'and I am wife to Hasan of the Beni Rus.'

She'd worn her hood thrown back with her black hair
loose and swinging heavily to her waist, no veil; her face
was strong and striking, as determined as her character.
She was in her middle twenties, Julianne had guessed,
and she carried innate authority as easily as her husband.
Likely she always had; it wasn't his rank that had invested
her.

Elisande had pulled off hood and veil with a huff of
relief, rumpled her flattened hair and said, 'I am Elisande
d'Albéry, granddaughter to the Princip of Surayon; this is
Julianne de Rance, daughter to the King's Shadow.' Then,
abandoning formality, she'd gone on, 'I think we met
before, Sherett, when I was living here a year since, or a
little longer. You weren't married then. You rode a black
mare and went hawking without permission, without an
escort, which had you in trouble with your menfolk . . .'

A laugh had greeted that. 'It did; but it achieved its purpose, it attracted the attention of Hasan. Unless it was the
horse that caught his eye. But I remember you, of course,
Lisan; and welcome back. Our house is yours, as it ever
was. My lady . . .?'

Slowly, Julianne had detached her veil and put back her
hood. She'd felt herself surveyed, summed up, weighed and
measured almost; and had returned that proud gaze
proudly, although she'd been able to feel every one of the
days and nights of hard travel and stress marked out on her
sore and filthy skin. When she'd pulled her own hair out

from under her robe, she'd heard the soft scatter of dry sand falling to the floor at her back.

Her wince had made Sherett laugh again. Not unkindly, but it had still left Julianne caught between a bristle and a blush. Which she'd resented, just enough to say, 'We have a message for you, from your lord . . .'

'I heard it,' which had answered the question only in part; Julianne still thought she would have been there and greeting them regardless. 'Pay him no mind; he is a man, and therefore foolish. Very foolish, in his dealings with women. But he listens to me, which is rare.'

'And you to him . . .?'

'On occasion. When he speaks sense – which is rare. Now come, Lisan, my lady—'

'Julianne. No more than that, please, Sherett.' Despite herself, she had swiftly lost hold of her resentment; this was a woman to deal with fairly. And to listen to, and learn from . . .

'Julianne, then. Come, you have sand in your hair and sand in all your joints, I know. We have oils to ease them and water to bathe dry eyes, sticks to work the grit out of your teeth. No doubt you can wash each other's backs, you will not need my thorns . . .'

In fact Sherett had joined them in the hammam, which had proved to be a series of chambers that varied from sticky-warm to roasting, with a shockingly cold plunge-pool to follow; as promised, it put to shame the Sultan's simple steam-room.

'The men hear rumours of this,' Sherett had said, almost chanting the words in rhythm with her strong fingers as they'd worked aromatic oil deep into Julianne's back, 'and they mock us for it; but it is simple to achieve, where there are braziers, rocks and water. Why make a virtue of denial, why live as paupers amongst such riches?'

'They think you will grow too soft to face the Sands,' Elisande had grunted, from where she'd lain stretched out on a shelf, half asleep in the seductive heat. *Too dry to sweat*, she'd called herself; too thin, Julianne thought rather. All her friend's bones were showing; and she'd been eating rapaciously since she came back from the djinn's country. She and Marron both, which had only made it more evident. They must have starved, living for a week on what little food one girl could carry. Elisande denied it, but Marron had infected her, Julianne thought, with more than his lack of interest in food . . .

'They had better not say so to me.'

'I don't suppose they'd dare,' Julianne had smiled gently, 'but they would think it in any case.'

'Of course they would; they are men. Worse, they are Sharai men; they think we were all born to suffer.'

'Oh, and were we not?'

'Perhaps. Perhaps so. Lie still, this suffering skin I can at least attend to . . .'

After the bath, the meal: fine cuts of tender meat, fresh fruit and bread and the miracle of clean, clear water. Julianne had eaten lightly, Elisande quickly; and then Sherett had given laughing permission for them to wander as they would. She laughed often, this confident woman; thinking of her man, Julianne was not surprised.

'Of course; this is your own home, for as long as you stay

with us. Go where you will, we have no secrets here. You do not need me for guide, and there's more pleasure in exploring alone. Besides, Lisan will remember every corner of this house. Ask for me, if there is anything you want.'

Only one thing Julianne wanted, that she did not have and hoped she might obtain; and that she had asked for already. 'A message may come, from my father . . .'

'If it comes, I will find you, Julianne. If it comes not – well, he is a man. A fine man, who may deserve his daughter; but a man none the less, and they are playing men-games in the council . . .'

Games which could lead to war – but Sherett knew that, for all her seeming scorn. Julianne had nodded, had caught hold of her friend's hand and led her away without another word.

Every passageway was rugged with long runners of that same hardwearing midnight-blue stuff from which the Sharai made their robes. For these rugs it had been plaited into ropes, which were coiled and interknotted and sewn together into fantastic designs. Julianne's eyes saw them vaguely, in the shifting shadows of the lamp she carried; her bare feet felt their textures exactly, and she delighted in them.

All the walls in passageways or chambers were hung with colour, bright banners of gold and green and red, some embroidered with the unspoken name of God, Elisande said, or else with a tribal sigil.

'If the Sharai can make such as this,' Julianne asked, fondling the silken swathes, 'why do they dress so drably? Oh, I grant you, these are practical in the desert,' and her hand plucked a little fitfully at the fresh robe she wore, that she'd been so grateful for an hour earlier, 'and thrifty no doubt, for a poor people; but here, where they dress their walls so gaily . . .'

'The women do the work,' Elisande said, touching her hand to the nearest embroidery with a gesture that was surprisingly reverent, that she must have learned by watching, 'but they do not weave the silk; they trade for that, with caravans from the east. These robes are traditional, laid down by centuries of custom; they believe that this is God's own colour, the colour of the sky behind the stars. It marks them out for what they are, a chosen people, chosen to live in a harsh land where weaker blood would perish. They are not a poor people, Julianne, never make that mistake; they have great wealth in store, here and in their tribal lands. They live in poverty by their own choice, because they think that life enriches them.'

'And yet they fight over goats and camels . . .'

'Oh, the Sharai will fight over anything. Including Outremer, unless my father and yours can dissuade them from it.'

That was a cold reminder, that they were not here to play; a reminder too of her father's supposed danger, that she had fled her new-made husband and a promised life of comfort to forestall. *Fled from trouble into trouble*, she thought wryly, thinking of Hasan; and shook her head determinedly. Her father would come to her when he would, if he would. They could talk then, have a *long* talk, about a great many things in this changing world. *If* he came. That was as it always had been, a question without a dependable answer. She had lived all her life in doubt of him, and been constantly surprised; he came unexpectedly and left without warning, and that was her definition of a father.

Which was why, when they eventually did have that talk, she was not going to apologise for any choice she'd made since his last dramatic departure. If he left her alone, she must act alone; and tonight she was going to play explorer, whether or not she ought . . .

She plunged through a heavy tapestry that hung across a doorway, and found herself in a room of chests and bags. Opening one at random, she pulled out a rich velvet robe – storm-grey, like Imber's eyes sometimes, when he was unhappy; she stifled the thought, before it could stifle her.

'I told you,' Elisande said from the doorway. 'Great wealth, but they don't make a show of it.'

'Then what is the point of it, what's it for? Why have such things' – and there were many of them, that her busy fingers found: dresses and chains and bangles, gold and silver plate in the chests where she flung them open in frustrated exposure – 'if they only hide them away?' Dresses were made to be worn and plates to use, by her lights, or they lost all purpose.

'They are to have, to keep. To possess. This land allows them little permanence; they have to keep moving, and take with them only what they can carry or feed. They set great store by ownership. Of their herds, which is why they raid for them; to steal from an enemy is to wound him worse than a sword-blade can. And of their women, which is why they keep them in seclusion. Though they are hardly alone in that. Julianne, why did your father have you raised in Marasson, when he is King's Shadow in Outremer?'

'Oh, I was a bargaining counter,' a possession, yes, a game-piece in a complex plan. 'He always meant to marry me where I could be most use, within the Kingdom: to make peace with a restless lord, to shift the balance of power, to strengthen a bond that was weak. Whatever made most sense to him, when I came of age. He thought it would be better if I was kept apart till then; he said it would protect me from the intrigues of the court, no man could use me or threaten me if I was a thousand miles away. I think there was more to it, though. If I came to Outremer as an innocent, I would be more pliable to his will; and also it prevented me from forming any attachment of my own, of course, which might have proved a terrible inconvenience.' *Oh, Imber . . .*

'Instead of which,' a quiet dry voice spoke at their back, 'you have found your own way to inconvenience me.'

Elisande gasped, and whirled around; Julianne was deeply proud of herself, that she did neither. She turned slowly, swept into the best courtly curtsey that she could manage in a Sharai robe, and rose laughing to say, 'You cannot be here, it is most utterly forbidden . . .!'

Here he was, though, her father: as ever appearing unannounced, when and where he was least looked for.

He looked well, she thought, tanned and fit, dressed simply in her favourite green. As she always was recently, she was momentarily surprised to find herself looking down at him; she had spent too little time in his company to grow accustomed to that, or else she always built him up bigger in her memory than he was in body.

He examined her with no less candour, and nodded a grudging satisfaction. All he said, though, was, 'You've grown thinner, Julianne – unless you've simply stretched a little further. Either one was unnecessary. The dress suits you.'

'I think the life suits me, father,' she said blithely. 'May I make you known to Elisande d'Albéry, granddaughter to the Princip of Surayon?' She used the same form that her friend did, always; she was never *daughter to Rudel.*

'I know who she is, girl,' her father grunted. Of course he knew, he knew everything; that was another definition of fathers. 'And her lineage. She's even thinner than you are. If that's some new fashion among the young, you should forswear it, both of you.'

But then he bowed, and smiled; took Elisande's hand and kissed it for all the world as though he could never behave other than gentlemanly, and said, 'I am a friend of your grandfather's, and of your father's; I hope I can be a friend to you too. Call on me, for any service you choose. I could never deny beauty.'

Elisande blushed, to Julianne's high delight. She recovered quickly, though, glancing over and saying acidly, 'Now *that's* what I call a father. He should give lessons.' Then, back to him again, 'Tell us, though – how did you get in here? Past the guards, and past Sherett too, which I think would be harder? No man is allowed in the women's quarters, not anyone, not ever . . .'

'It's no good, Elisande,' Julianne interrupted her. 'Never ask him a question beginning with "how", he'll give you no useful answer. Just an enigmatic smile and something that sounds like a quotation, only he turns out to be quoting himself. He'll tell you why, he'll talk to you for hours, why this and why that; but how is always his big secret. And this isn't worth wasting your breath on. He comes, he goes; that's all. He always has done. Nothing more to say.'

He smiled, enigmatically enough for anyone, and bowed to her for the compliment of her understanding. This time she didn't curtsey in response, she only watched the mockery and thought how mock it was. He had always been a serious man, though often and often she had seen him cloak that with frivolous manners or a foolish smile; it seemed to her suddenly that the core of him lay closer to the surface these days, and so the cloak was correspondingly gaudy. Like his coming here to the women's house, however it was that he had managed that: there was no point to it, except to add a fragment to his legend. The man who went where he would, heedless of bar or custom – but he could as easily have had her fetched to his own quarters, where they could have been comfortable and cosed together half the night, sharing journeys and anxieties and memories and more . . .

Instead he was here, and she thought that this would have to be a hasty meeting conducted in whispers. She was a little surprised, that he would think the adventure worth the risk; but he was after all her father, and surprising her was his especial interest.

Then the tapestry over the door billowed and was swept aside, and her heart sank; Sherett stepped through with a tray, and her heart plummeted. They were discovered already, no chance even for that secret and rapid exchange of views. She wondered what the penalty was, for a man who broke so strict a sequestration . . .

Sherett smiled brightly at the girls, somehow contriving not to see the man who stood so close by her elbow. 'I thought you two might enjoy a little *jereth*, to celebrate your safe arrival here.'

Julianne's father took the tray from her, playing the invisible gentleman; she added, 'No need to hurry. You will find us all in the kitchens, when you tire of your own company. Elisande knows the way.'

And then she was gone. The tapestry fluttered and fell still, while Julianne was still gaping at the place where she had been.

'Now that is a sensible woman,' her father said cheerfully, setting the tray down on a convenient chest. 'A better choice for Hasan than his first two wives; I told him so, indeed, while he was still considering the matter. I have high hopes of Sherett.'

Julianne said nothing, only watching as he poured out small measures of *jereth*. The jug was fine work, chased silver of a quality to outshine the plate inside the chests. The goblets matched the jug, and there were three of them on the tray.

He passed the first to Elisande; she took it gravely, with a little bob and, 'Thank you, sir. Oh – what am I to call you, please? If I say "sir" you have to call me "my lady", and I can't abide that. And "Shadow" is ridiculous, but if you have another title I've never heard it . . .'

'I renounced my titles,' he said, 'when the King appointed me his Shadow. My name is Coren.'

'Coren. Is it? I like that,' she said artlessly, playing the giddy girl with all the art she could muster.

He smiled gently, entirely undeceived; gave a goblet to Julianne and took the other for himself, saluted them both briefly, sipped and said, 'So. Tell me, then, everything that you have wrought or seen since I left you, Julianne, on the road to the Roq.'

So they did: they did it between them, telling their individual parts where their stories diverged and sharing the tale where they had shared in its shaping. If Julianne kept anything back, it was only trivial matter after all, what she was sure her father would dismiss as trivial; if Elisande did, there must still be secrets that girl had not yet told to her friend.

They told of their meeting on the road, and of their meeting with the djinni; of Marron and Sieur Anton, of Marshal Fulke and his call to arms, of Rudel's coming and the rescue of Redmond from the cells. They told how the Preceptor had sent them on towards Elessi, and how they had met the Barons Imber along the way; how they had fled, had encountered first the 'ifrit and then Jemel; how they had been caught and brought back, how Julianne had been married that same day. Neither said anything of the night that followed, how she had slept not with Imber but with Elisande. They tried with inadequate words to describe what had happened in the Tower of the King's Daughter, how they had collected the Daughter and been balked when they tried to go through to the land of the djinn; it was simpler but no easier to say what had happened after, when they had finally escaped the castle by means of Marron's ignorance and fury.

Their journey since, their separate journeys were swiftly covered. Much of what they'd said, perhaps most, Julianne was sure her father had known already; he showed no sign of that, though, listening in silence largely, his occasional questions only for clarity's sake where their tales disagreed.

'Well,' he said at last, 'you have at least married the man I chose for you, Julianne, though you seem to have tried your utmost to avoid it.'

'The djinni . . .' she said helplessly.

'Yes, the djinni. I have met your Djinni Khaldor, more than once; it takes more interest than the rest of its kind in the doings of mortal men. Even so, such an intervention is unusual. Unprecedented, I am inclined to say, though who knows the whole history of the djinn? It spoke to both of you, you say . . .'

'And sent us both here,' Elisande confirmed. 'Ultimately.'

'Ultimately, yes. Have the Sharai pestered you with questions, Elisande, as it predicted?'

'They have not. Although we've not been here half a day, yet; and it didn't say "pester". It said the questions would be a gift. I don't understand what it meant.'

'The djinn are always elliptical, but very seldom wrong; I think you may depend on the questions. Whether you would be wise to answer them is another matter. Until I know what they are, I cannot say. Enough, for now. We will talk again. Julianne, I must find some way to return you to your husband; I am afraid it will not be a happy homecoming, there has been too much damage done already, but between us we may contrive to mend the worst of it. I still have some respect for your diplomacy.'

If none for her wilfulness; so much passed unsaid, but not unnoted. 'The djinni said that you would be in danger . . .'

'I am grateful for your concern, but I am always in

danger. You know that. Less so here, frankly, among our enemies than I would be in Outremer, with friends. And Outremer's danger is great; I would risk much, more than my own life, to save the Kingdom. I wish Redmond were here, though. The Sharai respect old warriors; they respect my master, but not especially me. Nor Rudel – he has fought, but never under his own banner as a prince of his people. Spies and guisards command no respect at all. They will listen to him, but not be swayed. Without Redmond, the burden falls to me; so I cannot listen to your djinni's warning, even if I believed it to matter.'

'The djinn are very seldom wrong.' Elisande quoted his own words back at him; he reacted only with a smile, and a nod of farewell.

The tapestry covered the doorway closely, but it seemed barely to twitch as he passed through. Sometimes Julianne thought that he had no physical body at all, that he was as much a creature of spirit as the djinn were, all purpose and intent and hidden thought.

'Well,' Elisande said, 'what now?'

Julianne shrugged. 'There's no point asking the guards at the door, if they saw a man entering or leaving; they'd only laugh. Are there hidden gateways in the rock?'

'None that I know of, except that one we came down by, from the hills. Every child here knows of that. He came; he went. Does it matter how?'

She sounded like Julianne's father, dismissing the means and interested only in consequences. It was probably deliberate, a light teasing; Elisande was cat-curious, she must be aching to know the truth.

'I suppose not,' Julianne said, refusing to play along.

'We should go to find Sherett, and the other women. We're their guests; it's only polite to keep company with them.'

But Sherett came to find them, apparently as well-informed now as she had been earlier. She retrieved the tray – though not before Elisande had topped up her goblet, and Julianne's – and led them briskly down through the house. Towards the kitchens, presumably, where she'd said the women had gathered. Why the kitchens, after the evening meal and when the house was full of greater comforts, Julianne couldn't imagine.

On the way, Elisande asked, 'What would happen to a man who stole in here, and was caught?'

'He would not be a man for long,' Sherett said, chuckling wickedly. 'We would cut him and keep him, as a slave. It has happened, here and elsewhere, though not in my time. We are kind that way; the men would kill him, if we drove him out. The death of the scorpion, which is not kind at all.'

Julianne didn't particularly want to hear about it, but Sherett clearly wanted to tell; Elisande encouraged her. 'Scorpion? Painful but quick, at least . . .'

'Not necessarily. After the sting, yes, they die quickly; before it, they can live for hours.'

'Well, indeed. I myself have lived for years already, waiting for a scorpion to sting me . . .'

'You don't have one in your mouth.'

'Ah. No. But again, I would have thought that quick.'

'They use a small scorpion, which has been packed in ice and left for a day. It becomes slow, lethargic, even-tempered. Then it is placed in the offender's mouth, and his lips are sewn together. So it warms, it becomes active again.

At first it is hungry; then it is enraged. I am told that men have survived half a day by keeping it placid, by holding their tongue quite still while the scorpion feeds on it.'

'Ugh. I don't think I'd want to. If I'm going to die anyway, I'd rather have it over. I'd aggravate the thing, sooner than let it eat me.'

'Suicide is an offence against God.'

'*Suicide?*'

'Deliberately to anger a scorpion, knowing it will sting you – what else? It is the role of man to endure whatever God sends; when death must come, even in disgrace, it is still a man's duty to delay it as he can.'

Was there a touch of cynicism to Sherett's smile, as though she thought a woman might be wiser? Julianne thought there was. Or hoped so, at least; she had small patience with religious orthodoxy, and none at all where it preached a hopeless fatalism.

Down the stairs to the entrance-hall and down again, a narrow flight where the air was hot and heavy with smells of frying spices, clamorous with the clatter of pans and the high voices of women at work.

'The King's Shadow gives a feast tomorrow night,' Sherett explained, 'and so you find us busy. He gives the feast, but we must make it happen. Poor entertainment for you, to watch us cook; there are few of us, though, and I can spare none.'

Julianne's polite demurral was overridden by Elisande's declaration, 'You have two more sets of willing hands now. What can we do?'

'Nothing. You are our guests. Sit and talk with us if you will, but it would shame us to see you labour.'

'It would shame you more if the feast were ill-prepared, for lack of a little help; and it would shame us to sit idle while you worked. I at least have peeled onions and scrubbed pots in this kitchen before now, Sherett. And Julianne is a married woman, she needs to learn all the arts of womanhood. It is a guest's privilege to breach a custom where they choose. Give us tasks, or we will take them on ourselves in any case—'

'—And likely spoil what you do not spill. I have worked with clumsy girls before,' scowling momentously at them both. 'Still, I don't deny that any help is welcome,' and the scowl melted into a smile. 'Come in, then, and we will see if you can scrub to Yaman's satisfaction . . .'

The kitchen was small, airless and swelteringly hot, with open fires and ovens all stoked high and a dozen yammering women frenziedly chopping, kneading, basting. Julianne feared that she might soon regret Elisande's easy generosity; she was sure that she would soon want another bath. After so long in the desiccating Sands, she'd thought her body had forgotten how to sweat; two minutes in here showed her that she'd been wrong.

At least the scrubbing proved to have been an empty threat. Even Sherett deferred to another's authority in the kitchen, and was swiftly overruled. Yaman was the oldest woman there, wife to one of the tribal leaders and so doubly senior, and she was appalled by the very suggestion that guests in her house might wash dishes. It took another argument from Elisande to persuade her that they should work at all; eventually they were reluctantly permitted to occupy stools in the quietest corner and prepare a heap of garlic and ginger and turmeric root. Sherett was herself sent to the massive earthenware washpot – to Julianne's quiet pleasure, and Elisande's manifest glee – with a pile of roasting-trays to scour, though she quickly delegated that duty to a younger woman.

Julianne peeled and sliced, while Elisande pounded in a giant stone mortar, with a pestle that reached to her waist when its bulbous end was resting on the ground. It must in the past have been the source of a thousand lewd suggestions; Julianne thought it might have provoked a few more tonight, except that good manners towards visitors forestalled them. The older women eyed the way it rose and fell in Elisande's hands, to a steady thudding rhythm, and snickered quietly between themselves.

'I don't understand,' Julianne said quickly, before her friend could notice, 'how my father can be giving a feast for his hosts?' Sharai laws of hospitality were stricter even than those in Marasson, or so she'd understood; and in Marasson a guest could neither refuse a gift nor return a kindness without causing deep offence.

'Oh, it's a gesture, an ancient custom, a form of words that doesn't actually mean what it says. The host provides the feast, of course, or rather his women do,' with an expressive dash of her hand across her glistening brow. 'The guest can contribute nothing to it, except a speech. It actually costs the host dear, when it's done properly; he must slaughter some of his precious herd, and spices are expensive. He takes honour from it, though, from his openhandedness; which is why it happens, because honour is all that a guest is allowed to give his host.'

Put that way it made sense, she supposed, if you

accepted the slightly peculiar notion that it honoured your host to drive him to great expense. She thought it rather dishonoured the guest to do so, but then she was not Sharai. Neither was her father, of course; but he would use that custom and any other, to bring about the ends he sought. She thought it unlikely that a grand feast that a Patric had required them to pay for would influence any of the tribal sheikhs against making war on Outremer; again, though, she was not Sharai. Nor would she have the opportunity to hear her father's speech. That was likely the greater purpose for it, from his point of view; that man had a gilded tongue, when he chose to use it. Give him a well-fed and mellow audience and he just might sway them, or some of them at least.

Some, she feared, would not be mellowed by any amount of feasting in his name. He was yet a Patric and an unbeliever, one of those who occupied not only fruitful land worth fighting for but also the holiest sites of the Catari faith. The Sharai were a religious people; even Jemel still said his prayers morning and evening, despite his loyalty to another unbeliever. It was a holy war to which Hasan was calling the tribes; however persuasive her father's voice and Rudel's, Redmond's too perhaps if he came in time, she thought that the tribes would come in answer.

She thought of Imber riding to that war as he must, her bright and beautiful boy, foolish with dreams of honour of his own, and she wanted to weep.

She thought of Hasan, equally brave and equally driven, and didn't know what she wanted.

Her first sight of Imber had seized her heart, perhaps even her soul; she'd thought that he possessed her, mind and body, that he inhabited her skin now as certainly as she did. She'd thought that he would stand in her eye for ever, blond and tall and reliable as rock – changeable as rock changes, that was, in sunlight or shadow, starlight or dark: mutable of mood but quite untouched beneath – and be a bar to any other man. What need another, she'd thought, when Imber was her own and she was his?

She'd been wrong.

Her first sight of Hasan had gripped her like a hand of fire, hard and hot. She thought him beautiful as his land was beautiful, as a hawk is: rapacious, unforgiving, deadly and yet breathtaking, limitless, free. As wide as the ocean, she'd thought him in that moment, as high as the moon; and so very different from Imber, who was beautiful as a rose is beautiful, young and thorny and close-furled petal on petal, showing only the outermost colour and shielding the heart . . .

So very different, it seemed that she could be owned and claimed by both; or at least that each could have his own, his separate Julianne. Imber had lost nothing of her, she was still entirely his own – and yet there was another Julianne who ached for Hasan's touch, whose body thrilled in his presence, whose heart had sung when he'd spoken so lightly of his marrying her. *Alas, my lord, I am married already* – but to her it had not been a joke, and still was not. She was eternally married to Imber; and yet, and yet . . .

And yet she had promised to ride with Hasan, she remembered, in the early morning. Or no, she had demanded that promise of him; and how loyal was that to her wedded lord, her love? Perhaps she would grow into one of those women whose affairs were the gossip of the court at Marasson, who had a new passion every summer, whose husbands were more pitied than mocked . . .

She didn't believe it, though. She would not. She had too much self-respect; she would return to Imber at Elessi as her father had said, and she would mend what damage had been done by her running away, and she would be a faithful, loyal wife to her tender and doubtful baron, and so they would both be happy.

Before that, she would go riding with Hasan. Before that, she would stone these apricots Sherett was bringing her, now that they had finally worked all that garlic and ginger and turmeric into a soft and pungent mound . . .

At last they were chivvied out of the kitchen, and sent to bed like weary children. No second bath, she was too tired for that; only a quick, cool wash and she fell onto the pallet laid out for her, with Elisande beside.

'What happens in the morning?' she muttered, as the other girl put out the lamp.

'In the morning? I wake you, earlier than you want to be woken; I wash and groom you till you're beautiful, then waste it all behind a robe and veil that shows no more than your eyes. Then you wait like a tremulous maid, peering through the window-screens and refusing to eat, until Hasan brings your horse to the door. You mount, you murmur sharp-edged compliments at each other as you have these past days, and you ride away.'

'Alone?'

'Sweet, where do you think you are? Of course, not alone. A Patric and a Sharai, a warlord and a married lady — oh, no. If you were his captive, then perhaps; as you are his guest, you will both need chaperones. I ride with you, and he will bring some company to protect him from two such fearsome creatures as we are. Why, did you want to have him alone?'

'No, indeed. Why would I?'

A snort was all the answer she received to that. For a moment she was tempted to be childish, cruel even, to ask *did you enjoy your time alone with Marron, all those days . . .?* But she was too tired to fight, and too tired for the reconciliation after. She lay still and felt the numbness spread from feet and fingers, rising like an inexorable tide throughout her body; just before it reached her mind and took her off, she did wish fervently and truthfully to dream of Imber.

While the image behind her eyelids, the man who stood foursquare and certain of his place there was not so tall as Imber, darker, older . . .

Morning came, with Elisande's predictions one by one: dragged up in the half-light with her rebellious body shrieking for more sleep and her recreant mind for the shadows of dream to hide in, that this had come too soon, she wasn't ready, she didn't want to go . . .

And her friend's bullying her into washing and dressing and sitting still while she was petted and perfumed, while her hair was combed into order and brushed to a high gloss; and then her sitting on the window's ledge and peering out through the lattice, watching the gloomy pavement so far below and nibbling on a little fruit and refusing all breakfast else, because how could she possibly eat when her stomach was cramped with tension, when her thoughts were so dizzy between duty and longing, between one man and the other . . .?

There was constant movement along the pool's side, men and boys walking slowly this way and that; others were busy in the fields on the further bank, carrying water to the crops before the sun's first light could creep down the scarp to burn them dry. She watched and waited, in a frenzy of doubt and desire.

At last, at long last she saw the dim shapes of horses coming down from the stable, a line of them, some ridden and some led. Heard them too, the hard but quiet sounds of hooves on stone, a single sudden whinny that sang in the air, in her ears. That was what she wanted, she told herself firmly, all that she was craving: not the man's company at all but the height and liberty of a horseback ride, a strong responsive body beneath her and the curious communication she could achieve through reins and touch and voice, till human mind and animal worked almost as one, sharing the excitement of speed and discovery . . .

She tried to tell that to Elisande, and was laughed at; and then was hurried downstairs, down many stairs to the entrance hall where Sherett was waiting for them, already hooded and veiled, her black eyes mysterious and challenging today.

Her voice was sharp, as she told them to conceal their faces; her fingers were quick but delicate, adjusting the folds of their costumes with more grace than Elisande could manage.

'Are you coming with us? For the ride?' Julianne couldn't decide if she wanted that or not. Wisdom said yes, said *yes please, ride with your husband, so that I don't have to*;

but wisdom's was a cold voice, and she was too hot to heed it.

'Not I, girl. I have a feast to prepare, yes? I merely want a word with my lord, and then to see my guests on their way to their pleasure. Stand still and let me tighten this, shameless, or the wind will have your veil . . .'

When Sherett was finally satisfied, she led them out around the door-screen, into a cool breeze and the company of men.

Men, and horses. Five horses, and three men: and Hasan the first of those, sitting his mount a length or so ahead of the others and drawing her eyes inexorably to him.

He greeted her with a bow and a smile, and, 'You see? I keep my oath . . .'

'Prince, I never doubted you,' she said, and swept into a deep curtsey, deliberately Patric, alien to both the dress and the custom of these people.

'Lady, you relieve my mind. I chose this filly for you,' a young chestnut mare, short and restive, her breeding showing in every fine-boned line of her and her reins tied to his saddle-bow. 'Her name is Tezra, and she is eager for a run.'

'And so am I,' but first, even before making friends with her mount, she walked a little way further to bid good morning to his companions. He had chosen those, she guessed, with equal care: a quiet older man whose company promised much, and a blazingly handsome youth with dancing eyes whom she could appreciate as a work of art and beauty, who touched her heart not at all. She might wish him on Elisande, she thought, if that girl could possibly be persuaded to it; he might have been picked for exactly that purpose.

When she turned back, she saw Sherett at Hasan's stirrup. They were talking, too softly for her to overhear; they were not touching at all, but did not need to. Simply from the way he stooped in his saddle, the way she stretched up almost on tiptoe, she thought she could sense all that bound them together: the passion, the intelligence, the understanding and acceptance. *She is his wife, and I am someone else's* . . .

And yet he had two wives else, and Sherett accepted that. The others were not here and she was, which must count for something; but still, he was about to ride off for a morning's jaunt with another girl, and Sherett accepted that also.

A girl who is married to another man; in Sherett's eyes, that might make a difference. She doubted that it did in Hasan's.

Would a man with three wives already – and a relationship with one at least whose depth, whose true value was spelled out before her now, in every lineament of their two bodies – would such a man truly desire a fourth? Surely not; of a certainty he had been teasing only, praising her beauty in the most fulsome way he knew. *Tell me his name, that I may kill him* – that had undoubtedly been a joke. Though it might become a joke that acquired a grim reality, if Hasan were permitted the war that he craved so ardently . . .

She stroked Tezra's soft nose, and murmured endearments into the flickering ear. 'You're so beautiful,' which she was. 'I have another horse I love, but I could love you too,' which was true; and if only it were so easy to love two men, if only her culture or his would allow it ⋯

One of Hasan's companions – the young one, of course, Boraj of the easy grace and astonishing beauty – slid off his horse to help her mount. She thanked him, and took the reins from Hasan with no more than a tremor when his fingers quite advertently touched hers. She wondered what it was about this man, or else about her, that he could affect her so profoundly when she'd thought herself utterly given and claimed already; and found no answer in his strong face or his strong gaze. She turned her head aside to watch Boraj lift Elisande into the saddle of the other spare horse, a mare of gentler temper by the look of her.

Tezra fidgeted, tossing her head and shifting her feet on the rock walkway. Julianne spoke to her sternly, preaching the necessity of patience; then laughed and glanced forward. Sherett had stepped away from Hasan's side, she saw. As though that were the permission he'd been waiting for, he saluted her gravely, then beckoned the whole party forward.

As they picked their way slowly through the foot-traffic, Julianne watched the faces that they passed. Man and boy, occasional veiled woman or girl too young for such conformity, all gaped up at Hasan, pressing themselves back not to impede his progress.

She wasn't the only one, then. To be sure, he was the leader, he would attract first attention regardless of who came behind; but they kept their eyes on him long after he was past, swivelling their heads and sparing barely a glance for Julianne and the others.

Perhaps that was what she felt also, no more than the

common admiration for a man whose charisma was undeniable, whose fascination was irresistible, whose power and potency was patent. Only that because she was a girl, a foolish girl, married but not yet made wife to any man, her romantic soul twisted her sense of him into something more . . .

Perhaps. She yearned to believe that, but could not. She knew herself better; despised herself almost, for being so weak and foolish.

And having nothing she could do about that, yearned instead to kick Tezra into a mind-numbing gallop, to blast all such idiocy out of her head; and couldn't do that either, here where there was so little space between rock wall and water, and that space too full of people.

She trailed along behind Hasan, constantly tormented by the adulation that she saw and could not allow herself to replicate. Either as man or war-leader, he was not for her. Her frustration passed through inevitably to her mettlesome horse, so that she had to fight Tezra as she was fighting herself; to these skilled riders she must be looking incompetent or mismounted as she struggled to control the beast with reins and stirrups, to hold her to a steady walk. That only added to her frustration.

The long, long pool dwindled at last, as the valley's walls closed in on either side; she found herself riding a twisting path between them, a path that grew narrower at every turn until there was only a bare slit of sky far above, barely enough light to cast a shadow. This must be the siq Hasan had spoken of, the way Elisande would have preferred to bring her to Rhabat . . .

Here too there was traffic; they met a camel-train approaching, and hardly found room to squeeze their horses past the high swaying loads. Even the camels, Julianne thought balefully, turned their heads to watch Hasan as he passed.

At the far end of that winding defile – and it was far, perhaps half an hour's slow ride – the high walls that had towered above them broke down in masses of crumbling rock and shale. The horses picked their way delicately, where falling stones had invaded the path; as they came out into sunlight, viciously dazzling after so long in the dark, Julianne turned her head to look back. She saw a steep slope rising behind her, a chaos of tumbled slabs and shadow. If it weren't for that well-established path, she'd have no hope of finding the one sliver of darkness that masked the way through. Easy to understand how Rhabat had stayed hidden for so long, even from the Sharai.

'That is our shelter,' Hasan said softly. 'It cannot be climbed; every boy who comes here has tried it, but the rock shears away under your fingers, and leaves you clinging to dust. A dozen men with bows can defend the siq, and we can feed and water an army if we need to; but there is no water out here, if ever an army was led against us.'

No water, but there was still an army here. She gazed past him and saw a wide gravel plain dancing with light, where every separate stone seemed to glitter and burn under the sun. The plain was shrouded with shapeless black shadows, and she had to blink and rub her eyes to see them clearly. They were tents, vast tents, the homes of the nomadic tribes; each one could shelter dozens of men, and there were dozens of them, more, gathered in disorderly groups as far as she could squint against the glare.

'Every sheikh has come with his retinue,' Hasan went on, 'but only the sheikhs and their close supporters may come into Rhabat; the rest make camp here, and we supply them from our stores. Even so, there were not this many two days ago, and there will be more tomorrow. Word is spreading; the tribes are gathering, uninvited but welcome none the less. Welcome to me, at least. You may feel differently.'

'I don't know what I feel,' she confessed; which was true, except, 'Hasan, I don't want war . . .'

'I know; but war must come. Tomorrow, perhaps – who knows? It is as God wills it. Not today, though. Today, we can ride in peace. Will you come?'

And he kicked his stallion forward, hard. Julianne had no chance to refuse the challenge; Tezra responded on her own account, almost unseating her dithering rider with an explosive surge of speed.

Away from the stonefalls at the hill's margin, the pea gravel made good footing for the horses, hard and level. Julianne caught her balance, crouched low in the saddle and set herself and her mount to a grim chase. Hasan had the start on her – if a short one, thanks to Tezra – and he had a stronger horse beneath him; Tezra was lighter, though, all sinew, built for speed.

She was nimbler, too, quicker to weave her way between the clusters of tents; soon they were racing shoulder to shoulder with Hasan. He glanced across with a grin, and then expressively behind him; she risked a peek, and saw that they had far outpaced their companions.

Briefly she hesitated, thinking of what was proper, of his reputation and hers. In that moment he surged ahead again as Tezra slowed a little, sensing her doubts through the reins. Julianne gritted her teeth, drove in her heels and cried the horse on with a wild whoop. Devil take the proprieties; she might blush for it later, but she meant not to lose this race.

Neither did she, though that was by his kindness. Slowly Tezra gained ground on the bigger stallion, slowly they drew level with his withers, with his shoulder; then they were running head to head again, and all the vast desert lay open and empty before them, no more tents now, only an infinity to run in . . .

Except that Tezra was blowing hard suddenly, not her will but her stamina failing her. Hasan knew as soon as Julianne did, or so it seemed; he reined back his mount, drawing him smoothly from that headlong gallop to a canter, to a trot, to a walk. Gratefully, she did the same. She would have hated to force Tezra on beyond her strength, but she might have done it regardless. She wasn't sure she'd have had the resolution to call a halt before he did.

That wild ride had left her breathless too, but joyfully so. Exhilarated, flushed behind her veil – she could feel the blood burning in her cheeks, and was grateful also for Sherett's care to fix her clothing firmly. There was no one but Hasan to see here, and he at least would not have been shocked by a glimpse of her face, she was sure of that; but she was equally sure that she did not want that exposure. Not now, not like this. Her eyes must be enough of a giveaway . . .

His own eyes sparkled darkly, as he bowed extravagantly in the saddle. 'The race is yours, my lady.'

'No, not so! You checked your horse, but only out of courtesy . . .'

'Precisely so. He who will not press his advantage when he can is doomed to lose.'

He said it lightly but meant more by it, she thought: that this was a rare gallantry, that when it mattered more he would not be so weak.

She nodded, to tell him that she understood; and thought that he would turn his horse now, that they would go meekly and quietly back to rejoin their chaperones.

He was standing in his stirrups, though, and shielding his eyes as he gazed out across the limitless plain.

'Someone comes,' he grunted. 'One camel, riding fast. I have outrunners on all the approaches; I think we'll wait.'

Wait they did, sitting their stationary horses for so long that Elisande and the men tired of waiting themselves and came to join the raceaways. Boraj was dancing attendance on her friend, Julianne was delighted to notice, sidling his mount against hers and murmuring softly, offering her a drink from his flask. The stubborn girl only shook her head, though, and edged her horse away. Julianne sighed, and willed him silently to keep trying. *He who will not press his advantage* . . . And Boraj had one advantage at least, his spectacular looks. Elisande was susceptible to beauty, after all; and unclaimed, and likely to remain so, for all that she might wish it otherwise . . .

Weeks in the desert had not given Julianne desert eyes; Jemel would have seen it perhaps before Hasan did, Marron certainly. Slowly the little flicker of shadow that Hasan had declared to be a man drew closer, though, and resolved itself indeed to be a man, mounted on a running camel.

Closer still, and she revised that opinion. Not a man; ~ boy. She didn't know when Sharai lads were recognised as adult – when they killed their first enemy, most likely, and brought his head back in evidence – but surely it wasn't this young. The Sharai were a small people, by and large, and some of the men had shrill voices, good for carrying far in desert air; even so, this one couldn't be more than twelve. Emphatically, a boy.

Good for carrying messages, she thought, a light-framed boy; and on such a camel, made for speed as much as Tezra was. She recognised the lines of the beast, much like those the Sultan had displayed for them, Sildana's offspring and their confrères. It made sense, that the Sultan's racing stock should have been bred from such as this.

The boy saw Hasan's wave and came straight to him.

'Halm – you are well?'

Of course, Julianne thought with a touch of spite, such a consummate leader of men would know all his message-boys by name. How not?

'I am, Hasan. And you?'

And, of course, he'd encourage them to use his name unadorned: no title, no gesture of respect. That way the name acquires respect in itself, it accumulates weight that it still carries in night-time conversations around the fire, when the night's too cold for sleeping. This boy would half-worship the man, would certainly die for him, simply for being allowed to say his name like that, in this company . . .

They asked politely after each other's families – the boy's uncle had a poisoned foot, for which Hasan recommended

a hot poultice of camel-dung and a certain kind of cactus –
until Julianne began to wonder why the hurry, why the
racing-camel and the bird-boned rider if they were going to
delay the message another hour by talking? Might as well
have sent it on foot, or by tortoise. She'd had a tortoise
once, a pet tortoise that she'd raced against her friend's
along the palace corridors, a lettuce-leaf the prize . . .

Eventually, though, Hasan broke off the preliminaries.
'You have an errand to me, Halm?'

'Yes, Hasan,' and he sat straighter in his saddle to deliver
it, a soldier on duty reporting to his commandant. 'There
is a trader's caravan camped at the oasis of Tosin's Stone.
They meant to leave at first light, and will be here by
sunset; I left at midnight, to advise you.'

'That was well done. I will give your family a pigeon,
though, to spare you the ride next time. Which trader?'

'He is dead. The drovers are led by a Patric,' and the
boy's eyes found Julianne and Elisande, reading their breeding from their eyes alone, unless it was from the way they
sat their horses. 'An old man, a cripple; the drovers call
him father, and are anxious for him . . .'

'Redmond,' Elisande said. 'He would be a father to the
world, if it would let him; he was always my best substitute.
I told him he was taking on too much. And he must have
driven himself and them, to come this far so fast, only a day
behind us . . .'

'We were delayed,' Julianne reminded her. 'The Dancers
led us out of our way, and divided we were slower through
the Sands, besides having to battle with ghûls en route.' All
that was really for the boy's sake, to put a bulge in his oh-
so-experienced eyes and a gape in his dismissive, almost

contemptuous mouth. Only women and only Patrics, but they'd had more adventures in a week than he'd seen in his short lifetime . . .

Hasan nodded. 'Redmond indeed – and in time for your father's feast, Julianne, though he might be more weary than festive. He will be welcome, however he comes. We'd best take the news back now; a caravan of goods is no great matter, but the Red Earl deserves a better greeting. Besides, we should send a party to escort him in; he might be startled else, by the number of our gatewardens,' with a gesture back towards the proliferating tents. 'Halm, find your own people, and rest; the Kauram are camped to the south of the road. Tomorrow, come through the siq, say I sent for you; I will give you that bird.'

No doubt he would, but the pigeon was not the prize. Halm bowed, hand to heart and lips and forehead; then he rode away, his head high and his eyes starry. He would see Rhabat, by Hasan's personal word; even now he would be thinking that this was a story to tell his children and his grandchildren, how the greatest general of the age – the man who would win back Ascariel, no less! – had touched his life with blessing, for the slightest favour done.

Oh, Hasan was good at this, Julianne thought, wheeling her horse in his tail, riding in his dust. He would leave them all behind: defeated, hungry, bereft . . .

12

What Comes from the Water

Jemel walked slowly along the gully that led down to the Dead Waters, knowing that he was taking a risk, or more risks than one; his life might be the least of what he risked.

But his life was of little value to him anyway, and less if he lost anything more of what he valued more. And so he was here, his scimitar loose in its sheath and his bare feet silent in the shadows, his nose scenting rank salt and his ears straining for any sound ahead.

He could hear nothing, neither what he sought nor what he dreaded. So he stepped forward more confidently, less guardedly, remembering that he was after all Sharai and so not born to skulk, especially here in Rhabat. He came out from the deep darkness of the gully into the lesser shade of the narrow waterfront; the sea lay dark and still within the bay, brighter beyond under the glare of the afternoon sun. So much water made him simply uncomfortable, regardless of its sinister reputation or its more recent annexation. He stood gazing at it, snared by the quiescent threat of this place, almost amazed by his own courage in venturing here; and was startled by a more immediate threat, the mundane sound of steel drawn at his back.

He spun around and found himself facing two men of the Ashti, who stepped forward from a cave-mouth, each with a blade aimed at his heart. A boy lurked behind them, a lad, a runner of the same tribe, watching open-eyed the best excitement of his day so far.

Well, this had been one of the risks, the smallest risk Jemel had faced. Hasan was bound to have set guards here, after the report of 'ifrit in the water and his own encounter with the ghûls. Jemel had been lucky; the tribes would be sharing the duty, and it might have been the turn of the Saren to stand watch.

He kept his hands carefully far from the hilt of his weapon, and said, 'I am called Jemel.'

'We know who you are. What you are, tribeless,' replied one.

'Sand Dancer,' added the other. 'What do you want here?'

Perhaps he had not been so lucky after all; perhaps he should after all have stayed in the house of the Beni Rus, where he was safe. That had been the common advice, the instruction from Hasan. But a host could not give orders to his guest, and no one could command the obedience of a man without a tribe. Jemel would have obeyed Marron, reluctantly, if he'd added his voice to the clamour; but Marron had slipped away in other company, and without a word to his friend. And Jemel would not cower cravenly behind another man's guarded walls, he would not have that added to what was already being said about him . . .

'I came seeking the Ghost Walker,' he said. 'I was told that he had come this way.' A child had told him, a barefaced girl, awe and terror mingling in her voice; it had only added to his humiliation, that a crop-tending brat had known Marron's movements when he did not. Asking the question had been bitter enough; getting a reply had been almost worse.

'He did. With his woman.' The Ashti's voice betrayed the general confusion. The Ghost Walker was their prophecy made flesh, the talisman they'd waited centuries to see; and yet the boy who claimed that title was nothing of theirs, neither the company he chose to keep in defiance of all custom. There was no terror in this man, or none that he would show: again a mix of emotions, though, wonder and contempt uncomfortable partners.

'Him we passed through,' the other said. *With his woman*, implicitly, adding further to Jemel's gall. 'You, though – you are another matter. Why should we pass you?'

'Were you set here to watch the water, or to obstruct those with good reason to come this way?' That was temper only, and he regretted it immediately; if they challenged him, he could offer no good reason. His reasons didn't seem good even to him, only that the alternative was worse.

They gave him no answer at all; one said to the other, 'A tribeless man has no honour; he might be a spy for the 'ifrit. Or he is a Dancer, and they are forbidden this valley. If we slay him, we would at least earn the thanks of the Saren, perhaps of the whole council.'

'Does the gratitude of the Saren mean so much to the Ashti?' Jemel snapped back. Here he was on safer ground.

'Does the anger of the Ghost Walker mean so little? Or the dishonour of Hasan, who has named me friend and guest?'

This was posturing only, on both sides; they wouldn't kill him now, he was sure. Not without greater authority. A Saren guard might have done it without a thought, to please his sheikh; these might have done it in the moment of recognition, but not once they'd let him argue for his life.

'You should have stayed in Hasan's house,' one said sourly. 'You offend us all. But go, then. That way,' with a twitch of his scimitar's point. 'Run and speak with your master, tribeless. If you are wise, you will keep in his shadow hereafter, or else in Hasan's.'

If he'd been wise, he thought, he would not be here at all; or at least not tribeless, and not in Marron's retinue. Grief had made him reckless first, but it was not grief that drove him now. Nothing was as simple as it should have been. God had made his a simple people, or God and the desert between them; complexity confounded them, and Jemel was not immune to that.

He did not run, but walked along the waterfront, foolishly close to the edge; posturing again, but he allowed himself the indulgence. The guards were holding back, hiding in their cave at the gully's mouth, where rock walls offered some illusion of shelter. Let them see him bolder . . .

Let them see him eaten by 'ifrit, to know him no spy – but he did not believe he would be eaten. He found it hard to believe in the 'ifrit at all, because he had not been there with Marron—

—Or because Elisande had. As she was here, though not with Marron now. He found her at the open gateway to the rising tunnel, Rhabat's secret exit; she stood just outside its black maw, fretfully staring within.

'You showed him this?'

'Of course. He asked me to.'

Briefly, Jemel felt all of the Ashti's patent distrust of her. She was Patric, a friend maybe but still of the enemy and committed to its cause: its survival, its occupation of Catari land. She should never have been allowed here the once, let alone brought back; this gateway was a Sharai secret and precious to them, it should never have been taught to her . . .

It should never have been taught by her to Marron, but his reasons there were more obscure, and faltered before her gaze. Marron was also Patric, of course, also perhaps of the enemy; not committed to anything, though, so far as Jemel could tell, beyond the avoidance of war.

'And you let him go up alone?'

'He told me to. It's *dark* in there, Jemel. I didn't think to bring a torch, I didn't know what he wanted until he led me here. He said he could find his way without light, but I would slow him down . . .'

'Why has he gone up, what for?'

'I don't know, he didn't say.'

Is he coming back? was the question neither one of them wanted asked, for fear of the other offering an answer.

Nothing to do then but wait, and find out. Wait together, as they must: caught in a reluctant companionship, bonded by a mutual love that only touched each other at its fringes.

The Sharai could wait in patience, in silence when they must. So could she. Talking was always better, though, talking killed relentless time; how many nights had he talked through with Jazra in their youth, huddled together over a low flame without a blanket between them to keep back the bitter cold of the stars? Uncountable nights, immeasurably precious to him still. Talking with her could never mean so much, but he would talk if she would; the alternative was all but unbearable, to watch the dark and listen to its silence, to wonder if trust and need were both to be betrayed again. Marron had said more than once that his only skill lay in betrayal . . .

Jemel's eyes shifted, away from the shadows of the gateway to the shadows shifting on the lapping water. Nothing was moving there, except patterns of dark on the surface and below; he set his back to the rock so that he absolutely couldn't stare any longer into that tunnel, slid down to a comfortable squat and asked, 'What did you see, in the land of the djinn?'

What did you see, that I should have seen instead? was the real question, and she heard it clearly. 'Little,' she said, shrugging as she sat beside him, folding her legs neatly beneath the hem of her robe as his own people did. 'You went through first, you know what was there, the Pillar's elder brother; other than that, gold dust and golden rock, gold sky by day and night. It's not a land for looking at. There's little there, and little of what there is is extreme, or even actually interesting. Except that simply being there is fascinating. Like standing at a spring when you know it's the wellhead of a massive trading river, when you've spent all your life on its banks: to be at the source at last is mindshaking, even when the source is a trickle of clean water through a simple pasture and no more.'

Jemel had never seen a river such as she described, and

hardly knew what she meant; but he knew how he'd felt when he stood in that other world, and so he nodded. He'd thought he stood in the heart of the sun, and was not burned.

'What of the mountain that was flat at the peak?' This was all a tale already told. She had narrated the whole journey to the entire party before they reached Rhabat; but stories were made to be told again and again. And he wanted to hear it alone, to have at least some sense of sharing.

'It was hardly a mountain, Jemel, no great climb.' *You didn't miss that much.* 'I don't know what to tell you about it, else. It wasn't just flat, it didn't happen that way by nature. It had been cut off somehow and polished after, unless what did the cutting left it polished as it went. The surface was smooth as glass – smooth as ice, if ice is ever warm. And it got hot towards the centre, hard to walk on. Perhaps we should have run and slid across, like children, but it felt like a cathedral. Like a temple, somewhere holy . . .'

'What did it mean?'

'I don't know, Jemel. Nor does Marron. What did the needle mean? It was something they could do, perhaps, no more than that . . .'

Jemel shook his head. Everything must have a meaning; he believed absolutely in signs and portents and significance, only not in the ability of women to read what was written in the world. Works so great had to have a potency beyond their sheer scale. If he had seen and could not understand the blade – *the needle* she had called it, but she was a woman – perhaps that was only because he had not seen the mountaintop. A man might need to walk far in that land to penetrate its secrets. The week they'd been gone, she in the Ghost Walker's shadow – and fasting by the gaunt look of them and the hunger now, though they denied it – that week should have proved plenty, in both time and distance. Would have done, he was sure, had he been there in her stead. As he should have been, but for the mischance that had set her in his place, at Marron's side . . .

It had been more than mischance today, it had been Marron's choice, or hers. Almost he twisted his head, to seek the Ghost Walker fruitlessly in the dark; instead, again, he looked to the water.

'What is it,' he wondered aloud, 'that lives in there?'

'The 'ifrit,' she said, and shuddered.

'No, not those. Something more, something greater. This has been a place of evil for generations. Men used to sail these waters,' though it was hard for him to imagine, who had never seen a boat; he knew the words from stories, but he had no pictures in his mind. He waved his hand towards the evidence, storerooms in the cliffs and steps from the quayside that broke the surface of the sea and went on down into mystery. 'Now we watch them and whisper, and keep safe away.'

'They stink,' Elisande said, which was true but fell far short of the truth. 'They are dead; nothing lives there, nothing could. That's reason enough. The rest is story-telling, nothing more.'

'No,' again. If he'd known no better, he still would not have believed her; she had the shifty look of someone driven to a lie. Against her desire, perhaps, but lying none the less. 'Men have died, and been found dead on the shores. Dead in terror, or torn apart. Not many and not recently, but they are more than stories, they have graves.' Or tombs or cairns, crumbling rock-piles in the Sands to cover crumbling bones. 'You have lived in Rhabat, as I have not,' and he hated this, that he must ask a Patric for knowledge that was Sharai. He hated also to press her past her defensive lying, it was ill-mannered and worse, humiliating for them both; but if he could not have her share of Marron, he'd have whatever less he could take from her, and give her as little as he could in return. 'What do they say here? They must speak of the Dead Waters . . .' In the women's quarters, and elsewhere; she'd been a girl then, unveiled, licensed to roam. Girls were demons, he'd often thought: they tormented the boys and plagued the men, and nothing could be kept secret from them.

'Surely,' she said, her face tight against him. 'They say that they are dead.' And then, of a sudden, her expression changed: collapsed almost, like rock that had stood too long against the sand on the wind and was worn as thin as paper, too weak to hold its own light weight any longer. 'Oh, Jemel, I'm sorry. But you know what the djinni called me . . .?'

'Lisan of the Dead Waters.' He had not forgotten. He called her Lisan himself, these days, when he called her anything at all. His tongue could find its way around her full name if he chose, but he preferred to emphasise the distance that lay between them, that he was Sharai and she was not.

'Yes. I didn't understand it then, and I still don't; but now we're here, and I don't want it, I don't want even to think about it. I'd forgotten, I think, how rank these waters are. More than smell, but you said that. I came down here seldom, except when the children challenged me. And that was rare, they were scared themselves; but it was forbidden, and so we had to come. Besides, there was this,' a jerk of her head towards the open gateway, 'though we never explored far up there, either. Too dark, and too dull. The water was dull too, to be honest. If we stayed long enough to be brave, it was long enough to be bored. Nothing ever happened; we were never even caught by the adults, there wasn't a guard then. Why risk men, against a devil? That's what they say, in Rhabat: that a devil lives in the water, and takes whoever dares to come within its reach. Takes and torments them, body and soul – that's what they say, that the water's fouled by the souls of all its victims, which it keeps so that they'll never find their way to paradise. It's worse than death, they say; it's death and hell together.'

Jemel had – perhaps – stopped believing in paradise, and so in hell; he had stood however briefly in another world, and thought that two such might be enough for any man's faith to sustain. Belief was easy, for those who had not seen. Truth was heavier, and he could only carry so much in mind or heart. He said his prayers by rote now, and only when others were there to see it if he failed.

He could still believe in devils, though; that much was easy, where wickedness seemed to seep up through the damp stones, and hang in the very air he breathed. And if in devils, perhaps also in souls; he shuddered at the thought of it, being trapped past death in those murky waters.

Watching more alertly now, perhaps looking for souls among the shadows, he thought he saw solid shadows gather below the surface. It was hard to be sure, when the waters were more choppy suddenly – but they were choppy only in a small area above that cluster of black shadow, as though a wisp of wind stirred them only there. Or as if something were rising, disturbing them from below . . .

And moving too, moving swiftly now, sending little bubbles up to stir the surface as it, they headed cleanly for the steps.

Jemel leaped to his feet to cry a warning to the guards, drawing his scimitar and pointing it towards the broken arrowhead of ripples that was spreading slowly across the water.

Too slow, too late, and useless anyway; what could two men do, against a sudden eruption of ebony-shelled creatures from the deep? Too many to count, they scuttled up the steps like crabs, like giant crabs with claws like scything daggers; but they were growing, changing even as they climbed, swelling into something greater than those hard shells could contain. Their backs split open, and bony wings unfurled.

The guards shrieked like women, but neither of them ran. The boy ran, off into the gully as no doubt he'd been kept and told to do, but honour to the Ashti: the men stayed to face that dreadful onslaught with weapons drawn and ready, though they must have known their blades would be all but useless. One broke, indeed, on the back of a carapace; the other struck and skidded uselessly, was quickly seized and snapped between great claws.

Where two men could do nothing but die, three could do no more. Jemel made no move to join them in their deaths, felt only relief when Elisande grabbed his arm and hauled him back into the deep shadow of the gateway.

She at least had thought of something she could do; she cried out softly, up the curve of the tunnel.

'Marron! Come quickly, the 'ifrit are here . . .'

Whether the cry would reach him, who could tell? Marron had sharp ears, and the windings of the tunnel carried sound a long way before it died; but the tunnel climbed higher even than a voice could at full pitch, which hers was not. And he might have left it, Jemel thought; he might have opened the upper gateway — what other purpose could he have, after all? — and gone out onto the headland above. He might have gone altogether . . .

He had not. A scurry of light footfalls and he was there abruptly, not breathing hard, showing no sign of how far he'd come, whether he'd been one or a hundred turns above.

' 'Ifrit?'

'See . . .'

Dozens of them, scores now, shapeshifting from crab to airy monster that Jemel could give no name to. If they were aware of being watched they paid no heed, but took wing one by one till the sky was full of them, a black flock rising high and swiftly.

Silently, also. No cries came back from that dread gathering. Jemel cried out, though, as he felt his wrist seized with a grip he couldn't resist; and Marron cried too, as he forced the edge of the drawn scimitar across his forearm.

Elisande's turn to add her own voice, 'Marron, no . . .!'

A waste of breath: blood followed the blade, and the Daughter poured out of the wound.

Poured and rose, appearing as ever like drifting smoke but moving faster far than any smoke could in this heavy stillness, driving upward.

It chased after the 'ifrit like a dense, smudged arrow; but they flew faster, whipping at the air so savagely Jemel thought that he should feel the wind from their wings, even so far below.

Perhaps the Daughter did feel the turmoil of it, perhaps that was why it could make no headway, couldn't reach even the last straggler in the flock. Or perhaps it had simply gone too far; Marron seemed to be straining when Jemel glanced at him, his face tense and twisted with effort.

'Enough,' Elisande whispered, laying a tentative hand on his shoulder. 'You cannot reach them, call it back . . .'

He sighed, and nodded. Jemel looked up again and saw the Daughter pause, saw it hang for a moment, losing shape, as though it too felt the disappointment of defeat. Then it flowed down and back, insinuated itself into his bleeding arm and the wound sealed behind it, loose tails of leather drooping from the flesh like dark dead worms to show where Marron had slashed through the useless stitches in his haste.

'What were you trying to do?' Elisande demanded breathlessly. *Not to kill, surely?* There was shock in her voicelessness, as though that would be another betrayal, the worse for being so unlooked-for.

'I thought I might open a gateway that could catch a few of them, send some at least back where they came from. I brought them here,' bitterly, accusing himself, 'I might try to make amends. But I couldn't reach. I almost lost it, I thought, for a moment . . .'

That, they'd seen. It was a lesson learned, Jemel thought, and not to be lightly forgotten.

*

As ever Marron was fully recovered in his body, if still shaky in his mind. If he couldn't open one gateway, at least he could close another; he turned round and gripped the wide slab of rock that stood ajar at his back. One heave of his shoulders and it swung into place, the ancient mechanism so well-crafted that even so strong an effort couldn't make it slam or spring open against its locking. Once it was closed, only the closest examination could find the hairline cracks that distinguished door from rockface; not even the sharpest minds could calculate where and how it could be opened, if they weren't already privy to the secret.

Marron glanced at Jemel with seemingly both shame and triumph in his face, *I know now, although you did not show me.*

Despite his misgivings Jemel would have shown it, if he'd been asked. How not? He remembered having felt obscurely glad, though, that Marron couldn't slip that way without his guidance. He'd forgotten Elisande's familiarity with Rhabat. Now he would be anxious for as long as they were here, and drawing small comfort from the fact that she'd been left at the foot of the tunnel this first time, at least . . .

No blame to her, though. She gave Marron what he asked for, and Jemel would have done the same, as he always did. Not their fault, neither of their faults if Marron turned from one to the other alternately, seeming not to know which he wanted closest.

And this was distraction anyway, far from what mattered now. Jemel's eyes met hers and seemed to share the same recognition, as though her thoughts had marched in line with his; even Marron's neatness of mind, closing the door behind him, even that was only a delay, a way to fill a moment or two of time . . .

Enough. He gestured with his head, and led them forward; found Elisande unexpectedly at his elbow, where he'd expected her to take Marron's at his back.

'We should say the *khalat* for them, Jemel. We two, Marron doesn't know it . . .'

'I have heard it,' his voice, strained and reluctant. 'What is in me has heard it many times; I don't believe it knows how to forget. I will join you.'

There were many forms of the *khalat*: from complex sung choruses intended for a solemn funeral that could take as long as an hour to complete, to a brief prayer-chant that any lone warrior could remember, to sing his fallen comrade home in the midst of a battlefield if he must.

There were also inevitably variations between tribe and tribe, but with a strong voice to lead, any Sharai could follow and join in even the most elaborate rite. They all depended on the same few simple verses.

Elisande and Marron both looked to Jemel to lead them, she from where she was kneeling beside the bodies to do the woman's work, straightening the messy remnants and cloaking them as best she could with the ripped rags of their clothing. Marron stood back, coming no closer than he must for decency's sake; even that was too close, by the way his own blood – or that which was in his blood – responded to the stink of what was spilled, rushing vividly to his skin.

What *khalat* came most naturally to Jemel came from the Saren, inevitably, a soft call-and-response they would sing over two avowed brothers fallen together, as such brothers should. He had begun before he knew what he was doing. He choked on the words then and fell silent, heard his friends' mingled voices take it up – and joined them determinedly, saying Saren words over Ashti bodies and thinking all the while of another who was not here, who had lived and died Saren yet had not heard this in his death. Elisande had sung Jazra to his rest, a Patric voice in a Patric country, using what bastard version of the rite Jemel did not know . . .

He thought again of trapped souls in the water at their backs, of Jazra's soul perhaps trapped in that alien castle if Elisande had faltered or failed; and clamped his mind against Jazra and Elisande and all, focused only on being sure this *khalat* was properly sung. If there were no paradise, even if there were no souls, he could still give that much respect to the fallen.

He was so concentrated, indeed, that when they got to the end of it, when they'd chanted the final words together, he didn't know what to do or say next. Nor were his companions any help. Marron lifted his head to the sky and seemed to lose himself in silence, though even his far-seeing eyes could surely find no hint of black wings now, no sign of where the 'ifrit had gone. Elisande had blood on her hands; she glanced once towards the corrupted waters of the bay and made a visible decision to live with it for now, but then apparently could think of nothing else.

The sound of rushing footsteps in the gully, many of them, was relief to all three, Jemel thought. They turned as one, to see Hasan lead a group of men out onto the waterfront. The boy had got his message through, then. Some carried bows strung and ready, the rest had blades drawn; when they saw no immediate work for their weapons, they milled together in murmuring confusion, Kauram speaking with Beni Rus and Ib' Dharan, no distinction. That was Hasan's special gift, Jemel thought, to bring the tribes together at need, in a crisis; if he could only hold them so for a period of weeks or months, he must surely win his war against Outremer.

It had been that same gift of leadership, though, that had led to Jazra's death and Jemel's survival, his outcast condition now. Jemel could see the value of it, and still feel a surge of furious resentment.

Hasan came walking towards them; with the *khalat* he'd never said for Jazra still echoing in his head, Jemel took a pace forward to meet him.

Hasan checked, gazed at him appraisingly and said, 'There is blood on your blade, Jemel.'

Jemel hadn't realised even that his scimitar was still in his hand, let alone that he'd half-raised it as he had, the point a short thrust from Hasan's chest. He shook his head in bewilderment at himself, and muttered, 'The blood is Marron's. He unleashed the Daughter against the 'ifrit, but could not catch them . . .' *We did not face them at all,* but he felt no need to say that aloud; it was implicit, he thought, in his and his friends' survival.

'Where did they go?'

'Up. They flew, above the cliff . . .'

Hasan nodded and walked on, to stand above the bodies. Jemel hastened to wipe his scimitar – on his own robe, there was nothing else and he lacked Elisande's nice care for her clothes – and sheathe it before he followed.

Hasan noted how the bodies had been arranged, and thanked Elisande for it; then he asked, 'You said the *khalat* for them?'

'Yes,' Jemel confirmed – though no doubt the Ashti would say it again in their own preferred rite when they buried their men.

'Good. Thank you, Jemel. Thank you all . . .' His eyes seemed to count them off, though Jemel was sure that he had counted them already; there was no true surprise in his voice as he went on, 'You seem to be one short in your number. The Lady Julianne is not with you?'

Elisande laughed shortly before catching herself, seeming to realise that her news might not be so funny now. She made an effort to keep her voice light, even so, as she said, 'Julianne is becoming more adventurous, or less conventional. Her father has ridden with a small party, to meet Redmond on the road; they needed to speak, he said, before his feast tonight. Julianne went with him.'

'Indeed?' Hasan's voice had no trace of humour in it, only a grave disquiet. 'Are you sure? I saw them go; there were no women in the party.'

Nor should there have been, at such a time, for such a purpose; though it was clearly not the lack of propriety that so disturbed him.

Elisande was still trying to smile, but finding it harder now. 'No, she thought that would be inappropriate. She rode hooded and veiled against the sand, in the dress of a boy of the Beni Rus. I showed her how to wear it . . .'

If Hasan recognised the compliment inherent in the choice, he gave no sign of it. 'She should not be so far from the safety of Rhabat, with 'ifrit in the air. I had best go after them, with men who know the danger.'

'May I come?' The words were out of Jemel's mouth before he knew his own intent to say them. It meant leaving Marron, and the first time he had chosen to do so; it meant choosing Hasan, which he had sworn never to do again; it meant leaving Marron with Elisande, which was perhaps greater yet.

'If you will not stay in my house, you had better ride at my side. Swiftly, though, Jemel – fetch your bow, and meet us at the stables. Tell my people, I would welcome more company. You other two, these waters are not safe to linger by. Elisande, I expect Sherett would be glad of your help in the kitchen—'

Jemel didn't stay to see her reaction to that barely veiled order, nor allow himself so much as a breath of relief that Marron could not join her there; he ran. Back through the gully, which was peopled now with archers, better defence than swordsmen if the 'ifrit had come that way; past the first small pool and so to the bank of the greater, and on to the house of the Beni Rus. Hasan was seriously alarmed, he thought, and with good reason.

He cried the warning to those he met in the hallway – 'The 'ifrit have come out of the water, and are flying above Rhabat; Hasan rides, to protect the King's Shadow and his party. Bring bows!' – and raced up to the chamber he shared with Marron. It took only a moment to snatch up his bow and arrows, another to be sure of the one specially blessed by an imam, that had already proved itself sovereign and might again have to rescue Julianne from an 'ifrit. Even so, by the time he regained the hallway, he found a throng of men armed and ready.

He could not lead here; he named the stables as meeting-place and followed the surge. Hasan was there already, mounted and waiting, with a dozen men beside; the Beni Rus made up a dozen more. Others would follow, Hasan said, as the word spread; they dared not delay.

They kept to a fast trot as they rode the length of Rhabat, and all through the siq; the way was too narrow for any greater speed. Even so, it felt good to Jemel to have a horse beneath him again. The Sharai depended on their camels and treasured them accordingly, but it was on horseback that they felt truly alive. He understood Julianne's yearning; her disguise this afternoon needed no excuse. Hasan might blame her none the less, or Elisande for aiding her; Jemel didn't envy either girl his anger later. In truth, though, they couldn't have foreseen this danger. No one could . . .

Once beyond the siq Hasan kicked his horse into an immediate gallop, racing away from his followers. Giving chase with the rest, Jemel thought that this too should bring more men on their tail; the tribes camped here would be growing restive, with nothing to occupy them and sworn enemies in tents on every side. The peace of such a gathering was vulnerable at best; give them a chance of action without violating their oaths, and they'd seize it with glee.

Which would teach them perhaps that they could ride together, tribe beside tribe, and fight as one if it came to fighting, so long as they had a leader all would respect. Oh, Jemel thought, that man was subtle. Genuinely anxious, he had no doubt of that; but using the opportunity regardless, always keeping his eye on his ultimate goal, one army under his command to lead against the unbelievers . . .

Or perhaps that was his immediate goal, and his dream looked further. One kingdom, under his command? It would not be impossible. Nothing would be impossible, if he led the tribes successfully against Outremer. If he won back Ascariel for the Catari, if he set imams once more in the Dir'al Shahan, the high temple, he could demand the moon; the sheikhs would ask no more than how he wanted it, new or gibbous or at the full.

His horse outpaced them all, as did his urgency. Soon they stopped trying to catch up, and only kept their horses at a steady gallop in an effort not to lose too much more ground. Hasan rode for Julianne, though that was a complication Jemel couldn't understand, let alone untangle. Julianne was married, albeit by infidel rites before an infidel altar; the Sharai still respected such a marriage, and Hasan would not take or claim her against all custom. Still, he rode for Julianne; his men rode for him, and all these other men besides. So long as they could watch him, see him safe, they were content. Why kill their horses, for the sake of a few Patrics? They would ride, and ride hard, but not at his slaying speed.

So Jemel came through the troop, driven by his own concern for Julianne, and found that he led them after all, despite himself. Perhaps that would spur their pride, to be outstripped by a tribeless man; perhaps he could hurry them a little, just by riding a good horse well . . .

Focusing on that – on style and speed, on laying down a challenge to those behind – at first he misunderstood the sounds that overtook him. Confused cries and wordless yells, they might have been anything. Simple shouts of encouragement, furious protest when one eager horseman rode his beast too close to a tent and tangled its feet in the ropes – his was a rowdy people, and voices were for raising.

Jemel didn't bother to look back until he heard the high scream of a horse in agony. It might – almost – have been the cry of a horse falling, its legs tangled in tent-ropes; he didn't think it was.

Twisting in the saddle, he had time only to register terrible confusion, no time to understand it before dense shadow blocked the light. Too fast, too dark for a cloud, and there could be none in any case, not in this dry season; startled, he glanced up to see a vast black shape swoop towards him, the sun making a dazzle around its silhouette.

His idiot horse flung its ears back, its head high and reared in terror, lifting itself and him closer to the claws that were outstretched already, iron-black talons curling out of glossy black chitin.

No time to nock an arrow to the string; no time even to draw his scimitar and try to beat those claws aside. All he could do was slip a stirrup and let himself slide sideways, almost out of the saddle altogether, to put the horse's body between him and the monster's strike.

For a moment he lost sight of it, as he clung to his frantic mount with both hands on the saddle horn and one leg hooked over; then that swift shadow was directly overhead and talons scythed the empty air, a hand's span above the horse's plunging back.

A blast of hot, dry air with a metallic taste to it, like the air a blacksmith breathed, and it was gone. Jemel hauled himself back into the saddle and quieted the horse with brutal heels and hands, while he scanned the sky.

There it was, rising to the peak of its arc now – and there were others behind it, hovering and striking where they pleased among the tents.

It turned in the air, graceless but swift; folded its wings like a falcon, and dived again.

There was nothing else about it that was bird-like. No feathers, no hint of feather. It had kept the breastplate of a crab, or something like it; in the brief time that it had hung exposed, Jemel had seen the sun glisten off rounded ridges that none the less made up a single piece of armour.

The claws he'd seen, close enough to test their razor edge if he'd had a mind to it; the legs were long, too thin for such an ending, and bent wrongly.

Two fatter limbs thrust forward and up, with pincers like lobsters'. Between them was a head like a disc on a short rod, two red eyes set in the foremost edge; behind were those wings, bent before the wind now but he'd seen them stiff to thresh it, and he'd seen them shaped earlier, down on the waterfront. Long and narrow, sharp like knives, with a structure of slender bone like fingers overlaid with a fine skein of sheeny skin: more bat's than bird's wings, they looked not strong enough to bear that weight of wickedness, but nothing in the creature's making was natural or right.

It plummeted towards him, those spider-legs stretching far forward with their monstrous claws agape; again he had no time except to duck down the other side of the saddle.

His horse bucked mindlessly, then seemed to stretch itself impossibly high; Jemel lost all grip with his legs and felt himself dangling, swinging from his hands' locked grip about the horn.

He threw his head back and stared upward, to see those cruel talons sunk deep into the horse's skull. The 'ifrit's wings were spread wide and beating now, raising horse and man together; Jemel took a breath, and forced his desperate hands apart.

He fell, twisting in the air, to land hard on his back. The impact drove the breath from his body, so that he lay gasping, while the bizarre shape that was 'ifrit and hanging horse together filled his sight.

An instinct of self-preservation had him rolling to one side, before he knew that he could move. A second later the body of the horse came crashing massively to ground, just where he'd been sprawled a moment before.

He threw himself back against its shattered bulk, seeking to hide in its shadow while he slipped the bow from his shoulder and searched among the arrows in his belt. He had only four, and one was broken; the one he sought had special fletching, though, and his frenzied fingers found it by touch. It was blessedly sound, and whole. He fumbled it free and lifted his head to spot the 'ifrit.

It was circling high above, out of bowshot and looking for his movement, he thought, to stoop again. As he watched, though, he saw it distracted; he saw it turn and set its wings to dive, but not this time at him.

Scanning the near horizon to seek its new intent, he saw Hasan.

Hasan, who must at last have realised that he rode alone; who must have looked back, perhaps hearing some hint of the mayhem in the camp or else simply wondering how far behind his men were; who must have seen the lethal shadows diving and so had turned his horse – of course, what else would such a man do, what else could he do? – and come racing back to bring his sword and his authority to the battle.

To die with his men, Jemel thought grimly, and with all the men of all the tribes that were gathered here; because what good could one more sword do against creatures that were immune to mortal steel, and of what use was authority against chaos, against the turmoil of panic and terror . . .?

Well, he had one chance to learn.

Jemel stood up and ran a few paces forward, then set his feet and set his arrow to the string. He sighted along its shaft, tracking the 'ifrit in its swoop; no wind that mattered, nothing to allow for except the speed of that dive, but that was almost too fast, he barely had a moment to adjust . . .

He held his breath, and loosed the arrow. He saw it fly, like a rip in the air, he saw the 'ifrit stoop; he saw Hasan realise his danger, and rein back his horse. He saw that maddened animal rear, as the 'ifrit closed from above.

And then, at last, he saw his arrow strike.

It might have been the finest shot he'd ever made, unless the arrow had some special virtue on it to meet his aim and his intent, to find its target as well as to destroy.

It caught the 'ifrit in the body, driving deep between belly-armour and wing. A little lower, and even that arrow might have glanced harmlessly away; a little higher, it might have torn somewhat at the fabric of one wing, done nothing to save Hasan or his people or the world.

But it struck true, and buried itself to the fletching. The 'ifrit tumbled suddenly in the air, losing all its impetus, changed in a moment from lethal raptor to broken drone. It crashed to ground, and Jemel's ears hurt with the high, edgy sound of its shrilling. He'd heard that before, and knew what it meant; even so he slung his bow, drew his scimitar and sprinted forward.

Hasan had his horse controlled, but could neither leave it nor force it close to the fallen 'ifrit. Jemel had trouble enough with his own legs, that were threatening to rebel; but he wouldn't show weakness before that man of all men. It wasn't weakness in any case, only relief that he'd shot well, but Hasan might misunderstand . . .

So he ran all the way to the trembling, writhing monster, fighting against the awful hissing shriek of its distress. He'd done the same once before, but then he'd been sure of its death and his final stroke of the sword was for satisfaction and for show, no more. This time, the closer he got, the less certain he was. Its legs waved and tried to run against the ground, and could shift its body not a finger's length; its two massive claws threatened the wind; its head twisted and jerked on the short neck.

Perhaps he should wait, trust the arrow and the imam's words on head and shaft, hope that blessing would spread like poison through the 'ifrit's system and so kill it at last. Perhaps he should nock another arrow to his bow and try for its eyes, from a distance, from here where he was still safe. Certainly he should not overleap its kicking legs and come stupidly close. Within sword's reach meant within claw's reach also. Just because Hasan was watching, he didn't need to make public display of his own idiocy . . .

Just because Hasan was watching, of course, he did exactly that. One of those long wings lay stretched out on the tawny ground, fluttering the gravel; Jemel treated it as a ramp and a way of safety, and simply ran straight up it.

His bare feet found purchase on splayed ridges of bone or cartilage but only skidded on the slippery smoothness of the skin between, so that mounting to the creature's back was a harder scramble than he'd anticipated. The wing flexed beneath him, and nearly threw him off; it tried to beat upwards, but its own weight and his combined to keep it pinioned, though he had to stoop and use his hands for balance and grip, when he'd wanted to show his grace and courage by leaping lightfoot up it, like a tumbler leaping from horse to galloping horse.

As soon as he'd reached the wingroot and was standing astride the 'ifrit's spine – if it had one – one giant claw came groping blindly back to find him. He hewed at it with his sword; the blade rang falsely and juddered in his hand. So far as he could see, he hadn't marked the chitin.

That seemed to be the 'ifrit's final effort, though. The claw subsided and lay next its fellow on the gravel, too heavy to be held up any longer. The terrible screeing noise had faded to a whistle, sharp and harsh but barely whisper-loud; Jemel felt confident enough to walk forward along the broad back until he came to where the neck sprouted suddenly inflexible, overlapping rings of chitin, where the head still turned and jabbed the air. Head-high to him, and yet the neck seemed short, so big this creature really was. He'd been deceived, by flight and speed and distance; by memory too, perhaps, a little, because the crab-things that came out of the water had been no larger than a Patric knight's shield, and now they were the size of a Sharai tent, longer, wings the length of an evening shadow . . .

The head was straining to see him, he realised, and could not twist itself around so far. It was a flattish disc, like one rice-bowl or one round shield inverted upon another – and there was a budding, he saw, like a bubble under the chitin, just on the rim. It was swelling as he watched, and as he watched it opened like an iris, like an eye, and there was hot red underneath and it was indeed an eye, grown to find him.

That was as much shapeshifting as the 'ifrit could manage now, seemingly; and it was plenty enough for Jemel. He didn't need Hasan's shout to tell him that there was no time for foolishness here, nor for curiosity. The whistling had dwindled to little more than a sigh, a simple use of air with no sound added; he could hear again the screams and cries of the camp at his back, and knew that Hasan would be desperate to reach his men, for whatever little good he could do there. He knew too that Hasan would not leave him here. There was a task unfinished, and a debt to acknowledge . . .

So Jemel finished the task, with a single clean thrust of his blade through the 'ifrit's new-grown eye: deep and hard he thrust, near to the haft the blade sank and must have been close to scraping the further side of that strange skull. The head lolled as he withdrew, and then flopped down as the neck lost all its strength.

He saw a mist creep through the glossy black of the creature's armour, and it seemed to him as though it became thinner, lighter, more frail moment by moment. It didn't shatter under his weight, as he half thought it would;

instead it dissipated, frayed into the wind and was gone, as immaterial as shadow.

So he fell again, through where the thing had been, and landed awkwardly from sheer surprise; and had barely got to his feet before Hasan was there, still ahorseback.

'I owe you my life, Jemel. That was a fine shot.'

'It was necessary,' he replied simply.

'Perhaps. I hope God agrees with you, or it may have been wasted; we may lie and rot together, if these things don't eat us instead. Come, seize hold . . .'

Jemel gripped his stirrup, and Hasan kicked the horse away.

The first tug all but wrenched arm from shoulder; but every boy ran like this at his father's stirrup, or his elder brother's. Any unhorsed warrior would expect to. It was close to flying, Jemel thought, or close to the mythical magic boots of story; every leap carried him further and faster than he could run, so that he seemed to soar over the ground, barely touching toe to earth between each tremendous step.

That speed brought them back too soon to the congregation of tents, before Jemel was ready to stop flying. He was flying in his head also, washed with victory, and far from ready for the turmoil of defeat.

That this was defeat, he had no doubt. Hasan reined in his horse; Jemel stumbled at the abrupt halt, his feet staggering on ground that was suddenly hard and ungiving beneath him. He let go the stirrup, his arms wheeling for balance, and reeled a few paces before he caught it. Then he straightened slowly, staring at the chaos before him.

There was nothing, of course, that could have prepared the tribes for an attack from the sky. Even knowing that, though, the devastation that he saw numbed his mind. Tents flapped, torn and empty, or else lay collapsed like vast black skins atop their broken poles. Men, camels, horses ran mindlessly to and fro, their feet catching in the sprawled bodies of the fallen; and all the time they were harried from above, as the 'ifrit picked their targets and swooped, to rise again with a struggling, screaming victim in their grip. Sometimes that victim – man or beast it might be, they seemed to draw no difference – would fall quiet quickly, as talons bit deep into chest or head or belly; sometimes death would be delayed a little, while the 'ifrit climbed high into the air before it opened its claws. Sometimes the victims were still screaming as they fell.

Jemel knew it was useless, even as he pulled his bow from his shoulder and reached for an arrow. Others were doing the same; he saw their shafts rise, he saw them fall. It didn't matter whether they hit or missed their target, whether they struck belly-plate or seemingly fragile wing. With no power but bow's strength and man's strength behind them, they had no effect.

Still he drew, aimed and shot, only to be doing something. Hasan's hurry and his own fall to ground had driven any thought of his more lethal arrow from his mind; it would still be lying on the gravel somewhere behind him, potent and wasted.

He loosed all the arrows that he had, and saw them all fail, all fall. Then he slung his bow across his shoulder again and drew his sword, looking round for Hasan. All his oaths were forgotten; if he must die, if they all must, at least he would die defending that man, for his people's sake.

That man, he saw, was already the centre and focus of a small group, men of his own tribe and others. Hasan was the only one horsed; animals were as maddened as their riders by the stooping, swirling shadows that killed from above, and it took a master to control both himself and his mount.

As Jemel watched, Hasan stood in his stirrups and bellowed. It was the name of God he cried, that which all the Sharai knew and were forbidden to utter; for as far as his voice could reach, men turned to gape. That one word could cut through even panic and despair, to draw their attention to him.

He whirled his sword above his head in a gesture all could read, *come to me, gather about me . . .*

Whether it was Hasan's native authority, or simply the sight of someone, anyone taking charge, men came running. Not all, not immediately: some turned and bellowed in their turn, to spread the message further.

Jemel did the same, calling and beckoning, as loudly as he could; then he followed the general rush, to cluster in a dense pack around Hasan.

One man had made the difference; one man's clear sight could yet turn a rout, a disaster into an orderly withdrawal. At his urging they moved slowly, warily back from the tents and towards the siq that would bring them into the safety of Rhabat, their numbers growing every minute.

The soaring 'ifrit still fell on them, picking off those who were slow or too far distant and assailing the main band; but now they met a bristling hedge of blades lifted against them. Even unblessed weapons could batter clutching claws aside, if they could do no worse damage.

Men were still lost, plucked suddenly from the mass; Hasan himself was in most danger, sitting so much higher than those who surrounded him. Necessarily he made himself a target, even if he was not so already by virtue of who he was. A hundred voices warned him, though, of every diving 'ifrit. Most times he simply ducked, sliding down and around his saddle as Jemel had done before him, and so survived.

Once, though, Jemel saw him keep his seat, and swing his scimitar against the talons that reached for him and for no man else. Jemel saw the blade connect, and slice through the creature's legs when its claws were only a moment from Hasan's body. That blade must have been blessed at some time, and held its virtue still . . .

The wounded 'ifrit rose high above them, seeming to lose the solidity of its body. It didn't fade as they did in death but rather contracted, from nightmare creature to spinning coil of smoke. Jemel soon lost sight of it in his steady march among the throng, with the need to keep alert against the danger of others coming.

Others came, inevitably; they hung in the air, wings flailing to keep them out of sword's reach, while their long legs thrust and grabbed towards the men below. No arrows met them now; no one had space to draw a bow, even if there'd been any purpose to it. They could choose their intended victim unmolested; they chose Hasan so often, Jemel was sure that it was more than his height above the pack that drew them to him. Men had to cling to his horse's bridle on both sides, to keep the crazed animal from bolting; Hasan himself had to keep his blade flicking this way and that as they snatched at him time and again. Still he refused to dismount, though. Jemel thought he was right; even those on the margins of the group needed to see him, to hold them together in that slow retreat. If once they lost that sight, that certainty, they would break and run; and then more would die, dozens more, and it would be panic and terror that the remainder carried with them into Rhabat.

Instead they brought a victory of sorts, a grim and unlikely survival. Gradually the high walls of the siq closed around them, until there was no space, no wing-room for the hovering 'ifrit.

Discipline broke briefly, as that dense pack of men tried to squeeze into too narrow a road; voices threatened, men surged and shoved, blades flashed between tribe and tribe. Hasan cried them to order, though, and drove his horse through the throng, the flat of his scimitar beating left and right.

And so he led them on, and so they followed, several hundred men with scarcely one wounded among their number; but they left many, many dead behind them, and the way out of Rhabat was closed at their backs. They heard its closing, the thunder of falling rocks; a cloud of dust overswept them as they walked.

They were halfway back through the siq before Jemel remembered why he'd followed Hasan in the other direction just that short time ago; and realised that if they were shut in, then Julianne, her father, Redmond were equally shut out. If they were still alive at all . . .

13

Heights of Terror

Julianne hadn't dared ask for Tezra when she'd followed her father to the stables, with the half-dozen men who would accompany them. Her father had known about her disguise, of course — she would never have tried, never have dared to think of trying to hide the truth from him — and she'd thought that most likely the men knew too; but the stable-lads could not. She was tall enough to pass as a boy, but her voice might have made them wonder; her asking for a lady's mount would certainly have raised questions in their minds. Their gossip might have spread further than the stable yard, might have caused trouble for her father. She had perhaps been trespassing too much on his kindness already, with this escapade; the last thing she'd wanted was to have rumours reach the sheikhs, of how he'd blinked at such a breach of their customs.

Besides, there'd been the danger of Hasan's seeing them ride out. If he spotted Tezra in the party, he'd be sure to look closely at her rider. What he might do then she hadn't been able to guess, she'd only been sure that the consequences would have been public, and unpleasant. Hasan believed in the traditions of his people; he might, she thought, have other reasons too, for wanting to be assured of her safety.

So she'd kept quiet as the horses were saddled, and only sighed to herself when the lads had brought her a hard-mouthed, raw-boned little cob, fit mount for a boy permitted to ride with men. His name was Rubon, they'd told her; she'd nodded silently, and hauled herself swiftly onto his back before their dark, inquisitive eyes could see too far beneath her hood.

The party had ridden off, herself in a boy's proper station, last in line; and of course they had indeed met Hasan standing in the doorway of his tribal house to see them off. He had bowed to her father, had watched them all past; she'd kept her head down and her hands loose on the reins, trying to imitate the Sharai men's easy slouch in the saddle.

No summons at her back, no questions: she'd let out a breath she hadn't realised she'd been holding, and looked forward to the afternoon. An hour's riding, perhaps, before they met Redmond; another slow hour's return, telling her news and hearing his, sharing his thoughts and her father's. And of course escaping the call of duty, dull work in the hot kitchens. Yaman might make a show of reluctance at putting guests to work, but that was habit only; once past it she was a hard taskmistress, and seemed driven by demons today. Elisande had had her own plans of escape; Julianne might have gone with her, but her friend had made it rather obscurely transparent that those plans included Marron, had been formed indeed at his instigation. It had only been tactful to let her go alone, even if it was also courting trouble: young women were not ordinarily to be seen around Rhabat in male company. As an excuse, *he is the Ghost Walker* would be more likely to throw oil on the flames; particularly given this Ghost Walker, and this girl. *Patricularly*, she'd thought, and giggled to herself . . .

Once beyond the siq and the camping-grounds, they'd broken the strict order of their riding, so that she'd found herself at her father's side, while the other men followed at a discreet distance – far enough to let the two talk in private, far enough to swear that they'd heard no squeak of a female voice from their anonymous companion. She'd been grateful but anxious still, now that she'd started worrying; she'd asked, 'Who are these men? I can't read their tribal markings . . .'

'Can you not?' he'd replied dryly. 'You should learn, if you mean to spend time wandering their deserts. They are of the Ib' Dharan, my honour guard for the time I spend at Rhabat; which means of course that I am honoured to buy their services. If you are worried where their allegiance lies, don't be. I have it in my purse.'

That might not have stopped a whisper reaching their lord, that the Shadow's daughter had ridden out with the Shadow this day, in the dress of a boy; but he would likely say not a word, for fear of losing his own share of his men's income. Julianne had been reassured, and had tried once again simply to relax into the pleasures of riding slowly under a hot sun. Pleasure was what she'd come seeking, after all, pleasure in various guises; this was the simplest, this steady progress through a barren landscape, and it would have been such a shame to worry it to waste . . .

Her father had said little, the rhythms of riding seeming to lull him into a contemplative mood. He'd be thinking about his feast tonight, she'd guessed, and trying as ever to anticipate, to be ready to meet whatever came. He hated to be unprepared, always; which was why he could be so swift to change a plan, because he was ever ready to be redirected. Serving the King as he did, he had to be.

When he'd ridden half an hour without a word, she had taken her horse on a short distance ahead. Let him ponder in peace; she'd look for first signs of Redmond. His caravan should be coming into sight soon, surely, however unhurried its pace . . .

Either her father had been concerned to see her ride alone, or else she hadn't been the only one grown a little impatient; a couple of the Ib' Dharan had come cantering up beside her. Rather than oblige them to slow down to match her pace, she'd kicked Rubon into matching theirs. And they'd been young, those two, if not so young as she was, let alone as young as her dress implied; and they were bored with her father's stately progress, so much had been obvious. Nor would they ever have let themselves be outridden or outraced by a child, boy or girl . . .

So they'd raced, or near enough to it, along the broad and clear track. Nothing like that morning's head to head with Hasan, neither their mounts nor their minds could have managed the same focus of intent; this had been a wild, dusty, laughing scramble and no more, play entirely without purpose.

Remembering the morning's lesson, though, she'd given way gracefully and hauled her horse effortfully to a walk before the heat could sap his eagerness. The other two had swept past her, kicking up a storm of dust and sand which their abrupt halting had only made worse; choking on it even behind her veil, she'd turned her head and looked back to see just how far behind they'd left her father.

'We'd better wait,' she'd said as the young men came back to join her. Her voice had sounded thick and hoarse, almost boy-like to her own ears; they had nodded gravely, still not challenging her disguise.

They'd walked their hot mounts in slow circles, while the breeze blew the hanging dust away; and now, still waiting for the rest of the party to catch up, she shielded her eyes against the fierce light and squinted forward, thinking that she could just make out something, perhaps someone on the road ahead. Or just off the road, rather, a hint of shadow against the gravel's glare that could possibly be a caravan at rest. It was absolutely at the limit of her sight; it might only be a smudge of desiccated shrub, although she'd seen none so far and any growth on such a bare plain was likely to have been stripped long since, for forage or fuel.

It seemed a strange place for a caravan to pause, though, and a strange time for it, just a little distance short of better rest and water. She remembered that Redmond was still carrying old hurts, and without a companion from Surayon to ease them; the boy who'd brought the news of his coming had said the drovers were anxious about him. Perhaps he'd worsened, and was not fit to travel further today. Though if that were so, surely he'd have sent someone ahead to carry the news to Rhabat, perhaps to ask for a doctor; he wasn't too proud to know when he needed help.

Her father was laggardly, dawdling deliberately, she thought, to teach her not to be so impulsive. She turned to her companions and said, 'Is that the people we've come to find, can you see?'

She didn't bother to keep her voice gruff; they disregarded it manfully. Both looked where she pointed, one standing in his stirrups to see better; he said, 'There are camels there, and people moving.'

That must be them; if there'd been any other party headed for Rhabat, the boy surely would have mentioned it. Julianne wanted to ride on, to reach Redmond first and so turn the lesson back on her father. But she was nervous suddenly, afraid of what she might find in that curiously still group. Pure cowardice, but if there were bad news she'd rather not be the first to learn it. Besides, she might need to discard her disguise, if Redmond needed nursing. Better to do that with her father there, to shield her against any reaction from the drovers. They'd be accustomed to meeting women on the road, but a girl in boy's dress might be another matter . . .

So she lingered, and the young men with her, until at last her father joined them with the other riders at his back. She suppressed her fretful impatience under his austere gaze, and simply pointed.

'Look, there are people and camels, up ahead there. We think it's Redmond and his caravan . . .'

He peered, grunted, and nudged his mount into a brisker pace. She fell into place behind him, keeping her anxieties to herself; he could make his own assessment, he didn't need her to list the possibilities. He'd keep his thoughts to himself, in any case. He always had. Only his sudden haste betrayed him.

He led them at a sharp canter, over the remaining distance; she rode in his dust for a while, until it became so dense that she was riding blind, her every breath a cough. Then she moved up to his side. Her watering eyes cleared slowly; now she could see, and what she saw worried her intensely.

There were all the camels of the caravan, couched together and hobbled, as they would have been for a noonday rest. She could see men slumped against them too, as it might be their drovers sleeping through the heat. But noon was long past, they really should have been on the move by now; and the only figures moving among them were women, gowned and veiled. As it might be, as it might well be if Redmond really were too sick to finish the journey, if the men had handed his care over to a group of local women and were dozing the time away until he was fit to go on. If he ever was, today or any day, if they didn't leave his body by the road . . .

No, she was being stupid. Redmond's injuries had been well on the way to healing, before they parted; he might be, he must be tired and weak after a difficult journey, and torture left damage in the mind that would take a long time to scar over, but there was no reason to imagine him dead or dying. Exhausted, perhaps, too weary to sit a camel for a full day; no more. For sure, no more than that.

Nor would the women scurry so, over a dead body. Julianne could see a couple clearly now, coming away from

the caravan and trotting over to a string of scattered packs
and bundles at the roadside. Their belongings, where they
must have dropped them when the drovers called for help.
They crouched over one of the packs, took out a flask –
water, perhaps, or something stronger – and went hurrying
back, their tattered robes kicking up flurries of dust. They
spared barely a glance for the riders' rapid approach;
Julianne had only a glimpse of shrouded eyes behind long
veils. Peasant women, she thought, long familiar with the
type: shy and silent in the presence of strangers, with a
wisdom that belied their simplicity and a stubborn strength
that far surpassed her own. These at least she swore to know
better, if they had truly brought aid to Redmond. She had
tricks learned from her father, to overcome that shyness.
Offering them money would be an insult, but she could at
least learn their tribe and the name of their sheikh, she
could seek his favour for them . . .

She wheeled Rubon off the road and took him straight
towards the line of couched camels and resting men. The
beasts were restless, she saw, tossing their heads and straining at their hobbles; the drovers must be exhausted to sleep
through that. Likely they'd been smoking *khola*, to ease the
heat of the dreary day; she'd heard that that herb had a
bitter flavour but brought sweet dreams to its users.

Closer now, she could see over the camels' backs; and
yes, there was Redmond at last. He was sitting with his
back to a rock, and seemed to be sleeping too, while the
women fussed about him. Sleeping, or unconscious – perhaps he'd shared the drovers' pipes, to earn himself some
brief cease of pain.

Rubon shied suddenly, his hooves skidding on the

hard-packed gravel as he twisted violently away. Julianne cursed, and slipped perilously in the saddle before she caught her balance. Then she dragged at the reins, to haul the horse's head around. She'd seen nothing obvious to startle him, no bird flying up suddenly and no abrupt movement in the caravan; but an unknown animal could have unknown fears. Perhaps he simply didn't like camels . . .

She wasn't sure she liked the look of those camels herself, she thought, fighting to force Rubon closer. A foaming mouth and rolling eyes were common enough in an excited horse, but camels were more phlegmatic, or simply more difficult to overwork; she couldn't think what it would take to bring them to this condition. Poisoned water, perhaps? But then their drovers wouldn't be so relaxed. Abject terror might do it, but the same objection applied . . .

Abject terror was still her best guess, though. It was affecting Rubon too, by the way he planted all four feet firmly in the gravel and stood shaking beneath her, ears back and neck running with sweat. He would not go closer; and she didn't like to dismount and leave him in such a state, though she was desperate now to reach Redmond and find out how he was.

The men had got ahead of her, by dint of being patient; they had followed the road a little further and so approached from the other side of that line of camels, that wall she couldn't breach. She saw her father jump down from his horse and toss the reins to one of his companions; she saw the women make way for him, standing back to let him through to his old friend Redmond's side.

She wrenched furiously at Rubon's reins, meaning to

take him back and around to follow the men's wiser tracks, if she could only get him moving again. What had she meant to do in any case, jump him over the hobbled camels? Couched nose to tail as they were, there was no path between . . .

Before she could persuade or bully Rubon into taking a single step, though, one of those frenzied camels suddenly managed to break its hobble. It surged to its feet and galloped off blindly across the plain – while its drover simply toppled and lay flat and unresponsive in the sun.

Even *khola* couldn't do that to a man. Julianne turned her head to find her father. No need to cry a warning; he knew. As she watched, he laid his hand on Redmond's shoulder and nudged it gently.

The old man slid slowly sideways, and settled to the ground with his face in the dust. His fall left a dark wet streak on the reddish stone of the boulder he'd been leaned against; between his shoulderblades, Julianne thought his robe was hanging open down the length of a savage tear.

Then she realised that it was his back that had been torn open, through the robe; those were flaps of skin and flesh that gaped.

Much of his spine was missing.

She thought that the world had slowed calamitously around her; she thought that she was the only one still thinking. It felt almost as though she'd been granted a gift of prophecy that ran just half a moment ahead of its realisation, or else that her thoughts governed the actions of those she watched, as though she were dreaming and yet ordering the progress of the dream.

She thought there must be hoofprints in the gravel all around her father, and saw his head dart bird-like left and right to spy them out.

She thought he should understand by now, he had to, he wasn't usually so slow; she thought he should straighten and defend himself, and so he did, or tried to. But he was slow again, too slow in drawing his sword. She thought those supposed women must show themselves now for what they truly were; and saw it happen, saw them grow tall and monstrous, their ragged robes shredding as their bodies swelled. All but one loped towards the men who were still on horseback, who were struggling to control their panicked mounts; that other swung a dreadful arm, and clubbed her father across the back of his balding head.

She saw him lifted off the ground by the force of that blow, saw him fly some distance before he fell. She wished, she prayed, she willed him to stand up; but the sense of foreknowledge, almost of power had abandoned her already. He only lay sprawled and still, as still as Redmond, as any of the drovers . . .

Thrown back into the physical world, where men and horses were screaming and dying, where her father was brutally hurt and perhaps dying also if he weren't dead already, she wanted only to go to him: to stand above his body with knives in hand and shriek defiance at the ghûls.

In the maze of confusion and fear that her mind had suddenly become, focused only on that one small thing, her father's empty form, she forgot that she wasn't sitting Merissa or Tezra or any of the pliant, courageous ponies she used to ride. A horsewoman to her bones, she dug in her heels and concentrated eyes and thoughts on that jump, clean over the struggling camels that lay between her and her goal.

Rubon tossed his head, to remind her of the truth; she saw how his nostrils flared to smell the blood and terror she was trying to force him towards, and she thought too late that she should have left him here after all, she should have slid off and run the distance, it wasn't so far . . .

Too late because he was on the move already, kicked into it by her own heedless feet. Not where she had set him, that living barrier; he'd turned almost on the spot and was charging blindly in the opposite direction, over the plain that was so smooth and flat it might have been made for such running.

She threw all her weight against the reins, trying to drag him physically to a halt, but he had the bit between his teeth and his jaw locked tight; there would be no stopping him now.

If she jumped she'd break a leg at best, going so fast over such a surface. Nothing to do but sit tight and wait for him to tire, or else for the panic to fade in his mind, for his grip on the bit to slacken . . .

She twisted round in the saddle, trying to see what was happening behind her, and almost lost her seat as Rubon shied again, turning abruptly to the west. Trusting his instincts now, when that trust was little or no use to her and none at all to her father, she tried to see what had startled him. There were birds flocking and wheeling in the sky to the south, but they were far away. Or no, they couldn't be that far, they'd have to be dragons else; but still, black birds were surely nothing much to a horse so far gone in fear . . .

To a horse so far gone, she supposed, anything that

moved could be more cause for terror. Perhaps he was wise to turn into the sun, to run blind . . .

Perhaps not. He played literally into her hands by doing so; his pace slackened as the glare denied him even a clear sight of the ground he ran on, and she felt it through the reins as his teeth loosed the bit. One sharp tug, and she had control again. His mouth was hard, but not hard enough to resist her desperate strength. She hauled his head around by main force, and set him galloping back the way they had come.

This time, she was wiser. She murmured reassurance into his ears as soon as they started to flicker, hearing the sounds of battle ahead before she could; she let him slow to an uncertain walk, let him stop altogether before the scents of blood and death could overcome his courage, as they had before.

She had no thought of leaping off and sprinting forward now, to die beside her father. That had been a moment's yearning, a girl's stupid gesture, long since blown out of her head by the wind of that mad ride. She stretched high on Rubon's back for the best view she could achieve and watched numbly, wanting only to witness, to be a voice for others. If men had to die, they should not do so unregarded.

It would fall to her, she realised, to tell Elisande and Rudel of Redmond's death. That was a cruel twist after they had worked so hard to free him from the Roq, after he had come so far, so near to safety; briefly it felt almost worse than the loss of her own father.

But thoughts of her father brought back the memory of the djinni's voice. *You can save him, though it might be better if you did not.* Well, she had not; that might please the djinni, though she couldn't imagine how. Nor how she might have done it, unless she'd not paused to wait for him on the road, unless she'd ridden on and so found Redmond dead and died herself to warn him. That wasn't fair; how could she have known or guessed, how could she have seen ghûls in those women when more experienced heads than hers had not?

She caught a sob in her throat, swallowed hard against rising guilt and turned her mind deliberately back to follow her eyes, to witness.

The ghûls' sudden ambush had caught all the tribesmen unprepared, as it had her father; none had survived, that she could see. Bodies of men and horses lay scattered across the gravel, and the ghûls were shambling among the maddened camels now, slaying with claws and razor teeth. Some were pausing to feed, and not only on the bodies of the beasts.

If any tried to feed on her father, she thought she might yet do something stupid; but he lay yet where he had fallen, face down and seemingly untouched.

Close enough to see so much, she was also close enough to be seen; far enough away to have time to flee, though, she thought. She hoped, as more than one bloodied muzzle turned in her direction.

What would they see, though? A boy, on a pony. Offering no danger – and right enough there, alas – and offering no interest either; they had food in plenty, no reason to hunt for more. Besides, a fast pony could outrun a ghûl, at least a ghûl in that form, horse-headed but bandy-legged; Rubon she thought could outrun the wind, if it smelled of ghûl. They were dull creatures, or supposedly so, swift neither of thought nor limb. That was why they relied on guile to snare their victims, and fell back constantly on the appearance of a woman.

Well, it worked, so why not? Even on the intelligent, it worked. Even with one in the party who had met a ghûl all too recently, and shaped like a woman, too. Perhaps that was what the djinni had meant, that she should have been more alert, and so had failed it and her father both, and all her people too . . .

She could have mourned her father then, she could have broken down altogether; but at that moment she saw one of the ghûls leave its feeding, and go to stand above his body. She watched breathlessly, fearing to see it stoop, its jaws open; instead, though, she saw muscles ripple and surge along its back. She saw the sparse fur stretch, and split; she saw it raise its head and heard it keen as if in pain as dank wet matter slithered out of the opening wound. Slithered and spread, unfurled like distorted leaves – like a pair of leaves, rooted in its spine . . .

Wings, she realised at last, marvelling at the stupidity of her eyes; it had grown wings. And wafted them slowly now, as if in experiment or wonder. They dried rapidly in the hot sun; it beat them harder, and rose a hesitant length above the ground before dropping back.

As if satisfied with that, it reached its long arms down and hooked them into her father's clothing, perhaps through the clothing and into his flesh, she couldn't tell. Then it tossed its terrible head, flexed its wings, leaped into the air and flew.

*

She didn't understand; did it mean to play with the body as she'd seen young tercels do, dropping prey from on high, only to catch it again mid-air? And why him, why did it have to be him when there were so many bodies it might have chosen . . .?

Perhaps because he is not dead, she answered her own protesting question as Rubon flinched from the ghûl's shadow when it passed across them. Alone of all his company, it might be that he was still breathing; it might be that the ghûl would take him up and drop him and not catch him again before he struck the ground, and so for a second time she could see her failure, see her father fall.

But *why?* was still a question, and not answered yet. If they wanted him dead they had teeth, they had talons, they had used them many times today; and this change at least had seemed to hurt the creature. Why put itself through that without need – and why single out her father, whether for play or for special execution? Her father was special, of course, this had been a careful ambush and he must have been the target, all those other deaths were incidental; but—

Because he is not dead, and they do not want him dead. Or not them, but their masters. The ghûls served the will of the 'ifrit, they had stones in their tongues to force them to it; perhaps that keening cry had been not pain but protest. Or pain as punishment, perhaps those stones burned hotter if they delayed or disobeyed . . .

But, *he is not dead, and they do not want him dead* – that was enough. There would be time later to work out why the 'ifrit should want her father alive, whether it was for some dread purpose or simply to kill him for themselves, to be absolutely certain he was dead. That would be like seeing Redmond's body, worse than cruel; but even the chance of it could be put aside, for now.

Redmond's body, this moment, she would always regret; he deserved better than abandonment, the chance perhaps of a later hunt for bones. The living outrank the dead, though; she would have left her father – she thought, she hoped – to chase Redmond, or any survivor. She wheeled her willing horse around, away from the scene of slaughter, and set him to pursue that shadow across the plain.

The ghûl was heading westerly, into the sun, all but impossible to spot a dark fleck against that dazzling light; but its speeding shadow ran before them and all they had to do was chase it, no need to catch up. Julianne was still no more than a witness. The 'ifrit were in the Dead Waters; if the ghûl meant to deliver her father to them, it must fly over that high scarp that hid Rhabat, that lay between plain and sea. Without growing wings of her own, Julianne could not follow it then.

There was still the chance, though, of something unforeseen: an archer chance-met, to wound the ghûl and bring it down; a sudden storm of sand, a wind it could not fly against; a djinni . . .

Actually, she thought bitterly, the djinni was all her hope, and so she had none. The rest was foolish dreaming. Djinni Khaldor could save her father in a moment, but it would not. *It might be better if you did not*, it had said, which was a death sentence for him now, because without its help she could do nothing. A death sentence or worse, if the 'ifrit had other plans for him . . .

She reminded herself that the djinn did not interfere in

the affairs of men, except when it suited their mysterious interests; and then only to send her into heartache and despair, it seemed, from love to desire and from doubt to hopelessness.

Well, she would ride as far as she could follow the ghûl, to the hills' rise. She would watch it out of sight, and try not to think of her father; then she would go to the tribesmen camped before the siq, and tell them of the ghûls at their feasting by the road. Then she would go to Rhabat, and through Rhabat, and ask if anyone had seen a man dropped into the sea, and if he fell with a splash or were swallowed silently by something other than the water . . .

And so she rode, and the scarp rose before her, more cliff than hills, steep and broken. And the rapid shadow that she'd hunted was gone suddenly, swallowed by the still shadow of the land; but once in that shadow herself she could look up and not be dazed by light, she could see the cruciform of the ghûl in black silhouette against the sky, not beating its wings now but gliding. Gliding and dropping, growing just a little bigger in her sight. And surely it must be lower than the cliff's height now, and was not trying to lift itself and its burden back up into free air . . .

Suddenly slightly hopeful after all, she stared upward with a grim determination to be certain. Shadow against shadow now, as the creature approached the cliff, but still there was no mistaking the abrupt backbeat of its winds as it lifted a little, slowed in the air and so settled. Settled onto a ledge a long, long way up the face, near to the top: just where an eagle might settle to tear its prey apart in peace, inaccessible and safe . . .

But the ghûl wouldn't have borne the weight of her father so far, only to eat him now. Of a certainty, it wouldn't. Perhaps it was tired, if such creatures did tire; after struggling such a way on new and unfamiliar wings, it might need rest before it tackled overtopping the scarp. Or else this might be the appointed place, where it was told or forced to bring him. Why this side of the ridge she couldn't imagine, when the 'ifrit were in the Dead Waters; but there were things, she knew, that were beyond her imagining, and they still existed in the world. Because an idea made no sense to her, didn't mean it didn't make sense . . .

Whatever the ghûl's reasoning – if such creatures did reason – the fact remained: there the ghûl was, for now at least, and there also was her father. And here was she, and there was a long climb, an impossible climb between them. Hasan had said it was impossible, and that even without knowing how impossible such a climb, any climb would be for her.

And yet, and yet. The djinni had said *you can save him*, and she had to try. If it had said *you cannot save him*, still she would have had to try . . .

She slipped off Rubon's back and hobbled him quickly Sharai-fashion with the girdle of her robe, thinking even as she did so that it was like a declaration, *I'm going to fail here, I'll be coming back soon* . . .

Her knives she stowed safely, pointlessly in her hood; little use they'd be against a ghûl, even if she did find a way up and contrive to climb it. It was a gesture, no more, to counteract the hobble. *Knives cut hobbles*, she thought, and almost managed a giggle.

She could find nothing more to giggle at as she

approached the rubble at the foot of the cliff. At first she stumbled over loose shale, then larger chunks of rock that turned beneath her feet; then there were boulders the size of a chest that she must scramble up onto, and already she felt nervous, arms out for a balance that was never quite there so that she was teetering though both feet were firmly planted.

Then she was facing a wall of rocks the size of houses, and this was still detritus, pieces of the scarp that had fallen away. She lifted her head and looked up, and even in the dense shade she could see that the cliff didn't have one face, it had a thousand. Whatever god had built this ridge, the work had been done poorly; it must have begun to crumble almost before it had been finished. She could see deep cracks in it, and great overhangs where wind or rare rain had bitten a slab away; it defied her understanding of the world, that rock was a solid thing that could be trusted to endure, and only herself was weak and liable to falling.

Still, her father was up there, and in need of her; she had to try, before she could know that she'd failed. The rock might be as friable as stale bread, but at least there were plenty of holds on its rough surface; she stretched up, gripped with both hands and slotted one foot into a crack.

And stepped up, found another foothold by touch, put her weight on it – and felt it flake away beneath her, felt her hands slip at the sudden jerking shock and so slid down again, skinning her palms as she tried to cling to rock that grated before it fell to dust.

She stood where she had stood before, sniffing and swallowing hard against a threat of tears. This was only a boulder, albeit a massive one; she had to surmount it before she even reached the cliff-face proper. And there was so much of that, it stretched so high and the climb simply wasn't possible, even to one who was skilled at climbing; just the thought of it terrified her.

So brief an attempt didn't count as failure, though. She moved a step or two to the side, tried to read it with her eyes – *hold there and there, step there, stretch to that and hope, trust, pray that it would hold her* – and then reached out her stinging hands again.

Set her mind to climbing, tried to blank out all thought, all fear of a fall; took a tremulous breath, took a grip as firm as she could, as firm as she dared – and stayed, pressing her whole body against that insecure rock in a sudden shaking fit as she heard an unearthly voice speaking at her back.

'Daughter of the Shadow, you are no son of the rock, whatever your dress declares. You risk your life to no purpose; you need not hope to reach your father that way.'

Djinni, rot you, I know that – but oh, where have you been? When I needed you more even than I do now . . .? If it had come earlier, it could have saved Redmond's life, and the others'. To be fair, it would have needed to reach the caravan before she had, perhaps long before; but she felt no obligation to be fair.

She bit her tongue hard, till she tasted blood, to remind herself not to ask questions unless or until she simply had to; and pried her fingers slowly away from the rock, forced herself to turn around and stand straight, somehow managed a little bow before the slender twist of dust that was the djinni this time.

'Djinni Khaldor.' She struggled to keep her voice from trembling as her legs were, without conspicuous success.

'Your arrival is opportune. I know I cannot climb this cliff; and yet my father is in need of me,' in need of help at least, though preferably something better than her own, 'and you said yourself that I might save him, although I don't see how . . .'

'So you might, though perhaps you should not. Even a man such as he is expendable, at need. But you are human, and young, and will perhaps not see that as the djinn do. I may not raise you to the ledge where he lies, Julianne de Rance; if I touched your body, that touch would destroy you.'

Indeed, she had seen that; but, 'You could go there yourself, great one.'

'I could, though again I might not touch him. I could destroy the ghûl, and the 'ifrit when they come; but he would still be on the ledge, where no man or girl could reach him. I will not do that. What I can also do, what I will do if you ask it, is to bring you to a cliff that you can climb, if you have the courage.'

She doubted her courage for any climb, and she didn't understand; but she was used to bewilderment in this creature's conversation, and there had to be a point to it, surely.

'Very well,' she said, 'I do ask it.' Was that, did that count as a question? She couldn't decide; and had to grit her teeth at the djinni's countering laugh, sure that it was reading her doubts, perhaps her very thoughts.

'Prepare yourself, then.'

'Wait. One moment . . .' Wherever it took her, and for whatever purpose, she was fairly clear that she would not be coming back here; she couldn't leave Rubon hobbled in the desert.

She clambered down across the rocks and ran over to

where the horse was standing; took a little longer than a moment to unknot her girdle and tie it round her waist again, and then to fix the reins about the saddle-horn, so that they shouldn't trail on the ground and trip him. She slapped his neck, told him lies about his beauty and courage and gave him a firm push away, back towards the road. If he were sensible or lucky, he might find his way to safety; any Sharai would gladly take possession of a stray horse. She could do no more.

As soon as she saw him start to move, she hurried back towards the djinni. It had moved a little distance towards her, so she didn't need to scramble over the rubble of rocks again; as she drew close, it said, 'Stand still, do not fear – and do not reach for me, Julianne de Rance, if you value your own life and your father's.'

She nodded her understanding, stood stiffly with her hands clenched on the seams of her robe, and waited.

For what she didn't know, and was too slow or too distracted to guess. It drifted closer to her, and began to spin faster and to stretch itself, to climb higher into the sky until it was only an insubstantial thread before her eyes. She felt the wind of its spinning, as a breeze first and then a gathering storm, battering at her. She closed her eyes for a moment but liked that less; it felt like the first time she'd been drunk, the world gone dizzy around her.

Opening her eyes again, she thought that perhaps she hadn't; at first she could see nothing but darkness. Then a golden thread in darkness, a twisting thread of light, and that must be the djinni; except that it couldn't be, because it opened like an eye itself or like a pair of curtains drawing back, and all a golden landscape was before her.

And beside her, as the dark swept further round; and so behind her, and there was no dark at all. She stood in golden light on golden dust, and the djinni was a shimmer of air, no more, that she could see only peripherally, in the corner of her eye when she turned her head away.

When she turned her head away, she saw a cliff.

This one cast no shadow, except across her thoughts. *I will bring you to a cliff that you can climb* – and the djinn might not lie but they could certainly, most emphatically be wrong. She couldn't climb that thing. She simply couldn't.

It rose perhaps no higher than the broken ridge she'd been defeated by in the other world – and there at least was one small blessing, that she felt no need or urge to ask the djinni where they were; no question in her mind, she recognised Elisande's descriptions instantly – but this rose sheer, as though it had been punched up from bedrock by some almighty fist. The stone shimmered in the strange light, and looked completely smooth.

'Djinni, I can't . . .'

'If you do not,' it said, quite matter-of-fact, 'your father will die. Soon.'

She wanted to ask how, and how her climbing this would help him in another world; and bit the questions back just in time, her numbed mind fumbling for some other way to phrase them. 'I do not, I do not see that this will aid my father . . .' she said at last, only hoping that there was no suspicion of a query in her voice.

'When you reach the top, I can take you back. You will then be above him.'

She didn't see how that would help either, but there had to be a way. That was implicit.

So she steeled herself, and walked forward to the base of the cliff. No rubble here, to catch her feet and give her a premature taste of the fear to come. Only the level dust, running up to the great wall of rock.

When she reached to touch it, it was warm beneath her fingers although there was no sun to heat it. She snatched her hand back, startled; she'd forgotten what she'd been told, how the warmth of this world pervaded everything. How it rose from below, indeed, so that the underside of a turned rock would be hotter than the top. She wondered how hot this massive scarp must be inside, and decided she would be glad never to know.

This close, it didn't look so impossible, at least for any-one who could be confident high up, with nothing to catch her should she fall. Elisande might relish the challenge of it, she thought; as she would have done herself years ago, when she was young and carefree, when height delighted her past breathing.

Not now. Now she looked and saw ledges where strong fingers could grip, cracks where bare toes could find a pur-chase, her old skills of eye and judgement not deserting her; but already all she could think about was falling.

She tried to focus her mind on her father instead, on his imminent danger; but that was a distraction, it could be allowed no place in her head. She would need all her concentration to make this climb, higher and more dan-gerous than any she'd tackled in Marasson before she fell.

She bent and pulled her boots off, one by one; thought of stowing them in her hood along with her knives, but felt that that too would be a distracting weight. However light a burden, it would pull at her constantly, another reminder of the drop at her back . . .

So she tossed the boots aside, took one glance back but couldn't see the djinni, set fingers and toes to the rockface and began to climb.

At first, she thought that perhaps she could manage this after all. Her toes could find their holds by touch, she never needed to look down; and so long as she could just keep eyes and thoughts on her hands, her balance, her next move along her chosen route, then she'd be fine. Falling was all in the mind, she told herself quite firmly, and her mind was far too busy to fall. Besides, it wasn't climbing that terrified her, it was heights. She was a creature of such little faith, she had to see a thing to believe in it; and she couldn't see how high she'd come already, she couldn't see over her shoulder. There was only the wall of golden stone, a hand's-breadth from her nose. She'd been scared before and she might well be scared after, standing on the top and looking down; but for now there was nothing to be scared of. So long as she was holding on and moving up, so long as she could sight her grips and reach them, oh yes, she'd be fine. Why not . . .?

She thought it was the warmth of the rock that made her sweat so, fingers and face and feet and all her body else; she thought it was some phantom breeze that made her shiver when it played against her sweat-slick skin, though Elisande had said there never was a breeze in this bare land.

She thought it was the danger of a creeping darkness that she felt behind her back, and building. She didn't look to see — why waste the time, if time was precious? — but her friends had said that night rose rather than fell here, and she was sure that the light was dimming slowly, she was finding it harder and harder to see good holds above; and something certainly was reaching up for her, something insidious and deadly was clutching at the hanging hem of her robe, dragging at her shoulders, trying to pull her down.

She thought, she truly did think that it was only coming night; until it tugged that little harder, and her foot slipped off a ledge that was no more narrow nor any more slant than a hundred others she'd already trusted her weight to.

She didn't dangle, neither did she scream. Her other foot was firmly placed, both hands had solid grips, and this rock wasn't friable; she thought it would endure the ages. Just the one foot slipped, and the shock robbed her of any breath at all. It chased like bitter silver through her bones, killing-cold and deadly heavy.

She clung. No more than that, she clung; while all her body shuddered convulsively, entirely out of any control of hers. She pressed her face against the rock for greater contact, and felt how cold she was against its warmth, how she repelled its heat. Chill throbbed through her, exuded from her; she thought she might cool the world if she were here long enough. She thought she would be; she thought she'd never move again.

Until she fell, of course. She thought she would fall now, she was certain of it. There was nothing else that she could do.

She understood what was behind her now. Not the night: she'd been deluded, lying to herself, persuaded by her own deceit. All this time, as she'd been climbing so the drop below had been growing, the awareness of it had been growing like a hidden tumour in her mind. Now it had declared itself. It had seized her and she had seen it at last, unable to prevent herself from casting one wild look down as her foot had scrabbled for purchase; she had screwed her eyes shut in a helpless response, too late. All light below, but the darkness inside her skull offered no escape. It was there, and she could hear it calling to her, singing almost, seductive and terrible. All she had to do was let go, release her grip on the rock and so fall. A few seconds in the air and then an end, it would all be so easy . . .

She couldn't do it. Almost she wanted to, only to spare herself what was worse, dragging that tremendous weight of horror higher, feeling it grow heavier with every inching step when there was so far still to go and so little chance of ever reaching safety. But she couldn't do it, she couldn't unclamp her rigid fingers any more than she could lift a foot, either foot, to feel for another ledge. She was caught, frozen into immobility. There was a slow and perilous way up, another down; or there was a fast way down, and she could take none of them. Only hold and cling, and wait for the inevitable moment when at last her hands would cramp and spasm and so she would fall regardless and die in defeat, against her choice . . .

Until she heard the djinni's voice again, speaking close and quiet beside her ear.

'You should not linger, daughter of the Shadow.'

'It, it is too hard for me, spirit.' *I'm only mortal and my flesh has failed me, and my courage too.* 'I cannot move any further.'

'That is not true,' it said chidingly, 'though it may become true if you wait too long.'

'I dare not, then,' she whispered. 'I nearly fell . . .'

'Nearly to fall is not to fall. Your kind live always on the edge of death, a breath away from falling. You might have fallen; you did not fall. Nothing has changed.'

Oh, it was so wrong. Everything had changed, in a moment's clear sight of the emptiness below her. And yet it was right also. The world, both worlds were still as they had been in the moment before she slipped; she was still here on the cliff-face, her father was still in deadly danger and his saving in her hands, perhaps, only that her hands were locked and useless . . .

No, that wasn't true either. It was her mind that was locked, trapped in a childhood memory that had become an adult nightmare. If she didn't move, then she would fall; that was inevitable as sunrise even here, where no sun rose. If she fell, her father would die. Again, inevitable. She had begun this climb with no sense of hope, only a grim determination to attempt it. The point and purpose hadn't changed. She was tired now, and her fear had broken out of its cage; but to balance that she was halfway up at least, and maybe more.

Fear lied, she thought; it said she had the choice, to give up now rather than fail later. That wasn't true. Giving up – no, be honest, call it jumping – was no option for her; her body wouldn't do it, even if her mind had genuinely wanted to. Climb or fall, live or die, her only route was on and up. She'd lied to herself also, she'd tried to pretend that she could leave memory and fear behind in her necessity, or bury them so deep within her that she couldn't hear their cries. Truth had caught her out, truth had snared her;

but truth would lead her on. She would climb, and carry terror on her back for so long as she was able. She could do no more than that.

All she had to do was to begin, to move one foot – this foot, the right, the one that had slipped before. She lifted it slowly, tremblingly, and set it on the same little ledge it had slipped from, because there was none better that she could find by touch. Her toes tried to dig into the rock for a moment; she waited, focused, forced them to relax. Balance and judgement would take her to the top, not brute strength. She couldn't pit herself against the cliff and hope to win, any more than she could against the fall. They were both immeasurably older, immeasurably greater than she was; but they were neutral, for all that her fear said otherwise. If she could only trust her body as she used to, she might yet satisfy the djinni's faith in her. The djinn could see some aspect of the future; it would never have brought her to this, if failure were certain . . .

Her foot was in place, her hands were set; now she had to lift her left foot, and put her weight on the right. She had to do it now, or else she never would . . .

Because she had to, so she did. And found a crack she could wriggle her toes into, where the ball of her foot could rest upon the lip; and then she could slowly, slowly loose the fingers of her right hand, and stretch it up to find another hold.

She climbed, against the endless rise of the cliff above her and the endless suck of the fall beneath. She climbed, and sweated from the sheer exhausting effort of that climb; she squinted and groped for holds, and did not, could not believe what her body and her failing eyes were telling her when at last she dragged herself over the cliff's sharp edge and onto its plateau top. She crawled a little way, until her numb mind recognised that there was level ground below her; but then she only lay on it to rest a little while, before hauling herself onward as she thought she must.

It was the djinni who called her back to herself, as it had before, though this time its voice seemed to come from a greater distance, she had wandered so far from the world.

'Julianne de Rance,' it said, 'rise up, and be ready. Time moves differently in this world, but it moves yet; I cannot hold it still. Your father's peril draws nearer; if you would save him, you must do it now.'

Her father, yes. He had been the cause of all of this, hadn't he . . .?

It took an effort, a tremendous effort to let go of the rock she clung to, to trust the air; but she forced herself to her feet and found that she could after all stand without holding on, with nothing to hold on to. That was good enough, for now. She nodded to that slender twist of air that was the djinni, hanging upright here, where it had always seemed a little aslant in her own world.

'I am ready, djinni,' she said, though her voice was so faint and weary to her own ears that she thought it couldn't possibly believe her.

It did, or else its urgency was greater even than it had admitted. It spun itself into a tight cord; the wind of it whipped at her, battering her sweat-damp robe against her body, startlingly chill after the heat of exercise and the warmth of the rock she'd lain on, the warmth that was inherent in the very air.

This time she resolved not to close her eyes, but it made no difference. A sudden dark engulfed her, she felt dizzy and unrooted from the world, from either world; briefly she thought she was falling after all, and nearly betrayed herself by screaming.

Then the dark unfurled itself about her and she felt ground beneath her bare feet again, and the breath of a normal breeze. The first thing she saw was the sun, red and huge, close to setting in a glorious haze of purple and scarlet. As she turned, she realised that she was standing high on the scarp, that same scarp she'd been defeated by; the dangerous edge of it was only a few paces from her, and all the wide plain lay below. A pale line marked out the road; if she looked more carefully, if she peered and scanned, she thought she might spot Rubon's wandering, if he'd not found safety yet.

But if she looked that carefully she'd see the bodies of the afternoon, she'd see Redmond dead and unburied, or else what little that pack of hungry ghûls had left of him.

She looked for the djinni instead, and couldn't find it.

Her father, then: she must look for her father, and quickly. The djinni had been in haste; what irony if she wasted its efforts and her own, by dawdling now . . .

The lip of the scarp ran as far as she could see, to north and south. No telling from a glance in each direction, where below was the ridge where her father lay. Behind her there was a crumbling stump of rock that must once have been a pinnacle, that would have made a fine landmark even from the ground, from where she'd seen the ghûl set down; but it was too low now to be useful, she had no memory of it. She'd have to go right to the edge, and peer over; even then, the ledge she sought might be here or it might be a mile away or more.

Except that the djinni had been in haste. It could have put her anywhere; surely it must have put her close . . .

She walked slowly forward; nothing could have hurried her here, not the djinni, nor her own awareness of her father's peril. If she'd seen a squad of 'ifrit scurrying towards her across the bare plateau, she still would have measured her paces as though she were walking into a gale. Her conquering the climb hadn't conquered her nervousness of heights, only given her the courage to face it. With caution, with extreme caution . . .

The closer she drew to the edge, the slower her steps became. At least she kept moving, though, she didn't hesitate even when her legs began to tremble of their own accord, when she could see nothing ahead of her but the drop. She walked on, trying not to think how soft and uncertain this rock was, until her feet were absolutely on the lip; then she lowered her head by a tremendous effort of will and looked directly down.

And saw her father, saw the ghûl.

They were immediately below her, on a long and narrow ledge perhaps twenty, perhaps thirty feet down. She couldn't judge distance from above, when she daren't look too carefully. Her father lay stretched out, quite still; the ghûl had folded its wings and was hunkered down almost as far from him as it could get. Julianne thought that was deliberate. Even from this topmost and foreshortened view, even with the long, long fall below dizzying her eyes, she could see how it tossed its head as if in pain, she could hear how it sobbed to itself. It was in pain, or else cruelly, painfully frustrated. She thought it was likely slavering for meat, for the fresh meat it had won and carried to this height; but the control of the 'ifrit held fast, either on its body or its mind.

If it had been animal, she might have pitied it, almost. As it was not, as it was brute spirit and brutal with it, she need not.

She stepped back silently, hastily, before it could hear or smell or sense her presence. Then she sank down on her haunches, much as it had; and wanted to keen much as it was, and had to force herself to think.

The 'ifrit were coming, the djinni had said or at least implied as much; until then, clearly, the ghûl would stand guard. No hope, she thought, of tempting it away. Her only bait was herself, her only weapons two short knives that could do little damage, far too little from above against its massive skull or its hunched body and not much more face to face. It would have to be killed with one stroke; Elisande might chance a throw to its throat, but not Julianne. She might have earned the luck, but she doubted its delivery.

The rock was rough and gritty beneath her bare feet; there was a jagged stone under one heel, digging in. She shifted, and wondered briefly if she could drive the creature away by pelting it with pebbles. It wasn't a bird, though, to flee such a feeble attack. It had a mind, albeit a weak one; it had instructions, that were being viciously enforced . . .

She had to kill it, then. One swift and deadly blow, and she lacked the means. *You can save him*, but she couldn't see how; and that irritating stone was still there, sharp under her soft arch now, breaking her train of thought. She reached under her foot to force it out with her finger, and found it smaller than it had seemed, just a flake from that fallen pinnacle, most likely—

—and she rose suddenly, and turned to run to the heaped rubble of rock that crowded around the remaining stump. At first her ambition overreached her strength, she strained to lift a massive boulder and couldn't shift it; she tried something a little smaller and then smaller again, until she found the largest that she could carry. Whether it would be big enough she wasn't sure, but she could do no more.

She staggered back towards the edge, clutching the heavy rock against her chest. It was hard to be quiet, harder to be careful when it tugged so at her balance, trying to drag her forward; she leaned back against it, her feet groping blindly ahead of her.

Her toes found the lip before she'd expected it, reaching suddenly into emptiness. She snatched that foot back, and stood trembling for a moment under more than the weight of the rock. She peered over its rough mass, and found herself standing directly above her father; so she backed away, inched sideways as silently as she could, then tried the edge again.

Good: there was the ghûl. Another sideways shuffle, and it was beneath her. Her foot knocked down a little shower of dust, but it paid no attention, rapt as it was in its own misery.

Its head made a target that she hoped, she prayed she couldn't miss. She fought to hold the rock out with aching arms, so that it shouldn't catch the cliff-face and be deflected in its fall; nearly its weight pulled her down, but she let go just in time.

Suddenly free of it, her body and mind both tried to drag her back; but she danced her feet against that urge to safety, intent on watching the rock's fall.

It fell straight and true, as it had to, and impacted on the ghûl's skull with a soft, devastating sound.

The creature collapsed, all in a moment. The rock rolled off and then went on falling, down and down into the deep shadow below. The ghûl's slumped body lost its grip on the ledge and slipped off, to follow the rock.

Julianne had just a glimpse of its crushed head, before it was gone. If that wasn't enough, if it wasn't quite dead, then its crash to land should revive it; she had no great concern about that, though, and no time in any case to worry. It was almost night; there was nothing to say that the 'ifrit would come with the darkness, but they had to come sometime, and likely it would be soon.

Which meant she had to climb again, down to her father. Quickly, down an unstable cliff towards a narrow ledge, and in shadow so heavy that it might as well be night already . . .

She knelt, turned her back to the drop, lay flat on her belly and swung her legs over the edge.

There were plenty of cracks and ridges that her groping toes could feel, but she was hanging with all her weight on her elbows before she found one that she trusted, a little hollow in the rock where her whole foot could fit.

She didn't want to trust it long; nor the next foothold that she found, a projecting knub of stone that surely must fall sometime, so why not now, when she put her weight on it, when better?

By then only her hands clutched the lip of the cliff

above, and only briefly; she felt for holds and found them, and was committed.

And so quickly down, driven by anxiety that she tried to pretend was confidence restored. She could hear crackles and murmurs in the rock, she could feel it flake beneath her fingers, beneath her feet; soon she was scrambling in a constant fall of dust, grabbing at anything that seemed secure and finding nothing that was.

Her feet slipped and couldn't find a hold; she slid down the last ten feet or so, all her body stiffening in anticipation of a far, far greater fall; and landed with a jarring thud on the ledge, spread herself against the face and tried to embrace the entire cliff until the patter of falling stones had entirely ceased around her.

How she'd make the climb back up with her father a dead weight to carry, she couldn't imagine. First things first, though: and the first thing was to assure herself that he wasn't simply dead.

She inched along the ledge, face to the wall still, until she felt fabric against her foot. Then she worked her way down onto her knees, straddling his legs; and fumbled inside her robe to pull out the water-skin she carried, blessing Elisande's care in making certain it was there.

She moistened a corner of her veil, and wiped her father's face. There was at least a whisper of breath in him, she could feel it against her damp wrist; she poured water liberally over his head, and gasped her relief as his eyelids fluttered.

She put the mouth of the skin to his lips, dribbled a little water between them, and saw him swallow. His eyes opened, he shaped her name silently; she gave him another drink, then slipped her arm beneath his shoulders and helped him sit up.

'Careful,' she whispered, 'we're a long way up . . .'

'Too high for you, eh, Julianne?' No mockery in his dry voice, and no panic either, only a calm assessment as he gazed about him, blinking in the dim light.

'Much too high,' she agreed. 'And the 'ifrit are coming, soon, I think. It's not far to the top,' though it might be too far for both of them, 'but the rock crumbles under any weight . . .'

'Then we'd best not climb it. Give me your arm, and let me stand.'

That confused her, and she was briefly afraid that he was too confused to make sense of where they were, despite his words; but she had a lifetime's practice at trusting her father, and was only glad to cede authority to him, where it had always belonged.

He was slow to rise and shaky on his feet, clutching her arm with both hands. He took the outer side, though, leaving her the security of the wall, which reassured her further.

There was barely room on the ledge for the two of them to stand side by side, and she didn't see the point of it; there was nowhere to go, if they didn't attempt the climb.

But he said, 'Walk a little, slowly. Don't look down, and don't be afraid; you needn't look at all if you don't want to, close your eyes if that's easier for you.'

There was no question of her looking down, except at her feet on this dark and untrustworthy ledge, certainly no further down than that; nor was there any question of her closing her eyes. Whatever he meant to do, she meant to see it.

She matched her steps to his, slow and shuffling; and they'd gone no distance at all before her feet were washed with a softly golden light. She lifted her head in wonder, entirely trusting now, and found herself walking into a bright mist, as though an unnoticed door had opened to pass them through.

She thought perhaps they'd find the land of the djinn on the further side of that mist; and was wrong, knew herself to be wrong even before the light was gone. Her feet stumbled over loose rock and she all but shrieked, terror suddenly resurgent and her turn to clutch at her father.

He gave way beneath her, no strength in his legs; but they didn't fall, or only so far as the ground they stood on. She lay clutching at it, panting for breath, surprised to find the ledge so wide; and only slowly realised that this was not the ledge, it couldn't be. Her dazzled eyes distinguished shapes, shadows all around them, jumbled rocks and one black edifice; it took a time for her to recognise that as the stump, the broken pinnacle that had given her the weapon she needed against the ghûl. They were atop the scarp somehow, and her father was smiling at her, his teeth bright against the night.

'I couldn't bring us far,' he said, 'not far at all; and that's my limit for a while. My thoughts are still jangled. We've a walk ahead of us, I'm afraid, and the 'ifrit may find us on the way.'

Somehow, she couldn't care. If the 'ifrit found them, her miraculous father would undoubtedly whisk them both away on the wings of his will, no concern in the world . . .

Actually, she thought in all seriousness that he would, however tired or confused he claimed to be. He seemed as unconcerned as she felt, and that without any of the excuses that she had. She was elated, flying, the very opposite of falling; he was hurt and weakened and surely must be full of doubts and questions – if his last coherent memory were standing above the brutalised body of his old friend Redmond, how could he not be, finding himself high on a cliff and only his hypsophobic daughter for company ? – but yet he was entirely sanguine about the prospect of 'ifrit, even a host of 'ifrit falling upon them. He wouldn't be so casual about his life or hers, unless he knew that he could walk her out of danger.

Walk her out of one place, and into another, apparently without breaking sweat. Even the djinni had to work, to carry her between the worlds . . .

'So that's how you do it,' she murmured.

'Is it?'

'All that coming and going, and no one ever knowing where you are or where to look for you . . .'

'Oh, that. Sometimes, yes. Sometimes I'm just an old man in other clothes, and people don't quite see me. Coming or going.'

'I don't suppose you're going to tell me how you do it?'

'Change my dress.'

'You know what I mean.' She'd earned something more than the distraction of jokes, she thought; but the shape of his mind was elliptical, and perhaps he was giving her what knowledge she could use. Though she knew that much already; wasn't she in boys' clothing now? And hadn't she often and often slipped out of the palace in urchins' rags as a little girl, to play with her urchin friends?

'The King finds it useful,' he said, 'for his servant to

move swiftly sometimes, between place and place. Sometimes to move secretly. And so he has gifted me this power – if it is a gift. It can be a monstrous inconvenience, to be convenient to the King. You saw that yourself, on the road from Tallis.'

'You were called away,' she said slowly, remembering, 'and you rode into a furious light that terrified the horses; but that was nothing like this just now, what you did on the ledge . . .'

'I am nothing like the King. He can call me from Tallis to Ascariel, and open a road that I ride in moments, a month's journey in an eyeblink of time; I can carry you from where we were to where we are, and it exhausts me to do it.'

He didn't seem exhausted, he seemed stronger by the sentence, by the step. He walked beside her, one hand on her arm still but hardly leaning now, as much for company as strength; she thought how often she had walked so at his side, her hand tucked through his elbow, and wondered if he were also paying her a little tribute here, telling her that she had grown in more than inches since last they were together.

As ever with her father, it was impossible to be certain what he meant. He could be a snake that ate its own tail sometimes, so subtle that his secret messages consumed themselves in their own mystery.

The sun was gone, but the stars gave light enough for walking on this high plateau. Light enough for the 'ifrit to spot them, perhaps, that too, but she was still unworried. They were headed south, towards Rhabat, which meant towards the Dead Waters too, towards where the 'ifrit lurked, and she was still unworried.

'Julianne,' her father said, 'have you had much conversation with Hasan?'

'Not much, no.' Too much, and not enough; but those were both confessions, and she was a married woman. Her husband should hear it first if any man, but Imber never would, or not from her. She knew how deep a hurt could go with him, and wanted never to bruise those green eyes grey again.

If ever she saw those grey eyes green again, if ever he could find a way to take her back . . .

'Well. He is not a man to waste time with idle words. When he speaks, it is to the purpose; and he tells me he wants to marry you.'

'He told me that, too.' It was difficult to keep her voice as dry and airy as the breeze, as her father's was; but some things should be difficult. Concentration helped, it gave her a little distance from thoughts of Hasan, thoughts of Imber. 'I told him I was married already.' And he'd asked her husband's name, *that I may kill him.* She hadn't said it, she'd said something foolish instead. If he truly wanted to know, he could learn from someone else; she thought it likely that he did know by now, if he hadn't already known it then.

'Mmm. How did you get up onto that ledge?'

'Down, I came down, from up here. I climbed down . . .'

'Julianne, how did you get up here? You were on the plain with me, not so long ago.'

'I climbed,' another confession that she hadn't wanted to make, or not to him. No father should owe his daughter so much, and this one especially not. He ought to be untouchable, as he always had been; she hated to have seen him so defeated. 'Not this. The djinni took me through to its own country, and I climbed there. It said it couldn't just lift me to the ledge, I had to climb . . .'

'It didn't say that, Julianne. The djinn do not lie. It could have done that much, or a great deal more. It could simply have brought me down to you; it could have taken us both to Rhabat, or anywhere else in the world. What did it actually say?'

She thought back, listening to its voice in her memory. 'It said "may", it said *I may not raise you to the ledge*. It said if it touched my body, it would destroy me. That's true, I've seen it happen . . .'

'Indeed, that is true. It wouldn't have needed to touch you, though. It didn't touch you when it took you between the worlds, did it?'

'No . . .'

'No. Well, no doubt it had its reasons. Everything that djinni does is curious to me. Let us get on; it's a long way to Rhabat, when we have only feet to take us there.'

They walked for an hour or more, talking lightly of this and that, till the stars had drawn all heat out of the world and it was only the chill that made her shiver now. Gazing up at the great frosty blaze above her, she saw shadows cross it suddenly, like vast and deadly birds that couldn't be, like monstrous bats. She croaked, and pointed; her father looked, and nodded calmly.

' 'Ifrit,' he said.

'With wings?'

'Why not?'

Why not, indeed? Their bodies were an artifice in any case. And if a ghûl could grow wings, why not the 'ifrit?

'Perhaps they did not see us . . .'

'Perhaps not; but they will look. Time we were safe home, child. Besides, I'm already late for my own feast, which is unpardonable; and I find myself remarkably hungry.'

And so it was a shimmering cloud of light that they stepped into; and as they went, she wondered vexedly how long it was since her father could have done the same as he did now, just how far he'd made her walk to no apparent purpose. And why, because he never, ever did anything that had no purpose . . .

14

Out of the Shadows, Into the Dark

Elisande couldn't quite believe that this was happening.

She'd been in the kitchens when the news broke: dutifully where Hasan had sent her, pounding almonds grimly into paste and watching her own sweat drip into the mortar for added flavour. She had hoped vaguely that telling Sherett about what had happened at the water's edge might have won her some more interesting task; she'd been disappointed but not surprised when the only response was, 'Hasan will see your friends safe. Now come, if you will; we have only a few hours left to us, and we have missed your help already. And Julianne's . . .'

You have been playing like silly children, her harassed frown had said, *meddling with men's business when there was work to be done.* It had been true, too, at least by her lights; Elisande didn't want to see the world that way, but it was hard to resist. What she'd stolen for Julianne – a boy's clothes, and so an afternoon on horseback – had been precious to her friend; what she'd stolen for herself, time again and Marron's company to spend it with, had been perhaps more precious to her. No one could have predicted that the 'ifrit would choose that time to rise, and so make both their adventures seem foolhardy. Even so, though, a glimpse of Sherett's strained and weary face had made them both seem selfish at the least. Another woman would have been shocked, and angry too: two girls her guests, and one chooses to dress and ride with men while the other slips away to be private with a boy . . . Elisande had followed Sherett meekly to her labour, feeling glad to be taxed only with self-indulgence, and that obliquely.

An hour later, she'd not been meek; she'd been hot and tired, bored and resentful. Resenting Jemel, who was at least allowed to do something, to ride to Julianne's rescue if she should need it; resenting Marron, who could do exactly as he pleased and was no doubt doing exactly that, though she didn't know what it was; resenting Julianne for her borrowing of Elisande's tricks, for her meeting with Redmond, even for the risks that she was running.

Above all, Elisande had been busily and deeply resenting each and every one of the women who surged and jostled at her back, adding more at every moment to the steam, the heat and the cacophony of the kitchen. Real and deadly things were happening in the world just beyond their door, and they paid it no attention; that wide world belonged to men, and so they were cramped in this little space and frantically cooking for the later pleasure of those same men, and not one of them had seemed to feel any resentment of her own.

Even Sherett had been trained to accept this role and wouldn't challenge it, content to waste her strength and intelligence on the paltry matters with which she was permitted to concern herself. Even when the news had come, leaking back through the guards at the door: even when word had cut across the women's gabble, a single voice raised loud enough to silence all the others, still Sherett had only paused for a moment in her frenetic chopping, had only bowed her head to Yaman's sharp observation that more men in the valley meant more call on their stores and more work for them all.

'Ifrit had attacked the tribes, where they were camped before the siq; Hasan had rallied the survivors and brought them into Rhabat, but many had been killed and there was now no safe passage in or out. The party Hasan had been riding to protect – Redmond's caravan, Julianne, her father – had not been sighted, and was either stranded or lost . . .

Elisande had abandoned pestle and mortar, and headed for the door; Sherett had stopped her, with a hand tight on her elbow.

'Where are you going?'

'To the stables. You heard . . .'

'And so did you. You cannot pass the siq; what, will you fry 'ifrit with your glare, Elisande? Your friends are in God's hands now, or else in the hands of the Shadow, which are nearly as strong. Trust and pray, and return to your work; or if you cannot pray, trust Julianne's father and work anyway. Work will keep you from pacing and bothering people, when there is nothing you or anyone can do now. It will also keep you within my doors, where you belong. This is not the time to go blustering among the men.'

That she hadn't been able to argue with although she'd wanted to, or she'd wanted to go bluster regardless. She'd wanted to plague Hasan for details, how far had he got, had he really not seen any sign of those he pursued or those they'd gone in search of; she'd wanted urgently to check on Jemel, was he living or dead, was he hurt? Most urgently of all, she'd wanted to find Marron. There was one who could leave Rhabat, if he chose to. He could open a doorway, make the journey in another world and so come back beyond the danger. Surely, he would go. And if he went, when he went, she'd wanted to go with him. He might need her help, if any were hurt; he might need her courage in a fight. He should not go alone . . .

He should not, but it had seemed that he might have to. Sherett had refused to let her go.

'What, will you scour all of Rhabat in search of that one? He may be of your people, but he is half ours now, he is the Ghost Walker; where he goes, you may not follow. That is written.'

'I have been there already, Sherett.'

'Even so. What if he is gone already? He is no fool, he will take men if he needs them, better help than you could be.'

'He can be a fool,' she'd said, thinking of the shy boy she'd first known, who sometimes resurfaced even now. 'He might not ask, he might not think to ask . . .'

'Let his wisdom make the choice, Elisande. Every girl thinks her boy a fool. You would not find him in any case. There are thirty houses here, with thirty or forty rooms in each; will you invade them all? When there are men in each now, hundreds of unsettled men, and more in the huts across the valley? They would not welcome a wild girl. No, stay where you are truly needed.'

'To make a feast? How can you think of feasting? When the man who gives it is one of the missing . . .'

'I have not heard that the feast is cancelled; only that we must make more food for the hungry. The men abandoned their camps, they have nothing. And the man who gives the feast is the Shadow; he will not be missing long.'

'I thought I was your guest,' she'd grumbled, 'not your prisoner. Nor servant to your men . . .'

'Because you are my guest, I will care for you. Child. Here, under my eye. The care of children does not include letting them run headlong into stupidity or danger.'

'Don't call me that, I'm not a child . . .'

'No? Very well, then. Still less does proper care of a woman allow her to disgrace herself before men of my tribe or any other. You wear the dress of a Beni Rus, Elisande, and you will behave accordingly. I am sorry, girl,' she'd gone on more kindly, 'I do understand your distress, and your impatience; but there is no help for it, or none that you can give. We women learn to wait; sometimes what comes back to us is not what we have waited for. We learn to accept that, also. It is the most useful lesson the desert has to teach us. It would be easier to show you in the Sands, but I will do my best within these walls. Take this mortar, here, and these nuts . . .'

And so she had stayed, because she'd had to. She had mixed her paste with honey and whole nuts and saffron steeped in rose-water, to make sweets for the men to amuse their tongues and their bellies with after they had feasted, while they talked and drank coffee – which thought had struck her with another, suddenly. She hadn't considered it before, but of course someone must serve this feast to the men, all those grand sheikhs and warlords, and their coffee afterwards. The young men of their tribes might do it, but she'd fancied not. The young men might have helped with the preparation, and had not. In the desert, yes, at a meeting of men where the women were left with the herds; but here there were women enough if they worked, and what more were they for . . .?

She had checked with Sherett, standing on tiptoe to peer over that woman's shoulder as she spun sugar-syrup into a fantastic confection of towers above a cake of camels'-milk boiled stiff with honey.

'Of course, we will serve the food. Not you, though. I would not see my guests demeaned so far as that.'

'Sherett, I'm not so proud. And if you don't let me fetch and carry at the feast, Yaman will have me back here scrubbing dishes all evening, you know she will . . .'

Sherett had slapped stingingly at Elisande's hand, where she was dipping a finger into the hot sugar-syrup; then, laughing, 'Scrubbing or boiling rice for the new-come men. There will be work enough, that is certain. Can you behave, though, can you curb your tongue? We must be swift, and silent. A girl's voice has no place at such a feast; I will not have you disgrace us all.'

'Silent as the Sands, I swear it. It won't be the first time I've played servant. Truly, I'll be good.'

'Your father will be among the men. Would he not be shamed, to see his daughter at such a task?'

'Not he. He'll deem it fitting, and thank you for the lesson. He thinks me too forthright, too independent; he says I get above myself, and need knocking down . . .'

'A wise man, your father. Does he hope to see you married soon? He should do, you're ripe for it, girl. And there's one at least here who would offer for you, I hear.'

'Boraj? That pretty, laughing boy? Oh, please . . .' The only boy she wanted was as pretty, or nearly so, and solemn as rock; she couldn't remember having made him laugh, but a moment's smile from him was worth a day, no, a lifetime of the giggling, flattering Boraj.

'His father too would welcome it; and I think so would the Shadow. An alliance between Patric and Sharai, at this time – that would be no bad thing. Boraj's father has a strong voice among the sheikhs . . .'

Elisande had gazed at her doubtfully, an appeal already shaping itself on her tongue, *don't lend your voice to such a notion* – but she'd swallowed it in fury at herself, seeing how Sherett's eyes danced in the hot light.

'You're teasing me,' she'd scowled. 'And even if you weren't, my father will let me make my own choice.'

Would he? It was the custom in Surayon, she couldn't remember a girl ever being married against her will. If her father knew where her choice lay, though . . .

Well, it didn't matter. Her choice was hopeless; she was resigned to that. Nearly resigned, only tormenting herself by snatching at stray threads of fraying hope.

'I may join you tonight, then? You owe me, now . . .'

'Don't growl at me, girl – and don't sulk, those brows will show it above your veil. But yes, you may join us, if only to save your fingers from the scrubbing-sand. Don't thank me, you're sure to regret it later; for one thing, you may expect to see Boraj at the feast. I'll dress you up prettily, for his sake if no other's,' and her eyes had been sharp then, seeing too much. 'It would be a shame to let ourselves be outshone by the food we serve . . .'

Small chance of that: when they were finally finished in the kitchen, she'd been towed away to the baths by a crowd of women, and then up to a room that was gaudy with hanging dresses of silk and satin. Some had been so gossamer-thin, even she had thought them indecent; Sherett had made her blush, simply by fingering one of those with her eyes on Elisande and her lips seeming to shape the name of Boraj.

But the older woman had laughed then, claiming her victory, and turned aside to find another, a gown of heavy gold brocade.

'We will wear blue,' she'd said, 'as we always do; but you need not. This will suit your colouring admirably.'

'That will make me stand out like a lamp in the shadows. I'd rather not . . .'

'I insist. You may play the servant, Elisande, but you must dress as a guest. I won't have you hide among us. Let the men see you, and understand the courtesy you do them. It will reflect to your honour, and your father's also.'

She cared not a whit for her father's honour, nor her own; but the dress was lovely, falling over her skin like spun sunshine, warm and enfolding as woven flame. One touch, and it had stolen from her the capacity to argue.

In Roq de Rançon, she had played lady's-maid to Elisande; in Rhabat, where once she had played rapscallion, now she played serving-wench to a hall full of men.

She had only ever glimpsed the Chamber of Audience

when she'd been here before, peering through the doorway to decide that it was vast but dull, it had nothing to offer a youngster. Now she wanted to stand amazed by its height, its width, its decoration, its massive pillars hewn whole from the same rock that made the ceiling that they supported and the floor beneath her bare feet. Her soul cried out for time to stand and stare, but she had none; she could only snatch moments of wonder, an occasional pause in the shadows to gape upward or around.

It was the light that made the difference, she thought, more than any added years affecting her reactions. A child then, she felt a child still; she didn't understand how anyone could feel otherwise, enclosed within such an ageless weight of rock.

The hall was ablaze with light, torches in sconces on every wall and pillar and a leaping fire in a pit in the centre of the floor. There were veins in the rock of the walls which caught that light and ran with it, as though it were their lifeblood; they glittered and pulsed in rhythm with the hurrying women, whose deep blue robes shimmered as though there were starlight trapped in the silk. Even the men's drab desert dress seemed to quicken, while the skin glowed on their hands and faces; the dishes gleamed on the floor before them, and the food was jewelled.

And yet Elisande knew that she was the brightest thing in the hall that night; she shone as she scurried to and fro. Single or married or many times married, every man followed her with his eyes; she felt the weight of their gaze on her shoulders, heavier even than the weight of that roof so high above that even this much light couldn't reach it, and left it swathed with shadow.

Those young men privileged to be there, sons and nephews of the powerful, they called her to come to them, to fetch them bread and rice, meat and drink when there was plenty still before them. She chose not to acknowledge their brashness even by ignoring them; she served them as she served their elders, quickly and efficiently and with what they needed, nothing more.

Boraj was the loudest and the most obvious among them. Trading on earlier acquaintance he made great play of his soft eyes and lustrous hair, flirting with her so outrageously that in the end his father called him to order, loudly across the hall. He flushed at the raucous laughter that followed, as it had to; the looks he gave her after were quieter, but spoke of some more serious desire.

She treated those with the same disdain she had awarded his coarser efforts, and searched in vain to find Marron anywhere among the several score of men around the hall.

Her father she had no trouble finding; he sat among the sheikhs, higher even than Hasan, and spoke with them as an equal. He spoke to her not at all; she had better from his neighbours, soft words of thanks and occasional polite requests that she hurried to fulfil.

His silence towards her was nothing unusual, she had lived with it before and paid it back a hundred times, in contempt or vitriol. What was rare was to sense the disquiet that underlay the grave courtesy that he gave to his companions, if not to her: to sense it, and to share it. She was not accustomed to finding herself at one with her father. It had happened too much for her liking already on this journey, since its beginning indeed; she almost yearned for the old antagonism to run as it used to, far below the scornful surface.

Much like hers, his eyes shifted around the hall, following the shifting shadows as if seeking constantly for the arrival of those who were missing and much missed, much needed. Seeing that, she felt suddenly overwhelmed by the futility of this great feast. Its author was among the missing, as were two good friends of hers, the father of her soul and the friend of her heart; guests of these people who claimed to prize hospitality higher than their own lives, they were cut off at best, surely in danger. And yet their hosts feasted in their absence, and talked of nothing that mattered because that was the custom, not to speak of the day's business until the meal was done; and she couldn't believe that it was happening like this, it didn't seem real after all the desperate business of the day.

She wanted to break out, to protest, to fetch a horsewhip from the stables and drive them off to search, to rescue or revenge. She wanted to hurl a plate of glazed and roasted mutton across the floor, right in front of the sheikhs there, to splash them with its seething juices while she harangued them for their cowardice, their idleness, their discourtesy to guests. She wanted to forswear herself and all her promises, to humiliate Sherett and her father and anyone else there who thought she could or would behave herself under such provocation.

She could name three, perhaps four people whose good opinion she valued enough to hold herself in check for their sakes – and they were none of them there, and that was the point. Someone had to do something, and she was forbidden to, and none of these men apparently would, or not without urging. She was forbidden to do that too, but oh, they needed it . . .

She might have done it; she felt as close to it as she had to all the mad things she'd ever done in her life, that brief moment before she did them.

What held her back was Hasan, a sudden glimpse through custom and manners and normally iron control to the heart of him, the real man. His voice rose abruptly above the general babble; nothing unusual in that, the Sharai didn't feel they'd eaten well unless they'd had an argument for seasoning, and they didn't feel they'd argued well unless they'd shouted. But she heard him say, yell rather, '—And if she die, how then? She died in our care, and we left her blood unmarked in the Sands, shall we say so . . . ?'

A hush followed, sign of deep shock. Like everyone, she stared at Hasan; like everyone she saw him colour, saw him turn to the sheikhs and bow, seated as he was, hand on heart, profound apology.

He'd broken age-old tradition, and had made what amends were possible for such a breach; talk started up again all around the hall. No one laughed at Hasan, no one referred at all to that moment; they all politely turned their heads away, not to add to his embarrassment.

All but Elisande. She watched him, and saw that there was a third to be added to the list, that short list of her father and herself. Hasan was more than anxious; he was racked tight with tension, eating little and speaking less, speaking hardly at all since that outburst.

The time would come, when he could have his say and men would listen. If he could wait for that, then so could she; these lean men couldn't eat for ever, surely, though they showed no signs of slacking yet. She'd follow Hasan's lead, and only if he failed her would she bring shame on herself and all who loved her, by telling this whole gathering what she thought of them and their feast, their craven greed, their passivity. Their God too. He would not be immune to her tongue if they dared suggest that the fate of her friends lay in His hands now . . .

Determined on that, she threw herself back into the role of willing servant-girl until the time came. She gave special attention to Hasan, though she had almost to fight for that privilege, pushing ahead of other women equally keen; even here and even after he'd disgraced himself, it seemed that tribal prejudice wilted in the face of his fierce charisma. She could fear for her land and her people, she could fear deeply if she weren't so eager to see him use that power to claim and lead his own tonight.

With all her attention, all her hopes focused on him, she forgot to keep checking the entrance to the hall, against the fading chance of longed-for latecomers. It was the sudden stillness of the men she served that alerted her, the way their heads all turned toward the doorway, while the constant flow of voices all around her dwindled slowly into silence.

She straightened, backed away, finally allowed herself to look. Even as she did so, she was struggling to expect nothing that she wanted — and lost that struggle gladly, gave it up in a moment as she saw Marron striding down the centre of the hall. Jemel was with him, which answered one lingering question; but that was the least of what had troubled her all evening, or she hoped it was. She hoped she was not so petty.

The two boys came marching past the firepit, towards

where the sheikhs sat assembled with her father among them. She thought she was not the only one there whose breath was stilled in their bodies, as they waited for what might follow.

Properly it should be Coren de Rance who challenged the boys; this was his feast, after all. But of course he was not here. The sheikhs looked at each other, as though waiting for any one of them to claim precedence, so that the others could instantly deny it; it was not Julianne's father but her own who stood eventually, who spoke to them in his clear jongleur's voice, not loud but carrying, as all clear voices carried within this hall.

'You will have some good reason, Ghost Walker, I am sure, for disturbing the gathered tribes at their meal; I would be glad to hear it. You were not invited here, neither you, Jemel . . .'

Jemel scowled, as though it had been an insult to be omitted and another to be reminded of it; Marron only smiled.

'You need not talk to me as though I were a djinni, Rudel. It's safe to ask me questions. I know we were not invited, and I apologise for intruding; some number of your company would rather see me dead than living, let alone here among you.'

'That is a matter to be resolved another time,' Rudel said quietly, without disputing the fact or declaring his own position. Elisande thought she knew where he'd stand; another reason why she would always, always stand with Marron. 'Tell me now, why have you broken in on our feasting? What is so urgent that it could not wait an hour?'

It might be news of Julianne; it couldn't be good news,

though, or he'd have brought her with him. Wouldn't he? He was breaking custom simply by being here, he challenged the Sharai simply by existing; he'd have no hesitation in fetching a girl to stand before them, if that girl were their friend and freshly brought safe back.

Elisande listened, almost dreading to hear Julianne's name; and almost felt relief when Marron said, 'The imam in the high temple, who watches your hidden gateway for you – that man is dead, and an 'ifrit guards the gate now. We have been up, we have seen. If they attack the valley, there will be no escape that way. Or that may be the way they choose to come . . .'

'Perhaps; though sea or air might serve them better. Well, thank you, Marron, Jemel. You came to no harm?'

'None. The 'ifrit did not attack.' And neither of course did he.

'Curious, if it knew who you were; curious if it did not. They must be content to keep us penned, for now – though we are not, of course, with you here. We could all of us leave, at any time . . .'

'If the Ghost Walker opened a way to the land of the djinn,' one of the sheikhs said abruptly, 'the 'ifrit could slaughter us there. I will not lead my men into that.'

'There is more,' Marron added heavily. 'We have been there, Jemel and I; we met no 'ifrit, but we came back onto the road, and found Redmond's party. I am sorry, but they are dead, all of them. They met ghûls, by the look of it.'

It was cold news, coldly spoken; Elisande fought down a wave of sorrow. Later, she would mourn that old man as he deserved. For now, she had to hear what more had not been said yet.

'What of the King's Shadow, and his daughter?'

'There was no sign of them. There were many dead, including some Sharai of the Ib' Dharan, who may have been the men they rode with. The bodies had been desecrated, but we checked them all, and those two were not among them. Casting about, Jemel found the tracks of one horse that went away westward, that we thought it better not to follow.'

'Very well. Stay, both of you, eat if you are hungry. We must discuss this. Marron, would you go back, and take me and a number of men with you? It is a risk, perhaps, but I would like to bring their bodies here. We can at least give them an honourable burial, they have deserved that much of us.'

Marron nodded; Jemel took his arm and led him away, to the opposite side of the hall. Elisande watched, ready to go to them, to bully them both into eating, but she wasn't needed. One of the other women was ahead of her, with a plate of bread and meat; the two boys sat close together in a space apart from the men, and Jemel pressed food into Marron's hands before he took any for himself.

She sighed quietly, and tried not to keep looking over: not to see how their shoulders pressed one against the other, how neither of them shifted to give the other more room, how it was Marron who reached first to touch Jemel more deliberately, and not the other way around.

When the men were finally done with eating, there was coffee to be served. Elisande steeled herself, determined not to be a coward in this; she carried her tray towards her friends, greeted them with a determined smile that they should at least be able to read in her eyes – that might disguise what else they might have read there – and knelt carefully on the floor before them.

Jemel first: Marron could watch, and be reminded. She filled one tiny cup brimful of thick sweet coffee, and passed it to the Sharai. He took it with a nod, drained it and held it out. She refilled it, he drank again; and so a third time. He set the cup back on the tray, inverted, to show that he had had enough.

She poured another cup for Marron; when he took it from her, her fingers tingled at the touch of his. She had to fight not to snatch them back, nor to let them linger. She could feel Jemel's eyes on her, and struggled to play the perfect Sharai woman before him, veiled and submissive. It was all play, but not in any sense a game; they both knew that.

She wondered if Marron knew anything at all; he was so hard to read, since the Daughter had begun to change him. He smiled at her, though, as he imitated the way Jemel had drunk, the way men were drinking all around the hall as women carried coffee to them one by one. There was even perhaps a hint of mischief in his face as he took his third cup, as though he were thinking of a scandalous fourth.

She shook her head fractionally, *don't do it, Marron.* He was being watched, to see if he could follow custom at least this far; he faced trouble enough, he didn't need to add a trivial irritant to the offence of his presence, his very existence.

She moved on, from her friends to the nearest group of men; but couldn't resist one glance back as she went. His eyes were following her, but she saw Jemel reach for his hand and hold it loosely, and she saw how his head turned back immediately toward the Sharai.

Oh, Marron, she thought, heartbroken, *I'm sorry, I'm so sorry I couldn't be a boy for you . . .*

When they came, she was watching Marron again: one last look to last her through the night, because she'd not see him again before the morning. Some women would stay to serve tea or sherbet for as long as the men should call for it, but not her. Sherett was sending her away with most of the others.

'You need not scrub dishes,' she'd said, 'though they must. It's time to shed the servant, and be a guest again. Go to bed, Elisande – and thank you.'

And so she would go to bed, she thought; her bones ached with weariness. She wouldn't sleep, though. How could she sleep, when men were talking of taking war to her people, and there was only her father to stand against Hasan; when Marron was so very much in her head, so very much with Jemel; when Julianne and her father were still missing; when Redmond was dead and unburied, his body lying open to any desert scavenger and perhaps abused already?

She trailed miserably to the doorway, last in a line of women, and paused for one last lingering look back. The firelight had died to a low glow and some of the torches had burned out, but she could still see Marron in the shadows, Jemel's arm flung around his shoulders. As she watched, he lifted his head and gazed into the furthest corner of the hall. After a second, Jemel looked the same way.

And stiffened, half lifted his other arm to point. She couldn't hear what he said above the constant babble of other voices, but she saw his mouth working. Other men turned, as she did; she saw a misty gleam and two slow figures walking forward, arm in arm. One was taller than the other; something in the way they moved said that the taller was a woman, the shorter a man.

Something in the way they moved held her rigidly in place, before she started jerkily back towards them.

The strange light faded, but she could see them more clearly with it gone, as torchlight touched their faces; and she was running now, dodging between the men as they rose and stared.

She was swifter even than her father, though she'd had so much more distance to cover; she was first to reach Julianne, though her legs failed her at the last, stuttering to an awkward halt a couple of paces short of her friend.

Not tiredness had slowed her so, or dragged her to a stop. She wanted to hug, but was suddenly afraid to touch. Julianne looked exhausted, all too solidly there and feeling every ounce of her own weight; and yet the light shifted and she seemed to shift with it, she seemed ethereal almost, uncertain of her own skin's containment.

And a quick unnecessary glance confirmed what Elisande knew already, that there was no doorway in that corner they had come from . . .

'Are you real?' she whispered stupidly.

'I don't know. Am I? You tell me. Elisande, I climbed a mountain . . .'

And it was, it had to be the true Julianne who stepped away from her father and came unsteadily to Elisande, who clutched at her with hard hands. She felt the bite of nails through her silks, inarguably real; her voice choking on a protest that came out as half laugh, half sob, as she reached to peel the fingers gently away and found those nails chipped and broken, the skin of the palms roughly torn.

'Have you been breaking rocks with your bare hands, sweet?'

'No, I told you, I climbed a mountain—'

'Indeed? And where did you do that, lady, when all the mountains hereabouts have defeated me, and all men else?' It was Hasan, of course: appearing at Elisande's elbow and taking Julianne's hands from her. Dark thumbs worked gently over pale knuckles, as though they had a claim there that none could dispute. 'And why did you do it, why go climbing mountains when there were those here who were anxious about you?'

'It was in the other world, prince, the djinni took me. And I had to do it, I had to save my father . . .'

She looked back then to find him, but Elisande's own father had claimed the King's Shadow, taking his arm and steering him towards the sheikhs. Late for his own feast, but he had come at last; his slender back and Rudel's broad one said that there would be no place for the girls in their coming conversation.

By the same signs, though, Hasan's place was manifestly there and not here, with the man and not the daughter. His reluctance to leave her was more than seeming, Elisande thought, this was no lordling showing off his pretty manners in the court.

Go he must, though, and go he did, if not before touching Julianne's fingers to his lips. Patric-fashion, that was, and nothing Sharai about it; Elisande wondered if Julianne had any idea of its significance, with all these tribal leaders watching. Its significance to her, at least, seemed clear. Her hand lifted as if to hold him back, her throat worked as if to call him; how he managed to keep walking, not even to turn his head with such a summoning so close, Elisande could barely imagine. The determined strength in him was something terrible. When he set his mind to a task, it seemed that no one alive could deflect him from it. And yet he was not single-minded, he was able to set himself more tasks than one, when the need arose.

She thought it was a need, in him at least, if not in Julianne. For her it might only be a yearning; but Hasan was the perfectibility of a Sharai, he sought only what was necessary and would chase only where he was driven. She thought he'd never hunt for pleasure, only to eat.

Well, but he has a full larder already, one wife here and two more with his tents, wherever his tents are pitched. What need he another?

The answer was easy, of course, that it wasn't another wife he needed, it was Julianne. Why was another question, and she could put it off one more time, she thought; shrug it off for the moment, at least, to attend to her friend's more immediate comfort.

'That's a story I want to hear, sweet – but you can tell me later. You're here, you're safe, that's what counts. Are you hungry?'

'Elisande, I'm starving.'

Sherett was there suddenly, at her other side. Sent by a gesture from Hasan, perhaps – or perhaps not even needing to look for it, knowing his will or her own, or simply her duty. 'That we can take care of, if you're content with what small pickings the men have left. You too, Elisande, you need to eat now. Come with me, the pair of you . . .'

Between them they half led, half carried the stumbling Julianne out of the hall and into the clear night, along by the water to the women's quarters. The way was crowded with men, hurrying between the bright-lit houses or else gathered in small groups to talk; they made room for the women to pass, but jostled each other in a way that might lead to fights before the night was over, despite the tribal truce that supposedly governed Rhabat. They were nervous, watching the sky continually for shadows against the stars; many held bows ready-strung. Elisande at least was glad to pass the guards at the women's door, and come through to the comparative peace beyond.

She was desperate to hear Julianne's story, but food came first, food was urgent. Elisande recognised that same hunger in her friend that she'd brought back herself from the land of the djinn. Her own was with her yet, though its edge was duller now; and besides, it was late and she'd been serving delights all evening and never had the chance to snatch a mouthful . . .

'Small pickings' Sherett had said, but the woman lied. Nor had the leavings from the feast been distributed among the men outside, despite their need; the tireless Yaman and her cohorts must have given them plainer fare. Sherett brought the girls to the same long chamber where they'd eaten the previous night; they found it already full of women sitting quietly around a steaming array of dishes heaped high. Too weary to eat with any fervour, they were nibbling while they murmured softly between themselves.

Neither of the girls would let that restraint inhibit them; nor did they need Sherett's injunction to sit and eat, and save the talking till later. They headed for the nearest clear space they could see, and were reaching for food almost before they'd settled onto the carpet.

Flavour didn't matter, it was bulk alone that counted. They chewed and swallowed with frantic haste, and couldn't have spoken if they'd wanted to, so busy their mouths were. Not till she'd worked off that first demanding appetite did Elisande begin to taste what she was eating. Sherett passed her a bowl of rice bright with saffron, fragrant with spices, studded with chicken and almonds; she worked it into little balls with her fingers, popped one into Julianne's mouth and another into her own, and decided that this feast was none the worse for having been served and picked over once already. Time to slow down, time to enjoy both the food and her friend's simple company, uncomplicated by where she'd been or what she'd done; it was a time to feel truly appreciative of that custom that forbade earnest talk during a meal. Simply to have Julianne safe back was enough for now. Even Elisande's ever-burning curiosity faded to a glimmer under the combined effects of exhaustion, relief and a comfortably full stomach, especially when she had the chance to fill it fuller yet. Desert wisdom, that was, to eat whenever and as much as she could; it was some consolation to find that she could still be wise, in this at least . . .

Julianne outlasted her, even so. Sherett laughed at them both, even as she pressed them to another sweet, another little cake of pressed fruits and nuts. When at last Julianne cried for mercy, with a plea of imminent bursting, the older woman said, 'Come, then. I know you are tired, but it is not good to sleep too soon after a gorging, and you two have gorged like the children you are. Besides, Julianne is as filthy as a goat; and she has a story to tell, which Hasan has charged me to hear . . .'

She led them to the hammam. Elisande stripped off her gorgeous silk dress with only a brief pang of regret, then helped Julianne, who was fumbling with sore fingers at the ties of her robe. Baking-hot rocks cracked and split as Sherett transferred them with tongs from a glowing brazier to a tub of water; steam billowed about the girls, making their bodies gleam with sweat.

'Lie down, Julianne, here on this bench. I have oils which will soothe you, where you ache.'

Julianne stretched out obediently, her head cradled on her folded arms; she groaned softly under Sherett's hands, yelping occasionally as hard fingers dug deep into stiff muscle. Elisande grinned, and searched a crowded shelf until she found sharp files to attend to her friend's broken nails, balm for her skinned palms.

She knelt at the bench's end, took one of Julianne's abused hands and began her work.

'Tell us, then,' she said softly. 'You can talk and suffer, it'll take your mind off the pain. And you'll go to sleep else, however much she hurts you. Trust me, you will . . .'

Julianne told them a story about a ghûl with wings, a djinni and a mountain; but her mind was drifting between worlds, she told it briefly and badly. Eventually Sherett hauled her upright, and threw a bundle of dried herbs onto the brazier. Smoke mingled with the steam, adding a sharp, bitter perfume that had both girls coughing in chorus.

'Breathe deeply. It will clear your heads.'

'What, will it bring our brains out through our noses?' Elisande grumbled, rubbing at stinging eyes.

Sherett only laughed, and said again, 'Breathe deeply.'

After a minute, it was true, the weariness had lifted from Elisande's thoughts, if not her body. Julianne's voice had been slurring on the very edge of sleep, but it was brisker now as she said, 'I'm sorry. The Sharai value tales, I know, and I was spoiling mine. Redmond deserves a better eulogy than I can give him, and I did not see his death; but let me try again.'

This time they questioned her as she spoke, to draw out more detail; anything she'd seen or heard might prove to be important. When she talked of seeing Redmond dead, she wept a little, which brought tears to Elisande's eyes as well. At her first mention of the djinni, though, Elisande straightened her back, pushed away her sorrow to wait for a better time, and said, 'You didn't ask it any questions, did you?'

'No, love, I didn't.'

'Are you sure?'

'Positive, yes. It helped me, I think, not to do that.'

'It is not always a mistake,' Sherett said slowly, 'to put yourself in debt to a djinni. Sometimes the answer to the question is worth any price.'

'I got no answer worth the having, when I questioned this djinni,' Julianne replied.

Elisande snorted. 'You didn't put any question worth

the asking; but what it told us was still important. It sent us here.'

'Which cannot have been incidental,' Sherett said. 'And remember, the djinn do not lie. If you ask, they will tell you true. It's worth bearing in mind, children. Your paths cross this djinni's more often than is comfortable, but it clearly means you no harm.'

'No – but it can cause harm regardless,' Elisande retorted. 'Redmond is dead, who only came this way because of us.'

'Because of me,' Julianne corrected her. 'He said so. He would have gone to Surayon with me.'

'True, he would – and then come to Rhabat after you were safe. The ghûls wouldn't have killed him, no, or not today; but the desert might have done, or else his injuries. He knew the dangers, sweet, but he couldn't have kept away, where his voice might have helped our people live.'

Julianne gazed at her doubtfully. 'In which case his death was not the djinni's doing. Was it?' When Elisande gave her no answer, she shook her head and went on, 'In any case, I asked no question of the djinni this time. Even when I was terrified, I remembered that. And it gave me courage to finish the climb, although it was – equivocal, about what I did. It said again, it might be better to let my father die; and the djinn do not lie, so it meant that truly. But it helped me anyway. I don't understand it . . .'

'Why should you? You're human, and it is not. Just don't forget that it used you, it uses us both; and its uses are not for our good.'

'Julianne's father is alive,' Sherett said dryly, 'and I say that is good for both our peoples, whether my husband has his war or not. True, I have not the djinni's sight; but what the djinn see, of whatever future, they see dimly. That's why they are equivocal sometimes, Julianne. If you must ask a djinni questions, never ask it what's to come; it may deceive you without meaning to.'

'Be safe,' Elisande grunted, 'and never ask it anything at all. It might send you to the uttermost east next time, with me dragging along like an unwilling dog in your wake.'

Sherett smiled, and rose to her feet. 'Those who talk often with the djinn are not doomed to live safely. Go where it sends you, Julianne—'

'—And marry where I must. I know.' Her gaze met the older woman's, challengingly; Sherett's smile didn't falter, though it perhaps acquired a quizzical edge.

'Take your time here, children,' was all she said, 'linger as long as you please. There is cool juice to drink, in the pot on the shelf there. Lisan, your friend still has claws that need your attention.'

Then she was gone, a figure quickly lost in the steam. Julianne stared after her; Elisande reached for her friend's hand, where she hadn't finished working on her nails.

'Julianne,' she said quietly, with no tease at all in her voice, 'are you going to marry Hasan?'

'Oh, I expect so, yes. The day you marry Marron . . .'

Elisande's file twisted in her hand, came close to stabbing deep into Julianne's thumb; she barely caught it or herself in time. 'Claws indeed,' she murmured, working busily away. 'But I thought Marron was going to marry Jemel?'

'Not he, he's married already. To Sieur Anton d'Escrivey. Oh, Elisande, why's it all such a mess?'

'Ask the djinn, sweet, don't ask me. If it's that important to you, ask the djinn . . .'

'Perhaps I would, if I knew where to find one. Elisande, I'm sorry . . .'

'It doesn't matter.'

Of course it didn't matter, that was why she wasn't crying. Her face was only wet with sweat and Julianne couldn't see it anyway, she'd turned away deliberately to make sure. When she felt fingers stroking gently through her damp hair, it was just a sign of friendship, nothing more.

After such a day, such an evening, such a meal and such a bath, she should have slept as Julianne did beside her, like the dead. But Redmond was truly dead, and she couldn't forget that, she couldn't stop thinking about him as he had been, wise and kind, the father of her heart; she couldn't stop wondering how he had died, how terrible it had been, whether he'd felt much pain before the end. That old man had known too much pain in his life; he hadn't deserved such an ending, ripped away too soon for all of them, far too soon for the world which needed him maybe even more than she did.

And when she turned her thoughts away from him, there was always Marron waiting, and that was a different kind of need altogether and a different kind of loss. She was sure now that he was lost; Julianne's barbed reaction confirmed it to her. Which likely meant that he had never been there to be won, that she'd been a fool from the start; but he might, he just might have been foolish too. She thought he almost had been, those days they'd spent together in the land of the djinn. Another country, truly – here he was all Jemel's, when he was not all his own. Nothing of hers, whichever. He might not have realised that yet, but Jemel had, she thought.

So she turned between Redmond and Marron, and could face neither one of them, and couldn't shut them out; and so at last she rose up off her pallet and slipped quietly out of the chamber, anxious neither to wake Julianne nor to disturb anyone else in the house. She couldn't face questions, and she couldn't face company just now.

Occasional lights had been left burning through the corridors; by their kindness, memories of her time here before and an odd fumbling moment where the dark was too much for her eyes and her hands had to do their work for them, she came down to the hammam by ways that didn't take her through the central hall. She didn't at all trust Sherett not to be still watchful. She thought that woman could read minds, perhaps. For sure she read Julianne's; Elisande preferred to keep her thoughts private, and especially a night-time jaunt such as this.

The two girls had been last to bed, or last of those who would see a bed tonight. The hammam was still as they'd left it – promising each other that they'd tidy in the morning, knowing full well that come morning others would be up and tidying before them – with even their discarded clothes lying where they'd laid or dropped them. Her bright silk Elisande had folded and left neatly on a bench; Julianne's torn and dust-drenched desert robe, a boy's robe at that, had been simply abandoned on the floor, only kicked a little out of sight.

There was still a flicker of light in the lamps here,

enough for Elisande to find it without groping. She stooped to retrieve it, felt it damp under her grip – even here in the antechamber to the baths proper, the walls glistened with water, and there were pools in the uneven floor – but shrugged and pulled it on regardless, tying it swiftly with long-practised fingers. How often had she dressed as a boy? Times without number; and not only for reasons of disguise. It was quicker, easier, more practical by a distance . . .

Tonight, she had another reason yet. She pulled the hood up to cover her growing hair – then checked, scowled, and pulled it down again. Went to search that useful shelf in the hammam, and found a fine pair of scissors. No mirror, the Catari God had forbidden the making of images and the imams had ruled against reflections too; but she didn't need a mirror, she'd done this often enough by touch alone. And with a knife, too. These scissors were a luxury . . .

As she chopped, she thought of knives and wondered whether to go back for hers. Decided not, the added risk wasn't worth it. She felt half naked without them; but she'd have felt simply stupid padding entirely naked through the house with a blade in each hand like some God-sworn fanatic assassin. Perhaps, if she didn't have her knives, she'd be more likely to avoid any situation that might come down to knifework. That would be no bad thing. Tempers would be short and hot out there in the cold night; she'd be wise to tread carefully, if she trod as a boy.

Besides, she could always keep these fine sharp scissors in her sleeve, just in case of any trouble she couldn't duck away from . . .

At last she was done cutting, and there was more mess

for someone to find in the morning; something more for Julianne to be distressed by, she thought without a pang of guilt, and for Sherett to disapprove of. Let her, let them all. She very much wanted to be a boy again tonight, as best she could contrive it. For herself, though, this time, not for Marron. Which was all the pride she could find, and barely, perhaps barely enough.

She left all her hair where it lay in a circle on the floor, and walked out running her fingers through the rough crop on her scalp, as crude as any desert lad might wear it. Now there was only the guard at the door to be evaded, and that she could manage without fuss.

There were few children here at the moment, just as there had been few men beyond the sheikhs and their retinues, few women too; but all the children in Rhabat slept in the women's quarters. They had their own part of it, that they called the Children's House. The boys still resented it, though, from about the age of six until they were allowed to eat and sleep with their fathers, after their tenth birthday. Penned up by women, of course they sought to escape, to have wild adventures, particularly at night; of course the guards knew, and of course said nothing if they saw a figure slip out through an opened screen. They remembered their own boyhoods, and stood silent and blind.

Not only boys could be wild. Elisande had exploited their licence time and again during her time here, frustrated beyond endurance by the restrictions placed on her after the freedom she'd known in Surayon. Even though she'd been allowed to dress and run as a child here rather than a woman, still she'd needed to break out, to be unwatched and unprotected under the stars.

Alone or with like-minded friends, she'd followed this path so often: along the passage which was always well-lit for the sake of wakeful children, and into the boys' dormitory; on tiptoe between their pallets – wondering as she always had whether they truly were all asleep, or whether some were kindly snoring for the sake of their wandering sister, not to spoil her adventure – until she came to the window, the one particular window where somehow no adult ever seemed to notice that the barring screen was loose, and could be swung quite easily open, so . . .

They might have been more watchful of the children tonight, with the valley under siege and the skies so dangerous; but that very danger meant that the guards were watching the skies tonight, as were all the men who lingered along the poolside. No one seemed to mark her, as she slipped from the window and jumped to ground.

Hood up and head low for added security, she mingled quickly with the restive tribesmen as they surged aimlessly this way and that. She kept her elbows tight to her sides and dodged through the crowd, trying to avoid any contact for fear that it might be interpreted as a jostle; that kind of adventure she could well live without.

In truth, she wasn't really seeking any adventure at all. She'd only hoped to leave grief and misery behind her, in her vacated bed, as escape into sleep had proved impossible. Now that she was out and on the move, though, she found that she'd brought both with her. It was no great surprise. What she had tried to run from was inside her head, riding her thoughts with spurs and whip; even as she ducked and weaved, she felt the twin pains of her twin losses goading her.

If she couldn't sleep and she couldn't run, she might as well sit down. Her body felt as leaden as her spirits. She found a clear space by the water's edge and sank onto her haunches, hugging her knees against her chest like any Sharai lad out too late and trying to keep inconspicuous.

She didn't know why the men around her were twisting their necks to stare upward all the time. Even the imams hadn't been able to forbid the world from making its own reflections; she could see all the sky laid out before her, across the still surface of the pool. The stars glimmered like silver chasing on a blue-black blade; she looked for Redmond's face among their patterns, but couldn't find it.

Behind her, she heard voices:

'What of the Ghost Walker, then, what does he do to help us?'

'Nothing. What can he do?'

'He could see us all safe, he could take us out of this trap . . .'

'It is forbidden. Only the Sand Dancers may go with him, to the other world. You know that.'

'I know that they say that, not he. They speak against the imams – but there are none here, imams or Dancers. And I know that he has taken the tribeless one before this, and a girl.'

'The girl is of his own people, and does not respect our laws any more than he does. And I have heard that the tribeless one is a Dancer, or claims to be.'

'No matter what he claims, or what he is. The Ghost Walker does not follow the imams' teachings; so I say he could save us, if he chose.'

'But he chooses to dally with his tribeless boy instead,

that's the only one that he'll save. They're off together now, in this world or the other, it makes no difference to them. Nor to us. They play at lovers under the stars, while we wait for the 'ifrit.'

'Do they so?'

'Aye, I saw them. Heads together and holding hands, walking through our people as though they did not see us, eyes only for each other . . .'

You would have let them go as if you did not see them, Elisande thought furiously, *if you did not need him so . . .*

But she couldn't sit and listen to such talk, repeated again and again, as it must be in this forum of fear and despair. Nor could she challenge what they said, nor what they assumed: not without revealing herself, laying herself open to their scorn. A Patric girl caught playing at Sharai boy, trying to be what she was not, what he wanted – no. She had too much pride for that. And she had no defence to offer, for Marron. For all she knew, it might all be true; most of it certainly was.

She stayed silent, then, until they'd moved on; then she stood and moved on in her turn. *Running again*, she thought, withering herself under the lash of her own hot contempt; but she moved regardless. Restlessly, pointlessly, she wandered along past the stables, where she could hear horses whickering, infected with her own insomnia or their masters' anxiety; and so to the pool's end and further still, looking only to be private, to find some place where she could hear nothing but her own bitter thoughts.

She came through to the smaller pool, but there were men there too, sitting around fireglows in the trees' shadows: guards, she thought, against an attack from the gully that led to the Dead Waters. She stole past, hugging the rock wall to avoid their eyes and their suspicious questions, and went on.

There were guards in the gully too, but they had climbed high onto ledges from where they could shoot either up or down, whether the 'ifrit came from the air or the water. One spotted her and called out, 'You, boy – go back! This is no place to be foolish, and no time to be alone. Go back, and ask your father for a beating . . .'

She ignored him, trusting that he'd not come down after her. Nor did he; one moronic boy wasn't worth the risk of an adult warrior.

At the gully's end, where it opened onto the waterfront, she was afraid of meeting more guards on the ground, as she had before when she came here with Marron. That post had been abandoned, though; not even Hasan could order or persuade men, even his own men to stay so close to the Dead Waters after dark. Nor would it have been the fear of 'ifrit that backed their refusal, if he'd been so heedless as to give such orders.

She wondered if it was strange in her, to fear guards but not the legends of the Waters. The first would only send her back, the second might destroy her. But discovery meant humiliation, now and later; she thought she might almost prefer destruction. At least that would bring some sense of drama with it, a potent ending, even if it were terrible: something for the Sharai to weave a tale around. And perhaps she was after all looking for adventure, a match for Julianne's, to give a purpose to her being in Rhabat. *Lisan of the Dead Waters*, the djinni had called her; and here were the Waters, and here was she, and surely there should be some acknowledgement of that, surely something should *happen* . . .?

Oh, she was thinking wildly and acting worse, acting stupid. She could almost laugh at herself, for being so childish. Except that she'd forgotten how bad the air smelled out here, sick and sour; she'd choke, if she tried to laugh.

Breathing shallowly, she stooped to pick up a stone and skimmed it out across the water, watching how it bounced and skittered before it sank, how the ripples spread.

Well, she'd announced her presence now, she'd made her gesture. She could turn and go back at any moment she chose; she had no need to stand and watch those ripples die in the heavy water, nothing compelled her to wait breathlessly at the edge of the pavement there, scanning the dull, dark surface for any response. The djinn might not lie, but even they could be simply wrong, they didn't always see the future truly . . .

Wait she did, though, long after there seemed no point in waiting longer. Even the stars' reflection was blurred into drab pewter, on this poisoned water; she thought that was a symbol of her disappointment, now that she felt brave enough to be disappointed by the lack of any answer to her stone. Only a hint of breeze made any stir in that reflection; she was about ready to leave, when the thought suddenly struck her that there was no breeze here in this deep bay, the rank air moved not at all against her skin . . .

Startled, she stared and saw it again more clearly, a definite break in the ghost-band of the stars, a ruffle on the water. A zephyr, perhaps, visible only by its effect – but a zephyr did not have to be a wind . . .

She felt abruptly clammy-cold, deeply regretting her

bravado. She remembered the djinni, though, she remembered more than one djinn and the conversation earlier; she stood still, waiting, watching.

As it came closer, she saw that the disturbance was within the water, not above it. The surface rippled across a broad span, as far perhaps as both her arms could reach; the ripples seemed to grow more solid, as though the water were woven into coherent strands and those strands plaited together into an endless rope, the coils of it twisting down deep into the dark.

Then it rose like a pillar, like a shaft thrust up from below; the rope climbed the air and bound itself into a body three times her height and width, a body that shimmered darkly and stank worse than the air or the water had before.

This was death, the most intimately she'd ever faced it. Her mouth worked, she felt lips and jaw and tongue all move, but no sound came; she swallowed dryly and tried again, hurling words out as she had hurled that stone, hard and flat and low and with a tremendous effort of will, acting against everything that she knew was wise.

'Are you a djinni?'

Just that, four simple words; but they changed her world as they were designed to do, as they had to.

The creature stopped, in its relentless progress over or through that foul water. It was silent for a moment, she might almost have thought that it hesitated; then it said, 'Yes.'

Just as simple, just as direct. One word. Elisande felt it close about her like the jaws of a beetle, or the jaws of a trap.

She was no prey, though, it would not kill her now; if she were a victim, at least that was deliberately so. She was almost not pretending as she sat on the chill, slimy stone of the waterfront, folded her legs like a man and said, 'Well, then. Tell me your name and how you came to this, then say how I may serve you. I am called Elisande, though one of your kind has named me otherwise.'

A hiss, like an overboiling pot damping a fire; the water grew choppy for a moment all around where the djinni stood or balanced or was rooted, where its spinning darkness met the darkness of the sea.

'Perhaps I am not djinni now,' it said, and its voice was as murky as its substance, far from the high clarity of its kind. 'Once I was, and I was called Esren Filash Tachur; but the djinn are free, they wander where they will and are enslaved by no lesser creatures.'

'The djinn are changeless too, or so I've heard it. Gold does not lose its lustre, for being buried in the earth. You must have been in these waters for many years, Djinni Tachur; there are stories of you that have been told through generations.' *And each of them a cruel one*, but she had no need to say that; it would know.

'I have been centuries in these waters. I came for pleasure, because they were beautiful; now I am trapped here, and they are foul to me.'

'To us also.' She tried to think of the Dead Waters as a place of beauty, and could not do it. Perhaps they had been, though; perhaps the death had followed the djinni, and not the other way about.

'I have made them so,' it said, confirming. 'Nothing lives here, but I have killed it. Your kind, too, I have killed many of them. Some I asked for aid, I *asked* and still they would not give it, and so died. Now I do not ask, I simply kill. People come to me in my anger; they are stupid. You have said it, tales are told.'

'Indeed. I have heard them; and yet I came. We are a stupid people, perhaps. But I am in your debt, djinni, I acknowledge it, and I will pay your price. Tell me first, though, how it is that you are trapped. I had not known that anything could trap a djinni against its will or against its power . . .'

'Our will is our power, and so was I trapped. This lake, this puddle enchanted me; so small a thing, but I found it worth my time. I had enough of that, I thought, to choose to waste it here. And so I did, and welcomed all as though it were my home, as though I dwelt here like some mean spirit in a bond of flesh. Even the 'ifrit, when they came, I made them free of this water as though it were my own.

'I showed them my vanity, and so they snared me. They had intended it; the 'ifrit have some sense of what will come, as we do, though mine was darkened then. They penned me in a trap of my own making. I spread myself through all the water that this sea contains, and so they caught me, as a rock will catch a net and hold it.'

'I don't understand. What rock?' she asked, deliberately deepening her debt.

'A rock they had, that I had not seen: a stone, a pebble they had brought from my own world. A piece of the living land, that has great power here. They use the same to control their ghûls; I had never thought they might use that trick against a djinni. They dropped it into the water, into me; it lies at my heart, and I cannot touch it. It burns, it holds me here and binds me to their will. They have stolen that which makes me djinn, my freedom.'

'Tell me what it is that they would have you do.' Good: that was a command, and not a question. It was a hard game, this, a balance of power: to put herself in its debt but not too far too soon, to keep it well aware how much it needed her good will.

'Nothing, yet. They have only kept me here these many years, far from my land and my kind. Caged as I am, I cannot see beyond the moment; they have blinded me to what will come.' There was a hissing hatred in its voice; time itself could mean little to ageless spirit, but imprisonment within it must be bitter, worse surely than the physical containment. 'They are here now, though, in numbers, as they have not been before; I think they will use me soon.'

So did Elisande. She had a brief and terrible vision of the djinni's rising higher and broader than it was, as it surely could do: of its drawing up vast quantities of water and then hurtling like a dust-storm through the gully, dragging ever more water in its wake. It could fill the valley, she thought, flood Rhabat, drown every man penned in there. Why the 'ifrit would want that she couldn't imagine, how slaying a human army would satisfy any need of theirs; but they had made the pen and they held here a tool, a mighty weapon. It couldn't be coincidence.

'Djinni,' she said slowly, carefully, 'you have answered me two questions,' *and given me much information besides, but never mind that,* 'and I stand in your debt. I will help you, I will free you if I am able – but there is a further price. You must answer me one more question.'

Its body surged and shivered; she fought not to flinch from a hail of stinging water. 'Debtors do not bargain,' it said.

'I do. Come, you have faced this with others. Whether you begged or threatened, they refused you what you need.' She was guessing, but not wildly.

'They did. They died.'

'Even so. One more question, djinni; it is not so much to demand, in exchange for your freedom.'

'Very well, then. Ask.'

She took a breath, nerved herself to it, and spoke. 'If I free you from this bond, will you serve me instead? To do my bidding for a time, for a short time, here or elsewhere?'

All the waters of the bay were churning suddenly; the pillar of darkly solid sea loomed above her, spinning frenziedly. She had been spattered before; now she was soaked in a moment, gasping under a weight of falling water. She thought more might follow, she thought that in its rage it might engulf her altogether and so lose its hope and her own.

'Come,' she shouted, 'you have been enslaved for centuries; slay me now, and you may be a slave for ever. Or do as I ask for a little while, and then be free.' For how long? A day, a week, a year? No — it wasn't the length of service that enraged it, the djinn were all but immortal. Let it be for the period that she might be mourning Marron, then: a poor substitute, but something at least that she could call her own. 'For the length of my brief lifetime, djinni, come when I call for you and act at my command. Will you do that? I swear I'll not abuse the privilege, I'll take no more than I need from you. Now answer the question, and answer truly.'

It might, of course, answer her no; that would still be an answer. But then she might fail in the task that it set her, she might not try too hard. They were both gambling here, girl and djinni; she might fail anyway . . .

Eventually it spoke again, it gave the answer she sought. 'I will,' it said, no more than that.

'Very well, then. I stand in your debt,' and she did stand then, dragging herself up against the trembling in her legs and the drag of her saturated robe, the stinking chill of it setting all her skin to shiver. 'Tell me how to free you.'

'The stone lies deep in the water. Swim down, and bring it out.'

She opened her mouth – and closed it sharply on a question, took a moment to rephrase before she said, 'I do not know if I can dive that deeply; and I will never find one stone, in all this sea.'

'You will know it, when you see. I cannot touch the stone, but I can bring you to it.'

That at least she didn't doubt; whether she'd survive the swim was another matter. If she refused, though, it would kill her anyway; better to die trying.

Wondering just a little quite why she wanted a reluctant djinni for servant, she stripped off her sodden robe and let it fall. The djinni drew away, sinking its bulk down into the water again till there was only a slender column of dancing dark to mark its watchfulness.

The sea's surface fell still, lying dead and drear before her. She took slow, deep breaths, barely tasting the reek of the air against the sour tang of fear in her mouth; then she lifted her arms and dived cleanly, neatly into the Dead Waters.

And felt the djinni receive her, sucking her brutally down and down, into the uttermost dark.

15

Breaking Through

Marron had watched it all, from where he stood with Jemel
at the foot of the hidden stair.

Neither one of them had moved or spoken. Too far away
to help Elisande if the djinni attacked her, there was nothing they could do but witness, and be prepared to take the
news to her father – and to Julianne, which would be
worse, he thought – if it should come to that.

They saw her dive, and they saw also how the waters did
not close above her head: how they opened, rather, so that
it was as though she dived into a twisting funnel, a worm-
hole whose mouth writhed away across the bay and out
into the open sea, further than even Marron's eyes could
follow in the dark.

'Will she live?' Jemel asked, in a whisper.

'You know the djinn better than I.'

'I know not to trust them, although they do not lie; and
I know not to ask them questions. She did it deliberately.
Why did she do that?'

'Because she needed to,' Marron said briefly. For her people's sake, or for Jemel's? Perhaps; but he had seen her eyes on him at the feast, as he thought Jemel had not, and he understood a little of her turmoil. For her own sake, then, because she could: because she was distraught and desolate, because she would risk more than her life to win something, anything from this night of loss. *A gift of questions*, yes . . .

He could understand that. Who better? His eyes turned against his will towards the north, towards a man he could not see and should not ever see again; he dragged them back to find Jemel, there as he was sworn to be, anxious now about Elisande but still instantly aware of Marron's gaze and responding to it. Dark eyes huge and liquid in the dark, black hair and skin of bronze that would gleam gold under the sun, that was stretched over whipcord muscle and prominent bone, no spare flesh on him anywhere and yet he was constantly urging Marron to eat more, as bad as Elisande like that . . .

Her name brought a memory with it, that glimpse they'd had of her body as she dived, lean as any boy and as graceful. Thinking of bodies, thinking of boys, he thought of Aldo; and then, inevitably, of Sieur Anton, his only full-grown man, a body so different, scarred and strong and demanding . . .

He twisted around to stare into the dark of the open tunnel, to escape them all, even Jemel; and was not allowed to. Long fingers gripped his waist, a stubbled chin touched his cheek, a soft voice whispered, 'I am not so easily left behind, Ghost Walker. Not in this world.'

'You none of you are,' Marron muttered, grumbled

almost; but he was learning to accept his memories, as he was learning to be what he was. He leaned back into Jemel's resilience, accepted a kiss, barely hesitated before turning his head for another.

It was an effort then to tug himself free, to say, 'This is not what we came here for.'

'No – though everyone will think it was.'

'Will they? To the edge of the Dead Waters, to play boys' games with each other?'

'This is no game, Marron. The Sharai know that, if your people do not. And there is no privacy in all of Rhabat tonight.'

'And none for the Ghost Walker anywhere, where there are Sharai. My people call it no game but a sin, Jemel, a crime against the God. Men have died for it, and boys also. But we came to watch . . .'

To guard, because he did not believe that the 'ifrit had had no purpose in slaying the imam above. A guard was needful, but even Hasan would not listen; the men in the gully were enough, he'd said. And so Marron had come himself, and so Jemel, as ever at his side to watch with him – and to watch over him, of course, and perhaps simply to watch him also. Jemel could read his mind sometimes, he knew that Marron had looked at that climbing tunnel and thought of running.

Marron wouldn't do it now, when danger threatened his friends and all the people in Rhabat; but still he'd come back to the tunnel. It preyed on his mind. A way out of the valley, but 'ifrit had not blocked this as they had the siq, they had only seized and guarded it; a way into the valley, but 'ifrit did not need it, they could fly at will . . .

He wondered very much what else might be coming down that tunnel, and had stationed himself here against the chance of learning. Elisande had been a complete surprise; he thought perhaps she had surprised herself.

'We have two ways to watch now,' Jemel said.

'True. There's nothing else that we can do for Elisande; you look for her, I'll guard the gateway.'

He meant to move a few paces into the dark, perhaps up and around the first winding corner of the passage, to give him rest from more than Jemel's questing hands; he needed to feel those eyes not on him, he couldn't think under the weight of that implacable possession.

It was hard to move even such a little distance, though, and leave Jemel behind him. All the more reason to do it — *a delightful cage is still a cage, and soon turns dank and deadly: ask the djinni in the water there* — and swiftly: if he lingered over the walk, he thought Jemel might follow him. *What use is a guard who will not kill an enemy?* They'd had that argument already, more than once. He needed to be gone, suddenly and ruthlessly, if he wanted to be free of the other's company. Jemel couldn't follow him where no light burned.

But still, it was hard to do; and he'd taken no more than a step before he paused, and was briefly too glad of the chance. He'd heard something from the tunnel, a distant whisper, the rhythm of light feet; it took him a moment to remember what this meant, that it wasn't simply a gift for his sake, an excuse to stay out in the open with his friend.

This was what he'd been waiting for, what he'd been afraid of; what he'd been certain of, that something was coming and that it was not 'ifrit.

Some*one* was coming. Those were human steps. He concentrated, and was almost sure they were Sharai: bare feet for certain, backed by a man's breathing and the faint rustle of a rough woollen robe.

Jemel had heard nothing yet; his eyes were fixed on the water, looking for any sign of Elisande's returning. Marron reached out to touch his shoulder, and gestured him back with a jerk of the head. No words: the rising shaft before him carried sounds a great distance. No man's natural ears were as sharp as his, but even so he was cautious. He eased Dard from its sheath, glad to have that sword at his waist. With the speed and strength he borrowed from the Daughter, he could fight with a Sharai scimitar or any weapon else; but nothing felt so native to his hand, so well balanced, so much an extension of his arm. Besides, this blade had been given him by Sieur Anton. This blade had cut Sieur Anton, indeed, as the knight's blade Josette had cut him. There was a connection there that he treasured, dark though it was. And Dard's whole history was shadowed by betrayal. That was another connection; Marron felt bonded to the blade, body and soul.

That he had sworn never to kill again, with Dard or the Daughter or any weapon else, was a complication he would have to face time and again. The better he fought, he thought, the easier it should be; and so he was glad to have Dard in his hand, as he faced the tunnel's black mouth.

Glad to have Jemel at his back, too, a fine swordsman himself with no inhibitions about killing. Though it would be as much a betrayal of his oath to let his friend kill for him. Marron glanced over his shoulder and waved Jemel further off; the Sharai lad hesitated, before taking a few grudging steps backward. Oaths in conflict, Marron's and Jemel's; he wondered if all his life would be a series of betrayals, if he could ever find a hope of peace and trust.

There was the faintest glimmer of light in the tunnel now, fading the black to grey: the man coming carried a torch, or a lamp. Marron stepped to the side, not to stand too obviously in the gateway.

The glow grew, but then died abruptly before its source or its bearer were visible. No fool, this man, to bring a light out into the open, where there might be guards. No friend either, Sharai though he might be. But that had never been likely, with 'ifrit at the upper entrance to the passage.

Marron held Dard close to his side, to kill any glimmer of starlight on the steel. Not so the man in the tunnel: his blade was what Marron saw first, the curve of a drawn scimitar reflecting the glow of the sky. And then the figure that held it, edging out onto the pavement, cautious and alert. A hiss of breath, as the man must have seen Jemel outlined against the water; Marron moved immediately, to step between them.

Another hiss, this time of recognition. Marron had guessed already, who the man must be; now he knew.

The scimitar's point rose against him, just beyond Dard's reach; Morakh's voice rose behind it.

'Have you been waiting for me, Ghost Walker?'

'Why not? You are my servant, sworn and promised . . .'

'I give no more service to an unbeliever. You are a freak, a thief; what you have is not yours, and will be taken back. By your death, Patric.'

'Is that why you give your service to the 'ifrit instead?'

'The 'ifrit do not deny our God; and they will do what has been promised us, they will drive your people from our land. With me and mine among them, the Sand Dancers following a true Ghost Walker.'

'Come, then. Slay me, and take what you seek . . .'

Morakh laughed harshly, contemptuously. 'You are like their ghûls, an animal hard to kill. One cut, and I face not you but what you have stolen. I will kill you, thief, with the single blow that is needful; but not here, not yet. Not while you are on guard and ready to use my own against me. Instead . . .'

Instead he was gone, suddenly vanished, and Marron faced only the emptiness of air. He whirled around to cry a warning to Jemel, too late; he saw Morakh behind his friend, saw the scimitar flash across his throat, saw Jemel flail and stagger, and fall.

He plunged towards the Dancer, roaring, and could have killed then despite all his oaths. But Morakh disappeared again, and this time even Marron's eyes could not find him.

One raging stare around was all that he could spare. Seeing nothing that moved anywhere this side of the gully, he let the man go – *for now, for the moment, not for long* – and the sword too, and fell down beside Jemel.

It had been a hasty, almost a clumsy blow, and Jemel had been twisting away from the blade as it hacked; what might have half-severed his head – and had been meant to, surely – had in fact not cut near so deep.

Deep enough, though, Marron thought grimly, seeing how blood gushed from Jemel's torn throat, how he gasped desperately for air he could not draw.

The Daughter surged in Marron's veins, in response to so much blood. He fought it down with a desperate effort and ripped the sleeve from his robe with one hard tug, thinking as he did so that it was futile, that no bandage could hold such a wound together. Jemel was doomed, was all but dead already; anything he did would be only a gesture.

Still, he had to make the gesture. He reached to lift his friend's head, to slip the sleeve beneath his neck, and was startled to find how cold Jemel's skin felt against his fingers. Only the pulsing blood was warm. Swiftly he wrapped the sleeve around the dreadful gape of the wound, and knotted it as tight as he dared.

Jemel's lips moved, shaping a word he couldn't speak; Marron read not his own name, but Elisande's. *Lisan*, Jemel was saying.

Marron wouldn't spare even a moment of his friend's dying, to look round for any sign of the girl.

'Don't worry about Elisande,' he murmured, stroking Jemel's chill, sticky forehead while the Daughter raged in his body. 'The djinni will keep her alive, it needs her.'

Jemel was trembling now, shaking with cold or fear; Marron wrapped his arms around his friend, but they were as useless as his improvised bandage, which was already dark and sodden.

He couldn't stem the flow of blood, he couldn't help the hoarse, rattling breathing; all he wanted was to force some heat into Jemel's body, to give him some comfort as he died, and it seemed that he couldn't do that either. He saw the world through a cast of crimson, his ears roared with the Daughter's hectic thunder; suddenly he laid Jemel down again and snatched Dard up from where he'd dropped it.

He thrust the point into the wound on his arm, and gasped as the Daughter poured out. Pain followed, but he could manage that. He let the sword fall again, lifted Jemel again, opened a doorway and stepped through into the world of the djinn.

He didn't expect a miracle, he knew there was no healing to be found here. But there was warmth, at least, and light; Jemel needn't die in the bitter dark of the waterfront. Let him die in wonder, in a mystical and alien place. Perhaps Marron would bury him here too, say the *khalat* and only hope that Jemel's soul could find its own way home, while his body stayed for the djinn to ponder over. He had cut himself off from his tribe, from all his people, by his choice; let him be truly outcast, then, let him lie where none but the Ghost Walker could find him . . .

Marron stood in brightness, by the shore of a steaming golden sea. That was something for a man to look on, as he died. Perhaps that dying would be slower, here where time moved so strangely; or perhaps not. Marron bled more quickly in this world, so Jemel might also. That might be a blessing.

What was surely a blessing was the heat, striking into Marron's bones already. He found a great slab of rock, and laid Jemel atop it; and couldn't think what to do then, except to stand witness to his friend's death. But the Daughter still pulsed in the corner of his eye, in time with the blood that pulsed from his arm, the pain that wracked him now; he lifted his hand to call it back—

—and checked himself, remembering.

Lisan . . .

He'd been sorely wounded when he'd come through with Elisande, and she had healed him. She'd healed her father too, when he was struck by a killing arrow . . .

Had it been hard to leave Jemel before? It was cruelly hard now, knowing he might come back to emptiness, to absence. He resented every blink of his eyes, for fear that his friend might choose that moment to leave him.

He went, though, because he had to. Walking with his head twisted around, finding the Daughter with senses other than his eyes because he couldn't bear to take his eyes from Jemel a moment sooner than he must, he stepped backward through the doorway and was in darkness again, the land of the djinn only a dim, misty glow framed by the smoky red of the Daughter.

He turned to face the sea, seeing nothing but darkness; and cupped his hands about his mouth and bellowed her name, 'Elisande!' although he was sure that she would never hear him, wherever she was beneath that implacable surface.

He'd lied to Jemel, he wasn't at all confident of her safety, her survival even; all he had was hope. The djinni would try to keep her alive, for its own sake; but its body was close to immortal, hers was frail human flesh which it might not understand. Or she might simply fail to find or raise the stone that imprisoned it, and it was not likely to be patient with failure . . .

Marron saw nothing, heard nothing in response to his call. He glanced behind him, towards the gully, thinking of Morakh slipping unseen by the guards, a lethal servant to the 'ifrit; his greater duty might lie that way. If Jemel died without or despite Elisande, and some other died too because he'd lingered here, he'd have another burden of guilt to carry, and perhaps a great one.

But he couldn't abandon his friend so long as any whisper of chance remained to save him. It was the Sharai way to be loyal even in despair, and Jemel was his sworn companion; others must face their own risk. That was Sharai also: matters came out as they were written, or as their God decreed.

He lifted hands and voice again, 'Elisande! Come swiftly!'

Whether in answer or not, he didn't know and couldn't guess; but there was a surge beneath the water, and her body burst suddenly to the surface, shattering the murky image of the stars.

He thought she might be dead, she might have paid the djinni in full for failure; he could see no movement in her bobbing body. She floated face down, only her bare shoulders showing pale amid the rippling dark. Something buoyed her up, though, something propelled her toward the stone embankment where he stood; and as he watched, her head thrust upward and she gasped for air.

There were steps that led down into the water; they were bitter cold and slimy beneath his feet, but he plunged down till he stood waist-deep and ready to receive her.

She was pushed, almost, into his arms. The steps were cold, but she was colder: as cold as Jemel, he thought, and caught like his friend in that unworld between life and death. Her body was stiff, clenched around something that she clutched against her belly; her breathing came hard and irregular, as though she had forgotten the natural way of it and had to wait, to fight against the urge until she was desperate.

He carried her up, staggering a little under the weight, and laid her out on the pavement. Her robe was close, fallen in a pool of water; he wrung it out and rubbed feverishly at her back until at last she moved, stretching out and groaning, rolling over to lie belly-up. The thing she'd held fell from her grasp then; it was a stone the size of her head, and it glowed warmly golden in the night.

Marron reached to touch her stomach, and found it hot against his fingers. She opened her eyes, staring blindly up at him and gasping like a landed fish.

There was a sudden eruption from the sea; the djinni hung above them, a pillar of swirling water.

'Break it. Break the stone . . .'

It was half command, half plea. Marron had no thought to disobey; he glanced around, saw Dard and snatched it up. Held it reversed in his hand, and brought the hilt smashing down onto the stone with all the native strength he had. Not much, with the Daughter outside his body and his arm hurting terribly; but it was enough. The stone splintered into shards that skittered wildly across the pavement.

For a moment, Marron thought that the air, perhaps the world itself had split also, unless it was simply his head. There was a high and terrible scream, and he was knocked flat by a deluge of stinking water that washed all those shards back into the sea.

He pushed himself up one-handed, and gaped around. There were the cliffs, the gully, the sky, all as they had been; but there too was the djinni, bound no longer, a spinning rod that hovered in the air close by Elisande's head.

'I am free,' it said simply. Its voice was high and pure and clean; Marron wouldn't have recognised it. Pity its release hadn't cleansed the water, too . . .

'No,' he returned breathlessly. 'You are not free, you are sworn to Elisande. Wait, and serve.'

It said nothing, but it stayed; that was, that must be enough.

He turned to her, dragging her up from the stone. 'Can you stand?'

'No,' she whispered, clinging to him, making him hiss with pain as her fingers dug into his bleeding arm. 'Marron, I'm so cold . . .'

'I can take you where you will be warm. But you must come, Elisande. Jemel is wounded, dying; he may be dead already. If not, you might heal him, though he is dreadfully hurt.'

She whimpered, struggling for balance on unsteady legs. 'I feel so weak, I want healing myself – but I will try. Where is he?'

'In the land of the djinn. I took him. You will be stronger there, as you were before, for me. Come, we must hurry; Morakh is in Rhabat. I need to give warning, but I cannot leave you there. Nor can I leave the way open for you to return; I can't go far from the Daughter.'

'Wait.' She stood, frowning with the effort of thought; then said, 'Djinni, can you—'

'Lisan, do not ask me questions again. Even now. I said that I would serve you, for the debt I owe to you; you should not put yourself in my debt also.'

That startled them both; she took a precious moment to recover, before trying again. 'Djinni, you can travel at will between the worlds; I think you can take me too.'

'That is true.'

'Good. You take me, then, to where my friend is. Marron, take back the Daughter, and go. I will do what I can.'

He could ask no more. He touched his lips to hers in gratitude, tasting bitter water and her surprise in equal measure; then he left her, pausing only to press her robe into her hands with an incoherent mutter.

He was truly and unequivocally glad for once to have the Daughter back in his body, and not only or even largely for the relief from pain. He felt his senses reach out, as though he stood at the heart of an expanding bubble of under-standing. He didn't need to look behind him to see Elisande taken over to the other world. He could hear how fast the djinni spun, so fast it unpicked the threads that divided this from that, and forced a gap between; he felt it when that rupture came, like a hole torn in everything that was solid. He heard Elisande's squawk that wasn't truly driven by her voice, only by all the air being squeezed out of her as she was plucked up and flung through. He was smiling as he felt the rupture healed from the further side; that djinni would be obedient to its oath, but it was never going to make an amenable servant. Elisande had interest-ing times ahead, he thought . . .

And turned his thoughts deliberately away from Elisande, and so away from Jemel also. There was no more that he could do; life or death, it lay in her hands now, and no blame to her if she failed. The wound might have been too deep, or the delay too great in fetching her. She would do all that lay in her power, and she had no responsibility else.

That same delay was much on his mind now, and all blame to him if it caused more deaths than one. For all that stretch of his senses, he couldn't find Morakh: couldn't see him ahead in the gully, couldn't hear his footsteps padding in the dark, couldn't scent him on the still, dank air. He knew the desert smell of the man, but it was too dry, too dusty a scent to survive the teeming assault of this damp, enclosed space which funnelled the reek of the Dead Waters through to meet the rich perfumes of trees and pool beyond.

Besides, none of the guards admitted to having seen a man pass this way. Morakh must have done so, but Marron thought it likely that he'd shifted from one hidden crevice to the next, blinking in and out of presence; moving like that he wouldn't have left a clean trail of scent or print to follow.

He was going to be very, very hard to find in the teeming disorder that was Rhabat. Unless his actions marked him out, unless he made himself very, very easy to find; and more even than for their centuries of patience, the Sand Dancers were famous for their stealth.

Marron ran through the gully and out to the lesser pool with its attendant trees. There were men on guard here too, or there were meant to be; he found them all on their feet and massing together beyond the pool, where the high walls drew close again in a narrow defile that led through to Rhabat proper. Duty was warring against some greater distraction. Marron heard it more clearly than they possibly could, but even to him it was only noise, the sound of many men shouting, each individual voice losing its purpose under the sheer volume of the others.

He elbowed his way through the crowd, moving faster even than the rumour of his coming, so that it was only as he squeezed past that he was recognised. He left a clear path uselessly in his wake, where men pressed back from his star-shadow and whispered their name for him, *Ghost Walker*, half in awe and half revulsion.

Breaking through at last, he could run again, and did; through to the bank of the greater pool, that wide and shallow stretch of water that fronted all the houses of Rhabat.

Here again there was a crush of men, along that narrow front: too many and too tightly thronged for Marron to force even his slender body between, too hot to make way for him even if he'd shouted his arrival. There were blades drawn here, the traditional truce trembled on a knife's edge, and that knife was working.

The cause lay clear to be seen, a body floating in the pool. As Elisande's had, face down and shoulders showing; but this was a man in his tribal robes, not stripped for swimming, and the clear water was clouded all around him.

Marron looked in vain for any figure of authority, who might contrive to quell the building riot. It needed Hasan, and likely several sheikhs beside; he could see none. They'd be in the hall still, in council, or else dispersed by now to their several houses. Either way they'd be trapped, held withindoors by the same press of bodies that was frustrating him. Their names and ranks would pass them through at last, but that would be too late. Those blades were sparring now, but they'd be used in earnest soon, and even one more death would splinter this small army into a dozen battling factions, tribe against tribe.

Marron did the only thing that he could think of to do; he plunged feet-first into the pool.

The bed was slippery, and loose stones shifted under his weight, but his bare feet found purchase enough to keep him upright. The water rose to his chest, and had long since given up the heat it had stolen from a day's sun; he hardly felt its chill, though, with the Daughter warm in his blood. Warm and growing warmer, growing hot as he waded slowly towards the body.

The surging crowd fell slowly still, as he'd hoped it would, as his progress was marked and followed. Even those with weapons drawn drew back from instant fighting, though they didn't sheathe their blades; even the loudest voices dropped to a low murmur. Again he heard his title, *Ghost Walker* passed from mouth to mouth.

When he reached the body, he gripped its shoulders and rolled it over in the water. A man in his middle years, a hint of white in his dark beard; his head lolled back, to show the terrible gash in his throat. Marron struggled against thoughts of Jemel – was he living yet or dead already, had Elisande come too late? – and against the Daughter also, as it reacted fiercely to the blood that swirled around him. All the blood this body had contained, he thought, was in the water now.

He turned to face the staring line of men, hundreds there were, there must be, massed along that bank.

'You all know me,' he cried, 'you know what I am, and

you know that I owe allegiance to none of your tribes. Tell me, who is he?'

A dozen voices answered him, in chorus: 'Bensallah, of the Kauram.'

'Very well. How did this happen?'

This time the answers were more various. He had been slain, cowardly murdered, by the hand of the Ib' Dharan, or of the Saren, or of the Beni Rus. Knives and scimitars were raised again, as other voices heatedly denied the accusations.

'Enough!' Marron bellowed. 'Who saw him die?'

A babble that dwindled as Marron emphasised, 'I do mean saw him die, saw the blow, saw who made the blow. Who among you saw that?'

Silence followed; at last a single voice said, 'He was walking alone, towards his fellows. I saw, I saw a shadow rise behind him, and then he fell . . .'

'You saw a shadow. A shadow from what tribe, could you see that?'

'It is dark, Ghost Walker, and I was not close.'

'The eyes of the Sharai are sharp – or said to be.'

'None the less. I cannot say, I could not see.'

'Could you see the tribal ties of the victim, could you see his face?'

'Of course. I saw he was Kauram. And the attacker drew his head back, to use a knife; I saw then that it was Bensallah, I knew him.'

'You saw that clearly, but not even the dress of the attacker?'

'I – no, I did not.'

'Could it be that the attacker wore a black robe, with no tribal ties?'

A murmur ran through the crowd, at that; Marron lifted his voice above it.

'There is a Sand Dancer at large in Rhabat. He fights for the 'ifrit, and is here plainly to sow dissension among the tribes; you have seen how easy that is. Let all beware; there may be other killings. Do not blame your neighbour, blame your enemy.'

The murmur grew, while Marron waited; at last someone shouted, 'The tribeless one is a Sand Dancer, or claims to be.'

'He does not wear black,' another voice objected.

'Black, blue – what difference, in the dark? He is tribeless, his dress proclaims it. Where is he?'

Marron answered, with a roar. 'Jemel,' – and he used the name deliberately, to silence them – 'Jemel is in the land of the djinn where I left him, or else he is in paradise by now; I do not know. His throat was cut by the same hand that did this,' and he lifted the body out of the water to show how the head hung loose. 'We met the Sand Dancer by the Dead Waters; he would not fight with me, but he near slew Jemel. If you want his name, I can give it you. He is called Morakh; some of you may know that name.'

Many of them did, clearly, and knew enough to fear it. Marron saw a lot of sidelong glances as people checked the faces of those around them, some shuffling at the fringes of the pack; no one felt comfortable with their backs exposed.

And now, at last, here came Hasan, shouldering through to the water's edge. He leaped onto a rock that raised him above the mass, and lifted his arms to draw all eyes to him.

'You have heard,' he said, his voice booming back from

the high carved cliff. 'Those of you who have the watch, double your guard and watch each other's safety too; danger may not only come from above. Let some of the Kauram take their dead brother, and say the *khalat* over his bones. The rest, get you to where you are safe, within walls, with those who are known to you. The man who is alone in darkness will be most at risk; where there are eyes and lights, the Dancer will not dare to venture. Go!'

Swiftly – and amazingly, to Marron – they went. That was this man's power, to cut through allegiance and ancient grievance, to speak directly to all. Marron's voice they resented, even where it spoke patent truth; Hasan's they loved, because he was of their people and yet could transcend his tribal loyalties and their own.

Some few men lingered, close beside Hasan; those he spoke to quietly, while he beckoned Marron to bring Bensallah's body to the bank. He startled them all, Marron not excepted, by jumping into the water himself to help lift it out.

The tribesmen raised the dripping body between them, and bowed their heads to Hasan; one or two even managed a brief nod to Marron, before they hurried away with their burden.

Hasan laughed shortly, before he levered himself up onto the bank. He turned then and extended an arm down to Marron, who didn't need it but took it anyway, feeling the man's strength as he was hauled bodily out of the water.

'That was well done, Ghost Walker. You have my thanks.' His eyes said more: that he was surprised to find a Patric quelling a near-fatal riot in the Sharai army. Truly, now that he had time, Marron was surprised at himself. If he'd stopped to think – or if he'd still been certain where his fealty lay – he might have stood back and let them slaughter each other. He thought Rudel would have done that, at least, for the greater good of Outremer . . .

'It was you they listened to,' he muttered awkwardly, against Hasan's waiting.

'No. It was you they listened to; it was me they obeyed. They know that Morakh was of my tribe, before he took the Dancers' oaths. But you had convinced them already. Come, let's find dry clothes and get warm; we have much to talk about.'

More even than Hasan knew; Marron remembered Elisande, and the djinni in the water. But then, inevitably, he remembered Jemel.

'I have to see my friend . . .'

'Marron, you have said it; living or dead, Jemel is beyond any man's harm at the moment. Nor should you go anywhere alone, at the moment. You of all men are in the greatest danger.'

'And you,' Marron returned briefly, though he wanted to say more; he wanted to bless Hasan for using Jemel's name so easily. That too was the man's power, he thought, to find anyone's weakness and play upon it with quiet skill.

'I, too,' with another laugh. 'We should stay together, then; and I am going to my house, to change my dress and sit before my fire. With my friend, I hope,' and he laid an arm around Marron's shoulders and steered him off along the path, still talking. 'That water is cold, and the air is colder; I am chilled to the marrow. Do you feel it? At all? Or does what you carry shield you from such crude contact with the world? You are not shivering, as I am.'

Marron had to think about it, before he could frame a sensible answer. 'I am aware of it,' he said eventually, carefully. 'I know that I am wet, and cold – but I don't feel it as I used to, before. In the same way that I don't feel hungry, or thirsty, or tired. I don't feel anything truly . . .'

'That is not true,' Hasan observed. 'You feel anger and confusion, those I have seen in you. And you feel love, that is evident in your concern for Jemel. And for others, the remainder of your party. Do you know where Elisande is, by the way? Sherett tells me she is not in her bed. That disturbs me now; I had thought that she might be with you. Should I have her searched for?'

Marron shook his head slowly. 'She is with Jemel; I, uh, I sent her there. But you need not fear for Elisande; even here she'd be safer than any of us.' Unless the djinni sought a quick end to its service, by slaying her itself or letting another do it. She should give it explicit orders, to guard her life; he must remember to tell her, if she hadn't thought of that herself . . .

Hasan eyed him oddly. 'Would you care to explain that? A girl alone, secretly out of her quarters, how could she be safe?'

'She's not exactly alone any more, Hasan. I'll explain, yes – but let's get dry first. I may not feel the cold, but I can feel your shuddering.'

Hasan took Marron to his own quarters, a modest room with an immodest view: set high in the house of the Beni Rus, the long, narrow chamber looked out over the breadth of Rhabat and all its length, from gully to siq.

'The sheikh has fewer stairs to climb, and far more space

to play in,' Hasan said as Marron looked and looked, 'but from up here I command all the valley.'

How he meant that, Marron wasn't subtle enough to determine; but what he meant didn't matter, the reality was plain to see. Hasan commanded all the Sharai, except perhaps the council. He might yet be denied his war; Marron thought he might wage it anyway. The tribes might follow Hasan even without their leaders' blessing.

Hasan flung open a chest and plucked out a pair of robes. One he threw to Marron. 'Too broad for you, but belt it tightly, it'll do. I'm not much taller. I'll do the ties for you; my people will be upset if you wear it wrongly. Stupid to make a blood insult out of a matter of knots, but it's been so for a long time. They think they need these little things, to remain who they are. Times are changing; it frightens them, I think.'

A minute later, after he had rubbed himself vigorously dry with a linen towel and then belted and knotted his own fresh robe with swift, accomplished fingers, Hasan turned to help Marron – and checked his hands, cocked his head on one side, whistled softly through bright teeth.

'You learn quickly, Marron. That is exact.'

'I've been dressing Sharai for weeks now . . .'

'Not in the manner of a young man of the Beni Rus.'

'Well, Jemel showed me . . .'

'Even so, we have to beat these knots into our own boys; we don't let them out of the women's quarters until they're perfect, but it can still take weeks. You must tell me your secret, I'll pass it on to Sherett . . .'

He was teasing, Marron thought, he knew it was no secret. He still wanted to hear Marron say it, though, *the*

Daughter remembers where I do not, it works my fingers for me.

He wouldn't say that; he didn't like its implications. Instead he shook his head; Jemel sighed, slapped him on the shoulder and nudged him over to where the promised fire blazed.

'Whoever made this place,' he said, sinking down onto the rug-covered floor with a sigh of relief, 'they cut flues all through the rock, to keep us from smoking our own flesh. I offer prayers of gratitude for their souls every night that I am here, although I have no name to give them.'

He offered more earthly gratitude to the boy who came in then, with a tray of coffee and sweetmeats. Younger than Marron, the lad was trying so hard to seem nonchalant, as though it were an everyday chore to serve Hasan, and the Ghost Walker added nothing that mattered to the tedium of the task.

Hasan spoiled it, though, not taking the cup held out to him; he took the boy's chin instead, and lifted his face into the firelight. One eye was bruised and swollen, and one lip was cut; there seemed to be toothmarks in his cheek.

'Shall I send you back to the tents, or back to the women?'

'Hasan, no . . .'

'No more of this, then, you hear me? Practise your writing, make a list . . .'

'Yes, Hasan.'

That was all; a wave of the hand and the boy fled, Hasan grinning wickedly at his back.

Marron said, 'You couldn't send him to your tents, the way is blocked—'

'—And the women would not have him, he's too old. He knows that. But they fight, for the privilege of serving me. I endured it before, I did as much myself when I was young; but I won't have it now. This is no time for foolish games, they must draw up a rota and abide by it. Even the children I need fit. If Topar is so marked, imagine what the other lads must look like, the ones who didn't win. I must see them, in the morning; some might need the women truly, for their healing.'

'Ask for Elisande. If she's there, she has magic in her fingers. So does her father, though, if you can't find her.'

'I know; but Sherett's ointments are good enough for bleeding boys. We will have more use for the healers of Surayon, I fear. And why would I not be able to find Elisande? If Sherett had lost her, I'd simply ask for you. Someone will always know where the Ghost Walker went.'

Marron shook his head. 'She's not always with me.'

'Is she not? I was told so.'

He drew breath to deny it, foresaw the difficulties that might lead to, thought that instead he ought to tell Hasan about the djinni, which was surely more important – and then had no need to do either, as the air in one corner of the room suddenly twisted, with a glimmer that drew his eye and Hasan's also.

They watched in shared silence, while that little catch of light grew into a spinning pillar, the breeze of it tugging at their hair. Marron was breathless with tension, with a hope he dared not allow; it seemed an age before there was any further change, a tearing in the air beside the djinni, a softly golden glow with a shadow at its heart, a shadow that showed itself to be a girl as she walked forward into the room from somewhere else entirely.

The glow died, as that tear sealed itself behind her; Elisande stood blinking for a moment, then bobbed a little curtsey to Hasan and came straight to Marron.

She dropped to her knees beside him, and took both his hands in hers. She looked exhausted, her new-cropped hair matted and clinging to her scalp, but there was a feverish brightness in her bruised eyes.

'He didn't die, Marron. He didn't die . . .'

'Where is he?'

'Still there. Probably asleep, by now. He's too weak to walk, and I couldn't carry him. Esren could have brought him through, I think, but he's better there for now, so long as someone goes back to watch over him. I shouldn't have left him, really, but I wanted to tell you . . .'

He nodded and squeezed her hands in his, the best thanks that he could manage. Relief had muted him, he could find no words to say; and those few words seemed to have drained the last of her energy. She slumped beside him, rested her head against his shoulder and lapsed into silence. It was left to Hasan to fill the two cups of coffee, and to pass one to each of them.

'Drink,' he said softly. 'You need it, both of you. Elisande, this is the best news you could have brought; it is not only Marron who sees virtue in that young man. But you have brought another visitor with you, and I neglect it shamefully; will you introduce us?'

She drained the tiny cup, but shook her head when he moved to refill it, rousing herself with a visible effort.

'Forgive me, I was distracted . . . Hasan, this is Djinni Esren Filash Tachur. I freed it from the Dead Waters, where it had been trapped by the 'ifrit; it has sworn to serve me in recompense, but I have hopes that it will be my friend, and a friend to us all . . .'

'If it has helped to save Jemel's life, it is my friend already,' and Hasan rose to bow low to the spinning djinni. 'Djinni Tachur, you are truly welcome here.'

Its voice rang silver in that space, like the chiming of distant bells. 'I never thought to find any value in the friendship of humans, but there can be surprises even for the djinn; I could see nothing when I was held in the snare of the 'ifrit, in the Waters. I have been unravelled from the spirit-weft, so this is all like being remade new. It is interesting.'

Hasan bowed again. 'I am glad; and doubly so, that Elisande has such a protector.'

Marron stirred, glancing at her and remembering his earlier doubts. Hasan had carefully not called it a servant, but . . . 'Will it protect you?' he murmured. 'Have you told it to?'

'She has no need, Ghost Walker,' the djinni replied, when she did not. 'The djinn have their own honour. I swore to serve, and I will do that. No harm will come to her, that I can prevent.'

That was good enough. Marron put his arm around Elisande, because he thought she wanted him to; as she subsided against him with a soft sigh, he said, 'Tell me of Jemel, how he was, how he is now.' Alive, he knew, and that had briefly been enough; now he wanted more, he wanted to share every moment that she'd spent with him and he had not.

Elisande whispered again, 'He didn't die. I thought he would, for a while I thought he'd take me with him, I was so deep inside him and trying so hard; something was sucking at the pair of us and I think it was death, I think it must have been. But he's stubborn, that boy, or he's just got something worth living for,' and her hand stroked his arm while her eyes flicked away from his face, to rest for a moment on the djinni. 'He fought it more than I did, I don't know where he found the strength, there was none in his body; and at last it just went away. Then I could work on him, I could start to mend what was broken. He needs more, but not now; sleep is better, for a while. He will be fine, Marron, if nothing else harms him. He shouldn't be alone, though, there are 'ifrit in that world who may find him; I ought to go back . . .'

'No, not you. You should rest; I'll go. I cannot heal,' *I can heal nothing*, 'but I can watch him while he sleeps.'

He pulled himself away from her, and saw the resignation in her face as he did so. For a moment he hesitated, but only for a moment. Hasan said briskly, 'Yes, go, Marron. You can bring Jemel back when he wakes, if he seems enough recovered. Elisande, you I forbid; you need more than a cup of coffee to restore you. And I would be unhappy if you took Djinni Tachur away from me so quickly; I would like to hear both how it came to be trapped by the 'ifrit, and how you rescued it.'

He clapped his hands sharply, twice; there was a scurry of steps beyond the doorway, and the same boy who'd brought the coffee appeared there, gaping soundlessly between the djinni and the unveiled girl.

'Topar, fetch a beaker of juice for the Lady Lisan, and

some food; she has a starveling look. And bring her a clean robe, too. One of your own; you are much of her size, and I cannot send her back to Sherett looking like that.' The robe she wore had dried in the warmth of the other world, but it was wrinkled and filthy, smelling of sweat and foul water. 'If you don't object, my lady?'

'I object to this,' she said, fingering the stains on her robe. 'As do you; I can see your nostrils working. Thank you, Topar, I would be honoured to borrow your clothes. And a bowl of water, if you could fetch one? If you can carry so much . . .?'

'Of course, my lady,' though he'd need several more hands to do it in a single trip.

'Get help,' Hasan ordered brusquely. 'I'm sure there must be some other boy awake in this house. Bleeding from the nose, most likely.'

Topar was struggling not to grin, as he left; Marron followed him out, not struggling at all against the bubbling elation inside him.

'Topar!'

'Yes, uh, Ghost Walker?'

'When you come back, stay with Hasan and the lady. For her honour's sake, they should have a better chaperone than the djinni. And when she leaves, remind him of his own order, that no one should be alone while the Dancer is abroad. You have heard about the Sand Dancer?'

'Yes, Ghost Walker . . .'

'Good. Hasan's safety lies in your hands, then. Lend me your knife for a moment.' He had his own in his belt, and Dard too; but he felt skittish and ridiculous, more than willing to give the boy a thrill.

Topar drew his knife and handed it to Marron hilt-first, with a puzzled frown. Marron pricked his arm delicately, gave the blade back and gestured the boy to a safe distance as the Daughter smoked up from his blood.

He opened a gateway right there in the corridor and stepped through to the other world, giving Topar a cheerful wave on the way.

He found himself standing before a cliff that was quite unmarked by any man's carving, that made a glittering match to the cliff of Rhabat. As always in this world, his arm bled more freely and the pain was greater; he closed the gateway quickly and drew the Daughter back into his wound to stifle it.

Then he ran, his feet as light and foolish as his thoughts. He coursed across the hard-packed dust, along the base of the cliff and through the winding defile beyond, where the opposite wall of this valley closed in; and so came to that same sea that he had seen before, its waters seething as though something monstrous dwelt beneath the surface. Marron spared it barely a glance; he looked along the shore, and there lay Jemel, on the same slab where he had laid him but naked now, his blood-weltered robe tossed to one side.

Elisande must have done that, he thought, approaching more slowly now. She worked best skin to skin; he pictured her lying full-length atop Jemel, her short body stretched against his, and felt a moment of stupid jealousy for her having come first to where he had never yet been. He quelled it in fury at himself — she was surely entitled if anyone was, for the pain his own desire caused her; besides, she'd lain so with him in this world, so why not with Jemel? – and walked up to stand beside his friend.

She had taken his makeshift bandage from Jemel's throat, too. Marron stared in wonder at what he could see there, the livid scar that would mark Jemel for ever now as a man who had been called back miraculously from death. It was almost a match for his own scars, though Jemel's would lose that fresh-made look soon enough, while one of Marron's never would. For the moment, at least, it made them brothers; and it was his marked arm that Marron reached out with, to lay his fingers lightly on Jemel's neck.

He could feel a pulse beneath the tender, brutalised skin, too weak to please him but he rejoiced none the less; that beat of blood was a victory in itself, against Morakh and all his kind. Marron thought he could stand there for hours, for days, only counting the rhythm of it as he gazed down at his friend's face, at the lean body below. The scar was a badge of honour, but Jemel didn't need it; his strength, his character was laid out there for Marron to read in every muscle and every showing bone.

When his eyes moved back to the face again, he saw that Jemel's eyes were open, and his mouth was smiling faintly.

'Jemel . . . How do you feel?'

He didn't really expect an answer, the question was only noise; his spirits were so running over, something had to spill out.

After a while, though, that smile moved, shaping words without ever losing its own shape. There was not much more breath in the Sharai's voice now than there had been before, when his throat was gaping open, but Marron was still caught by the marvel of there being any at all. If Jemel had been here and Marron had been back in the home-lands, at the further end of the other world, he thought he'd still have heard each syllable.

'I feel tired . . . Was I dead?'

'No. Almost. Morakh tried to send you, but you wouldn't go.'

'Someone pulled me back, then, I remember that . . .'

'Elisande. But she said it was you holding on, she said you saved them both, she'd have gone with you if you hadn't held on. Too stubborn to die, she said.'

'Lisan. Yes. I remember her. I thought she pulled me out.' He closed his eyes for a moment, leaving Marron bereft; then they opened again, and his smile stretched. 'She lay beside me. I remember the touch of her, telling me that I still had a body. I had forgotten, I think.'

Marron nodded, not unhappy that he should remember that. She'd worked so hard to save Jemel, even at the risk of her own life and to the sure loss of her happiness; she deserved to have it acknowledged, by him more than anyone. By him and Marron both.

'Marron?'

'Yes?'

'Lie with me.'

Marron blinked, not understanding or else refusing to understand. 'What, are you cold? Your robe is here . . .'

'No, fool. But I have been in cold places, and Lisan, this world, they can only warm my body. I have been wait-ing for you.'

'You've been sleeping.'

'That's what I said. Take off your robe, and lie down with me. There is an ice-chip in my heart.'

That was a thing that Marron knew about; he carried several and had thought Jemel might make another, dying for his sake, because they'd been together. Not even the living Jemel could melt those that remained, he thought, or never had thus far. But this was a new Jemel, remade – if roughly made, with his seam showing – and asking for what he never had before. Demanding, rather. This was a barrier breached, and who knew what might happen on the further side . . .?

Marron slipped his robe off slowly, and lay down on the rock beside his friend.

It was hard and hot against his skin, but he was only distantly aware of that. Jemel was vulnerable where he was not, and Jemel was not even sweating. He moved for the first time, rolling into Marron's arms, and his skin was warm and dusty, strangely scented with the sharp dry odour of this country. His body settled languidly, as though his bones were too heavy for his own muscles to carry, though he felt strangely light to Marron; his head fell onto Marron's shoulder, and he sighed faintly.

'You are the first man who has held me so since Jazra, the first I have wanted to; but that is not so long. Do I betray his memory, and all our oaths?'

'*No!*' explosively; and then, more quietly, 'I do not think the living owe very much to the dead, Jemel.' *And I am the master-betrayer of us two, and my master is not even dead . . .*

'I owe him vengeance, that at least. Perhaps that's why I did not choose to follow him, if Elisande is right, that I was fighting; perhaps I have to live, to face Anton d'Escrivey and claim the death-price. Perhaps it wasn't you I came back for . . .'

But his own fingers called him a liar, tracing the patterns of Marron's bones across his skin; his lips, his tongue did the same.

'Give me your breath, Marron, to melt this ice-core that is in me . . .'

Can you do the same for me? Marron thought not; his heart was colder, reminded of Jemel's fixed purpose to slay Sieur Anton. At the same time, though, heart and body and all were quickened by Jemel's touch, heated as the rock could not heat them, nor the sun in the other world. His own hands moved in response, wary of his friend's weakness at first and then more forceful as Jemel snorted, 'I am not made of glass,' and proved it with fingers that were suddenly as hard as glass, teeth that seemed as sharp.

Marron broke away only briefly, levering himself up on his elbows to gain a little distance, just enough to say, 'What if a djinni come by? Or an 'ifrit?'

'What if they do? The djinn do not care about men; the 'ifrit – well, I have frightened death off once already. I will pull faces over your shoulder, and the 'ifrit will go away.'

And his arm curled up around Marron's neck and pulled his head down, hard.

Not so very tired after all, Jemel: unless he stole vigour from Marron, to turn from lazy cat to lion.

It was Marron who was indolent after, content to be a cushion to his friend against the roughness of the rock; it was Jemel who lifted his head – too soon! – to say, 'Now we are both men again. And being men, we should go back to our own world where we belong.'

'You should sleep,' Marron protested in a mutter, meaning *let me sleep, and wake again to find you at my side.* He hadn't slept for how long? He couldn't work it out; this world was turning dark, but his own had been dark a long time before he came here. He'd thought he would never feel tired again, with the Daughter always wakeful in his blood; he'd been wrong.

'Marron, I have slept. I could sleep more, yes – but sleep is like a little death, and I have been too close to his brother to seek him out so soon. We should go back,' again. 'You are the Ghost Walker; you may be needed.'

'Elisande can find me. She has a djinni to ride.'

'I remember it, I think; there was something behind her, something she clung to as she pulled me out. Something powerful: did she say she was afraid of falling? She need not have been, it would have held her back. I thought it might have been you. But however that is, she has her duty and you have yours. And I mine: I am servant to the Ghost Walker, and will nudge him when he strays.' And did, with long fingers that felt all bone now, no tender touch at all. 'Come, up! Open us a door, and take us home.'

Marron rose reluctantly, under the scourge of those fingers. He dressed himself, then looked at his friend and said, 'Will you wear this?' He lifted Jemel's discarded robe, which was stiff and caked with blood. Even dried and dead, that touch made the Daughter wake inside him, driving down his lethargy. 'Or go naked, under all men's eyes?'

Jemel laughed recklessly. 'Do I care? Give it me.'

He took the robe and knotted it loosely around his

waist, like a kilt for decency's sake. 'This will do. Now
prick yourself, or shall I do it for you . . .?'

No need for that; but he did hold Marron's hand, his left
hand, while the right did the necessary knifework; and
didn't let go even while the hot red smoke poured out,
while the blood ran.

They came back to a wakeful world, the bay in shadow as it
almost always was but the sea to the north running with
sunlight. Marron thought the water looked a little clearer
than he'd seen it before, and the air smelled a little less bad.
Innate honesty forced him to confess to himself that it might
simply be walking handfast with Jemel that coloured his
judgement, but it was possible too that, freed of their furious
captive, the Dead Waters were already beginning to recover.

There was no one to be seen on the waterfront. Jemel
retrieved his weapons from where they'd been left lying
when he fell, reclaimed Marron's hand determinedly and
tugged him on through the gully. Here they walked under
men's eyes, and Jemel at least walked with pride; Marron
had to struggle against an old resurgent shame, the abiding
taint of his upbringing.

One of the guards called down to them, a message from
Hasan: would they please seek him out in the Chamber of
Audience, where he was meeting with the sheikhs?

'You see?' Jemel said, vindicated. 'We are looked for;
and you would have slept through their counsels, sluggard.
While I famished, for lack of food.'

'If it had been urgent,' Marron repeated, 'he would have
sent Elisande.'

'Women don't carry messages.'

'That one would. Or she'd have sent her djinni.'

'The *djinn* don't carry *messages*!'

'That one would, if she sent it.'

'Marron, has the world remade itself completely, while I slept?'

Not itself; it remade you, or she did. But he shook his head, laughing, and said, 'It's the price of freedom, for the djinni: that it serve her instead of the 'ifrit. Don't you remember?'

'Yes – but she said she wouldn't abuse it. To send a djinni with a message, that would be an outrage . . .'

'Between the worlds, where she can't go without it? I'd do that, Jemel. In her place, I'd do it gladly. Think how the djinn have had her running to and fro, with no explanation. I guess we know why now, they wanted her here to free Tachur; but she's entitled to claim her price, full measure . . .'

'No. Would you give orders to a saint, or to an angel?'

They argued as they walked, but it was all words, all superficial. Deeper, Marron was delighted simply to have the chance to waste time with Jemel, to argue pointlessly; deeper yet, he was thinking that Elisande was exactly the right person to have released the djinni and secured its service. She'd spent time in the desert with the tribes, enough to know to be wary – though it had reminded her when she slipped, and he'd been surprised; her face had shown him just how surprised she was – but still she was Patric at heart, she wouldn't give it the unquestioning respect it would have drawn from Jemel, Hasan, any of the Sharai. She would use it where its attributes were useful, whether or not it was fitting for a djinni to be so used.

At the house of the Beni Rus, Marron veered in through the doorway, dragging his friend with him.

'The Chamber of Audience, the message said,' Jemel protested.

'I know; but you're hungry, you said. And you're naked, near enough. Or had you forgotten? You don't dress as a tribesman any more, but that's no reason to dress as a beggar in rags.'

Jemel glanced down at his improvised kilt, and giggled. 'You're right – the sheikhs would try again to kill me, I think, if I went before them like this. I had forgotten. I'll find a robe, Marron, if you find the food. Enough for two, you need to eat too.'

True, he did; and if he felt hungry suddenly, Jemel must be ravenous. Marron went scouting downstairs, where the boys slept. There if anywhere, he reasoned, he'd find food.

He found more than that, he found wide-eyed wonder and a desperate eagerness to please. There were unsuspected advantages to being the Ghost Walker, he thought, grinning privately as lads little younger than himself fell over themselves in their hurry to fetch bread and fruit and hunks of cold meat, all that was left of the morning meal. Hasan had eaten at dawn with the other men, he learned, and had then been summoned; he'd left his message here too, for Marron and Jemel to follow. There was other news to explain his urgency: three more men had died in the night despite all precautions, their throats savagely slit from behind. All were of different tribes, no one had seen their attacker.

The boys had been told to stay here in their den, and guard themselves and each other. Out of curiosity, Marron asked after Topar and was shown a heap of blankets in a corner; he could just make out a tousled head amidst the bundle, where that boy lay dead to the world, sleeping off the excitements of his night. Marron yawned, and shook his head against a sudden longing for his own bed. If the Sharai commander could go a night without sleep, as Hasan surely had, then so could the Ghost Walker . . .

He enlisted a couple of boys to carry the food and a pitcher of water back up to the hallway, where Jemel stood waiting, wet-headed and clean and decently dressed. They ate on their feet, quickly and rapaciously; then Marron calmly took the pitcher and tipped what was left in it over his own head. The boys gaped, while Jemel cackled. Marron shook water out of his ears, seized his friend's hand and led him out into the sunshine.

Small groups of men were gathered along the poolside to watch them as they went. There was no crush this morning, no intermingling of the tribes. No confrontations either, that Marron could detect: only nervousness, tension, a sullen distrust. Discipline was holding, but for how long? If Morakh wasn't found soon, some hothead would cease believing in a phantom Sand Dancer, when enemies of long standing were all too visible and only a knife's cast away . . .

They hadn't yet reached the doorway to the great hall they were bound for when they saw a man go running in, with a bow clutched in his hand.

They glanced at each other, sharing a single thought. 'All the archers should be on guard, or resting,' Jemel muttered. Marron simply grunted. He wanted to run after the man, but restrained himself with an effort; his place was ambiguous enough already, and Jemel's was worse. Better not to antagonise the sheikhs by bursting in unannounced, with hot demands for news. If there was trouble, they'd learn it soon enough . . .

And did, the simplest way: by meeting Hasan at the doorway, as he came hurrying out with the archer trailing him, breathless and shamefaced.

Hasan greeted them with a roar, 'Where have you *been*? No, don't answer, I know where you've been. Forgive my impatience, but I could have wished to have you back an hour since. Jemel, I am none the less pleased to see you on your feet. We have Elisande to thank for that, I know. Are you fit?'

All this without breaking stride: they had to hasten to keep up with him.

'Fit enough,' Jemel gasped, though the sudden weakness in his voice betrayed the lie. Hasan's gaze was ruthless in response.

'You look half dead, boy. I'd send you back to the house to rest and Elisande to tend you further, except that she is sleeping and I may have need of you too soon.' His eyes moved to Marron, who read the message clearly: it was he Hasan might need, but the man doubted his commitment, if he were separated from Jemel. Even a Ghost Walker reluctant to kill might kill regardless, to protect his friend . . .

'Hasan,' he demanded, 'what has happened?'

' 'Ifrit have been flying above the siq, and these lackwits,' with a jerk of his head back towards the hangdog archer, 'have been loosing at them, and never thought to send a message until one was out of arrows . . .'

'We slew some,' the man muttered defensively.

'Aye, and missed many, or else hit with unblessed arrows that could do no harm. They have spent all the hope we had; without an imam here, we had to preserve our few effective weapons. I *told* them that . . .'

And of course they had not listened, or had forgotten when the monstrous shadows of the 'ifrit came swooping at them out of the sky. Marron could understand both the archers and Hasan's fury. He'd heard from Jemel how an unsanctified blade would simply skitter off the creatures' armour, how it needed a pure stroke into an undefended eye to slay them. With the rare potent arrows lost, how many men would the 'ifrit pick off on the wing, how many more would die trying to make that desperate thrust when they came in to land?

That was Hasan's fear, clearly: that invulnerable monsters would destroy his nascent army before ever it had the chance to march. He was running now, abandoning any image of the good commander's unhurried self-control in his urge to see what damage, what danger faced his men.

Marron could have paced him or outpaced him all the way; Jemel, not. So Marron held his friend back when he tried to run, said, 'No, be patient. Desert wisdom, Jemel – don't spend your strength.'

A sidelong glance, and, 'Did you learn that from her?'

'Or from you, I don't remember. You both preach desert at me, as though it were the source of all knowledge.'

'All that matters, in the Sands. Important here, too. You're right, we needn't rush. I don't believe this is our day to die, but if it is the 'ifrit will wait for us.'

So they walked the siq, while the sounds of running feet

faded ahead of them. Straining to follow those rhythms, Marron thought that perhaps the 'ifrit were doing exactly that, were waiting; he could hear no noises else, no sounds of battle.

They caught up with Hasan at the point where the siq was blocked, near at its end. The Sharai was pacing in the deep shadow, glaring up at a wall of loose rubble ripped from the constricting walls of rock. Men stood in an uncertain huddle, a little distance off and watching him; others – those still with some arrows left, presumably – were stationed on ledges as high as they could safely climb.

Above, above them all, what little sky Marron could see was clear blue and still, host to nothing that flew. Any birds, he thought, must have been frightened away by the 'ifrit; would be crouching probably in cracks and crevices all along the siq, the best shelter they could find. Certainly they weren't singing, any more than they were flying. There was heavy silence this side of the rockfall, broken only by the soft grate of pebbles under Hasan's restless feet.

'They are no fools, these 'ifrit,' Hasan said at last, speaking to Marron but meaning to be overheard by the withering tone of his voice, meaning to be fully understood, *the 'ifrit are no fools, but these men of mine* . . . 'A couple of dives to fright 'em, then they just drifted on the wind, just within bowshot. And watched, and let the arrows slip by. Counted them, maybe, if 'ifrit can count, or looked for the ones that could harm them if they can tell 'em apart. I don't know. But these dung-heads kept on shooting. They say they killed a few, but they can't show me bodies, because they fell beyond the siq. That's no matter, the 'ifrit fade from this world when they die, there would be no bodies; but they can't reclaim the arrows either.

'The only body they have shown me,' with a shadowed glance towards what lay heaped beside a boulder by the path, what looked at first like a bundle of rags and no more, that reminded Marron of Topar asleep in his corner, 'is the lad I left with them as a runner. They did send him, but an 'ifrit brought him back to them. They say they didn't think to send another, until Hosim here was out of arrows; I say they were all afraid, and stayed where they were safer until the 'ifrit withdrew. Marron, I need to know where the 'ifrit are now, and what they are doing. Can you find them for me?'

He could, perhaps. The rockslide was beyond climbing, even for him; but he could call up the Daughter and pass it by in the other world, come back to see beyond. He thought he might not need to, though.

'Listen,' he said. 'Don't you hear?'

'What? I hear nothing . . .' Hasan's voice died even as he said it, as it became untrue: as he began to hear what was already clear to Marron, the sound of stones slipping and falling, just a short way out of sight. No man could climb that treacherous heap of rock, perhaps, but it seemed that something could. From the other side, still out of sight, it was certain that something was.

Hasan gestured, and they began to fall back from the foot of the steep slope. Whatever came down, best to meet it on level ground, and not in a cloud of dust and a hail of falling scree.

Two of the men broke away, going to retrieve the body of the dead boy; Marron nodded, and stepped aside to let them pass. Little they could do in any case, with unblessed blades against 'ifrit, whatever form the creatures came in. Little any of them could do, in all honesty. Hasan's scimitar had been blessed, by Jemel's report; but he was one man, and couldn't be risked alone. He was too valuable. Without his leadership, the Sharai would splinter into factions, and their fighting strength would be dissipated.

Which Hasan knew, it seemed. He drew his blade, but made no move to set himself forward of the others. Instead he called after the men with the body, 'Hurry back, and alert the tribes! Tell them to be ready, with spears where they have them. We will try to delay what comes . . .'

Delay would be the most that they could manage, Marron thought, even before he saw the creatures that breasted the height of the wall of tumbled rock before them.

They were 'ifrit, there could be no doubt of that, the glossy black armour of their bodies betrayed them; but these were 'ifrit as he had never seen nor heard of them before. Learning perhaps from the way they'd been beaten off as winged marauders, realising perhaps that flight would be useless in the warren of narrow passageways that was Rhabat, they had remade themselves in a shape designed to be more deadly.

Worms, Marron thought, *giant worms* – but these were worms with overlapping rings of impervious chitin to protect them, with their scorching red eyes buried deep behind great gaping mouths that chewed on air, that strained to chew on more solid flesh.

They rippled over the rockfall and began to slither down, dislodging vast boulders as they came, crushed rock rising in a cloud of powder all about them to speak to the tremendous mass of their new bodies.

'How did they get so heavy?' Jemel whispered. Marron had no answer for him; they'd been half hollow before, or had seemed so, by the ease they had in taking wing and their speed through the air. If these things grew wings, still they'd never fly.

It was hard to judge in all the dust and horror of their coming, but their backs stood perhaps a man's height above the ground and ran perhaps the length of a dozen men laid head to foot, before tapering to a rounded tail. Hasan was right to call for spears, Marron thought, and right too to be backing away now as all the men were, as Marron was himself. Dard was in his right hand, but his left was locked securely on Jemel's sleeve, just in case. Anyone who tried to be a hero, who flung himself forward, would meet those working mouths before ever he came within a sword's thrust of a vulnerable eye.

Retreat only delayed the inevitable, though. The 'ifrit moved slowly in this shape, but their advance was inexorable. Marron had a vision of what would happen when they broke out into Rhabat, how all the gathered men – and the women, Elisande, Julianne – would have nowhere to run. How they'd pack into the houses, and be trapped there; how those bodies would squirm in through the doorways, how those mouths would find meat at last, while useless weapons battered against impregnable armour . . .

'Marron!' Hasan called out. 'Can you slow them, at least, can you block the siq?'

He could try. He let go of Jemel's sleeve, trusting his friend not to be stupid, not to waste his life; he touched

Dard's bitter edge to the wound on his forearm, and drew the Daughter out. He shaped it into a gateway that filled the siq from wall to wall; if the 'ifrit tried to pass through it, they would find themselves back in the land of the djinn.

He stood waiting, while Jemel and Hasan stood with him, while the other men massed behind. They were all blind now, seeing nothing but the golden shimmer of another country ahead of them, encased in a crimson frame; Marron listened, and heard something that at first he did not understand. A slow crunching, very different from the rumbling, scraping sounds of 'ifrit bodies dragging over stone . . .

Uncertainly, he gestured his companions back. Neither of them actually moved, unless Jemel came a little closer to his side.

The noise grew steadily louder, *closer* he thought in bewilderment; it seemed to be coming from inside the rock itself, he could see wind-blown sand sift down from ledges, little flakes of stone fall away . . .

Worms, he thought suddenly, belatedly; and thrust Jemel behind him as he waved Dard in a frantic sweep as though to drive Hasan away, as rock shattered and fell like a sheet of crystal, as the great head of an 'ifrit burst out through the wall of the siq before him.

It was so close, so dreadfully close. He could see how the mouth was made in three parts, great beaks that opened wide and slammed together, that opened again to reach for him. He could see all the way into the creature's gullet, monstrous plates that ground together, that could pulverise rock, that would make short work of a man. Such a foul throat ought to reek, but did not; the scent of the thing was dry and sharp, not unpleasant – for a bizarre moment an image of Jemel came to his mind, Jemel in the other world, scented with that golden dust . . .

He could never remember having closed the gateway, even at the time he was sure he hadn't done that; but the Daughter was suddenly there, a misty red haze hanging in the air between him and the 'ifrit. A flicker of brighter light caught his eye, and that was Jemel's sword desperately slashing over his shoulder, trying to defend him. It wasn't the blade that had the 'ifrit's mouth suddenly snapping shut, though, that drove it back into the tunnel it had chewed. It knew its own strength, as it knew its own peril; the Daughter was what it feared, and rightly so. A single thought from Marron, a momentary summoning of his will, and that frail-seeming mist would have swept forward to engulf, to destroy . . .

He did gather his will, after a moment's thought; he did send the Daughter to destroy. But he sent it upward, against the rock, backing away as he did so and dragging Jemel with him.

Where the Daughter touched, the face of the wall splintered. He drove it in more forcefully and great cracks appeared, running wide and deep; a little nudge more, and a massive slab broke away and fell crashingly to ground, blocking the hole where the 'ifrit had eaten through.

That would hold it back only briefly, but long enough, he hoped. Long enough at least for him to do the same on the other side of the siq, where another 'ifrit was breaking out of the wall.

More were coming in single file along the path, now that it was no longer blocked. They seemed hesitant, however, having once seen the Daughter. They and their brothers inside the rock stood clearly in fear of it, and wisely so; how long that fear would last, how long they would take to realise that it would not be wielded directly against them, Marron couldn't guess.

He moved further down the siq, to where a sharp angle took them out of sight; there he used the Daughter furiously against the rock, creating another landslip as crude and brutal as the 'ifrits' own that had first closed this narrow road. Not as effective, alas, not to creatures who could chew their way through solid rock, but it would buy time . . .

Jemel coughed, spat out the dust of the fall and said, 'Marron, not even 'ifrit . . .?'

'I'm sorry. Not even 'ifrit.' They were living, intelligent, never mind that they were malign; he wouldn't, couldn't stand and slaughter again.

'To save Rhabat, and all these people?'

'There's got to be another way, Jemel. I can't do it.' With a sword he might fight if he had to – indeed he already had, to save Elisande, though he had failed with Dard as he failed in so much – but with the Daughter, never.

As he drew it back into his body to quell the burning pain of his arm, he heard muttered voices at his back, 'He is Patric, he wants us all dead. All but his friends, he will take them to safety and leave us to perish . . .'

Nothing he could say against that, only prove it untrue by staying and dying uselessly among them; he was determined suddenly to do that if he must, not to be a traitor once more. He had betrayed his own people too often; perhaps he betrayed his enemies too by refusing to kill for them, but he would not abandon them now.

Hasan tried to kill the talk by coming to stand with Marron, by throwing an arm about his shoulders and turning him away from the rockfall, saying, 'Come, you have done what you can. If you had killed one, the rest would simply have tunnelled all the way through to Rhabat; you could not reach them inside the rock.'

Even Hasan, though, had a doubtful look in his eye, a look that said *even one dead would have been a help, and you might have killed many before they escaped you.*

Marron couldn't dispute any of that, aloud or silently eye to eye or even to himself, in the privacy of his own head. It made no difference, in any case. Right or wrong, he was what he was, what the Daughter and his life had made of him: he was a man with a strength he dared not use, and he thought that was worse than being weak.

It was a lot worse than being as Jemel was, treacherously hurt and nobly scarred by it, bravely come from his sickbed to face what battle there might be. It seemed strange, absurd, perverse to Marron that the hurt man should help the whole, that the exhausted should lend strength to the inexhaustible; but that's how it was. Jemel slipped his shoulder under Marron's and wrapped an arm around his waist, and it was true support he offered.

'If you come to the Sharai, you must endure gossip,' he murmured. 'You can feed them truth,' and his mouth was so close to Marron's ear it was almost kissing, surely stoking the fires he described, 'or you can listen to their lies; there are no other choices. Do what you must, don't let their whispers drive you.'

Marron smiled thinly. 'I will not.' He could not, rather: not in this.

'One thing, though: if a man calls you a coward to your face, you must kill him, Marron. They will kill you, else; and there will be a mob of them, too many even for you unless you run to the other world, and how would I find you then?'

'I would find you,' he said, *if you wanted finding, if the disgrace was not too much even for you.* 'But if a man calls me coward, Jemel, I will take him to the other world – and leave him there, if his apologies aren't deep enough to please me.'

Some quiet part of him was watching, listening in, gaping in astonishment that they could smile together when such danger threatened at their backs. But the 'ifrit were some little distance behind them now, still behind his rockfall, Marron thought; at least he couldn't hear any pursuit. Fear of the Daughter was delaying them, he guessed; even spirit creatures perhaps had to work, to sustain their courage against the chance of death.

So he and Jemel walked a quiet, shadowed path, two young men bound together by more than clinging arms and close-pressed heads, walking a little apart from their companions; and was it really such a wonder, if their talk drifted away from terror and towards a dreaming hope?

They came back to reality soon enough, too soon. Marron heard other voices, other footsteps coming towards them, from around another bend in the siq. He cocked his head to listen, and thought he could identify a couple of the newcomers. The others quickened their pace, as they too caught the sounds of company; Marron held Jemel back, just a little.

By the time they reached the bend, Hasan was deep in

conversation with Rudel and the King's Shadow. Those two had brought half a dozen men with them, each armed with a long spear; Hasan's archers were already past those and hurrying on, evidently anxious to be clear of this narrow way before the 'ifrit reappeared.

'Marron, Jemel . . .' Hasan beckoned them forward, to join the conference. 'The sheikhs are organising their people, in the open ground beyond the siq; they will need time, though, and it is our task to supply it. We must delay the 'ifrit longer, if we can.'

Marron glanced up at the high walls that overhung them. 'I can block the path again, if you want me to. That slows them down, especially if they think they might find me waiting when they come through.'

'If you destroy this path altogether,' Rudel said harshly, 'then we are truly trapped, and only the 'ifrit can make a way through.'

They were trapped already, Marron thought, and had been since the siq was first closed. He opened his mouth to say so, and was forestalled.

'If the siq is destroyed,' Hasan said, 'then Rhabat will die, whatever happens to us who are here now; and more than the Sharai need Rhabat.' He glanced at Julianne's father, who nodded his agreement.

'Thank you, Marron, but I think we need other means, if we can find them. My own skills are no longer warlike, but I can make shift when I must; and I have scores to settle with these 'ifrit, for myself and for Redmond. Keep with us, lad, but hold your hand until you have to use it. Pulling down the walls of a house is the last resort of a desperate defence.'

Marron thought that their case was indeed desperate, if they were dependent on an old man who hadn't made war for forty years. Even when that old man was the King's Shadow; they were far outside the King's realm now.

Rudel was there too, though, with a grim cast to his face and any ambiguity set aside. He had his own daughter to protect, and his own close friendship with Redmond to avenge. Marron had seen him fight before, both with a sword and with fire. Swords were no use here, but whether it was craft or magic, that fire might prove a blessing.

It was Rudel and Hasan between them who decided where to make their stand, where the siq ran straight for a short way. Hasan took a spear himself; Rudel stood at his side, his hands already working in his satchel, while the other spearsmen were ranked behind. Jemel argued to take his place among them, but there was no spare weapon; Marron dragged him to the rear, to wait and watch beside Julianne's father.

They didn't have to wait long. As ever, Marron was first to hear what was coming; he warned the others, and saw them ready themselves before the first 'ifrit showed around the corner.

It heaved its rock-heavy bulk towards them, its body flexing as it came, its great mouth agape. Hasan murmured, 'Wait, wait . . . Now!'

Rudel flung a ball of matter that burst into flame as it flew, flaring white against the shadow of the walls. A perfect cast, or else guided by some power the man had to control it: it soared past the open mouth and struck one of the creature's deep-set eyes.

The 'ifrit reared up, hissing, as the fire bit and clung;

Hasan was already sprinting forward, the spear raised high in both hands. Marron heard more than one of the Sharai choke down a cry, and Jemel shifted anxiously, seeing how their precious leader risked himself.

Hasan was only a few paces short of the raging 'ifrit when its head crashed back to earth. He might have thrown the spear then, but did not; for certainty's sake, he plunged on and drove it into the flaming eye-socket with all the strength of his body behind his thrust.

The shaft sank in the length of a man's arm, or further. The 'ifrit shrieked; the beaks of its mouth clashed together as its head tossed blindly. Hasan hung onto the spear, seeking to work it deeper while every man who watched was willing him to jump clear and hurry back.

His feet were lifted clean off the ground as the monster reared again; he was tossed from side to side while the spear-butt bent beneath his weight; he was battered cruelly against the canyon wall, and still he clung on. At last, the 'ifrit slumped to ground again. Hasan braced his feet firmly and leaned all his weight on the spear, forcing it in further yet, until flames leaped back at him and the shaft snapped. Marron saw the red glow die in the creature's other eye. Its mouth-parts moved one final time, biting on emptiness; then its so-solid body dissolved slowly into smoke and dust, and was gone.

Hasan threw aside the charred butt of the spear, cried a challenge to the next 'ifrit that was already visible at the corner, and came running to rejoin Rudel.

'That was foolish,' the older man said quietly.

'It was necessary.'

'Once, perhaps. You have shown them now, that the

thing can be done; remember that your people need you, we all need you if we are to survive this day.'

'Should I stand back and let some other man run the risk in my place?'

'Yes,' Rudel said simply. 'You are the commander; you must learn to command, as well as to lead. Here comes another, but this one is not for you.'

One of the spearsmen strode forward, shouldering Hasan aside. 'You are a great warrior,' he grunted, 'but the Beni Rus may not claim all the glory. I am Shorif of the Saren; wizard, throw your fireball.'

'Very well; though it is not wizardry, and I have only a little left of what is necessary. Hasan, we need another plan. Shorif, be ready, and beware – and do not linger as this madman did, after you have made your thrust. If the creature is wounded only, that may be as well; it might block its broodmates' progress, for a while.'

'A wounded animal is more dangerous,' Shorif said flatly.

'The 'ifrit are not animals, and wounded or whole, they are deadly. Beware!'

'I know him,' Jemel murmured, as Rudel shaped to throw, Shorif to run. 'He will try to kill swifter than Hasan did, for his pride's sake and his tribe.'

And so would you, Marron thought, *though you have no tribe now; and so would any Sharai . . .*

The fireball soared through the air, and struck again beneath the ridge of the eye; Rudel could say what he liked, but there was wizardry for sure in his aim, if not in the ball's constitution. Like Hasan before him, Shorif was on the move almost before the ball had been thrown, and had covered the best part of the distance before it struck. He trailed the spear behind him as he ran, ready to hurl it straight-armed, direct and true. Pride indeed, Marron thought, to come so close and then to trust a cast, to stand unarmed before the creature after . . .

Where the first 'ifrit had raised its body skyward in the pain of burning, though, this one twisted aside to lash its head against the rock wall. The fire blazed on, and it whistled in its agony; but its still-seeing eye fell on Shorif. He cried out despairingly, and hurled the spear towards that eye. And missed his mark, striking only glossy armour as the massive head lunged towards him.

The spear clattered harmlessly away, and was lost; the man stood immobile for a lethal moment, and the 'ifrit's mouth closed around him.

Marron wanted to look away, and could not. He saw Shorif sucked into that appalling gullet, heard his final scream, heard it abruptly cut off as the beaks snapped together.

One more death for him to answer for, one more that he might have prevented. He wanted to push his way through to the front and plead to be allowed to bring the walls down now; he wanted to do it without permission, to save any more deaths. Delay the 'ifrit long enough, and he could save them all or try to, he could take them out of the valley's trap at least . . .

But Rudel had his wounded monster now, that unnatural fire lodged in its eye; and it was doing what he'd predicted, writhing around in its agony and blocking the path as well as any rockfall. There were other 'ifrit crowding behind, but they couldn't pass, and its lashing body prevented their attempts to mount and slide over it.

That might have been the best that the men could hope for, they might have pulled back then to join the tribes in an ordered defence of the siq's narrow mouth. Something caught Marron's attention, though, a sudden noise breaking through his bitter self-accusation. He stared wildly at one near wall and then the other; he yelled, 'Back! Get back!'

The men turned slowly. There was no time to explain, and he was beyond words anyway; Dard in hand, he gestured at the rock where it closed in on both sides of the path, *there* and *there* . . .

As he pointed, so they heard it too, dull ears reacting too late and dull minds lagging even behind that. They had hardly begun to move before the 'ifrit broke through.

Marron seized the man closest to him and wrenched him away, flinging him to safety. A gleaming black beak scythed through the space where he had been and caught another, piercing his ribcage; Marron heard the shocking crunch of bone. There was no other sound; the man died without even the chance to scream his death to the heedless rock that had betrayed him.

The 'ifrit rose up, struck down, and its huge mouth engulfed another man, spear and all. The air was full of screaming now, as this and the other wreaked their terror. By intent or lucky chance, they had divided the party; Hasan and Rudel were trapped, between them and their wounded, burning broodmate.

The path was open, at Marron's back. The man he'd saved had already fled that way; he could follow, if he chose. So could Jemel, and the King's Shadow. He turned, to tell them to run; but at that moment one of the 'ifrit turned also, its head rose like a snake's head poised to strike, and its jaws reached for Jemel.

Who did not run, of course; who stood with scimitar poised, ready to make a vain and useless thrust towards the creature's unreachable eye.

Ahead almost of Marron's thought, Dard had done the work for him. His arm was bleeding, the Daughter filled his sight. He could have hurled it in an instant, straight into the 'ifrit's mouth and down that grinding gullet; it could have torn the thing apart from within.

Could have done, and did not.

Just for an eyeblink he hesitated, a battleground of oath and instinct, of yearning and fury and self-disgust; and in that moment, the chance was lost.

Slowly, he drew the Daughter back. It was unnecessary now.

Something else had intervened, where he could not. The 'ifrit's terrible head swung from side to side, as if blindly seeking what it could not see; when it struck rock its jaws opened and began to close, and Marron could see how those three beaks carved through the stone like knives through cheese, how swiftly the creature chewed its way into the wall.

Briefly, that was all that he could look at. Then he turned his head, and saw Jemel still rooted where he was, where he had been; and found Julianne's father standing just behind him, smiling faintly.

'Thank you . . .' he whispered.

The King's Shadow shook his head a little. 'A young man shouldn't get into the habit of breaking vows,' he said. 'You have too much to deal with already. If you kill again, you'll loathe yourself for it; but you'll also lose your fear of killing. If once, why not a dozen times more, a hundred? I would hate to see that, for the world's sake. Your friend needs your company, I think. Be swift.'

Marron was swift to reach Jemel, slow to find words: 'Jemel, I'm sorry . . .' *Sorry I didn't want to kill for you, even for you; I would have done, but the Shadow beat me to it, and I'm sorry for that too, that you needed anyone else to rescue you when I was there . . .*

Jemel shook his head. 'An oath is an oath,' he said softly. 'It would be more dishonourable to break it for me than for others, now. What did he do?'

'I'm not sure. Confused the creature's mind, hid you from its senses, sent it away. The Surayonnaise can cloud a man's sight; I didn't know what the King's Shadow could do, but . . .'

'No one knows what the King's Shadow can do. Look now, see what Hasan can do . . .'

There was, of course, another 'ifrit. Marron had all but forgotten; Jemel had not. Hasan was the other side of it, unreachable.

Marron thought again of sending an 'ifrit to the other world uninvited, or of dropping a doorway beyond it, to offer the trapped men an escape; but neither was needed. For once Jemel had been swifter, to see what was happening.

Hasan had shepherded Rudel behind him, and was using his scimitar like a butcher, hacking at the 'ifrit. Beak or armour, it made no difference: where that blade touched, it cut through. Pieces of the creature fell away, to fray to nothing like smoke in a breeze.

'His sword was blessed long ago, I think,' Jemel said,

standing relaxed and easy, utterly untroubled now. 'He is a man who plans, who thinks ahead.'

That was rare among the Sharai, a part of what made Hasan the man he was, with the power that he had. Behind Rudel, the wounded 'ifrit was dying now, as that mystical fire burned ever deeper into its body. Hasan hewed, chopped, finally thrust deep; his victim thrashed and died and was gone, and the men hurried through where it had been.

'Enough,' Hasan said, breathing heavily. 'Well done, all. Back now, back to join our people; we can do no more here.'

They had done no more than survive, Marron thought, and delay the 'ifrit a little; what more could they do in the open, where many of the creatures could come at them at once, where they were more but useful weapons were so few . . .?

Where the siq debouched into the valley proper, they found all the forces of Rhabat drawn up in battle array, each tribe beneath its separate banner and behind its own sheikh. That surely wouldn't have been Hasan's choice, but he had come too late. When the time came, Marron thought, the tribes would fight independently and flee independently, as they always had. His own people would never have won Outremer without that weakness in their enemy; the 'ifrit he thought would have won Rhabat regardless, but it would come easier to them now than it might have done.

Hasan was already running from sheikh to sheikh, trying and failing to persuade them to draw their men together.

Rudel stood watching; sensing Marron's eye on him, he turned to say, 'Their pride is their strength, and their great failure; but I think it will make no difference today. This is a battle lost before it is fought. Marron, it is stupid to blame yourself for not doing what you cannot do; but if you do no more, will you at least save Julianne, and my daughter? The King's Shadow can save himself . . .'

'I will save whoever I can,' he said in reply. 'You, too . . .'

'No. It is hopeless, but I think I have to stay. I have some power yet, that I can use. So too does Coren, but he is wise enough to leave at the last, I think, where I am not.'

Marron could think of nothing to say; he nodded a reluctant agreement and turned to Jemel, who said, 'These are my people. I want to stay, to fight . . .'

'With what? And with whom, where will you stand to die? The Saren will not have you.'

'With Hasan.'

'Hasan will stand with his tribe, I think, the sheikhs have denied him any other choice. The Beni Rus will not have you either, or not willingly. Jemel, if nothing else,' and this was cruel to both of them, but it had to be said, 'remember your oath. Your two oaths – to serve me, and to face Sieur Anton. Die here, and you fail both.'

Jemel just looked at him, agonised; it was Julianne's father who saved the moment, saying, 'Come with me, both of you. You too, Rudel. The Kauram and the Ib' Dharan have left such a space between them, there is plenty of room for us.'

So they stood alone in the line, four men who had no other place and perhaps no place at all in the battle to come, except that they had chosen to stand among sworn enemies against a greater evil. On every side Marron could hear the murmurs of the tribes, men bidding good luck and farewell to their brothers in arms, courage and fatalism mixed. None that he heard expected to live, they wanted only to die with honour and to have that death reported, to have someone else survive to say the *khalat* for their souls. Marron thought that might be him – but only if he could say it with his friends. If he couldn't save the girls, if he couldn't save Jemel he thought he might stay himself, and die with them. If the Daughter would let him die; he wasn't at all sure about that . . .

Like every man there they stood and waited, gazing across fifty paces of open, rocky ground to the rough cliff where the siq began. They waited longer than Marron had expected; Hasan might have had time to arrange the tribes to his own design, if the sheikhs hadn't set their men so hurriedly.

At last, though, a shadow moved through the shadows of the siq, and came out into sunlight. Many of the men were having their first sight of an 'ifrit, in any form; a hissing whisper coursed down the line.

All along the cliff-face, wiry shrubs started to shake, loose rocks fell in a hail of dust and pebbles; 'ifrit came issuing monstrously from new-made tunnels, a dozen, a score of them rippling out at once, while more came from the siq. A single voice shrieked at the sight; no one laughed.

A few desultory arrows flew; those that hit their marks bounced off. There was still Rudel's fire, but he had little left, he'd said; there was Hasan's sword, perhaps some few other blades that had been blessed. How many 'ifrit could one man kill? Or a dozen men, if there were so many? Not enough, for sure.

Someone ran forward with a spear, stabbing up towards a glowing eye; the 'ifrit swung its head almost contemptuously, broke the spear and broke the man too, Marron thought, sending him sprawling into the path of another monster. That one didn't even bother to bite; it simply rolled over the man, crushing him utterly beneath its massive weight.

The tribes were shifting in their places, muttering hoarsely and casting wild glances around. Marron wondered how long it would be now before the first spirit broke, before these bravest of men began to run.

16

After the Flood

Just as it was impossible – for Julianne, at least – to look at Marron without seeing the Daughter in his blood, even when his back was turned or his eyes were closed to hide that demonic crimson cast, so she was finding it increasingly hard to look at Elisande without seeing the djinni.

It wasn't always there, at least physically, in so far as a little twist of light and dust could ever be called physical. Even in its absence, though, it seemed to lurk around her friend: a glint in Elisande's eye, an abstraction in her voice. Certainly it was never further than a spoken word away; she had only to say its name and there it was, hovering to do her bidding, the perfect servant. *Esren* she called it, though it was Djinni Tachur to Julianne and every person else.

Like an old servant it assumed privileges, though its service was less than a full day old; Julianne had already found cause to resent its elliptical rudeness. She wondered if she were perhaps becoming jealous. But no, that was absurd. Elisande had been hopelessly preoccupied with

Marron for weeks, and she'd never minded that. She should be glad, if anything, that Elisande had a distraction suddenly, another focus for her thoughts now that Marron was so evidently lost to her. And such a distraction, such a servant, a guarantee of strength and security for life: she should be deeply glad of that.

And yet she was resentful, and her native honesty forced her to admit that it was more than the djinni's manner that upset her, and more too than Elisande's interest in her new companion. That was natural, inevitable, and no genuine threat. She thought that the truth lay deeper, that companionship was the key. The Daughter was no kind of comfortable companion, but Marron had Jemel now to content him, if that boy could ever be content. Elisande had lost him or given him up, but she had the djinni to occupy her in his stead, not a substitute perhaps but a clear fascination. And what did Julianne have for herself, what had she gained in this short summer? A husband forced on her, whom she had loved and lost too quickly, almost in a single day; and with the hurt of that still fresh she had found another man whom she could love, she thought. Not instead of Imber, never that, but in addition – and what an addition! Imber or Hasan, either one would make a companion to give value to a girl's life, worth a lifetime's delighted study; and the one she had taken possession of and then fled from between a night and a morning, while the other she could not have at all. Hasan's being married already, to Sherett and others too, that was apparently no obstacle; but her being married – albeit in name only, and in reality for just that one desolate, abandoned night – was a fact inescapable and insurmountable. Raised in a distant country among people other than her own, with her mother dead and her father constantly away, she thought that all her life had been a search for companionship; and now she saw her friends achieving what she so deeply yearned for, and the taste of that was bitter to her. That she understood herself so well, that she resented her own ungenerous resentment, only added to her gall.

Having to be grateful to the djinni made it worse yet. The creature's ability to transfer Elisande between the worlds had helped to save Jemel's life, and she was of course grateful for that; it had done both girls more immediate service, though, and she was savagely grateful for this too.

Elisande had been deeply asleep when word came through Sherett of the 'ifrits' attacking in the siq. Julianne had woken her straight away with the news, and the first thing her friend had done had been to summon the djinni and disappear, having it convey her all around the valley while Julianne could do nothing but stay in the confines of the women's quarters, helping Sherett to organise salves and bandages against a hoped-for need.

Elisande had returned to report, accurate knowledge to offset rumour and imagination, which was gift enough. Then the two girls had come back up to their chamber, in hopes of watching together the progress of the battle. Their window was firmly screened, though, as every window was, and they hadn't been able to shift the heavy shutter. Its ornate piercings gave them glimpses of the valley, but no view. After a minute's struggle Elisande had pulled her away and spoken to the djinni, 'Esren, if you please . . .'

One brief touch of the little wisp that was the djinni's visible body, and the wood had splintered, the entire screen had fallen out.

And now they sat tightly together in the embrasure, seeing clearly; and even in her overriding anxiety Julianne found a corner of her mind that was grateful for the chance, and another corner that resented the source of its supply. The djinni floated outside the room, on a level with the window and very much in eyeshot, calmly fifty feet above the ground. She thought it was goading her deliberately and disdained to look directly at it, let alone to look directly down.

Besides, Hasan was out there. From up here, they could see all the way to the mouth of the siq if they leaned perilously out of the window, as they did. She could see how the tribes were mustered, a small army but numbers were unimportant, ten times as many men would make no difference if the 'ifrit didn't suffer when they were struck; she couldn't see Hasan until the last few figures came running out of the siq. There he was, of course, the last to leave, where else? And with him Marron and Jemel, Rudel, her father – all of them down there and she'd forgotten that they would be, she hadn't thought to ask Sherett; only about Hasan, and no wonder the woman had given her another of those looks before she answered.

There they all were, though; and all safe, at least for the moment. Saved to die under her eye, she thought grimly, seeing how they joined the ranks of warriors, even her father who hadn't been a warrior since before she was born, and long before.

He was a powerful man, though, he could work miracles at will; and Rudel too, and Marron. Between them, surely, there was something they could do . . .?

*

She watched almost in hope as the first 'ifrit appeared, thinking there would be gouts of flame, perhaps, and monsters dying. There were men who died, she saw that, a few; and one little flare of fire from Rudel, that seemed to madden one of the 'ifrit but not to kill. It plunged into a block of men, threshing and roaring; its cries were thinned by distance but Julianne could hear them even so, as she heard the screaming of the men it caught or rolled upon. Some fled in terror, some assailed its flanks with scimitars that might as well have been dull boughs of wood, for all the damage they could do. She wondered if it were better to be craven or stupidly bold, to live with crippling shame or die with useless honour; she knew what Hasan's answer would be, and dreaded to see it come.

After that, after she'd seen the banners fall and the bodies lie broken, after she'd seen how the running men infected others from other tribes, how fragile their pride and courage were – after that, she no longer hoped for magic. She saw those ponderous and lethal creatures, how many there were and how immune to human weapons' scratchings, and she didn't blame the men at all for running. But where could they run to? She saw how many of the monsters came bursting out of the cliff-face; if they could chew a path through rock, there would be no shelter for anyone anywhere in Rhabat.

'Cowards,' Elisande muttered, dashing furious tears from her eyes. 'All my life they've told me how brave they were, these damn Sharai, how they love to die in battle; and look at them . . .'

'Don't be hard, love,' *though that's my Hasan they're*

abandoning there, as well as your Marron. 'As well try to stand against a rockfall, or a flood . . .'

Elisande stiffened abruptly, and her eyes went to the djinni. 'I think the 'ifrit meant to use Esren to flood the valley, to kill us all that way, did I say?'

'No, but . . .' But she hadn't thought about the djinni; how slow could she be? She held her breath, tried not to hope, couldn't help it as Elisande spoke cautiously.

'Esren, tell me what would happen if you tried to destroy the 'ifrit, as you are.'

'I would destroy myself. They have made themselves earthbound bodies, but they are still spirit within. Spirit cannot touch spirit, without a cloak for shield.'

It was more than disappointment to Julianne, it was defeat, utter desolation; but not it seemed to Elisande. She said, 'Take me,' and squirmed to her feet in the embrasure, and stepped out into the air.

Julianne screamed and made a snatch at her, but couldn't reach. Elisande was standing on the wind beside the djinni, wind made visible, streaks of pattern and strange colour swirling around her feet.

'Julianne,' frowning, absorbed, 'are you *coming*? Hurry!'

'What? No, you're insane, I can't . . .'

'Oh, come on, sweet,' and she held a hand out towards the window, towards a frantic, clinging Julianne. 'Esren won't let you fall. Tell her, Esren . . .'

'Daughter of the King's Shadow, I will not let you fall.'

And they did not lie, and so she could believe it; and it was better protection than the other djinni had offered her, when it had made her climb so much higher than this. And Hasan, her father, people she loved were down below, in deadly danger, and still she couldn't move. Not till Elisande reached in and gripped her under the armpits, and tugged hard.

'I was scared at first,' she said, hauling bodily, 'but this is solid ground, or feels it. And we haven't got *time*, Julianne, people are *dying* down there . . .'

And they were, more now, too many; and somehow Julianne managed not to fight her friend, not to flail and kick. And so found herself standing on solid air; and no, it did not feel like solid ground, it had more give in it than that. It was like that floor they'd stood on or that bridge they'd climbed inside the Tower of the King's Daughter, firm underfoot but somehow yielding also. As in that place, there were colours in it that she couldn't name. She yearned for the mist that had wreathed them then, to hide her from where she stood above the world; lacking that, she screwed her eyes tight shut, and clung to Elisande.

'Elisande, what are we *doing*?'

'Going down.'

'We could have used the stairs . . .'

'No time. Esren, take us to the battlefield, please. Julianne, listen. We're riding a djinni, near enough, that should attract attention; but we're only a pair of girls, we're going to have to yell at them.'

'Yell what?'

'Tell them to run,' Elisande said bluntly, 'those that aren't already. Tell them to get up high, tell them to climb. Stairs or rocks, doesn't matter, just so long as they're out of reach . . .'

Even if the men would listen, Julianne thought, it would

make no difference. Those 'ifrit ate rock; any stair too narrow for their bulk, they could chew the walls wider. Any pinnacle too steep, they could chew the base away until it fell.

Elisande was determined, though. At a word from her, the djinni took them swooping down towards the battle; wind whipped at Julianne's face. She squeaked, and tightened her grip on her friend.

'Julianne, I can't breathe . . .'

'Neither can I.'

She did slacken her hold, though, just a little. As the noise of the wind died in her ears, she heard instead the sounds of fighting – or the sounds of failure, rather, the sounds of defeat and death. She cracked her eyes open and saw the gleaming body of an 'ifrit heaving itself along directly below; it held one man skewered in its jaws, while others fled before it.

Something like silence fell among the tribes, as they saw two women floating on a cloud of colour, it must seem to them, with a djinni spinning alongside.

Hasan's voice cried loud, against that hush: 'Back, all! Back to the houses, and we will try to defend the doors! We can do no good here . . .'

Him they would listen to. Elisande added her own voice, even as men began to turn and run. 'Not the doors – climb higher, as high as you can! Climb high, and trust . . .'

Julianne didn't need to say a word; nor did she have time, as Elisande ordered, 'To the Dead Waters now, Esren.'

They flew away, skimming above the heads of the fleeing men; Julianne wanted to close her eyes again, against that dizzying landscape. She loved speed, but not like this, with nothing beneath her and nothing to hold to except her tense, excited friend. People were not made to go so fast, she thought, with so little support.

Elisande was screwing her head around, trying to make out what was happening behind them even as the scene dwindled. 'Will they listen, will they do as I said?'

'I don't know. You gave them no reason . . .'

'The 'ifrit would have heard too. I'd trust Hasan, but I don't know if he'll trust me . . .'

Julianne couldn't answer that; she knew her man too little, less well perhaps than Elisande, who at least understood the Sharai.

The djinni soared above the narrow gully, giving them a view of the bare, sere heights which Julianne quickly turned her face away from. Elisande was gazing forward, her eyes fixed on the Waters.

'Well, they must trust and so must we,' she said, 'we dare not linger. Esren, set us down here.'

Here was the cliff-edge, high above the storage-caverns and the waterfront, with no way down. Julianne didn't protest, she was only too glad to have good rock beneath her feet again; she slumped rather than sat, hugging her knees to save herself from hugging the ground. Every muscle in her body was shaking; it was an effort even to lift her head, to watch her friend. She didn't understand at all what Elisande meant to do, or why she had had them brought to this place. They were safe from the 'ifrit, true, unless there were any left a-wing, which there didn't seem to be; the sky was clear from one horizon to the other. But she couldn't have meant only to see them safe, she wouldn't have abandoned everyone else . . .

'Esren, do what the 'ifrit would have had you do. Draw up the Dead Waters, as much as you can take, and make a flood to wash the valley clean.'

'Lisan, I could take it all.'

Amazingly, she laughed. 'Well, not that much, perhaps; I don't want to drown my friends. Take enough, though. Make a waterspout, make a storm. And tell me you can kill the 'ifrit that way . . .'

'I can kill the 'ifrit that way,' it said, echoing the rhythms of her own voice mockingly.

'Good. Then go and do it.'

The djinni dropped from Julianne's sight, down below the edge of the cliff. Elisande beckoned, 'Come and see. It's all right, I won't let you fall.'

'Elisande, I *climbed* a cliff, remember? Higher than this, it was . . .'

And it hadn't cured her fear, whatever she might pretend, only taught her that fear could be overcome under a pressing need, that her will could be stronger than her terror. And so it was now, under no stronger need than her friend's urging and her own curiosity; she came slowly to her feet and stood beside Elisande, gripping her hand tightly as she looked down.

She was only just in time to find the djinni, a distant glint of light that she lost quickly among the glints of sunlight on water. There was a momentary eddy, where it must have insinuated itself beneath the surface; then there was nothing but the vast sea. She wondered briefly how it must be feeling, returning to its age-old prison; but she didn't know if the djinn did feel things that way, and she had more urgent questions anyway.

'Elisande, I don't understand. The 'ifrit can grow wings, and fly . . .'

'Not now. At least, I don't think so. You saw them; they've changed, become huge, and they've been eating rock. That ought to weigh them down. What kind of wingspan would they need, to lift those bodies? I'm sure they can't do it in time . . .'

She didn't sound sure at all, but the djinni had. It still didn't make sense to Julianne.

'Well, perhaps not – but they can live in water, we know that too.'

'Yes – but again, they'd need to change from what they are. I don't think they'll have time. And if I'm right, they won't drown anyway. They'll be crushed. Remember what Esren said, spirit can't touch spirit – but they've made themselves those bodies, and it can do the same, it can make itself a body from the water. When they meet – well, I wouldn't like to be an 'ifrit. That djinni hates them, Julianne. Watch, and trust . . .'

She found it hard, but there was nothing more that she could do. She thrust her doubts aside, and did watch; and saw something greater than an eddy build within the water, saw the surface sucked down into a giant whirlpool. Out of its centre a pillar rose, a massive spinning cone, balanced on its point. It grew broader and higher, sucking up the dark water until the bay below was quite dry, its murky floor exposed; then it moved. It went smashing into the wharf, shattering stone. Julianne didn't see it disappear into the gully, even with her new-found courage she wouldn't lean over as far as Elisande was leaning; but she did see how it pulled more water in its train in a great surge, a wave that battered at the cliff so hard that she swore she could feel it shake the rock she stood on.

A moment later the sound of that meeting rolled up and rolled over her, carried her physically back from the edge and sat her down, hard. That was how it felt, at least: a sound more solid than anything she'd encountered in her life, a sound like a wave itself, felt rather than heard, thudding deep into her bones; the impact of it was impossible to withstand. It passed on, and left utter silence behind it, as though it had stolen all the sound there was. She blinked around, and was meanly glad to see Elisande sprawled in the dust at her side.

Elisande was gaping like a stranded fish, her mouth opening and closing, saying nothing. It took a moment for Julianne to recognise shapes on her friend's lips, to realise she was trying to speak. She laughed – and couldn't hear herself laughing, could only feel it in her throat. Slowly, it dawned on her that she was deaf.

Elisande had made the same discovery, by the way she was poking fingers into her ears and waggling them about. She looked absurd, but Julianne was far from laughing now. She pressed her hands against her own ears, and found that they hurt. Elisande was looking at her fingertips; she raised them to show Julianne the wet red stains of blood.

Julianne pushed herself to her feet and staggered unexpectedly, couldn't catch her balance, had to sit down again in a hurry. She stared wildly at Elisande, and mouthed, *what's happened to us?*

Elisande shrugged, and got cautiously to her knees. She reached across to take Julianne's hands, gripping tightly. They stood up together, supporting each other when they wobbled; it felt like a victory simply to be upright in a strangely dizzying world.

Walking was harder, but they managed it in a slow and unsteady fashion, arms linked like two drunkards, each a prop to the other. At Elisande's tugging insistence, they headed towards the gully.

Julianne wouldn't go close to the edge, she felt too unsafe; even from a little distance, though, they could see dark and turbulent water frothing white as it raced through the narrow canyon. It must have been reaching halfway up those high walls, perhaps more.

Staring down into that hectic moil, she felt as giddy as she had before, when it had been she who was rushing in the djinni's immaterial grasp. She needed to close her eyes again; better yet, she needed to sit down again, and did.

And lay back on good firm rock, and kept her eyes closed against the sun, and felt entirely alone, cut off; and thought it was not so bad, she could live like this. For a short time, for an hour, say. A lifetime might be harder. But her life would be grim in any case, and at least she'd be spared recriminations. She thought Imber would keep her out of kindness now, so she would at least have him to look at. And no need to make dreary, meaningless conversation with other women to pass their time or hers, no need to twist and spy for her father's manipulative schemes . . .

She lay and baked in her isolation, even Elisande left her alone, and she was almost content. Picturing a future in Elessi — *the poor deaf baroness, struck down in the midst of her own folly, such a goodness of the baron to take her back* — she managed almost not to think about Hasan, almost not to wonder what had happened in the valley: whether the men had reached safety in time, because for sure there had not been much time given them; whether they would have climbed high enough, because they'd had no real warning and that water was monstrously deep; whether Hasan had taken the time or trouble to save himself, because he would certainly have been last to leave the field to the 'ifrit and last to set his foot on a flight of steps, herding all his men before him.

Well, it didn't matter. Living or dead, she had to give him up. Perhaps she should be practising now to be a good Elessan hereafter: perhaps she should be hoping that the gathered Sharai were all drowned, and Hasan most particularly so, as he was the only man who could make an army of them. Perhaps – but she was suddenly tired of it all, and too drained to try. She lay and baked, and managed almost not to think at all.

Slowly, slowly the world came back to find her.

It came first as a white hissing, that she took a little time to notice and a little longer to identify as sound. It seemed to be entirely inside her head, and she wondered if this were common among the deaf, that they should hear noises of their own to compensate for losing any other.

It grew louder, though, too loud to live with, surely; perhaps this was what happened to mad people, she thought, that their heads filled with sounds that they could not abide. This was a rushing, thundering noise, that she thought would lift and float her and carry her off, it was so deep and so intense; and even then, it took her a foolishly long time to understand. Memory did it for her in the end, a triggered snatch of a similar roaring and a picture with it:

of course, the great falls in the river at Marasson. Water in a dreadful hurry, pounding at rock in its haste. What she was hearing was the sea still gushing through the gorge as the djinni pulled it, still flooding into Rhabat and *oh, let Hasan have climbed high, high . . .*

There was something else she could hear, apart from water. She could hear voices, though she couldn't make out their words.

She opened her eyes, squinted into the light, saw Elisande sitting cross-legged and talking: talking as much with her hands as with her voice, admittedly, but she was at least talking.

The man she was talking to was Julianne's father. She could only see his back and the shadow it cast, but that was plenty. The King's Shadow they called him, but the one he carried was his alone.

She sat up cautiously, finding the world steadier than it had been, or else herself steadier within it. If Elisande said anything about her, she didn't hear it; if one of those expansive hands paused to make a smaller gesture, *your daughter's awake*, she didn't see it. Perhaps he simply knew. At any rate he turned, he smiled and beckoned, and she crawled uncertainly to his side as she had not since she was a child, and a small child at that.

He put a hand out and stroked her hair, tangling his fingers in it, as he had not since she was a child. 'Can you hear me, little one?'

She could, though he sounded not quiet but strangely distant yet, and muffled by the constant roar of water; she was glad to be watching his face, to read what his lips said while she listened.

She nodded, and tried a word in answer; but her first 'yes' seemed to come out silent, and her second was a bellow that made him flinch, that rang unpleasantly inside her own head.

Elisande laughed, came to her side and cupped her hands over Julianne's ears for a moment.

She felt warmth, an intimate touch that spread all through her, mind and body; and when Elisande took her hands away, the world seemed back in balance. The only trouble that she had in hearing was the way the water's surge overrode all noises else, drowning normal voices . . .

She didn't want to think about drowning. But the question was so very much there in her head, she had to ask it.

'How was it in the valley when the waters came, father? Did you have time to see everyone safe?'

He smiled wryly. 'I think the waters came as a relief after the djinni, Julianne – at least to the 'ifrit. But no, we couldn't get everyone to safety. I had half an idea what Elisande meant to do, and Hasan took his cue from me; even so, though, there were too many sheikhs with their own ideas, and too much confusion. There were still men milling about on the valley floor; the djinni avoided them, but the water did not. I saw some men go under. I had to, ah, walk to safety myself, in the end; my boots are wet.'

She understood him perfectly. He meant that he had stayed to usher or command as many men as possible out of the water's reach, he had lingered too long too far from safety, he had been forced to use his magic to convey himself out of danger as the flood lapped at his heels.

'What of the others?' she asked. 'Rudel, Marron? Jemel?'

He smiled; she thought perhaps he understood her just

as perfectly. 'Rudel I last saw bullying a number of the sheikhs up onto a ledge above the water's rise; I think they will be marooned there for some time, and I think he will not stop talking until the flood recedes. It is probably a waste of breath, but breath is cheap and I can't think of a finer way to waste it. Marron had his arm cut even before the water came; he had the Daughter dancing attendance on him, while he waited for Jemel to be ready to be rescued. I think you need not be concerned about those two.'

'And Hasan?'

'Ah, now Hasan was more stubborn, he didn't want to move till all his men were safe, which they never would have been. In the end I had to drag him along with me. He's standing behind you, girl.'

She gaped; Elisande giggled, and let her gaze flick past Julianne's shoulder. Something in her face suggested she'd been fighting the desire for a while now.

Julianne wished she could have turned round like a lady and stood up like the baroness she was, with dignity and poise; she feared that she had turned like a child demanding gratification, and then scrambled to her feet like a hoyden. A whip of wind brought her hair wildly across her face, the only veil she could pretend to.

It didn't matter. He was there, standing in profile to her as he gazed towards the valley, a commander snatched away from his war; but he turned to face her as she rose, and was just a man whom she couldn't believe that she wanted, nor that he wanted her. They were two utterly different disbeliefs, utterly opposed to each other; and the one burned shame into her cheeks, while the other was simply refuted by the avid look in his eyes.

She yearned to respond to that, to hurtle into his arms. But now when she wanted it least, all her father's training came back to her under his eyes; she sank into a ridiculous curtsey, and said, 'I am glad to see you safe, my lord. I had been afraid for your welfare.'

'And I for yours,' he returned. 'Lady.'

Oh, every inch the lady now, when she ached to be otherwise; she thought he was teasing her, though, as well as speaking true. She managed to find a little acid under her tongue to answer him with, as she whispered, 'Prince . . .'

He smiled, and held his hands out to her. Nothing could have held her back then: not her father's disapproving eye, not her friend's fascination, not the brutal, lashing memory of Imber's face, the echo of his voice, the shadow of his fingers' touch on hers.

Still, she thought she would only grip Hasan's hands and exchange barbed courtesies, no more. What more could they do? This was no time for dalliance, it would be absurd . . .

Neither did he dally. He seized her wrists, so that she could feel her own pulse against his fingers' pressure; she could have counted its racing beat, but that she seemed to have forgotten how to count. In his closeness he absorbed her, he made her stupid, senseless, a thing of body and desire and nothing else: no thought at all, no history.

This was his strength, to steal heart and mind together; and other men's wives too, seemingly, where he chose. She had no choice in this, or else she had made it already, and days ago. He drew her close and she did hurtle that last little distance between them, a very long way.

His arms received her and claimed her, while his mouth possessed her. For the first time in her life she tasted passion, and returned it. If a quiet voice somewhere in her head whispered Imber's name again, it was soon lost in the tumult of her body's hunger, and his response.

When at last her arms recalled their duty, uncoiled themselves from his neck and pushed him back – and they had to work to achieve that, against his obstinacy – it was bizarrely not her husband whom she offered as excuse.

'If,' she gasped, 'if Sherett were to see us, or hear about this—'

'—She would be shocked by your shamelessness, but not surprised at either one of us. Be easy, little one, Julianne,' and there was something in the mere way he named her that made her shudder, unless it was his hands' grip around her waist, 'lady. The first time I saw you I said that I would marry you, remember? Sherett knows. She will welcome you to my household.'

'You did say that, prince. And I said that I was married already . . .'

'You lied. You are no more married than your friend there, Lisan. She told me how it was. They forced you to it, in the absence of your father; they said their words over you, but your man refused you on your wedding night, and you have not been with him since. By our laws, that is no marriage.'

When had that happened, when had Elisande betrayed her? She'd find out; but in the meantime, she was bereft of words. He was right, of course. Even by the laws of her own people, a marriage unconsummated could be annulled without stigma, and both parties would be free to marry again. She hated the thought of her Imber – *hers!* – being wed to any woman else; and yet, and yet . . . She had fled him, and now she loved another. Loved them both, she thought, husband and new man too; but could not have them both, and Imber might renounce her in any case, might have done so already, word of it might be chasing her across the desert. Better surely to have one than neither . . .

She temporised; said, 'You must speak to my father, prince . . .'

'Lady, I have done so already. He has no quarrel with me over this.'

What, had all her world conspired behind her back? She could have been angry, if she hadn't so wanted to weep over her lost boy, *oh, Imber, I'm sorry* . . .

'Then you must allow me to speak to him,' she said stiffly, hoping that he would think her angry, would not see how she was fighting tears.

'Lady, I would allow you the world if it were mine to give. Go, speak with him, he is there . . .'

She hadn't meant right this minute; she needed time, and he wasn't allowing her any. She said, 'Prince, you were in the midst of a battle, before my father plucked you out. Should you not be concerned with that, rather than with adding another woman to your harem?'

He didn't so much as wince, though she had meant that to bite deep. He said, 'Lady, I should be, and I will be. But I saw the djinni come, which you did not. I saw how it assailed the 'ifrit, ahead of the flood; I do not believe that it left one living. You are right, I should go and see, to be sure; but I will not move one step from this place, until I have my answer. Julianne, enough delay. Will you wed me, or no?'

Again, her name in his voice melted her entirely. She pined for Imber, but still said, 'Hasan, if my father permit it, I will.'

He smiled, and kissed her again: lightly this time, a fleeting warmth that still whispered of the fires that had scorched her before. Then he released her and turned away, as if knowing that she could not move before he did.

Ignoring Elisande's wide grin, she walked back to where her father stood watching and said, 'What do you mean to do now, old man – reclaim me from Elessi, in favour of a better offer elsewhere?'

The bitterness in her voice was deliberate, because he would have done exactly that against her own wishes, if he had seen advantage in it; or else he would have forbidden it despite patent desire in her, if it ran contrary to the best interests of his scheming. She was all too conscious of being trade goods in a marketplace. She had been raised to understand that, and had long since schooled herself to acceptance. Even so, she didn't feel inclined to make it too easy for her father. At least no easier than she had already, unwittingly, under the web of that dark, hypnotic spider who had snared her. Having shown how deep she was entangled, she had small chance of persuading him that a protest was anything more than token. She felt like a woman offered diamonds, protesting at the mine; it could hardly carry conviction. But oh, she did wish sometimes to find some poniard sharp enough to pierce all his layers of disguise and dig its way through to the small twisted leathery heart of him, just to test whether it truly had any feeling at all . . .

He looked at her in that neutral manner that had always greeted her temper, that used when she was a child to make her angrier than she had been before; it spoiled all the fun of a tantrum, to see its monumental lack of effect. This time, though, it wasn't his own detachment he offered her; he was only quoting.

'Go where you are sent, Julianne, and marry where you must.'

That robbed her of any intent of her own, as so often he had before; this time she was robbed almost of breath, for a moment. 'Do you think, do you think that's what the djinni meant . . .?'

'Child, who can know what a djinni means? If Elisande spends too much time with her Djinni Tachur, she may learn something of what drives it, or what it seeks to achieve; if she does, though, it will have been too much time, and she will be the lesser for the expense of it.'

'Your prophecies are more oblique than the djinni's,' she grumbled.

'But more accurate. It sees clearly what might happen; I see only vaguely, but what I see is certain. Shall we make your djinni happy, Julianne, shall we say that you must marry again, marry here, marry Hasan?'

'You're not seriously offering me the choice?'

'I am hoping that you would choose what I can offer. I think the evidence supports my hope. Child, do you want that man or not?'

'Yes,' she said, on a sigh. 'May the God forgive me,' *and Imber, somehow, sometime,* 'but I do. Even a part-share, I'll share him with Sherett.' *He'll be sharing me, after all, some part of me will always yearn elsewhere.* 'Can I truly have him?'

'Your marriage to the heir of Elessi would have brought you major influence, perhaps in twenty years, if that young baron doesn't get himself killed meanwhile; it was a prize worth the play. Your marriage to Hasan of the Beni Rus may bring peace between our peoples. Not immediately – I'm afraid that Hasan must have his war, there is nothing we can do now to prevent it – but sooner than it would otherwise have come. You may prevent his razing Outremer. Julianne, you can have him, yes. I think that you must.'

Which was what she had known all along. She nodded, a compact concluded. So small a gesture, and yet it meant so much: a rift irreparable torn between herself and her own country – how would this be seen, back in Elessi? That she fled her new-made husband and ran to the arms of a Sharai; and she could dispute nothing in that hard summary – and herself a sacrifice again, for that country's good. A willing sacrifice, to be sure, but she must go under the knife none the less. For once she appreciated her father's foresight in raising her in a far-off land, although it wasn't this that he'd foreseen. She was at least accustomed to living among strangers, and she wouldn't lose friendships by that cutting-off; she had none in Outremer.

Except Elisande, of course. That one she would not lose, come what might. Though she still might scarify her for sharing with Hasan what should have been kept private, the secrets of a desolate wedding-night . . .

Julianne turned to find her, perhaps to confront her; and found herself forestalled by the simplest of tactics, a kiss on the cheek and an anxious, 'Will you be happy, Julianne? I think you could be . . .'

'So do I,' she said on a sigh. If anyone could ever be happy, with a constant blade in their heart. Perhaps that was only the adult condition, though: they were all acquiring them, Elisande and Marron, Jemel, herself . . . 'You shouldn't have told him, though, Elisande.'

'Should I not? He only asked me for confirmation; he'd guessed already, from something that you said before. And if my betraying a confidence is the price of your happiness, sweet, it's worth the paying.'

I could have been as happy otherwise, I could have been happy with Imber too . . . But Elisande might never have guessed at that. She'd known all Julianne's doubts before they'd met the baron, she'd helped her try to evade that meeting and try to escape afterwards, try again and succeed at last. The verity of Imber, the way he'd snared Julianne's soul at her first sight of him – that had never been confessed, and Elisande might simply not have seen it. Hasan had done the same, but publicly, for all to see.

Julianne wondered if she would always be a wanton, desiring one new man after another. She couldn't quite believe it of herself; but perhaps every girl expected to be chaste, before discovering the reality of men. Well, however wayward her character should prove, she thought she could depend on Hasan and Sherett between them to keep her modest in body, if not in mind . . .

'One thing,' Elisande murmured, slipping an arm around her waist. 'I think you can be sure with that man, that he won't be leaving you to sleep with me tonight . . .'

'Elisande!' Her heart seemed to skitter frenziedly at the words, the image, the anticipation – and better Hasan than Imber, perhaps, better a man than an inexperienced boy? – so that it took her mind a little while to catch up with the full import of what her friend had said. 'Tonight? What do you mean, tonight?'

'Oh, I think you're in for another hasty marriage, sweet. Don't you? Look at them.'

To be sure, Hasan and her father had their heads locked together in talk; but, 'They might as easily be making plans for next month, or next year . . .'

Elisande shook her head. 'These things happen quickly; the Sharai do not linger. Life is too uncertain to delay. And they're nomads, remember. Who knows when two wandering families might meet again? Besides, your father's as unpredictable as Hasan. He has to be there, as head of your family; that's more than custom, it's the law. Him or his representative, male and blood,' which meant it had to be him, she had none other. 'Will he still be here tomorrow, even, can you swear to that? Can he?'

No, of course he couldn't, and neither could she. If the King summoned him again, he would go on the instant and without a word.

He glanced round then, sensing their eyes on him, perhaps; he said, 'Elisande, can you tell your djinni that it has done enough, and that we would be grateful if it would put the sea to bed again?'

Elisande nodded, her eyes bright with pleasure at his phrasing. She spoke the djinni's name, quietly but firmly, 'Esren!' and it was there, dancing attendance in the air.

'Esren, turn the waters around now.'

'I have done so already,' it said, its voice chiming coldly in Julianne's ears. 'The 'ifrit are no more, and the siq has been cleared of its rockfalls. Some of the water went that way; what remains is running back. I have removed the bodies of the dead men, and set them together in a place that I found, that seemed fitting. I will not have those waters corrupted further.'

'Esren, you're a marvel.'

'I am a djinni,' it said simply, 'and so marvellous to you, who are less than I. To my own kind I must be a mockery, for having been snared so by the 'ifrit, who are greater than you but still less than we. Any one of the djinn could have freed me at any time, and they would not.'

That was interesting, Julianne thought. It served to explain both the djinni's sour disposition and the service it offered to her friend, over and above the terms of its promise. If it felt betrayed by its own, it must feel a corresponding gratitude to her, and might prove a better companion even than Julianne had hoped.

'I would not say that the 'ifrit are greater than humans,' Elisande growled, in high indignation.

'Nevertheless, it is true. They are spirit; you are flesh. They demean themselves by taking form in this world, and so I could destroy them when I did the same; your bodies demean you with every moment that you wear them, and yet you cannot let them slip.'

'We have spirit,' Julianne suggested, 'as well as flesh.'

'If that were so, the two should be divisible. I have taken many bodies from the water; leave them where they are or set them otherwise, they will still rot. I do not believe they are uninhabited houses, whose owners have moved elsewhere.'

'That is what we are taught.'

'It may be that you are taught lies or ignorance, daughter of the King's Shadow. I travelled widely between the worlds, before I was penned in; I never found a human spirit that thrived beyond its body.'

'It may be that the djinn do not know all that there is to know,' Elisande said snappishly, 'or go everywhere that there is to go. I have been in two worlds, yours and ours;

perhaps when I leave this body, I will find that there is another yet, and that you are still bound to my service.'

'That would be an interesting lesson, Lisan, for both of us. I do not foresee its happening, however.'

Do you foresee her death? The question hung in the air, unasked by either girl but very present; Julianne was glad when her father's voice cut through their silence, before Elisande could yield to the temptation of finding another way to phrase it.

'Children, haven't you learned yet not to debate philosophy with the djinn? It is a thankless exercise. Like fathers, they assume a higher wisdom, and cannot be shaken from it. Julianne, a word with you.'

More than one word, in fact, but yet not many: remarkably few, to change utterly the course of a girl's life.

As Elisande had predicted, the wedding was to be that night. 'Before the sheikhs can recover from the shocks of the day,' her father said, 'and seek to forbid it.'

'Would they do that?'

'Some might try. They see too much that is Patric already, what with Rudel's and my invasion of their council, and Marron's misappropriation of their prophecy. That in particular is a great confusion to them. If their war leader marry a Patric girl – and not just any girl, not a nameless captive taken in a raid but the daughter of the King's Shadow, no less – they may feel they are being consciously acted against. As they are, in truth; but Hasan will have you, and I will not pass up that opportunity. Even at the cost of another feast,' he added heavily, 'and this time one that I must pay for.'

She surprised herself by laughing, feeling a wash of genuine merriment overtake her. 'Even Yaman and Sherett together couldn't make a feast in an afternoon,' she consoled him, 'even if the kitchens weren't flooded, which they must be.'

'Mmm. I don't know if the djinni will have left them so. Perhaps; it has a peculiar affinity with water, and may not see the problem. But a feast there must be, even if it's only stale bread seasoned with good wishes and a little affection. That would certainly be cheaper. The Sharai are generous to their guests, but rapacious in business . . . Ah, don't worry, girl,' seeing her expression, 'it won't be as you think. Its people may have survived, but this has been a disaster for Rhabat. Most of the stores were in cellars; the crops are lost and the land has been drenched with salt water, much of the livestock will have drowned. We'll all be on desert commons tonight, and for nights to come. Whatever the women can conjure up – and it may seriously be little more than bread and dried fruit – we will call a feast, and I will pay them handsomely for it. But everyone will share the same, you'll see. The sheikhs will eat with their men, and all the tribes will eat with me. And see you married to Hasan, and who knows? Some at least may see Outremer married to Sharai, and get to thinking. We can help them a little, perhaps, by the way we dress you. I must speak to Sherett . . .'

'Then you'll have to wait,' she said, 'at least a little, unless you want to swim. The djinni may have turned the water round, but listen, it's pouring yet.'

He smiled at her, a little wearily, as he always had done when she was being particularly stupid. 'Julianne, I could walk dry-shod and directly into Sherett's private chamber; I've done it before. You know that. Or Elisande's djinni could carry us down in glory, to the general amazement of all. But I'd rather not draw any more attention than we need just now; we've given the sheikhs cause to be grateful to us, or rather Elisande has, and that's humiliation enough. Patrics and guests, and we protected them where they were helpless . . . Better not to make a public display of talents, after that. Not if we want to ease this marriage past them unprotested. Hasan will have trouble with them after, mind; but you shelter behind your veil, shelter behind Sherett and the most trouble you'll have will be with their wives. Though that's trouble enough, I grant you . . .'

'I can take it. I practically grew up in the Emperor's harem back in Marasson, remember.'

'Did you? I thought I forbade you even to visit that house?'

'Of course you did. So of course I went there as often as I could – which meant often, with you being away so much. They made such a fuss of me, sweets and kisses and all the gossip, it was wonderful. I used to carry messages for the new girls sometimes, to a soldier or a lordling who'd caught their eye.'

'Julianne! That's a capital offence, for the messenger as much as the girl . . .'

'Not for me. I was daughter of the King's Shadow, the Emperor himself wouldn't risk your anger by beheading your only child – and besides, I wasn't stupid even then. Even if the girl could write, I wouldn't take a paper. Just a message I could remember, and a token – a scented hand-kerchief, a flower, anything that might have been my own.'

'And if you'd been betrayed, by a soldier or a lordling . . .?'

'It would have meant their heads too; they wouldn't be so foolish. And why spoil the game, in any case? That court thrives on intrigue, and the girls' affairs are the least part of it. It was the older women I watched more, they were much more interesting. I was a child, but you taught me well – I could see how they fought for influence, how they undermined each other, how they manipulated every whisper that came their way. They were like a collective mother to me,' she said, smiling at him brightly. 'I learned from them as much as I did from you. So I'm fairly sure I can survive the scheming in the women's quarters, even if it's all turned against me. It won't last long, anyway; whatever happens, whether they go to war or back to their tents, the tribes won't linger here.'

Indeed they wouldn't. Couldn't, rather: Rhabat could not sustain them. Julianne had heard what her father said about stores and crops, but her mind had been on marriage – on marriages, rather, on hope forsaken and hope cautiously reborn – and she hadn't given any thought to the reality of what he'd been describing. She had seen floods before, she had pictures in her memory to call on; but she'd been a child then, and it was only ever the poor who suffered in Marasson. She'd gaped from rooftops at dark rivers flowing through what used to be streets, and had been too young to feel anything other than the thrilling wonder of it all.

Now, though – now she stood high and vulnerable and exposed on the plateau above Rhabat, gazed down on turbulent waters and could see nothing but the devastation they had wrought.

As the djinni had promised, the sea was receding, back

to its own bed again; as she had heard, it was not yet gone, and not yet finished doing damage.

They followed a goat-path that tracked along beside the rift. Where it was narrow, the water-level had dropped far enough that she couldn't see it without going right to the edge; Elisande did that, she did not. Enough that she could hear it, still roaring and echoing within the confines of the gully.

Where the rift broadened, where there had been that first quiet pool amid its stand of trees, the flood was quieter but inescapable, a seething mass that ran from wall to wall. A few surviving trees still showed their tops above the surface, bent and straining; as she watched, one more was swept away, tumbling in the water to show how it had not broken but been plucked up, roots and all. Wiser to be weak, she thought, to snap at the trunk and lose all your topgrowth and still have at least the hope of growing again.

She followed the tree out of sight, seeing how it broke too late against the rock, how currents ripped it asunder; then she moved her gaze effortfully against the flow, to where the gully walls closed in again. A cataract was gushing there, driven by the weight of so much water at its back. Julianne's eyes were drawn further, though, to her first sight of the valley beyond.

It lay open and empty before her, as she had never seen it before and had never thought to see it. The waters were retreating like a slow tide; some of the higher terraces on the far side were visible, stripped of their crops and washed down to bedrock in places. Where some soil still clung, even from this distance she could see white streaks of salt against its sodden black, and knew it would be barren for generations.

She could also see a charnel-heap of drowned horses, camels, other animals. That must have been the djinni's work, plucking them from the water in an excess of tidiness. She remembered that it had done the same for the dead men, but had set them somewhere else in a rare gesture of courtesy. Briefly she wondered where, as it had not said; but momentary curiosity was drowned itself by a sudden pang of distress for little Tezra and Sildana too, who must surely have been trapped in the stables, and so died in that overwhelming flood. Rubon had been lucky to escape it, if he hadn't met some worse fate instead, out in the desert . . .

All else in the valley was still inundated under a sheet of dark, reflective water. Smooth as silk it appeared from this height, drawn tight and creased where it funnelled into the gully, only a little lacy along its lapping edges. All the high doorways in the cliff-face were still submerged; a stain on the rose-pink rock above showed the extent of the flood's reach. There was movement at some of the upper windows, Julianne saw, faces showing. For the first time in years she was glad to be up high and not contained down there, where the stink of the water must be dreadful within the houses. There would be no escape, until the flood had retreated a great deal further.

'Perhaps,' she heard her father say musingly to Hasan, 'this is not such a good night to hold a wedding?'

'It is the best night possible,' came the swift reply. 'We must move tomorrow, and no one can say when we will come together again at Rhabat; we have lost this place, for a while. How better to bid it farewell, than with a wedding? And one that does not set the tribes at each other's throats for jealousy, that it was one girl and not another who was chosen . . .'

'It may set all the tribes together at your throat.'

'No,' Hasan laughed. 'I am Hasan; they will forgive me this. Besides, they have all seen your daughter, they will understand.'

'And envy you?'

'What man could not? She is a treasure. But a foreign treasure, so it will not be a case of knives. We fight only over our own. And truly, Coren, we need this. We have won a victory, true – but at a cost greater than the victory was worth. We don't even know what we were fighting for. Why would the 'ifrit want Rhabat, what use would it be to them when they have their own country? They are malicious, dangerous – but never like this, never organised, never an army. We have kept them out, but driven ourselves out too in the doing of it; the siq will be choked with rubble despite the djinni's efforts, I doubt we'll be able to walk out without climbing, and this ground will not yield again in my lifetime. We have lost the heart of our land, or at least seen it grievously hurt. And we have lost friends too, many animals, and much pride. We fought and died; it was a girl and a djinni had to save us. If we give the tribes nothing more to talk about tonight, they will talk about all of this, and victory will become defeat. If we give them a wedding and call their rations a feast, they will dance all night and look to a new morning.'

'And when that morning come, they'll be too tired to move before noon. I have been to Sharai weddings. But you're right, of course. Let me talk a little with my daughter . . .'

He took Julianne by the elbow and led her aside. Sharp

eyes followed them, and not only Hasan's; Elisande was interested, and Julianne wondered how good a djinni's hearing might be. Perfect, very likely. It could probably hear a whisper from the wrong side of a thunderstorm, if it chose. No point warning her father, then. Besides, she had no secrets from Elisande, except the one.

'So it begins,' her father said. 'Hasan means every word of what he says – and yet he is also looking ahead, pursuing his dream. If Rhabat is closed to the Sharai, all the more reason for them to seek Ascariel. He will work that image into their heads tonight, the golden city won to replace the rosen that has been lost. If the tribes scatter back to their own lands, then he loses all he's achieved and more; this was their only neutral territory, and the sheikhs won't come again if they go away thinking this a disaster.

'If he can keep these men together as the kernel of his army, if he can give them a vision, something to fight for that they understand – then he wins, and he will in the end win Outremer. You might help to prevent that. At such a marriage, at such a time, you may be privileged to sit with the sheikhs. No point your preaching against the war, you are a woman and would not be listened to; besides, it would be seen as deep disloyalty, to argue against your husband. Bad enough at any time, it is not done among these people, and you'd best find a curb for your wilfulness, daughter; Hasan may grant you some leeway, but Sherett will not. In public, on your wedding-night, even he would be outraged. Still, what you can legitimately do, you can play on their attachment to Rhabat. Stress its beauty, remind them of its importance as a place of trade and conference, plead with them not to abandon it. That would be more than fitting, it would be quite winning in a girl newly married into their culture. The land here will not support them as it used to do, but they can bring in fresh stores, and men to clear the siq of what rubble the floods have left. Give them this as a project, and they will be less keen to go to war; they may lose sight of Ascariel altogether, at least for a time. Or if they're quarrelsome – and they may well be so, tribal loyalties could be resurgent after a battle that's left them nothing to count but their losses – you might quietly feed their tempers, to encourage an open break and dispersal in the morning. You know how to do that with subtlety. Anything, to counter Hasan's keeping them united and focused on Outremer.'

'You're asking me to act against my husband,' she said, spelling it out forcefully, brutally, 'from the very moment that we're married?'

'Yes. Of course. For the sake of both our peoples, Julianne, his and ours. That's why I agreed to this match.'

She knew that, none better; but still resented his easy assumption of her compliance. If she were going to marry Hasan – and she was, she really was, though she couldn't quite believe it yet – she wouldn't willingly do it as a spy or a secret enemy. Hasan had chosen her for her own sake, and that was what she wanted to give him: herself, uncomplicated by her father's plots.

And yet he was right, any influence she had she must use, and quickly. Loyalties struggled within her, loyalties to two peoples she hardly knew, two lands she had hardly seen. In theory it was simple and obvious to decide for peace and against war; in practice it meant beginning this new marriage, this new life in dishonesty and guile, where she wanted to bring only trust and wonder and an eager, aching desire.

'Father, if it must be done – will you leave me to do it my own way?' *And not beginning tonight, please, let me have just one night . . .*

'You won't have such an opportunity again, to work on the sheikhs of all the tribes together. And don't think you can lure Hasan out of his intent with sweets, child; he has conceived a passion for you, true, but his other passion burns hotter and deeper by far. That one will not prove vulnerable to soft entreaty, even to please you.'

No. That she believed. She sighed, and said, 'Well, Rhabat was wonderful, and should be so again. And the Sharai do need it. That much I may do with honour, if I can. The rest – we'll see how things fall out tonight.'

'Good enough. Don't forget, though, this is what I trained you for, Julianne. Use the skills you have, don't make a waste of all those years.'

Well, she was determined not to do that. But she was determined too to be more than a tool of her father's making, as she was to be more than her husband's plaything, his junior wife. She hoped to show them both, these strong men, that she had strengths of her own, and ideas too. She had seen her friends develop strangely, grow into an uncertain independence; she would not willingly give herself into another's possession now. After this night she would be a girl no longer; she intended to be a woman of character, a figure who commanded respect.

They lingered on the height there, speaking little as they watched the waters dwindle. Eventually they saw movement below, men wading knee-deep between the houses;

for appearance's sake they waited longer, until the last of the flood had drained away.

Then, 'No hidden stairs down from here, Hasan?' Elisande enquired.

'None that I know of. We are on the wrong side of the ravine to use that passage we descended by before; and I would not take you that way in any case. Marron found an 'ifrit at the tunnel's head, and it may be there yet. Your djinni will not have reached so high with its waterplay.'

'If it's there yet, my djinni could deal with it; but no, that's a long and a dull way down. Will you ride with me, Hasan, or walk with the King's Shadow? Julianne will walk, I think . . .'

'Julianne will walk, you know,' she said immediately. 'Hasan, come with us? If she wants to float about in mid-air, let her do that; but let her do it alone, she deserves no better company.'

He smiled, and shook his head. 'Go you with your father, Julianne, this last time before you are mine. If I let Lisan carry me – or the Djinni Tachur, rather – I may at least prevent her making too wild a show of herself.'

For a moment, Julianne thought her friend was going to pull a face at him; instead she drew herself up haughtily, at least as high as she could manage, and tried to wither him with a glare.

'How if I make a show of you, though, Hasan? A much-married man on the eve of another wedding, skidding around the sky with a girl, unchaperoned . . .?'

'Hardly that, with a djinni in attendance. And who knows what mischief you might not get up to, if I let you go alone and unattended? I am with you, Lisan, never doubt it.'

Listening to them banter, Julianne thought how much tidier things would have been if it were Elisande he meant to marry tonight. For all of them: Hasan would have acquired a woman of power and a wicked companion, while Julianne's father would still have had his spy; Elisande would have had someone to look to beyond Marron, an end to pining and a meaningful role, while she – she could have stayed half-married to her delightful boy, with the promise of that other half to come when at last she found her way back to him again. No divided loyalties, no private agony of doubt . . .

But life had lost its tidiness, long ago it seemed; even her smooth father could be ruffled sometimes. As when he took her hand and led her through a golden nimbus into the discreet shadows of the gully below – and found himself standing ankle-deep in sticky, stinking mud.

She could have laughed at the disgusted expression on his face, the way he sought too late to lift his clothes above the clinging muck; she could have gagged at the smell of it herself, or shuddered at its chilly touch as it oozed through the seams of her boots. Instead she seized the moment and said, 'Father, I know this marriage is politically convenient to you, and you've taken care already to say how you want me to behave, how I should use all the skills you've given me. There's only one thing missing now.'

'Is there?' he murmured distractedly, as he picked his way fastidiously through the mud. 'What's that?'

'You haven't wished me happy.' *And I'm your only child and you're treating me exactly like a tool, a thing you made for a specific purpose; and I should be used to it by now, but I just don't believe that you care . . .*

'Oh, Julianne.' He stopped, turned, stared up at her. 'Have I not? I'm so sorry. Blame it on the confusions of the day; I've been too caught up in trying to see through this tangled web of events and consequences. I yearn so much for a djinni's sight of what may come, sometimes I forget what I am, a man and a father . . .'

It was a gracious apology, and she might almost have believed it earnest if she hadn't known him too well, if she couldn't see him already working out what effect this moment might have in the future. She'd never thought of it that way before, but he was entirely right: he would kill, she thought, for the foreknowledge of the djinn, unreliable though it was. Or for anything that would gift him a greater understanding, that would make him a better servant to his King. She'd never doubted that he held her in affection; she was sure that he would wish her happy, so long as that happiness didn't come at the expense of his wider goals. If the survival of Outremer depended upon her utter misery, she was certain that she knew which way his choice would fall . . .

Still, she tried not to show that in her smile; and she would have welcomed his hug, his kiss for they were meant to be, signs of a love that was quite genuine, if they had come. That they were interrupted by the djinni's abrupt descent was no injury. The intent had been there, and that was what mattered. She had touched as deep within her father as she could reach, and the block she'd encountered was nothing new and carried no blame.

She watched them come down, her friend and her husband-to-be, seeming to stand alone on a platform of air turned solid, while the djinni was only a shimmer in the dusky light; she was half inclined to suggest that she and her father join them, that they all be wafted through to Rhabat above the invasive mud. Discretion was all very well, but the price of it here was vile.

Hasan forestalled her, though, jumping down onto none-too-solid ground. She heard the squelch as his bare feet landed, and had to fight to suppress a giggle. She was perhaps none too successful; the look he gave her was imperious and intended to be crushing. Except that she refused to be crushed, could not be crushed by him. She returned his gaze undaunted, and heard the smile in his voice as he turned to give his hand to Elisande.

'Be careful, Lisan, this is slippery. Ill footing for a lady, I fear . . .'

Fit for Julianne, he was implying meanly, and her soul rejoiced. She didn't need her father's good wishes, nor a djinni's foresight; she needed nothing more than him. Even the ache of Imber's loss she could bear, so long as she had Hasan.

Elisande dismissed the djinni, discretion again, before they waded through the mud into the open valley. Hasan was greeted with joy, by men who'd thought him lost; Julianne could sense how quickly the news would travel between the tribes, *Hasan is safe, we have our leader still . . .*

He stayed with them, though, all the way to the door of the women's house. She'd been wondering whom he would tell first, about his intentions for that night; and was answered when Sherett came out to greet them, when he took her elbow and spoke privately to her.

She knew her man, clearly, or else they had discussed this already; there was no surprise on her face as she glanced across. No caution either, no disapproval, if not exactly the welcome that Julianne was hoping for. She looked harassed more than anything, a woman with burdens enough already being confronted with something more.

Julianne steeled herself, and hastened over to join them. 'Sherett, it was not my idea to have this happen tonight . . .' Or at all, if she were honest: it had only been a dream of desire, that she'd never thought could possibly turn real.

Sherett's veil hid her mouth, but not her eyes; the sudden smile was easy to read, as she gripped Julianne's hands and said, 'That I could have guessed. It is this man who has no patience, who must see everything done at once. It means that the hall must be cleaned, and Yaman must somehow gather food enough for a feast, although we have no kitchens and no stores; but what is that to him? He has decided, he will wed tonight, and so we women must scrub and glean. Go, then,' to her husband, whose mouth was twitching against his evident iron control, 'show those fool men you are still breathing, for what use that is, and give them something else to shout about.' And more soberly, 'Visit the wounded, Hasan. We carried them up to the gallery when the waters came; there are few enough survived that far, and I doubt if any will live the night.'

'I will,' he said, 'and thank you, Sherett. You are a jewel.'

'Aye, and I must make another shine tonight. Come then, girl,' with a sharp tug on Julianne's wrists, 'we have a great deal to do, and little enough time for it. Besides everything else, I will be blamed if you do not look your part tonight.'

Absurdly, Julianne hesitated. 'Uh, my feet are filthy, I don't want to trek mud through the house . . .'

Sherett laughed shortly. 'Julianne, there is mud through half the house already. And the baths are unusable, and we have no fires and no clean water to waste. We must make shift somehow. Will you *come* . . .?'

They made shift in an upper room, with wet cloths and ungenerous ewers of cool water that Elisande ferried from a cistern, she said, that collected the rare rainwater when it fell on the plateau above. The channels didn't extend as far as the ravine where they'd been standing earlier to look down on the valley, but she said there was an intricate network cut into the rock, funnelling the runoff away before the returning sun could steal it. Every house had its cistern, water stored against a sudden need; Julianne would be surprised, she said, how much rain the system gathered in a year . . .

Julianne was surprised that the system existed at all. She asked how long it had taken the Sharai to create it.

Sherett snorted; Elisande said, 'The Sharai do not build, sweet. Neither do they dig. They just use what they can find or seize.'

'What God brings us,' Sherett said firmly.

'It's the same thing. Isn't it? God set this in my path, for me to find; God gave my enemy into my hand, so that I might seize what he had. Anyway, Julianne, whoever built Rhabat built the water-system above it. A small people they must have been, unless they used their children for the work. The brats here have a game, where they wriggle into the ducts to sneak from house to house. They get lost, or get stuck in some tight angle, and have to yell for help; and it's always the girls who are sent in to look for them. Boys get too big to fit.'

'Not true,' from Sherett. 'The main channels, at least, a man can squeeze along; they have done so, trying to find their way here. We do send the girls in after lost children, and to keep the channels clear; but that is partly to prevent boys learning what we would prefer men not to know.'

'Does any man ever make it this far?' Elisande wanted to know.

'It has happened,' Sherett said primly. And said no more; Julianne wondered if Hasan had ever squirmed his way damp and breathless through the dark, to court her privately. Or some other man, perhaps, before Hasan . . .? She would ask, she thought; but not yet. After the ceremony, perhaps, when they were bonded wife and wife to the same husband . . .

The idea of that ought to seem so strange, she thought; and yet it did not. It had never been her people's custom for a man to take more than one wife, but she'd grown up among people whose custom it was; she'd never for a moment imagined that she would marry within that custom, but she found herself quite comfortable with the thought. Possessiveness had always been a puzzle to her. She could share Hasan with this woman, and not feel jealous or deprived. There were other wives too, older, but they seemed to be of little account; they were not in Rhabat, and she hadn't even heard their names yet. Perhaps it was only the smugness of the new favourite, but she thought she could discount them. Sherett never, but there would never be the need. She hoped . . .

'Tell me about the ceremony,' she said, realising suddenly that she knew nothing about the wedding-rites of the Sharai. 'Will you be there?'

'Of course. Everyone will be there. And how could I not? That's my husband you're marrying. I must present you, ready for his taking – and you will be presentable, girl, if I have to scrub every inch of skin off and drench you with orangewater after. Lisan, there is still mud beneath those toenails.'

'I know it. I can smell it, too – unless that's coming from my own feet. Hold still, Julianne, this pick is sharp, and you can't get blood on your wedding-dress. It's supposed to be bad luck. Symbolic, I suppose . . .'

'Indeed you cannot,' Sherett confirmed. 'Silly girls have been known to cut themselves deliberately, to delay a match they do not want. In the Sands, within the tribe, very silly girls have been married naked; the men lose patience with such games.'

Well, at least she wasn't silly, or not in that way; she'd sooner hasten than delay. She was nervous, of course, but it was anticipation and not nervousness that made her skin shiver. She thought Sherett knew that, from the thoughtful glances that those shivers drew.

She had a silly question, though, knew its foolishness before she asked it; the answer should have been obvious and was not, or not to her.

'If there are no priests, no imams in Rhabat, how can we be married? Who conducts the service?'

Sherett had taken a rough comb of bone to her wet hair, to tease out tangles that the wind had made; she paused in her work now, and her voice sounded genuinely bewildered as she said, 'What have imams to do with a marriage?'

Julianne was too stunned to offer any answer. Elisande had to rescue them both, sitting back on her heels to say,

'Julianne, sweet, this is not Outremer. It's not even a Catari town, where the imams might hold sway. The Sharai rarely see a priest from one year's end to the next; they say their own prayers in their own way, and deal with God on their own terms. He doesn't have much of a place in wedding arrangements. There's nothing that happens in the Sands – or in Rhabat, or anywhere the Sharai pitch their tents or lay their blankets out – that needs an imam's endorsement.'

'Indeed not,' Sherett affirmed with vigour. 'Why would there be? They are fat men; they know little of our lives, and nothing that is useful.'

They know how to make a weapon proof against 'ifrit, Julianne thought. But she was wise enough to know an insult when she heard it, and to recognise prejudice when it was backed by bile; she said mildly, 'How is the ceremony conducted, then, if not by a priest, as ours are?' *And how are we married, if not before the God and under His law, as I was . . .?*

'It's a marketplace,' Elisande said cheerfully. 'They are much more honest here, they don't disguise the true nature of the event. Sherett and I will make you look as precious as we can, then hide your worst disfigurements behind a veil and disguise your earthy odours with a bucket or two of perfume. Your father hands you over to Hasan, who gives him the price agreed, which is certainly not what you've cost him to rear; the crowd sucks air through its teeth and shakes its head and agrees with itself that poor Hasan's been monstrously overcharged. They have a really nice time, and so do you, because both sides give you presents. In return you give your father his freedom from you, which can't come a moment too soon for any man with an expensive daughter. What you give to Hasan, of course, is your own affair . . .'

Julianne snorted in indignation, put a foot on her friend's shoulder and sent her sprawling across the floor, where she lay curled up and cackling in high delight with herself.

'Stop it, the pair of you!' Sherett ordered, snapping a wet cloth at them that stung where it struck. 'We don't have time for childishness. Julianne, I will tell you how the wedding will be. Your part is not difficult, but it must be done perfectly or you will shame me and your father both. And what shames me shames Hasan, what shames Hasan before the tribes shames all the Beni Rus . . .'

Julianne sighed. 'Teach me, then, Sherett.' She thought that that this would become a familiar cry, that some considerable part of their life together might be devoted to Sherett's teaching her how not to shame their husband. She would try to be a dutiful wife and sister-wife, as she had tried to be a dutiful daughter; and if she must break out and be wild sometimes – and she would, she thought, as she always had – she would be wild with Hasan and perhaps with Sherett too, they could all be wild together. If those two had forgotten how, well, she'd just have to teach them . . .

Julianne did feel something like an animal being prepared for market, before Sherett was content with her. Nor was Elisande spared, despite her grumbles; even her rough-hewn hair had to be trimmed into respectability, although her head would be decently covered for the feast.

As soon as they were both approved, they were taken to

the store of fine clothes that was hoarded here, that the flood had not reached. Julianne's father could have had no chance to speak to Sherett, as he had promised, but it wasn't necessary; their thoughts echoed each other's, unless long tradition simply overruled any other factors.

'You are not of our people, Julianne, but you should dress as we do now, and go barefoot to your wedding. A bride may wear silk, but it must be of our own colour, to honour God's choice of us; the tribes will be glad to see you respect our customs.'

Julianne was nothing loath. The gown Sherett picked out for her was deepest blue, so dark it looked almost black except where it sheened in the lamplight; it was simply but beautifully cut, slipping like oil over her skin to hug her tall slender figure. Even without a mirror, she knew she looked well in it. She didn't need Elisande's silent applause, though she smiled her gratitude for it.

Elisande would have her own role in the ceremony – 'as you have neither mother nor sister to stand with you, Julianne, you may have your friend' – but was left free to choose her own robe, while Sherett slipped away to supervise the preparations.

She made a dressing-up game of it, trying on a dozen different gowns and parading them for Julianne's approval, each one more exotic than the last. When she had her friend reduced to a state of helpless giggles, she shrugged off the skimpy satin that had induced it and said, 'That's better, you were looking altogether too solemnly blue. The dress suits you, Julianne, but the mood does not. Help me now, find something quiet. It's you the men must be looking at tonight . . .'

Between them they chose a crimson gown of watered silk, fine enough to satisfy even Julianne's pampered tastes and dark enough to meet Elisande's insistence that she not outshine the bride. 'I'll catch no eyes in this,' she said, stroking her palms over the fabric. 'I'll feel wonderful, but no man will come close enough to know it. Not like you, sweet. Your Hasan will be hard pressed to keep his hands off you, even under Sherett's eye. Later, though . . .'

'Don't joke, Elisande.'

'I'm not joking. It's what you want, isn't it?'

'Oh, yes. It's what I want,' more even than she had wanted it before, when Imber had refused her, that dreadful night of misunderstanding. 'But I don't want to talk about it. No secret, but it should be left private even so.'

'Sorry,' her friend said, grinning insouciantly and looking not sorry at all. 'I wonder where they'll put you? He can't come here, but I'm not sure you can go to him either, a woman alone in a house of men. We never had a wedding, the times I was here. Perhaps they have a special place – or perhaps you will go to the Beni Rus but Sherett will come with you and sleep across your doorway like a page-boy. She'd keep you private, that one, the men must be terrified of her. I know I am. I pity Hasan, caught between the two of you; not to mention his other pair, back in his tents. No one ever does mention them, have you noticed? I expect they're busy doing what good wives do, raising children. Sherett's given him a couple already, did you know? She told me that. He'll expect them from you, too. And soon. Tonight you can enjoy yourselves, but it'll turn earnest soon enough . . .'

'Elisande, stop. No more. Please? Whatever happens, it'll be according to custom. That's good enough for me.

And – Elisande, there'll be a man for you too, if you want one. I'm sure there will.'

'Perhaps – but not the one I want. Still,' smiling slyly, mercurial as ever, 'at least Rudel won't choose my man for me, eh? That much I can be sure of. We don't do that in Surayon; and even if we did, he knows I'd refuse, just to spite him.'

'Oh, your poor father. Elisande, my love, isn't it time for you two to make some peace between you? It's cruel, the way you treat him, when you're all the family that he has . . .'

'Cruel, is it? It was more cruel, the way he treated my mother. He abandoned her, and she died. I watched her *die*, Julianne . . .'

'He didn't know. He'd have come back, if he'd known.'

'He should have known, he should have seen it in her. He had time enough to realise what it did to her, every time he went away. Don't ask me to forgive him, Julianne. I can't.'

'Yes, you can. And I do ask it. He hurts, Elisande, as badly as you do. He mourns her just as much.'

'What, has he told you? Have you been talking about me? Or her?'

'No,' or only a little, 'but I've heard his song. It needs no more. Elisande, for my sake, then, if not your own? Please?'

Elisande only shook her head, but there was perhaps doubt in her eyes, the moment before she hid them.

Julianne could say no more; it was a blessing, she thought, that Sherett chose that moment to come back, before the silence could grow oppressive.

*

Both girls were coached rigorously in what would be expected of them at the ceremony. That turned out to be a blessing also, even if it didn't seem so at the time. Julianne had thought that getting married would be easy; she'd done it before, after all, and had found it simple enough. It was the being married after that had been hard on her.

This time, though – this time it was more than a girl's natural nervousness in front of strangers that dragged at her heels, slowing her steps as she walked towards what she wanted. It was more than Imber also, though he would be a chain she must carry for a long time, she thought, and possibly for ever: first love brutally betrayed, wilfully betrayed again and again without ever losing its sense of aching wonder.

It was more than two people who were to marry here, it was two cultures that were or likely would be shortly at war, and she had duties that went far beyond making a success of the marriage. She had her father at the one side to remind her of that; she had Elisande at the other to remind her unwittingly of the last time, of Imber; she had Sherett ahead to lead her, to remind her of how alien these people were to whom she was giving herself.

Small wonder if she walked slowly, heavily towards her future, she could forgive herself that. She found it harder to accept her trembling fingers, the greater shudders that seized her body and shortened her breath. They were nothing to do with the political situation or her particular, peculiar circumstances, and all to do with Hasan: just the thought, the anticipation of him and this night to come. He was a man, she reminded herself furiously, no more than that. He was a man and she was a girl, it was natural and inevitable that they should join together in the dark, as thousands did and had done each night since the beginning; and still she couldn't stop the shivers coming. She wanted to take hold of Elisande's hand, to see if that warm grip could suppress them, but her friend might think her fearful. She was not afraid, not that, and would not be thought so.

Her father had decreed that this time – 'to save your pretty dresses, children' – they didn't need to wade through the crusting mud outside. He was the King's Shadow, after all, famous for appearing out of nowhere, and she was his daughter; drama would be expected, the tribes disappointed if it were denied them. This once, they must play to their audience.

Even so, he had asked Elisande not to summon her djinni tonight. That was unnecessary – she'd already made it plain to Julianne that she would do nothing to steal any glory from her friend – but she'd accepted the admonition with a nod and no protest. How they made their entrance was in his hands, and his alone.

His arrival in the women's quarters had raised not an eyebrow between the three of them; his smile as he arranged them in their proper order, as he gestured to Sherett to lead them off along the corridor, suggested that more than eyebrows would be raised shortly among the men of the Sharai where they were gathered in the Chamber of Audience.

They walked – slowly, oh so slowly, as Julianne struggled under her many burdens – and a golden light enveloped them as they went. The walls that had been so close about them were lost in the dark beyond that light, but not merely hidden: taken away, Julianne thought, removed, or else she and her companions had been removed from within the walls.

Briefly they seemed to be nowhere, in a space that had no place in any world. The light they walked in her father had brought with him, be it created or stolen from elsewhere; it wasn't native here. Nothing was, or could be. There was no ground that she could feel beneath her feet, no taste of air, no touch of wind; again she wanted to grope for Elisande's hand. And did not, and was glad a moment later when the smaller girl's fingers touched hers, touched and clung.

'Now,' her father's voice sounded strange, thin and muffled though he stood almost shoulder to shoulder with her, 'try not to startle, as we come through. Concentrate on startling the men. Grace and elegance, Julianne, and trust me. I'd have walked through fire, to wed your mother; would you do less, to achieve the man you want?'

The darkness faded to shadow, and grew form; sounds of voices swelled up all around them. But there were noises closer, hisses and sharp cracks from beneath their feet, it seemed; and the darkness left them but the light did not, it grew brighter if anything, flickered and flared about them as they walked.

And as they walked, those voices went away again, fell silent one by one. Julianne could see little through the fierce walls of light that encompassed her, but she could feel the weight of many men's stares upon her.

And stiffened her shoulders against them, raised her head; and so perhaps took a little longer than Elisande to realise quite where they were.

In the Chamber of Audience, of course, that much she knew; but there were pillars on all sides, men on all sides, no wall on either hand; her father had brought them into the middle of the hall, then, spurning discretion altogether.

But, the middle of the hall – not an open floor, no . . .

In the middle of the hall was a firepit, and they were walking through it.

All the length of the firepit they walked, perhaps the length of three tall men laid head to foot, with boots and helmets too; and the fire licked about them all the way, and not a hair was singed, not a bare foot was blistered or even scuffed with ash.

It was all illusion, Julianne thought, just a conjuring-trick. If they were truly walking in the fire she should be treading on shifting logs and cinders, and was not. If she looked down, she thought she'd see her feet walking on a cloudy light, that same soft nimbus that had brought them here, that she could still see like a pale swathe around Sherett ahead of her. The flames would hide it from the staring men, perhaps; or if they caught some glimpse, it could only add to the legend of this moment, *the firelight wrapped itself about them, and would not let them burn . . .*

They came to the end of the firepit, and stepped out onto solid floor; Julianne felt a sudden heat at her back and wanted to hurry now, but was restrained by her father's hand on her elbow.

Seeing the hall clearly for the first time, she saw how crowded it was, packed with men sitting, men standing behind, all gaping. The only clear space was where they were, where the sheikhs sat in a group before them.

On his feet in the centre of that group was Hasan. She let out a soft, slow breath, and stopped walking; stopped thinking almost, focused eyes and mind entirely on him.

He hadn't looked at her, not yet. He'd said something to Sherett, but she had missed it; she heard his wife's response, though, ringing strongly through the silence.

'Husband, as you commanded me, I have brought you the girl of your desire.'

'Wife, you bring me more than ever I could deserve.'

He set his hands on Sherett's shoulders, and kissed her brow; she stepped aside and beckoned Julianne forward, with her supporters.

And now it was easy, thanks to Sherett's careful rehearsal. She could never have improvised her way through a ceremony like this, it was so at variance with every wedding she'd ever sat through, and she would probably never have kept her temper. She knew what was coming, though, phase by phase and almost moment by moment. She could stand – much like a prize cow at market, yes, but it didn't matter – and keep her eyes fixed on Hasan, as his were fixed on her. No touching yet, but that didn't matter either. The very air between them throbbed with a tension unresolved. Her body shivered in response, and he must have seen, her gown hugged her skin so closely. Well, let him see, let him know; there would come a time for touching later, when he would learn more intimately the effect that he had on her. No hope of disguising it then, so why worry now?

She stood proud and silent while he and her father bickered over her value. It was all show, all ritual; the true price was already agreed, and everyone present knew it. She stood – still proud, still silent – while the inevitable objection was raised, that she was married already. That was Elisande's cue to testify that she was virgin still, that her supposed marriage was a mockery. Her friend played the part to perfection; her father confirmed that the wedding had been performed in haste and in his absence. She didn't have to say a word. Imber – *oh, Imber* – was dismissed with grunts and shrugs, all the divorce that she needed.

Only once did she depart from what had been drilled into her, and only in a small way, though it meant much to her. It was her one chance to speak, and Sherett had told her that she could say what she liked; it was good form for the girl to weep and wail and plead, to seem reluctant to leave her father's care. She wouldn't do that, but when at last – after she had already been bought and sold, all terms agreed – Hasan turned to her and said, 'Will it please you, then, to be my wife?' she had her answer ready.

'If it please you. Prince.'

Just the one unexpected word, added to a dutiful text; it made him blink none the less, and add a few words of his own.

'It pleases me very much. Lady.'

And he took her shoulders and kissed her on the forehead, as he had done with Sherett; her skin burned so at his touch, she hardly heard the great shout that went up all around, hardly realised that she was again a married woman.

Her father left her, to join the sheikhs; Elisande and Sherett took her to one side, to where they would be permitted this once to sit and eat with the men. Among the men, at least – not close enough to speak with any of them. *Sorry, father . . .*

'Well,' Elisande murmured, ever sharp, 'do you feel wed?'

She shook her head. 'Not without a priest's say-so, how could I?'

'You will,' Sherett assured her, and she struggled to suppress another shudder, for fear that they should misunderstand it.

As host, her father made a clever little speech, praising all present for their valour against the 'ifrit before ever he praised his daughter or her new-made husband. He added that in honour of the occasion, city girl wedded to desert lord, they would eat only desert food tonight, 'to give her a taste for it.'

A ripple of laughter ran around the hall. No one was deceived, they all knew the true reason, but they were glad to hear him make a joke of it.

In fact, the feast was not so sparse as he'd suggested. There was meat in plenty, though they must have slaughtered half the surviving herds to supply it; there was fresh-baked bread for all, though Yaman must have begged flour from every careful man who carried his own supply, and Julianne couldn't imagine what she'd done for an oven. No grit in it, and no charring: it was far from desert bread.

And there was fruit and toasted almonds, plenty enough for a feast even without the flasks of *jereth* that were passed from hand to hand to give a touch of splendour to the occasion. The women were brought their own, with beakers to drink from. Julianne had eaten little, as befitted a new bride, but she sipped gladly and eyed Hasan over the brim of her cup. She couldn't take her eyes from him; she had tried, but they kept drifting back of their own accord. It was manifest that Sherett approved; it was, she supposed, inevitable that Elisande would tease.

'Look your fill, girl. He'll be too close for seeing soon, and the lights'll be out.'

Julianne wished she'd been trained to control her blushing as well as her tongue. As the one was impossible, though, she decided to let the other loose. 'Oh, and I suppose you've not been looking for Marron, in all this scrimmage?'

Elisande just glowered at her. Instantly sorry, Julianne changed tack rapidly. 'Anyway, I thought you said there'd be presents for me?'

'That's right.'

'So where are they, then?'

'A man cannot give presents to another's wife,' Sherett said, sounding genuinely shocked. 'After the meal, Hasan will receive the bride-gifts on your behalf.'

'Oh. Yes, of course he would. And what, he gives them to me later?'

'No. He gives them into my charge, as the senior wife present. You are a girl yet, Julianne, and girls should be modest; a young wife should not flaunt gold before her elders. I will decide when you are ready to receive your gifts. In the meantime, they will be stowed with our other treasures.'

'Oh,' again. But yes, that sounded truly Sharai: to hoard wealth, rather than display it. 'Um, do I actually have a chance to see them, before you lock them away?'

Sherett laughed. 'Greedy child. Yes, you do. They will be brought to your room tonight, and you may play to your heart's content until the morning.'

Somehow, she had made that sound implicitly plural, and inherently lewd. Julianne's cheeks were on fire again, goaded by Elisande's speaking silence. Ah, well. They might guess, but they couldn't possibly know. For once she blessed the secrecy of the veil.

None of the men made any approach to them during the meal; it would be improper, Julianne supposed, to address a woman in her husband's presence. She saw Rudel suddenly, sitting among the sheikhs where she was sure he had not been before. He might legitimately have come across to speak to his daughter – but of course he would not do that, nor would Elisande welcome it if he did.

One of the serving-women came with a tray, to clear their dishes away; as she knelt to her work, she said, 'I have a message for you, Julianne. From the bearded Patric.'

'Rudel?'

'Yes. He asks me to tell you that the Ghost Walker has returned, with the tribeless one. That one is sick still from his wound, and Rudel has treated him. He sleeps now, and the Ghost Walker stays with him.'

That wasn't a message for Julianne. She glanced aside, to be sure that Elisande had heard, and caught her staring at her father. If there were a message in the look, Julianne couldn't read it.

She sighed, and turned her eyes back to Hasan.

As with most feasts Julianne had attended in her life, it was hard to say exactly when the meal was over; the bread and meat were long gone, but men still nibbled from bowls of nuts and candied fruits. She had no appetite even to nibble; she did peel an orange by touch, but set it aside uneaten as she saw the sheikhs lean over to Hasan one by one, passing him small things that gleamed and sometimes sparkled in the light. He thanked each man formally, and gave the gift courteous attention before placing it on a tray before him and turning to receive the next.

'This will take a long time,' Sherett said, 'and it is not good for you to watch. You are too acquisitive, Julianne. Come, we will leave now and see you to your chamber.'

Was she acquisitive? She didn't think so – except in the matter of husbands, of course. Talking about the presents had been a distraction, no more. She didn't want to go, but that had nothing to do with the increasing mound of gifts.

She stood, though, practising obedience, and looked back only once as Sherett led them out. She couldn't catch Hasan's eye, but her father looked up and blew her a rare kiss. That warmed her heart, though it did not quell its fluttering.

This time they did have to brave the mud outside, as Elisande was still honouring her promise not to call for the djinni. A path of sorts had been cleared alongside the foul and stinking pool, but their feet and the hems of their dresses were still filthy before they came to the house of the Beni Rus.

There were guards at the doorway as ever, but they bowed the women through. Well, that answered one question, at least; she would spend her wedding-night in the house of her husband. Perhaps it should never have been a question. Would Sherett stay, would Elisande? Surely not;

the Sharai might conduct their marriages like a cattle-mart, but they had a strong sense of what was decent. Privacy must be vital, in a world of tents . . .

Some effort had clearly been made to clean the hallway; Sherett dabbled her bare feet in a bowl set there for the purpose, and instructed the other two to do the same.

This house was plainer by far than the women's; there were no rugs in the passageways, and no hangings on the walls. That gave her a better chance to admire the architecture, she supposed, which was magnificent; but she really wasn't in the mood to gawp at elaborate mouldings or wonder how they'd worked the rock so finely. Besides, Sherett was unlikely to encourage dawdling . . .

Indeed, she hurried the girls up several flights of stairs, and so into a high room where a dull fire and the dim light of a single oil-lamp in the window were barely enough to show them how simple the furnishings were. Rugs on the floor, and a fur-covered pallet; a low table with folding legs with a plain stool set beside it, one large chest with an intricate lock, on which stood another bowl of water with towels beside. Julianne guessed that Hasan's tent would look a lot like this inside.

'Good,' Sherett said. 'Lift that bowl down, Lisan, and help Julianne to wash her feet properly; she must be clean, to greet Hasan when he comes.'

They did as they were told. When they were finished, Julianne gazed uncertainly at the murky water and said, 'Should I ask for another bowl, for Hasan?'

'You cannot give orders in this house, girl. Our husband will ask for water if he needs it; and you will wash his feet.'

Rebellion stirred momentarily, pride warring with obedience. Thinking about it, though, she gave a submissive nod, which served also to hide her expression from the sharp eyes of her companions. She thought she might find some fun in washing Hasan's feet, as a preliminary . . .

'Now, out of that robe, Julianne. It is dirty; and besides, silk is for public show, not for the bedchamber.'

'Oh? And how then shall I greet our husband, when he comes?'

'In your bride-gifts, of course,' Elisande suggested wickedly. Julianne's temper flared for a moment, and was lost in a sudden surge of giggles as she pictured herself clad in gold and jewellery and nothing else. Shyness had no place between husband and wife, between Hasan and her tonight; but even so . . .

Sherett simply snorted, threw up the lid of the chest and drew out a simple woollen robe, Sharai blue of course.

'You will greet him as a modest maiden, dressed in the style of your own tribe and his. Lisan can teach you the ties.'

She knew them already. Her fingers were unaccountably clumsy tonight, but Sherett watched closely, and finally nodded her satisfaction.

'Now the veil, so. You need not hood your hair in your husband's house, but it is his privilege to reveal your face. Well, we are done. Be good, girl; give him pleasure, and he will give it you a hundredfold. I know my man. Ours.' Surprisingly she kissed her then, as Hasan had done, formally on the forehead. 'You will have a wait; use it to prepare yourself, in peace. We will leave you now.'

'What, all unchaperoned in a house of men?' Julianne was fighting to keep her voice light, but a quaver betrayed her.

'In your husband's house, you need none. What, do you suppose I bring a chaperone when I come to the Beni Rus? Every man here would die for you tonight, Julianne. Be easy.'

She hadn't actually been nervous of the men, but she said no more. Elisande hugged her fiercely, pushed both their veils aside for a warmer kiss than Sherett's had been, and then rearranged Julianne's for her with fingers that fumbled just a little.

'Julianne . . .' She sounded suddenly more tearful than teasing. 'Enjoy him, and be happy. I will miss you . . .'

It only struck Julianne then that their paths must part here, tonight; she would follow her husband in the morning, and Elisande – she didn't know what Elisande would do, or where go.

Her friend hurried out of the room, though, before she could ask questions. Likely Elisande had no answers, and feared to be asked. Her choices must be few. She could trail Marron like a dog, perhaps, and be miserable; or travel with her father and be worse than miserable, snared in that old and weary passion that twisted both of them out of their true character . . .

Time passed. She explored the room from corner to corner, and found nothing in it that she had not already seen; she explored the trunk and found nothing in it but clothing, all dull to her fingers and drab to her eyes.

She gazed out of the window, and saw all the valley dark; she twisted her head to look up at the stars for a while, but that made her neck ache and taught her nothing. She had no talent to read the future in the constellations, nor in anything else. Like her father, she briefly longed for a djinni's foresight; but it had been a djinni's foresight that had brought her to this, and she was still uncertain whether she had gained or lost by it.

She had gained trinkets, at least, when she was allowed them. It took two men to carry the great tray of wedding-gifts into the room; they set it down on the chest, bowed to her Sharai-style, with graceful hands, and said they would stand guard outside the door until Hasan should come.

Oh, let him hurry, she thought, kneeling beside the chest to toy with the heaped adornments.

Necklets, armlets, anklets, chains of heavy gold; other work that was more ornate, tiny boxes of finest filigree studded with gems and strung on a delicate chain to be worn at the waist, if she were ever permitted to wear them . . .

She tried on some pretty bangles despite Sherett's in-junction, and admired the look and feel of them on her arms. And thought, *nomads wear their wealth – except for the Sharai, who store it in secret. As they will store me, veiled and hidden from the world. Hasan has bought me – and paid too much, the fool! – and will keep me as a treasure, one of his several treasures . . .*

She let the bangles slip, listened to their clatter as they fell back onto the pile, watched one tumble onto the carpet and reached out to retrieve it.

And then, just then heard the soft hiss of a man's breath at her back; and thought Hasan had come for her at last, at long last, and had found her unprepared, weltering in misery.

And took a moment before she turned to greet him, trying to have a smile ready for when he lifted back her veil—

—and in that moment felt a hand close like iron on her throat, and heard a sour voice whisper, 'You think he has you, and you him? No, you are wrong, girl. I have you now . . .'

The room was growing darker yet, as her mind grew dizzy. She opened her mouth to scream, and found no breath to do it with; she wrenched her head around in a desperate effort, and saw Morakh's face too close to hers, far too close but the walls it seemed were closer and the ceiling was coming down so fast, and suddenly there was no floor beneath her and nothing she could do but fall, and oh, she was so afraid of falling . . .